Camellia Creek

Also by Charlsie Russell

The Devil's Bastard

Wolf Dawson

Epico Bayou

River's Bend

Camellia Creek

A Novel

Charlsie Russell

Loblolly Writer's House
Gulfport, Mississippi

Loblolly Writer's House
P.O. Box 7438
Gulfport, MS 39506-7438
Visit our website at www.loblollywritershouse.com

First Edition: May 2013

This book is a work of fiction. Names, characters, and incidents are products of the author's imagination. Any resemblance to actual events or persons is coincidental. Any scenes depicting actual historical persons are fictitious.

Library of Congress Control Number: 2013905463
Russell, Charlsie.
    Camellia creek: a novel

    ISBN 978-0-9769824-4-9
    1. Historical – Fiction

Book design by Lucretia Gibson
Copy editor, Nancy McDowell

Printed and bound in the United States of America.

For Phillip Sherrod Young,
Private, Company G,
"The Mississippi Volunteers of Pontotoc County,"
Third Battalion, Mississippi Infantry,
C. S. A.

And

For all those who wore the gray
And those who loved them and still do
The sons of those who framed the Constitution
Those very ones who kept it true
The final breath of our Founding Fathers' nation
Of all the things that make me proud
To be an American, and there are many,
I'm proudest to be descended from you

Charlsie Russell

Guide to Characters

Eli Calhoon - ex-Lt. Col., Confederate States Army (CSA), owner of Camellia Creek Plantation
Alice Shelton - Orphaned heiress recently arrived in post-war Mississippi
Seth Parker - Maj., United States Marines Corps, assigned to the United States Army (USA)
Isabel Hays - Owner of The Pink Lady in Rodney, old friend of the Calhoons
Holland & Rosalind Calhoon - Eli Calhoon's parents, both deceased
Andrew Calhoon - Eli Calhoon's older brother, died in the war
Laura Calhoon Blackledge - Andrew's widow, Eli Calhoon's lover
Hannah Calhoon - Eli Calhoon's younger sister, died of yellow fever during the war
Naomi Polk - Rosalind Calhoon's sister, Eli Calhoon's aunt, long a fixture at Camellia Creek
Jacob Shelton - Alice Shelton's father, died in the war
    Jason and Michael Shelton - His sons, Alice's brothers, both died in the war
Peter Franklin - Alice Shelton's uncle, ex-Union soldier, speculator, lusts for Camellila Creek
    Betty Franklin - Peter's wife, Alice Shelton's aunt, Jacob Shelton's sister
      Cassie Franklin - Peter and Betty's daughter, Alice Shelton's cousin
Eustacia "Stacy" Franklin - Peter Franklin's dependent sister-in-law
    Jonathan Franklin - Eustacia's son, Peter Franklin's nephew
Rebecca Mackey - Isabel Hays' daughter, a war widow
Poynter Cummings - Editor of *The Port Gibson Chronicle*
Tobias Holbein - Eli Calhoon's lawyer in Rodney, Mississippi
Doctor Ephraim Lester - Doctor and coroner, Claiborne County, Mississippi
Caw Pruitt - Freeborn Negro, ex-CSA, neighbor of Eli Calhoon
Alexander Wilson - Lt. Col., United States Army Corps of Engineers
Thomas McKee - 2d Lt., United States Army Corps of Engineers

Camellia Creek's Negroes

Elvira Hinny - Auntie Elvie, freedwoman and midwife, nursemaid to Eli Calhoon
Brim Solomon - Freedman and childhood companion of Eli Calhoon
    Sally and Samuel Solomon - Brim's wife and son
Rosie Walton - Freedwoman, orphan, from Camellia Creek
Buck Pike - Freedman in the employ of Eli Calhoon

Eli Calhoon's friends and neighbors, ex-Confederates

Wayne Hale	*Dilbert Bowen*	*Hiram Cleaver*
May Hale - His wife	*Jake and Ben* - His sons	*Adam* - His son

Seth Parker's Troops from the Mississippi Native Guard, USA

Capt. Jubal Summers - ex-United States Colored Troops, New York

Sgt. Frank Zachary	*Pvt. Lawson*
Cpl. Peters	*Pvt. Ball*
Cpl. Daws	*Pvt. Spain*
Pvt. Price	*Pvt. Hand*

Alan Guthrie - U. S. Treasury agent murdered in Hinds County, Mississippi
Jocelyn LeBlanc - Mulatto beauty, long dead, whose restless spirit allegedly haunts Camellia
      Creek Plantation

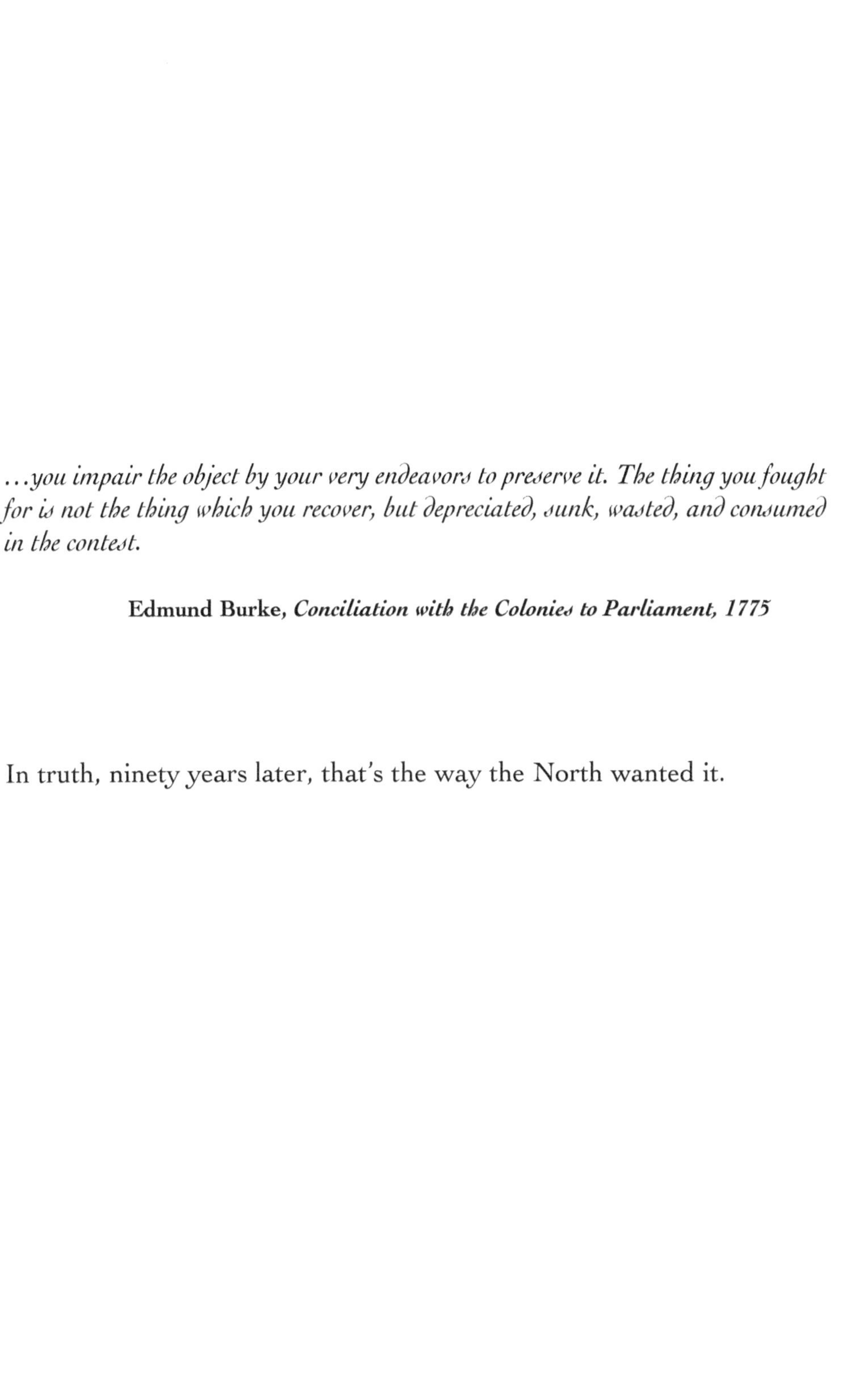

…you impair the object by your very endeavors to preserve it. The thing you fought for is not the thing which you recover, but depreciated, sunk, wasted, and consumed in the contest.

Edmund Burke, *Conciliation with the Colonies to Parliament, 1775*

In truth, ninety years later, that's the way the North wanted it.

Chapter One

"Our land ends here, follows the creek just beyond that tree line. He's holding on to his river-front property as long as he can, but if the rebel states have to pay all those back years in Federal taxes, I don't know how long he'll manage."

Eustacia Franklin said something typically self-righteous in response to Uncle Peter's remarks, and Aunt Betty murmured a platitude focused on the misfortunes of others. Mrs. Franklin took offense at that and launched into another sermon on sinners reaping what they'd sown.

Alice Shelton, late of Ohio by way of Chicago, crept farther into the woods, away from the rough dirt road that had brought Peter Franklin and his extended family to the site of his new property, one hundred fifty acres of rich, black-soil farmland. They'd come to the end of it, but what Uncle Pete had wanted Aunt Betty to see, to get a grasp for, was the lovely site not far from the Mississippi. A house nearby sat on what remained of the owner's land. The site, some distance from the river, was situated near a spring-fed creek and shrouded by cool woods and a wild flower garden. Uncle Peter wanted that house.

Alice wanted nothing.

Eustacia Franklin's shrill voice faded. Aunt Betty had ceased to talk, and Alice gathered, from what she could hear behind her, that Uncle Pete had moved away from his dead brother's wife and was now speaking to his nephew Jonathan, Eustacia's adult son, on the benefits of cotton planting. She hoped her uncle's excitement would hold Jonathan's interest for a while.

Alice breathed in clean air. It had rained last night and the ground was a sodden carpet of brown and yellow leaves, leaves from other Novembers. She stopped and looked up. Here, in war-ravaged Mississippi, fall had only now begun to color the foliage. Gently she exhaled, and her breath formed a soft mist against the mosaic of forest green and clear blue sky. This was a pleasing spot, a luscious contrast of light and shadow, pierced by sun-fractured raindrops. Quiet, serene, but cloistered, like the peaceful seclusion of a forgotten grave.

Uncle Peter's voice grew softer, but Eustacia raged on about God's swift justice, if four years permeated with losses that could not be recouped could be considered either swift or just.

Raising the hem of her sun-mottled dress, Alice moved to the crystal creek, its turbulent rapids sparkling like fireflies in the filtered sunlight. The sedgy bank indicated the stream had flooded with last night's downpour, and she saw no place to cross without soaking her feet and skirt. Just as well since her uncle said the creek represented his property line. Thus thwarted, she removed a glove and squatted, and cupping her hand, she drew a drink from the icy water. Sweet, she thought. A bitter reminder that life goes on.

Vision blurred by tears, Alice shook the water from her cold fingers and watched—she frowned—the droplets pit the now placid surface of the creek, and on that mirrored surface, the reflection of a young woman reached for her across the water.

Alice jerked her head up, then rose and stumbled back two steps. No one stood on the opposite bank. The hackles rose along her spine. No one, at least, that she could see.

She blinked, blur and tears forgotten. The creek flowed along as it had before, its surface too turbulent to reflect anything but light and the muted colors of the forest.

Hesitant to get close to the water now, Alice bent forward to make sure she'd really not seen anything. An image of herself, perhaps, beckoning her to oblivion?

She took another step back, thinking it prudent to leave this place, but reluctant to turn her back on the stream. When she did look up, ready to bolt, she caught her breath. Across the torrid creek, a man stood a far stone's throw away, too distant to have been what she saw in the water, but close enough for her to know he watched her. She returned his stare and hoped he, proud dressed in butternut, was too far away to see the tear tickling her cheek. For that reason alone she did not wipe it away. They stood, watching each other, until she broke eye contact and glanced down the length of him. He was tall and lean. Two dead rabbits were tied to his belt, and he held a rifle in his right hand. A hunter, a poacher, or the owner of this land, which her uncle, still to be heard talking to Jonathan Franklin some distance away, lusted for? If the latter, she was embarrassed this person overheard their conversation.

Momentarily, he raised his hand to his hat and tipped the cover in silent salute. She noted the braid of faded gold on his coat sleeve. A Confederate officer and, undoubtedly, the owner.

He turned his back and walked away.

"Alice?" Aunt Betty called.

"I'm here," she called over her shoulder and swiped at the errant tear. Except for her aunt, their party still milled about in the sunlit clearing where the road ended. For sure Betty Franklin was eager to escape her protesting sister-in-law. In that, Alice's search for brief solitude would find favor, though Alice was sure her aunt's gratitude would be overshadowed by a gentle admonishment. Aunt Betty worried over her niece's emotional frailty and feared, Alice knew, the nature of the solitude Alice sought.

Alice looked back across the stream, but the man had disappeared. There'd been another son, Alice knew. The older of the two brothers died in combat. This person—her gaze scoured the area—must have been the younger one…or a ghost.

"What…?"

Alice jumped at her aunt's voice, and Betty Franklin pulled her close. "I'm sorry, darling. I didn't mean to frighten you."

"You came up so quickly, that's all."

Her aunt glanced at the stream. "What are you doing over here, sweetness?"

"Exploring your new farm. It's nice here, don't you think?"

"Yes," Aunt Betty said, glancing first at the stream, then looping an arm through Alice's. "Is the water deep?" She guided Alice back toward the clearing.

"Not very, I don't think." Alice sneaked a last peek at the sparkling brook as she moved away. "Do you think the owner will give up his home?"

"Peter thinks he may have little choice, given the situation here."

Eli Calhoon stood his rifle against the fireplace and stretched. The fire was out, the chopped wood wet. He needed to cut more, anyway. Obviously, Doolan Mills wasn't coming back to work.

"And where have you been all morning?"

He managed a nonchalant pivot and faced her. Laura Ménier Calhoon Blackledge grew more beautiful every time he laid eyes on her, and he was laying eyes on her often of late.

"Hunting." His eyes raked her black-clad body. "I liked the way you were dressed earlier. I thought mourning was over?"

Pulling on the satin bow beneath her chin, she smiled and reached for the hat atop her golden tresses. "Not after only six days."

"And five nights, the last of which I spent with you."

"And I thought I'd spend tonight with you."

"So mourning is over."

"A respectable woman must keep up the pretense."

"How long are you planning it to last this time, Laura?"

"If I waited six months after Andy to wed Albert, I think I can weather the disgrace and wed you after five, don't you?"

"If I were of a mind to wed."

"Oh, you are, darling," she said.

Albert and pretense aside, she'd mourned Andy less than a week after they'd buried him. At the time Eli had justified the desecration of his brother's memory as duty to the wife, mutual need in the wake of shared grief. And Laura had, after all, been his until Andy had stolen her, all too willingly, away. To his credit, Eli had planned for them to wed before his furlough ended. Now he recalled his sleeping with Laura so soon after Andy's death with self-disgust. He didn't know how Laura remembered their impropriety, but he was pretty sure it wasn't with disgust.

"Do you mourn Albert at all?" he asked.

She tugged a glove off her slender fingers. "I was good to him until the end."

Not exactly what he'd asked. He pursed his lips, and Laura tossed the hat and gloves onto the battered table he'd pieced back together last month.

"He died happy, Eli."

"Fond memories from healthier times?"

Gracefully, she raised her arms and began extracting the pins that held her flaxen tresses in place.

"You think I can't make a bedridden man happy, darling?" she said, finger-combing her curls. "I missed you this morning."

"I had to get some things done early."

"Early?" She laughed. "You left in the middle of the night."

"Couldn't sleep."

She smiled, then spun, arms wide to take in the house. "Well, you shouldn't have that problem here…with me to comfort you."

Only because he wasn't going to allow "here" to become a habit.

"Comfort isn't what I want from you Laura."

Gazing at him now through half-closed lids, the smile still plastered on her lips, she draped a golden lock over her shoulder and reached for the high collar of her dress. "Do tell."

He stepped to her, and her smile blossomed.

"You look good in black," he said.

"You told me that years ago, remember?"

Yes, he remembered.

She had her top two buttons undone, and his groin tightened.

"Not many women look as good in mourning as you do, and

I see women in mourning no matter which direction I look these days. Personally speaking, there's one I'd very much like to get out of black crepe."

She giggled and stepped back when he reached for her. Button number three, then four. "Would she happen to be tall and blonde?"

"Petite, and I believe her hair is dark red. Auburn, I think you'd call it." He was on her, crushing her back against the wall and pressing his hardness against her pelvis.

She pushed him. "Who?"

Eli covered her lips with his and forced his tongue inside. Heat seeped between his legs. Laura twisted her head. "You bastard, let me go."

"Tell me this, *darling*—understanding I already know the answer—can a bedridden man make you happy?"

Her struggle stopped, and he dipped his head to suckle her neck. Docile now, she lifted her chin to give him easy access.

"There is no petite redhead, is there?"

He chuckled and reached for her skirt, drawing it up in the front and pushing her pantaloons down.

"Please, Eli, I want—"

He swallowed her words with another kiss, then said, "I know what you want, and there'll be plenty of time after. Right now I want you."

She arched back when he stroked her, rolling her head, eyes shut, against the wall. "I passed Aunt Naomi on the way in… Oh God," she said and opened her legs wider. "That feels good, Eli."

He reached for the top button on his britches. "And did she speak?"

"She gave me a look fit to kill, but didn't say a word." Laura placed her hands on his shoulders and moved her pelvis against his invading fingers. "She's yet to offer a word of sympathy for Albert's death."

Laura was having trouble talking and breathing at the same time. She really should shut up.

Again he shifted his weight and braced so that he held her

firmly against the wall. "She's mad at me for taking my rabbits to Elvie to cook."

Laura moaned, at the same time trying, as best she could in yards of crepe, to circle her legs around him. "Some things never change, do they?"

"Yes," he said hoarsely. With his exploring hand, he pushed her thighs wider beneath the voluminous skirt and petticoats. "Things get worse." He gritted his teeth with his thrust, and she cried out. "But some things do get better." Even if they last only a moment.

He buried his face against her throat and rocked against her, leaving her panting, her nails clawing his shoulders. He grunted when he climaxed and pulled out of her, spilling his seed against her thigh.

"You didn't have to do that," she said, distaste permeating each word. "Finding myself in the family way is no longer a problem."

He breathed out, then relaxed while the last wave of pleasure eased through his body. Sated, he wrapped his arms around her shoulders, rendering her helpless in his hold, and looked her in the eye.

"Petite and redheaded. She is, I do believe, a Yankee."

Chapter Two

"**Y**ou say things like that because you're still angry with me."

Laura's back was to him, her lovely derrière snug against his thigh beneath the quilt. He rubbed his forehead with the heel of his hand. "Laura," he said, "I've had you twice in as many hours, and fulfilled your most wicked desires. I am at this moment quite content. In no way am I angry with you."

"And I can continue to keep you content," she said, rolling over so she could see him.

There was all manner of contentment. "No, you can't."

She sat up. "You're being impossible."

"I've enjoyed the day, darlin', and I know you have, too. I see no reason why, if you should desire it, our relationship cannot continue as is."

"Well, it can't. I'm not the town whore." With a provocative glint in her eye, she flattened her palm on his chest, then began to swirl an index finger through his chest hair. "We don't have to wait five months."

"My, my, what would the congregation say?"

"Not nearly as much as they'll say if they find out about our present liaison. You know I can't afford the risk."

"So the answer is you don't wish to continue our relationship."

She stopped the motion of her finger. "I want us to marry immediately."

"I've told you, Laura, I'm not gonna marry you."

She stared at him momentarily, then laid her head on his breast and pressed closer. "I'm sorry you were hurt, but I did what I had to do. Stop punishing me."

"What I'm doing is enjoying you. My desire to wed you ended in the fall of '62 when I accepted what a fickle, selfish woman you are."

"I don't believe you."

"You should."

She raised her head, and his gaze found hers. "Look at it from my point of view," she said. "Andrew was dead—"

"You see, you should have married me when you first said you would. You wouldn't be a widow today."

She squirmed closer, and he felt her head on his shoulder. They'd napped for a bit. The afternoon waned, and the house was growing cold. He still hadn't chopped any firewood.

"We were so young," she said.

"And Andrew was heir to Camellia Creek."

"My father wanted me to marry Andrew."

"Because he was heir to Camellia Creek. But," he continued, purposely inserting an amused lilt to his words, "more importantly, you liked the idea of being mistress of Camellia Creek."

"And I will be, because that's what you—"

"Which brings us to poor, recently departed Albert."

"He had a railroad, Eli."

"You refused to marry me after Andy was killed."

"For the love of heaven, your brother had been dead less than three weeks."

"So you waited six months and wed Blackledge."

"You could have been dead within that length of time."

"Then you could have still married Blackledge."

"He was..."

"More solvent," Eli finished for her. Eli's father had sunk a lot of money into the Confederacy, leaving Camellia Creek little to fall back on as the war strained resources. "The farm's destitute and there's little prospect for improvement in the near term. Even if I married you now, you might not be mistress of Camellia Creek for long."

Again she raised her head. "You see, you do understand. My father was sick. A woman has to look out for herself."

"Oh, I figured that all out one rainy afternoon in a man-made ditch in Tennessee when Paul Phelps returned from furlough and told me he'd danced at your wedding." Eli smirked. "I had a minié ball in my side. Not life-threatening if you don't count the blood loss, but it sure hurt like hell once the numbness wore off."

She found the scar with fingers that Eli just recently realized had become quite adept.

"I'm sorry," she said.

Yes, she probably was, but she would forget her sorrow as soon as the omission favored her.

"And how's that railroad you jilted me for?"

She glared at him, then laughed when he smiled.

"Ah," he said, "the misfortunes of war."

Gently, she touched his breast. "You know, Albert never swore allegiance to the Confederacy."

Good for him.

"I believe if I knew how to go about it, I might be able to make a claim to the Federals for that railroad." Laura rubbed the back of her thumb over his nipple, and he moved, forcing her up. Thank goodness he'd killed dinner earlier, else he'd be too worn out to scrounge any up. If his good fortune held, Elvie had fried those rabbits and brought his portion to the cookhouse.

"We could marry," she said. Beneath the covers, she drew her knees up. "You'd get the railroad. What do you think?"

He tossed back the quilt and brought his legs over the side of the bed, then reached for his britches before looking over his shoulder at her. "Darlin', you are delusional. I most assuredly did swear an oath of allegiance to the Confederacy."

"Now you'll swear one to the United States."

Eli stood to pull up his pants. "There's not enough left of the United States my fathers forged to swear allegiance to."

"Of course there is. You must—"

"It's not going to be that simple."

"But we've got a new constitution and an elected legislature—"

"And a governor the President hasn't pardoned yet. Toss me my shirt."

"But he—"

"Johnson has serious problems and a corrupt, vindictive Congress containing too many radical Republicans opposed to him." He took the shirt she offered and pulled it over his head. "This isn't over yet, Laura, not by a long shot."

He stuffed his cotton undershirt into the waistband of his pants, then sat back on the bed to put on a dirty sock. "What you need to do, sweetheart, in addition to getting out of bed so we can eat, is find yourself one of those Federals."

Yep, you are exactly what one of those bastards deserves.

"Hear tell you're sellin' off land," Dilbert Bowen said to Eli after shaking Hiram Cleaver's hand. Hiram retook his seat and Eli motioned Dilbert onto the settee beside Wayne Hale, who'd already reclaimed his perch. Eli hoped the couch held the both of 'em. He'd fashioned a replacement leg for the thing just last week. So far it was sitting level.

"I recently sold Peter Franklin a hundred and fifty acres of bottomland. You know him, a Northerner. He and his family moved into the Stanchion place late summer."

"I know about 'em," Hiram said. "Emma worked for 'em when they first got here. The missus said she couldn't find reliable help, but my Emma says Mrs. Franklin didn't want darkies working in her house. Thinks she's warmed to 'em a little bit now."

"Hmm...," Dilbert said. "I hear her daughter don't share in that dislike."

"Abolitionist?" Wayne asked.

"Despite their 'rhe-tor-ic'," Hiram enunciated, "there's plenty of *them* don't like the Negro."

"Ain't that simple," Dilbert said. "Rumor has it the daughter likes them Nigra soldiers."

Eli frowned. "Who'd you hear that from?"

"Doolan Mills. One of them bastards he was rollin' dice with up in Vicksburg told 'im that a lieutenant in the Louisiana Loyal Guard claims he diddled 'er on the boat south." Dilbert looked to the floor on the other side of Wayne. "Push that homebrew my way, will ya?"

Wayne shoved the clay jug toward Dilbert. "Rubbin' our noses in it lyin' with a white woman," Wayne said, "then braggin' about it."

"They're talking amongst themselves," Eli said, "and she sure isn't the first white woman to sleep willingly with a Negro man."

"Whores and prostitutes," Wayne said.

Dilbert handed the jug to Eli and rose. "Doolan was talkin' to me, son," he said to Eli, then made his way to the fireplace into which he spat tobacco. Smoke hissed in consonance with the sparks that shot up the chimney.

Eli was on the verge of concluding that Doolan was turning out to be a problem. He took a swig of the corn whiskey, not his first of the evening. Wayne had brought it, and good God it was bad.

"Can't understand why a white woman would do that," Hiram said.

Dilbert retook his seat. "Curiosity, I reckon."

"Curiosity about what?" Wayne asked, and if the look on his face meant anything, the man's question was honest.

"Performance," Eli answered.

Wayne twisted his head Eli's direction. "You always were a smart-ass, Eli."

He shrugged. "Some women enjoy sex, too."

"Only whores enjoy sex. That's why they're whores, and they can damn well enjoy it with their own kind."

Eli studied him a moment, then said, "That's a real peculiar notion you have regarding women and sex."

Wayne started to say something, but Hiram chuckled. "Yeah, I don't think that's right either, Wayne, but I do agree with you they should be whorin' with their own kind."

"Whether they do or they don't," Dilbert said, "I know them blue-butted hypocrites well enough to tell ya that kinda behavior ain't gonna be no more acceptable to them up there than it is to us down here."

"Maybe less so," Eli said. "And from what I've seen of Peter Franklin, if his daughter is sleeping with any man out of wedlock, I think he'd be bothered."

"Franklin made it to first sergeant with the 72nd Illinois," Hiram added. "He's likely to up and shoot the bastard, if the fool don't keep his mouth shut."

"Needs to shoot the damn woman," Wayne said.

"Well, we know *he* could get away with shootin' the nigger," Dilbert said, retaking his seat. "Any one of us would be hanged."

"He'd get away with shootin' the woman as far as I'm concerned," Wayne said.

Eli took one more swallow of the whiskey before passing the jug to Hiram. "How's May, Wayne?"

The man snorted.

"Emma says she's been feelin' poorly." Hiram passed the jug on to Wayne without imbibing.

"She's better," Wayne said and looked at Eli. "Brim back?"

"Nope."

"I could sure use my mule."

"He oughtn't have done that, Eli," Dilbert said, "run off with Wayne's mule."

"Not like that boy to do such a thing," Hiram said. "Not like him one bit.

"Dammit," Dilbert said, "we don't know what any of 'em is liable to up and do anymore." He looked at Eli, and Eli grimaced. They were all three looking at him.

"I haven't seen him since I got back," he said, and his gaze rested on Wayne. "And I have no idea why he did what he did. You'd know the answer to that better'n anybody, Wayne. But when he comes home, I'll ask him."

Wayne studied him a moment, then pursed his lips. "Figured he'd already be back now that you're home." Wayne looked away. "Might mean he ain't comin' back."

"Ain't no tellin'," Hiram said, "what with the freedmen believin' everything not yet burned or stolen is gonna be divided among 'em come Christmas."

"That's them colored soldiers fillin' their heads with that," Dilbert said. "Need to get 'em out of this state."

"Or outa them blue uniforms," Hiram said.

Eli focused on Hiram. "Which one's Franklin's daughter?"

"The frizzy-haired blonde with the gap between her two front teeth."

Eli hadn't seen any of 'em close enough to detect a gap, but he was relieved the woman of interest wasn't the petite redhead. "Got any gossip to spread on the dark-headed one?"

"Nothing untoward, if that's what you mean. Emma said she was quiet, standoffish. Emma wondered about her some. Said her aunt was always worrying after her like she weren't right. The daughter appeared not to have a care in the world. A bit spoiled, Emma thought, but well-mannered. Both girls were always polite to her.

"Anyways, the niece's daddy was Mrs. Franklin's brother. Him and his two boys died in the war. The daddy was a widower. That's how the girl come to be with the Franklins."

"Husband?"

Hiram shook his head. "Don't think she was ever wed, Eli."

"Abolitionist?" he asked.

"I don't think Franklin and his womenfolk so much, don't know about the niece, the Shelton girl, but Emma would come home madder'n a cat dipped in coal oil on account of that widow woman, Franklin's sister-in-law. Apparently she's one of them self-righteous types who tries to compete with Stowe in her degree of ignorance and hate mongering."

"What's she doin' with 'em?" Dilbert asked.

"She was married to Franklin's brother," Eli said. He knew that much from Franklin. "The younger man is her son and Peter Franklin's nephew. Franklin has no sons of his own, so he's more or less adopted his nephew."

"Well then," Hiram said, "that makes sense."

"What makes sense?" Eli asked.

"Emma kinda got the feelin' Franklin was pushing a union between his nephew and his wife's niece."

"I've heard that," Eli said. "The girl's about to come into a fortune."

Wayne snorted. "Well, now it really do make sense, don't it? Where'd you hear that, Eli?"

"In a place where a lady's name should not be mentioned."

Hiram guffawed, and Wayne straightened in his chair. "And where would that be?"

Dilbert said, "Do we care?"

Eli cared plenty, and the fact Jon Franklin was mentioning his supposed intended, and her worth, in a whorehouse implied a fissure—and shoot, significant fortunes were hard to come by.

"What do you think of the menfolk?" Hiram asked Eli.

Jackasses, but Jon Franklin was more than an ass, and his being more made him something less in the "decent human" department. "Peter Franklin thinks he's gonna improve productivity over and beyond what we've been doing for the past century and a half. He's trying to draw his nephew into the venture, but my impression is that the younger Franklin's not interested."

"Yeah, they know so damn much," Hiram said, his voice bitter. "Their attitude is Southerners don't deserve the South, and it will be better in their hands."

Dilbert grinned. "You sold Franklin that bottom patch north of the creek?"

"Yep." Eli hadn't missed the gleam in Dilbert's old eyes. "I told him it was about cottoned out. Told him he should go with corn. Didn't seem to disturb him any. He's after the house."

"Your house?" Hiram asked.

Eli glanced at him, then turned back to Dilbert, who was watching him with knowing eyes. Significant fortunes and fair turnarounds. "Yep."

"Nice place your granddaddy picked, but for the threat of flood."

Dilbert reached for the earthenware jug. "How you feel about them wantin' it, son?"

Eli tightened his lips. Dilbert's hand was on the jug, but he didn't move to drink.

"As is, the house has never flooded, but I'll open that hollow to the Mississippi myself," Eli said, "before I'll let a Northerner take my family home."

Dilbert gave him a satisfied nod and raised the jug. Hiram grunted. "Wait till they move in, then open it."

Wayne blew out what sounded like a breath of disgust. "You may not have to give the place to the river if you can hold out. Don't know what he thinks he's gonna raise, but that fool is liable to fall flat on his face with any crop if he don't come up with some labor."

Wayne Hale locked his tired gaze on Eli. Hale looked older than his years. War and worry had drained him. Once he'd been handsome, and by most accounts, gallant. He was brave in battle, but Eli was beginning to suspect other faults, things that had nothing to do with bravery or honesty or loyalty, but disturbing nonetheless. Nothing, however, that kept Eli from asking him here tonight.

"And that brings me back to Brim Solomon," Wayne continued. "Your hand contracted with me to help gather my fall crop, then start clearing the fields for planting after Christmas."

Eli rubbed his temples. His head hurt. For a full month, Doolan Mills had done a half-assed job for him, then disappeared with his first pay. But it was more than Eli needing Brim home, he *wanted* him home. If he'd taken Wayne's mule, he had a good reason, and Eli was curious to know what that reason was.

"Brim's not my hand anymore."

"I know it." Wayne leaned against the back of the settee and closed his eyes. "I was makin' a point. If we don't get some crops in the field and somebody workin' 'em, we're all gonna starve, freedmen included."

"I think they'll come to realize that in a year or two."

They had finally, albeit indirectly, broached the reason he'd drawn them here to begin with. Briefly, his gaze passed over each face, mostly aged and all tired, worried. Each was a veteran of the Confederacy, tried and true. He and Wayne Hale, fourteen years Eli's senior at forty-two, had volunteered at the start of hostilities.

Dilbert and Hiram, now both pushing sixty, though they looked well into their seventies, had never floundered when conscripted. By that time, Grant and Sherman had ravaged the south central and western part of the state, and Vicksburg had fallen. For them all, it had become fight or die. Well, they'd fought, but hadn't died, not yet. But the fight wasn't over.

"In the meantime," Eli said, "I say we generate some income."

Chapter Three

Dilbert caught Eli's eye. "How?" the older man asked for them all.

"Cotton, gentlemen."

Dilbert leaned forward on the settee. "You ain't talkin' about plantin' it, are you?" Wayne narrowed his gaze on Dilbert before looking at Eli.

"Indeed I'm not," Eli said and smiled at Wayne. "I'm talking about cotton that's already been picked, ginned, and baled. I'm talking about taking our cotton back from the people who have stolen it from us."

Hiram made a sibilant sound. "I don't know, Eli. We don't need more trouble with the Federals."

"All we got is trouble with the Federals," Dilbert said softly.

"Yeah, but—"

"I'm not talking about stealing from the Federal cotton stores, Hiram. I'm talking about stealing from those bastards robbing their own government."

"Dammit, Eli, one of them Treasury agents was kilt a few weeks ago. You can bet them blue bellies are lookin' for a Southerner to blame."

"Well," Wayne said, "did a Southerner do it?"

Each man looked at another, then to the next. The other three finally rested their eyes on Eli.

"I didn't kill him," he said.

"Me neither," Wayne said, "and I'd tell you if I had."

"Listen," Eli said, "they're killin' one another. Some of these agents and a company's worth of the Yankee officers left in this state are dallying in the cotton market. Confiscated Confederate government cotton isn't in the hands of the Federal government. It's in the hands of crooked Federal agents."

"Hell, it ain't only Confederate government cotton they're takin'. Lowell Henderson's cotton was taken last month—"

"Yeah," Hiram interrupted Dilbert, "but Lowell's going to get his back."

Wayne sat forward so fast the settee's bum leg scraped loudly on the wood floor. "And all the slave owners are gonna be compensated for their niggers. Only way Lowell will see any recompense for what was taken is if he can prove he never had any dealings with the Confederate government. Which,"—Wayne nodded his head emphatically—"he couldn't even if he never had, which he did. Routinely."

Dilbert sighed. "We all did. It was our government, same as the Federal government was theirs. Nobody's questioning them."

Eli laughed, honestly amused. "That's 'cause they backed the winning side."

Wayne leaned back in his chair. "Always the smart-ass, Eli."

"I'm a realist."

"Bullshit," Dilbert said. "You're still clingin', son."

"Maybe so, but I *realize* when reality kicks me in the butt. The point I was trying to make when I suggested stealing cotton, Hiram made for me when he mentioned that murdered agent. These people are greedy. No Southerner killed that man, one of his cohorts did it."

"That or he was honest, and he was about to turn the thieves in," Dilbert said.

Eli nodded. "That's possible, too. But what I'm trying to get across is if they're dealing with stolen cotton, that cotton, in the eyes of the Federal government, doesn't exist, does it? The thieves can't exactly call out the dogs on us, can they?"

"Depends on how many of those 'dogs' are involved," Hiram said.

"You're right." Eli blew out a breath. Dilbert extended him the jug, but he waved it away. "I'm offering this ploy under the assumption that though dishonesty is running rampant among the Yankee officers and Treasury agents assigned to this state, the majority are still honest, at least to one another's face."

"I'm for considerin' it," Dilbert said.

Hiram rubbed the back of his neck. "Do you know where they're stashin' it?"

"The old Fletcher warehouse west of town."

Dilbert nodded. "Off the Rodney Road?"

"Yes. Federal agents stockpile cotton there, daily, it seems of late. Every fortnight they move it to Jackson's landing over that old road that led to the mill. Riverboat meets 'em. The *Lucky Lilly*. They load the cotton, and she heads south." Eli breathed in. "Two weeks later she's back."

"They do this at night?" Wayne asked.

"Start before midnight."

"You've seen 'em?"

"That's how I know about it. Been watching their antics since shortly after I got back."

"Coon huntin'?" Dilbert piped out.

"Trouble sleeping. The nights have gotten too quiet here at Camellia Creek."

"Just tryin' to rile you, boy."

"I'm about riled out."

"Yeah," Hiram said, "sounds like it, you wantin' to raid a Union warehouse full of contraband and all."

"Said I was 'riled out,' not ready to curl up and die. Anyways, didn't take me long to figure out they were moving illegal con-signments of cotton."

"How do ya know they're storing it in Fletcher's warehouse?"

"Hiram, dammit, I followed the empty wagons back to town that first night."

Wayne was studying him as if he didn't quite believe him, but Eli didn't care. He had indeed skulked about in the dead of night searching for opportunity. "I've watched what happens at that warehouse during the day, too." Eli glanced at the men. He had their attention. "It's nigh stocked again. We can take that cotton, friends."

"It would be a onetime shot," Wayne said, reaching for the jug.

Dilbert rubbed his unshaved chin. "How many wagons?"

"Four big army wagons, but they make two runs starting about midnight till right before dawn."

"How many men?"

"The four drivers and two shotguns, one each on the lead and rear wagons."

"Soldiers?"

Eli frowned. "Soldiers and civilian. I think the civilian are Treasury."

"Means some of Wood's officers are involved for sure, if not Wood hisself."

"Yep," Eli said. Hiram was anxious about this, Eli knew, but he was coming around, else he'd have left before he heard too much. Eli looked at Dilbert. "We'll need Jake and Ben"—then let his gaze slip to Hiram—"and Adam. What do you think, they're your boys?"

Dilbert nodded. "They've been baptized under fire. I know they'll be game."

"I'll think about bringing Adam in, Eli. This ain't easy for me. I was damn happy he made it through the war."

Wayne set the jug down, frowned, then drummed his fingers on the table.

"How many men stay behind at the warehouse?" Hiram asked.

"Two."

Wayne smiled. "Checked this out pretty good, haven't you?"

"I—"

"What do you think the men on the *Lucky Lilly* will do if the wagons don't show up?" Hiram asked.

"I know what I'd do," Wayne said. He shifted in his seat to get a better bead on Hiram. "I'd assume my cohorts had been caught and haul my ass away from Jackson's landing before the troops showed up."

Eli nodded in agreement.

Hiram shook his head and smiled. "Well, hell, I say we take them wagons before they get as far as Lake Elizabeth. I'm sleepin' on Adam, though." He looked Eli in the eye. "Where you plannin' on puttin' the stuff?"

"Old Ferris plantation house west of me. Growth has retaken it. No one but us locals know about it. Then we go back and…"

Eli was watching Hiram, who had refocused his attention over Eli's shoulder to something in the dining room. Dilbert looked behind him, as did Wayne. Eli turned around as the other men stood. Then he started up, too, as Laura, dressed in a blue wool coat, stepped up behind him. She had her hand on his shoulder and was guiding him back into his seat before he was full on his feet.

"Don't get up, and please, gentlemen, do be seated. I didn't mean to interrupt. I simply stopped by to see Eli."

With that, she smiled, a bit too suggestively, and Eli flexed his jaw.

"My goodness, Wayne, how is May doing? I saw her in Port Gibson a few days ago. She looked a bit peaked. Said she fell."

"Off the back porch, but she's gettin' around better now, thank you."

Laura waved a hand at the three men. "Please, do resume your business. Mine can wait. Hiram, I haven't seen you in months, I swear."

Eli rolled his eyes.

"How's Emma and the kids? Y'all making it all right with the present unpleasantness?"

Present unpleasantness Eli's ass, and what was she doing here now? Well hell, he already knew the answer to that, but more importantly, how much had she overheard? And her being a daughter of the Old South, did it really matter?"

"They're well, but things are tough, Miss Laura."

"Oh, I do so know," she said and placed a hand over her heart.

Hiram cleared his throat. "I was sorry to hear about your mister. How're you makin' out?"

"Why, thank you for asking, kind sir." She squeezed Eli's shoulder. "I'm finding comfort with my family."

The only family she had left was him, if one considered an ex-brother-in-law family, and they all knew it. He reached up and covered the slender fingers kneading his shoulder.

"Laura, darlin'," he said sweetly, "could you make us some of that awful coffee. We're about done here." He looked up and winked. "Then we can discuss whatever your business might be."

Her reciprocating smile could have been less obvious. The other men would have caught her innuendo, but then, he suspected she meant for them to. All four males rose again when she left, then retook their seats, except for Eli who remained standing until he was sure the back door had closed behind her and she was on the breezeway.

"Albert Blackledge lost everything when Sherman took Meridian," Hiram said.

Dilbert reached for the jug. "I think he really lost *everything* when that marauder ripped out miles of track south of Jackson."

Wayne snickered. "You might say he'd already given up everything when he married sweet Laura."

Dilbert glanced at Eli, who was retaking his seat. "Better to Laura than Sherman," the older man said.

"So," Wayne said, "Laura lost the railroad to Sherman."

"That's what she tells me." Eli was ready to get off the subject of Laura and wondered if any of these men would ask what each knew better than to bring up.

"She part of this cotton thing?" Wayne asked.

"She knows nothing."

"Might want to keep it that way."

"I intend to, Hiram."

"Women talk. Women get angry."

Eli rubbed his temples.

"And…" Dilbert's voice, but he didn't continue.

Eli looked at him. "And what?"

A grin spread across Dilbert's face. "And it appears keepin' things a secret ain't too important to Laura these days."

"I'm thinking she's putting her stock in the power of public expectations," Eli said. "Are we agreed on the cotton?"

"What are we going to do with the men we're taking it from?" Hiram asked.

"Need to kill 'em," Wayne answered.

"For sure that would shut 'em up for good."

Hiram made a sibilant sound. "Dilbert, I—"

"We can't make any noise," Wayne said, and he looked at Eli as if seeking agreement. "We've got to make sure they don't get a shot off, so we're going to have to knife 'em."

This time, Hiram blew out a breath and rose.

Dilbert shook his head. "I can shoot 'em, but I ain't no good with a knife."

"And in case you two haven't noticed"—Hiram glanced at Wayne then settled his gaze on Eli—"me and Dilbert ain't young men anymore."

"Your boys are young," Wayne said.

"Adam ain't—"

"Hiram, sit down," Eli said. "Killing 'em would be stupid unless we think we'll have time to hide their carcasses where they'll never be found. The Federals can make a case with a bunch of their men dead. If the men are alive, however, said men can't say anything, not to the authorities anyway. Theoretically, we can assume proper authority won't even know what has happened. What we need to do is incapacitate the bastards and keep them out of the way six hours. That's all."

Dilbert snickered. "That's all?"

Chapter Four

Headquarters, Department of Mississippi Southwest, Vicksburg, Mississippi, November 1865

Seth Parker hadn't made it inside the citadel the first week of July 1863 when the Gibraltar of the Confederacy had fallen to Grant, but he was here now. He was sure things must have improved since then. For certain, some of the people were friendlier. He hadn't come across even one, as a matter of fact, who was out and out unfriendly, and no one was lobbing cannon balls or grapeshot at him.

And there were a lot of blue uniforms, most covering black skin.

He glanced at the Negro private, sitting at the desk outside the office, he'd been told, of Colonel Malcolm Byrnes, United States Army. This young man looked sharp enough, but the two privates who'd rendered him a rifle salute as he entered the building were scruffy. Scruffy soldiers were the norm, and skin color made no difference.

The soldier rose, glanced at Seth's uniform, then rendered him a hesitant salute as if not sure he should. Seth returned the greeting and passed him papers. "Major Seth Parker, United States Marines. I've been assigned to Colonel Byrnes."

"I was wonderin'…"

Seth grinned. "I noticed. Is the colonel in?"

"Is he expectin' you, suh?"

"Yes, but I'm early, Private…?"

"Taylor, suh, Private Taylor." He smiled with a gentle shake of his head. "An' da colonel, he's been a might cantak'ris this mawnin'."

"Unless he's given you specific instructions he's not to be disturbed, I'm confident he'll want to see me."

"He did tell me to leave 'im alone." Taylor glanced at the closed door. "But he says dat to me every mawnin'." With that, Taylor approached the door and knocked, while Seth squelched the urge to overtake the man and burst through the door on his own. Instead, he followed close behind, hoping Malcolm's desk was situated so the man would see him at the door.

The private made no move toward the doorknob. Impatient, Seth grabbed it and pushed the door wide with the gruff "What?" from inside.

Private Taylor started to speak when Malcolm Byrnes looked up, grinned, then tossed his pen onto the desk top.

"Get your sorry ass in here."

Beside him, Seth sensed the private stiffen. He patted the man on the shoulder and stepped around him. "He's talking to me, Taylor."

The man drew in a relieved breath, nodded, and slid out of the way. Malcolm was already up, moving around his desk, hand outstretched. "Hell, you look fit. Army's taking good care of you?"

Seth snorted. "Only since the Navy abandoned me to it last month."

Malcolm laughed. Seth pushed the door shut and grasped his senior's hand.

"Welcome back to Mississippi."

"I saw all of Mississippi I wanted to see two years ago."

"You'll find things a little better."

The room was large. Judging by the faded sign outside, the building had once been an apothecary, this back room probably the owner's office. A cool breeze passed through a partially opened window and fanned the pull of a yellowed window shade.

"I came through Meridian and Jackson. Calmer might be a more appropriate description than better."

The painted floorboards groaned when Malcolm turned and started back to his desk. The man was shorter than Seth by a head. In the two years since Seth had last seen him, he'd developed a bit of a paunch and added a lot of gray to his dark hair. "There was a war on, Seth."

"I remember. Nothing like putting Clausewitz to the test and seeing how it all pans out."

"Yeah, well, it worked."

With the finesse of a butcher who believed himself a surgeon, but Seth said only, "I guess it did."

Malcolm released an audible sigh. "Their grand strategy cost them the war."

"Their lack of a navy cost them the war."

Ah, there was Malcolm's relaxed smile. Seth's teasing prick, though spoken in truth—a navy would have helped that grand strategy—had lightened the mood, and he determined to keep it there. The United States Army was drunk on victory and power. He needed to remember that.

"You think that's all it would have taken?"

Seth grinned. "Not a doubt in my mind."

Malcolm snorted. "Sit."

Seth walked to the chair indicated in front of the desk, but waited to take his seat until Malcolm had done so. Situating himself comfortably, he smoothed his hand along the worn leather arm of his chair. "You're a bit off post."

"Only a couple of blocks. I'm heading a new special office under internal affairs. General needed to find me space fast."

"Confiscated?"

"Abandoned. 'Confiscation' was my means for getting you here."

Seth was a little bitter about that. He looked up to find his military senior, a friend, watching him from behind half-closed lids. He was equally annoyed and flattered. "I could have gone home, you know. Daddy could use the help. I was torn between resigning my commission and accepting these orders."

"I thank you for coming."

"My application to Treasury was denied. It's my understanding General Slocum was behind it."

"Most assuredly." Malcolm sat straight and rubbed the back of his neck. "Look, I know you're angry over my intervention. I honestly had nothing to do with pulling your application to Treasury. It was the general's prerogative. I requested you, and I sent that request up the chain. Personally I didn't care if you came as a Treasury agent or as a mid-grade officer, but Slocum preferred a military officer. His relief, General Wood, concurs."

Seth purposefully kept his expression blank, and Malcolm breathed in. "Slocum was aware of your record, now Wood is. For both Slocum and Wood, military discipline is the problem. Treasury agents are a bit too autonomous."

"There are a lot of colored troops outside. Are they the problem?"

Malcolm opened his eyes wide with what Seth knew to be faux shock. "They are a problem, yes, but not the problem that brought you here. The coloreds you see are Native Guards, ex-slaves. Locals. They're a bad influence on the freedmen, telling them not to work on their old farms and that the government is going to take care of them. They're undermining the labor force, and the South isn't going to get back on its feet without a lot of hard work from everybody."

"You've got white officers, why would you need me?"

"Because those white officers are the problem." Malcolm shot him a walleyed glance. "Too many of them, along with Treasury agents, are reaping the spoils of war."

"Confiscated cotton?"

Malcolm nodded. "So, you're aware?"

"It's a problem throughout the occupied states."

"But here the ante's been upped. A Treasury agent was murdered last month east of Port Gibson, other side of the Hinds County line. The man was the nephew of a wealthy Republican contributor out of New York. Washington has its own turmoil and intrigue. Powers that be are making an issue of this."

"A potential 'policy' issue," Seth said.

Malcolm looked across at him. "I want the murder solved, so we can get on with putting this war behind us."

This war wasn't going to be behind them for a long, long time, and if Seth gave any credence to half of what his father feared, it never would.

"You know security and discipline," Malcolm continued. "You know cotton markets, and I know you'll make an effort to use the colored troops for something other than a means of irritating Southern whites. Your second will be a Negro captain…"

Seth frowned, and Malcolm held up a hand.

"In this particular case you can trust him more than you could a white junior officer, and after you've served in this mess, you ought to be a top pick for Treasury."

"Or I'll be so rich I'll never have to work again."

The colonel's lips tightened. "Be as sarcastic as you want, *Major* Parker, but I trust you. Trusted you with my life, in fact, and was rewarded."

Well hardly, as Seth's saving Malcolm Byrne's life had been inadvertent. The trust had come after.

Malcolm raised an inexorable index finger, as Seth had seen him do a hundred times, and pointed it at him. "I know you won't let me, General Wood, the Marines, or your country down. The very fact you're sitting across from me right now, you horse's ass, proves that."

"Southerner kill the agent?"

"Washington would love to think so, but I'm not sure, and the only men I have to investigate the killing could very well be the ones who committed the crime, and if the killer is an army officer or two, I know you'll enjoy arresting them.

"The agent was killed on the Natchez Trace between Clinton and Port Gibson. He'd been working in the Hinds and Madison County area, but he boarded in Port Gibson. That was a good central location for him, giving him access to the Jackson area and easy access to the river at Rodney. From there he had a quicker route south to Natchez and north to here. I don't know what the man was up to when he was killed. Don't know if he was involved with thievery, trying to circumvent thievery, or was just an innocent bystander in something unrelated. All I know for sure is that in addition to being a U.S. agent he was important to that Republican crony and now they're screaming for someone to blame his death on, preferably a Southerner.

"There's a whorehouse in Rodney. Just about the only business left there. It's an impressive establishment, and of late it caters to a number of Wood's officers. Guthrie was known to visit. My gut tells me that charming den of iniquity might very well be the place where a great deal of illegal activity is hatched."

"Is the proprietor—"

"Proprietress, and in answer to your unfinished question, I don't know, but I suspect she knows something, even if she's not directly involved. Seth, this woman has been around a long time. She has Whig contacts going back to the '30s and they range from one end of the Mississippi to the other. She knows powerful people, dangerous people."

"The '30s? How old is she?"

"She's in her fifties, but doesn't look it. She is a mature beauty."

Seth narrowed his eyes. "You know her?"

Malcolm grinned. "I've met her, and from that, you may construe that I've been inside the establishment. Reconnoitering the places where my men spend their free time, you know?" The grin had disappeared, and Malcolm leaned back in his chair. "I speak the truth. I don't think she rents herself out often, not anymore certainly. Don't know if she ever did. She was the mistress of a very wealthy planter. He died years ago. There's one daughter. Don't know much about her, but she's a war widow, and she lives on what is left of her late husband's estate in Madison County. I've never seen her."

"The proprietress' name?"

"Isabel Leigh Hays. Her house is called The Pink Lady. Can't miss it. You can see it from the river. Her clientele refer to it as The Pink Pussy."

"I feel better about this assignment already."

"Be careful in dealing with 'Madam' Hays. She's smart, savvy, and I believe, no stranger to dangerous situations. The truth is I don't know that those whore-mongering soldiers who loll around her girls don't give away more than they get."

"And my detail?"

"Captain Jubal Summers is your second in command. He joined the 20th Infantry in New York, but left when his enlistment was up. Came down to join the fray in '63—he has a free-born aunt in Warrenton. He's a member of the 53rd Colored Infantry Regiment. He's literate, articulate, and dedicated.

"Per my instruction, he provided me names of twenty-five coloreds who he thought would serve you well. I weeded out ten. That leaves fifteen from which you and he can sit down and choose eight. In addition to you and Summers, that gives you a troop of ten. Don't dally."

Malcolm rose and Seth did, too.

"When do I meet him?"

"You're two days early, but we should find him in the Negro barracks. I've commandeered quarters for all of you at the Port Gibson Hotel. Best spot in town. The owner has managed to make it somewhat accommodating. Port Gibson still stands, but it's lacking some creature comforts."

"We payin' for the hotel?"

"You mean are you paying?"

"I mean is the United States Government paying?"

Malcolm's eyes hardened, as well they should have because Seth's challenge was there. "Like I said, I commandeered."

"I want to know where I stand in the eyes of the local populace, Malcolm."

"You stand as an unconditional conqueror."

Seth laughed, not pleasantly. "We stand as royal, arrogant bastards who have already shredded the Constitution to bits."

Malcolm dropped his eyes and reached for his pipe, lying in a tray on his desk. "You sound like you might believe that yourself," he said softly.

"I want a voucher."

"You'll have one for your meals," Malcolm said agreeably and knocked the tobacco from his pipe bowl into his hand.

"And for the rooms, Malcolm."

This time the man's hard gaze met his eyes, but Seth held steady. "The goddamned Army isn't bivouacking me in a hotel in Mississippi with nine colored troopers and the proprietor having no expectation of reimbursement. I've got to work with those people out there. Even payin' 'em their due, it's not gonna be easy."

Chapter Five

Eli brought the hoe down. This time, it caught in soil he believed half-frozen, and when he yanked, the dead plant pulled free.

"You shouldn't be doin' dat..."

Eli jerked his head around and straightened.

"...not till afta Christmastime." Brim Solomon grinned at him. "Damn, Eli, what you thinkin'? You done gone off an' fo'got eva'thing you eva learned."

"It's my understandin' this field has missed a couple of 'after Christmastimes.'" Eli dropped the hoe, then pulled the glove from his right hand. "Where the hell have you been?"

Brim stepped toward him, his slouch hat hiding his eyes in shadow, but not the smile on his face.

"I need to be harvestin' a fall crop of collards right now," Eli continued, extending his hand in welcome. "Not clearin' this cotton patch. And you need to be helpin' me."

Brim took Eli's hand, at the same time sweeping the hat from his head. Eli dragged him into a hug. Brim returned it. "I know it, Eli. I do. I know it. Dat's why I'm here. I wanna come home."

"Well, come on. I figured you were holdin' out for Christmas when the lands are supposed to be divvied up."

Brim hesitated, then chuckled. "Dey really gonna do dat, you think?"

Eli shot him a look, then turned back for his hoe. "I don't know what the hell is gonna happen. It's my understanding they're talkin' confiscated and abandoned property, but if they do decide to 'confiscate' mine, I want you to bury my bullet-riddled body at the foot of that mound overlooking the creek where you and me used to hunt for arrowheads, 'cause no bastard, colored or white, dressed in blue, is gonna take me out of Camellia Creek alive." He looked back at Brim. "Will you do that?"

Brim rocked back on his heels and smiled. "Sho' I will, but I reckon dat's all hogwash anyways."

Eli reckoned so, too, but he was no longer sure of anything. From his point of view, the Republican infestation that now called itself the Congress of the United States, along with its leader, had for the last four years interpreted Constitutional right with impunity and always to suit itself. He grabbed up the hoe. The South was to blame, too. In succumbing to its own pride with secession, no matter how much its right to do so, then losing the war that had been sure to follow, it left itself, and any hope for the United States, as they in the South had perceived it to be, vulnerable to the carrion fowl now gathering strength against President Johnson.

"What's this I hear about you contracting out to Wayne Hale, then leaving him high and dry and taking his mule to boot?"

"Yeah, I took his mule. Still gots it, too. I'll bring it wif me when I come back. Me an' you'll use it."

Eli started back toward him, hoe in hand. He punched him in the shoulder. "You know I can't do that."

Brim fell in step beside him, and they trudged back toward the house, a good mile away.

"Den I'll sell 'im an' buy me an' you a new one, but Josephus sho' is a fine ole mule."

"Who gave 'im that name, you or Wayne?"

"Me, befo' I eva took 'im. Beast a body spends whole days wif needs a name. Gotta call 'im somethin'."

Eli looked at him and finally laughed. Brim made him laugh. Brim had always made him laugh, ever since they'd been small. "Where'd you get that coat from, a Yankee billy goat?"

"Might be moth-eaten, but sho' beats doin' wifout."

"Freedman's Bureau not helping you?"

"Dey do, but it's done got too crowded in Vicksburg, Eli. Sally she's 'bout to have another baby, and Sammy, he's kept an earache since Octoba. Sally wants to come home, no matter what dem nigger soldiers say. Be close to Aunt Elvira and her medicine."

Eli grinned at him. "Go fishin'?"

A big smile contorted Brim's face. "Fo' sho' go fishin'. You and me like always."

Eli rubbed his chin. He needed to find that razor on the back porch; he hadn't shaved in two days.

"Then y'all come on home, sooner the better."

"What 'bout dat mule?"

"You need to return it to Hale."

"Ain't no way I'm gonna do dat."

Eli blew out a breath, and the air misted. He didn't stop walking, though he was tempted to so he could face the man. "What happened between you two?"—Eli grinned—"Or were you just in love with his mule?"

Brim gave him a slow, easy smile. "Naw, I ain't in love wif no mule, Eli. Didn't know where you'd got off to, but Mr. Wayne sayd he put me to work on a fall crop."

"And?"

"An' dat be fine. Worked fo' 'im five days. Hard, too, and give his damn mule a name as a bonus. Neva b'lieved dem Yankees gonna give us you white folks' land, not even da abandoned part. Dey might take it fo' demselves, but I neva thought dey'd give me any."

"But they love you, Brim." He'd spoke the words with some exaggeration and Brim might very well have picked up on the sarcasm. If he did, he ignored it.

"Some say dey do, but most look down on darkies. I seen it, like I ain't neva seen it from nobody. More'n likely dey wanna spit on da likes of us, but dey need us to spite you."

"So they might give you the land."

"Well, yeah, dat would spite you, but I'm not believin' it."

"So what soured between you and Wayne Hale?"

"He beats Miss May. Beats 'er bad."

Eli's gut twisted. He'd suspected that had happened once,

years ago, before the war, but he'd never known for sure, and May never said anything to anyone. But she'd grown reclusive as her and Wayne's marriage continued.

Brim chuckled softly. "Remember how when you an' me was little, an' we fished way up da creek?"

Eli remembered.

"We'd take da white perch and bream we caught up to 'er daddy's farm 'cause you thought she be so purty, an' sometimes she'd bring us shawtbread an' cream butta. You remember?"

"Yeah."

"An' you recall dat time you tol' 'er you was gonna grow up and marry 'er? Shoot, we couldn'ta been no mor'n five or six. An' she laugh an' say she gonna marry Wayne Hale, but she hope she had a little boy jus' like you."

"And you said, 'and a little darkie just like me.'"

"An' she sayd yes, and we both thought we was da bes' things since hot sauce on collards."

Eli frowned. "She never did have her little boy."

"She neva had any chil'en a'tall, an' I can tell ya why."

Eli gave him a side glance, the warmth of the upcoming house less important now.

"He beats da babies outa her."

"What?"

"When he gets 'er wif chil', he say da baby ain't his an' beats her till she loses it."

Eli broke out in a sweat, and for a moment, he thought he'd be sick. "Are you sure of that?"

"Dammit"—Brim did stop and turned on him. Eli stopped too—"you think I could make somethin' like dat up? I could neva think up such on my own. Can't b'lieve a man murderin' his own babies like dat, though I know some do, even afta dey bawn. Yeah, Eli, I'm sho'."

Eli tugged Brim's worn jacket and nodded to the house. He was chilled now to the bone, but it had little to do with the leaden, November sky and much to do with cold on sweat. "What happened?"

"I come back to da house from da field late one day in Septemba. Heard 'im in da cookhouse rantin' and ravin' an' cussin' her whorin'. Heard hittin' an' her cryin', beggin' 'im to stop. I run on up da pawch steps, not wantin' to get involved in fool white folks' stuff, you know dat. Knocked loud, too. Made lotsa racket, hopin' dey'd stop fightin'. Dey didn't, so I opened da door, an' he was beatin' da devil outa her. I saw him hit 'er belly, but 'er face be bloodied, too. I couldn't turn an' leave. I swear, I thought he was gonna kill 'er, an' it be *Miss May*."

"You tried to break it up?"

"I did try, but he were crazy. I couldn't stop 'im. I swear, at da time, I don't know if he even know'd I was der pullin' on 'im."

Eli stepped on the bottom stair leading to his front porch. The plank was weak and gave, but only a little. Brim followed close behind.

"He pushed me away an' went back to hittin' her."

Eli turned the knob and pushed open the casement door, its shattered glass boarded up, then stepped aside and motioned Brim in.

"Grabbed a cast-iron skillet off da stove and smashed it 'ginst his head."

"Knocked him out?"

"Second blow did."

Christ. "I think Aunt Naomi is out in the kitchen. I'll see if I can scrounge us up some hot coffee. Get a fire started, will ya?"

Minutes later Eli was thawing out and waiting patiently while Naomi Polk fussed around them. He knew she didn't like him in the dining room with Brim. Brim should be out in the cookhouse as far as she was concerned, but Eli didn't care. Brim Solomon had enjoyed free run of Camellia Creek since he'd been old enough to walk, and though at times it had been hard to throttle her, Aunt Naomi's influence had always been tempered by the ole master. That wasn't about to change now that Eli was sole proprietor of the farm.

He stood and glanced out the undamaged set of doors he'd taken from Hannah's old room to replace those in the dining room smashed by marauding Yankees two years earlier. He was more comfortable being able to see the comings and goings in the cookhouse than the lake out front, hence he'd installed them here. Hannah's was the only set of casement doors not damaged by the invaders, and he was in no position to buy new ones.

When he was sure his aunt was back inside the cookhouse, he sat down to find Brim grinning at him.

"See much of Miss Elvie?" Brim asked.

"You know better than me that she's kept to her cabin pretty much since Daddy's death."

"Yeah, yo' Aunt Naomi moved right back in when Massa Holland died, an' Miss Elvie skedaddled back to da quawta."

"I sent Aunt Naomi back to her place when I got home, but she's still over this way most days."

"She gonna be able to keep dat house in town?"

"Hope so. Daddy bought it outright, but the taxes will be comin' due. Don't know if I'll be able to handle them, but I guess I will or she'll find a way to move back in here permanent."

"Mama used to say it was yo' daddy she wanted, but now I'm thinkin' it's da house…or you."

Eli narrowed his eyes on him, then said, "You left the area after you knocked out Wayne?"

"Borrowed Uncle Buck's wagon, packed up Sally an' Sam, an' took off. Wanted to take Miss May to da doc or Miss Elvie befo' I went, but she weren't havin' none 'a dat, and she seemed real worried I get outa der befo' Mr. Wayne come around. I don't think she wants folks to know what he's been doin' to 'er, but I'm thinkin' Aunt Elvie knows."

"She's probably afraid some people might believe she was pregnant by another man."

"I don't b'lieve it, do you?"

"No." But what did he really know? "I can't imagine doing that to a woman even if it were true."

Brim shook his head before taking a sip of the steaming coffee. Eli, in turn, wrapped his hand around the chipped cup and luxuriated in the warmth enveloping his frigid fingers.

"What would make 'im like dat? You know?"

He really didn't, and it sickened him now, knowing sweet, pretty May Mallory, his boyhood dream, had lived with abuse all these years. Sweet Jesus, for the past four, she must've prayed a Yankee bullet would take the man.

"So you stole his mule?"

"Took the mule as pay. Sun still gonna come up da next mawnin', Eli, no matter what. I know'd he wouldn't pay me afta what I done."

"He asked me where you were. I thought he wanted you to fulfill your contract…and bring his mule back."

"Fulfill my contract, hell. Scared 'a dat man, Eli. Mor'n likely he wants to kill me."

"Well, as far as we know, he's never directed his madness toward anyone other than May. You bring 'fine ole' Josephus back. We'll return him, and that should be the end of that." Eli didn't know yet what he'd do about May.

"What about da contract?"

"I'll tell him it's abrogated. Doolan Mills left me clearin' cotton fields by myself, and I never gave him cause to knock me upside the head with a skillet. Appears nonfullfillment of contracts is the norm."

Chapter Six

Alice Shelton kicked the back door shut with her foot. Her cousin Cassie Franklin, holding the door to the dining room, giggled. "Hurry, while it's hot!"

When Alice entered, the three men sitting at the candlelit table scrambled to their feet. Even Aunt Betty rose with a lovely smile, getting out of the way so Alice could place the tureen in the center of the table. "I'm sure," Alice said, nodding to her Uncle Peter, "they had a better system than what we're using."

"I'm certain they did not," Eustacia Franklin said, still seated. "Slaves cooked their food, then set it on the buffet along with fine china. The slaves brought the made plates to the table."

"Not so unlike we did it in Chicago, Eustacia," Aunt Betty said and retook her seat. "Or you in New York, if I recall."

"I think Aunt Stacy is partly right." Cassie clasped her hands in front of her, looked proudly over the beautiful table she helped set, then waved a hand in the direction of the well-equipped sideboard. "The buffet did hold the dishes and silver, but according to Rose, the food was set on the table, and the diners helped themselves."

Eustacia sighed. "My point is we did not suffer our servants to traipse back and forth outside, regardless of ill weather, to serve us, and we would have paid them if they did. Free labor, indeed."

"Hardly free. It's always been my under—"

"They were poorly fed and clothed, Betty, lived in shanties, and were generally worked to death. I wonder sometimes if you think at all, or simply listen to these people's platitudes on the virtues of slavery. And where is that girl Rose?"

Alice, in the process of placing fresh-baked bread and butter on the table, looked at her aunt. Livid was a good description.

"She's sick," Betty spat out, "and with which Southerners do you pre —"

"Sick with what?" Eustacia peeked beneath the linen cloth covering the bread and blessed it with a noncommittal look. "I do hope it's not catching."

Alice thought for a moment Aunt Betty would spring from her chair and throttle the woman.

"She's going to have a baby, Aunt Stacy." Cassie caught Alice's eye and made a face.

"Oh? I didn't realize that. I thought she was fat."

"Why would you assume the child to be fat," Aunt Betty said, "when you repeatedly state how undernourished she'd been in the care of her master?"

Eustacia blinked at her sister-in-law, and Aunt Betty glared back. "Dear me, Betty, you react as if I have offended *you*."

Aunt Betty rolled her eyes, and Uncle Peter bent down to touch her arm. "A point well taken, my love," he said pleasantly. The man was trying to keep the peace and had done a credible job, with a few exceptions, since Eustacia and Jon had joined them in Mississippi. The crux was that Eustacia grew more taxing the more she settled in. "Betty is correct in spirit, Eustacia."

"And from what I've seen," Captain Nathan Simmons said as Cassie circled behind her father, "many of the slave owners themselves lived in hovels." Cassie graced Nathan with a charming smile and took the seat he offered. Sweet, happy Cassie.

Jonathan Franklin pulled out the chair on his left and waited for Alice. Aunt Betty made a habit of seating them together now — at Uncle Peter's request, her aunt had told her. Her uncle hoped companionship with Jon would bring Alice out of her shell, but Aunt Betty warned her he hoped for more than that.

Once Alice was seated, the men resumed their places, and Uncle Peter shot her a big smile. "Split-pea soup, if my nose does not deceive me."

"Your nose is correct once again, Uncle Pete."

Cassie turned to Nathan, sandwiched between her and Alice. "Alice makes wonderful split-pea soup. I always asked her to make it for me when I visited Uncle Jake's during the summer."

Aunt Betty stretched her hand across the linen-draped table. Steeling herself, Alice reached out and twined her fingers with those of her father's sister. "It was Jacob's favorite," the woman said.

Alice's quivering smile forced her to squint, and her vision blurred. Aunt Betty squeezed her hand and with a tearful smile of her own added, "Today is his birthday."

Uncle Peter looked first to Aunt Betty, then Alice. "Today's the…" He appeared to calculate the date in his head, then he laughed. "Well, so it is, isn't it?"

Alice nodded and bowed her head.

"It certainly is," Aunt Betty said. Then drawing a breath, she released Alice's hand and reached for the bowl sitting in front of Uncle Peter. "The soup is in his honor. Fresh-baked bread and churned butter to start. Alice has worked all day on this dinner."

"And we are the fortunate benefactors," Uncle Peter said, nodding his head in anticipation while Aunt Betty filled his bowl.

"Indeed," Jonathan said.

Emotions checked, Alice turned to find Jonathan watching her with a tender look in his eye. The man's attempts to befriend her had increased of late, but Alice was put off by what Cassie referred to as his feeble display of courtship. Other than a handsome visage, she found little to admire in Jon Franklin, not that she'd searched. More importantly, there was only one reason any young man would consider her good company of late.

After her aunt served Uncle Peter, Alice reached for Jon's bowl. "I thought, perhaps, we could pretend he was here."

"And he could be," Cassie sang out, "him, Jase, and Mike."

Across the table from Alice, Eustacia grunted, and Cassie's eyes widened. "They could be," she said, looking first at her father, then Nathan beside her. The latter nodded in agreement.

"Indeed, they could, my sweet innocent," Uncle Peter said. "Now, let us bow our heads."

Alice lowered her chin, but she did not close her eyes, defiant of the supplication despite Uncle Peter's warm reference to the memory of Jacob Shelton and his two sons, Jason and Michael, and she did not join in the chorus of "amens" at the conclusion of grace. For the past seven months, quiet acquiescence was Alice's only contribution to prayer.

She looked up to find Betty Franklin studying her, concern etched on the woman's pretty face. Alice smiled in reassurance and shared her smile with Uncle Peter—silent thanks for remembering her father and brothers. Then, with a heavy heart, she watched Peter Franklin lift a spoonful of what would always be Jacob Shelton's split-pea soup to his lips. A moment later he winked at her. "Delicious."

"To speak of ghosts is sacrilegious. Goodness"—Eustacia glanced at the empty spot between her and Aunt Betty—"I feared you were going to suggest we set another place, Cassie."

Alice narrowed her eyes on the jowly woman. There sat another cause for Alice's reluctance to encourage Jon Franklin. The woman looked up and caught Alice's perusal. Then, as if catering to Alice, she pulled her filled bowl in front of her, situated her linen napkin in her lap, and dove in. "Needs salt and pepper, Alice dear, but overall it's tasty."

Aunt Betty slapped the salt and pepper shakers down in front of the woman. "Here, Eustacia, 'dear.' Fix it to suit yourself."

Uncle Peter cleared his throat. "Is there cake?"

Alice could care less if the horrid biddy liked her soup. The woman never approved a single dish that Alice was aware of, no matter the cook, and Eustacia Franklin would do well to miss a few meals anyway. She opened her mouth to say so.

"Alice?" her uncle prodded.

She bit her tongue and turned to him

"Is there cake?" Again, he stuck his spoon in his mouth and made much ado about smacking his lips. Alice relaxed.

"Pound cake with lemon glaze."

"That's my favorite. Was it Jacob's, too?"

"Coconut was his first choice, but I couldn't find coconut."

"Godforsaken place must pay for its sins."

Alice's heart skipped a beat. She absolutely could not tolerate the harridan Franklin tonight.

Cassie said, "We're the ones missing the coconut cake, Aunt Stacy. Not them."

"Perhaps we're paying for our sins," Aunt Betty quipped.

"No," Jonathan said and laughed. "We're making *them* pay for our sins."

Alice looked at him and wondered if he considered himself clever. Then dismissing him and his tasteless humor, Alice sipped soup from her own spoon. Jacob Shelton would have showered her with adulation (he did with every meal, no matter how horrible it might have tasted) while her brothers would have teased her about not using dirty dishwater next time. Years ago, when the war was still young and packaged with the promise of a quick end, she'd dreamed of the night her men would come home and they'd all sit down to a dinner of her split-pea soup. She'd held to the dream. For nearly three years she'd held to it, until the day the dream was shattered. Then its shards were shattered, and in the end, the last of those shards had been pulverized, and the night she dreamed of could never be.

Alice jumped with the clink of Eustacia Franklin's spoon in her empty bowl. The woman pushed her dishes away and turned, sweet-faced, to Uncle Peter.

"What did you mean earlier?"

He blinked at her. "I beg your pardon?"

"When Betty—"

"With the possible exception of my own dear mother's, this is the best split-pea soup I've ever tasted, Alice."

Alice looked to her side and watched Nathan hold up a finger. "*Possible* exception, I said."

She smiled. "Thank you."

Eustacia cleared her throat, and Alice glanced her way. The dowager widow had focused her stern visage on Nathan. When the widow Franklin spoke, particularly on subjects she considered of import, that was to be the only conversation at the table. Nathan mumbled an apology, and Eustacia turned her attention back to Uncle Peter.

"When Betty contradicted me about the care of Negro slaves in this part of the country."

Alice cut a piece of bread from the loaf and watched her uncle set first his spoon, then his napkin, on either side of his bowl. He didn't want to have this discussion any more than the rest of them wished to listen to it.

"Eustacia," he said finally, "even putting aside the issue of man's inhumanity to man, which you are so quick to assume is characteristic of all Southerners, a slave constituted a significant investment to the owner. To say that he did not make some effort to care for his property would be like saying I do not feed my horse."

"A human being is not a horse."

"I qualified my argument," he said. "We are speaking of property, humanity aside."

"You cannot put humanity aside."

"Of course, you can't, Eustacia," Aunt Betty broke in. "That being said, why do you assume Southerners did?"

"There are documented cases—"

"There are documented cases of men beating their wives to death in every state of the Union," Uncle Peter said to Eustacia before looking pointedly at Aunt Betty. A subtle indicator, no doubt, he wished to handle this alone. "That is not, however, the norm."

In her own mind, Alice substituted sisters-in-law for wives and snickered. Eustacia Franklin witnessed her amusement and raised a haughty chin. "And what do you know of it, girl? Did you join in the movement against slavery?"

Aunt Betty leaned toward the woman. "Don't start this."

"I gave it little thought," Alice said.

Betty Franklin straightened in her seat. "Alice, honey, you don't need—"

"And look what it has cost you."

"Slavery?"

Eustacia closed her eyes and shuddered as if under some heavy emotional burden. "No, my dear, your indifference to it. Your father and brothers' indifference to it."

Alice's throbbing heart lodged in her throat.

"It was a national disgrace, and people chose to ignore it."

"It's gone, Mother. We should change the subject," Jonathan said and reached for the bread in front of Alice.

Eustacia Franklin stopped him with a look. "Do not interrupt me."

Alice clenched her fists, crushing the fine linen napkin with stiff fingers. Slowly she raised her hand from her lap and placed the napkin next to her plate.

Aunt Betty, watching Alice's every move, stilled. "Eustacia, you've said quite enough."

"'Enough,' Betty?" The woman removed the spoon from her empty bowl and plopped it, rather hard, on the table. "This girl needs to understand that the abomination and her people's callous indifference to it has cost her her family."

"Peter?" her aunt pleaded.

"Eustacia, please, lets —"

"I had a house to run," Alice said, "and a farm to help my father with. Papa used to say if abolitionists had enough honest work to do, they wouldn't be so determined to mold the rest of the world into their vision of it and demand everyone else go along."

The woman narrowed her eyes on Alice. "Your father agreed with slavery?"

Alice sucked in a breath. "'Damned fanatics' he called you, to be specific, and he most certainly did not participate in slavery, nor did he partake in many things other people did. What he did believe in was preserving the Union and in obeying the law."

Her aunt pushed her chair back from the table. "Alice, honey, don't worry about —"

"The law was wrong."

"Peter, please," Aunt Betty said, "stop this."

"Because you say so?" Alice blurted at Eustacia.

"Alice, enough!" Uncle Peter said. "Eustacia, be quiet."

"God says so."

Alice's mouth opened slightly. Where had *He* said so?

Eustacia tightened her lips and held her head high. "And this war was righteous. Not only was it righteous, it was God's punishment, I now realize." The woman glanced up at Aunt Betty standing dumbstruck beside her, then slid her gaze to Uncle Peter. "God's punishment against the entire nation for allowing such a sin to continue as long as it did."

"More than six hundred thousand men gave their lives in this war," Alice said, enunciating carefully because her body was shaking. "And you think it was because God was punishing us for slavery?"

"There is absolutely no doubt in my mind that the recent war is the direct result of our most grievous sin against our fellow man. And our late, great president, Abraham Lincoln, thought so, too. Obviously, you have not read his second inaugural address, *Miss* Shelton."

Alice rose slowly. "You do not worship God, Mrs. Franklin. You worship a monster."

"Alice, sit down." Uncle Peter rose when she didn't obey.

Eyes not on Peter Franklin, but on Eustacia, Alice said, "You, and people like you, are monsters, and now you've created God in your own image."

The woman blinked at Alice then, hand on her chest, looked at Uncle Peter. "Well, I never."

"Alice," he said, "apologize and sit back down."

She turned to him, then looked down at her hands, clinging to the table edge. The linen tablecloth she laid out an hour ago in honor of her father's birthday had scrunched beneath her fingers. Good Lord, her aching arms were the only things holding her up. In disbelief, she again looked at her uncle—apologize?—then glanced at her aunt, staring at her with pale-faced sympathy. Alice blinked and focused back on the hate-filled woman who waited for her to…what? Apologize?

"Mrs. Franklin…"

Smug-faced, Eustacia Franklin cocked her head. Alice drew in a breath. "You are, Mrs. Franklin, no better than a whore-mother—"

Beside her, Jon Franklin stirred. "Alice, I really must—"

"And would be exactly that except for the fact you lacked even the strength of character to risk your own son to your self-righteous cause, choosing instead to sacrifice other people's sons and brothers"—tears were blurring her vision, and she leaned over Jon's place setting to bring herself within inches of the despised face—"and *fathers* to your bloodthirsty monster of a god." Jonathan stood and grabbed her arm, but she yanked free and straightened. From the corner of her eye, she could see her aunt had raised a hand, which now covered her mouth. Alice squared her shoulders and held her head proudly. "To create a world of dubious quality made the more so by your presence in it. At this moment, you hateful creature, I hope there is a hell because there is absolutely no doubt in my mind that the God I once loved will cast you into it."

Jonathan Franklin clutched the edge of the table. "Really, Alice, you go too far."

Eustacia Franklin's beady eyes teared, and she started fanning herself, repeating, "Oh my, oh my, oh my."

At the other end of the table Uncle Peter groaned, and when Alice looked his way he was raking a hand over his face. He dropped his hand and glared at her.

"Leave my table."

Of course she should. For weeks, for his sake, the rest of the family had sidestepped Eustacia Franklin's unyielding and flawed opinions—slavery was her primary cause, but certainly not her only one. Alice had annihilated their disciplined efforts in minutes.

She glanced at Cassie, who gave her a small smile, but when the girl started to rise, her father ordered her to sit. Clumsily, Alice pushed her chair out of the way. Jonathan reached over to help, and she stepped around him. Clear of the table, she ran for the door.

Behind her, she heard her aunt tell Uncle Peter not to try to stop *her*. With a sob, Alice surged out of the dining room, through the back door, and onto the wraparound porch circling their rented farmhouse two miles west of Port Gibson.

"Alice, honey, wait!"

Halfway to the exterior stairs leading to the upper portico and the solace of her and Cassie's bedroom, Alice stopped. Lanterns hung at each end of the long porch, providing a little light to ward off the darkness of the chilly night. Alice wrapped her arms around herself and turned.

Bathed in lamplight from the central hall, Betty Franklin, guardian to a rude, foul-tempered, and generally thankless niece, stood outside the open back door. Alice felt her chin pucker. "I'm sorry."

Her aunt pulled the door shut behind her. "Oh, honey, I'm the one who's sorry. Jacob's birthday dinner is ruined."

The shadowy form of her aunt blurred, and Alice tried to blink away the tears.

"Papa and Jason and Michael died to keep the Union to-gether, not to fulfill that woman's perception of God's demands." Her aunt watched her with what appeared to be mute grief and understanding. And to a great extent, the woman did understand. Alice had lost a father and two brothers; Aunt Betty, a brother and two nephews. "I remember Papa fearing trouble would come if the Republicans won the presidency." Alice stepped toward her aunt. "Did President Lincoln really think like that woman said?"

Her aunt's mouth opened to speak, but then she held her hands out, palms up, bewildered it seemed. Alice took that to mean she didn't know, and if she did, she wouldn't say so to Alice.

"If he did, then I understand why these people were driven to leave the Union, and I'll never forgive him that."

"Honey, President Lincoln didn't intend what happened. He had his beliefs and wanted a peaceful resolution to the issue. It was the South—"

"Don't you see, Aunt Betty? I want to hate Southerners and the South. I want to believe they were irrational and hell-bent on destroying the country. I want to be happy the evils of slavery are ended, but when I listen to that person in there, it's as if to her, none of that mattered. That in her mind the purpose of the war was a purging through destruction, a sick fanaticism, and then I wonder if I even understand what evil really is. Is it her?" She blinked. "Or God?" She covered her mouth to ward off a sob. "Is it us?"

Clearly shaken, Betty Franklin breathed in, then grasped Alice by the shoulders and gently shook her. "Remember that your father and brothers fought to preserve the Union, and the Union is saved."

"When half of it doesn't even want to belong?"

Betty held up a staying hand. "It doesn't matter. It's saved."

"That doesn't make sense to me."

The back door rattled, and both she and her aunt watched it open and Uncle Peter step onto the porch.

"Elizabeth?" he called. He saw her, then Alice, whom he pierced with a look. "Get to your room."

"I'm sorry for my—"

"Right now! Tomorrow you can apologize to Eustacia."

Heat washed over Alice, a hot flash of hatred that seared her soul. She locked eyes with him, tight-lipped behind Aunt Betty. She loved Uncle Pete, but…

"If that horrid woman was your sister by blood I would not apologize to her."

He stepped around Aunt Betty, and Alice braced.

"You are in my home. My brother's wife and son are now dependent on me. I cannot abide disrespect on the part of youth to their elders. It undermines my household and society in turn. If you cannot bring yourself to adhere to my terms while you live under my roof and eat the food I provide you, then I will ask you to leave."

Aunt Betty brought one hand to her mouth. With the other, she touched his sleeve. He shook her off.

Leave? And go where? Alice drew in a breath. It really didn't matter. She was dead inside anyway. "Very well, I'll go." She watched his face change. Whether it was shock, relief, remorse, she couldn't tell. "I'm sure, under the circumstances, there must be a way to break the trust. Pritchard will find a way since I'm no longer welcome in your home."

"No," Aunt Betty said, turning on Uncle Peter. "Stop this, right now."

At first he said nothing, then appeared to come to himself. "I have to think of Cassie in this."

"Cassie, ha!"

"I cannot have Alice undermining me in front of my daughter, Elizabeth." He started around her.

"Stay where you are, husband." She whirled on Alice. "Go on up to your room. Enough has been said in your presence."

Yes, it had. Worse yet, too much had been said from her own lips. She nodded. She really had no desire to leave Uncle Peter and Aunt Betty's home, and leaving the resolution of this crisis in her aunt's hands seemed the most prudent thing to do at the moment. She spun around and hurried to the stairs at the end of the porch. There she froze.

The Confederate officer she'd seen in the woods on the other side of Camellia Creek stood at the bottom of the steps leading up to the porch. As he had that morning, days ago, he tipped his hat in silent greeting. Heavens, how much had he heard of this horrible squabble?

"Alice?" her aunt said.

Alice raised her chin and glared down at the man, partially hidden in shadow. She swore he smirked, then he started up the stairs.

"We have company."

"Oh?"

Alice didn't give an inch, holding her ground until he stopped on the next to the top step and looked down at her from half a head higher.

"Mr. Calhoon," Uncle Peter said. Alice discerned irritation in her uncle's voice, and she was sure this Mr. Calhoon must have heard it, too.

"Your sister-in-law opened the front door," Calhoon said, never dropping his eyes from Alice's. "She said I should come around back. I have your document."

Alice studied his face, his jaw lean and clean shaven, his eyes glinting in the lantern light, despite the shadow cast by his hat. He had a slightly cleft chin, straight nose, and a broad mouth, relaxed, Alice was sure, compared to hers. She noted the yellow collar on his worn frock coat, the pairs of stars.

"Skulking around, Colonel, reliving past nights spent sneaking up on unsuspecting campfires."

"Alice, for goodness' sake, haven't you caused enough discord tonight?" Uncle Peter said, moving up behind her. Alice heard the rustle of Aunt Betty's skirt.

"I announced my arrival with a rebel yell, Miss. The Yankees crapped their britches and took off runnin'. That's why I'm still here."

"I consider your prowess in battle overstated, sir, else *I* would not be here."

She sensed him tense. Anger, aggression...? Challenge?

"Turned out there were too many of you to scare off."

The quality of his voice had changed, softened. She swallowed, wishing she'd not seen this man. She'd fought and lost enough tonight and had yet to appease those she'd already angered. "Is that so?" She looked past him and feigned a search of the yard. "Where's your horse?" Confident he no longer had his "precious" cavalry horse, she sought to get his goat. Truly, she hoped a Negro private in the Union Army had confiscated it.

"He's out front. As I said, *I* was sent to the back door."

Her uncle grabbed her arm and shoved her toward the stairs. "We've much to discuss, young lady, but I'm done with you and your antics tonight."

Alice didn't look back.

But Eli watched her, the sweet scent of lemon and lavender fading with her retreat, and he listened to the swish of her black crepe skirt as she climbed the stairs, then cocked his head just enough to peek between the footers for a glimpse of white petti-coat.

"How dare you?"

Eli jumped at Mrs. Franklin's voice, but when he looked, he realized it was Franklin she addressed.

"Elizabeth, we'll talk about this later."

"When I've calmed! Well, I'm not going to calm, Peter. Not this time. You've taken appeasement with that woman too far."

"Elizabeth," he said, turning his back on her and walking away, "we have a guest."

"We do not have a guest," she said, on his heel. "We have a man who has inadvertently walked into a hornet's nest, and unless he has the good sense to leave right now, he will remain in the middle of it until I've had my say."

Eli turned to go.

"Mr. Calhoon," Franklin said, "my apologies."

"I can leave this in the kitchen if you want."

"No, please wait. I'd hoped to talk to you about my labor."

Labor problems, he meant. Well, there was damn little Eli could suggest on that. It was Franklin's own "confiscated" forces telling the Negroes not to work.

"This won't take but a minute."

Franklin should have been watching his wife. Eli sure was, and the woman was more-than-a-minute upset.

"You are correct, Peter, this will only take a moment."

Peter Franklin clenched his teeth and stuck a finger under his wife's nose. "She ruined a pleasant dinner. She…"

The lovely Mrs. Franklin hit the finger. She didn't swat or slap the finger, she hit it. Eli stepped around the corner of the house, out of sight, but not out of earshot. He'd have left, but he did want to hand over this piece of paper and be done with Franklin and his nephew.

"She didn't ruin dinner. She made dinner. Dinner in honor of her father's, my brother's, birthday. He would have been fifty-four, Peter.

Fifty-four with many good years in front of him. The person who ruined dinner was that selfish, self-centered—"

"Betty, honey, calm down, she'll hear you."

"Termagant," she screamed out.

"Good Lord."

"That self-righteous hypocrite who dared to suggest my brother's and his sons' sacrifice to their nation was God's punishment for their not believing in the dissolution of slavery with the same fanatical zeal as she, while at the same time, she purchased her son's deferment from the fray. God's love, Peter, what's wrong with you?"

Eli heard a muted slap and surmised Mrs. Franklin had hit her husband. He figured if Franklin were the type man to hit his wife, he'd have done so by now.

"She contributed nothing to the nightmare she and thousands like her are responsible for."

"Elizabeth, you cannot blame—"

"Oh, yes, I can. The least they can do is accept some of the responsibility for what they've done, instead of looking over the carnage they've created and railing about what a damn good job God has done on us all.

"Eustacia never once experienced night after sleepless night, Peter, wondering if the man she loved would come home."

"Many abolitionist families did, Betty."

Franklin's voice had softened, while his missus' dripped with emotion. Eli heard scuffling, then a soft grunt.

"Not nearly as many as should have, and Eustacia didn't. And it is Eustacia who dared to impose her sick concepts of God on my niece's grief. Heaven knows that relationship was already bad enough."

Eli heard a floorboard groan in tandem with the rustle of Mrs. Franklin's dress.

"Do you have any idea what it's like to read about a battle in the paper one morning where thousands, even several thousands of men have perished, then wait for days and days for a telegram or a letter or a unit member to come to your door telling you someone you loved is lost?"

Franklin murmured something Eli couldn't decipher.

"And about the time you're sure word is not going to come, there's another battle in another place, and another newspaper report, on and on,

month after month, year after year. Do you know what it's like? Do you really think it was so hard sitting out in the rain and the heat and the snow and the filth while the dirt ate at your skin and the vermin sucked your cold, heartless blood? Well, you knew you were alive. The more you suffered, the more you knew you were alive. I didn't. My suffering was in my soul.

"No! Don't you dare touch me. I never received that news, Peter. You came back to me, I'm happy to say, though for the life of me at this moment"—her voice broke—*"I don't know why. But that girl upstairs received the news. Three times she received it. Twice within ten days of each other and once only seven months ago. She's still not over the shock, and you know that. You know how I worry for her. How can you stand in front of me now and side with that woman!"*

"It was the lack of re—"

"Respect? Respect Alice's grief, damn you! Good Lord, the war was over. We thought Michael was on his way home."

Betty Franklin really started crying then, and Eli forced out a breath. He wished he had left this porch.

"So I'll give you a choice as to who you want to leave this house, husband. Either Alice goes or Eustacia does, because Alice is not apologizing to that woman. But understand this, if you choose Alice, I'm going with her, and you can get your sister-in-law, who I should add, drove your poor brother into an early grave, to warm your damn bed."

Eli heard the woman move, quick footfalls followed by the sudden swish of skirts, the squeak of a door.

"And another thing. You don't have to worry about what Eustacia might have overheard, because I intend to say everything I just said to you to her face to make sure she did not miss one word."

Silence followed the slamming of the back door. Then Eli heard the approach of heavy footfalls along the length of the porch. He leaned one shoulder against the corner of the house and waited for Franklin to step into his line of sight. After a moment he did, a tall, handsome man with blue eyes and a thick head of wavy hair, mostly silver. Premature if the man's overall fitness and tone were indicators. That gray hair could have been the war showing, and Eli couldn't help but wonder when he would turn gray.

"I hoped you'd left," Franklin said.

"You asked me to stay." Eli handed him the folded paper. "Your deed. I filed it."

"Thank you." Franklin gave him a sheepish look. "I do apologize for my family's behavior."

"No need. Once we had happy homes here in the South, too." Eli straightened. "Franklin?"

"Yes?"

"I've had pretty good looks at both those women, your wife and sister-in-law, I mean."

Franklin frowned.

"If I were you, I'd let Alice stay."

Chapter Seven

"Where are you trying to get to?"

"To Aunt Elvie, Massa Eli."

Eli sat back on his heels and again tried to place the girl. "What's your name?"

"I'm Rosie, Dolly's girl. Don't you rememba me?"

He cocked his head and studied her face, then grinned. "Do now. Aunt Naomi told me you were working for the Franklins."

She smiled, a bright toothy thing despite her difficulties. "Yes, suh, been wo'kin' fo' dem folks, but I been sick and dis mawnin' dat ole fat one say I should jus' go on back to da fahm I come from till I birth dis baby an' might not should come back a'tall 'cause dey didn't have no place fo' no squallin' chil' I'd be wantin' dem to feed."

Yep, Franklin's sister-in-law was a fine, Christian woman, but as much as he despised them as a group, he didn't think she was a true abolitionist. From what he'd seen and heard about her, up to the present — he looked at Rosie — he figured the woman to be one of those who needed something to cause trouble as long as she wasn't inconvenienced by it. Southern slavery had been the biggest cause going as of late.

The girl had been talking away since he found her hunkered in the road — jus' restin' she'd said, but blood was pooling beneath her squat, and she was noticeably pregnant. Eli recalled little Rosie had always been a talker. Of all the more recent young'uns watched over in the kitchen, she'd been the one who drove her mama, the cook, crazy, and Dolly's agitation had caused Hannah to laugh till she cried.

Eli wrapped an arm around her shoulder; the second he

slipped under her knees. She'd been a child of eight or nine when he'd left for war over four years ago. Naomi hadn't told him the girl was pregnant, and he wondered if she knew, but couldn't imagine she didn't.

"How long have you been bleeding?"

"Started jus' now. Been feelin' po' fo' a while though, an' dis mawnin', I gots pains in my back, an' when I didn't get to da kitchen early, dat ole woman made brekfes' hersef. Tol' me I bes' go. Thought 'bout waitin' for Miz Betty to tell me to git, but I be hurtin' so, thought I might shouldn't wait. Went to Miss Naomi's, but she weren't der, so I started home to Camellia Creek. Hope Aunt Elvie's der 'cause dis bleedin's scarin' me."

"Miss Naomi was at the farm when I left." Eli straightened, the girl in his arms. He wished she'd waited for Naomi to get back. She didn't need to be on her feet.

"Aunt Naomi told me Gus took you with him when he left, but you came back soon after. She told me you said he sent you home and you don't know what happened to him after that."

She tightened her arms around his neck and pressed her body close to his. He sensed her action wasn't caused by his prying. She was chilled, and she hurt. He waited till she relaxed some- what and said, "Miss Naomi and Aunt Elvie say you wouldn't talk about why he sent you home. As a matter of fact, they said at first you didn't talk much about anything. They're thinking some- thing bad happened."

He turned and found Johnny partaking of the grass on the side of the road. "I could sure use Gus right now. I'll go get him if you'll tell me where he is."

Other than her labored breathing, she didn't make a sound. "Who got you with child, Rose?" he asked, and when she didn't respond, he said, "You haven't made a peep in at least two min- utes. You're gonna bust wide open, Rosie, Rosie, blackie toesie."

She leaned back, eyes shimmering, and laughed. "You rememba dat?"

Her daddy had created the nonsense ditty, but it had been her mother Dolly who Eli repeatedly heard recite it to her baby while she tried to work around her in the kitchen. "Yeah," he said, "I remember that." Rose was watching him, her eyes full of trust, and he hesitated, not sure how best to proceed. He opted to go with his gut. To this girl, he was the "ole massa" now. "Is your daddy dead?"

With no hesitation, she nodded and started to cry. "Dem men dat got me wif dis baby shot 'im back las' springtime."

Them. More than one. His stomach soured. Marauders and deserters were running rampant over the state and had been for months. Hell, for years. Why hadn't Gus stayed home or, at least, left the girl where she had some modicum of safety?

"Daddy, he try an' stop 'em. He know'd what dey wanted to do wif me. I didn't, not den."

Eli whistled, and the horse lumbered toward them. "Where did it happen?"

"We was goin' to Jackson. Daddy say he wanted to fin' wo'k, but I done heah Miss Elvie tell 'im all he know'd be fahmin' an' fo' 'im to jus' keep wo'kin' Camellia Creek till you come home."

"I'm going to set you in the saddle."

She nodded, and when he did, he noted the amount of blood on the front of his frock coat. She wasn't bleeding, she was hemorrhaging. He climbed up behind the girl, who was now shivering uncontrollably in a clean, but ragged coat. The coat should be warm enough, but her dress was summer cotton and came halfway up to her knee. Eli wrapped his arms around her and pulled her against him for warmth. The day was leaden and the intermittent north wind, freezing.

"But Daddy tol' 'er none of us know'd if you'd come home. An' we didn't, Massa Eli. Back den we didn't know if you even be alive."

"How many were there?"

"How many?"

"The men who found you, how many were there?"

"Five, I think. I don't know fo' sho' 'cause dey did what dey did to me ova and ova"—her breath started to come in little pants, and he jostled her gently between his arms.

"It's all right. I know. You don't need to tell me more."

She sobbed suddenly, and Eli hugged her tight, inadvertently tugging the reins. Johnny snorted and shook his head in defiance. Immediately, Eli righted his mistake and coaxed the gelding forward.

"Daddy and me was spendin' da night in a shack by da road. Nobody lived der no mo'. Dats where dey come up on us. Dey was on patrol, dey sayd."

His sour stomach suddenly held the weight of a brick. "On patrol?"

"Dat's what dey sayd."

Whoever the bastards were, they were in federally-occupied territory, not that that would have made a difference to them.

"Dey ask what daddy was doin' der wif a girl like me. Asked if he'd stole me. He tol' 'em no. Sayd I was his li'l girl an' he'd lef' da plantation like da nigger soldiers in Vicksburg done tol' 'im he could, 'cause he be free now.

"Dem soldiers sayd dat was so, and den one of 'em laughed and sayd it was dem we owed fo' our freedom. Dat man looked at me. Daddy sayd 'no Lawd, no you ain't'…" Her bottom lip was trembling, making if hard for her to speak. "Den I hear da shot. I screamed an' ran fo' 'im, but dey…dey g-g-grabbed—"

She hid her face against his chest, and he took the reins in one hand and rubbed her back with the other. "Hush," he said, "don't say any more."

Instead, she tensed. "Lawdy, Massa Eli, it hurtin' so."

A contraction, without a doubt, and after a good full minute she lifted her head. "I can feel da blood just arushin' outa me."

"We're almost home."

She appeared to make note of their location, then said. "We goin' to da big house?"

"Yep, Miss Naomi should still be there. Then I'll get Aunt Elvie."

"Da hurtin' done stopped again."

He figured the respite wouldn't last long.

"Rosie, did those men wear uniforms?"

"Dey uniform be blue. Dose mens be Yankees, Massa Eli, from up nawth, like dem dat kilt ole massa and to'e up Camellia Creek."

There was a colored private outside the door of the *Port Gibson Chronicle* when Alice arrived mid-morning. He surprised her. Not because he was Negro, but because, simply, he was there. He looked at her, and she looked at him, and truth was she wasn't sure she needed to speak to him at all. Uncomfortable, she asked, "Is there some reason I shouldn't enter, Private?"

He seemed taken aback by that. "No, ma'am, not dat I know of. My officers and sergeant be inside talkin' to da newspaperman. Dey lef me heah."

"To guard the door?"

"Didn't say so. Jus' tol' me to wait."

She looked at the doorknob, thinking perhaps he would open it for her. When he didn't, she reached for it herself. That brought him to action, and he grabbed the knob before she touched it, positioned himself between her and the door, and asked, "You wantin' to see da newspaperman, too?"

"Yes."

"Might be I should ask 'em if it be okay fo' you to come in?"

Alice nodded, more comfortable with that suggestion than bursting in on who knows what. She'd seen Union troops in and out of Port Gibson. Officers manned the Freedman's Bureau in Claiborne County, and Uncle Peter often invited one or more to join them for dinner, but the nearest garrison in the area was at Vicksburg. She had no idea why these were here or what she might be walking into beyond that door.

The private stuck his head in, and she calmed herself by brushing water from the shoulders of her cape. The heavy skies had let loose on her halfway to town, and sopped her outer clothing during the long walk in a steady rain. She stomped the mud from her boots, not winter gear, but fashionable leather footwear, and they had leaked. Her toes stung.

The man looked over his shoulder at her, then opened the

door wider and stepped in. He moved aside and motioned for her to enter. "Warm in heah. You best come on. I don't see 'em."

Indeed, the front room was empty and dim despite raised shades. This day offered no sunshine, and no lamps were lit. A spool-turned bench sat behind the door, and he suggested she sit, at the same time eyeing a door behind a short counter. In the left corner of the room, a potbellied stove glowed, emitting warmth, and Alice considered forgoing the comfort of the bench for that of the fire.

The private hesitated outside the closed door, unsure, she sensed, of what to do next. Goodness knows she didn't want this trip in to Port Gibson to be worthless. Given a choice, she'd wait hours for the man. "Don't disturb them, Private…?

Yes, it was a pregnant pause and by the look on his face, her interest in his name must have surprised him. "I be Private Ball, ma'am."

"Don't disturb them"—she smiled—"Private Ball. If you think it would be all right, I'll wait right here until they're done."

"Dey been inside awhile."

And Alice could hear them beyond that door, and she feared that made Private Ball even more anxious since he was clearly unsure she should be overhearing their discussion.

"Where is your home?" she asked, more to make polite conversation than out of curiosity.

"Mizz'ssippi. Bawn and raised up in Warren County."

"Oh, I—"

The door flew open and Private Ball snapped to attention. A Negro officer glared at him, started to speak, then caught sight of her on the bench. He narrowed his eyes and turned back to his private. "May I ask your purpose, Ball?"

"Dis lady ask to talk to da newspaperman, so I opened—"

"I wanted to see the editor, Captain." Alice hastened to her feet. "Private Ball said you hadn't asked not to be disturbed, and I requested permission to wait rather than leave or interrupt your meeting."

Inside the room, a chair growled across the wood floor and

after a moment another man in an unfamiliar military uniform appeared behind the captain. This man was white.

"What's going on?" he asked pleasantly before settling his gaze on her. Alice didn't desire this attention…or scrutiny. "I'm sorry"—she looked at the sleeve of his blouse, then found his collar—"Major…?

He nodded. "Correct. Major Seth Parker, United States Marines."

"Ah."

"I noted your confusion, Mrs.…?"

"Shelton, Miss Alice Shelton."

"And how may we be of service, *Miss* Shelton?"

"I didn't mean to create a fuss." A little more comfortable now, she approached him and extended a black-gloved hand and what she hoped was a pleasant smile. Pleasant enough she guessed, because he smiled in turn, an expression that reached his green eyes, and he took her hand. "I wished only"—she glanced around the major to the balding, sallow-faced man who had moved up and stepped to one side of him—"to speak to the editor. Would that be you, sir?"

"Poynter Cummings," the new man said, then gave her hand a firm shake when she offered it. Alice looked back up and met the handsome major's eyes, then returned her gaze to Mr. Cummings. "I came in to town in hopes of finding a copy of President Lincoln's most recent inaugural address."

"I'm sorry, Miss Shelton. I haven't one. The paper has only been back in operation since this past July." He turned to the major and added, "Citizens are still finding pieces of my original type in the street and bringing it to me."

Alice swallowed. He referred, of course, to the havoc Union troops created when they invaded this area in 1863. "I'm happy you're back in operation, Mr. Cummings, and thank you for your time"—she swept the room with her gaze so as to include them all—"gentlemen." She turned to the door, wanting nothing now but to get out of this place, out of Port Gibson, and back to her and Cassie's secluded little bedroom outside town.

"I have a copy, Miss Shelton, and I would be happy to lend it to you."

Her heart skipped a beat, and she pivoted. The tall, sandy-haired major had a pleasant voice and, based on his dimpled smile, a gregarious personality.

"For a price."

Her spirits plummeted with the sudden realization he regarded her a Southern woman desperate for favor. Well, she'd seen enough of these Southern women to know if she were wearing widow's weeds and hadn't been raised in a brothel, odds were she'd starve before committing to the price of favors. She raised her chin. "And what, sir, would that price be?"

His brace was subtle, but she did note it, then he smiled and moved around her to reach for his cover on a peg by the door. "Lunch, Miss Shelton. That's all. I want to buy you lunch."

He reached for her elbow and guided her to the door at the same time issuing instructions to his captain. Captain Summers, he called him.

Seth told her the printed speech was in his hotel room, and he sensed that prospect made her uneasy. He would not have been able to lure her upstairs, even if that had been his intent, which it wasn't. Hoping to relieve her anxiety, he left her in the lobby, on a worn, but what he knew to be comfortable, upholstered chair next to the wood-burning stove, and went upstairs to retrieve it. She was cold, and he wondered how far she'd walked to find a copy of the speech. He was even more curious as to why it interested her. Finally coaxing her out of her woolen cape, and assuring himself she was indeed dressed in mourning, he left her reading while he went into the dining room to reserve a table. That didn't take long given the economic woes of the town and the day's inclement weather. He lingered there, periodically peeking into the lobby until he was sure he'd given the lovely *Miss* Shelton time to digest Lincoln's address. The speech had not been a long one and had met mixed reaction, mostly unfavorable.

"Would you tell me whom you are mourning?" he said, taking

his seat beside her at the table. He watched as she unfolded her napkin, then he did the same. He glanced from her surreptitiously bowed head to the napkin she was arranging in her lap. Answering must be difficult for her, and he regretted asking. Absently he perused the hodgepodge of tables and chairs occupying the room he'd been pacing the last ten minutes. But the dining room's walls were newly painted and its window glass sparkled. The panes were probably new, too, a legacy of senseless vandalism.

She looked up. "My father and brothers," she said strongly. "Well, officially just one of my two brothers this time."

"What unit?" The question slipped out. He didn't know why he asked. He now knew her monastic trappings weren't for a lover or fiancé. Ghosts were hard to fight.

"Company J, 78th Ohio," she answered, then laughed at what must have been the look on his face.

"So, that's what elicited a pretty smile for a blue uniform. And here I thought I was winning over the vanquished."

"A rather odd blue uniform, and I am sorry to disappoint you."

"I'm not disappointed, only surprised. Why are you here?"

"I'm with my aunt, my father's sister, and her family, the Franklins west of town. Uncle Peter has rented a house here, until he can acquire the land he desires."

"Prices are cheap."

"It's not only that. Uncle Peter likes it down here. He likes the winters. They're much milder, he says, than Chicago's."

"Yes, they are."

The wife of the owner, a mature woman with tired eyes and a sour expression approached them. "Two lunch specials," he said before she asked.

"Shall I charge the government for your guest?" she asked.

"I'll pay for hers."

The woman pivoted and headed back to the kitchen. Seth refocused on Alice Shelton. "The summers make up for it. Has he spent a summer here?"

"April 1863 until August of that year. My father and brothers were here, too. After Vicksburg fell, Uncle Peter went west. Papa, Jason, and Mike went east."

"They were with Sherman?"

She nodded. "Michael was with him all the way to the sea. Papa and Jason's journey ended at Atlanta." She fidgeted with something in her lap, probably her napkin, and he gave her a moment.

"Have you gotten to know many of the locals?"

"I've pretty much kept to home."

He'd been about to tell her she should probably keep her menfolks' association with Sherman to herself, but now was not the time. "I'm sorry for your losses, Miss Shelton."

"Alice, and thank you."

"I was in the area from May until the end of June, 1863."

"Perhaps you knew one another?"

He smiled. "There were a lot of us, but I am aware of your uncle outside town."

"Oh?"

"I'm working here, Alice, and it behooves me to know who around here might be friend or foe."

"I do believe you can consider Uncle Pete a friend."

"I counted on that."

"Uncle Pete had a cousin stationed in Vicksburg until recently. He had no sooner walked through his door back home when he received a letter from this person telling him land in Mississippi was selling cheap. So Uncle Pete packed us all up, and here we are."

"He's a farmer?"

"He was raised on a farm in Illinois until he was twelve. That's when his father died. His older brother moved the family to Chicago. Uncle Peter finished school and became a somewhat successful accountant. He invests in things."

"In this case, Southern land?"

"Real estate's a favorite, but I really think he wants to be a gentleman farmer."

"Does he realize gentlemen farmers require labor?"

"He's trying to hire freedmen."

"I'm afraid he may be disappointed."

"I believe he already is. You don't think the Negro will work, do you?"

"Not in the spirit your uncle envisions."

"You mean paying them a fair wage?

"And what's considered a fair wage to a Northern investor?"

"I..." She touched her fingers to her lips. "I don't know. Do you agree with slavery then?"

"I'm a Kentuckian, Alice. My father and his father before him were Whigs. My family still has thirty-two darkies who aren't sure what to do next. At present, they're on the farm. My father feeds them, he clothes them, he provides their shelter and medicine. Now he has to pay them. He can't do all that. The entire system has to change. The destruction caused by the war is catastrophic to this region, but in the long term, this shift in labor will probably prove much worse. The common people in the north don't understand that, nor do I believe they care. It's delusional to believe the ex-slave will work in the glow of his newfound freedom for poorer return."

She swallowed, and Seth realized this young woman didn't know how to proceed.

The proprietress placed a plate in front of Alice, then him. "Enjoy your meal," she said, and Alice smiled her thanks.

"Would you like to say grace?" he asked.

"No, but I will listen to you if you do."

He picked up his fork and loaded it with black-eyed peas. Alice looked at her plate, picked at a piece of fried okra and took a bite. "You're not used to Southern cooking," he said.

"I am, and I like okra."

He watched her take another bite, then a sip of water. "Did you find in President Lincoln's speech what you were looking for?" he asked.

"I found no comfort in it, if that's what you mean?"

"Comfort?"

"That's my attempt at tact. From what you've just told me, you didn't fight for the United States to end slavery."

"I fought for the United States…" he swallowed and studied the distant wall…because his neighbors, and hence, his family, hedged their bets when hostilities commenced.

"You're no doubt aware Kentucky was torn in its loyalties. My family believed its interests would be best served by remaining a part of the United States. As for the fight, I attended the Naval Academy and was commissioned a second lieutenant in the Marines in '59. Duty, not slavery, drove my resolve."

"I don't know what angered my father more, the abolitionists, the Republicans, or the South for secession. That's why he and my brothers fought, to preserve the Union. President Lincoln's speech disturbs me terribly."

He started to tell her it had disturbed a lot of people, but she set her fork down and, to his dismay, blinked back tears.

"My father and brothers are dead. I refuse to believe the war was God's punishment on this nation. It's as if Lincoln was saying I've led my nation to disaster, taking more than 600,000 of her young men to their deaths as penance to God to absolve us of the sin of slavery. If he truly felt that way, then he took office believing it was his duty, as God's instrument, to destroy his people."

Lord, she was upset. Seth hadn't been particularly impressed with the speech, but he did find Alice's interpretation painfully skewed.

"He didn't take office with a premeditated plan to wage war, Alice, and our people are not destroyed, simply bloodied. And we still have the nation your father and brothers died for."

"Do we?"

No, he knew they didn't, but this young woman didn't need to be lectured on the intricacies of Constitutional interpretation, state rights, or the abusive power of central government. She needed to believe what her loved ones had died for was still there, united under one flag, even if that flag no longer represented the spirit of its founding document.

"It's stronger now," he said.

She frowned at him and started to shake her head. Immediately he reached for the hand that had held her fork. The other remained in her lap. "It will be," he said.

She hadn't cried, thank goodness, and he wished more than anything he hadn't pushed her interest in that speech at their first meeting. But he hadn't realized what drove her. "I'm sorry," she said. "I've behaved terribly and ruined your luncheon."

"No, you haven't. I think you're filled with grief, and I've found our conversation stimulating."

"It's not as if I'm the only one, is it?" She looked around the sparsely occupied dining room. "In some ways, being here in the South helps. I'm surrounded by grief that's deeper than mine."

He wasn't sure grief deeper than hers was what she needed. "I would agree theirs is as deep, but not necessarily deeper."

"They've lost not only loved ones, but their way of life."

And the despised enemy had his heel on their necks. "Do you share grief with them or find their misfortune a comfort?"

She studied him. "As in vengeance, you mean?"

"Yes."

She dropped her eyes. "My father and oldest brother died together. Goodness, it was only a year ago this past July. They died the same day, but I learned of Josh's death first. I received a letter from Michael ten days after that Papa was gone, too. The official letter from the War Department came two weeks later.

"General Taylor had already surrendered in the west when news came of Michael. He'd been killed in North Carolina shortly before Lee surrendered to General Grant. Aunt Betty and I were sitting in the parlor, when the knock came at the door. I looked out the window and saw a blue uniform on the front porch stoop. I was so sure it was him come home."

She couldn't manage the tears this time, and he reached into his breast pocket for a handkerchief, but she was already wiping her nose with her napkin.

"It was one of my father's old friends from the unit. He came up from Ohio personally to tell me and Aunt Betty."

Alice looked up at the ceiling and gave a little laugh, all the while blinking back tears. "I almost lost my mind that time. Poor Aunt Betty still thinks I've lost it, and I fear she thinks I'll never find it again."

She straightened and looked him in the eye. "As you must also. In answer to your question, I want to hate these people. I want to hate them with all my heart, but I can't. I think it's because I've lost my capacity to feel."

Again he offered his handkerchief. "If you'd lost your capacity to feel, Alice, you'd not need my handkerchief at this moment. And please take it. You'll have to wash it, and that will give me an excuse to see you again. That's how crazy I think you are."

Chapter Eight

Eli scraped the mud from his boots and opened the door. Elvira Hinny, her gray head covered with a colorful kerchief, turned from her wash pot on the stove and gave him a grim look.

"I used the back of the piano for the lid."

"I'd hoped we might be able to salvage that," Aunt Naomi said. She stood in front of the sink, washing the coffeepot. Lips tight, she looked over her shoulder at him before pushing a tendril of hair behind her ear. She'd been blonde in her youth, but now her hair was streaked with gray, giving her a washed-out and haggard look. He had no memory of her young.

Eli lifted the ladle from its nail on the rough wall, checked it for unwanted bugs, and dipped it in the bucket of fresh water on the counter near the cookhouse's back door. "There was no way I could have repaired that thing."

Naomi sighed. "You're probably right, but I'd held out hope since it was your mother's."

The water did little to relieve the lump in his throat, and he returned the ladle to its nail. Outside, a soft rain pattered against the roof. The dreary room was, at least, warm and smelled cleanly of lye. He removed his coat and hung it on a peg near the door. Elvie told him she'd get the blood out.

"How old was she?" he asked.

"Turned thirteen in July."

So she'd only been twelve when five grown men raped her. He swallowed hard, "ova and ova."

Aunt Naomi moved to the pantry. "Has Brim left yet?"

The room was wide, but appeared bigger given its sparse furnishings. Once it had been a fine kitchen. Eli looked across it now and met his aunt's gaze. "He's at the graveyard diggin'. We're puttin' her beside her mama. He won't leave till we have her in the ground. I'm gonna need help with the casket."

"Needs to get off the road with that wagon before dark."

"He realizes that. We're goin' as fast as we can."

Beside him, Miss Elvie sniffed, and he moved closer to place an arm around her withered shoulders. She continued to stir the steaming cauldron with a stick. After a moment she fished out a white sheet to check the bloodstains.

"Damn dem's God-fearin' Yankee souls. Yo' daddy wouldn't let no man touch him's female slaves till dey be seventeen. *Seventeen* and he'd a kilt any man dat raped 'em." Elvira blinked back tears. "Girl don't need to be doin' no birthin' till she be a woman full-growed, no matter what her color. Yo mama taught 'im dat and made 'im believe it."

"She learned that from Papa Jack," Naomi said, moving up behind them.

"Sho' she did," Miss Elvie said, nodding. "She learn dat up in Tennessee from Papa Jack. I agrees with you on dat, missy, I do. Papa Jack he be a good massa."

Naomi gently touched his arm. "I'm gonna make us some coffee. Auntie, you put the peas—"

"Peas and collards already on." Miss Elvie twisted her head over her shoulder and looked at Naomi. "An' I'll do up co'nbread d'rectly. Don't need to be tellin' me to do it."

Naomi turned her back on the woman, and Elvie's lips tightened. "Need to be worryin' where we gonna hang dese sheets so dey'll dry in dis rain."

"I'll string the cord. If we keep the oven going, they'll dry soon enough."

Eli didn't know if they had enough dry wood to keep the oven going, and he didn't care at this point. Despite the cookhouse's warmth, a chill pervaded his bones. Right now he didn't care if he ate—Laura stepped through the cookhouse door leading from the breezeway—or if the sheets dried for that matter.

"I've got her and that poor little babe cleaned up as best I can." Laura glanced at him, then turned to Aunt Naomi searching in the cupboard. "What should I dress her in?" Naomi had her back to her and didn't appear to be paying attention. "Auntie Elvie, what do you think?"

"Runnin' outa sheets."

Naomi turned and briefly passed her gaze over Eli before bringing it to rest on Laura. "I saved the parlor curtains after the Yankees came that time. We draped Holland in one. The others are in the wardrobe in your and Andrew's old room."

"That will look nice in the coffin, but I hate to put that bloody dress back on her, and we'll have to do something with the baby."

"Hannah's dresses?" Elvira said, turning to look not at Laura, but at Naomi.

"We might need—"

"Oh, Aunt Naomi, yes," Laura said, a sad smile lighting her pretty face. "The purple one. Remember what a fuss Rosie always made over Hannah every time she wore it?"

Naomi nodded, resigned it seemed. Eli knew she'd planned to protest using one of Hannah's dresses for the burial, but she'd obviously changed her mind. "I recall, too, Hannah telling her once that she would give it to her when she was big enough to wear it."

Elvira turned from her wash, her glistening eyes belying the big smile on her face. "And oh, missy, she were da happiest li'l thing when Hannah tol' 'er dat. She run all da way from dis kitchen to my bean patch to tell me." Suddenly the old black woman let go of the stick and covered her face. Eli started to embrace her, but then thought better of it. She was crying for Rosie and for Hannah and for who knew what else. He listened to the rain on the roof. His whole damn world was crying and probably would be for a long, long time.

Elvira wiped her eyes with her kerchief, blew her nose, then looked at him. "I think young missy would like dat, too."

Eli looked at Laura across the room and nodded.

Naomi tossed the cord to the table. "Where did you scrounge this up from?"

"Brim brought it from Vicksburg."

"Any other goodies he brought us?"

"Farm implements mostly. Got 'em from the Freedman's Bureau."

Aunt Naomi drew in a shaky breath. "This awful day reminds me of the one when Rosalind died."

At the stove, Miss Elvie stopped stirring.

"Good Lord," Naomi said, "I can't recall a happy day at Camellia Creek since I don't know when." She looked at him. "Day you were born, I guess."

Eli could remember happy days since then. Maybe even one or two since 1861, but once they'd been plentiful.

Naomi pulled out a weathered side chair, its cane seat worn, then sat at the table and started unwrapping the cord. She again glanced at Eli.

"Then your father commenced misbehaving."

Elvie glared at Naomi's back. Eli was in no mood to listen to his aunt berate his father, and if the topic had long grown old for him, that was nothing compared to what it had become to Auntie Elvie, who'd been hearing the woe since he'd been a shirttail boy.

"I wonder," Naomi mused, "why a man loses interest in a woman after she has a child."

He'd been that arbitrary child to which Naomi referred, Rosalind Polk Calhoon's second baby. His birth had been precarious, and, truth was, his mother should have never risked another pregnancy.

"Perhaps the woman is the one who loses interest," he said sagely. "From what I saw today, I can see why giving birth would quickly lose its appeal for a woman."

"Your father was a philanderer," Aunt Naomi said.

His father had been a man, nothing more. It had been Rosalind's steadfast refusal to accept her husband's infidelity as an acceptable part of married life that had been the deviation and, in the end, her downfall. She'd forgiven his trespass, then kept her man at home in her bed. The result had been a third child, Hannah.

"He never forgave himself, her dying hating him."

Miss Elvie slammed her stick against the table with a crack that made Naomi Polk jump, primarily because she'd been concentrating on untying the cord and not paying attention to the person whose ire she was purposely trying to roust.

"Quit tellin' 'im dat."

"I'm speakin' the truth."

"No you ain't. But even if yo' lie be true, you've no business tellin' a chil' 'im's mama hate da daddy."

Naomi rose from her place at the table. "For nigh on forty years you've forgotten your place in this household."

"I always know'd my place in dis household, missy. Holland Calhoon neva made you one. Dat's what's botherin' you."

Eli watched his aunt's right fist clench, and Miss Elvie picked up her stick. Naomi was tall, Elvira a little thing, her vulnerability made the more so by her advancing years, but she did have the damn stick.

In an instant, he'd forced himself between the two and grabbed Naomi's wrist. At the same time, he barked over his shoulder at Elvie, "Put it down." Given where he'd insinuated himself, he was the person most likely to get hit.

Naomi jerked her wrist from his grasp and stepped back. At the same time, Eli twisted and snatched the stick from Elvie's hand.

"She was my sister," Naomi said.

"An' my missy. I know'd everythin' she felt an' everythin' she did to keep 'er husban' in 'er bed. Only thing hurt Holland Calhoon was knowin' da birthin' of his baby kilt her. You don't know nothin', you hateful, jealous ole woman."

"If you think I'm gonna stand here —"

"Massa's back home. Yo' reign as mistress of Camellia Creek be ova once mo'."

Good Lord, why did men live with women, period?

"Aunt Naomi, go help Laura find that dress."

Naomi hesitated.

"Go," he said. "I don't want to hear any more of this."

She went. Elvie returned to the pot on the stove and held out her hand for her stick. He gave it to her. "Why do you let her rile you like that?"

"Hmmph!" She started stirring. "You be da one she's testin'."

"I ignore her." Eli joined her at the stove and touched the forgotten coffeepot. Hot.

"Yo' cain't igno' 'er. She wantin' to move back heah. Scared to def you gonna wed Miz Laura."

"You want coffee?"

"I do, thankee, suh. You gonna wed 'er?"

He moved to the cupboard and found two cups.

"Both 'em 'spectin' you will," she said when he returned to the stove.

He poured her a cup, and she stopped her stirring to take it from him.

"You lettin' her share yo' bed?"

"I've told her I won't marry her, Elvie. She's not a child. Now I wish you'd shut up and mind your own business."

"What if you git her wif chil'?"

"I'll bring her to you."

Elvira shook her head, then set her cup aside. "She won't come. She gets a baby in 'er belly, it's 'cause she wants to."

"I imagine you're right. I'd marry her, then she'd come to you." He looked at the woman and found her watching him. "I'm not going to get her pregnant, Auntie, don't worry."

"Why won't you marry 'er? Sho' set yo' Aunt Naomi to huffin' if you did."

"I don't want to listen to her huff."

"You loved Miz Laura once."

"Or thought I did. Either way, I don't love her any longer." Eli scratched his neck, then walked to the table. He'd sit a bit before going back out in the cold.

"You like her."

"Some things about her, yes, but those 'likes' have become specialized."

"She been a big he'p here today."

Yes, she had been. He thought of her in that back bedroom right now dressing Rose Walton in a dress that was probably still too big for her.

Laura had been waiting on him in the parlor when he carried Rosie through Camellia Creek's back door. He'd left Rosie in her and Naomi's care and fetched Aunt Elvie from the quarter. For two hours the three women had struggled to save Rosie and her baby, who Elvie told him when he'd described the bleeding, was already dead. Forty-five minutes after the birth of her stillborn son, Rosie died from loss of blood. Nope, this had not been the entertainment Laura had expected when she'd come visiting.

"Dis batch 'bout done. Sho' wish we was doin' dis outside."

But it was too wet and too cold.

"Rain filled dem barrels yet?"

Eli nodded. "I'll pour this out, you start fillin' pails."

"When we gonna get da pump fixed?"

"Don't know, they tore it up pretty good."

"Gonna patch the tank?"

He'd climbed up in it three days ago. "That thing will never hold water again."

"Dey had demselves a right good time shootin' it up and watchin' the water spurt out." Elvie fished the first clean sheet from the pot and transferred it to a worn-out basket. They all had to be rinsed. "Need to get da line up, too," she said.

"I will. Elvie?"

She turned her wizened body his way.

"Do you know of any more disasters that have befallen my people?"

Her eyes filled with tears. "Ain't no tellin'. Yo' darkies been driftin' away since massa died. Gus he be da las' one, if you don't count Brim leavin'. Only person eva did talk good sense to Gus be Dolly. I tol' him nots to go, weren't safe nowheres, but he wouldn't listen. He shoulda neva took dat girl off."

"Why didn't you get rid of that baby? Surely she didn't want it."

"She wouldn't say what happen to 'er, an' I sho' didn't know 'bout no babe. Don't 'magine she did either at first. Didn't even know she be ole enough to git a babe in 'er. Nimi got 'er dat wo'k wif da Franklin's 'cause we know'd she'd get enough to eat der. By da time we found out 'bout da babe, it be too late to get it outa 'er wif'out riskin' her dyin' fo' sho'."

Chapter Nine

"Wherever did you find him?" Cassie dropped the curtain and looked at Alice, who'd just opened their bedroom door. "From this vantage point"—and she nodded to the window—"he's divine."

So why, instead of spying from the bedroom window, hadn't Cassie come down and met the handsome Seth Parker who had escorted her home—in a commandeered buggy, no less? Shyness was not one of Cassie's virtues.

"I met him at the newspaper office," Alice said and closed the door behind her. "Aunt Betty said you needed to talk to me. Are you not feeling well?"

"I'm not." Cassie closed her eyes a moment. "Did you find a copy of the address?"

Alice tossed her hat on their quilt-covered bed and pulled off a glove. "Major Parker provided me one."

"Is that the name of the dashing young man who escorted you home?"

"Seth Parker, and he's a major in the Marines of all things. I'd never met one before, a marine, I mean. He's working on something here. He didn't tell me what, but I think he's grateful for the opportunity to meet Uncle Peter."

Cassie stepped away from the window and gently touched her cheek. "You really think he befriended you just to meet Papa?"

In spite of herself, Alice smiled. "I think that's why he volunteered to bring me home." She held out her hands and twisted her hips, making her skirts swish. "Look at me. I look like a drowned rat. I looked as awful when he first laid eyes on me."

"You're beautiful, but you must get out of mourning."

Self-consciously, Alice caught a tendril of hair and attempted to tuck it inside the bun at the nape of her neck. She settled on forcing it behind her ear.

Cassie sighed. "What did you think of it?"

"The address?"

"I would not refer to the man as an 'it', Alice. He's not a dog that followed you home."

No, he certainly was not. Alice stepped to the window and pulled back the lace sheers. The rain continued to wash fall color from the surrounding woods, and skeletal limbs had emerged from the palette of golds, reds, and yellows that only days ago had fought so hard to brighten her gray world. This afternoon dreary grayness pervaded everything.

Fall came late here. What had once been her farm in Ohio probably had already seen its first dusting of snow.

"I'm afraid the thing read to me as your Aunt Eustacia said."

"But the words did not offer you the same comfort?"

"They tripled my hopelessness for the terrible waste."

"Oh, Alice."

She let the curtain fall back into place. "I feel better now, after discussing the speech with Seth."

Cassie's eyes widened, and she smiled. "'Seth,' is it?"

"He's still with Uncle Peter." Tossing her other glove onto the bed, Alice snagged Cassie's hand. "Come down and meet him."

Cassie resisted the tug. "No," she said, "I'll meet him later. Mama will be up in a moment, and I have something I must confess to you." She bit her bottom lip. "This is hard for me, Alice. Very hard, for I fear you will think less of me."

"Don't be silly."

Cassie burst into tears, and Alice's heart surged into her throat. She stepped toward her cousin, who averted her face. "I'm not being silly. This is a matter of serious concern."

"I'm sorry, darling"—Alice reached for Cassie's hands, and she pulled her around so the girl again faced her. "I only meant there is nothing you could have done to make me think less of you."

Cassie laughed shortly. "Love me less, you mean, but there is much I could do to make you think less of me, and I fear I've done so. I know Papa will." Cassie covered her face with her hands. "Alice, he must never know. I would die. Mother is devastated."

"Tell me then, so we can get on with fixing it."

Cassie laughed and cried, then hugged her. "I'm pregnant."

The words did take Alice's breath away, but only for an instant. For several years now, she'd suspected her cousin's often too easy familiarity with the opposite sex would lead to this.

"Nathan?" she asked.

Cassie shook her head. That would mean Edward back in Chicago…maybe Miles, but he'd been so long ago. No, definitely not Miles. "Edward?"

"No."

Out of guesses, Alice waited.

"Lieutenant Bradford."

Alice frowned.

"I met him on the boat. He got on in St. Louis."

Alice still couldn't place him, but she wouldn't worry about that now. If she'd slept with the man between St. Louis and Vicksburg, then her pregnancy was not that far advanced. "Cassie, have you slept with Nathan?"

"Yes," she said and blew out a breath.

"Have you considered telling—"

"Oh, Alice, I wouldn't be above such a ploy, but it simply will not work."

"Then where is this Bradford stationed?"

"I believe he was continuing south to New Orleans."

"Then perhaps we need to tell him."

Cassie held out her hands. "For what purpose?"

"Well, you slept with him. You must have found him appealing, and he you. He might consider…"

Cassie was already shaking her head.

"He's married?" Alice asked.

"I don't think so," Cassie said with a snort, "but to tell you the truth, I don't know."

"But, Cassie why would you—"

"Why? Alice, have you no idea what it's like to feel a man's skin pressed against yours, to surrender to his strength when he holds you to his will, and you give your body to him?" Cassie rubbed her arms, now folded across her breasts, and looked away. "I like men, Alice. I enjoy lying with them. This Bradford was different—I'd heard things...."

Cassie closed her eyes. "I hardly knew him, but I slept with him purely for sex just to see...." She blinked her eyes open. "That in itself was exciting, but I must stop this behavior."

Yes, she must.

"Nathan has asked me to marry him."

"And you care enough not to dupe him?"

"I can't dupe him." Cassie sobbed. "Lieutenant Bradford is a Negro."

Alice clenched her jaw to keep her mouth from falling open.

"So you see it would be impossible to fool Nathan."

Dumbfounded, Alice nodded. Lord, now Cassie was staring at her. The poor girl thought she was judging her. Perhaps she was judging, but not harshly.

Behind her, the door opened, and Alice turned and watched Aunt Betty quietly close it.

"You know?" she asked Alice.

"Yes."

"Everything?"

Alice looked at Cassie, who nodded in response. "What are we to do?" Alice asked.

"I see no other way, but to end the pregnancy."

Bile soured Alice's stomach. "That's too dangerous, Aunt Betty."

"I know it's dangerous," she said and pulled Cassie into a hug. She reached out and tugged Alice into the circle. "But I fear Cassie's life will be ruined otherwise. Did she tell you Nathan has asked her to marry him?"

"She did." And that should have been such happy news.

"No one, *no one* must know of this," Cassie said.

Alice grabbed her aunt's arm. "You don't mean for us to attempt this ourselves, do you? We need a doctor."

"A midwife," Aunt Betty said and wrapped an arm around Alice's shoulders.

"Elvira Hinny," Cassie said. "Rosie told me about her."

"You told Rose you needed a—"

"Oh, good Lord, Alice, do you take me for an idiot? I fished the information out of her while talking about her pregnancy."

"The woman lives in an old slave cabin three miles west of here," Aunt Betty said. "I went to see her two days ago."

"I think a doctor would be safer."

"Regarding Cassie's physical safety, I agree, but for discretionary reasons, a local doctor is out of the question."

"Do you know anything about this Hinny woman other than she gets rid of unwanted babies?"

"From what Rosie told me," Cassie said, "she's a miracle worker."

"Which means she's a witch."

"She's a healer and a midwife, nothing more," Aunt Betty said, "and she appears to be somewhat of a recluse."

Alice shook her head. "I think we need to talk to Rosie more."

Aunt Betty sat at the foot of the bed and tugged Alice down beside her. "I know you're worried about this, darling, and so am I, but I've been weighing everything since Cassie told me four days ago. Given the circumstances and Cassie's wish her father not know, a desire with which I concur, this *is* the safest course. Pregnancy is not the healthiest state for a woman under any circumstances, and as far as our talking to Rose, which would at best be indiscreet, Eustacia has run her off."

"But why?"

"She was late with breakfast this morning," Cassie said.

The anger Alice had experienced the night before kindled anew. "You told her just last night Rose was sick. Has that woman ever taken a good look at the girl? She's little more than a child. This pregnancy is hard on her, and she has no family."

"She's from nearby," Aunt Betty said. "I went to Miss Polk's place. I thought the girl might have gone back there, since that's who brought her to us in the first place. No one was home. In Rose's case, I'm reluctant to terminate her for indiscretion, so I'll reinstate her once we've found her. In the meantime, we still have Cassie's problem to contend with."

"And when do we plan to do that?"

"Tonight."

Alice's quick intake of air caused her to choke. "Tonight?"

"After Peter and I retire. Eustacia should be in bed by eight, and I trust Jonathan will leave after supper."

"Why must—"

"Tonight, Alice. Cassie has the morning sickness, and your Uncle Peter is beginning to pay attention. Right now, he thinks her ill health is due to the change in diet. I don't want him to suspect otherwise, and it's what Elvira Hinny and I agreed to. She's expecting you."

You? Meaning Cassie and her?

Aunt Betty patted her skirt pocket, stood, then pulled out a piece of paper. She sat back down. "I drew a map."

Alice's hopes that they'd take more time to think this out had amounted to naught. "Are you not going to be there?"

Cassie sobbed. "Papa would miss Mama if she were to disappear from his bed in the middle of the night."

Oh, dear.

"Believe me, Alice. I want to be there."

"I want you there, Mama"—Cassie took her mother's hand—"but I know it's not prudent."

Torn though she was, Alice took the map from Aunt Betty. Cassie could die tonight. What would they tell Uncle Peter then?

"I hope the rain lasts till morning," Aunt Betty said. "I didn't plan it, but the bad weather should improve the chances you won't run across anyone on the road during the wee hours. Once you turn off the Port Gibson-Rodney road, the route should be deserted."

Alice looked up from the diagram. "We should walk."

Cassie frowned at her.

"That way we can get off the road should we happen on any-one."

"Alice is right."

"But we'll have to get home. I can't imagine Cassie walking three—"

"I'll bring the wagon for you in the morning after Peter leaves the house. We should be home long before he returns for lunch. He'll never know you were gone." Her aunt covered Alice's hand and pressed. "You will go with Cassie, then?"

"You know you don't need to ask that."

On her left, the mattress gave as Cassie sat, sandwiching Alice between her and Aunt Betty, the two people who'd kept her sane this past year and a half; they were all she had left.

"I'm so sorry, darling," Cassie said with some difficulty, at the same time taking Alice's free hand in hers. "When your handsome major brought you home today, he'd put color back into your cheeks for the first time since I can't remember when. Now I've driven it out again."

Chapter Ten

A hand closed on Eli's shoulder.

"You told us not to let ya kill any of these bastards," Dilbert said, raising his voice in deference to the rain. "He ain't makin' no noise, boy. I think he's out."

Eli rose and took a step back before wiping the rain out of his eyes with the hood he'd crafted to hide his face. He hadn't worn it.

Yep, the whoreson was out or doing a damn fine job playin' possum. Eli removed the gauntlet from his right hand and flexed his fingers. The cold rain felt good on his aching knuckles and miserable down the back of his neck.

"Hey," he hollered to Ben, "do you see my hat?"

He removed the other glove, stuffed the pair in his boot, and squatted beside his victim. This was the last man down. Good thing, too, 'cause Eli had botched his attack in the rain, not quite putting the man out with the ax handle he'd picked as his weapon of choice tonight. In the ensuing struggle, he'd lost the thing and ended up using his fists to finish the job. This had been a long, hard day, and he had a long night in front of him.

Wayne Hale was coming around the bend, a lantern swinging at his side. Back up the road from where he came, Hiram, his son Adam, and Dilbert's older boy Jake waited with the three other wagons and their unconscious drivers and guard.

An hour ago, he and Wayne had hidden in the woods off the road and watched this wagon train, loaded with confiscated Confederate cotton, move from an isolated warehouse on the outskirts of Port Gibson and onto the Rodney-Port Gibson Road. On the three occasions Eli had reconnoitered this movement of contraband, the drivers hadn't used a light, relying on the steadfast mules to lead the way in the dark. But on those nights, the moon and stars visible above the canopy of trees shrouding the road had relieved human anxiety. This night boasted no moon and no stars, just a cold, relentless rain—and the lead wagon bore a single lantern. Given the bleakness of the elements, Eli had considered the cotton thieves might not move the stuff at all. But they had, and they'd been considerate enough to provide their attackers light to boot.

Two miles west of where it started, no longer following the main route to Rodney, the guiding light rounded a narrow bend on the back road and disappeared from the sight of the trailing wagons. As planned, Eli's group ambushed the last wagon, the one with a shotgun, and the middle two wagons simultaneously. Beyond the element of surprise, Eli, Wayne, Hiram, and Dilbert—and the latter two's offspring—had an advantage over the Federals manning the wagons. They knew these woods, and they knew this ancient, timeworn road—they'd known where to stage their attack. This might not be the cavalry, Eli mused, but guerilla warfare had its place.

Four men total had manned those last three wagons, one driver for each, plus the shotgun. That shotgun had gotten out one rain-muffled shout when he realized they were being attacked, but by the time the driver of the lead wagon and his guard realized something was wrong, Ben Bowen was snuffing the sole lantern and Eli had knocked out the guard. The driver now lay at Eli's feet.

"Any of 'em conscious?" he called to Wayne above the downpour.

"One was stirrin'. I knocked him in the head again. Sure we don't want to get rid of 'em for good?"

"That'd be a mistake." Eli tossed one of the man's boots aside. "Wagon ready?"

"And loaded 'cept for your two here."

Eli started peeling off the man's blue britches. They were wet, and Dilbert helped. Ben moved up beside them and plopped Eli's hat back on his head. Eli straightened it. His back was soaked. "This fella's a captain," he called out. "He the senior man?"

"Got a major back there and another captain," Wayne said.

Eli nodded to the man Dilbert already had stripped and hogtied. "The two shotguns appear to be civilian."

"Ya think them are Treasury agents, Daddy?" Ben asked.

Dilbert draped an arm around the boy's neck and spit tobacco on the downed man's chest. "Ain't no tellin', son."

"Whatever they are, we're puttin' an end to their thievin' careers," Wayne said, then helped Eli flip the man onto his stomach. Eli pulled his wrists together.

"Maybe, but they're like cockroaches in the walls; there's too many of 'em. They're gonna be contaminating things for a long, long time." Eli tested the binding, then looked up at Dilbert. "Who's gonna guard 'em?"

"Jake."

"Good. Let's get these two in the buckboard and stow their asses away. We've got a lot of cotton to move before sunup."

"*I*'ll get her, I promise." Alice released Cassie's hand and rose from the chair next to the narrow bed in Elvira Hinny's two-room cabin. Miss Hinny, small, aged, and by all appearances fragile, followed her out of the room.

"She be all right, girl. Ain't no need to get her mama now."

Alice raised shaking fingers to her lips and closed her eyes. "You are certain the bleeding is not abnormal?"

"Chil', you cain't 'magine da blood flows from a body bleedin' to def. Dat girl ain't los' nothin' but dat baby she didn't want."

Through the door, Alice could hear Cassie crying, her sobs echoed with mumbles of "Mama." More than pain and fear, Alice figured. Remorse, sorrow...? Cassie needed Aunt Betty.

"Do you have any idea of the time?"

"Pas' midnight, but still got aways to go befo' da sun comes up."

"My Aunt Betty won't be here till way past breakfast as we have it planned now."

Alice looked back at the closed door and bit her lip. Outside the rain pounded; inside Cassie softly wailed. There had been so much blood after…and still she bled. What if this old woman were wrong? What if Cassie bled to death calling for her mother and she, Alice, simply sat at her side doing nothing.

Alice reached for the gloves she'd laid atop Miss Hinny's stove. They were still damp. Her wet cape hung next to Cassie's on a peg inside Miss Hinny's cabin. She pulled it down.

"You ain't got no business out alone, missy. Things ain't like dey used to be here, and dat white girl, she be fine."

"I'm sure you must be right, Miss Hinny, but I have to go. I told her I would." Alice reached for the tin lantern on the floor beneath Cassie's cape and lit it. Coming, it had blown out on them twice; the weather was worse now.

A gust of wind misted her body when she opened the door. She'd been so relieved to have escaped nature's misery when she and Cassie arrived less than an hour ago. Miss Hinny's cabin was warm and smelled of wood soaked with life. Though much smaller, it reminded her of her Ohio home.

Alice ventured onto the porch and looked into the yard, scarcely visible beyond the shimmering curtain of rain reflecting the light from her lantern. She shuddered from cold…and the thought of the dark road. She didn't want to go.

"Wait," the old woman cried over the pouring rain, then turned back inside. Seconds later she returned to the door with a floppy slouch hat in her hand. "My old massa give it to me. Be his fo' a long, long time. I want it back come mawnin'. Ain't nothin' can take its place."

She considered not taking the headgear, considering its apparent emotional value, but with only the cape hood to protect her, the rain had at times rendered her almost blind en route. She looked at the frail old woman, hat in hand and arm outstretched. The offer was considerate, and Alice would not refuse the kindness. "Thank you," she hollered and took the hat.

"I'll give dat girl somethin' to ease her mind. Pro'bly sleep till you get back. Don't make no sense a'tall you goin' out in dis."

"I know," Alice said, placing the hat on her head, then raising her chin enough so that she could see beneath the low-hanging brim. "But I have little left to live for. That girl in there is one of them."

The Negress grunted and stepped back inside. "You watch yo'sef."

Alice stepped into the churning night and immediately floundered in the quagmire of the grassless yard. She'd be doing well to watch her step, much less the rest of her. Tonight, at least, she wore her winter clothing, and the odds were slim to none she'd meet anyone out and about in this weather. She figured that was what Miss Hinny really meant.

They'd taken over an hour getting here. Given the elements, she'd give herself an hour and a half to reach home. But first, she needed to find the road.

Seth felt Captain Jubal Summers settle into place beside him. "They ain't comin'," Jubal said.

The man was probably right, but Seth wasn't quite ready to give up. "Could be the weather holdin' 'em up."

"Could be Cummings lied to you."

Seth shifted his gaze from the dimly-lit form of the *Lucky Lilly* a hundred yards in front of him and tried to make Summers out. "Could have, but I don't think so." The newspaperman had his own agenda, but lying to Seth in this instance would not have been smart, and he figured Cummings knew that. Then again, Cummings might have figured Seth as disreputable as the other men Cummings had come into contact with, the ones he'd betrayed when he volunteered information on this particular shipment of cotton.

"The men cold?" he asked.

Summers was not only quiet, he was still. Frigid with cold or disbelief at the absurdity of the question? Seth would've laughed if he weren't so damn miserable himself, lying here in the mud of a near-jungle patch of woods at the edge of the rising Mississippi. All of 'em were soaked and getting wetter by the minute.

"Didn't know how cold it got down here till I came," Summers said.

"It's the damp makes it feel that way, I think." Seth stirred, then punched his second in command. "Movement on the landing. You see it?"

Summers moved in the darkness. "Sure do. Hear that old engine singing, too."

Which said plenty, because the pouring, pounding rain hindered not only sight, but sound. "They're castin' off." Prudent of 'em, too. It was after two in the morning. If he'd been skipper of that boat, he'd have been long gone an hour ago. From what Seth understood of the operation, the *Lucky Lilly* should have received at least one load of cotton by now. Obviously the crew had expected the operation to go on as usual, despite the weather. Whatever had spooked the cotton movers, the ship hadn't been made privy to it.

Summers chuckled. "Few minutes ago I heard Spain tellin' Frank Zachary how happy he was to be chosen by you for this duty, so he can spend nights out enjoyin' the countryside. All of 'em gonna be pleased knowin' how much this loiterin' in the rain was worth it."

"I know from their records they've experienced worse tactical bungles."

"Think they were hopin' those were over with the war."

The ship's gaslights floated between the branches of scraggly brush, and over the roar of the rain the churning of the paddle-wheel picked up speed.

"Weren't we all?" Seth said, grinding his knees into the wet ground as he pushed himself to his feet. His legs were so cold and stiff, he scarcely noted the additional discomfort.

"Yo," Summers called in a harsh whisper, drawing the troop of eight scattered soldiers from their hiding places.

Seth's gut feeling was that someone had betrayed his ambush, someone he was working with at headquarters, or even in Claiborne County. Someone intimately involved in the lucrative, illegal trade of confiscated Confederate cotton. Seth sensed his dark-skin troops around him. There were few white officers he trusted in this cotton matter, but he trusted his Negro captain and the men the two of them had handpicked between them.

"What now, Major?" Jubal asked.

Seth shook the water from his kepi and placed it back on his wet head. "Well, Captain, I guess we better head back up the road and see what we can find out about that elusive cotton."

Chapter Eleven

Two in the morning, Alice figured, at the earliest. She wasn't absolutely positive she hadn't lost her way. She should have come to the Rodney-Port Gibson road by now. There were other narrow, tree-shrouded byways branching off this one, and she'd started to worry that she'd followed one such. Perhaps she'd have to stop and wait, in the pouring rain, for sunup—and if she were lost, and if a search party had to be drummed up for her...all would be lost to explanation.

Alice swung the lantern, then held her drenched skirt to one side before carefully picking her way through oozing mud to side-step another puddle. Despite being work boots, they'd finally begun to leak. Her feet were frozen, and she doubted she'd ever get the mud stain out of the hem of this dress.

The wind gusted, and she grabbed for the slouch hat Miss Hinny had loaned her. A low howl echoed the wind, not the first she'd heard this night, and she looked over her shoulder, back down the tunnel of trees hanging low over both sides of the road. She couldn't see the leafy canopy or the thick woods to either side of her, but she knew they were there. She shivered, as much from the atmosphere as the elements, and squashing the hat tight on her head, she hunched her shoulders and waved the lantern over the river of road, only to stop abruptly when the light flickered. The wind had blown it out once already, and relighting the thing, in the dark and the rain, had been nerve-racking, not to mention near impossible.

The flame steadied and so did her heart. Head bowed, her eyes focused on the ground, her ears oblivious to everything but the driving rain through the autumn leaves, she started forward, then recoiled with a small cry when the brim of her hat brushed something in front of her. Bringing one hand to her mouth, she raised the lantern with the other and found herself looking up into the bright eyes of what was, at that moment, the scarifying face of a mule.

Dilbert had stopped the caravan when he saw the light, then told Ben to walk back and tell the others there was a problem meandering their way. For a minute or so, the cotton thieves had huddled behind the first wagon and watched the light close on them, then Hiram sent Adam and Ben back to stand guard at the rear wagon.

Even on a night as dark and nasty as this one, Eli could see it was a woman. He thought she'd sensed their presence when she'd stopped in the road, but that hadn't been the case. Upon them now, she raised the lantern and looked at the second mule, then bent to one side and peered down the length of the beast to the wagon. Beside him, Dilbert shifted slightly. Eli was fairly certain she couldn't see them in the dark. The woman moved directly in front of the mules. All he could see now was her lantern light refracted by raindrops in front of the lead wagon.

"Checking the other side," Wayne whispered behind him.

"Who is it?" Hiram asked.

Eli thought at first it might be Miss Elvie, considering this person's size and the road she was on, but he knew now that it wasn't. She reappeared, raised the lantern...

"She's gonna bolt," Wayne cried.

The woman dropped the lantern, snuffing the light, and Eli surged from his hiding place. She'd almost made it into the woods when she stopped, and he ran into her, mired on the side of the road in the same ditch that now ambushed him. The collision forced them to the embankment, him to one side and slightly on top of her. She twisted, then lashed out. He managed to get hold of a flailing arm, while she tried to push herself up the saturated embankment with her foot. He slipped, and she broke free, but when she rolled back to her stomach and started up the embankment, and what she must have thought was safety in the woods, he found her waist in the dark, pulled her off the ground, and yanked her to him, her back against his chest.

"Let me go!"

She didn't stop fighting, arching her spine, then kicking back, totally ineffective given the volume of sodden clothing weighing her down. She twisted, and Eli sensed she was going for his face. He caught the offending arm with her first harmless blow, spun her, and brought her arm behind her back.

"Somebody cover up and get me a lantern over here," he cried, then twisted her arm a little higher and let go of her waist. With his free hand, he covered his face with the bandana he wore around his neck.

She growled and tried to stomp his feet, but she couldn't see any better than he could, and her mode of dress, not to mention the significant differences in their size and strength, had her at a disadvantage. Moments later a shrouded man, Hiram, he realized, held up the light in the pelting rain, and Eli whipped the hat from her head. Hot damn and pepper jam!

He turned her so her arm was no longer pinned behind her, but he didn't let her go. "Why, Miss Shelton," he said, yanking the kerchief from the bridge of his nose, "whatever are you doing out on a night like tonight?"

She wiped the rain from her eyes with her free hand and stared at him, then her nostrils flared. Yep, she recognized him.

"That Franklin's niece?" Wayne said from somewhere behind Hiram.

"Don't anybody use names and don't let our little friend here see your faces."

"She sees yours."

Yes she did, but he didn't care. "Miss Shelton and I know each other, gentlemen."

Wayne snickered. "You do?"

Of course, Wayne probably didn't know quite what to make of that, but the man would back him. So would Dilbert and Hiram for that matter. "We do, indeed," Eli said.

"Let go of me."

He did, and she held her hand out for the hat, which he raised out of her reach. She glared at him. "It's not mine. I promised to return it."

He brought his arm down and studied the hat in the light, then handed the thing to her. "Put it back on, Alice, darlin'"—her dark eyes glinted, and he grinned—"you're getting all wet."

An understatement, to be sure. Water streamed down her beautiful face, moistening her lips and plastering loose curls against her smooth skin. He didn't know how effective that woolen cape of hers had been at keeping her dry, but his gut feeling was she was soaked to the bone. "You're a mess."

She looked down at herself, covered in mud and sand and dead leaves, then looked up and squashed the hat down on her head.

"I thank you for that compliment. I'll be on my way now."

He laughed. "Where are you going?"

She stepped back, but twisted around as her foot sank ankle deep in the flood-swollen ditch skirting the road. She pulled herself out. "Home."

"To your uncle's house?"

"Yes."

"I don't know that you'd make it by yourself."

"As always, it's been a pleasure seeing you, Mr. Calhoon, and I don't care what you think you know."

"You should," Wayne said.

He followed her eyes to the lantern, then to his three companions huddled around it. All wore the masks they'd made to hide their faces in this eventuality. He watched her swallow. They made a frightening bunch in the yellow glow of lantern light. She sidestepped, putting him between her and them. Despite her brave front, she was scared to death, and obviously he was the lesser of two evils.

"She ain't goin' home," Wayne said.

Eli turned and looked at her, hiding behind him. No, she couldn't go home, even if he'd wanted her to, which he didn't.

Alice Shelton met his eyes.

"I know," he said, and watched her tongue lick raindrops from her bottom lip. She backed up, one step closer to the woods. Hiram moved closer to his side, holding the lantern high. "Don't try," Eli told her. "You can't get away."

"Please," she said, her eyes brimming with tears. "I only want to go home."

Now she was getting too scared for his taste. "Why aren't you already at home?" In a warm, dry bed.

She closed her mouth and stood there.

"Not talkin', huh?"

"Must be some good reason for a proper young lady to be out on a night like this," Dilbert said.

"Yeah," Wayne said, "and it ain't 'proper.'"

She'd been looking at the ominous group as they talked. Now her wide eyes settled back on him. "I need my aunt's help, that's all."

"Honey," Wayne said, "you need more help than your aunt can give you right now."

She glanced in the direction of Wayne's voice, then back to Eli. "What does that person mean?"

"We aren't letting you go anywhere."

Wayne again, and Eli squelched the urge to reprimand him.

"You've stumbled upon us, that's what he means."

She looked in the general direction of the wagons, unseen in the rain-drenched dark. "I don't know what you're doing. I don't care. I've got to get to my aunt. There's a Negro girl. She works for us. I've been looking for her, and I found her."

Eli tensed, and anticipating what was about to follow, he asked, "What's wrong with her?"

"She's going to have a baby. I'm afraid she's going to die."

"Does this girl have a name?"

She opened her mouth to speak, and he knew she didn't know what to do. It had probably just occurred to her he might know Rosie, and he knew without a doubt that was the girl Alice Shelton was referring to.

"Rose Walton."

Eli snagged her wrist. For a moment, she resisted his tug, then followed on his heel as he pulled her around the men standing in the road. "And what would your aunt do if you dragged her out on a night like this?"

She didn't answer.

"You can't take—"

"I'm not," he said, cutting Wayne off. "Do try to keep up, Miss Shelton."

He led her out of the circle of light and called to the guard to let them know it was him coming. He walked faster, sensing the wagons lined up in the road more than seeing them. Dragging her along behind him, for all intents blind, she bumped into him twice.

"Where are you taking me?" she said with the second bump, about the same time Hiram, lantern in hand, caught up with them. Eli reached for Johnny's reins, tied to the last wagon.

"Why, to introduce you to my horse, Miss Shelton. The one you were curious about." He dropped her wrist to swing himself into the saddle, then nodded to Wayne, silly-looking covered with a pillowcase. "Hand her up."

She looked around quickly, but Wayne had her caught from behind and in the air before she could react. Eli settled her in front of him.

"Y'all can finish this up without me?"

Dilbert stepped forward. "If it means we don't have to shoot no woman, we can."

The girl was still in front of him, and Eli was glad Dilbert had clarified her precarious situation. Should keep her quiet, at least for a little while. He talked softly to the gelding when the horse shied, and settling the big animal, Eli pulled his own makeshift mask from his pocket. "Take your hat off for a minute, Miss Shelton. I'm covering your face, eyeholes to the back. Leave it alone and I won't tie your hands, do you understand?"

She nodded.

"And don't try anything funny," he said slipping the case over her head, then an arm around her waist. He pulled her close and noted how rigid she'd become, trying to hold herself away from him. "Yankees haven't sat real well with me for a long, long time, and you're not sitting any better at the moment."

'Course she would have sat better if she'd loosened up a bit.

Chapter Twelve

iss Elvie took the hat and motioned Eli through the door. "Where dat girl be?"

"At Camellia Creek. She's safe. What was she doing here?"

"She got lost?"

"I was out and about. Ran across her at the crossroad. What did she need from you, Auntie?"

Miss Elvie stepped softly to the door leading to her second room. She cracked it ajar, and Eli peeked inside.

"The Franklin girl?"

"Had a baby she wanted rid of," Elvie said and pulled the door shut. "Wanted 'er mama. Da one you got went to fetch 'er."

"Does the mother know they'd come here?"

"Yassuh. Gather da daddy don't though. Mama gonna pick 'em up later in the mawnin'. Reckon she won't be by till den since you stopped dat girl gettin' home tonight."

Eli tugged a buff gauntlet onto his hand. "When the mother gets here, tell her what happened. Tell her the girl got lost and wandered onto my place. Tell her I'm flooded in and will bring her niece home when the creek goes down." He looked Elvira Hinny in the eye. "Tell her she'll be fine."

"What you up to, boy?"

"No good, Auntie, no good a'tall. But I'm afraid that's the only way we're going to survive these bastards now."

"Dat girl you gots ain't no Yankee bastard, Eli."

"No, she's not. But neither were our women at Port Gibson or Jackson or Meridian or…" He clenched his teeth so hard it hurt. "Neither was Becky or little Rosie. The pretty Miss Shelton is a damn sight luckier than our womenfolk were."

⋑·⋐

100

*H*e was gone and had been, Alice reckoned, for about half an hour. He'd told her to stay inside, make herself at home — such as it was, and he had emphasized that point. Camellia Creek was an island, he said. There was no way off it now in this rain, and it would be foolish for her to try.

That they really could be on an island, she didn't question. Toward the end of her impromptu ride, she'd felt the horse hesitate, then lower its head and lumber down a slope. Adept handling by this Eli Calhoon person was the only thing that kept her on the horse. Seconds later, she'd felt frigid water past her knee. She'd been unable to escape the stream short of pulling her legs up and scrunching against him, and that was something she'd refused to do. Back on solid ground, he'd pulled the pillowcase from her head. Why he'd bothered with the blindfold, she didn't know, because the night was black as pitch, and blindfolded or not, she'd had no idea where he was taking her. But now she knew where she was. Well, sort of. Though her uncle had seen the house called Camellia Creek, she had never been here.

What she did question was there being no way off the island. Eli Calhoon was off it, or at least she assumed he was, and they'd gotten onto it. And his route in might very well explain the inexplicable blindfold.

Hurricane lamp in hand, Alice wandered from one spacious room to the next, not so much looking for him, as confirming he wasn't in the rambling house. The structure stood almost a full story off the ground — to accommodate flooding on stormy nights such as this, she surmised. The eight, first-floor rooms, four across the front and four along the back, each boasted double casement doors and mullioned windows, mostly broken and boarded now, opening onto a broad veranda that circled the house. A wide, central foyer, with a stairway leading off the hallway at its back, divided the front rooms into blocks of two rooms each. The rear stairway led to two upper, low-ceilinged bedrooms.

The footer creaked when she alighted from the bottom step into the foyer, and she swept her damp skirt aside to gaze at the heart-pine floor, smooth and dark after years of wear and wax. Alice held the lantern high to peruse the expansive foyer with its high plaster walls and stamped ceiling. Despite the cracks and dingy hues, the house's rich moldings and faded wallpaper boasted of tasteful beauty and an opulent history.

A lovely cobalt blue lamp burned on a table next to a wing-backed chair in the room where he'd brought her when they arrived. The waning fire he started shortly thereafter licked lazily at the logs inside the hearth. Alice moved to the fireplace and prodded the glowing stack of wood with a poker. The fire blazed anew, and she set the poker aside. Overhead, distant thunder grumbled above the steady, drenching rain. The wind had shifted, oddly enough, and now came, she was almost certain, from the south.

He had taken enough time to show her to a bedroom. His sister's, he said, and her dresses still hung in the wardrobe. They were too big for her, he told Alice, but not by much, and at least they were dry. Alice hadn't looked at them. Except for the bottom third of her voluminous skirt and petticoats, her dress was clean and mostly dry beneath her cape, which he insisted she remove before entering the house. She admitted her own clothing felt a bit clammy against her lower extremities, but the discomfort was nothing she couldn't live with for a little while.

He hung her cape by the front door and draped her gloves on a rack near the hearth. She wondered if they were dry now, then considered removing her boots and stockings and warming her feet in front of the fire. She decided against it. Time was awasting, and if her only concern had been escaping this man, she mightn't have given much thought to her fate. Mr. Calhoon had neither threatened nor frightened her since that initial meeting on the road. Truth was, he and his cohorts seemed more concerned with what she might have seen than doing her harm, and she would probably be better off minding what he said rather than trying to escape…and failing that, anger him.

Still, what did he mean to accomplish by keeping her here and, more importantly, what was Cassie's condition?

Alice looked around the room one more time, a battered beauty, warm and even comfortable, then made her way onto the porch and called Calhoon's name above the pounding rain. Only thunder replied. Though discouraged by the worsening elements, she told herself she should be thankful it had been a lightning strike and not the forceful Mr. Calhoon that had answered. She donned her cape, then searched for a suitable lantern to take into the stormy night. She couldn't find Miss Hinny's hat.

Alice was sorry she'd left. Ten minutes from the house, the "distant" thunderstorm moved in with the all too familiar pelting rain, reinforced now with skeletal fingers of light that etched their way across the black heavens, followed by earth-shattering thunder that tested her resolve. Peeling the soused gloves from hands numb with cold, she squatted and struggled to relight the failed lantern. This was the second time since leaving the refuge of Eli Calhoon's house that the gusting wind had snuffed her shuddering light, leaving her alone in drenched darkness with brief flashes of ominous shadows for company.

Twice, matches spat, sparked, then flashed out before she could find the wick inside the protected glass. The third caught, and in relief she placed both hands around the lamp for warmth, then stuffed her wet gloves inside a pocket.

A low moan forced its way through the angry night and invaded her senses. Loud enough to be heard over the tempest, the disconcerting sound was still soft enough for her to try to convince herself she'd imagined it. Unsure, she rose slowly, her security lantern at her side. She considered returning to the house, but one look over her shoulder left her doubtful she could find her way.

She looked to the ground, then to the fluttering yellow light that provided small comfort against almost complete darkness—except perhaps to lead Eli Calhoon to her, assuming he even wanted to recover her. She actually wished he'd appear at this moment. Again the moan. This time it swelled into an ominous wail, and she couldn't deny she'd heard it. She considered the light she held in her hand. It could lead something other than Eli Calhoon to her as well.

And what would that be, you silly goose? Shoring up her backbone seemed a viable alternative to dousing her only light, and holding the hood tight beneath her chin, she tilted her face to the drenching rain and listened to the trees churning in the wind. The wind. Yes, the wind in the trees, nothing more.

Lightning struck close enough to expand the air with blinding light and heat that left her hair on end. Not four feet in front of Alice, the macabre form of a woman hung from a limb. Alice screamed, and covering her ears to muffle the simultaneous thunder shattering what remained of her senses, she dropped the lantern, squelching its tentative flame.

Sudden darkness, but still the pounding rain. Alice forced herself to be calmer, then braced when lightning re-illuminated the sky, and again she pressed her hands over her ears to quell the thunder.

The woman swung in the wind, a ghastly sight.

Total darkness. Alice dropped her hands and rushed to help the poor creature hanging from the tree. In the dark, she collided with the trunk, then scraped her palm against the wet bark when she slipped. Again lightning lit the sky. Alice twisted her face up to orient herself in reference to the limb from which the body hung. Nothing swayed beneath it.

She let go of the trunk to brush water from her eyes and fell backward, then cried out with a shock of pain that numbed her derrière. The lightning flickered out, leaving her in darkness. Her lower extremities nearly numb from pain, she forced a hand beneath her and touched a tree root projecting above the ground. She'd landed on her butt bone. With shaking arms, she pushed herself up and stood on tingling legs. But for her petticoats that root might have temporarily paralyzed her.

Alice swept the hood from her head, and bottom aching, she stepped back, nearly toppling once more. Steadier now, she stared up until another flash of lightning confirmed the body was gone.

With some difficulty she found the lantern, then cursed the contrariness of the night when the rain snuffed her match. The wick caught on her second try.

There was no more lightning, only distant thunder, but the rain did not relent. She walked round and round the tree, moving away from it in ever-widening circles, searching for the body. Not far from the tree, she stepped in water. Holding the lantern high, she saw she'd stumbled upon a raging current and could go no farther. If she had seen a body hanging from that tree, maybe this flood had taken it. Though how it got down.... Alice shuddered. Suddenly, she wanted to leave this place.

Alice skirted the raging stream in the darkness until thickening woods turned her from its banks, to the south she figured, or east. The only thing she was sure of is that she turned back to her left. Hopelessly disoriented in the dark, her bruised bottom aching, she found dubious refuge beneath a tree to await daylight, which would come late, given the elements. Whatever Cassie's fate, it was sealed now. Miss Hinny would not have known she was intercepted, her aunt would not have known she'd been on her way during the wee hours of the night. No one would even worry about her until her aunt arrived at Miss Hinny's home mid-morning to find her gone. Alice closed her eyes and wept. Lord, she hoped Aunt Betty didn't find her daughter dead.

When the black faded to early-morning gray, she rose and continued on the way she'd decided for herself. In places where she could see through the brush on her right, a large stream flowed, near out of its banks. She knew enough of the lay of the land and the plantation Eli Calhoon owned—the one her uncle wanted—to guess that stream was Bayou Pierre. Within three-quarters of an hour, picking her way over sodden leaves and twigs and between brush and blackberry, she came to a large lake, covered in places with green scum and placid except for the now slow rain drops marring its surface. Abundant cypress grew throughout the lake, climbing fifty or more feet, sentinels against a gray sky.

When she came to the place where a body of water—she

guessed it was Camellia Creek—had overflowed its banks and was emptying into the lake, she at last saw the house and breathed a sigh of relief. Indeed, on nights like this past one, this place was an island.

A cold wind buffeted her. She was drenched and cold, and thoroughly miserable. Her aunt would be coming for her and Cassie in a few hours and no one, except a bunch of renegades, knew where she was.

First light. A gruff and rumpled Poynter Cummings held the lantern and turned in a full circle, looking at what Seth Parker already knew to be, except for sixteen wet army mules, four large wagons, and two beaten, but now conscious—and sullen—junior officers, an empty warehouse. Seth had roused Cummings about four. Hell yes, he'd got him up. He and his troop had spent all night in the frigid rain for nothin'. None of them were happy.

"Yesterday afternoon this warehouse was a good quarter filled with baled cotton."

"Well, it's gone," Seth countered, "and it didn't go down river aboard the *Lucky Lilly* like you told me it would. And if you knew where the stuff was stored all along, why the hell didn't you tell me? I could have watched it."

Cummings said nothing.

"Maybe he wanted us distracted last night, Major." Summers might have been talking to Seth, but he kept his eyes fixed on Cummings.

"Mr. Cummings," Seth said, "do you know where the missing cotton is?"

Cummings looked at Seth, glared at Summers, then turned on his heel. "What missing cotton?"

The warehouse door squeaked open about the same time Cummings reached it. Private Ball entered; Cummings waited. "Major," Ball said, "Sergeant Zachary sent me. Wants ya to know we found"—he stared at the two battered men on the ground behind Seth—"six men stripped down to dem's drawers in da wheelhouse of dat burnt-out mill down Bayou Pierre a-ways."

"Alive?" Seth asked.

"Beat unconscious, but we got 'em all woke up. Dey's pukin' all over demsefs. Dey was covered with canvas, a moanin' and a groanin'." Ball turned to Summers, and a big grin lit his face. "Hogtied officers dey is. Boots, pants, even dey's socks be gone." He nodded at the two on the ground. "Dem officers, too?"

One of the two, Lieutenant Jenkins he'd said his name was, glared at Ball, then bent over and puked. The other, Second Lieutenant Henderson, watched him a moment, then fell back in the dirt and closed his eyes. Both had taken pretty good blows to the head. Neither was providing much in the way of useful information, at least not yet.

Cummings had meandered back their way. "Six. With these two that makes eight and should account for all of 'em."

"I'm surprised whoever did this didn't kill 'em," Jubal said.

Seth swung the wide door open and stepped out to a cold, dreary day. At least the rain had stopped. "I'm sure they weren't spared out of love for humankind. Prudence more likely. Guess I better get out there."

Cummings followed them out. "Take your time, Major. I can assure you that when you ask the victims what happened, they won't say one damn thing more than those two in there."

"Yeah, but if I can get 'em separated quick enough, they might not be able to get their story straight, whatever it is."

Chapter Thirteen

The house was quiet. Too quiet, and when Eli poked his head into the parlor, the cold fireplace all but confirmed what he suspected. A quick holler and look in Hannah's room verified his fear. The girl had flown. Chest tight, he started through the dining room to the back porch. Evidence indicated she'd been gone for hours, and if she tried to get across that creek she was probably drowned by now, her body sucked into the undercurrents of Bayou Pierre en route the Mississippi, never to be seen again.

The tragic waste of a beautiful woman aside, he could already feel the censure in Aunt Elvie's eyes, though he didn't figure she'd ever believe he'd killed the girl. Then there were Wayne, Hiram and Dilbert, and the boys. The latter bunch wouldn't believe him a woman killer; he wasn't sure about Wayne, but no matter what they thought, he'd told him the word was, should the subject of Alice Shelton come up—and he'd implied gossip—the girl was with him and had been through the night. That's why she was on the road—she was coming to him. That story sat fine with them. When he'd left them at the old Ferris place less than an hour ago, he'd wanted them to repeat the lie. Now his purposeful deceit could well-nigh get him hanged.

Eli pulled the back door shut behind him and raced down the breezeway and into the cookhouse. Maybe he'd find her lost somewhere on his....

He breathed a sigh of relief when he almost ran her over outside the cookhouse door. The first thing she did was raise her pretty chin in haughty defiance, but nothing could disguise the contrition in her gray eyes. As for himself, he was hard put not to hug her, but he managed and held the door wide for her to enter.

"Nice walk, Miss Shelton?"

She raised the hem of her sodden skirt and stepped onto the stoop before entering the building. She hadn't put on dry clothes hours ago when he'd first brought her here. She had to be freezing.

"I see you didn't get far."

"I've been out all night," she snapped.

"Most of the night was gone by the time I got you here. Couldn't find your way off, could you? You should have listened to me."

"It occurred to me, sir, that you'd found a way off." She slammed the cold lantern onto the rough-hewn kitchen table. "Surely you would have credited me with trying."

"I credited you with the good sense to stay warm and dry, but then that was a foolish thought on my part, considering I found you out in the wee hours of the morning on a deserted road in the middle of a storm."

He stepped around her and made his way to the door opposite, the one leading to the breezeway and the house. "Come on, let's try and get you warm."

"I'm fine, and I would like to get warm and dry in my own home, thank you."

Except for her fussing, she offered no resistance, and once inside the house proper, she pushed the hood from her head and unbuttoned the drenched cape as she trudged in the general direction of the front door.

"Here," he said, taking the thing from her. "You get inside the front room."

The damn front room was no warmer than the cookhouse or the foyer thanks to the fool woman's allowing the fire to go out. He rummaged in his bedroom and found her a quilt before he squatted by the fire. There were still some hot coals. Kindling, a couple of fresh logs, and a little coaxing and the flames blazed anew.

Finally, he stood and removed his own cover, but not his frock coat. It was worn in places, its piping tarnished, but it was wool and warm. Elvie had gotten Rosie's blood out of it. He glanced behind him at Alice Shelton holding his half-folded quilt in front of her and watching him. But at the moment, the most special thing about his gray frock coat with its "CSA" buttons was that his lovely Yankee captive hated it. He smiled at her.

"How far did you get?"

Her eyes widened. "I walked around the entire home site, I assume. From one 'moat' to the next."

From Camellia Creek, to Bayou Pierre, and to the lake. If that were true, and she had no reason to lie, she had indeed been out almost since he left her.

"You were out in the thunderstorm?"

"Yes."

He stepped around her and sat in a wingback chair. If she wouldn't sit, he sure would.

"There was something very strange."

She was very strange, wandering around in a thunderstorm, in an unfamiliar place, all alone. He waited.

"I hesitate to tell you. I fear you'll think I'm mad."

He laughed. "Miss Shelton, I already think you mad. Go ahead and tell me."

"There was a woman, hanging from a tree. She was there and then she wasn't."

She fidgeted beneath his perusal. "Where?" he finally asked.

With one hand, she twisted the quilt over her breasts, but held out the palm of the other. "I don't know, somewhere"—she waved her free hand toward the back part of the house—"out that way."

He dragged his booted feet up from where he'd stretched out in front of the fire and leaned forward. "Who told you the story?"

She jerked her head around and faced him. "What story?"

"The ghost story of Camellia Creek."

He swore he saw her shudder, then she pulled the quilt around her. She was wet and cold, and she needed to get out of that dress.

"I have never heard such a story."

"Rosie?" He frowned and wondered if little Rosie even knew the story, but of course she did, had to have heard it a thousand times growing up, as much as she had grown up.

"N-no." She appeared taken aback. Whether it was because he doubted her word or her sudden realization that he actually knew Rosie, he wasn't sure. "I didn't know there was a ghost associated with this place?"

"Well, there is, and I suspect you've heard about it."

She narrowed her eyes on him. "Please, pray tell, why I should make myself part of such a story even if I had heard it?"

"To irritate me."

"Or to amuse myself? I assure you, I am in the mood to do neither, and if I wished to irritate you, I would find a much better way to do it than throwing myself in the middle of your ghost story. And how would I know that would irritate you?"

He leaned back. He didn't believe in the damn ghost. He absolutely refused to believe she'd seen anything. "Perhaps you heard the story and then, running around out there in the dark, you became distraught and frightened yourself."

"I can assure you, I am capable of becoming distraught, but not when I'm trying to escape the clutches of a kidnapper, and I could hardly have frightened myself since I was unaware of such a story being part of the folklore of this place."

She'd moved and stood glaring down at him.

"What did she look like?"

Alice Shelton's pretty mouth dropped open. Immediately she closed it, and appearing slightly flustered, she stretched her neck to one side, closed her eyes, and stuck her tongue out of the corner of her mouth.

"We've already established she was hanging. What did she look like?"

"I only saw her when the lightning struck, but her hair was dark and curly and fell around her face, and I must assume down her back." Her eyes opened wider. "It was dry. There was no way her hair could have been dry, is there?" She stared at him as if inviting confirmation.

He shrugged his shoulders. "What was she wearing?"

Looking away, she touched the tip of her tongue against her upper lip, then shook an index finger in his direction. "Something dark, forest green silk perhaps, a voluminous skirt. It was a dress. I think in life she must have been beautiful."

Now her imagination was getting the better of her. "Jocelyn LeBlanc."

She pressed the quilt to her at the same time she looked at him. "I'm sorry?"

"Jocelyn LeBlanc. That's the name of the ghost. Unless of course you did see some poor soul hanging from a tree last night."

Alice dropped in the wing chair opposite him, and he noticed her wince. "So she is real?"

"Jocelyn LeBlanc was real a quarter of a century ago. Are you all right?"

"I'm fine. Then what—"

"What happened to her last night?"

She blinked at him. "Oh, I tried to get to the limb to help her. I slipped, and by the time I got up and lightning had struck again, nothing was there. I thought she'd fallen into the water—"

"So, you were near the creek?"

"Yes," she said, "I thought somehow—"

"You're not the first person to have seen her, Miss Shelton, and did you fall on your bottom?"

"I did, but I assure you there's naught to be concerned with. Who else has seen her?"

"A number of people over the years. Always on stormy nights."

"But it wasn't storming the night she died." She'd said the words softly and turned to stare at the fire.

"Why do you say that?" She was right, but he wondered how she knew—and if that knowing verified she had indeed been aware of the story before last night.

"As I said, her hair was dry." Alice turned back to him, and asked, "What happened to her?"

"It was suicide."

"Why did she kill herself?"

Eli stretched his shoulders. He was tired. Yesterday had been emotionally taxing, the long night physically exhausting. He regarded the young woman sitting across from him, an expectant look in her big gray eyes. Alice Shelton was a living, breathing beauty. After the night she'd spent, she should look like hell. She was the one redeeming thing, with the possible exception of the cotton he and his cohorts had stowed at the old Ferris place, that made the misery of the past twenty-four hours worth it. Right now, he was gambling she was his biggest coup.

"Story goes she killed herself when my father broke off his relationship with her."

"Your father was her lover?"

"So people say, and she was pregnant."

"Where was your mother?"

"Dead. My brother Andrew was seven. I was three, and my baby sister Hannah was around a year old. My mother died giving birth to her."

"Your father didn't wish to marry again?"

"I don't think he wished to marry Jocelyn."

"Then she killed herself out of shame?"

"A broken heart."

She frowned at him, and he grimaced.

"Jocelyn was an eighteen-year-old woman of mixed blood, Miss Shelton. She had dark, wavy hair and tawny eyes, and I'm told she loved my forty-year-old father more than life itself. But my father had loved my mother with as much passion as Jocelyn loved him, and Mama had only been dead a year. He didn't want the suffocating love Jocelyn offered. He took her home."

"But she was here when she died."

"She returned, without his knowledge, and hanged herself from that tree."

"But—"

"My father never discussed his and Jocelyn's relationship with me. I asked him once. I was twelve. He said, 'Son, none of it is true, and I won't speak of it again.' He apparently told

Andrew and later Hannah the same thing, and he never did speak of it again. Not with us, anyway."

Incredulity marred her features. "Are you telling me people actually see that woman's ghost hanging from a tree, your father *told* you 'none of it is true', and you've never mustered the curiosity to uncover what really happened to her?"

"My father never made it clear what part of the story wasn't true, but something was true because she did kill herself."

"Are you sure?"

"I didn't watch her jump off that limb if that's your question."

"Why doesn't she rest?"

"Miss Shelton, you are asking me to explain something I don't even believe exists, but for the sake of argument I offer that she was unhappy, and since she took the life God gave her, maybe she can't."

Alice flexed her jaw. "She would have killed herself to punish your father."

"Rather extreme, don't you think?"

"Upset people don't think rationally. Did your father appear guilt-ridden?"

"I told you, he never talked of it."

"Could he have killed her?"

He frowned. "Why would he have done that?"

"Because of the baby."

"Jocelyn wasn't raised like you. She was the granddaughter of a prostitute and she, like her mother before her, was illegitimate, and my father would not have killed her because of the baby."

"He would have acknowledged a baby of mixed blood?"

"He may or may not have given it his name, but my father would have cared for it in every other way. Such mixes are not unusual and as far as the child looking black"—he leaned forward—"have you taken a good look at the people down here, Miss? Some of the most attractive are of mixed color. The crux of the matter is that my father didn't love her, and he didn't want to be with her any longer."

He watched the movement of her lovely throat as she swallowed. "I am sure you must be right, Mr. Calhoon."

He stood and moved forward to poke the fire.

"Surely her presence disturbs you?"

"Miss Shelton, she materialized for you, not me. You find out what's bothering her."

She rose and unfolded the quilt before draping it over her shoulders. "You consider this amusing?"

"I don't know what people see out there on that tree. I do not believe in ghosts. Perhaps there is some form of energy left in the air and when elements are right—"

"Such as the storm?"

"Always a storm...that energy can be seen."

"In the form of the woman?"

"Yes."

He saw her shudder for sure this time. "And you do not find that frightening?"

"It's frightening only because we don't understand it."

"If there's energy, Mr. Calhoon, it's the energy that comes from life."

"Now you're talking about a soul."

"Yes," she said, "a soul, so we are right back where we started from."

"With a ghost?" he asked and retook his seat.

"If you believe in the energy, you believe in the ghost."

He smiled slowly, watching her all the while. "So would you like to tell me what you were doing out last night on the Camellia Creek Road?"

Her eyes flashed. "Would you like to tell me what you were doing?"

"Stealing confiscated cotton from the Federals."

She sucked in a breath, and he leaned back, satisfied. "Your turn."

"I told you. I was helping Rosie."

"You took her to Miss Hinny?"

He watched as she pursed her lips. That's right—think, girl, think. And he knew she was thinking she had possibly stuck her foot in her mouth, as indeed she had. Moreover, she was debating on what she should say next, if anything, because whatever she said might thrust her petite foot a little farther down her slender, white throat.

"You know Miss Hinny?" she said finally.

"Indeed I do. She stood between my mother's legs and caught me when I was rudely thrust from the womb. She was there when my brother was born four years before that and when my sister came less than two years later. My mother died with her head in *Miss Hinny's* lap."

"I am sorry." She had reddened, and he figured that was due to the image of his birth.

"Sorry for my mother or for your prevarication?"

"For your mother, you oaf. I owe you no explanation for why I was out last night."

"You do not. In fact, I don't require you to say anything further."

She looked away. "Good."

"However, I will tell you that Rosie died in the room next to this one"—he nodded to the wall behind him—"early yesterday afternoon."

Anxiety washed over her features, plain as sunlight on a clear summer morning. He wasn't sure at first if it was because she'd been found out or if it was for Rosie.

"What happened?"

"She went into labor—"

Alice moved suddenly and the quilt fell off her shoulders and into the chair. He stilled, watching her.

"She was only six months pregnant."

He swallowed, moved by the censure in her voice. "According to Miss Elvie, the afterbirth separated from the womb. The baby was stillborn, Rosie bled to death."

The auburn-haired beauty closed her eyes tight. "What was it?"

What was it?

She opened her eyes. "The baby. What was the baby?"

"A boy."

He watched as she turned to the fire. Momentarily she placed a small hand against the mantle. "She hadn't been feeling well for several days, but Aunt Betty felt she was only tired."

"She told me your other aunt ran her off yesterday morning."

"That other woman is not my aunt. That woman was married to my Uncle Peter's brother, and yes, she considered Rosie lazy, and she did run her off, but Aunt Betty intended to find her and bring her home."

"Well, she made it home, Miss Shelton. Lord God, I wish she'd never left."

He rose. He needed a drink and all the hell he had was that damn awful corn mash Wayne had brought along three days before.

"She lived here?"

"Odd she would have never mentioned Camellia Creek to y'all. She loved to talk."

Alice waved a hand. "She probably did. I've spent most of my time here in Mississippi in my room."

He raised his brow. "Well, you've managed to get yourself out and about now, haven't you, Miss? Rosie's father was my daddy's lead driver when we had enough slaves to warrant one. Her mother was the cook after my sister assumed responsibility for the house." He pulled the jug out of the battered commode sitting against the wall behind his chair. "Her father took her away with him in May after you Federals moved in to stay with your dubious ideas of freedom and what is best for the Southern Negro and for the rest of the goddamn world, I reckon." He slammed the cabinet door shut and straightened.

"Ideals of freedom are what our country was founded on."

"You might do well to consider the foundation was flawed from the start, because slavery was flourishing when the North signed on to the Constitution—not counting that we in the South fought more than our share of the vicious battles that made the nation a reality." He pulled the cork from the jug and drank. Shit, the stuff was bad, and he set the jug on top of the commode with a loud thunk as heat spread across his chest and nausea swelled his stomach.

"That did not make it right."

"It didn't make it wrong, either. It simply was, and it came with the nation. In fact, considering Mother England's role in our whole sordid history, you could probably argue very well there wouldn't have been a United States without it."

"You yanked them out of their African home—"

"They were no more yanked out of their African home than I was yanked out of my Scottish one. The Negroes you see all around you, Miss Shelton, were born here and raised here. They're as much a part of the South as I am—and as much a part of the United States, since you Northerners insist, as you are." Eli laughed bitterly. "We'll see how quick you hypocrites will be to support that cause or do you plan to isolate them in the South and leave us stuck with doing your patronizing dirty work? So much for the Negro's life, liberty, and pursuit of happiness."

The lovely Miss Shelton made a sibilant sound. "They should have never been brought here."

Whether she intended those silly words to be philosophical, Eli didn't know, but they underscored everything he believed wrong with the North's stance on slavery. Maybe none of them, his people and Miss Shelton's included, should have come here. "Well, at this moment in time," he said, "I tend to agree with you. They could still be in Africa happily enslaving one another, and my father could have farmed land one fifth what he did. Most of the South would still be in the hands of the French and the Indians and you Yankees would still be wearing linens and wools, all cuddled together in your little east-coast hamlets, that's assuming Mother England's foothold in North America would have even survived."

"Oh, right, Mr. Calhoon, this nation was built on cotton!"

"The nation that used to be was built on hard work and greed, and no small amount of the latter resides up North. You talk of slavery. Have you ever visited the tenements housing the immigrant workers up North or looked at their working conditions? The only thing that spares that squalor the honor of its true name is the pittance the greedy employers toss at those people and dare to call fair wage for an honest day's labor." He leaned forward, and she stiffened. "And there is no master to provide them decent shelter, food, or medicine, and a few hours off when their work day is done, much less days of leisure, and I can guarantee you it will only get worse, because there is nothing now to stand in those bastards' way.

"My father, and the vast majority of Southern slave owners, provided for their people." He leaned back. "Now they have the likes of your uncle and his sister-in-law to care for them."

Perhaps he was being unfair, at least in the case of Peter Franklin, but he was angry.

She looked away and said softly, "Why must you be so condescending toward them, to think of them as children?"

"Well, that's better than some of the things we've been accused of, and for all intents and purposes they are children."

"They are not. They are adult, human men and women who have a right to decide for themselves."

Eli blew out a breath. "I'm in no position to argue that point, now am I? You people know it all." Relatively sure he wasn't going to puke that sour mash back up, he maneuvered around her and found his chair. "And you should be happy to know they are making their own decisions, with a little heartfelt guidance from the occupying forces, that being to leave their plantation owners and do nothing. If they continue on this course, the whole South will starve, them included."

She sat back down, more carefully this time, and he couldn't help but wonder if she considered this an intellectual discussion. "They simply need time to adjust to this new life," she said.

"Their life isn't new. It's the same old life. They work or they starve, only now the decision is theirs to make alone. There is no one to do it for them, and no one to feed them when day is done." He threw out his hands. "Or there won't be once Northerners realize they're footin' the bill."

"Well, they must be paid."

Eli made a conscious effort to keep his jaw from dropping. "With what? The South is gutted. What little is left your people are stealing, and there won't be any money until a crop comes in."

She opened her mouth to speak, but he laughed at her.

"Then maybe we'll be able to pay them that aforementioned pittance. But"—he interrupted her when she again tried to say something—"they can't survive off it."

She straightened suddenly. "Your argument sounds like the same old story you've told for the past one hundred—"

"Closer to two hundred."

She glared at him and started to continue, but he raised his hand. "I have no desire to discuss the virtues of Southern slavery relative to history and the rest of the world, including the Northern section of the Union, with anyone of your ilk."

He watched as her fingers clenched the arms of her chair. "You know nothing of my ilk, Mr. Calhoon."

"I've got a pretty good dose of your ilk sitting here listening to you."

"I was attempting to have a reasonable discussion with you."

Eli drew in a breath. "A reasonable discussion? Miss Shelton, more than six hundred thousand men are dead, not to mention the women and children—of both races—who perished, here in the South, as a direct result of the North's aggression. My family is gone, and my way of life destroyed and every effort I make to reconstitute something from the ashes is tramped down by a bunch of heathen hypocrites who do not even understand what the hell they're talkin' about."

"Why?" she hollered at him, and for a moment she took him aback. "Because I don't understand the virtues of slavery?" She rose. "Well, I don't care to understand slavery, and I don't have to any longer, because it's gone."

"It sure is." He looked into the fire, but he knew she wasn't done with him. He'd struck a chord, and he knew he had when he mentioned those six hundred thousand dead, but the words were out of his mouth before he thought.

"You're not the only one who suffered losses in this conflict."

God, her voice was trembling. He did not want to deal with this.

"You are the ones who seceded—"

"Rather than live with radicals and religious fanatics who held personal conversations with God regarding the abomination that was the South."

Her eyes widened with that, and he believed he must have struck another chord, but this time he wasn't sure which one.

"I don't care about whether or not the South was an abomination, and I don't care about God's opinions on slavery."

He guessed that was good.

"You would have destroyed the Union."

"And to save it you destroyed the Republic."

"We saved it!"

"Union be damned. The Republic our forefathers created is gone."

"The Union is whole."

"More a slough for greedy pigs to wallow in, but it's not the nation forged by the Constitution."

She shook her head in overt refusal to accept what he was telling her. "What matters is the nation is united."

"What your father and brothers died for no longer exists, Miss Shelton."

Her eyes were glistening. "Maybe they died for something greater than what was?"

"And maybe they died in vain. Pity your father isn't around so you could discuss it with him." Cruel, yes, but he was trying to be, wanted to be. He stared her down and somehow she managed to blink back all but one tear, which she swiped at as she turned away. She glanced once at the fire, then, not looking at him, she started toward the foyer and, he assumed, Hannah's room.

"Mr. Calhoon?"

He turned from where he sat, legs stretched out, heart raging, staring at the fire. She stood at the threshold and watched him. He didn't respond, but invited her to continue with a look.

"Are you the father of Rosie's baby?"

That corn mash soured in his stomach. "I beg your pardon?"

"Well, she came back here and I thought, perhaps…"

"Miss Shelton," he said, sinking his fingers into the chair arm as he pulled himself into proper sitting position, "I prefer my women full-grown."

She nodded. "My apologies"—little of his tension dissipated—"but I understand slave owners were sometimes notorious for taking liberties with their female slaves."

"And their male ones, no doubt, depending on the master's sexual proclivity."

Her eyes widened as she watched him rise from the chair.

"However, I was rarely made privy to any such goings-on."

She stepped backwards into the hall as he grabbed her wrist and pushed her the short distance to Hannah's room, only letting her go when she was inside.

"But I can tell you that Rosie didn't know who exactly was the father of her child. The man was one of five Union soldiers, on patrol they claimed, who found her and her daddy in a shack somewhere between here and Jackson. That's where her father was taking her to enjoy the fruits of their newfound freedom."

Alice Shelton, stock-still and wide-eyed, was staring at him as if he had lost his mind. And maybe he had. He fisted his hands and sucked in a breath.

"They raped her over and over next to her dead father, whom they shot when he tried to stop them."

She closed her eyes and, lips trembling, said, "They were colored?"

"Ah, your prejudice is shining through, Miss Shelton. They were white. They told her she owed them for her freedom." Eli grabbed the doorknob, more to hold himself steady. Then saying to hell with it, he slammed the panel back against the wall. Alice Shelton cringed and bowed her head when he lunged her way. But he didn't touch her.

"They defiled and humiliated her in ways they would have never done to a white woman, because from their bigoted point of view, her dark skin made her of less value, her hopes and young dreams less important. A lower animal."

And he had to stop, because his voice caught, and he waited until he'd regained some sort of control over himself.

"She meant something to me, something beyond mere property. Their crime, in and of itself, was a violation of Southern law and ethics." He grasped Alice's arm and shook her so she would look at him. "Do you know what would have happened before the war had white men done that to another man's slave?"

She shook her head, but he had to credit her, because she met his eyes and held them, and he was railing like a damn lunatic.

"A man of breeding would have never done it. White trash I can't rule out, but I can assure you the whoresons would have met their maker, and they'd have never seen the inside of a courtroom en route. Now we've got renegades of all sorts on the loose, including bastards in blue, and we aren't even allowed to raise a militia to protect ourselves."

He drew a cleansing breath and stared at her, rigid and wide-eyed, her breathing rapid. She was scared. He had her pushed up against the side of the bed, and he towered over her. He let go of her, and she folded her arms over her breasts. He knew what she feared, because his mind had taken him to that dark place, too. Impossible for it not to with the erection pressing against the buttons on his trousers. How simple rape would be. He stepped back, looked at the bed, then at her, cowering in front of him.

"I not only like my women full grown, I like them willing." He turned from her and again took the white-enameled doorknob in his hand, pulling the door as he stepped into the hall. "But if you don't get out of that monastic attire, I will rip it off you and make you put on dry clothes, and I'll take that opportunity to check your bruised derrière while I'm at it."

He slammed the door behind him.

Chapter Fourteen

"Do you think he'll have her home before lunchtime?" Betty Franklin asked.

Elvira Hinny stepped forward on the porch and peered at the sky. "Rain's 'bout stopped. If it do, maybe, but doubt it. Take time fo' dat ole crick to go down."

"By supper?"

The old black woman shrugged. "Might." She started for the cabin door. "Dat girl safe 'nuff wif dat man. No need fo' you to worry."

Alice's being safe with Eli Calhoon was only part of Betty's concern.

From the doorway, Miss Hinny nodded at Cassie, who stood near the porch steps. "Dat Miss Alice didn't need to go out las' night. I done took good care 'a you."

Cassie reddened—thank God there was still blood in her—then gave Betty a sheepish look. "I was a bit selfish last night, Mama, wasn't I?"

Cassie was a sweet and, in many ways, thoughtful child; however, to call her selfish when it came to her impulses was an understatement.

Betty glanced back to the old woman at the door, then dug into her reticule and pulled out a five-dollar greenback. She'd already paid the woman the agreed price for the operation. "For your discretion."

Miss Hinny looked at the note. She didn't take it. "My what?"

"Not to speak of this," Cassie said.

The old woman studied Cassie, then looked at the note. "I ain't neva talked 'bout no white woman's business, nigger woman either fo' dat matter. You done paid me, and I ain't needin' to be tol' how I'm s'posed to act." Her gaze settled back on Cassie. "Next time you get yo'sef with chil', girl, you make sho' you be likin' dat baby's daddy. No tellin' who might be doin' dis job on you. Sho' won't be me. Might not do as good as me, and you might bleed to def."

Cassie bristled. "Thank you so much for your unsolicited advice, and I intend to."

Miss Hinny snorted. Quickly folding the five dollar U.S. note in her fingers, Betty reached out and took the old withered hand. "You take this as added thanks for your special care. I know you can use the money." Then she grabbed Cassie's elbow and pulled her down the single step into the muddy yard. "Do not say another word."

Behind her, she heard the door close, and Betty, her hand still around Cassie's arm, glanced over her shoulder to confirm the old woman had gone inside.

"I don't need to be told I made a mistake by the likes of her."

Betty looked up at the cold November sky. A hint of blue briefly disclosed itself amidst the surging gray clouds, and a wisp of smoke curling from Miss Hinny's fireplace unfurled in a gust of November wind.

"She's right. Whether or not she had the right to say it is another matter."

"It was the way she said it. The contemptuous way she looked at me."

"I believe that has more to do with her personality than anything else." Betty pulled her boot from the mud beneath the wagon step, then helped Cassie climb up. "Have you considered perhaps that she said what she did for your own well-being and nothing more?"

No longer careful where she stepped, the hem of her skirt caked with mud, Betty made her way around the mule team and climbed into the wagon beside her daughter. Good Lord, this was a mess, literally as well as figuratively.

From under the seat, she pulled out a wool blanket and

handed it to Cassie. No doubt her blood was low. The child must be freezing; her cape was still damp from her walk here last night with Alice.

"I'm worried about what she might say," Betty said and picked up the reins.

"I'm sorry I lost my temper."

"I'm even more worried about that Calhoon man."

"That's who Papa bought the land from, isn't it?"

"Yes. More importantly, that's the owner of the house your father wants so badly."

Beside her, Cassie cuddled beneath the blanket. "Do you think Miss Hinny told him anything, Mama?"

Betty heard the anxiety in Cassie's voice. Once she would have reassured—perhaps that was part of the problem, she always reassured her daughter when what she should have done was beat her with a stick.

Betty flicked the reins, then turned the mules. "I've only met him. Your father doesn't have a good feel for the man one way or the other. He sought Miss Hinny out last night to tell her he had Alice. How did he know to go to her?"

"Alice told him?"

"I don't think she would have, not willingly. Alice isn't stupid and neither is he. This is what that Hinny woman does. Anyone from around here would know that. It wouldn't have been hard at that point for him to figure out what you two were doing here."

"You think he hurt Alice to make her tell?"

"Perhaps just frightened her. Your father feels he's bitter and resentful—"

"We are taking his land, Mama."

Betty twisted her head so that she looked directly at Cassie. "Your father paid the man good, hard cash for that land. Calhoon warned him the land was 'cottoned-out' and subject to flood."

"So he's honest."

"He'll be honest when he tells everyone around Port Gibson you had an abortion. What I was going to say is your father feels he is resentful of Peter's wanting Camellia Creek. He also disparages your father's proposals regarding working the land in the spring. Blames the South's labor problem on Northerners."

"Well, we did free their poor workers." Cassie grabbed her arm and held on as the wagon swayed its way over the deeply rutted road, now little more than a shallow, muddy stream bed. "What do you fear he'll do, Mama?"

"At best he could cause us some embarrassment. At worst he could resort to blackmail. Your father has money."

"Mama," Cassie said, squeezing her arm, "I can't bear the thought of Papa knowing. I could give up Nathan. He won't want to marry me if he finds out, but I couldn't stand Papa knowing."

"Calhoon couldn't possibly know the worst part. We've that to be thankful for." Betty's gloved fingers strangled the reins. "Whatever were you thinking, sending Alice back out last night? Have you no good sense at all left in your body?"

Cassie let go her mother's arm and covered her face. "I'm sorry. I was scared. I was hurting so bad. I was cold and afraid, and Mama, there was so much blood." She uncovered her tear-streaked face and stared at Betty. "I could feel it rushing out of me. I thought I was gonna die, and all I could think of was never seeing you again."

Betty loosened her hold on the reins and breathed in. "I'm sorry, darling, but we seemed so close to succeeding in this, and when I arrived to find Alice gone…and with this man—and I figure he knows what happened—and we cannot trust him. I'm worried sick.

"And as far as your father is concerned, you'll be better off him discovering your indiscretion than Nathan. Your father will always be your father. He will forgive you, but once Nathan walks away, he's gone. And I swear, Cassie, you'll not find another young man as handsome and agreeable to you as that one." She looked at Cassie, dry-eyed now beside her. "We can tell your father Alice is in town doing more of her research—he's happy she's showing interest in something again. That lie will serve well for the noon meal, but I don't know what I shall do if Calhoon doesn't have her home by suppertime."

"Papa will think she's gone to meet that Seth Parker."

"Go on, now," Betty cried when one of the mules hesitated at a pool of muddy water filling the road. She rose and gave the reins a hard flick. "Go on." A cold north wind buffeted her, and she sat down hard when the mules advanced and the wagon lurched. In quick succession, Betty swayed gently the other way and hit Cassie at the shoulder. The mules lumbered forward.

"Let him think that. He felt a regard for Major Parker when Alice brought him home."

"Grudging, for sure. Papa's scared to death someone other than Jonathan will catch her eye."

"I fear he's dreaming if he believes Alice would ever marry Jonathan, and I can't imagine your Aunt Eustacia accepting the match—"

"Especially after the things Alice said to her the other night."

Betty laughed, and it felt good. "Could you imagine Alice having Eustacia Franklin as her mother-in-law?"

"Poor Alice."

"Poor Jonathan. I doubt even the Erskine fortune would be enough to make the ensuing discord worth it."

"Oh, Mama, with Alice's money, Jon would never be at home anyway."

Poynter Cummings handed Seth a mug of coffee. At the same time the man nodded for Jubal Summers to take a seat, then poured him a cup from the pot sitting atop the wood-burning stove in his small office. Seth took a sip of the hot brew and got comfortable. He remained cold from the inside out.

"I didn't say anything to anyone," Cummings said, circling behind his desk and taking a seat. He looked Seth in the eye. "You may not realize it, Major, but I have a lot less love for those men than I do for you, and believe me when I say I do not hold you particularly dear."

No, he didn't. Seth had always known that. Cummings had been upfront, except for that matter of the warehouse, and respectful even to Jubal, who Seth instinctively knew the man resented answering to for even an instant. Poynter Cummings had not acknowledged that he knew of the warehouse, he'd told Seth after, because he hadn't been ready to give up everything he did know, and, he said, he sure hadn't expected the Federal thieves to be robbed last night.

"I think it's safe to assume the thieves were robbed by other thieves."

"Who you could be working with," Jubal said.

"In what capacity do you assume, *Captain* Summers? I had a tentative working relationship with Alan Guthrie weeks ago. That source is now dead. I don't know why Guthrie was killed, but I'm hoping the answer will make a good story." Cummings' jaw clenched, and he turned back to Seth. "That's why I'm working with you, and that's the only reason."

Except maybe to save his own life. Seth had no idea how deep these cotton scams ran, but the murder of the Treasury agent had upped the ante. Seth nodded. "Drink your coffee, Jubal."

Cummings wasn't scared, he was angry. Angry that they doubted him—angry the Negro officer was questioning him. Then again, Seth couldn't be sure the man's countenance would have been any different if Jubal Summers had been white. His uniform would still be blue. Personally, Seth's gut feeling was Cummings was telling the truth, but he also had to consider he might not be. Right now he'd like to know where that missing cotton was. After that, his choice would be a warm bed and a pretty woman to share it with. But sleep first, then the woman. He took another sip of coffee and allowed his tired thoughts to drift to Miss Alice Shelton.

He forced her aside and studied Cummings. "Your friend Isabel Hays?"

Cummings shrugged. "As far as I know, she's nothing more than a source of information."

Of information gathering he meant. How involved was the lovely madam, if at all? Cummings swore he didn't know. Disingenuous at best.

"What now?" Jubal asked when they stepped onto the porch.

Seth pulled his frock coat closed, then cursed when they rounded the corner of the building and a gust of cold wind assailed them. Jubal put his forage cap on his head.

"Get some sleep. The men get breakfast?"

Jubal nodded. "I imagine Zachary has 'em fed and tucked in already."

"Any trouble with the locals?"

"Not so far."

"Good, I want us focused on our job. On the surface this might look like simple theft, but there's more. One man is already dead."

"*I* wasn't sure you'd ever come out of that room again."

Alice was looking at his back. He hadn't turned or flinched or done anything to acknowledge her presence since she'd spied him squatting out here, a stick in his hand, and she was surprised he knew she was there. He appeared to be studying the charred remains of what had been a large building roughly fifty yards in back of his kitchen. The barn, if she were to guess.

"I truly am sorry about Rosie, Mr. Calhoon."

"I know you are." Still in a squat, he twisted and looked at her. "Open your cape and let me see."

She resented having yielded to his demand to change from her wet dress, but given she had, to continue complying now was easier than arguing. She unbuttoned her cape, and he gave her a long perusal.

"You look good in blue."

Her cheeks warmed. A compliment had not been expected, and he smiled, as if he could read her mind.

"You have many faults, Miss Shelton. Your looks, however, aren't one of 'em."

He wasn't reading her mind, only the color in her cheeks. "Thank you." Immediately she regretted acknowledging the compliment, more out of contrariness than anything else.

"The pleasure is mine," he said and turned away. He whipped the stick, end over end, away from him and rose, long and tall.

His cavalry boots were scuffed, his uniform worn, but his hat sat nicely atop his head, and it irked her to admit he made a handsome man. "I wish I could be as approving of the color you wear."

He pivoted on one heel, and she raised her chin in faux defiance. She wanted to kick herself for provoking him. He came closer, rubbed his chin, and began to circle her. "It's a little big on you."

She had to hold the skirt high to keep from tripping on the hem. "Your sister was tall?"

"Not really. Most people are tall relative to you."

His walking around her made her nervous, and she looked over her shoulder to find him still gazing at her. "An insult, Mr. Calhoon?"

"Not nearly as great as yours, Miss Shelton, if that's what I had intended, but petite women don't offend me in any way. In fact," he said, leaning closer, "they appeal to me."

"Not ones in blue, surely," she said and rebuttoned her cape. Uncomfortable with his freshness, she moved to where he'd been squatting. In the wet dirt, he'd drawn the rough outline of a building. "A new barn?"

"When I can afford one."

"And will your stolen cotton afford you one?"

"Probably."

She turned on him. "Why did you tell me what you'd done?"

"Because you asked me."

"You were trying to provoke me into telling you why I was out."

"And you made up a lie."

"Aren't you afraid I'll tell proper authorities about the stolen cotton?"

"You already know you can't do that."

She could hear her heart pounding in her ears. "Why?" she said, less forcefully than she would have liked.

He pushed his hat back, freeing his eyes from shadow and stepped closer. "Because if you talk, I'll talk, and from what Miss Hinny told me, you don't want me talking."

She studied his eyes, trying to gauge his intent. They were blue, dark blue, and he was very confident she would not betray him. She looked away.

"We burned your barn?"

She heard him come closer, but he didn't crowd her. "Yes, you did. Shot holes in the water tank, wrecked the kitchen, and knocked most of the doors and windows out of the main house, not to mention wanton destruction of vintage furnishings and the theft of family heirlooms. Generations of a family's history plundered by drunken backwoodsmen from the Ohio. *You* wreaked havoc with the place, Miss Shelton, and every town and other farm around here. For almost two full years you wreaked senseless, merciless havoc all over this area."

She regretted her use of the pronoun. The all encompassing "we" in reference to her and hers wasn't nearly so glorious in cases such as these as it was in reading about victory in battle.

"You would have burned the main house, too, but the well-disciplined lieutenant in charge of his plundering soldiers found out my pregnant sister was inside dying of yellow fever."

"I am sorry."

"No need to be," he said, stepping around her. "At least not on account of your boys-in-blue's regard for my sister. The fever took her. The troop left the house as you see it—I take that back, we have cleaned up a little bit—they were scared to stay inside once they knew about the sickness."

"Do you really think you would have been any better had you been the victors and not us?"

"The beauty of retrospect." He wasn't looking at her, but had turned and faced the house, and he spoke, as if to himself. "We should have taken the war north immediately. But"—he turned and found her. "The whole point of our secession was to divest ourselves of you Northerners. There was nothing of you we wanted, save our independence." He waved his hand at what was left of his barn. "You may not have noticed, but the war took place in the South. There's a reason for that."

"You started it."

"Ah, if the cause of wars were only so simple as who fired the first shot. But to address your rather naive understanding of events, Fort Sumter was part of South Carolina. South Carolina had seceded, not to mention the federal lease was up. Your government, after numerous warnings, refused to surrender it. Yes, we attacked first, but you provoked us with your illegal occupation and subsequent attempt to resupply it."

"And I must assume you consider the present occupation equally illegal."

He flexed his jaw, before curling his wide mouth into a grin. "As a matter of fact, I do. But we have no shots left to fire, not directly anyway." He looked her up and down. "The unwilling bride raped in her bridal bed."

Lord, he was horrid. "So the bride steals cotton?"

"The cotton the despotic husband stole from her. Yes, ma'am, I'm stealing the South's own cotton back from the thieves who stole it from the father of all thieves, your Yankee government."

"The cotton to which I believe you refer is confiscated cotton that used to belong to the now defunct Confederate government."

"Some of it."

"Then it's part of…." She blinked at him, then turned away.

"Cat got your tongue, Miss Shelton?"

Prudence had indeed gotten the better of her.

"The spoils of war. Is that what you were going to say?"

"Reconstruction will take a lot of money—"

"The money from that confiscated cotton is filling the pockets of dishonest Union officials. Me"—he stepped into her line of sight and nodded to the rubble that had been his barn—"I've got real reconstruction to take care of."

"I'd rather not hear any more details of your illegal dealings, Mr. Calhoon."

He shrugged. He was no longer looking at her, but looking out to where his barn had stood, then to the woods beyond. She had no idea what thoughts were in his head, what his intentions were.

"When are you going to let me go?"

He found her gaze, then momentarily held out his hand. "Come with me."

She looked at his outstretched palm, then met his eyes. "I do not wish to hold your hand, sir."

"Think how horrible it must be for the unwilling bride, Miss Shelton." He dropped his hand. "And how satisfying for the hate-filled groom."

A tremor moved through her.

"Follow me, then. If I meant you physical harm, I assure you, I'd have already inflicted it."

Flippant, she'd asked if he were walking her home, and he'd smiled at that. They walked five minutes, she reckoned, well behind the house and roughly along the same path she'd taken hours before. Since she hadn't been able to see at the time, she couldn't be sure. The day was cold and blustery. Still overcast, but here and there, between the near-barren branches of oak and gum, patches of blue sky tried to break through the gray. The leaf-covered ground was sodden, as were the wild shrubs and prickly vines that pulled at her cape and the hem of Eli Calhoon's sister's dress hanging from under it. He didn't offer his hand again, though a couple of times she could have used it. Once he did take hold of her waist and lifted her across a mud hole spanning the way.

He stopped at the edge of a flowing creek in a section of woods now glinting in mottled sunlight, and he pointed. "There."

She came up beside him and pushed the hood from her head.

"You see the middle of that stream?"

The thing looked more like a raging river.

"This is Camellia Creek. See where those little rapids are?"

"Yes."

"That's about where you were standing that day I first saw you."

She narrowed her gaze, then looked up at him.

"Hard to believe, isn't it?"

Yes, it was. That first day she'd seen Camellia Creek, she'd considered finding a place to forge it until she'd seen that strange reflection in the water, then this man on the other side. Today, she'd need a boat to cross. "It always does this?"

"Only when there's a lot of rain. November's been hard this year. Spring is always bad. It's overflowed into Lake Elizabeth, too."

"That's the old river channel?"

"A few centuries or more ago we reckon, but sometimes, when the spring floods come, we speculate the old Mississippi might take her back again someday."

Alice looked at him. "What of your house?"

He started walking along the turbulent creek. "River-front property, I hope."

"You don't think the river would flood—"

"It's a concern, but if you noticed, the house is built on a knoll. A geologist told my grandfather, when he built the house"—he looked over his shoulder at Alice, following behind him—"in 1811, that the knoll was the original river bank. If the Mississippi comes that way, and doesn't take the creek west and south, which would be ideal, the house will be on the northern bank of a river channel."

"Would you be in Louisiana?"

"I'm not sure how that would all pan out, but if there ended up being two channels, and I think that's how it would be initially, I'd be on an island, still in Mississippi."

He watched as she moved away from him and the bank, back to the cow path. He had purposefully led her this way, wondering if she'd recognize the place. It appeared she did, because she whirled on him suddenly, widened her eyes when she caught him watching her, then waved a glove-covered hand at the huge oak not fifteen yards in front of her. "That is the tree."

Indeed, it was the one Jocelyn LeBlanc had hanged herself from.

Pretty, petite Alice Shelton didn't wait for him to respond, but immediately set off toward it, then circled the thing. It was a gigantic live oak, centuries old by all estimates, and ghost or not, he and Andrew and their friends had played on it extensively as kids.

"Which limb?" he asked when she reappeared on the other side of the tree.

She pointed. "That one," she answered, without hesitation.

He came forward, looking not at her, but at the limb. "And if I told you that is not the limb?"

She stumbled over a tree root getting to him, then, appearing quite confident, she straightened. "Then I'd say you are trying to trick me or you don't know what you're talking about. That is the limb she was hanging from."

He drew in a breath, looked back at the tree limb, then to her. "You are correct, Miss Shelton. That's the tree limb from which Miss LeBlanc was found dangling by her lovely neck, twenty-five years ago."

Alice Shelton smiled at him. A warm, satisfied smile. He believed that was the first time he'd ever seen her do so. Certainly it was the first one she'd granted him.

"She wants something."

"I beg your pardon?"

Alice looked at the limb. "She can't rest. She wants something."

Chapter Fifteen

"Did you see her before she left this morning?" Peter asked.

"No." Lord, had that been the right response? "She was gone before I rose, as she was yesterday."

"Did Cassie see her?"

"She told me she had."

"For heaven's sake, Betty, did she indicate to Cassie where she was going?"

Betty placed an empty plate in front of her husband, then one in front of her sister-in-law. "To town, dear." She reached across Eustacia to hand Jonathan his.

"Where in town, did Cassie say?"

Betty took her seat beside Peter. "She did not, but I didn't ask. I told you Cassie doesn't feel well. She wanted to sleep."

Peter shot her a look of discomfort, then glanced at Jonathan. Betty had told her husband it was Cassie's time of the month and she was suffering severe cramping. Peter had taken her at her word, not wanting to discuss Cassie's condition further. Betty had known that would be the case.

Eustacia took a sip of water. "I heard some stirring late last night. Alice's absence so early in the morning disturbs me, also."

Peter waved a fork in his hand. "I think I'll wake Cassie after lunch, Betty. Just to see if Alice said anything to her this morning. I'm surprised you're not more concerned over her absence."

Instead of responding, Betty Franklin reached for the bowl of black-eyed peas and spooned a helping onto her husband's plate. He scowled.

"I've never liked these things. This is what the masters fed their slaves."

"I believe the darkies fed 'these things' to themselves. One such cooks for us now. The peas are good when prepared properly, which I imagine accounts for your previous distaste."

He gave her a doubtful glance.

"Oh, for goodness' sake, Peter, you were raised on beans. Eat them."

"Baked beans, black beans—"

"Eat them. Everyone in the South eats them."

He picked up a fork, then looked at Jonathan's clean plate. "You agree with me, nephew?"

"He agrees to eat what is put in front of him or do without," Eustacia said.

Jonathan dutifully began to help himself to rice and peas. "Best eat up, Uncle Pete, or we will as likely as not be doing our own cooking."

"Well said, Jon dear." Betty watched her husband stick a forkful of peas and rice in his mouth. After a moment he poked out his bottom lip and nodded. "You see," she said, taking her seat beside him, "I knew an old Illinois farm boy would like them."

"Perhaps the key is in the cooking. Now, why aren't you more concerned over Alice?"

"Because I see no reason to be. I thought you were pleased she's finally getting out."

"I'd be more pleased if her 'getting out' focused more on a social life and less with the war."

Which meant the obtuse rock wanted the girl to respond to Jon Franklin's self-centered wooing. "Perhaps you should have thought of that before you brought her to a place where the war is visible no matter which direction she looks."

"She's trying to determine the cause of the conflict," Jonathan said.

Betty looked over to find him dabbing the corner of his mouth with a napkin. All three of them, in fact, had turned his way. He shrugged. "That's the only reason she's ventured forth. Surely I'm not the only one who realizes that?"

"I've explained the reason for the war to her," Eustacia said. "You see how she reacts to me."

Betty picked up her fork. "What she's trying to understand, Eustacia, is the existence of people like you, and the poisonous influence—"

Peter cleared his throat, shot Betty a warning glance, then turned to his nephew. "I'm pleased you're sensitive to Alice's depth of feeling, Jonathan. Have you tried to explain events to her?"

Oh, good God. To do that, Jonathan would have to understand events himself, not to mention Alice gave Jonathan as little time as she could manage and stay within the realm of politeness. Alice had no respect for the handsome young man who had evaded the draft with the last of his dead father's money. Betty had repeatedly tried to explain that to Peter. Her husband, however, saw nothing but a good match for his beloved brother's son and his much-loved niece by marriage…heiress to a fortune.

"No, Uncle, she doesn't discuss such issues with me, and to tell you the truth, I have no interest in discussing them with her. I'm baffled by a young woman who wallows in something as inappropriate as the causes of war." Jonathan found Betty's eye, then he poised, his fork filled with peas halfway to his mouth, and he shifted his gaze to Peter. "I admit my growing frustration."

Peter looked at Betty. "You should talk to her."

She should pour that bowl of peas over Peter's head. Instead, Betty set her fork beside her plate and smiled. "I don't think that will be necessary, darling. Actually, I believe that handsome major"—she frowned and leaned closer to her husband—"what was his name?"

Peter stared at her. Quickly she raised a finger. "Parker. Seth Parker. You remember? He brought her home yesterday." She picked her fork up and returned to her plate. "He and she had a lovely discussion, apparently, about President Lincoln's inaugural address yesterday at lunch. The speech Eustacia so kindly brought to her attention the night of Jacob's birthday." Betty laughed pleasantly. "She glowed when he brought her home."

She raised a brow when Peter didn't answer. "Don't you agree, dear?"

"Parker did impress me, but he didn't mention a discussion on Lincoln."

"Well, Alice sure did." Betty nodded at Jonathan, who hadn't moved since she'd brought up Seth Parker. Betty turned and smiled at Eustacia, who also watched her. "She seemed to me more content than I'd seen her in a while. I do believe they'd agreed to further their political discussion. Perhaps that's where she is today."

"With him?" Peter said, rather sternly. "Where?"

Oh dear. Perhaps she'd overdone it. Her intent had been to knock the wind out of Jonathan's sails, not set Peter's to billowing.

"They lunched yesterday at the Port Gibson Hotel."

"That," he said, "is where his rooms are."

Dammit, sometimes this man she loved was an absolute ass. Betty slammed her fork to the table with a loud clap. "What are you thinking, husband?"

Peter blinked, then returned to his plate. "Noth —"

"That they can't lunch all day, Betty," Eustacia said. "That's what he's thinking."

Betty turned slowly in her seat so that she could see the woman sitting beside her. "But Alice can find comfort discussing the war with a knowledgeable individual who gives credence to her interest and concerns."

Eustacia smirked, then gave her son a smug, I-told-you-so look. "Perhaps she's simply finding comfort."

"That's quite enough, Eustacia!"

Betty jerked around to face Peter. He'd boomed the words, actually boomed them, and just in time, because Betty had been about to light into the woman.

Seeking defense, no doubt, Eustacia swallowed, and looked to her son, who simply shook his head at his mother. The silent admonition revived her. "That girl is not right for you, son."

"No woman is right for me, Mother."

Jonathan pulled the corner of his napkin from his shirt collar and laid it beside his plate. He wanted to talk to Peter in private, Betty could tell. Well, her tossing Seth Parker in the ring had succeeded in curbing his assurance that he had no competition for Alice; she felt very good about that. She'd also provoked a bellow from Peter to his horrid sister-in-law, but Betty feared the reason was because the same nasty thought Eustacia implied had crossed his mind, too. The very idea someone else would jump to the same conclusion had him livid…and worried. Goodness, what would he do if he found out she was really with that insurrectionist Calhoon and had been a good part of the night?

"You should be more persistent," Peter said to Jonathan. "More persuasive. Alice was raised by three men. Strong, forceful men. That's what she respects."

She respects a man who does his duty, Betty thought as she watched Jonathan's eyes harden. From everything she'd heard of him, he'd been quite the dandy with the ladies back in New York. His charm had not worked on the grieving Alice, however, and he'd quickly lost interest, that is until a concerned Peter, worried that Alice's vulnerability and grief, in tandem with her significant fortune, left her vulnerable to "men of prey." Peter had immediately decided the safest course for Alice would be to wed someone he trusted, his own dear nephew, and he'd suggested Jonathan woo her. Peter had never come out and told Betty he'd suggested Jonathan do that, but she was certain he had. Regardless, Peter had confided his hopes to her when he suggested the two would make an excellent couple, if Alice would but rekindle her charm. Jon Franklin, of course, would take her, charming or not, but Betty told Peter at the time Alice would never agree to marry the man.

Chapter Sixteen

"There is no sugar," Calhoon told Alice.

She glanced at the man, sighed, then pulled out a battered spindle-back chair, its cane seat mended with cow hide, and sat. He had a good fire blazing in the cook stove, and the kitchen was relatively warm. Between cracks in the boarded windows, the sun streaked through, and bits and pieces of shadow from the trees in the yard danced along the countertops and walls opposite the windows. "No cream either?"

"It's my understanding there hasn't been a cow on this place since the summer of 1863."

And of course, that was because the Federals had taken it. "There are dairies, are there not?"

"Not, but you are correct. There are places one could go to buy milk if one wished. I, however"—and he clenched his teeth with the sip of the hot brew—"prefer my coffee black."

She preferred hers with cream and sugar. She looked at the steaming liquid, dark and thick and greasy. He'd admitted to her he'd first brewed it yesterday. He could afford to waste nothing.

Well, she wouldn't give even the appearance of a spoiled Yankee conqueror whining at being forced to live as the vanquished did. She took a sip, and her stomach roiled. She glanced at him, watching her, but kept her face expressionless—at least she tried to.

"It will warm your innards, Miss Shelton."

She looked away, rolled her lips, and took another sip. "Yes, it does. I'm sure one could get used to it in time."

"Cornbread is in the oven. It's good with pea juice over it."

"You don't even have the peas?"

"I have the peas. Cold collards, too."

She stretched her arms out on the table. She had no appetite, and the one she might have mustered that awful day-old coffee had repelled. "I thank you for your invitation to luncheon, Mr. Calhoon"—he smiled at that—"but I know my family is worried about me. I want to go home."

"Your aunt knows where you are. I'll take you home when the creek goes down."

"It must be before…" She looked away.

"Before what?"

She took another swig of coffee.

"Would you like corn mash?" He laughed at her responding glare.

"It must be before supper."

"Before your uncle gets home, you mean."

"Yes, darn you. Before my uncle gets home. I'd rather not explain you to him."

"*Me*, Miss Shelton? No, what you mean is you'd have to tell him why you were out—"

The back door of the cookhouse, the one that exited into the yard instead of the breezeway leading to the house, opened. Alice looked around Eli Calhoon, equally surprised if his expression meant anything.

A woman stepped in carrying a cloth-covered platter. She didn't look up, but turned away and shut the door. "I brought you some fried"—she saw Alice, stared a moment, then shifted her gaze to Calhoon, who'd rose with the woman's entry.

"'Chicken,' I hope you were gonna say."

The rather tall woman, well into her middle years, appeared dumbfounded, and Alice was certain this person was as shocked as she.

"Is it?" Calhoon asked.

"Yes, chicken." The woman's voice was deceptively soft, decidedly feminine. She locked her gaze on Alice and approached the table, at the same time tugging beneath her chin at the tie to her bonnet. She set the platter on the opposite end of the table from where Alice sat and Calhoon stood, then she reached up and uncovered fair hair, washed with gray.

"Miss Shelton," Calhoon said, "my aunt, Naomi Polk. She makes the best fried chicken in Mississippi."

Alice could care less about the fried chicken at this point. "How do you do? And where did you come from?"

The woman knit her graying eyebrows.

"Have you always been on the island?" Alice asked and rose.

The woman turned to Calhoon with a perplexed expression. "What island?"

"She's referring to Camellia Creek in the rain."

Miss Polk looked at Alice. "The water goes down pretty fast once the rain stops."

Alice found Calhoon, who gave her an innocent look, then refocused on his aunt. "You walked the back way?" he asked.

"Doctor Lester was on his way to Vicksburg. He brought me as far as the bridge."

"What bridge?" Alice croaked out.

The woman looked her up and down. "The question is, young woman, what are you doing here?"

Oh, how Alice wanted to tell this woman she was being held against her will by the woman's horrid nephew, but Eli Calhoon could easily turn the tables on her. He answered instead.

"Suffice it to say she was marooned by the storm."

His Aunt Naomi appeared to appraise him. "She's been with you all night?"

"She has."

He didn't elaborate, and Alice's heart began to thump. "My stay was innocent, I assure you."

Alice heard Calhoon sigh, and she looked at him. He gave her a subtle shake of his head and said to his aunt, "Indeed it was." His agreement sounded as feeble as her protest, in retrospect, sounded shallow.

The older woman, her eyes on Alice, was unbuttoning her coat with jerky movements. "And what innocent reason would bring a young woman to an unmarried man's home in the night?"

Calhoon shifted his weight, and the woman glanced his way. She shrugged, then said, "I don't care who slept in whose bed."

"No one slept!" Alice cried.

That Naomi person's mouth dropped open, and Alice's cheeks heated.

"Miss Shelton," Calhoon said, "you really would be better off not speaking."

"What's she doing here?" the woman snapped, at the same time slapping her cloth bonnet onto the table.

"She's my guest."

Alice focused on Calhoon. His voice had become one of authority, and the older woman's tight lips relaxed. She removed her coat and draped it over a chair. "You are the Franklins' niece?" she asked, more civilly. Now Alice recalled the woman's name. She's the one who'd sent Rosie to them back in August.

"Yes, Alice Shelton." She would have extended her hand, but that was the older woman's prerogative, and Naomi Polk made no such effort. Instead, the woman fumbled with a wisp of hair that had fallen out of her chignon, then turned her back on her. "You have cornbread baking?" the woman asked Calhoon, and Alice looked at him, suspecting suddenly he'd expected this person to appear.

"She smells it," he said, as if he'd noted her accusation.

"Oh." Alice licked her parched lips. She had been rude when Naomi Polk came through the door—more concerned with how the woman had gotten here despite the high water when she herself supposedly could not leave because of said water.

"I apologize, Miss Polk. I fear I got off to a bad start with you, but I was surprised to see you arrive when"—Alice shot Calhoon a glare—"I've been told all morning I couldn't leave because of flooding."

The woman gave her an insincere smile. "Then I must assume my nephew enjoyed your company and is not done with you."

Alice tensed.

"Sit down, Miss Shelton," Calhoon said softly.

She blinked at him.

"You'll do more damage—to your cause—with continued protest." He nodded to the chair. "Trust me. Sit down and keep quiet."

Trust you? Her heart was thumping relentlessly in her ears. She looked to the woman, who had started back toward them, her hands wrapped around a set of dishes. Naomi Polk set the stack of four on the table with a clatter, glared at Alice, then turned on Calhoon. "You're playing with fire here. What do you mean bringing the likes of this person into your father's house and dressing her in your sister's clothes?"

Alice felt the color drain from her face.

"My house, Aunt Naomi, and I'll bring the likes of whoever I please into it."

Likes? Likes of what? A whore or a Yankee? Worse yet, a Yankee whore? Nausea worse than that engendered by the black coffee turned Alice's stomach. She was torn between sitting and leaving the kitchen. Calhoon pulled back her chair. "Sit," he said, and she did.

Plate in hand, the nasty women stomped to the stove, folded up a towel, and yanked open the oven door. "Looks done."

"It probably is," he replied curtly.

Alice watched the woman pull out a cast-iron skillet, loosen the bread with a knife, then flip it into the plate. She dropped the skillet on a burner with a clang, then proceeded to slip the knife under one edge of the bread.

Calhoon retrieved a jar of greens from a curtain-covered larder and unscrewed the lid. "There are peas on the stove," he told his aunt.

Moments later, Alice stared at a heavy helping of Southern food. The chicken looked delicious, but the thought of eating this Polk woman's food, after what she'd implied, grated on her. That this total stranger would immediately conclude she had come to this place by design to sleep with Eli Calhoon was inconceivable to Alice.

No, it hadn't been Naomi Polk's conclusion that chafed Alice. What else should the woman construe? It had been this woman's response to that conclusion, her self-righteous judgment of "Alice the whore," assuming Alice were a whore, and Alice could not plausibly deny the woman's conviction without jeopardizing Cassie.

Calhoon leaned her way. "Eat, Miss Shelton. You're going to need your stamina."

She looked at him.

"I'll take you home afterwards," he said.

Chapter Seventeen

It was afterwards all right. Almost two hours afterwards. Alice had attempted to help Aunt Naomi clean up after the meal, but the hateful being had snubbed her and told her to go change out of Hannah's dress so she could leave. She had left the kitchen, and she had changed. By the time she went in search of Calhoon, he'd disappeared, but sweet Aunt Naomi told her he'd gone to get a wagon so he could take her home. What else he'd done while he was gone, and Alice suspected he purposefully prolonged his return, she didn't know, but he did come back with his horse hitched to a wagon.

Aunt Naomi, he told her on the drive back to the Stanchion place, was his mother's older sister, half-sibling actually. She had managed the household for several years following Rosalind Calhoon's death, but Calhoon's father had eventually bought her a house in town. Nevertheless, she was more or less a fixture at Camellia Creek. She'd been the person to occupy it after his father and sister died. Naomi, Calhoon told Alice, often took liberties. Her position in and loyalty to the family granted her that, and normally he was tolerant of her.

The woman's implying Alice was a whore was a bit too much liberty in Alice's opinion, but she didn't say that to Calhoon. He'd warned her at the kitchen table to stop talking, and from that, Alice gathered the woman was a vengeful old gossip, and since the truth of her night spent with Eli Calhoon did her and hers more harm than the woman's believing Alice was Calhoon's lady friend, she'd kept her mouth shut for the duration of the meal. She had thanked the cook; Alice was a well-mannered lady friend after all.

But the events of the early afternoon waned in importance when Calhoon turned the wagon onto the narrow road that led to Peter Franklin's rented house. She'd asked that he stop and let her walk on home, but he'd refused, and when she'd asked him why not, he hadn't answered.

"You are purposefully trying to cause trouble."

He turned his head slightly so he could see her beside him. "There is something I want. It's not trouble, though I think it's going to take some trouble to get it."

"Money," she breathed out as the porch, partially hidden by the pine and oak trees trimming the road, came into view. "You intend to black…"

He frowned at her. "Blackmail your uncle because of his daughter, you mean?"

She tightened her lips. Heart racing she turned in the seat to face him. "Please, I beg you. Cassie would rather die than have her father know she was pregnant. He still thinks of her as an innocent child."

The hint of a smile graced Calhoon's handsome mouth. "The only innocent child in your uncle's house, I fear, is you."

She stared at him, then focused forward as the wagon entered the clearing where the house sat. Alice's right hand, ungloved, palm sweating, clasped the wagon seat to her right. The front door, some distance away, flew open, and Peter Franklin stepped onto the porch and stared. Then he bellowed her name.

"Late leaving after lunch," Calhoon quipped, pulling on the reins. "Or home early for supper, do you think?"

Alice's mouth had gone dry. She didn't look at Calhoon, though his jerky movements belied the amusement in his voice. He stood. Surprised, she looked at him. He'd stopped the wagon a good thirty yards from the house.

"What's wrong?" she asked.

"Nothing. Things are righter than I'd expected."

She leaned back as he stepped over her bent legs.

"That surprises me, given how my luck's run lately. Come on," he said, jumping to the ground on her side of the wagon.

Confused, she rose to follow, and he swept her from the wagon, then pushed her against its side and leaned into her. Opening her eyes wide, she looked up at him, then pushed at his shoulders.

On the other side of the wagon, she again heard her Uncle Peter yell for her. She turned to his voice.

"Listen to me, Alice," Calhoon said.

She didn't look at him, but again pushed at his shoulders, trying to see her angry uncle. The wagon hid her and Calhoon from view. "I've got to go."

Calhoon shook her roughly. "Look at me, now."

His voice was clipped and hard. She did as he said.

"I know everything."

She twisted her fingers into the woolen shoulders of his frock coat. What did he mean he knew everything? Breathing through her mouth, she stared at him, and he brought his face close to hers.

"Everything," he repeated.

"What do you mean?"

"Alice!"

She turned at her uncle's voice. He stood rigid, watching them, not ten yards away. Calhoon didn't look at him. Instead he brought his lips over Alice's ear. "I know the color of the baby Cassie destroyed."

Calhoon pulled back at the same moment she whipped her head back around to face him. She squeezed his shoulders as hard as she could, wishing with all her might he could feel her pinches, but the coat protected him, she knew it did, just as the damn truth did.

"I've compromised you, honey."

"C-comp-pro—"

He was nodding at her. "That's right," he enunciated slowly. "Com-pro-mised *you.*"

She frowned at him.

"What the devil is going on here?" Peter Franklin bellowed.

She blinked at Calhoon. "Why?"

He smiled. "Money."

"Alice?" her uncle ground out.

She pushed once again at Calhoon's shoulders. This time he relented slightly. She turned and squinted at Uncle Peter. He was mad, but even if he had a gun in his hand, she didn't think it would have fazed her. She waved a staying hand at him, and he darkened. But she turned back to Calhoon. "You want my grandmother's fortune."

"Whoever's it is."

Out of the corner of her eye, she could see her uncle moving toward them.

"You let me handle this, Alice," Calhoon said in a deceptively soft voice. He turned toward her rapidly approaching uncle.

"What the hell do you think you're doing with my niece, Calhoon?"

Alice flinched at the vehemence in Peter Franklin's voice.

Calhoon wrapped his gauntlet covered hand around Alice's bicep. "Franklin," he said, "we need to talk."

Uncle Peter had ordered her upstairs, but Aunt Betty and Cassie intercepted her in the front foyer as the older man ushered Eli Calhoon down the hall and into his study. Uncle Peter slammed the door behind them at the same time Aunt Betty grabbed Alice's hand and pulled her back out on the porch.

"Are you all right?" Aunt Betty said.

Alice nodded.

"Why did he take so long getting you back here?"

Quietly, Cassie stepped outside with them. Alice turned to her and caressed her cheek. "Are you recovering?"

"Yes," Aunt Betty hissed, drawing her daughter around her, then directing her to a hodge-podge group of chairs at one end of the porch. Aunt Betty looked back into the foyer and pulled the front door closed. "Lord, I hope Eustacia doesn't come out here."

Alice figured the time to be near three. Eustacia Franklin always napped after lunch. Alice took Cassie's hand and sat in a worn spindle-back chair beside her cousin.

"You haven't told Uncle Peter anything about Cassie, have you?"

"No," her aunt said, smoothing the back of her skirt before sitting in her old Boston rocker. "He thinks she's having a bad monthly flux."

Alice studied Cassie's pale face. The girl caught her watching and gave her a tearful smile. "I'm fine, but it truly is the worst flow I've ever had."

Aunt Betty blew out a breath. "God's love, Alice, what happened to you?"

She'd left Miss Hinny's for her aunt, stumbled on a group of Confederate thieves stealing Federal cotton, and now had ruined her life, such as it was. She swallowed and said, "I got lost."

Her aunt cocked her head.

"I ended up with Mr. Calhoon, Aunt Betty."

"That much I knew."

"Did Uncle Peter know where I was?"

"Not until you two drove up just now."

Alice gave Cassie a smile she didn't feel. "I was hoping he left after lunch."

"He did, but came back early when he couldn't find you."

"He went looking for me?"

Aunt Betty threw her hands up in exasperation. "At lunch, I told him you'd left early to do some research in town, then I made the ghastly error, provoked though I was by that conceited ass Jonathan, that perhaps Major Parker was helping you."

"With research?"

"On the war, Alice. Really, I had little else to come up with, and you've been so preoccupied…well, to make a long story short, he took that to mean you were at the major's quarters."

Seth. Alice felt her bottom lip tremble. Some things are simply not meant to be.

"At the hotel, he learned the major was in his room, sleeping."

Alice kept focused on her aunt, who shook her head mournfully. "It was after one in the afternoon, so you can imagine what your uncle thought that to mean."

"He thought—"

"Lord, yes, apparently. He told me he went upstairs to invite the major to dinner, but, darling, God only knows what really happened. I can just see Peter banging on the door and once he got inside, checking under the bed and in the wardrobe, and even out the window. I'm certain Major Parker considers him a lunatic."

Under those circumstances, it was probably as well if she never saw Seth Parker again. Alice felt Cassie's fingers squeeze hers. "It will be all right. I'm sure Mama is imagining the very worst."

Alice blinked back tears. "It doesn't matter."

"Of course it does," Cassie said, moving closer to her. "I know you really…"

Alice looked at her, and she stopped talking.

"What's wrong, darling?" her aunt said, taking Alice's free hand. "Did…did Calhoon do anything—"

"Elvira Hinny was his slave."

"I beg your pardon?"

"Miss Hinny belonged to the Calhoons before the war."

"But she's free, now, surely—"

Aunt Betty motioned for Cassie to be quiet, and Alice met her aunt's concerned gaze. A soft breeze blew a wisp of Alice's disheveled hair across her nose. She tucked it behind her ear. The day was cold, but the setting sun warmed the front porch. After a moment, Aunt Betty closed her eyes tight, and Alice knew she understood.

"She was Eli Calhoon's mother's slave. She attended his birth and the birth of his brother before him and their younger sister Hannah. The mother died when Hannah was born. I think the woman more or less raised the two littlest ones, at least when they were very small."

"She…?"

Alice looked at Cassie. "Given a choice of loyalty between us and Calhoon, Calhoon will win."

"So he does know," Aunt Betty said quietly.

Alice nodded.

"Is that what he's talking to your uncle about?"

To Alice's left, Cassie sobbed. Alice turned to her in time to see her cover her mouth. "He won't tell," she said.

"He won't tell for a price, you mean?"

Alice returned her gaze to her aunt. "Yes."

Aunt Betty rocked her chair forward, drawing herself as close to Alice as she could. "And the price?"

"I believe he's offering to marry me."

"Offering?" her aunt said curtly.

"He's compromised me."

Her aunt sat up, rocking the chair back. "What did he do?"

Oh for goodness' sake. Would she never learn to think before she spoke? "He didn't *do* anything, Aunt Betty. He didn't have to. To Uncle Peter and anyone else who knows I was there last night, it would appear I met the man after dark and spent the night willingly with him."

"Your uncle would never agree to your marrying him, even if he thought you did have relations with him. We'll simply have to tell Peter the truth."

Beside Alice, Cassie started to cry. "Calhoon will tell everyone," she said, "even Nathan." She reached inside the pocket of her cotton gown and pulled out a handkerchief.

"Cassie, I will not allow Alice to be forced into this union."

The girl nodded, then blew her nose. "I know."

Aunt Betty reached out and squeezed her daughter's hand. "And Nathan would not be the first man to forgive a woman for an indiscretion."

"Calhoon knows the color of the baby," Alice said.

Cassie and Aunt Betty turned to her in tandem. After a moment, Aunt Betty asked, "How could he?"

"I didn't tell him, and I don't know how he knows, but he does."

Alice braced when the door opened and Eli Calhoon stepped onto the porch. He looked around and saw them there. His eyes rested on Alice. "Your secret is safe."

Aunt Betty started to rise, but Alice was quicker and pushed her back with a gentle nudge. "Let me talk to him."

He stopped on the second step and waited for her to come to him.

"You told my uncle nothing?"

"I told your uncle nothing…about your cousin or about you and me."

"There is nothing about you and me."

"Oh, but he thinks there is."

"You are a bastard."

His eyes hardened, despite the smile that formed on his mouth. "Be careful, sweetheart, you may very well be at my mercy."

Inside the house, Uncle Peter called for Jonathan.

Calhoon reached for her hand and brought it to his lips. "The unwilling bride. You'll see things from the other side now." He kissed her fingers before she could jerk her hand away. He did not seem particularly offended by the slight, but his voice became serious. "He plans to marry you off to his nephew as spoiled goods, not knowing, of course, the decision is yours, not his."

Uncle Peter again hollered for Jonathan, and Calhoon looked at the closed front door. "You know, Alice"—for the first time it registered he'd begun calling her by her given name—"I know Jonathan Franklin, and I know about Jonathan Franklin. He isn't man enough for you."

She glared at him.

"I'll give you until tomorrow evening to make up your mind."

The door rattled open. "Has anyone seen…?"

With a curse, Uncle Peter stepped full outside. "Please leave, Calhoon. And I told you, young woman, to get to your room."

Alice didn't miss his reference to her as "young woman." He always addressed both her and Cassie as "young lady" when he was angry. She swallowed. She'd gone down a peg in his eyes.

She looked to Calhoon one more time.

"Tomorrow evening," he said softly, and he turned and walked away.

Chapter Eighteen

Alice shot Aunt Betty a sad smile, then closed the bedroom door. Her aunt sat at the foot of the bed. Cassie lay propped on pillows at its head. It was after nine in the evening. Alice had eaten supper in her room, alone. Her uncle had summoned her less than a quarter hour ago.

"He wants me to marry Jonathan," she said, sitting beside her aunt.

"He has wanted that for months. In his mind, his handsome nephew and his lovely young niece make a perfect match."

"And being married to Jonathan will ensure that my grandparents' fortune is safe from unprincipled men such as Calhoon."

"Yes, he's discussed unprincipled men with me, too."

"I would rather die than be married to Jon Franklin, Aunt Betty."

The woman hugged her. "I know. I've tried to tell Peter he's unsuitable for you. He is, I do believe, grateful to Calhoon for expediting this."

"Has Jon agreed to the marriage?" Cassie asked softly.

Alice looked around her aunt and found Cassie's pale face. "Yes."

"Of course he has." Aunt Betty smirked. "He's doing Alice a service."

"Can you imagine Eustacia Franklin's reaction to her son's marrying me to protect my reputation?"

"She'll expect you to show homage while she helps him spend your money."

Cassie giggled, though not with her usual mirth. "I can just see Jon and Aunt Stacy fighting over Alice's fortune."

Aunt Betty looked at Alice. "Did you tell your Uncle Peter you did not sleep with Calhoon?"

"I respectfully declined to acknowledge any relationship with the man."

"What did Peter say to that?"

"He said that was the same thing Calhoon said in reference to me."

Aunt Betty drew her lips tight. "And offered to marry you in the same breath—implying, of course, that he had indeed had carnal knowledge of you and was doing the honorable thing."

Cassie let out a stuttered breath. "What are we going to do?"

Alice stood. "There's only one thing to do."

"Kill him."

Alice blinked at her aunt, who released a short laugh. "I'm joking, dear. What we have to do is tell Peter the truth."

Alice watched as Cassie averted her face, then said, "If you do, Uncle Peter may very well attempt to kill Calhoon himself."

"We could hope," Aunt Betty said.

"I don't think Calhoon will die easily, Aunt Betty. We could end up losing Uncle Peter instead, and"—her voice broke—"I'm tired of losing people I love."

Her aunt enveloped her in her arms. "I know, I know." She pushed Alice back to arm's length and gave her a tearful smile. "We'll sleep on the situation. Perhaps a solution will present itself overnight."

"*I* told Uncle Pete that for his sake I am willing to make the sacrifice."

Jonathan moved around Peter Franklin's desk, and Alice watched him pull out the swivel chair and sit in her presence, leaving her to stand before him like a shamed child.

He'd knocked on her and Cassie's door around ten this evening. Uncle Peter and Aunt Betty had retired to their bedroom. Jonathan's mother, Alice knew, would have retired shortly after supper. Jonathan was a night owl. Night after night for the past two months, she and Cassie had lain in their dark room and listened to him sneak off when most folks were hitting the hay. He rarely partook of breakfast. Sometimes a day, even two, would pass before they saw him in the house again. His mother excused him as an early riser, out being productive, but Alice had long suspected he hadn't returned from wherever it was he went at night. Tomcattin', her father would have called it.

Jonathan pulled his legs into the kneehole, then rested his chin on his fingers, aligned steeple fashion, his elbows on the desk top. "I had hoped to give our love time to grow, time for you to recover from the grief caused by the loss of your father and brothers. I was foolish, leaving you prey to an opportunist. You were vulnerable, of course, but I'd never considered you weak or lacking in moral judgment. An error on my part. Now I must make things right."

Alice studied the arrogant fool. For all his ruthlessness, Calhoon was, at least, honest to her face.

"My mother will present a minor problem." He slapped the desk with his palms. "I can handle that, but I expect you to get along with her."

She opened her mouth to speak, but he held up one long index finger, warning her to keep quiet. "You tend to be waspish, my dear."

Alice frowned.

"You will learn to curb that. I won't tolerate the two of you bickering in my house, and she *is* the elder and my mother."

"Have you told her you plan to marry me?"

"I have not. We'll do it together, tomorrow evening."

"I think you should tell her, Jonathan, that you are sacrific-ing yourself to spare the honor of a fallen woman — for your dear uncle, of course. She should accept that considering how good he's been to the two of you."

He blinked, then studied her with hard eyes. Looking for sarcasm, no doubt. It was there, but he wasn't sure, nor, she doubted, would he have the courage to challenge her at this point even if he was. He rolled his lips together. "Telling her of our impending nuptials is something you and I will do as one."

She closed her eyes and nodded. "I am resigned."

"Good." Jon Franklin rose, then he smiled at her. A consolation, she thought, to make her feel he'd forgiven her trespass. "You can go back to your room. I know Uncle Peter has you confined." He grinned at that—levity. Not only had he forgiven her, everything was all right now. "Uncle Peter will be pleased. Together you and I will convince Mother. There's no reason to bring up your indiscretion."

"I fear she's already aware of it. It would be difficult to keep such a thing secret in this household, particularly with my absence all day. And everyone knows who brought me home."

"She believes you were researching the cause of the war."

Alice laughed, and he appeared to like that. "By interviewing the enemy?" she said.

He shrugged. "Why not?"

Bullshit. She turned her back on him. "Goodnight, Jon."

"I'd like us wed by the end of the week," he called to her.

She stopped, her hand on the doorknob, and gave her head a half twist. "You'll have my answer tomorrow."

"I'm not haggling over the date, Alice. I want us wed by the end of the week."

"*D*o you think he'll stop sowing his wild oats once you're wed?" Cassie asked.

Alice stood at the foot of their bed, holding back the curtain. Cassie sat on the mattress, leaning forward. Together they watched Jonathan Franklin, lantern hanging at his side, stroll to the barn.

The room was dark, their reconnoitering undetectable from the ground below. Alice dropped the curtain and stepped from the window. "If I wed him, Cassie, do you think that will protect you from Calhoon's wagging tongue?"

Cassie turned from the window, then found her pillow near the headboard. "Did you have to tell Jonathan about me?"

"Of course not, and don't you ever. Good Lord, it's better Uncle Peter know than him. Uncle Peter loves you. No matter how hurt he might be by your behavior, he'll protect your secret. Jonathan would divulge it the moment it proved to his advantage to do so." She plopped on her side of the bed. "Do you understand me, Cassie? Don't *ever*, no matter what, let Jonathan know what you did."

"I do understand." She drew in a breath. "What are we to do?"

"Like your mother said, we'll sleep on it. Perhaps a solution will present itself by morning."

"Maybe Mr. Calhoon will be eaten by an alligator tonight," Cassie said.

A silly solution, but Alice figured Cassie was merely emphasizing the hopelessness of their situation. Better would be another of his enemies killing him, surely a man such as he had....

Without warning, the scent of his soap and the crush of his body invaded Alice's memory. Her stomach clenched. Such a senseless waste that would be. She closed her eyes tight. Waste upon waste. Years of waste.

Shortly after eleven, Aunt Betty tiptoed in and gave Cassie laudanum. The girl was bleeding and enduring cramps, and on top of her physical complaints, she was thoroughly depressed with the day's turn of events...and perhaps with thoughts of the baby whose life she'd taken.

Her aunt's timely ministrations to Cassie worked well for her, because despite the fact she'd had no rest the night before, Alice couldn't have slept if she'd wanted. She packed her carpetbag in the dark. The solution would present itself, as her aunt had suggested, and that solution was her acquiescing to Eli Calhoon's demands and marrying him. And why not? She saw no reason to let someone she cared about be hurt when she was in a position to prevent it.

Chapter Nineteen

Calhoon came out on the porch when they drove up. Briefly he met Alice's gaze, then said to the Negro driver, "You're up early."

"Oh, yeah, Eli, Samuel's up every mawnin' befo' sunup."

Calhoon started down the stairs, then reached for the little boy sitting beside Alice in the back of the wagon. "Hard to think of you as a daddy," he said walking back to the driver. He handed the boy up to the father. "Welcome home, Sarah."

In the wagon seat, the light-skinned Negress waved. "Sho' glad to be heah. Thank'ee, massa Eli."

Calhoon started back for Alice, but she jumped down on her own. "Call me Eli, Sarah. We don't want these damn Yankees roamin' around to think I'm terrorizin' you into submission."

Sarah looked at Alice and laughed.

"You didn't travel overnight from Vicksburg did you?" Calhoon asked the man, at the same time drawing Alice away from the wagon.

"Naw, stayed wif Uncle Jessie las' night. We was fine."

"How is he?"

"Cold got 'im down some. Had a big pot o' collards, though. Po'k in 'em, too. Got it from da Bureau up in Waw'en County."

Alice watched as Brim Solomon, who'd told her his full name, tossed Calhoon her bag. The man nodded at her. "Picked 'er up 'bout a mile back. Said she be comin' to you. Guess she be tellin' da truth, huh?"

Calhoon gave him a two-fingered salute. "She was."

"Shouldn't let a woman be walkin' dese roads alone, Eli. Ain't safe no mo'."

Calhoon nodded. "And she knows that, too. I'll have another talk with her. Never know what brigand's liable to pick her up and run off with her." He gave her an appraising look, then turned back to Mr. Solomon. "Miss Elvie says your daddy's old cabin is cleaned out."

Brim Solomon reached for the reins. "Dats where we's headed."

"I'm leavin' the farm this morning. I'll be gone overnight."

The colored man's gaze darted to her. "She gonna be here?"

"She's goin' with me."

"In dat wagon?"

"Not much choice unless I take Johnny and borrow your mule for her."

Mr. Solomon looked from her to Calhoon. "Ya know ole Doc Lester has yo' daddy's carriage."

Alice watched Calhoon's forehead furrow.

"Miss Naomi done gone to fetch 'im fo' young miss da night yo' daddy be kilt. Dey didn't get back 'ere till afta dem Fed'rals come and gone."

Alice's stomach tensed.

"He drove it back to town next mawnin' afta Miss Hannah died." Mr. Solomon shrugged. "Dey'd burned da carriage house, so Miss Naomi told 'im to keep it, 'cause dem Yanks broke da wheels on da doc's da month befo'. Ya know he'd give it back."

The doc would need it to get around still. "I'll ask him about it, but I'm not going in to Port Gibson to get it today."

Again Solomon glanced at Alice, and she thanked him for the ride. He responded with a nod.

Calhoon looked at her as the Solomons' wagon, creaking and groaning, rolled away. "You're early," he said.

She blinked at him, and it struck her she was completely exhausted, emotionally as well as physically. "You were so certain I'd come?"

"Sure," he said, rubbing his chin. "Got up and shaved. I've been looking for you since first light."

❖

But he hadn't been. Oh, he'd been up since before dawn, but he hadn't known if she would show up today or any day. He'd made some good guesses and, apparently, sound assumptions. He glanced at her in those damn mourning weeds, then motioned her toward the porch steps.

"You look tired."

She raised the hem of her skirt a bit and started up the stairs.

"Couldn't sleep?" he asked when she didn't answer.

"No."

"When did you leave your house?"

"About four."

"You really shouldn't be on these roads alone."

She'd reached the porch and, in obvious frustration, whirled on him. "And what would you have had me do? You gave me an ultimatum. I could hardly ask Uncle Peter to bring me."

"Or Jonathan either, I would imagine." They needed to get moving. "Anyone know you're gone?"

She shook her head and started toward the side door. "Doubtful. I left a note for Aunt Betty beside Cassie. Uncle Peter always wakes and leaves before anyone else. Aunt Betty won't be up before eight. Normally she doesn't check on Cassie and me until after nine, but she might this morning because she gave Cassie laudanum last night."

"The kitchen's warm," he said, and turned her toward the back of the house instead of through it. "There's buttermilk this morning and cornbread."

She questioned him with a look.

"We mix 'em together. It's good, and you need to eat."

She needed to sleep, too, but she wouldn't get much of that today.

Chapter Twenty

When Eli got to the back road that would have taken him north, he turned south and wound his way until he picked up the Port Gibson-Rodney Road, on which he turned west, toward Rodney, on the river in Jefferson County.

He and his prospective bride had left before eight, but in this lumbering wagon they'd be near noon reaching Rodney, where they'd flag down a packet to Natchez, the city where he intended them to marry. He was pretty certain Peter Franklin would attempt to thwart the nuptials if given a chance, whether or not it was Alice's or Cassie's reputation at stake. He'd be a bit quicker to do so, Eli reckoned, if it were Alice's name being sullied, and Eli was relatively certain Franklin still didn't know it was his daughter's indiscretion, not his niece's, that had left Alice vulnerable to the likes of a Southern rogue. Alice had made the sacrifice and not, he now knew because Alice had told him so, with Betty Franklin's blessing.

"Will your Aunt Betty tell your uncle about Cassie when she reads your note?"

She squirmed on the wagon seat, hard, he knew, despite the extra blanket he'd brought along to cushion her derrière. "I don't think you need to worry about them following us, Mr. Calhoon."

"What exactly did you put in the note?"

Tree branches, many still bearing sparse remnants of summer's foliage, reached over the road to form a scraggly canopy, draping them in mottled shade. Alice pulled a second blanket tighter around her. "I told her that by the time she read the note, I'd be long gone." She looked him in the eye. "She has no idea what time I left the house. I begged her not to tell Uncle Peter anything except that I wanted to marry you. To tell him anything else would make my sacrifice worthless."

He nodded. "Well said. Worthless sacrifices are something I know about. At least you'll be spared that."

She shot him a look of silent contempt. "I assured her you will pay dearly for what you're doing."

"Well, Alice, seems that's all I've been doing lately—paying for my mistakes, or sins if you druther, but given the prospectus, I'd say you are one of the surest bets I've made in years."

"How did you know about my fortune?"

"You told me. Yes, you did," he continued when she frowned at him. "On the night you asked about my horse." In point of fact, most of what he knew about Alice's fortune he'd overheard from that ass, Jon Franklin.

Still wearing that frown, she looked away.

"You and your uncle were arguing. Apparently you'd had a disagreement with his sister-in-law and had behaved rudely."

"I remember," she said softly. "But I only mentioned the trust." She turned her head sharply and looked at him. "And I wasn't even talking to you."

He blew out a breath, honestly tickled. "It was out whether you were talking to me or not."

She seemed instantly alert, and that said a lot given how tired her eyes were, how pale her skin. "I can't help but wonder if you know how much I'm worth."

He smiled at her. He really had no idea how much money was in that trust, but he figured if Jon Franklin would marry her for it, it was significant. "Enough."

She flexed her jaw. "How do you know?"

"Your uncle's actions."

She breathed in.

"And only moments ago you mentioned 'fortune.' 'Fortune,' Alice. Think about that. The word conjures all sorts of things to a man whose country and home have been ravaged by an invading army."

"Have you considered, as traitors, you deserved what you got?"

"Traitors to what? What we did was in accordance with the Constitution. What you people did violated it. You have, in fact, been violating it for decades. And as far as 'deserving what you get,' Alice darlin', that works both ways."

Her heart beat against her breast bone. That he deserved her, did he mean? Or did he intend to show her what was deserved lay in the hands of the stronger and that true deserts had nothing to do with anything but physical might and hoped-for mercy. Mercy that might not be granted.

"How did your father die?"

He had leaned forward, his forearms resting on his thighs. Now he sat up and stared straight ahead.

Alice swallowed. "Did he die of yellow fever also?"

He shifted his weight on the seat and looked at her. "You're showing interest in things I'd rather not talk about."

She raised her chin. "I'm about to be married to you, Mr. Calhoon. I am merely trying to figure out the true depth of your feelings for me."

"My hatred for all things Northern, you mean?"

"Exactly."

He flicked the reins and the horse's gait quickened. He did that periodically. Fast pace, then give the beast a rest. She knew they were making good time; her aching bottom testified to it.

"My father argued against secession. He wanted to weather the radicals up north, yet again, but it never ended and was growing worse. He may have opposed secession, but there was no question as to where his loyalties, and those of his sons, lay when war came.

"At the time he died, he'd given a fortune to the war effort, one son and"—he looked at her—"one son-in-law—"

"Hannah's husband?"

"Killed in Tennessee three months earlier." He gave her an oblique glance. "Can I continue?"

"I'm sorry. Please do."

"And I was in Tennessee with the 20th Mississippi—"

"That was your cavalry unit?"

She must have noted the look he gave her, because she bit her bottom lip, then said, "I apologize once again."

He sighed and looked over Johnny's head down the road. "Actually, mounted infantry. We—"

"The new name for the old dragoons. My…"

She watched him flex his jaw, and she turned away.

"Correct," he said. "We called ourselves the Butterfield Grays after the fella who formed us up here in Claiborne County.

"This whole area was pretty much at the mercy of the Federals, who routinely raided the local populace, wrecking homes and towns. They'd come in like locusts, take everything they could get their hands on. Anything they couldn't carry off they'd destroy or vandalize. White troops would come in one day and plunder. They'd leave the coloreds outside town and let them come in the next for whatever was left. 'Bout time folks would get restocked, the bastards would come again. Routine, calculated Federal policy. The victims were, for the most part, women, children, old men and the sick. In August of 1863 a Union troop came to Camellia Creek for plunder. They intended to burn the rest. That's the destruction you saw."

He didn't continue, so she decided he was done. "You said they stopped when they realized Hannah was inside."

"They got in. They stopped at the door to her room because of the fever. Fortunately they weren't so depraved as to burn the house with her in it." He looked at her. "If she'd been well, pregnant or not, they'd have taken her out and burned the house, and God only knows what else they might have done to her."

Alice thought of her father and brothers. There was no way he would make her believe they would have ever participated in such an event.

"Your father, what—"

"One of the troopers hit him in the head with a rifle butt when he tried to stop them from entering the dining room from the back porch. That was before they knew about the fever. Daddy never regained consciousness."

"How old was he?"

"Sixty-two."

"I'm sorry for —"

"Don't sympathize with me, Alice," he said. "It'll weaken you, and you're going to need all the strength you can muster."

"*M*rs. Shadwell, Alice Shelton."

Alice nodded to the older woman, then took the hand Mrs. Shadwell offered.

"Soon to be Alice Calhoon," Eli continued, "and I absolutely refuse to wed a woman dressed in mourning."

His *fiancée* skewered him with a look, and he added, "Despite how fitting she may find it."

Mrs. Shadwell's delighted smile faded to a confused frown. Her gaze darted from Alice to him, then back to Alice. She again took Alice's hand. "Sudden, is it. Well, my dear, these things happen, especially in troubled times."

Alice was staring at the woman, and for a moment, Eli feared she was going to blurt out something rude. Poor Penny Shadwell wouldn't deserve that.

"She is reluctant, Miss Penny. She fears we're rushing into this marriage and wishes to wait, but she's lit a fire in my loins, which can only be quenched by her."

Penny Shadwell's cheeks reddened, but her smile returned. "Goodness, Eli, hush, you sound like your father."

She turned to Alice and started to say something supportive, he was sure, but before one more word uttered forth, Alice smiled sweetly and said, "He's marrying me for my money."

Miss Penny clamped her mouth shut, glanced at Eli, then turned back to Alice. "Then don't marry him, dear."

"I've lit a fire in her, too, and she fears losing control of me."

"The latter part of his statement is true, Mrs. Shadwell."

Plump and pretty still, despite her middle years, Penny Shadwell laughed. "I fear you'll do best simply to quench the fire, my dear, because I know of no woman who's been able to control a Calhoon man. I think that's what makes them so lovable."

"There's few of us left," he said, stepping between Alice and the effervescent Penny. "She looks good in blue—"

"Oh," the woman said with a quick wave of her hand. She moved along the wall where she'd hung finished dresses. "I have a lovely pale, pale blue flannel. It's been hanging here for three years." She pulled it from the rack. "A bit out of style, perhaps, but"—she shrugged and smiled sadly at Alice—"fashion hasn't been of much concern in Rodney for a while."

He liked the dress, pale blue—hell, almost gray, but he didn't say that to Alice, because he knew she'd turn it down if he did. It had lace and pearl buttons and a nice little white collar. She'd look good in it. He looked back down the way he'd come and saw her watching.

"I'll let you and her decide, Miss Penny." He started to the door. "I only know that when I get back here in an hour"—and he returned Alice's glare when he passed her by—"she'd better be out of widow's weeds."

"An hour?"

"Yes, ma'am," he said, stopping and turning in the open door. He glanced around the spartan shop. "Swamped with work are you?" He had, in fact, banged on her door to get her to open up. Penny Shadwell lived and worked in her shop on Church Street. These days she opened only on request, and he could tell by appearances that clients were rare.

Miss Penny folded the dress over one arm, put her hands on her hips and looked Alice over head to foot. "She's very small, Eli. The dress will take alterations."

"I'll make it worth your while."

The seamstress eyed him sheepishly, and he grinned. "With my bride's money."

Alice jerked her head around to face him. He wiped the grin away and regarded her coolly. "Make her pretty for me, Miss Penny. This is a big day in our lives.

"You'll be here when I get back?" he asked Alice.

"I will. I can't very well leave without killing you first."

⋙•⋘

"Have you had enough time to find out if it's gonna be worth it?" Eli asked.

"If I'd been gathering that information only since I got your telegram yesterday, the answer would be 'I don't know.' But it's a funny thing about that Erskine fortune…"

Tobias Holbein pointed to a padded chair in front of his desk, and Eli sat. Its seat was soft and felt darn good, and Eli wondered where Toby had come by it. He looked at the man. "What about it?"

"Isabel came to me a few weeks ago and asked me the same question you did. Seems she has a client who plans to use that money, or at least part of it, to maneuver his way into some venture to which she is privy."

"Jon Franklin."

His lawyer wriggled his eyebrows. "That's the name. Implied he was about to fall heir to it."

"Did Isabel tell you what the venture was?"

"She did not, and under present conditions, I'm smart enough not to ask. Federal officers, Treasury agents, old-line Whigs, Chicago goons. Who knows what she's up to or who she's working with."

"Were you able to tell her anything?"

Toby smiled. "This morning, as a matter of fact. Timely, she told me, because this Franklin informed her just last night he'd be married to the girl by the end of the week."

"Did you say anything to her regarding my interest?"

"I did not. I'm kinda curious myself as to how all this is gonna play out."

Eli sat forward. "How much?"

"Will the round figure of two hundred twenty-five thousand U.S. dollars pay those back taxes on Camellia Creek?"

Hell, yes. Put up a new barn, new water tank. Shoot, he might finally put in a gas pit and pump gas into the house.

"Am I going to be able to get my hands on it?"

"As soon as she's your wife, it's yours along with a little paperwork."

Eli was raised in a patriarchal society, but he swore at this moment, if he ever had a daughter, he'd damn well protect her better than this.

"From what I've been able to find out, old man Erskine believed in the male line. He disowned his daughter when she married against his will."

"Alice Shelton's father?"

"Yes. Miss Shelton's mother and father met at a party in upstate New York. He was a cadet at West Point—"

"He was regular army?"

"Left after fulfilling his second tour of duty. Took his wife and two sons back to his family farm in Ohio. They added the daughter there. His wife wasn't strong. Army life was hard on her. She died young anyway."

"Erskine, the maternal grandfather, died in 1858. He and his wife had adopted a deceased cousin's son. That boy was supposed to inherit everything when he reached his majority, but he died in 1861 of pneumonia. He was only seventeen."

"What about Erskine's two grandsons?"

"When I said disowned the daughter, I mean disowned everything about the daughter."

Seemed a little extreme to Eli, but...

"Anyway, old lady Erskine, the grandmother, apparently did not share her husband's incapacity to forgive. Her daughter was long dead, but after her ward died, she had her attorney rewrite the will so that upon her death, the business would be liquidated and her grandchildren would inherit the cash. The boys would have inherited outright, but the girl's portion was written as stipulated. Her spouse would get the money when she wed or she would get it, if she could hold out until she reached twenty-five."

And, of course, it was socially unacceptable for a woman to remain unwed until she was twenty-five.

"Now, instead of a third of the fortune, she's getting it all."

"You found all this out from the firm holding the trust?"

"What I found out from the lawyers responsible for the trust is its value, and the fact that once documentation is received that

Alice Shelton is wed—by that I mean a recorded marriage license—her spouse can set up an account at his local bank and start writing checks covered by the Bank of New York. The rest of this gossip I found out from an old friend in New York and the contacts I've made among the Federals here and in Vicksburg—one being Jonathan Franklin, who doesn't know how to keep his mouth shut. Apparently he thinks he's got first dibs on that girl."

"Well, I've got the girl. Do you know what business Erskine was in?"

"Textiles," Holbein answered.

"I had a feeling." Eli curved his mouth into a grin. "Reaping the benefits of slave labor one step away from the filthy act. I guess that's okay."

"We already know the majority thought it was okay. Erskine wasn't an abolitionist, Eli."

"I didn't figure he was."

Toby sobered. "Alice Shelton is agreeable to this?"

"Reluctantly."

The erstwhile Rodney solicitor pulled off his glasses and tossed them to the desk. He was a short, stout, jowly Humpty-Dumpty image of a man, right down to his balding head. He studied Eli, then leaned back in his swivel chair. It squeaked. "I've been a friend to your family for a long time. I loved your father like a brother. Do—"

"Did you ever read Machiavelli, Toby?"

He sighed heavily. "No."

"Daddy did."

"He read a lot of things, but he was not a ruthless man."

Eli smiled. "Pragmatic. I think in these times, he would have considered the requirement 'pragmatic.'"

"Are you going to be able to live with yourself?"

"I'm hardly the first person to marry for economic reasons."

"Economic. That's a nice way of putting it."

Eli started to stand. Toby swiveled and pulled himself back into the knee hole. "But there should be a mutual agreement between parties."

"There is."

"Coercion is not a mutual agreement."

"What makes you think I'm coercing her?"

"You said she was reluctant. That kind of gives it away."

Eli shrugged.

"She's a Northerner, dammit, Eli."

"Yep, she is."

"How do you feel about her?"

Eli gripped the arms of the chair. "Why your concern for this woman? They wanted the South in the Union, well, they've got it, on their terms. I want her, and I've got her, on my terms. I find the fact that she's from the North, and at my mercy, particularly sweet. Not much compensation for Dixie as a whole, but"—he jabbed his thumb into his chest—"for this particular little chunk of it, it's a satisfying feeling."

"She lost a father and two brothers, Eli. How does she feel about you?"

"I don't care."

"Does the fact that her father and brothers were members of the 78th Ohio make it more satisfying?"

Eli stilled.

"Sherman, Eli, from Vicksburg through Meridian all the way to the sea."

A brick settled in Eli's gut and pressed down hard. Toby must have sensed it. "You don't have to do this, son."

"It doesn't matter."

"An enemy within. She could turn you in if she learns you're up to anything."

Eli's mouth dropped open in faux surprise. "And what would I be up to? Besides, with all her money I don't have to be 'up to' anything now."

Toby snorted. "What does she look like?"

"Suffice it to say, it won't be a burden to consummate the marriage." Eli rose. "Now I'd best mosey on over to Isabel's and tell her she shouldn't be counting too much on Jon Franklin's investment."

He arrived around midnight," Isabel Leigh Hays told Eli. "A tad late for him, but not very. Lately, he's here two or three nights a week." She graced him with a side glance. "Haven't seen much of you."

"I'm broke." Eli stood at the front of the central hall dividing Isabel's secluded home. Across the entry foyer and into the parlor, he watched Jon Franklin, his tie off and shirt unbuttoned, lolling on a red velvet settee and enjoying a libation and the attention of a scantily-clad woman with whom Eli was not familiar.

"He did take time to knock on my office door and update me on his fiscal prospects."

Eli's gaze shifted to Isabel, and she smiled. Isabel was a flaxen-haired, blue-eyed beauty, smart and sophisticated. She had the manners, the bearing, and, when the occasion required, the modest taste of the most genteel of Southern women. Once she'd been mistress to a wealthy plantation owner, a married man with legitimate children. He'd died years before the war, leaving her this spacious townhouse on a bluff overlooking the Mississippi. Isabel also had one child, an equally lovely daughter, grown now and a war widow, the final offspring of a man whose life had been mostly fortunate.

Isabel's gaze drifted back to the red settee. "That's Cheri with her hand inside his britches. She's become a personal favorite of his."

"Has she now?"

"She's a favorite of a number of my clients." Playfully, Isabel batted her lashes. She was older than his mother would have been, but she didn't look it. "You should try her," she said.

"But she's taken."

Isabel laughed—a lovely sound. "He's running a tab—sex and spirits. I do believe the spirits are about to do him in, and Cheri will be ready for a change of pace."

"His 'fiscal prospects' refer to a poke?"

"You want to buy in?"

"Has *he* put anything up yet?"

"No, but *he* has contacts and a modicum of credibility."

"The Erskine fortune."

"That's what he says," she answered, then raised a brow. Isabel had a natural talent for business, and Eli knew, because his daddy had made mention of it years ago, she would never be at the mercy of any one man again.

"What," Eli asked, "has he told you about his relationship with the girl who comes with the Erskine fortune?"

"That she's a somewhat foolish little chit who too readily fell victim to his charms. He says they are to wed by the end of the week, at which time her fortune will be available to him. He celebrated his upcoming nuptials last night upstairs with Cheri. He's a pig."

Five other men were in that room, all Union officers if their various states of undress indicated anything. Occasionally one would show fleeting interest in the antics of Cheri and the obviously intoxicated Franklin. "Who else is in there with him?"

The beautiful Isabel Hays peeked around the corner. "I don't know that they're 'with him' per se, but to answer your question, Neville Forks. He's a full colonel stationed at headquarters in Vicksburg. We see him about once a month. Have for the past two years. Major Dicks, Major Hampton, Lieutenant Colonel Wills, and Captain Simpson." She stopped her perusal and looked at Eli. "They're all regulars, from time to time."

"They're associates with Franklin in this need for a poke?"

"Implying they're all my associates?"

"Are they?"

"Well, Eli, honey, you know damn good and well they are all associates of mine in some capacity or another. I see no reason for you to know more than that."

"Are they associates of Peter Franklin?"

"Who?"

"Has the senior Mr. Franklin ever visited you?"

"Why are you here, Eli?"

Eli set his cavalry hat on his head and looked into the parlor. This time Jon Franklin saw him. Eli turned back to Isabel. "It had come to my attention that Franklin was flashing the Erskine fortune underneath your lovely nose. I came to let you know, just so you don't get yourself in a bind, not to count on it too much."

He started toward the parlor entrance, and a haughty grin spread across Jon Franklin's pretty face. He rose with Eli's approach. "Well, well, the man to whom I owe my good fortune. Was she worth a onetime—"

Eli drew back, then threw his fist forward. His knuckles smashed into the bastard's face with a crunch that left Eli's hand smarting and his arm numb past his elbow. The settee toppled over, Franklin in it. The pretty Cheri squealed and jumped to one side, into the colonel, whatever his name was, sloshing his whiskey. He cursed at the same time one of the casually dressed captains laughed. A major rose from the chair he'd been relaxing in, smoking a cigar.

Eli rubbed the knuckles on his right hand. Franklin didn't move, neither did anyone else, as a matter of fact, until the tall colonel pivoted his way. He took in Eli's uniform, up one side and down the other. The remaining major rose more slowly. Eli felt Isabel's hand on his arm. "Cheri," she said, "check Jon."

The girl moved around the fallen settee, squatted, and wriggled the fallen man's head from side to side. He groaned. "He's all right." She raised her big brown eyes to Eli, then shifted her gaze to Isabel. "Slugged him good, but he was 'bout ready to pass out anyway."

The last major to rise stepped forward. He was a big, barrel-chested fella and appeared to be trouble. "What the hell do you think you're doin' here?" he said to Eli.

All of them were looking at him now, and inwardly, Eli cursed himself. "Excuse the interruption, gentlemen, jealousy got the best of me."

"Of what? Our victory?" the looking-for-trouble major said.

Eli tensed, but Isabel squeezed his arm as the belligerent major took another step forward. Isabel stepped between him and Eli. "Your victory, Mark." She pointed to Jon Franklin, out cold on the back of the downed settee. "Not his. At least Colonel

Calhoon had the courage to fight for his country. That's more than the man on the floor. The colonel is leaving now before any more damage is done to my"—she gave them all a brilliant smile—"pleasure palace." She was already dragging Eli from the room. "Mary Margaret," she called to a pretty redhead coming down the stairs, "get in there with Mark Dicks and make him happy." Isabel pushed Eli down the central hall, then all but shoved him out the back door. "What the hell are you thinking?"

He stopped, turned, and kissed her on the cheek. "Sorry, I couldn't help myself." He turned and started down the back alley, all too familiar to him. "I'll tell you everything in a couple of days."

Chapter Twenty-one

"To love, honor, and cherish —"

"I absolutely refuse to repeat those words," Alice snapped.

The preacher bridled. Behind him, his wife clasped her hands in front of her and stepped forward. Alice swallowed, glanced at Calhoon, who stood stiffly by her side watching her, then looked back at the Methodist preacher.

"My dear Miss Shelton," Mrs. Percy said softly. "Are you sure you want to be here?"

Alice blinked back tears. No, she didn't want to be here. First off, they were in a church — she looked at Calhoon in his Confederate finery, a brushed and pressed and generally immaculate shell jacket, but still gray with all its piping and gold trim and… and…. She raised a chin and glared at him. He just stared back with a grim set to his mouth and a warning in his eye. She'd asked him not to wear it, but he said this was one of the most important days of his life and he would wear it. And he did. She sucked in a stuttered breath and turned to Mrs. Percy. "I'm sorry. It's simply that I am so happy, I'm overwhelmed." She looked at Mr. Percy. "Could you read the words and allow me to say 'I do,' please?"

He nodded, proceeded to do as she asked, and when she'd responded, he turned to Calhoon. "Now, son, are you sure *you* want to be here?"

Well, he said he did. And he said his vows. And after it was all over he pecked her gently on the lips, thanked the preacher and his missus, then took her gloved hand and led her from the church.

It was late afternoon, and they were in Natchez. Before the

boat docked, she'd noted Calhoon's anxiety. That had made her anxious in turn, and she'd wondered what their sleeping arrangements would be if they couldn't wed till morning. Both their worries had proved for naught. They'd made it to the courthouse shortly before closing. He'd file the license in the morning, he'd told her, "if," he'd said with a wink, "he wanted to keep her."

Outside, he swung her black cape over her shoulders, shrouding the pretty blue dress in black. Fitting. He offered her his hand. She looked at it. "Take it," he said, "and get used to it. You'll be getting a lot more of me than my hand."

The devil take him! But she did place her hand in his, then looked up at the remaining foliage on the deciduous trees, its brilliance muted by the recent rain. He led her up the walk and out of the churchyard.

"I understand the animosity to my uniform, but what do you have against the church? I asked you specifically if you were of any particular denomination."

"And I told you I didn't want to marry in a church."

He opened the gate and held it as he guided her through it, onto the city walk. Natchez was a lovely town, untouched by the physical ravages of war. Behind her, she heard the gate close with a gentle pat, and Calhoon started them toward the center of town.

"A marriage should begin in a church."

She tugged at her hand. "Let me go," she said, "I want to button my cape." He let go of her then. The long day had waned. It was still daylight, the sun hanging just above the distant blue-hazed pines of Louisiana across the river. The temperature was chilly. "And our marriage is a joke. Why, under the circumstances, would you require God's sanctity of it?"

"It is not a joke, and I do."

She looked at him. "You care about what people think?"

He took her hand again. "That, too. I don't want any doubts when it comes to my"—he turned and looked pointedly at her—"property."

She sneered, and she hoped she looked perfectly awful when she did. "You go to hell, Mr. Calhoon."

"I probably will, *Mrs.* Calhoon."

Again she pulled on her hand. "And I will do my best to ensure"—she grunted when he wouldn't let go—"you know what you have in store…." She gave up with a snort.

He rubbed her knuckles with the back of his thumb. "Yes?"

"What you have in store for you while you are still alive on this earth."

"That can work both ways, Alice."

"Oh? Well, God has already created my hell on earth."

"I haven't even gotten you home yet."

"And I haven't even begun complaining a-about you."

Her voice had broken, and he must have noticed, because he turned and looked at her directly. Sucking in a breath, she averted her face from his scrutiny. "God hates me," she said. Conjuring anger to conquer the pain she didn't want to share with him, she stopped quickly and this time jerked her hand free. "But it doesn't matter," she said, folding her arms over her breast, "because I hate Him, too. That's why I didn't want to be married in that church. And if you do kill me, please grant me my one request, and that is, do not bury me in hallowed ground."

Chapter Twenty-two

Not to worry, Eli told her. If he killed her, he'd throw her carcass in the river. Maybe those weren't the words she needed to hear, but they were the ones he needed to give. She was emotional and tired and he still, somehow, had to consummate this marriage. It would be too easily annulled otherwise. Seeing her in that pale blue dress back in Rodney had pushed her father and brothers' marching with Sherman to the back of his mind, but he couldn't afford to let her get under his skin. Showing too much in the way of feeling would be a mistake. And actually, she hadn't seemed upset by his response. His words, in fact, seemed to pull her together when she appeared on the verge of falling apart.

"You bathed?" she said.

He looked up from his meal and found her watching him. "And shaved and got my hair cut—at a free-black barber's who I've gone to off and on for the past twenty-five years."

He saw the subtle movement of her throat when she swallowed. "Is that how old you are? Twenty-five?"

"Twenty-eight. Born February tenth 1837. I waited until I'd grown some hair to visit the barber."

"I am—"

"Nineteen."

She drew a long breath and picked up her fork. "Would you like the date or do you already know that, too?"

"Fifth of May, 1846."

She studied him, and he cocked his head.

"I thought I might like to buy you a present."

"With my money?"

"My money. You belong to me, now."

She stuck her fork into a mountain of rice. "You are vermin, Mr. Calhoon."

"A deer tick on an ole hound dog." He laughed. "You know what's funny, Alice...?"

She stuck the laden fork in her mouth and didn't even look his way.

"Your maternal grandfather acquired his wealth manufacturing cotton cloth. Think about that. He purchased raw, Southern cotton—perhaps some of my very own, grown by my beaten and oppressed slaves—and he got rich off of it. He ate candlelit dinners at New York's finest restaurants with your elegantly-clad grandmother at his side, while my poor slaves, each night, returned to their cabins for black-eyed peas, which they ate with their fingers straight from the pot. That's if I were generous. Then they washed and nursed the bloody lashes on their backs with burning tonic and prepared to suffer through the next day."

"Why don't you shut up, Mr. Calhoon?"

He shrugged and focused on his beef. "Simply pointing out the injustice of it all, darlin'. And would you stop calling me Mr. Calhoon?"

"Very well, Calhoon."

"My name is Eli."

"I know your darn name." She looked around with what seemed a sudden interest in her surroundings, then waved a fork in the air. "Is it my money that's paying for all this?" She met his gaze, then flicked her hands over the bodice of her dress. "And for my bridal trousseau?"

With feigned boredom, he returned to his roast. "No."

Leaning closer, she whispered harshly, "The stolen cotton money?"

He leaned over, too. "The money I got from selling your uncle depleted bottom land."

She sat back quickly, he in a more leisurely manner. He grinned.

"You are unethical."

He speared a forkful of green beans, a smile on his lips and a laugh in his chest. "I told your uncle the problems with the land. He didn't care. It bordered the house on the north, and he wants the house. I figure in a year or two he'll want to sell it back."

"And you'll buy it?"

He pursed his lips. "Probably. That tract was part of my grandfather's original purchase, but I'm really only attached to the homesite, and he *ain't* gettin' that."

She didn't respond, but returned to her plate and ate in earnest. Eli wondered if she were pondering the fact she was the reason her uncle would not get Camellia Creek. He wouldn't lose it now, not with her money to back him. Momentarily, he pushed his plate back. Alice Shelton Calhoon. She was a pretty little thing despite her disagreeable mood, and he didn't fault her that.

He watched her chew a piece of roast. He'd cleaned his plate five minutes ago, and most portions of her meal were still in front of her. No appetite, he wagered. He didn't want to rush her, but didn't want to spend his wedding night in the dining room, either.

"Are you done, Alice?"

She looked at his empty plate. "Can we have dessert?"

That breathlessness he'd heard in her voice two nights ago at Camellia Creek permeated her words; she was scared to go upstairs with him.

"Pecan pie?"

"Yes," she said.

"I imagine they already have it baked. You won't postpone the inevitable too long."

She screwed up her mouth, then sprang from her chair and, tossing her napkin beside her plate, said, "Very well, deny me dessert. Let's go."

Surprised as he was by her reaction, he didn't bother to rise with her. "I'll buy you a piece of pecan pie."

"I don't even like pecan pie."

"Something else then?" he said pleasantly.

She rubbed her hands over her arms and looked around the moderately-filled dining room. "Please," she said, bending closer to him. "You're making a scene. Get up and let's go."

Eli glanced around the room, gently lit by glowing wall sconces and a massive, candlelit crystal chandelier. Despite nightfall, the hour was early and the crowded hotel's dining room had yet to suffer its busiest time of day. Planters, some still monied, others barely solvent but with pardons in hand, overflowed the hotels of Mississippi's premier cotton port, ready to begin business anew. He'd been fortunate to secure them a room here, the advantage of his father's forty-year tie to an old Whig family from Kentucky.

Their young waiter moved silently across the carpeted floor and nodded when Eli handed him the signed bill. Except for the astute waiter, none of the clientele seemed to notice Alice standing at the table. Eli would have laughed at her, but feared she really might put on a show then. He pushed his chair back, stood, and pulled her seat away from her. She stepped from the table.

*M*oney and property, and mistreated slaves and the irony of it all. Calhoon was sticking in the knife and turning it. The knife prick wasn't what worried her, though. That of his manhood did. He would take her virginity and gloat with the victory of it. He'd have his way about everything then. She glared at his back clothed in gray. She'd married him. Stood by a man dressed in a Confederate uniform while her father and brothers, draped in the stars and stripes, cursed her from above.

He straightened. On the table beside the bed, a kerosene lamp glowed, bathing the quilted comforter in soft yellow light. Calhoon turned and looked at her standing in the doorway. He nodded to a door on the other side of the bed. "We have a bath, running water even. This is the best hotel in Natchez." He offered her a hand. "Come on in the room, Alice."

His hand was warm when it closed on hers, and he pulled her inside, then locked the door behind her. Her pitiful carpetbag was next to his in the corner, on the polished floor at the edge of the Aubusson carpet. She had a woolen nightdress inside, but it wasn't new and it wasn't white.

She hated him.

He sighed and stepped in front of her. Briefly his eyes, black in the golden light, studied her. Lord he was handsome, at least there was that. She could hate him, and he be ugly, and she would still have to sleep with him.

Gently he took the cape out of her arms and hung it in the wardrobe. "The register seems to be blowing good. Are you warm enough?"

"Yes." In point of fact, her entire body was trembling, and instinctively, she rubbed her arms. He frowned at her. Well, she wasn't about to give him the satisfaction of knowing she was scared to death. Scared and angry and frustrated.

He walked back to her and took her by the shoulders. "If you're not cold, what then?"

She wasn't sure what she would have said, and fortunately, she didn't have to. He pulled her to him and wrapped her in his arms.

"Sometimes it helps to be held, Alice."

Her eyes filled with tears, and she squeezed them tight shut. "Must—"

He pushed her back abruptly, but not roughly. "Yes."

She missed his warmth and his strength, so freely offered, then quickly denied. "Afraid someone will bang on the door and stop the reaping of your reward?"

He stepped back. "The money is the reward."

"You just have to march over me to get it, like...."

"A war analogy, Alice?"

"Isn't our marriage a war analogy?" She bit her bottom lip. "You describe it so."

"You were going to say 'like Sherman marching through Georgia.' Well, he marched through Mississippi on his way, so you shouldn't bring him up."

He turned away. One of the gold stars on his collar glittered in the lamplight, and she stiffened. "The war is all around me."

He stopped with her words and pivoted. She braced.

"You forced me to wed you in that uniform. Do you intend to keep it on while you consummate the marriage, too?"

"It's a thought. I might even put my hat back on."

"Oh," she said haughtily, "and your gauntlets. And keep your boots on, too, as a final touch."

He emitted a low whistle. "The boots most assuredly, but not the gauntlets. I'm looking forward to the feel of your breasts in my hands."

She wanted to cry, but instead, she narrowed her eyes. "Well," she said, with what she hoped was an arrogant toss of her head, "I intend to enjoy your hands on my breasts, the warmth of your skin against mine." She took a step closer. "The feel of your hard body when you hold me."

He went slack-jaw for an instant, then recovered, but not before she realized the effect her words had on him. Her feeling of impending doom dissipated, if her anxiety did not, and she could live with the anxiety, because now she realized he didn't know it was there. He watched her as if she'd bewitched him, and all she'd done was paraphrase the words Cassie had said to her two days ago.

He moved his shoulders and removed the pristine jacket. Eyes wide, she watched as he stepped toward her, dipped his head, and took her in his arms. She threaded her own around his waist and felt the taut muscles in his back at the same time his mouth covered hers. His lips were warm and firm, he tickled hers with his tongue. She pulled back and furrowed her brow.

"Part your lips," he said softly. She did and continued to watch him.

He smiled. "Close your eyes."

She did that too. His lips caressed hers before his tongue entered her mouth. Surprised, she bucked slightly, but he held her steady. After a moment, she followed his lead, and the kiss deepened. Warmth flowed from her breasts and pooled between her legs. She had never been kissed before, really kissed.

He pulled his head away and sucked in a breath. Resting his forearms on her shoulders, he caressed her cheeks with the back of his thumbs, his face very close to hers. She blinked at him.

"It's the anger, isn't it?" she said, raising her arms to circle his neck. "The anger drives the passion and passion heats the soul?" She didn't know where those words had come from. Cassie had never spoken anything like them. She searched his eyes, inscrutable, studying her. "I'm angry. You're angry. I can see it in your eyes."

He swallowed hard as his gaze moved over her face. Gently, he kissed her again.

"My soul's on fire, Calhoon. Is yours?"

He groaned. This time his kiss was brutal, but its passion fed the burning inside her. He crushed her against him, and she tightened her arms around his neck, and her breasts tingled, sweet torture, against her leather corset. "Help me put out the fire," she said when he broke the kiss. "You will do that, won't you?"

*Y*es, and his with it, though how long they'd keep it out, he didn't know. He gave her one more passionate kiss before reaching to his side and yanking down the bedcovers. She wanted the fire out? Well, his petite Yankee beauty was going to get the instrument he'd use to snuff it. She'd turned the tables on him, and he wasn't sure how he felt about that. His cock suffered more than he could ever recall. Not even the prospect of holding Laura in the wake of Andrew's death matched his need tonight.

He situated the pillows, and when he straightened and turned back to her, he bumped her. She'd moved closer to him. Heat, lust…?

No, he realized, what she sought was comfort. He could see it in her big gray eyes. She hid it well, but her timidity was shining through. Childlike, she held up her arms, he assumed to be held, but he wrapped his own beneath hers and started unbuttoning that pretty blue dress he liked so much.

"Skin against skin, Alice," he whispered. "Your request, remember?"

Eli froze when she reached for the top button on his shirt. In fact, she finished his shirt as far as the waistband of his britches before he completed her dress. Done with her, he pulled the shirttail from his pants, unbuttoned its last two buttons, and removed his dress shirt. When he finally pulled his undershirt over his head, he found her watching him with a mix of anxiety and curiosity. Not the morbid curiosity one experiences when seeing the body of a man torn apart in combat, but one of nervous anticipation. Wonder, he thought, might describe her look best, and it occurred to him she liked what she saw. He tossed the undershirt away. "You can touch me if you like."

Her gaze jerked to his, and her nostrils flared. He'd meant to put her at ease, but the firm set of her jaw told him she'd taken his words as a challenge. Regardless, his miscue worked, for she stepped closer and touched a rib. He managed to squelch a groan, but not a deep breath. Apparently encouraged, she shifted closer, at the same time flattening a palm against the bodice of her dress, which slipped slightly at the shoulders, and she brushed her hand up to his breast. She stopped short of his nipple, and he cocked an eyebrow. Her lips tightened. "Am I expected to do everything," she blurted, eyes brimming, "because I don't know what to do next."

He pulled away the hand she was using to hold her dress in place, then slid his thumbs beneath the blue flannel at her shoulders — her skin felt like silk — and he pushed the bodice down her arms, exposing an enticing bust trussed in a dark corset. When her dress gathered at her feet, he pulled the bow securing her petticoat. It joined the dress on the floor, and he wrapped his hand around his bride's upper arm and pushed her crossways onto the bed. She lay face up, and he maneuvered himself comfortably beside her, then reached for the top hook on her corset.

"I'll do it," she said, staying his hand.

"I started undressing you, and I'll finish it."

"Could you blow out the lantern first?"

"The reason I want to undress you is because I want to look at you. Move your hand."

Curling her fingers into a loose fist, she pulled her hand away and laid it beside her head, then watched as he unfastened the top hook, then the second, and finally the third.

"It occurs to me you've experience removing a lady's corset."

Eli glanced at her. "From the look of the thing, it appeared simple enough." He reached inside the stiff garment and cupped a breast. She closed her eyes.

To pretend it wasn't happening? To pretend he was someone other than who he was? Well, he wanted her to know who touched her, wanted her to see him when he caressed and finally entered her. "Look at me," he said.

Her eyes opened. Gazing on her face, he feathered his thumb over her nipple. Her lips parted with a sweet sigh. He swallowed hard, then pushed the corset open and savored her breasts. Again he found her eyes. "You're beautiful." Her quick smile didn't hide her trembling lips, and when she started to fidget beneath his scrutiny, he relieved her by tugging on the undergarment. She shifted so he could pull it from under her, then he dipped his head over her bosom.

Alice gasped when his lips touched her nipple, then arched when he drew on it; and the heady combination of lavender-scented skin in his nostrils and its salty taste on his tongue left him primed to explode.

Calhoon's tongue explored her breast, leaving a wet swath in tandem with a delicious shudder, and her heartbeat quickened when she felt him pull the satin bow at the waistband of her pantaloons. He kissed her when she tried to rise, then reached inside her pantaloons to splay a palm over her belly.

"Your skin is so soft."

His voice served to calm her, and she wondered if he realized that—like a damn cavalry officer talking to his skittish horse. She considered asking him to slow his pace, but he'd agreed to none of her requests so far. She'd not make another. Resolved, she watched as he sat up and pulled off one of her shoes, then the other, and her heart stampeded when he pulled down her pantaloons.

He stopped her when she started to curl into a fetal ball, and his dark eyes roamed over her body. After a moment, she covered her breasts with her arms. He met her eyes when she did that, but he didn't reprimand her. Instead he wrapped his hand around an ankle, before smoothing his hand up her stocking to her knee. When he ventured above the garter and touched her inner thigh, Alice moaned, and he looked at her.

"We'll leave your stockings and garters on," he said, then dropped her leg and rose over her. "I like how it looks."

Naked with garters, did he mean, or what he perceived to be terror on her face? Before he could lower himself on top of her, she brushed his right breast with her thumb. When he made no move to stop her, she sat up and teased the nipple with the tip of her tongue, imitating his actions, wondering if her touch and tongue were as effective on him as his were on her. He responded with a gentle shudder, one of pleasure, she thought. Thus encouraged, she circled her arms around his neck and nuzzled him below the ear.

He twisted his head and found her lips. A moment later he crushed her to the mattress, his kiss deepening and his hand stroking her womanhood, effectively thwarting her brief advance. Alice wanted to fight him, to scratch his back, to bite his skin, but despite the force he exerted, his touch was gentle. His finger entered her. She hadn't expected that, and she reached for the offending hand.

"Stop," he said softly. "I need to know how tight you are."

"You want to know if I've ever been with a man."

He pulled back. "I know you're a virgin."

"Now you do."

He brushed her hair back. "I always knew."

She squirmed, wanting to put her legs together. He countered by pressing the heel of his hand against her womanhood. "What happened to your intention to enjoy my naked flesh pressed against yours?"

"You're not naked, I am, and it's your preoccupation..." His hand moved against her, and her mind wandered.

"Yes?" he coaxed, then kissed her neck.

"...with my virtue."

"Virtue is nothing to be ashamed of. It's a special..." He

frowned as if he remembered all of a sudden what they were talking about. "Alice, do you really think I could have relations with you and not figure out you were a virgin?"

"I'd hoped it wouldn't matter."

He studied her a long moment, then gently reinserted his finger into her. She turned from his scrutiny. "It bothers you, *my* taking your virginity?"

She brought her head around and her torso off the bed, but before she could shove him, he'd caught her to him, and he held her there with one arm.

"This is what it's like for a man to see his land invaded, his home ransacked and belongings stolen by a bunch of bastards who claim you are supposed to share a nation with them, a way of life. Common beliefs and values."

She pushed, but he caught her by the back of the head and held her while he kissed her. She growled at him, but there was nothing she could do short of physically fighting him now—and she knew she couldn't win—and the thought of his achieving victory by forcing her was abhorrent.

"To see your women raped, your children left to starve, generations of hard work go up in flames at the hands of men who have less honor in their whole being than you've got in a pimple on your behind."

Still holding her tight, he began to pull the combs and pins from her hair. He drew a lock over her shoulder and it curled around her breast, then he placed his face between her neck and that cascading lock and breathed in. "God, I love your hair."

She relaxed against his hold, and he reciprocated in kind, pulling back to look at her.

"The victor here is more merciful."

That was not the point. The point was he was the victor, and he knew it.

"I've yet to surrender, Calhoon," she said and grabbed the waistband of his britches and yanked.

He hadn't unbuckled his belt, so nothing more happened than to draw a grunt out of him. They were eye to eye, and he returned her stare with wide-eyed amusement. "That's *because* the victor is more merciful."

"Take off your pants!"

He started to push her back, but this time she did hit him, hard in the shoulder. "Flesh against flesh, remember? I can't have that with those britches on."

"Lie back," he said. He spoke in an accommodating manner, so she did. He unbuckled the belt, then unbuttoned his britches, and he pushed them and the drawers underneath over his hips.

And she tensed at the sight of him.

"My pants are as low as they're going at the moment."

She started to protest, but he pressed his index finger against her lips. "Hush. When you're in bed with a man, he doesn't want to talk, and leaving my boots on isn't symbolic."

He rolled to her side, then returned his hand between her legs. "I can't stop and take them off now, darlin'. You've made it impossible with your demands for flesh on flesh."

He tickled her ear with his tongue and at the same time moved his thumb against her sex. Her brain numbed with the warmth spreading through her body. Calhoon shifted over her and thrust. She cried out, but she wasn't sure if her cry was the result of the burning pain or scorching pleasure, and from his reaction, it really didn't matter. He held her derrière tight to his pelvis until the last of her spasms subsided. "Damn," he said and looked at her.

"I want you to know that my virginity was mine to *give*."

He kissed her neck. "I know that. The question is why you chose to do so." Then he laid her back and started to move against her.

"Where was your brother killed?"

Eli opened his eyes in the darkness and sighed.

"Please tell me."

"Why do you insist on bringing up things best left forgotten?"

"The war's been over seven months. No one's forgotten."

"Shiloh."

She tensed slightly. "My father—"

"I don't want to talk about this, Alice."

She stirred beside him. "I just wondered if—"

"We met on a bloody battlefield somewhere?" he said, and he hoped his voice sounded as cold as he felt.

She was like a rock beside him. Not a movement, not a sound. Then she said, "That would be awful, wouldn't it?"

"Quit worrying about it."

She moved then, very suddenly, and he knew she'd turned to face him in the dark. "It's all right for you to rub it in. To tell me how sweet victory is after you've known me."

"I didn't do that."

"You think it."

He smiled in the dark. It damn well had been sweet. All the more so because he'd made her enjoy him—and despite her brave front, she hadn't wanted to enjoy his touch. It angered her that she had.

"You may have won the battle," she said as if she could read his mind, "but I won the war." She plopped down on the pillow. "Just like we won the last one."

Damn, damn, damn. He seized a soft shoulder and forced her to her back. "Trying to rile me, sweetheart?"

"I'm trying to talk to you."

"I don't want to talk to you. I sure don't want to talk to you about the war."

She pushed against his chest. He couldn't see her in the dark, but he could feel her, sense her. "Don't you want to try and—"

She whimpered when he curled his fingers into her pubic mound. She was soft and moist, and he knew she had to be sore. "I think you're purposefully trying to anger me."

"Why would I?"

"To spark the passion you spoke of."

"You are a fool."

He probably was, foolish at least. He was feeling his own weariness from their lovemaking—though his swelling cock belied that. "I'm going to let you go this time."

He felt her arm around his neck, and she shifted her body beneath his. The faint scent of lavender tickled his senses, and her musk enveloped him. His John Willy hardened in need.

"And how am I to sleep," she said, drawing him to her, "with all this anger stored up?"

Chapter Twenty-three

Alice strained, but managed to get the pail on the counter. Water sloshed over her apron for the third time. Both the effort and the drenching told her she was filling the thing too full, but the more water brought from the well, the fewer trips to be made.

Naomi Polk's gaze moved to the mess on the floor. Alice challenged her with a look, then turned to the cast-iron sink. She did not care what the woman thought. The floor was filthy, the sink was filthy, the whole darn kitchen had been filthy before she'd started cleaning it, so her spilling water on the floor really didn't matter one bit.

"Has he said when he intends to get the pump fixed?" Alice asked her.

Aunt Naomi snorted.

Alice rinsed a dirty rag in the clean water. She'd talk to him herself. This was her horrible kitchen now, and she'd darn well get it serviceable.

Naomi didn't expand on her unladylike snort, and watching her from the corner of her eye, Alice knew the woman hadn't moved either. She was simply standing there, looking at her. Wondering why, no doubt, she had married Calhoon. Why with all that money she supposedly had, she'd be scrubbing cabinets, counters — clenching her teeth, Alice slammed the wet rag to her feet — *the filthy floor*. She dropped to her knees and wiped up the sloshed water, then gagged at the crusted remains of a cockroach she inadvertently dragged from beneath the counter.

She shook it off her rag and rose. The floor needed a better sweeping before she attempted to mop it, and tossing the rag back into the pail of fresh water, Alice made a halfhearted attempt to dry her hands on her wet apron. Heavens, she was tired.

"How did you get him to marry you?"

Alice jerked her head around and studied the woman with interest. Obviously Calhoon had told her nothing about her grandparent's fortune, or anything at all.

"I paid him to marry me," she said.

"Paid him?"

"Yes, and in return I get sex."

The woman's eyes narrowed.

"He has to make love to me every day. That's the agreement."

"What did you pay him?"

She could not believe this woman, but despite her irritation, she smiled. "Sex. I sleep with him every day in return." She sneered, a mask to hide the emotion in her face. "Hasn't he told you? We're passionately in love."

Alice reached behind her and untied her apron. She'd endured as much cleaning and as much Naomi Polk as she could for today. She turned her back on the woman, who appeared totally unmoved by her provocative words and totally unconvinced, and headed for the breezeway door. Alice didn't think Naomi Polk was stupid, but the woman sure considered herself to hold a significant place here at Camellia Creek, and she didn't appear pleased with Alice's intrusion into it. Calhoon's aunt was different from, but every bit as unpleasant as, Eustacia Bellingham Franklin.

Dappled sunlight danced on the skirt of Alice's cotton dress. The morning was chilly, but not nearly as cold as the one two days ago when they'd set out for Rodney. She pulled the cookhouse door shut behind her. Calhoon told her when they checked out of the hotel in Natchez yesterday, she in her blue wedding dress, that he didn't want to see her in mourning anymore, and they proceeded to the Emporium, where he told her to find some suitable clothing. Goodness knows there was little shopping to be done in Port Gibson, and even less in Rodney or Grand Gulf.

Alice took "suitable" to mean practical. All her choices had required hemming, but she told him she could do that at home. In truth, she preferred to make her dresses—store-bought ones small enough to fit were usually too tight through the bust—and to Calhoon's credit, he'd taken her to a general store before they left Natchez (she needed thread anyway), where she'd found a number of bland cotton bolts with enough cloth for several patterns. She purchased a bolt of gray wool, too, to make him a new coat, sans piping and CSA buttons, but didn't tell him its purpose.

Stepping from the breezeway, she crossed the back porch and pushed the dining-room door open. Inside, she leaned against it. What was she going to do about supper? The kitchen was serviceable, except for the floor, but there was little food in the larder—at least little she knew how to cook, and she absolutely refused to ask Naomi Polk how to prepare any of it.

Calhoon stuck his head through the dining-room door and looked at her. "You've company, darlin'."

She didn't miss the lilt he'd placed on *darlin'*. She straightened and started to follow him, but in his place, her Aunt Betty emerged.

"Are you all right?" she said.

"Yes." And Alice smiled, pleased beyond measure at the presence of her aunt.

"Oh, honey," Aunt Betty choked out without warning, and Alice rushed around the table. Her aunt did likewise and crushed Alice to her bosom, the buttons of Betty Franklin's fashionable walking dress pressing into her cheek. Alice closed her eyes tight. For years now her aunt had been her source of comfort. Dry-eyed this time, Alice pulled back.

"Uncle Peter?"

Aunt Betty shook her head.

"You haven't told him about Cassie, have you?"

"No, but I—"

"Don't ever. He's not going to try and do anything, is he?"

"No, sweet. Right now he says he never wants to see your face again."

Alice felt the color drain from her face.

Aunt Betty must have seen it, because she lifted a gloved hand and stroked Alice's cheek. "And that is why in time, I must tell him the truth."

Alice's vision blurred. "It will do no good. Best to give him time, and maybe he'll forgive me."

Her aunt looked around. "Could we sit somewhere and—"

"Oh, yes, I'm sorry." Alice pulled out a rough-hewn chair. The Federal raiders had moved from the kitchen into the dining room. That had been before they knew there was fever in the house. Few useable pieces of what had once been—and Alice knew this because the buffet had survived battered, but intact— a beautiful cherry set remained. "Could I get you some coffee?"

"No," her aunt said, reaching for the bow to her bonnet as she took her seat. A moment later, she set the hat on the table beside her and patted the table top, indicating Alice should sit beside her. "Washington plans to disband all the Negro troops in Mississippi by summer. Nathan's not sure when he'll be leaving, but he plans to stay in the Army and hopes for a posting in the west. If he receives orders soon, he and Cassie could wed immediately."

Alice reached out and covered her aunt's hand. "She could be far away."

Aunt Betty waved her free hand in dismissal. "I hope she'll be far from anyone else who might possibly know what she did, and that will be the end to the whole sordid affair."

For Cassie, her aunt meant.

"What I fear most is Nathan will leave without her and never send for her, but if he does, you'll still be close. Despite the fact Peter will most assuredly not get Camellia Creek now, he intends to stay down here. That's why I must eventually tell him what you did was to protect us, not defy him."

Alice shook her head. "It will only increase the animosity he has for Calhoon."

Aunt Betty's lips tightened. "I really don't care if he feels enmity for that bastard, Alice."

"Please, Aunt Betty, remember he's my husband, and I don't want trouble between them."

Her aunt sighed, then the woman's gaze pierced hers. "How is he treating you?"

"He's been very kind and considerate. Don't worry about me. Everything is going to be all right."

"Peter received a telegram this morning from Pritchard asking him to confirm you've wed. He tells me that once the custodians receive validating documents confirming your marriage, he will be removed as your guardian."

"Calhoon filed the license yesterday morning in Natchez. He sent a telegram shortly after."

"To Pritchard and Sons?"

"To his lawyer, I think."

"All he wanted was the money."

"I told you that." Alice curled her lips. "And he finds great pleasure in Grandfather Erskine's fortune coming from the textile industry."

Betty Franklin frowned.

"He considers us hypocrites on the issue of slavery."

"Oh, the devil with slavery. What does he say regarding the Union they would have destroyed?"

"He says the North betrayed the Constitution and has destroyed the republic."

"Dear God, I'll never understand how these people think. And now he intends to make you suffer for it?"

"He intends to survive."

"Oh, darling, I don't see how you can ever be happy with this person." Her aunt twisted her wrist and grasped the hand Alice had covered hers with. "I doubt you are even safe. Perhaps you should come home."

*A*lice watched her aunt settle into the buggy seat. She'd told her, she would not be coming home. Cassie's reputation was not yet guaranteed, but worse, Uncle Peter "never wanted to see her face again." That hurt. Alice thought perhaps that's exactly what her father would say to her if he could. But wasn't that what her maternal grandfather had said to his own daughter?

But her mother had married her father willingly, for love. "Sugar."

"Sugar?" her aunt asked, at the same time reaching for the buggy reins. "I thought something a bit more enduring."

"Salt then?" Alice said, then laughed lightly.

Her aunt shook her head, and Alice breathed in. Enduring? Something to keep for a lifetime in memory of her wedding to Eli Calhoon. "Sugar is all I want, Aunt Betty."

"I'm certain he'll be able to afford sugar now. Salt, too."

Well, she wasn't going to ask her aunt to come up with a milk cow. Aunt Betty flicked the reins, and Alice watched until the carriage crossed the narrow wooden bridge over Lake Elizabeth and disappeared around a cypress-shrouded bend. With one last unseen wave, she turned and started to the house.

"Kind and considerate? That's not the impression you've given me of my prowess."

Alice looked up the porch steps. Calhoon, dressed in britches and a white shirt, stood on the porch watching her. The hated coat was gone, the day had warmed, but his hat sat handsomely on his head. His eyes were concealed in the shadow cast by its brim, but his wide, sculpted mouth verified the amusement his tone had hinted at.

"I indicated nothing to you," she said, raising the hem of her skirt and starting up the stairs.

"Without saying a word, darlin'."

Alice glared at him, and he smiled. "It was the sweet sounds you made."

She dropped her eyes, but when she reached the top step, he moved in front of her. "And you are home."

"How long did you eavesdrop?"

"I heard most everything."

"Then you know Uncle Peter will not have me."

She started around him, and he grasped her arm. "I never once said I'd divulge Cassie's little tryst if you didn't marry me."

She narrowed her eyes on him, then reached for the door. "Yes, you did." She stepped into the dim entry.

"No, I did not," he said, closing the door behind him when he followed her into the house.

"*Yes*, you did."

"Think back."

She did, or she tried. She couldn't remember his exact words, but she was sure he'd threatened to expose Cassie's indiscretion if she didn't marry him.

He touched her arm when she stopped. "I've never told on a lady—or whatever she might be—in my life."

She drew a breath through her nostrils, then released it. "Like you didn't tell my uncle you'd slept with me while you kept me prisoner here against my will?"

"Correct, I did not."

"But you left him with the belief you had."

He moved into the parlor and tossed his hat on the settee. "Of course, I did."

"Just like you led me to believe you'd expose Cassie unless I married you?"

Heart pounding, she watched him squat in front of the commode and pull out the bottle of bourbon he'd brought back with them from Natchez. He poured himself a shot, stuffed the cork back in the bottle, then raised the glass to her in arrogant salute. "And you fell for it. Think. The choice you had to make was between me and Jon Franklin."

She clenched her fists to her side and stalked to him. "Only because you put me in that position."

He looked down at her, threw back the drink, then set the shot glass on the table. "Correct. I never threatened to expose Cassie."

"And what, pray tell, would you have done if I'd not fallen for your...your—"

"Ruse?"

"That will do."

"I'd have really compromised you."

She squinted at him. "You want me to believe you never kiss and tell, but you would have raped me?"

"Seduced you."

He stepped around her. "Close your mouth, sweetheart."

"You could have never seduced me."

He stopped short and looked back at her. "I had my doubts, too, given your animosity to the uniform I wear. Of course, that made the challenge so much greater. I had no idea how easy it would have been."

*H*e caught her fist as it glanced off his jaw, but she'd have got him with her left if he'd moved any slower. He'd meant his words to make her mad, and they should have, but when her guttural growls faded into frustrated sobs, he realized she was hurting — more due to Peter Franklin's disowning her, Eli reckoned, than his own provocation. He twisted her arms over her head, and now they crisscrossed her breasts, her back against his chest. It took some energy to control her, his arms over her shoulders to hold hers immobile. She screamed once for him to let her go. At the same time she kicked back with her feet, but his boots protected his shins for the most part.

"Stop it, Alice."

She strained.

"Stop it." He gentled his voice. There was little more he could do short of saying he was sorry and, dammit, that was something he wouldn't do. Betty Franklin had referred to him as a bastard and then dared to suggest Alice "come home." Well, Alice was his. Alice and Alice's money. They and theirs had come South to take what they could; they were not one damned bit better than him — he and his had always said that. Well, they'd won an unjust war and considered themselves saints. He'd won Alice and considered himself a dog; the difference being he was honest, and they were the same greedy, thieving pigs they'd ever been.

Pain pierced his forearm, and he hissed as she bore down harder with her teeth. He squeezed her tighter. "Stop it, Alice, and I won't beat the shit out of you. I'll give you the bite."

❧

She did stop, more because of the taste of blood in her mouth than his threats. He relaxed his hold, then finally released her when she demanded it one more time.

And she ran, not because she feared he would beat her, but because she didn't want him to see her cry—or worse yet—make her want him, want his body—then condone their horrible behavior by having relations.

She tripped on the back steps, but righted herself when her foot touched the ground, and surged forward again. The sun was bright, the weather nice, but the pounding in her head and the ache in her chest nullified life's simple pleasantries.

She forced herself faster, running into a gentle breeze that cooled her flaming cheeks. Dear God, she'd brought his blood. For all his emotional cruelty, he'd never hurt her physically.

Chest burning, Alice stopped short and blinked at the oak, the one Jocelyn LeBlanc allegedly hanged herself on. Just beyond, Camellia Creek rushed along, still higher than that first time she'd seen it, but well inside its banks. She had no idea she'd come this far from the house.

Alice swiped at her eyes. She was ashamed of her wantonness, of her tears, of allowing him to provoke her.

Gaze fixed on the limb that had held Jocelyn's body, Alice moved forward. She touched the tree's rough trunk, then with a soft sob, sank to the ground and leaned back against it. Bright red flowers adorned a shrub several yards away. A dozen like it lined the creek.

Camellias, Calhoon told her that morning he'd brought her out here to show her the swollen creek, progeny of the plants the first mistress of this place had planted during the last half of the previous century. She had been English, her husband a tobacco farmer from Virginia who'd come here during British times after the French and Indian War. She'd abandoned the farm sometime after her husband's death in 1788, the Natchez district no longer British, but Spanish. She had not been related to the Calhoons, her legacy being the farm's name and the flowering shrubs from which its name derived.

Alice leaned forward. A distant camellia did too, and she reached for it, now, oddly, only an arm's length away…

A disconcerting wail whistled through the trees, and Alice, hand outstretched, stilled, then stood when a shadow fell over her. The notable tree limb was within her grasp, as if she'd grown ten feet. *Or*, and she looked to the ground, the tree had shrunk.

A sudden gust of wind billowed Alice's cotton skirt and petticoats and scattered fall leaves all around her, and in its wake, doom fell over her, stifling her very breath. She gasped for air, then whirled, sensing a threat behind her.

The quiet creek glinted in the sunlight and the bright red of the camellias filled her senses. As quickly as they'd come, the wind and that sense of doom dissipated, as if the unknown threat were in retreat.

Heartbeat still erratic, but breathing now steady, Alice turned back to the tree and, with a shaking hand, reached for the limb in front of her face. She caught only air, and when she blinked, she found the gnarled limb was above her, well out of her reach; exactly where it was supposed to be.

Alice stepped back and turned, ready again to quit this place. She froze, one hand over her heart.

In point of fact, Calhoon's presence did more to ground her in reality than anything she could have done for herself. "What are you doing here?" she cried.

He cocked his head. "Looking for you."

She moved her hand to her throat. "For what purpose?"

"I wondered where you'd gone."

"Why?"

"I wanted to make sure you hadn't done something we'd both be sorry for."

She tamped down the desire to reach out to him, but she did step closer. Her head was pounding worse than ever. "Such as?"

He appeared to search the ground around her. "Try to leave me."

"What are you looking for?"

"A rope."

"That's in very poor taste," she said.

"Indeed it is."

She looked back over her shoulder. "Does that tree look all right to you?"

"All right?"

The thing appeared perfectly normal to her now; relative to the ground, she was where she should be.

"Did you hear the cry?" she asked.

"I heard the wind. What's wrong with the tree?"

"No, it wasn't the wind."

"What do you think is wrong with the tree?" he repeated, enunciating as if his patience were wearing thin.

"There are only buds on the camellias now," she said, not looking at him.

"They're winter bloomers."

"They had blooms before you came."

"Alice?"

She turned to his frowning face and said, "Jocelyn liked this place, didn't she?"

He released an audible sigh, then looked around him. "I can remember she used to bring me and Andy here. She played with us for hours. In the summer, she let us get in the creek. Darn thing is spring-fed and it's cold, but we loved it. We could get away with more when we were with Jocelyn. Aunt Naomi was a stick-in-the-mud." He shrugged. "Yes, I imagine she did like this place. We all did."

Alice looked over the scene, so calm and peaceful…and normal now. Carefully, keeping her focus on the area surrounding the huge oak, she stepped in back of him, putting him between her and whatever was wrong here. She felt him shift his body, following her movement with his eyes.

"I saw her that first day," she said.

"You told me."

"No, the very first day. That day I saw you across the creek. Her reflection was on the water, and she was watching me." Alice moistened her lips with her tongue. "She was alive."

"Alive?"

"As she was in life. Not dead like she appeared when I saw her hanging from the tree."

Alice hoped he understood, but the look on his face told her only that she had his full attention. No doubt he thought her mad. She reached for his hand.

"She was watching me as if she knew me."

Her fingers were like ice. He flattened his palm to hers and wrapped his hand around it. "What happened here?"

She blinked. "I can't explain it."

"Try."

She twisted her wrist, curling his forearm to get a better look. He'd rolled his shirtsleeve down to cover the bite, and now a spot of blood stained it. "Did you clean that?"

"Not yet."

She started working the sleeve up, but he pulled his arm away.

"Did you see Jocelyn again?"

"I didn't see her. Everything was normal when I got here. Then all of a sudden I became disoriented. The limb on the tree wasn't where it should have been." She looked at the ground. "*I* wasn't where I should have been. And there was a shadow."

"That doesn't sound like a haunting."

"And what do you know of hauntings?"

"Obviously, not as much as you, but sounds to me like you were dreaming."

She touched his forearm, and he swore what he saw in her eyes was hope.

"No," she said, the hope he'd seen in those beautiful gray eyes fading. "I heard her, too."

He pivoted so that he faced her straight on. "I told you, that was the wind."

"The darkness?"

"The shadow of the tree maybe?"

"It was more like the entire world darkened."

"A cloud passing over the sun?"

"Darker."

"We're back to a dream."

He watched as she bit her bottom lip. She was studying him as if trying to ascertain whether he could be right. Finally, she said, "It was Jocelyn."

"Believe what you want." He reached for her arm. "I think you need food and rest."

"How long were you here?"

She didn't fight his hold, but turned with him.

"Long enough to see you looking around like you weren't sure where you were. I figured you just woke up from a nightmare."

She stopped and pulled her arm away. "There was something behind me, a threat of some sort. It changed its mind."

He had been about to take her arm again. Now he hesitated. "I was in back of you, remember?"

She looked back at the tree. "*It* was in back of me. Over here," she said and started in the direction she was pointing.

"A noise?"

"No, I didn't hear anything. I sensed it, something in the woods."

Inwardly he cursed, but he followed.

"Something had Jocelyn worried," Alice said and moved behind and to one side of the tree and into the encroaching woods surrounding this place where Jocelyn LeBlanc had died.

"Worried her?" he asked.

"Yes."

He joined her in the brush. "What are you looking for, Alice?"

"Something or someone was here. Jocelyn knew it. She was angry or frightened."

"Something frightened *her*? Maybe she was angry at you."

That was possible, wasn't it? Perhaps Jocelyn didn't like her coming to this spot. Worse yet, maybe the ghost resented another woman being mistress of Camellia Creek, though at the moment Alice felt like anything but mistress of this place. But she hadn't felt threatened by the strange, disorienting changes to the physical place, only confused. The sense of threat, in tandem with the otherworldly wail, is what frightened her.

"Maybe she was frightened for me."

Alice looked up suddenly and stared at Calhoon, and he stopped short. Then, as if he read her mind, he said, "If you're thinking I was the threat, where's that sense of impending doom now? Besides"—and he waved a hand—"I was over that way, remember? You fell asleep and had a bad dream. That strange gust of wind woke—"

"You felt that gust?"

"I did."

"You didn't think it odd, coming out of nowhere?"

"I've felt many a wind in my day. I can't recall ever considering any of them 'odd,' as you put it. The wind just blows." He looked around. "There's nothing here to hurt you."

She flexed her jaw, then took one last look around. "Something's not right about this place, Calhoon."

"I fear you are correct," he said, turning her toward the house. "But I'm fixing to take her home."

Eli tossed his hat on top of the desk and yanked its top drawer open. The marauders of 1863 had pulled the drawers from his father's custom-made desk and managed to smash all but two. Eli had rebuilt, or tried to, the narrow center one, but now the thing stuck after a good rain, and it'd been raining a lot.

He pushed this morning's receipts aside. He needed to get over to Rodney, preferably this afternoon, to check with Toby regarding Alice's trust, and he needed to talk to Isabel.

"You've wed?"

Laura's snarl was more accusation than question.

Disguising his surprise, he looked up. "I did," he said, giving her a brief perusal before pulling his ledger from the drawer.

"Why?"

"Because I wanted to." He dropped the ledger on the desk, and Laura came full into the room.

"You did this to spite me."

"Actually I gave you no consideration at all."

"You're lying."

"No, I'm not. I've told you since I returned I wasn't going to marry you." He wanted to sit, but decided that might not be prudent.

Pretty, pretty Laura. Jaw tense, skin pale, she strode to him, then stopped in front of where he'd moved in front of the desk—closer to him than he liked. "I absolutely cannot believe you've done this," she said.

Folding his arms across his chest, he sat on the desk's corner. "Believe it."

"What are you going to do with her?"

He laughed. "What do you mean, what am I going to do with her?"

"Do you expect me to believe you love her?"

"Neither love nor your expectations concern me."

Her nostrils flared. "Surely you don't think I'll continue our relationship under these conditions."

He shrugged. "I've given no consideration to that either." Eli braced against the fury in her eyes.

"Oh, now I know that's not true."

"Do you?"

With a gentle tilt of her head and a softened gaze, Laura parted her lips in tender promise. She reached out and touched his thigh just above the knee. "Tell me she can make you feel the way I do."

He caught her hand halfway to his crotch, and he kissed it. "I'm not telling you anything."

She jerked her hand from his. "You're punishing me because of Andy and Albert."

He sighed. "I give you little thought at all anymore except when you walk through one of my doors."

"Well, I'm through the door."

"Indeed you are. Now that you're here, you—"

"Can go home."

Laura twisted her head with the interruption, and Eli lifted his eyes to the study entrance. Alice stood there, a bowl of steaming water in her hands. Laura turned, but not before he saw the smile forming on her mouth.

"Oh, Eli, this must be the lovely bride. I can smell the stench of Yankee all the way over here."

Alice flashed him a look, then returned her gaze to Laura, who had placed her hands on her hips and now sashayed toward Alice. Laura would be wearing that bowl of hot water if she weren't careful.

"What you smell is the scent of Calhoon all over me, and that's killing you, isn't it?"

Eli blinked. The only thing possibly better than Alice's words would have been the look on Laura's face, which he couldn't see.

Laura pivoted. Briefly she glared at him, then turned back to Alice. "She's rich, isn't she?"

Eli was watching that bowl of water. He figured it was no longer hot enough to do any permanent damage to Laura, but he wasn't sure. "Go home, Laura."

"Married her for money, didn't you, darling?" She turned half a step, the crepe of her mourning dress whispering against her petticoats. "You see how easy it is?"

"Any doubts I ever had, you dispelled years ago."

Laura sidestepped farther from Alice, who had come fully into the room. Her instincts for survival always had been strong.

"He's a ruthless man, honey," Laura said, her words now directed at Alice. "Did he tell you what happened to Andy?"

Eli's gut clenched, and he pushed away from the desk. Alice raised a haughty chin. "Watch your mouth," he said to Laura.

Laura never took her eyes off Alice, who was turning slowly, watching every step of Laura's retreat. "He died in combat," Laura said to her. "Eli supposedly was covering his back."

He wiped his sweating palms on his thighs. "Get the hell out of here, Laura."

Laura blinked at him and kept moving. "She needs to know the truth, Eli honey." The willowy blonde stopped in the doorway. "She needs to know how far you'll go to have me, up to and including killing your brother." Laura disappeared through the door.

Alice reacted before he could, but she didn't use the bowl of water. She somehow managed to set that down before charging after the intruder, who squealed when Alice slammed into her at the front door. Laura tried to correct her balance, took two more steps across the porch, then lost her footing on the top step and half fell, half ran down the stairs. On the bottom footer, she steadied herself against the newel post and glared at Alice on the porch, eight steps above. Laura grabbed the handrail and started back up. Alice would have started down the steps, but Eli seized her around the waist. He could feel her heart pounding with the same force that marked his own, but Laura had a full head on her and he'd guess close to twenty pounds. And Laura could be downright mean.

He swung the struggling Alice to his side. "Go home now," he ordered Laura.

"Afraid I'll hurt her?"

"I'm afraid I'll hurt you. Get out of here."

She raised her pretty face, marred now by a hateful sneer, and laughed. "You think I didn't know."

"I think you have delusions about any number of things. I'd never kill any man for you, last of all my brother."

Laura maneuvered, trying to see Alice, he guessed. He still had ahold of her, but she'd ceased her struggle.

"False words for your bride, Eli," Laura called out. "You'll never get me out of your system."

"Git yourself away from Camellia Creek!"

Eli jerked to his left. Aunt Naomi, tall and gaunt as Lincoln, stood at the north corner of the porch, glaring at Laura.

"This is none of your business," Laura called to her.

"You're making a fool of yourself. You don't belong here at Camellia Creek, you never did. Now Eli has told you to go. You git."

Laura hesitated, but only briefly. Then she turned on her heel and strutted to her carriage. "As if you did belong here, you old biddy," Laura called over her shoulder. She climbed up and looked back at Eli. "I'm the only woman who can make you happy, darling. I can also make you very unhappy. You're going to be sorry you did this."

Chapter Twenty-four

lice tore herself from his grasp and stomped through the door. Briefly he watched her back, then met the eyes of Aunt Naomi, still standing at the end of the porch. He turned to the house and headed after Alice.

She'd returned to his office and her bowl of water. She didn't speak to him when he came in the room, but instead reached for his injured arm, then rolled his shirtsleeve up. Once the bite was exposed, she tugged his arm over the bowl, picked up a brown, nondescript bottle, and poured—

"Whoa," he cried, grabbing the neck of the bottle at the same time the liquid scorched the wound. "That stuff burns."

"It's supposed to. That's the germs dying."

She never looked up.

"Bullshit, that's my skin dying. How could I feel the germs' pain?"

She looked up then. "Hmm, well, I never thought about that."

"What is that?"

"Some sort of liniment. Brim gave it to me. He says you use it on the animals."

"Good Lord, woman."

She'd dipped the rag in the now tepid water and started cleaning the wound. She wasn't being too gentle about it either.

"I don't know what you'd have me use. You've no supplies at all that I can find around this place, and when I ask your horrid aunt anything, she looks at me as if I have two heads. At least Brim is helpful."

"Helpful, my ass. Did you tell him you needed this stuff for me?"

"I told him you had a cut that needed cleaning."

Eli nodded. "He gave you that on purpose to make me holler. He's not who you go to for medicinal supplies. Aunt Naomi takes care of household items."

"She has her own house in Port Gibson."

"Yes, but she's always helped out here. Besides, we haven't had much money."

"Well, you do now, don't you?" She jerked her gaze to his. "I'm the mistress of this place. You insisted."

"Do you want to buy supplies?"

"Yes, and I want her out of my kitchen."

Aunt Naomi and the kitchen had been a problem for a long, long time. "Are you sure you want to cook?"

"I like to cook."

"She's a damn good cook."

"I don't only want her out of my kitchen, I want her out of my house."

"She is out of the house."

"She is not," Alice ground out. "She's rude, insulting, and belittling, and I never know when I turn around if she'll be there glaring at me."

Eli started rolling down his sleeve. "She'll get used to you."

"And learn to tolerate me?"

"Maybe you could learn to tolerate her."

Her eyes welled tears, and inwardly he cursed. "I don't want to learn to tolerate her," she said.

Eli turned his back on her.

"Or maybe you don't intend to have me around long?" she said softly.

He'd wondered how long it would take her to get back to Laura.

"What is Laura to you to come into this house and threaten me?"

He turned on his heel. "She didn't threaten you."

The wet rag dangling from one hand, she folded her arms across those lovely, ample breasts. "I beg to differ. Her telling me that the only reason you married me was for my money—which, of course, I already knew—and that you would go to any lengths to spend the rest of your life with her is a dire warning for me to leave Camellia Creek before you dispose of me."

He smirked. "I can't very well just let you go without the risk of losing your inheritance, can I?"

Alice huffed out a breath, then reached for the bowl. "Brim said to tell you he'd found the rope."

"Where…?"

He stopped when he caught the look in her eye.

"Why were you looking for a rope?"

"I sent Brim into Port Gibson to get some farm supplies this morning. We need to prepare the fields for spring planting after Christmas."

"You need a rope for planting?"

"Rope is handy on the farm, Alice, and it's hard to find lately."

She breathed in. "Why did you need it this morning?"

She looked up when he didn't answer. "Why did you need the rope, Calhoon? You followed me into the woods and you were—"

"I didn't need the damn thing, Alice. I wanted to know where it was. It wasn't with the things he bought."

He sought the button on his sleeve. "When you ran off, I decided to let you go, blow off steam. Brim was back, so I went out there to see what he'd been able to find and figure out what we'd have to go to Vicksburg for. He was lookin' for the rope. He said he'd gotten it and now he couldn't find it." Eli tightened his jaw. "Then I thought about you runnin' off to that clearing, and I decided I'd make sure you didn't have it."

She stared at him. "You thought I'd gone out there to hang myself?"

"Not until the rope turned up missing."

"Well," she said, with a haughty shake of her head, "apparently he'd missed it under the wagon seat."

"Mystery solved." Maybe, but she didn't seem quite satisfied. "If I'd planned to use that rope on you, sweetheart, it wouldn't have been to hang you."

She furrowed her brow, but didn't say anything. Giving the matter some thought, he figured.

"Do you want a demonstration?"

"I do not," she spat. "Is Laura your lover?"

"Not anymore."

She threw her arms out in supplication. "Did you kill your brother?"

Nausea swelled his stomach, and he considered not answering her at all. "I did not," he said finally.

She slammed the rag into the water, sloshing it over him, her, and the table on which the bowl sat. "Like you didn't threaten to expose Cassie unless I married you?"

"My God!" he exploded, "I didn't say I wasn't responsible for his death. I simply said I didn't kill him."

She was staring at him with wide eyes and a trembling bottom lip. The color was back out of her cheeks, too. Clenching his teeth, he sucked in a breath.

"I'm not telling you or her or anyone a damn thing about my brother's death." He hoped the look he gave her conveyed the anger he felt at this moment. "Suffice it to say it was a Yankee bullet that killed him."

For sure she was going to burst into tears, and he steeled himself to the inevitable. Instead she narrowed her eyes. "Fine, keep your treacherous secrets and your damn lovers, I don't care." She yanked up the towel, then the bowl, the washrag dripping over the rim. "But if you intend to kill me, you had better realize that my Aunt Betty will be aware of the threat you pose, and you certainly better come up with something more original than hanging me from that oak tree out yonder."

He stepped forward and knocked the bowl out of her hands. Alice jumped back with a small cry as the bowl clanged upside down on the floor between them. "Then I guess if I'm going to kill you, I'd better do it quick, before you get the word out on me."

She whimpered as he kicked away the bowl and pulled her roughly into his arms. He kissed her, then pulled back to gauge her response. She was still scared, but weakening. Again he kissed her, this time passionately—and she responded. He eased his hold enough to bring his right hand around and fondle a breast. "But you know what?" he asked, lips against her ear.

"What?" she whispered, her breath catching.

"I think I'll have you one more time before I do it, and if you please me again, I'll grant you another reprieve."

Chapter Twenty-five

"E-l-i, honey." Savannah Sutton—he'd always suspected that was not her real name—was on him like a fly on sugar water. She kissed him long and slow, rubbing her breasts on the buttons of his frock coat. "Heard you caused a little ruckus the other day, baby, and now you show up on our doorstep days after we hear tell you wed." She pulled back, swaying at the hips, her hands on his shoulder. She pouted. "Sorry, huh?"

"She has money." He smiled and kept his hand on the small of her back. "I can afford you again."

Savannah winked, a clear indicator of her astute skepticism. She was a tall, buxom blonde, pretty when made up, with full lips, bright red with rouge, and slightly crooked teeth. Her eyes, a tad too close together, were blue and matched the shimmering taffeta of her low-cut gown. She smelled of gardenia and tobacco—he'd known her to indulge in cigars with an accommodating gentleman—and she tasted of whiskey.

Beside them, raven-haired Charlotte, a pleasingly plump little whore of what Eli thought was probably Creole descent, blew him a kiss.

"I need to see Isabel. Is she up?"

"Sure, honey, it's not that early. Things'll be pickin' up here pretty soon."

On cue, the door down the wide hall of the elegant town home opened, and the proprietress peeked out of her office and met his eye. She scowled and started his way, down the red- and gold-wallpapered hall. This house had never suffered one instance of abuse from the invading Yankees.

Savannah sidled close. "I'm free," she whispered in his ear.

He turned to her and grinned. "Free?"

"Available, sweetie pie." She slapped his thigh with a manicured hand and a coquettish smile. "You know damn well what I mean."

"Considering what you pulled off a few days ago," Isabel said, "I can't believe you're back here already." She stood at the foyer entrance, her hand braced on the garish wall. Afternoon sunlight from a back window glinted off her golden hair.

He dropped his hand from Savannah's corseted waist and stepped toward Isabel.

"Are any of the witnesses here?" he asked softly.

"The boisterous major, but he's tucked safely away upstairs." She smiled. "From what I've been able to piece together, she was with you that day, wasn't she?"

"At Penny Shadwell's being fitted for her wedding dress. We left for Adams County and a marriage license shortly after I left here."

"Well, you sure tore Jonathan Franklin's little playhouse up. I lost a serious investor, sweetie, unless you want his stake?"

"I doubt he was a serious investor except in his own mind. What did he say to you after he came to?"

She shrugged. "He wasn't out long. When he left here, with a severe headache and weak stomach I might add, he was still thinking his nuptials would take place before the end of the week. I haven't seen him since we got word you wed the beautiful heiress and not him. He can't ante up, and the poor darlin' has fallen out of favor."

"Your favor?"

"My associates'." She held her hands out, palm up. "I still have my primary business here to consider. Paying customers, especially handsome ones, are always welcome, and when it comes to sex, the more foolish the better. Of course, I'm not sure he can even afford my girls any longer. Admittedly, I've been floating him for the last two months in anticipation of his windfall."

"That might be why you haven't seen him lately."

"Maybe, but I think it's primarily his pride. He was quite the braggart regarding his relationship with that 'silly twit Alice Shelton'"—she held up a finger—"his words, not mine, who he'd swept off her feet. Of course, the word's now out as to who really swept her off her feet."

Isabel looked over her shoulder at Savannah, out of earshot, but waiting. "You've a business arrangement with Savannah?"

"I need to get back home tonight, and I'm having dinner with Toby at six. I'm here on other business."

Isabel looked past him, to Savannah, and gave her a curt nod.

Savannah swayed at the parlor door and mouthed to him, "Find me later," then disappeared into the room. Charlotte followed.

"You've been garnering assets?" Isabel said.

"More like taking advantage of my opportunities."

She turned and started back down the hall. "Your daddy would be proud."

Pope Alexander VI would have been proud. Eli wasn't so sure about Holland Calhoon.

Chapter Twenty-six

"**Y**our source proved good."

Seth Parker glanced at Jubal Summers. "Yes it did." He looked around the old plantation house, its front room filled with cotton. He figured the derelict hadn't been inhabited for twenty years, maybe more. The windows were mostly out and in the adjoining room, one could see past the ceiling into the attic, then the roof, all the way to clear blue sky, darkening now with dusk. Private Ball had fallen through one of the porch steps, but he'd been more shaken than hurt.

Like primordial jungle, the woods along the Mississippi had reclaimed the house, but from the front porch, he could still catch glimpses of sunlight glinting off the river. This had been a pretty place in its day, and he wondered what happened to cause its owner to abandon it.

Today it belonged to no one. Mark Ellis, the most recent owner, had died of yellow fever the year the war began. His widow survived him by three years. Both his sons had died in Confederate service before their mother passed on.

But that family had lived in a modest cabin southeast of Grand Gulf, and though they must have been aware this place existed, they obviously had no interest in reviving it.

"Should we wait till they try to move it?"

Seth looked around him. The woods were dimming with the sunset, but he'd be hard put to catch anyone watching them even in broad daylight. Not when he was dealing with people who knew this area. "I doubt they'll try to move it now."

Summers followed his gaze. "You think they seen us come in here?"

Seth shrugged. "Probably, but it doesn't matter. I've got the names of the individuals." He looked over his shoulder at Frank Zachary. "I want three men left here. Have 'em relieved around midnight."

"Yes, suh."

"We gonna arrest the thieves?" Jubal asked.

Seth turned away. "Not for this. We're confiscating this cotton for the Federal government, but there's nothing to say it already belonged to us when it was moved here.

"Besides," he said to Summers, "We're looking for Alan Guthrie's killer, or killers, not cotton."

"How much you thinkin' dis stuff's worth, Frank?"

Private Ball had been addressing Sergeant Zachary, but Seth spun and snapped, "Plenty. And I want every damn bit of it accounted for and documented right now, and what's here come morning, when I bring wagons in, sure as hell better match the documentation I sign off tonight."

Chapter Twenty-seven

Alice woke, trembling. Had the wail been part of a dream? Or had it invaded her sleep? All was quiet now, but for her beating heart. She rolled to her back. She didn't recall a dream.

It wasn't late. She figured she'd been sleeping under an hour, and she, exhausted, had retired shortly after sundown. Eli was gone. He'd told her he'd be back late.

Lightning flashed through the cracks of piecemeal lumber boarding the smashed windows. Seconds later, soft thunder rumbled. A gust of wind roared through the trees. Then stillness.

Did the storm bring the ghost or did the ghost bring the storm?

A whisper rose on the wind, and Alice braced. Faint. Distant. Coming....

Her heart beat with the staccato pattern of a galloping horse. She reached beside her, hoping he'd sneaked in, knowing he could have never crawled into bed beside her without her waking.

Closer, growing, wailing. The scream invaded the room and swelled, swirled, then dipped. *Get out! Get out! Get out!*

Her bare feet hit the cold floor. She threw open her bedroom door and, feeling her way along the wall, scrambled the short distance down the hall to the stairwell, then up.

The endless wail chased her, urging her faster.

She stumbled, righted herself, went on.

The scream surged up the stairwell, violent and frigid like a blizzard across a fallow Ohio cornfield.

On the landing, she fumbled for the first door on the left. The knob turned, unhindered. With a garbled cry, she pushed the panel open, stepped inside and closed the door. Hands behind her still clutching the knob, she leaned against the door.

Silence.

All she heard was labored breathing. Her breathing.

Alice closed her eyes and swallowed. "Miss Elvie?"

She heard someone stir and opened her eyes. This room was brighter. No boards covered the upstairs windows. Lightning flashed and Alice saw the old woman sitting up in bed. "Dat you, girl?"

Immediately, she was away from the door, then on the bed as the lightning snuffed out. The room was dark again, but not pitch black. Not like downstairs.

"Yes, it's me, Miss Elvie. It's Alice."

Miss Elvie reached out and touched her. "What's wrong wif you?"

Alice grasped the gnarled fingers of one old hand. "Did you hear it?"

Outside the wind moaned woefully around the corner of the house, and Alice stilled.

"Dat?"

"It's different now."

"Only sounds diff'rent up heah, but it jus' be da wind."

Not *that* different. Alice breathed in. "It was a wail, inside the house." She sat back. "It was Jocelyn."

"Jocelyn? Jocelyn LeBlanc?" The old woman moved. "Let me lights a—"

"No." Alice squeezed the hand she held tighter. "She was warning me."

"Wawnin' you?" Miss Elvie whispered in the dark.

"Warning me to get out of that room."

"Yo' bedroom?"

"Yes, something is going—"

"Shh," the old woman said and pulled Alice a tiny bit closer.

A soft squeak. Almost imperceptible.

"Dat be da back do'h."

Alice didn't think she'd have heard it, but for the old woman.

"For years when my missy lived and some afta she die, when the chil'en be small, I listened fo' it. Listened durin' da wah, too, on dem nights I slept in da big house afta Hannah got sick. Listened fo' thieves and rabble gettin' in."

Alice started to move. Miss Elvie stilled her. Below them, a floorboard squeaked.

"In yo' bedroom now," the woman said.

Alice's heart was pounding in her head. Her chest and shoulders ached.

Seconds passed, then a minute, perhaps two, and during that time, Alice scarcely breathed. She didn't move, nor did the old woman. They sat on the bed, huddled, their fingers tangled.

A muffled noise below.

Without warning, lightning struck close outside and thunder shook the house. Alice jumped. Miss Elvie grasped her, and they clung to each other as the lightning flickered out. Downstairs the movements quickened. Floorboards groaned. Alice turned in the direction of the bedroom door. "Oh, God," she said softly.

Quiet.

"Waitin' on somethin'," Miss Elvie whispered.

Outside the wind picked up, but almost immediately its groans were drowned by pouring rain, which muted warning sounds they needed to hear. Alice shivered. The old woman fumbled with the quilts, but her effort was fruitless because Alice sat atop the covers. The icy chill of the room washed over her.

"Move over so's…"

She didn't finish, and Alice didn't move. "Did you hear that?" But Alice knew she had.

"Movin' 'bout ag'in."

"I fear it's coming up the stairs."

Chapter Twenty-eight

Eli lit a match. The bed was empty, and he cursed. He stood there a moment, then found the lamp on the table and managed to remove the chimney before the flame burned his fingers. He shook the match out and began again, this time lighting the lamp. Darn her.

Overhead, a joist moaned.

Lamp in hand, he left the room, called her name, then started up the stairs.

Alice turned into the stairwell and almost collided with Calhoon. Bareheaded, lamp in hand, he glowed ominously in the lamplight, his dark hair wet and plastered to his scalp. He'd removed his coat, and the britches covering his thigh were wet. He stood in stocking feet.

"What are you doing up here?" he asked.

"I was with Miss Elvie."

He looked over her head, into the dark hall. Alice turned and followed his eyes. Miss Elvie was there, two steps behind her.

"Sleeping?" Calhoon asked and started back down; she followed.

"No." From the bottom step, Alice gave Camellia Creek's cavernous entry a glance.

In front of her, he asked, "Where's Aunt Naomi?"

Alice stepped into the hall. "I didn't ask her. Miss Elvira said she'd stay."

That brought little response. He turned away. "Why were you upstairs?"

"Jocelyn woke me."

He looked over his shoulder at her. "The wind woke you, so you went upstairs to Elvie. I used to do that."

"Jocelyn woke me to warn me."

He disappeared into the parlor. "Warn you?"

She quickened her pace after him. "Calhoon, was it you in the house the whole time?"

He gave her a silly look. "I just now came in to find you were not where you were supposed to be."

"Someone came in the back door not fifteen minutes ago. I'd locked it before I went to bed. You unlocked it. It had to be you."

He stopped near the settee and glanced first at her, then to Elvie who trailed her. "I came in five minutes ago. The door was not locked."

Alice looked to Elvie who'd come up beside her. "Did you unlock the back door?"

"No, ma'am. I don't lock, an' I don't unlock dat back do'h."

Still holding the lamp, he brushed past them, lighting the way through the dining room to the back door, where he held up the lamp. The skeleton key hung from its nail by the door. He squatted, and Alice knelt beside him. The beautiful heart-pine flooring was dull now with years of wax, the painted threshold in need of a good sweeping, but she didn't see anything on the floor to indicate a stranger had crossed here tonight. But what would that have been, anyway?

From where he poised, lamp in hand, Calhoon looked at her. "When you locked the door, did you try it?"

She squinted and tried to recall.

"Do you remember?"

"I'm sure I must have."

He rose from his crouch. "But you're not sure, are you?"

"No, but someone came. Someone who meant me harm." She touched his arm. "Jocelyn wanted me out of that room."

He didn't say anything.

"You don't believe me?"

He started back through the dark house toward their bedroom, her and Miss Elvie on his heels. "I believe you and Elvie heard someone, but that was, no doubt, me." He set the lamp in its place beside their bed and turned up the wick. "But I don't believe Jocelyn told you to get out of this room." The bed stretched out before them, its mussed covers awash in yellow light and long shadows, which moved when one of them did. He cocked his head. "Looks like someone's been bouncing on this thing."

Alice tightened her lips. "When I went to bed, I didn't even pull down your side. Someone else messed it up."

"Or in your panic to get out of here, you messed it up."

Lord, she had been frightened, and she had exited his side, the side closest to the door.

Calhoon twisted in the direction of Miss Elvie. "Did you hear the ghost?"

"I heard da wail, same I have fo' yeahs an' yeahs."

Alice stepped closer to Calhoon. "She didn't hear what I heard. The wail was more a whisper." She straightened, anger surging through her blood, "I swear," she said firmly, "it was in this room."

Eli kneeled on one knee and looked under the bed. "The ghost talked to you?"

Alice held her hands out, palms up. "She didn't tell me with words. The warning was here"—she tapped on her temple—"in my head."

He studied her, then cast a questioning look at Miss Elvie.

"Don't know," the woman answered. "Nobody or nothin' said anythin' to me, but I know'd dat girl was scared to def when her gots to me. Scared me, too. Den you or somebody come in dis house."

"Auntie," he said and pointed at Alice, "the night she and Cassie Franklin came to you wanting to get rid of Cassie's baby, did you tell Alice anything about the ghost?"

Alice clenched her fists and stepped forward, but Calhoon held a palm up. "Don't you say a word." He looked back at Miss Elvie. After a moment, the old woman tightened her lips and shook her head.

"No, suh."

"You're sure?"

"Sho' I am, boy."

Alice waved her arms in the direction of the bed. "Do you think I'm making all this up?"

"I'm trying to rule out the role of the damn ghost, Alice." He'd raised his voice, not in anger it seemed, but more to dominate the conversation. "I think there should be more concern with who came in here tonight than you hallucinating about a spook."

"I'm not hallucinating."

"Fine, but the ghost doesn't worry me too much." He rolled his eyes. "Especially if you think she's on your side. Why would she be, do you think?"

"Why not?"

"Why would she be trying to protect you?"

Alice rubbed her forehead. "I'm a threat somehow, I guess."

"To her?"

Alice twisted her face and raised her voice an octave. "No, not to her. She needs me, and I don't know why."

"Why would she need you? You just showed up here."

"Because I listen to her," she yelled at him, then nodded her head vigorously, doing her damnedest now to maintain her composure. She raised her hand and poked him in the chest with an index finger, and he stepped back. "That's it. I *listen* when she tries to communicate. For the past twenty-five years the rest of you people have ignored her. That's why"—her voice caught—"she talks to me. I listen."

Calhoon dipped his face and stared into her eyes. Then he said, "She's keeping you safe so she'll have somebody to talk to?"

"Quit making fun of me. I don't know what she wants, but she wants something."

He blew out a breath and turned. Miss Elvie stood apart from them, withered and small, her body clad in a white gown, her gray hair, plaited, free of the kerchief she wore during the day. She held the single candle she'd used to make her way down the stairs. "Girl could be right 'bout da ghost, Eli."

"Good Lord," he said, and turned away.

"But I agree wif you, da thing we needs to be thinkin' 'bout right now is less Jocelyn and what she be wantin' and mo' what caused her to 'communicate' wif Miss Alice tonight.

"And Mr. Bowen he come lookin' for you 'bout suppa'time. You was gone. Missy she was cleanin' da fish Brim brought us."

"He didn't say what he wanted?"

"No, he didn't. Sayd he'd come back later. I tol' 'im you'd be late."

Eli nodded, then turned on his heel and looked at Alice. "You clean fish?"

"And fillet them."

"Well, hell, honey, if Jocelyn was warnin' you about me, rest assured you've nothin' more to worry about now, 'cause knowin' that, I'd be a fool to get rid of a treasure like you."

Chapter Twenty-nine

Eli looked at the down pillow folded onto itself, then picked it up and fluffed it back into shape before tossing it in place on Alice's side of the bed. Outside, the rain pounded. It was well past ten now. Miss Elvie had gone back to her room, and he gave thanks he got here without having to swim that lake. God, he wished the only thing weighing on his mind right now was Camellia Creek, the bayou, and the Mississippi and whether he had until the next rain or fifty years to try and fix the looming flood. Fix the raging torrents. The idea was as presumptuous as winning the war. Dilbert Bowen's visit was a worry, too, and Eli wondered what had brought him to the house. Of course it was getting late now, and with the weather, he kinda figured he wouldn't be seein' Dilbert till morning.

"You know, Alice, she could have taken her life and still be trying to communicate with you now."

"Why would she?"

"Something to do. Eternity is a long time to be bored."

She turned from where she stood brushing her hair in front of Hannah's old rosewood chest of drawers. "Oh, Calhoon, when we die, we go somewhere else and rest. If she's still here, she's not at peace. She's not staying around looking for something...." All of a sudden, his bride thrust her chin, and he knew she must have sensed his amusement. "You're making fun of me again."

He folded his arms over his chest. "You know, people have made observations in regards to the old darkies being able to communicate with the dead. Something to the effect that such abilities are veiled from the educated and revealed to those who are more akin to children."

Alice narrowed her eyes. "Yes, that's how you like to think of your women and your slaves. Well, you've got a ghost at Camellia Creek, Calhoon, and you're too stupid to realize it because you know so darn much." She returned to the mirror and continued brushing her hair. Lord, he loved her hair. She tilted the oval mirror and caught his eye.

He smirked, then sauntered her way, her watching him reflected in the mirror. She was dressed in white cotton flannel, the gown's long sleeves gathered at the wrist. The feminine night dress had a scoop neck, its top button undone.

Tired yes, but he could probably muster up a second wind.

He slid his arms under hers and wrapped them around her waist, then pulled her back against him. The house was chilled, her body warm. She looked away as she lay the brush down and picked up her bottle of perfume. Looking up, she again found his reflected gaze. She tossed her head to the side and placed a touch of scent behind one ear. He sank his face into her neck. Her hair brushed his cheek.

"You feel so good, smell so good."

"Thank you. It's lavender."

"I know."

"Yours smells good, too," she said, turning in his arms. "Gardenia, if I'm not mistaken."

His gut knotted, and he saw her bottom lip tremble.

"Let me go, Calhoon."

He dropped his hands, lead hammers now at the ends of his arms. She stepped away.

"A lover?" she asked.

"I had business with an old family friend in Rodney."

Her laugh was haughty. "An old family friend?"

"Yes."

"Who?"

"She doesn't concern you."

Alice's nostrils flared. He wanted to tangle his fingers in that luscious hair and yank, force that angry mouth open, ravage it, then ravish her.

Shut her up.

"Is she an ex-mistress?"

"Ex? If that were the case, you'd have no problem with her tonight, would you?"

"Is she your mistress then?"

"I have no mistress."

"So you're spending my money on whores?"

"*My* money. You are *my* wife."

"I wish you'd remembered that earlier."

"I never forget it."

Her eyes widened, no tears, thank God, but her chin was puckering.

"Then your having a wife means nothing to you?" She enunciated carefully in a small voice.

"Having you means a great deal, not the least of which is financial."

"Damn your black soul, Calhoon."

"I don't like you questioning me, Alice."

Her eyes flashed. Good. He could deal with anger easier than hurt.

"I don't care. If your relationship is innocent you should have no problem telling me who the woman is."

"It's not about the woman, it's about where I was, and it does not concern you."

"But you do."

"No more than I can help it."

She clamped her mouth shut in what he expected was shock, then drew herself up proudly and walked away from him. He stayed put. "Go sleep somewhere else."

"No."

She whirled on him, her lovely mouth twisted into a snarl. "And you are no more a concern to me than I allow you to be! Go back to Rodney and sleep with your 'family friend.'"

"It's raining."

A choked growl escaped her throat. "Then go sleep upstairs. I don't care where you go, but get away from me."

He stepped toward her, and she brought her petite body to full height and clenched the fists hanging at her sides. "If you come within the length of my arm, I swear I will sock you."

He stopped.

"How would you feel about me behaving in a similar manner?"

"What do you mean by 'a similar manner?'" he asked, but he knew what she meant.

"Leaving the smell of my perfume on another man."

Momentarily he stared at her, then watched her raise her chin in blatant provocation.

"Don't ever do it."

"If you care no more for me than you do for my feelings, why should you care?"

He stepped closer. "It's a matter of *my* honor."

In the soft glow of lantern light and the room's shadows, he glimpsed her sudden move, but didn't realize the significance until his jaw exploded, his head whipped to the right, and his face commenced throbbing. Slack-jawed, he turned slowly and stared at her, eyes wide and bright, her body braced for whatever retaliation he would mete out. Well, she had warned him to stay back.

He shut his mouth and, watching her so as to ward off another blow, raised his hand to his face and rubbed the ache. "Obviously you wanted a different answer."

"Yes, I did, and you and your honor can go to hell." She sucked in a stuttered breath. "Was it you?"

"Was it me, what?"

"Were you the one who entered the room earlier? Was it you Jocelyn warned me about?"

"Is she warning you now?"

"You can't kill me now. Miss Elvie knows you're here."

"What makes you think Elvie wouldn't be on my side?"

"I know she wouldn't."

"No, you don't."

She closed her eyes and asked softly, "Why are you being so horrid?"

He did touch her then, gently running an index finger over her shoulder and down the sleeve covering her arm. "Could have something to do with your accusing me of unfaithfulness, then of planning to kill you."

She shrugged her shoulder, and he dropped his hand. "I've just now accused you of the latter," she said, "but why else would you leave the warm embrace of a 'family friend' and come out in a storm?"

"To kill you for sure."

She reached for her pillow. "If you won't go, I'll sleep upstairs."

"Have you considered I simply wanted to be with you?"

Encouraged by a hesitant shake of her head, he wrapped his arms around her. "It's that simple, Alice," he said, placing his chin atop her head to calm her. She did, at least, relent in the defiant shaking of her head.

"There's still the gardenia."

"It's on my clothes." He squeezed her tighter. "I could take them off."

She tried to pull away. He kissed her ear.

"If you were to hug me, then I would smell like lavender."

"You are not amusing, Calhoon." She tore free.

He sighed. "I don't want us sleeping apart. Go to bed. I'll stay on my side, you on yours, but think about this, Alice. You smell gardenia on me, but you don't smell another woman."

<h1 style="text-align:center">Chapter Thirty</h1>

"**A**re you asleep?" Alice asked.

"No," Calhoon answered.

"Did you lock the doors?"

Alice felt him roll onto his back. "The two still working."

She hadn't smelled sex on him, that was true. The biggest fault she could hold against him was his refusal to tell her where he'd been and the name of the 'old family friend' who smelled of gardenia. Now the cold house and residual fear from whatever had invaded their bedroom earlier ate away at her anger. She shuddered. She'd lain awake over an hour and knew by the stillness of his body he had, too. She wanted to be held.

"Brim told me your daddy gave him that nickname."

He moved again, and she knew he faced her back. "When we were small. He was named after the fish, *b-r-e-a-m*, but we spell his name *b-r-i-m*."

"He told me he was named after the fish. Told me he always thought white perch tastier, but just a little."

At her back, Calhoon moved closer to her. She anticipated his arm across her waist, then felt it, and she snuggled her derrière against his pelvis. "Brim was easier to say, I reckon. Calling him 'white perch' every time we wanted him would have been a mouthful. Besides, Daddy was fond of bream and *Aloquitious* was sure fond of catching 'em. After he got older, he'd leave the fields after the noon meal and come sauntering up to the house. Daddy'd be on the porch, digesting his lunch. 'Ole massa,' he'd say, 'I figure you wantin' fish for suppa mor'n you want cotton chopped.' Daddy would laugh and most times he'd let him go fishing if the field work was on schedule."

"And you'd go with him?"

Calhoon snorted and tugged her closer. "Rarely. After I got older, I had lessons or work to do of my own. Despite what you Northerners think, we didn't sit on our asses and drink mint juleps all day."

No, they ran a farm, often large, even complex ones, and despite their use of slave labor, the labor wasn't free. Slaves were expensive and their owners, most owners, she had to admit, given the subjective success of the institution across the South, invested much to their care and well being—to include, sometimes, an emotional investment.

"Who gave him that name?"

"I just—"

"Aloquitious."

Calhoon snuggled his nose beneath her ear and breathed in. "His mama."

"She died?"

"Years ago, long before the war."

"His papa?"

"He's gone, too. Drowned in the spring of '55 trying to pull his swamped mule out of the rapidly-rising Camellia Creek. He was by himself. We didn't realize he was in trouble till it was too late."

"Were there brothers and sisters?"

Calhoon chuckled in her ear. "What's your interest in Brim Solomon?"

He'd brought them fish this afternoon, caught too many for his family, he told Alice, and he'd already given Miss Elvie some. Alice had cleaned them—Naomi Polk had stuck her head out the cookhouse door long enough to tell her only a stupid woman ever learned to clean fish, squirrel, or rabbit.

"He seems fond of you."

Calhoon kissed her ear, then searched for a breast. "Is that what piques your curiosity, that he's fond of me? Some folks are."

Through the cotton cloth of her nightgown, he gently brushed a nipple, and she stifled a groan.

"You're fond of me."

She rolled onto her back to hasten his lips on hers. "Sometimes."

He raised the heavy covers, then maneuvered his body over hers. "Like now," he said and kissed her.

Lord, yes, like now. His hands moved over her body for the second time today. They had made love—that was the first time he'd used that expression with her—after that Laura person had left.

In the parlor, the front door clamored. Calhoon cursed, then she sensed him sit up. She rolled from beneath him and sat, too. Someone was at the door, pounding and calling her husband's name. "It's all right," he said softly, and touched her shoulder. The tension she'd sensed in him moments before was gone. "You stay here."

Eli closed his office door. He hoped Alice stayed in bed.

Dilbert, slouch hat in hand and dripping as he went, made his way to the worn chair in front of the desk. Beads of water clung to his wool jacket, which hung open, and his worn boots left a trail of wet leaves on the floor. He smelled of tobacco, bay rum, and the damp cold outside. He needed a shave, but that wasn't out of the ordinary. "I'm sorry to drag you outa bed with this. Told Auntie Elvie I'd be back."

Eli flopped into his chair. "She told me, but with the weather, figured you'd wait till tomorrow. Was the bridge swamped?"

"Naw, ain't rained that much. Federals found our cotton."

"Well, shit," Eli said, "when did they show up?"

Dilbert shrugged. "Late this afternoon."

"I wonder—"

"Wayne's sayin' Brim Solomon told 'em."

Eli stared at Dilbert. "Did Wayne see him there?"

"Wayne weren't even there, Eli. I was checkin' on things and I seen 'em, and no, I didn't see Brim."

"Brim doesn't even know about the cotton, and even if he did, he'd never betray me."

Dilbert leaned back. "Wayne sure as hell seems to think Brim would betray him. He's still angry about Brim leavin' him high and dry late summer."

"It wasn't Brim, not about the cotton."

"Well," Dilbert said, turning his hat over and over in his hands, "I didn't think so either."

"I'll talk to Wayne. He's got a bee up his butt, and I don't want any more trouble between him and Brim." Eli looked across the desk to find Dilbert studying him. "What?"

"Could it 'a been your wife?"

Eli's mouth went dry. "She didn't know about the cotton either." Well, hell, yes she did—he'd told her.

"Beggin' your pardon, Eli Calhoon, but we was movin' that cotton the very night you brought her to your place. Me and Hiram said so at the time we believed you were a lot more pleased at catchin' her than you was with stealin' that cotton."

"I sure was, Dilbert, and I still am. Even if she did realize we were stealing cotton that night, she has no idea where we took it."

"We were on the—"

"We were at the crossroad, and she was lost. She couldn't have known which way we were going."

"Well, it was fifty-fifty weren't it? Check one way, then the other. Anybody round here knows these parts coulda figured it out."

"She's not from around here, and she hasn't had the opportunity to talk to anyone who is." Other than "dear" Aunt Betty.

Dilbert blew out a breath, then seemed to relax. He hadn't relished suggesting it was Alice who'd betrayed them, and Eli appreciated that. "What do ya think them Federals is gonna do?"

"Confiscate our cotton."

"They'll arrest us?"

"For what?" Eli sat forward. "Look, that was the beauty of the heist to begin with. The men who had the cotton never entered it on a Federal manifest. Assuming the Federals even know who we are, they can't prove we were in possession of stolen U.S. property."

"You sure?"

"I am." At least he was pretty sure. Given the way things were working around here, he couldn't really guarantee lack of evidence would keep them from being arrested. The Constitution the Yankees had betrayed and trampled on waging war against the South sure wouldn't be any more important to them now than it had been four years ago. He shot Dilbert a sheepish grin, and Dilbert narrowed his eyes. "I hope," Eli said.

Dilbert slapped his hat against his thigh. "That's damn great, Eli."

"Don't worry about it until they come for you."

"I'll shoot the bastards."

"Don't. They can't hold you, but they sure as hell can hang you."

"*W*hat's happened?"

She was facing the door, her eyes wide. The coal oil lamp beside their bed highlighted the outline of her delicious body, draped in white flannel. He closed the bedroom door.

"Did you tell anyone about my cotton?"

"They've found your cotton?"

He nodded and stepped around her to sit on the foot of the bed. "Did you say anything to anyone?"

"No," she said and sat beside him. He looked at her, studying her face for any indication she was lying to him. He was pretty sure she wouldn't be able to hide a falsehood. She wasn't able to endure much of his scrutiny either. "I wouldn't have told anyone, Calhoon. I was too afraid you'd betray Cassie."

"I told you—"

"This morning," she said, coming off the bed. "Who have I seen to tell since then, other than your horrid aunt and your girl-friend, and you heard the conversation I had with Laura—and you claim to have listened to everything I told Aunt Betty."

Most of it, yes. "You're sure you didn't say anything to your Uncle Peter the night I took you home?"

"The last thing on my mind that night was your thievery. I

don't think I even gave it a thought. Was that the authorities just now?"

"Not hardly."

"Are you in trouble?"

"Not yet." He reached for her arm and yanked her to him, then fell back and pulled her with him. "Tell me this, would you be happy if I were in trouble?"

He felt a shudder course through her. Fear or passion? he wasn't sure. "Could I visit you in prison…"

He wasn't hearing this.

"…when I wanted you, I mean? Actually, that might prove quite suitable. I wouldn't have to put up —"

She ended with a little "poof" when he crushed her to him, then he rolled over, pinning her beneath him. Lord, he was tired, but she felt so damn good. "Tell me this, darlin'. If there'd been no Cassie, would you have betrayed me?"

She struggled to push him off her. "I can't breathe."

He raised a bit. "Would you?"

"I wouldn't be here."

"Honey, I told you, you were doomed from the start. You would have been here come hell or high water." He swallowed whatever protest she might have mustered with a passionate kiss, and she retaliated by curling her nails into his shoulders.

"Let me up," she demanded when he pulled back.

He kissed her jaw. "Vengeance is so sweet."

She punched him, rather hard he noted, and he laughed.

He reached for the hem of her nightgown, and she squealed.

"That's right, sweetheart," he said, "I'm going to punish you again."

His last thrust coincided with her cry of pleasure, his echoing curse a tender caress. He told her he'd never climaxed at the same time as his partner. She certainly never had, and she wondered what it meant, this wonderful, warm physical attraction he held for her. In the beginning she'd thought to use her surrender for survival. He would have his way with her, and she'd leave him to think she enjoyed sex, for pleasure, as a man did, or a Cassie, sure all the while she wouldn't. That way he couldn't use possessing her as a token of conquest. But truth was she did surrender to his touch.

Chapter Thirty-one

Eli opened his eyes to a night dark as death and listened for a recurrence of the shot, the sound of hooves.

The scent of his woman returned him from the battlefield.

"What's wrong?" Alice whispered.

He'd wakened her, or the shot had. "Did you hear anything?"

"You cried out."

Had he? He rolled onto his back.

Another shot rent the night, and he sat straight up. Rifle. He felt her sit up beside him and pull the covers around her. They were both naked.

"What's happening out there?"

He swallowed. The shots came from some distance away, but still too close. "I don't know." He threw the covers aside. The room was cold, the bare floor like ice. He searched for his pants.

A light flickered.

"Put it out!"

She snuffed it, and he heard her rise from the bed. She was moving around, getting dressed, he hoped.

He buttoned his britches, pulled his undershirt over his head, and found his shirt on the floor.

"Eli," Elvie called from the stairwell, "der be a fire in da quawta!"

He was out their bedroom door and bounding up the stairs. He almost ran into Elvie, hurrying down. "Where?" he asked.

She led him to the small bedroom across from hers and to its undamaged window.

His heart slammed against his chest. "Jesus."

Elvie moved out of his way. Alice, just starting up the stairs, had to jump to avoid his running into her. "There's a fire in the slaves' quarters," he told her, but he could have been more specific. Already back to the table by their bed, he yanked open the top drawer and took out his revolver, then tucked it inside his waistband. "Get me some light." Where the hell were his boots?

He heard her scurrying, and in seconds she had the coal oil lamp burning. He found the boots.

Alice left the room and returned with his coat as he pushed down on his second heel. "You stay here," he said, taking the coat. Her mouth dropped open, and he figured she was about to protest. "Your rifle," was all she said.

"I'll get it."

Elvie all but beat Calhoon out the door. Alice stayed only long enough to dress properly and grab an old work jacket Calhoon kept on the mud porch. The sun was coming up, but the morning was cold and she could see her breath. From the back porch, she looked at the rough lean-to where Calhoon kept Johnny. The horse was gone.

Alice wasn't sure where she was going or how far, but she assumed she was to use the road that led to Elvira Hinny's home, and she wondered if it was the old woman's house that had burned. But how did that explain the gunshots?

It was good light by the time she passed Elvie's cabin, quiet and undamaged in the misty dawn, but wood smoke hung heavy in air laced with a sickening sweet odor that slowed her pace and warned her to proceed cautiously. She'd run part of the way, and taking a deep breath at this point filled her stomach more with bile than her lungs with air.

"Don't go in der, don't you dare. Too hot an' you know it an' not a thing you can do."

Elvie's voice. They were around the next bend in the road. Alice, heart pumping and head throbbing, hiked her skirts and started to run again. She slowed, then dropped her skirts when Elvie came into view. A cabin sat in a clearing, for all intents and purposes a duplicate of Elvie's. It was built off the ground, a narrow, covered porch running its width, a door in the middle. Calhoon stood on the top step, his bare hand against a support post, which held up the roof—the section covering the porch was still mostly standing, as was the front wall of the house. The roof covering the house proper, however, had collapsed. Smoke spiraled upward, then dispersed against a rosy early morning sky.

"We'll get 'em later," Miss Elvie said, "when we get he'p out heah."

Calhoon stepped onto the porch anyway, glancing up once to appraise the roof. Alice ran forward. There appeared to be no fire where he stood, but flames licked here and there among the smoldering embers on the side she could see. The interior of the house was gutted.

She reached Miss Elvie's side at the same moment Calhoon peeked inside. The old woman put a hand on her arm and silently warned her to go no farther. Alice watched her husband.

"He's here by the door. Roof's on 'im."

"Shots got 'im, you know dat," Miss Elvie said to him. "You see Sarah or Sammy?"

This was the Solomon family's cabin.

Alice heard her husband draw a breath. "No," he said after a long moment, "floor's collapsed here, it's under the roof. They're probably on the ground."

"Lawd, Lawd, Lawd," Miss Elvie said under her breath, and she turned away. "You come on down now. I'll go get Buck. His hearin's bad, only reason he ain't already heah."

Alice watched Calhoon step inside and started after him. Immediately, Elvie turned and grabbed her arm. "Eli," she hollered, "git outa der. You gonna git hurt, an' git yo' young wife hurt."

He jerked around and saw her.

"Git down before she comes up der tryin' to he'p you. I'm goin' fo' Buck."

"I told you to stay home," he said, jumping from the porch. He looked haggard, tired, drained. He stepped around her.

"I couldn't stay home, not knowing what had happened." She followed him around the side of the house.

"Brim and his wife and son are dead. Their cabin has been destroyed by fire. That's what's happened."

It hardly ended there, but given the emotion in his voice, now was not the time to push him.

He stopped at the back rear corner of the cabin. This entire section of the house was gone, the floor on the ground covered by the charcoal timbers, embers, and glowing ash of what had been the roof and the side and rear walls. "Sarah had wanted to come home," he said. He looked away, and Alice watched him raise his sleeve to his nose. "This is what she came back to."

Alice couldn't say anything, she had no idea what had happened, but she did know Brim had been murdered, and his wife and son with him. The gunshots, further referenced by Miss Elvie, testified to that.

"Goddamn it, Brim shouldn't have come back here."

Alice stepped closer to him and touched his arm.

He turned his head so he could see her over his shoulder. "I want you to go back to the house."

She couldn't. These people had to be recovered and buried.

He must have seen the refusal in her eyes. "Go home."

She stuck her chin out, then turned her back on him. "I am home."

*M*iss Elvie and a visibly shaken Buck returned within half an hour. Alice stayed away from Calhoon. He was angry at her for not doing what he told her, but this was where she belonged.

Miss Elvie said something to him that added to his agitation. Minutes later she confided to Alice that Buck's neighbor had sent his boy to Port Gibson to tell the Federals. "Tol' Eli. He's mad as can be. Tol' 'im Buck didn't have nothin' to do wif it. Dat man lives up da road a piece had walked down to Buck's when he heard the ruckus. Was der when I gots der. He be an uppity nigger and say da Federals ain't gonna stand fo' murderin' freedmen an' dey gots to know."

"And what's wrong with them knowing? Surely Calhoon wants the culprit caught."

"He do, but he wants to take care of it himsef."

"Does he know who did this?"

Miss Elvie shrugged. "You bes' talk to yo' husband. I ain't tellin' you, even if I know'd."

Calhoon and Buck got Brim out of the doorway. They'd let the fire cool a bit, she heard them say, before searching for Sarah and the little boy. He'd been such a sweet little thing with a bright smile and wide eyes in his dark face. He'd told Alice the morning she'd hitched a ride with them that he wanted a sister.

Now he was dead. He'd only been three years old. His sibling, whatever it would have been, died in its mother's womb. Alice glanced at Calhoon sitting on the bottom step of the porch, head bowed, arms resting on his thighs. Brim Solomon, covered by one of Camellia Creek's few remaining bed sheets, lay stretched out before him.

Her grieving husband knew who'd done this and, for some reason, blamed himself.

She started toward him. Not to ask what she knew he would not tell her, but to be with him.

She was almost there when the solemn air was disturbed by the creaks and groans of a rickety wagon coming around the bend. Two men sat in it. Ignoring her, Calhoon rose and started their way. Judging from his demeanor, he knew them.

One jumped down, yanking his hat from his head and shaking his head in humble remorse. The other, securing the mules' reins, seemed equally aggrieved.

"Eli," the first man said, "I'm sorry, son."

"I knew somethin' bad was gonna come of this," the second said, coming around the mules. "I felt it when I come to you last night."

Their late night visitor. Alice took a step closer, and the first man looked at her.

"Have you talked to him?" Calhoon asked.

"No," the second man said. "Not since yesterday."

Calhoon looked at the first. "Hiram?"

"Nope, and he wouldn't've told either of us if he was gonna do this, you know that, Eli. He know'd how you felt about Brim."

Calhoon started around them, toward Johnny, munching on grass at the edge of the woods across the road."

The first man pivoted with him. "He was just so upset about the loss of that cotton." He started after Calhoon, who stopped short and whistled. The horse started his way.

The second man narrowed his eyes on her. "Somebody talked 'bout that cotton, Eli. Wayne, he blamed Brim."

Alice's heart lodged in her throat at the accusation in the man's voice, not to mention his glare, and she recalled Calhoon's question from the night before. She turned to her husband, and his eyes met hers, then he shifted his gaze. "Dilbert, what happened here this morning hasn't got a thing to do with that cotton. Wayne's problem with Brim came before that, and you know it."

Dilbert looked at Calhoon, who'd caught up Johnny's reins.

"Blaming Brim for turning us in was a fabrication on Wayne's part. It gave him an excuse for…"

He couldn't go on. Alice knew it, whether the others did or not, and he waved his arm in the air to encompass the gruesome scene behind them.

Hiram took a step after him. "Where you goin', boy?"

"Where do you think I'm going?"

Dilbert, no longer preoccupied with her or her speculated role in the loss of their stolen cotton, strode after Calhoon. "No, you ain't."

"I'm gonna kill the son of a bitch," she heard him say. He already had one foot in the stirrup.

"No," she cried and charged after them. She got to Calhoon the same time Dilbert did.

"Let the authorities handle this, Eli," Hiram hollered from close behind them.

Calhoon swung his leg over Johnny's rump and settled into the saddle.

"Sure," Dilbert said, "they'll take care of this. One thing them Yankee bastards might prove good for."

"I'll be damned…," Calhoon ground out, his gaze passing over Hiram and Dilbert, before settling on Alice.

"Please," she said, placing her hand on his boot, "you'll be hanged."

"…before I'll turn in a fellow Confederate to the Federals."

"So you'll do it yourself?" she screamed at him.

"That's how it's always been. Now let go of my leg and go home like I told you to."

"Brim is not your property any longer."

"He was my *friend*. Now, he's dead." He pulled his boot out of the stirrup to shake her off. "You, however, are my property, and your purpose in my household is to conform to what I demand of you." He leaned low over the saddle. "Your money and your body, Alice. That's all. Fortunately for you, no more is desired. Now let go of me."

He might as well have slapped her. No matter how close he'd brought his face to hers, there was no way his friends could not have heard his words. She released him and stepped back, shocked too stupid to speak, even if she'd been able without breaking down in tears.

She looked in the general direction of his departing back, but nothing registered until she turned back to the two men, now looking at her.

"You best not be sayin' anything to anyone, Mrs. Calhoon."

She narrowed her eyes on the speaker. "Mr. Dilbert, I believe?"

He straightened and glared at her. "Dilbert Bowen."

"Well, Mr. Dilbert Bowen, go screw your mules."

Chapter Thirty-two

The porch creaked beneath Eli's weight, the only sound he heard. He did knock. He didn't figure Wayne was waiting to ambush him; else he'd have never done what he did to begin with.

It was after ten in the morning, but no one answered the door. The day had turned out nice, though scarcely noticeable to Eli. After giving whomever a chance to answer, he turned the knob and stepped into the dim entry.

The house, an enclosed dogtrot, was chilly inside, no fires lit, and he could see straight through to the back door.

"May?" Eli flexed his jaw. He couldn't bring himself to call out the given name of a man he was about to kill.

He glanced in the rooms on either side of the dogtrot, then exited the back and made his way to the kitchen.

May sat on the floor behind the kitchen's partially opened back door. He went to her and said her name. When she didn't respond, he touched her shoulder and knelt on one knee beside her. She turned to him then, her bruised and bloodied face brightening with a grotesque smile, well-meant but contorted from the beating. She placed a cold hand over the one he'd laid on her shoulder. "Eli, honey, it's so good to see you."

He touched her battered cheek, and she closed her eyes and leaned into his palm. Then she started to cry. "He killed Brim this morning," she said.

"I know."

She opened her eyes, one near swollen shut, and straightened. "Of course you do. That's why you're here."

"Where is he?"

"Out at the woodpile. Came back at dawn and said we needed

wood. Said we'd sit by the fire and talk about things." Her gaze returned to the yard. "He always said that after he hit me. That meant he wanted to make love." Bitterness had hardened her voice, and she turned and looked him in the eye. Lucid. When he'd first seen her, he hadn't been sure. "Would you want to make love to something you'd just did this to?"

He couldn't have, wouldn't have.

She focused outside when he didn't answer. "Make love. Make another baby to beat out of me."

Eli wanted to ask her why he did that. One day maybe he would, but now was not the time.

"I got to where I visited Elvie before he could find out. Over time, I didn't want to have his baby anyway." She twisted her head and looked at him with one good eye. "Did she tell you?"

"If she had I'd've killed him a long time ago. She was closed-mouthed when it came to 'white-woman's business,' she called it."

"She told me I'd die if I didn't stop. There was three she got rid of for me. The rest he beat out of me."

Eli shuddered, and May drew in a breath.

"Lord, I had so hoped a Yankee bullet would take him. As many good men as they killed, and they kept missing him. Worthless bunch."

Wayne had been a good soldier. He'd been a good farmer. Why the hell hadn't he been a good husband…and father?"

May reached up and touched Eli's cheek. "You grew into such a handsome man." Tears filled the one eye not swollen shut. "I wish you had been ten years older or me younger. Maybe I could have made your childhood dream come true." She dropped her hand and turned away. "I can't believe our sweet, sweet Brim is dead."

"And Sarah and their boy."

She turned her head and stared at him.

"He burned the house, May. They didn't get out."

Again she looked away. "He brought me fish late yesterday mornin'. Wayne saw him, but didn't approach him. I thought everything might be all right since you returned the mule."

"Brim had seen too much of what was happening here."

"Wayne accused me of layin' with him," she said, as if she'd not heard him.

"With Brim?"

"Oh yes." She laughed sadly. "Can you imagine that?"

"Did he always accuse you of such, May? Is that —"

She was already nodding her head. "From the start."

She'd been married to him for twenty years. Of course, for the past four he'd been mostly gone.

"That's why he killed the babies. He said they weren't his."

Eli squeezed her shoulder. "I'm gonna take care of everything, May."

She smiled and nodded. "I know you will, Eli. You're a good man, but we can't bring Brim back, can we?"

Pressure filled the space behind his eyes, but he swallowed the lump in his throat and rose. "Is he armed?"

"His rifle's in the house. His handgun's beside him."

Eli wrapped his fingers around the barrel of Wayne Hale's Colt, reared back, then threw the gun as far as he could into the relatively peaceful waters of the Mississippi. He hoped Wayne's weighted carcass sank as well as the pistol would, but too many times the river had given up its dead. He moved back up the old pier. Donnegan's landing the place was called. Once, years before the war, this old plantation site had been a hubbub of activity, but yellow fever had taken the family in the early forties; the house had burned two years later. The land was now part of Camellia Creek. A paddle wheeler hadn't stopped here in a quarter of a century, and Eli was thankful what was left of the pier had held him. The current was strong in this spot, and the farther he'd been able to get Wayne's body from the bank, the better.

He reached for Johnny's reins. "Lighter load goin' back, old son." He mounted and patted the gelding's neck. He hadn't wanted to dispose of the body in broad daylight, but he'd had little choice given the authorities were already on the trail because of the stolen cotton and a nosey neighbor.

He glanced around the misty forest, pierced by long rays of sunlight. Despite the intrinsic danger of being seen, there was peace here in the shadows. Maybe, in its watery grave, Wayne's sick soul would find some, too.

"You think you can't get away from da smell of it," Miss Elvie told Alice. "Seems to stay in yo' hair an' on yo' skin fo'evah. Think really it's all in yo' mem'ry."

Locked like a nightmare inside your head.

"Bend down now, else I'll get you wet, den you'll be cold. Soon as we done wif yo' hair, you can git yo'sef a baf inside, and I'll give you one 'a my cotton dresses. Dey worn, but clean, an' smell only 'a soap."

"Thank you."

Rinse water rushed through the tresses Miss Elvie had helped her shampoo. Alice closed her eyes and her mouth, and managed to protect her nostrils, pinched closed beneath a thumb and index finger, though it was there that the sickening scent of burned human flesh lingered and where the cleansing rinse would do the most good, if only it could.

"Don't move, der's still soap. You gots a thick head 'a hair, girl."

And curly. She'd have a devil of a time getting the tangles out without her rinse.

"Der now, think I gots it all." The Negress handed her a worn cotton towel. Alice straightened. Sweet agony and Lord, it felt good.

"I could wait to change until I get home."

"It be all right. I know you be sick to yo' stomach. I'll wash da one you wearin' and you can gib mine back."

Rubbing her hair dry, Alice followed her into the house. "I didn't think slaves had a large wardrobe."

"Two sets a yeah, winter and summer." Miss Elvie looked at her. "But heah we was always passed down clothes from da main house. Same lotsa places. Some of us earned our own money an' bought extras, an' we still had da past yeahs' old sets."

When Alice closed the plank door, she noticed the hat the Negress had given her a few nights ago to protect her from the rain. Elvie'd worn it all day. "I see you got your hat back."

Miss Elvie glanced over her shoulder.

"Eli brought it back not real long afta you left wif it." The woman lifted the top to a rough wooden chest and squatted. "Belonged to him's daddy fo' yeahs and yeahs."

He'd known from the time he'd caught her on the side of the road she'd been to Elvira Hinny's. Alice walked toward the old woman, rummaging in the box.

"You inherited it." She'd spoken matter-of-factly, sure that was the case.

Miss Elvie pulled out a neatly folded garment. "Had it fo' long time befo' Hollan' Calhoon died, if dat's what you mean. Him always gib me da ole one when him gots a new one. Done dat eva since I come back to da fields." She handed a dress to Alice. "Neva even wo' dis one. Made fo' a girl. Warm flannel."

Alice shook it out. "Let me guess. It belonged to Hannah?"

"Yes'm it did. Got lots of 'er eva'day things. She gib some of her fancy dresses to da young girls and womens."

The dress was burnt orange, simply cut with a skirt gathered at the waist. It's long, full sleeves were caught with wide cuffs, which buttoned at the wrist. The bodice was gathered and buttoned in the back; the collar was muslin. Despite the fact Alice feared the color would clash with her hair, she told Miss Elvie it was lovely—as it truly was—and thanked her for the opportunity to change.

"Was the last Mr. Calhoon your lover?"

"Might as well ask if Eli be my lover to ask such a thing."

"I'm sorry. I'd heard that—"

"Calhoons neva touched dem's slaves."

"But some masters did?"

"Yes, but not Eli or Andrew or dem's daddy." She closed the lid of her box, then checked the pot hanging inside the fireplace. "Water'll be hot soon. We needs to untangle dat mess of hair you gots." She motioned Alice into a chair by the fire. The room was small and close, the door shut because of the cold. The only window was in the other room.

"Eli's granddaddy come 'ere not long afta da Spanish lef'. Raised him's son, and Massa Holland passed it on to him's boys, not to be layin' wif dem's nigger women."

Alice assumed—she gritted her teeth against the pull of Miss Elvie's comb—some sort of bigotry.

"During him's young days, da granddaddy, I'm tol', took him a fancy to one of him's light-skinned slaves. Put her to work in da big house. House slaves always thinkin' demsefs better'n fieldhands. Well, dis woman already lain wif ole massa Calhoon's best hand an' dat man considered 'er his. Fine fo'man dat man was to hear Massa Holland's tellin' of da tale. Best him's daddy eva had. Well, dat hand wanted to run away wif dis woman afta ole massa took 'er."

Ouch. Alice hissed between her teeth, but she didn't complain. Having Miss Elvie comb out those tangles was certainly easier than her having to do it.

"But dis woman, she didn't wanna go."

"She was afraid."

Elvira Hinny snorted. "Maybe, or maybe she liked being *priv'leged.*"

Alice grimaced with another painful yank on her scalp. "Don't you think he forced her to sleep with him?"

"Could've, but women be women, missy, don't matter da color of dem's skin. Dey know how to get what dey wants outa a man. Keep da massa happy, he keep you happy."

"And her Negro male friend, the foreman?"

"Fo' sho' he weren't happy. Jealousy don't know no bounds when it comes to skin color neitha. When she wouldn't leave wif 'im, he kilt 'er an' he were hanged. Whole mess cost ole man Calhoon two slaves—two of him's fav'rits. From den on, he tol' him's chil'en not eva to be sleepin' wif any of dem's slave family. Strict 'bout dat, too."

Alice glanced over her shoulder. "What about his wife?"

Elvira stroked Alice's wet hair and shrugged. "Don't know.

Some women dey don't care. Happy dem's husbands leave 'em alone. My missy—"

"Rosalind Calhoon, you mean?"

Miss Elvira ran the comb, unhindered through Alice's hair. "Yes'm, Eli's mama, Rosalind. She were my missy."

Which explained not only Elvira Hinny's being there when Andrew, Eli, and Hannah were born and her holding Rosalind Calhoon when she died but also the ease with which Aunt Elvie assumed responsibility for Alice's hair and bath.

"She didn't want 'er man sleepin' wif nobody but her. She an' Massa Holland fought ova dat jus' one time."

"Did she have her way?"

"Best we all know she did."

"And when she died, he sent you to the fields?"

"Afta a bit, he did, but was me who asked 'im if I could go."

"But I thought working in the big—"

"I hated it der afta my missy died, Naomi tryin' to take ova eva'thin'. I run dat house up till my Rosalind died. Sho' didn't need no he'p from da likes 'a Nimi."

"You call Naomi Polk Nimi?"

"Yes'm, dat be what 'er mama and daddy called 'er. Know'd 'er all 'er life. Ole Massa Polk, Papa Jack we call'd 'im, brought me in from da field when I were fou'teen to be Rosalind's nursemaid. She be newly bawn. Nimi be five, had 'er own nursemaid. When my missy wed Holland Calhoon, I come 'ere wif 'er from Tennessee."

"As did Naomi Polk?"

Again Miss Elvie brought the comb through her hair. "She come later, afta her daddy died. Farm in Tennessee went to Papa Jack's cousin from Kentucky. Da Polks pass dem's lands to dem's menfolks as long as dey able. Massa Holland took Nimi in, bein' she was unwed."

Instead of a distant cousin taking her. That made sense.

"Nimi, she considered she inherited da woman's place at Camellia Creek afta my missy died."

"And you didn't want to work for her?"

The old woman stroked Alice's rapidly drying hair. "We'll wrap it back up while you git yo' baf, and I wouldn't work fo' 'er, not afta so long. Life fo' me was ter'ble in dat house. Field be wide-open and free. Darkies could talk when dey wants, take a rest when dey wants. Oh, Miss Alice, I'd fo'got how much better it be in da field.

"Many a lunch time in da late fall befo' Christmas when der weren't much to do, Massa Holland would come to my cabin and eat wif me. We'd talk 'bout da young'uns and my missy an' pas' times." She walked to Alice's front, pulling her hair up with a towel. "Sho' did make Nimi mad cause he do dat."

"And she stayed at his house all those years?"

"Yes'm, but she had 'er own bed, if dat's what you wond'rin' 'bout. Massa Holland needed someone to run da house an' he didn't feel right 'bout tossin' 'er out, an' he couldn't have two women der wif one bein' 'er. Finally got 'er a house in Pawt Gibson when Hannah turned fou'teen. One woman too many he tol' me, an' he be too old to deal wif 'em.

"Spent mo' time at da big house when Hannah become missy. Her I could work fo'."

Chapter Thirty-three

Eli eyed Major Seth Parker, United States Marines, and his Negro captain and sergeant, who were, Eli noted, Army. He stepped onto the porch. He'd be damned before he invited them into his house.

"A Major Dyer from the Freedman's Bureau was here about one. He said we could bury the bodies."

"He told me. Have you buried them?" Parker asked.

"We're planning a reading in a little bit."

"I'd like to see them."

Eli swallowed. It was already getting late, and friends were gathering, those left around, anyway. He wanted to get Brim and his little family in the ground. "You're welcome to. We've got 'em laid out in one of the slave cabins. Elvira Hinny and my wife have been taking turns sitting with them."

"You know what happened?"

Yep, and that was more than this major was going to learn from him. "Someone woke Brim Solomon before dawn this morning, shot him twice, once through the heart, and torched his cabin. His wife, who was five months pregnant, and his three-year-old boy did not get out."

"Fire could have started before he was shot," the captain said.

"My gut is that's probably how it happened, and that's what woke Brim up. When he tried to get his family out, he was met at the door with a rifle."

"Do you know who did it?" Parker asked.

"I didn't see what happened."

"That's not what I asked."

"But that's the only answer I can give you."

This Seth Parker, a tall, nice-looking man, studied him. "You mean that's the only answer you'll give."

"Correct."

The captain shifted his weight, and Eli glanced at his dark, defiant…assuming face.

"I have a source that tells me you were involved in a cotton theft five nights ago."

"Who's your source, Major?"

Parker smiled, almost friendly, as if he'd heard a joke. And he had. "You know I'm not going to divulge my source."

"Then I don't know anything about any cotton."

"You and three others. Rumor has it that some culprits in that theft believe it was Brim Solomon who divulged the whereabouts of the cotton."

Eli raised his eyebrows in mock surprise.

"Were you angry with Mr. Solomon, Colonel Calhoon?"

Eli folded his arms over his chest, drew in a long breath, and let it out. *Angry at Brim?*

"You know, Major, I've been mad at Brim any number of times. The last time I remember being mad enough to kill him, I was ten, he was eleven. I accidentally killed Auntie Elvie's rooster with my new slingshot. Brim thought that was so damn funny, he ran off and told the cook, who immediately told my father, who whupped my butt. Worse part was, though, Daddy gave my slingshot to Brim with the understanding he not use it anywhere around any of the slaves' chickens."

Again the captain fidgeted, but Parker simply nodded. "I've already talked to a Mr. Hiram Cleaver and Dilbert Bowen."

Eli cocked his head to one side and waited.

"They were at the Solomon house this morning?"

"They were."

"Why?" Parker asked.

"Surely you asked them."

The major pursed his lips. "We're looking for Wayne Hale."

Eli's gut tensed. He didn't think Hiram and Dilbert would have told them he'd killed Wayne.

"Do you have any idea where he is?" Parker continued.

"At present, Major Parker, I can honestly swear I do not." Damn, he wished he knew what Dilbert and Hiram had told these men, but he was smart enough to know he'd tell the major more trying to circumvent his questions than by saying nothing. The major, studying him intently now, was fishing. He knew he had Eli at a disadvantage, and that angered Eli to no end.

"Cal—"

His name died on Alice's lips. He turned to the back corner of the porch. The other men looked that way also.

"*I*'m sorry." Alice swallowed. She felt like a fool interrupting these men. She absolutely hated being the center of attention, and at the moment, four pairs of eyes watched her. The worst part was, one of those pairs, the pair that had displayed pleasant surprise, quickly clouded by confusion, belonged to the handsome Seth Parker.

Calhoon, reluctantly it appeared, held out his hand to her. "Major, my—"

"Miss Shelton, what a pleasant surprise," Parker said, sweeping the forage-looking hat from his head.

She nodded. "Likewise."

He turned to Calhoon, then back at her. "What...?"

"She's my wife," Calhoon said.

Alice heard the tension in her husband's voice. Her stomach quaked with it, and she wondered what the untimely presence of these Federals meant. She stopped next to Calhoon. Seth stood ramrod stiff in front of her, the Negro soldiers on either side of him.

The handsome major released a breath. "You married him?"

She steeled herself to the disappointment written on his face and held out her hand to him, but before he could take it, Calhoon's arm snared her around the waist and yanked her back against his chest.

"Under duress, I assure you, Major," he said and shifted her to his side. He kept his arm around her waist.

Seth's gaze moved to Calhoon's arm, and he stared. Alice looked down.

"Passion's kiss," Calhoon said. Apparently her husband had noticed Seth's interest, too.

With shaking fingers, Alice twisted Calhoon's wrist, so she could see the forearm exposed by his rolled-up sleeve. As she suspected, the clearly delineated bite mark, bruised and ugly, stared back at her.

"Are you all right here?" Seth asked her.

"Of course," she said, peeling Calhoon's arm away. "He's the one with the bite."

"*B*ut you'll not find a mark on her, Major."

Throat dry, Seth stared at this Eli Calhoon person, seeing him now in a completely new light. This man had wooed and married, almost overnight it appeared, the girl he'd been interested in getting to know better. Bile soured his stomach.

Calhoon stepped back, giving pretty little Alice some room. "The major and his troop, sweetheart, are here on a matter of some stolen cotton," the man said. "Apparently, they are now also involved in investigating the Solomon murders."

"Oh," she said, turning to find Calhoon behind her, "and have you been able to help them?"

Seth tucked his kepi under his arm. He needed to get her alone and find out what the hell was happening out here.

"Unfortunately, no."

"Do you know what happened, Alice?" Seth asked.

Tears filled her eyes. "I only know that someone shot Brim and burned the house down on top of his wife and son. I-I"—she glanced back at Calhoon. Whether seeking guidance or wishing he were somewhere else, Seth didn't know, but he'd like to find out.

"What?" he said gently.

She shook her head.

"Would you like to talk to me alone?" Seth asked. He wanted to get her out of here now, and he had the authority to do it.

She twisted her head back around to her husband. Calhoon looked at her calmly, then at him. "You can talk to her in my office, Major."

Alice blinked at Calhoon, who said, "It's all right, Alice. He thinks I'm intimidating you."

The son of a bitch was intimidating her, and he continued to intimidate despite his apparent agreeableness.

Calhoon pushed the door open. "Show him the way," he told his wife. Alice passed him with a questioning look, and Seth, one step behind her, stopped and looked Calhoon in the eye. "You've coached her?"

"We've scarcely spoken a word to each other since the thing with the Solomons happened."

"You're so sure she won't betray you?"

Calhoon glanced at Alice, watching them both. "I don't have anything to be worried about." Then he stepped forward, blocking Sergeant Zachary's entry into the house. Jubal Summers, one step behind Zachary, stopped short. "I thought you wanted to speak to my wife alone, Parker?"

Jubal Summers stepped to one side of Zachary and glared at Calhoon. The latter smiled.

"You know, Captain, Negroes of every possible sex and age have walked and run and worked and played in the halls of this house, and for the last four years I've fought side by side with many a Negro soldier. It's not the color of your skin that makes you unwelcome here. It's the color of your goddamn uniform."

Jubal Summers had bristled, but Frank Zachary appeared to take Calhoon's inhospitality in stride. Seth would have accepted it easier as well, but he was too worried about Alice to feel anything but dislike for one Eli Calhoon, Lieutenant Colonel, Confederate States Army. Seth told his men to wait outside, and he'd followed Alice to Calhoon's office.

"They all seemed to think a man named Wayne Hale killed Brim," Alice said. "I know for a fact my husband had no part. He was in bed with me. We woke together when we heard the shots."

"That doesn't mean he wasn't involved."

She shook her head and sat down hard in the chair near the desk. "He loved Brim Solomon."

"We can't find Wayne Hale. Sent my captain up to his house this morning. He talked to his wife, said someone had beaten her up real good, but Hale was gone and she claimed she had no idea where he was."

Alice was staring at him. "You don't think Calhoon beat her to make her tell him where her husband is, do you?"

God, Seth couldn't take this. He kneeled in front of her. "Has he hit you?"

"No."

"Has he threatened you?"

"Not my person, no."

Seth frowned. "He forced you to marry him."

"He convinced me to marry him," she said carefully.

"He blackmailed you."

She hesitated. "No."

He clenched his fists. He just might shake the truth out of her himself. "Then why did you do it?"

"We came to a mutual agreement."

"That benefited him," he said, pushing himself to his feet.

"It was to both our advantages."

"Tell me what your advantage was."

She smiled sadly. "That would defeat the purpose."

He had something on her, for sure. "Do you want out of this marriage?"

For a moment she sat there contemplating his question and, he imagined, weighing the consequences of her answer. Finally, she said, "No."

The handsome Seth Parker drew in a long breath and turned from her. Her gut knotted slightly. Alice hated disappointing him, but she had little choice now. She'd had no idea his interest in her went beyond a polite amusement, and she was surprised by his concern.

"Do you know anything about the stolen cotton?"

Her heart was pounding in her ears and silently she cursed Eli Calhoon for so flippantly divulging his activities that first night he'd brought her here. She swallowed. "What will happen to him?"

Seth pivoted and looked at her.

She jutted her chin out. She'd said the wrong thing. Well, she was a poor liar. Calhoon knew that. Why he'd volunteered to let Seth talk to her alone she couldn't begin to guess.

"He told me he stole cotton that dishonest Federal officers had stolen."

"Has he ever mentioned a man named Alan Guthrie?"

"No, who is he?"

"A Treasury agent found murdered north of Port Gibson a number of weeks ago."

"You think Calhoon killed him?"

"I have no idea what the man is up to, Alice, and I hate the fact that you're involved with him. Did he kill Wayne Hale?"

She stifled a gasp. He'd spoken quickly, no doubt his question meant to take her by surprise, but she forced herself calm and sat forward. "You don't even know for sure he's dead."

No, he didn't, and thank goodness Alice had been astute enough to point that out, because she didn't know what she would have told him had she tried to give a legitimate answer to his question. That Wayne Hale person deserved to be dead and in hell as far as she was concerned, and no matter how cruel his emotional abuse toward her might become, she didn't want Eli Calhoon hanged for it. Still, he couldn't take the law (in this lawless, post-war South) into his own hands.

"His questions were mostly about you and me, weren't they?" Calhoon asked.

Alice turned and studied her husband sitting behind his desk. He flexed his jaw, so cocksure of himself.

"Well?"

"Have you ever heard of a man named Alan Guthrie?"

"Treasury agent, murdered not too long ago. He was killed near Clinton, I think, but made his home in Port Gibson."

She rose from where she sat in front of his desk, same spot she'd been in since she entered this room with Seth Parker three quarters of an hour ago. "Did you do it?"

"Does he think I did it?"

There was no surprise or denial or anger in his voice. She was tired of being questioned and intimidated by men who made a habit of answering her questions with questions of their own. "I don't care what he thinks. I want to know."

A funny look crossed his face, something between curiosity and amusement. "Guthrie was dead before I got back into the cotton business, Alice. Now, I care if Parker thinks I did it."

She fell back into the chair. "He doesn't know, but he can't rule you out." She bit her bottom lip. "I told him what you told me about that cotton."

"I thought you might."

She fisted her hands in her lap. "What do you mean? Did you think I'd purposely betray you?"

He shrugged. "You did."

"I did not," she hollered at him. She was more angry at herself than anything. "I messed up. I was worried about what would happen to you."

"So you told him I stole the cotton."

"No. He…he —"

"Has no case."

She relaxed, at least a little. "I beg your pardon?"

"I told you. We stole the cotton from men who stole it from your thieving government. There's no record of the stuff ever belonging to the United States. Therefore, no one can accuse me of stealing it — except the first set of thieves, who have to keep their mouths shut if they know what's good for them." Calhoon folded his arms on the desk. "Parker's looking for a killer, not cotton."

"Guthrie's killer?"

He nodded. "And my guess has always been that Guthrie's killer is a Federal officer or another agent."

Alice licked her lips. "Would you have killed him for cotton?"

He gave his head a tiny shake. "You never know when to stop asking questions do you, sweetheart?"

"It's one thing to kill for a friend," she said carefully. "It's another to kill for greed."

"Or in self-defense. There is nothing to say this Guthrie was a nice person, and yes, depending on the circumstances, I'm more than capable of killing a crooked Federal agent."

She searched his eyes trying to determine the veracity of his words. She feared what she found was truth. Still, being capable of killing and actually doing it were two different things. With a mild shudder, she looked away.

"Alice, what did you tell him about me and Wayne Hale?"

Chapter Thirty-four

A brisk November wind whipped a strand of hair from beneath Alice's bonnet. She pulled the hair out of her eyes and pushed it behind her ear. Calhoon stood solemn beside her. He'd made silent note of the mourning dress she'd donned for the occasion, but had said nothing. He wore his Confederate frock coat fully buttoned and held his hat at his side. Alice had reached for his hand during the reading. He'd squeezed hers gently, then dropped it and sidled away from her. She'd offered no more comfort.

The Negro preacher closed his Bible and looked to her husband, who nodded before walking forward to shake the man's hand. Calhoon passed him something, recompense she imagined, and thanked him. The Reverend Marshall, as he'd been introduced to her, was yet another inhabitant of the surrounding area whom the Calhoons and their slaves had known all their lives.

Aunt Naomi Polk stepped up to Calhoon and said something to him. He pivoted and locked his gaze on something behind her. Alice turned. At the fringe of the tiny, unkempt cemetery stood Laura Blackledge, dressed in the familiar black that Alice recalled from their first meeting. Her hair was pulled up beneath her hat, and when Calhoon reached her, she raised the black veil covering her face.

Alice drew a calming breath as he took the woman's right arm and turned her from the graveyard. Laura covered her face with both hands, then laid her head against his chest. He stopped a moment while she wept, then urged her forward.

"She grew up with the Calhoon boys," Naomi said in Alice's ear. "She used to tag after Eli and Brim when they were all small. I'm sure she would have wanted to know about the burial."

Alice shifted her gaze to Naomi. "Obviously she did know."

The woman started around her, and Alice turned with her, trying to keep one eye on the spinster and the other on Calhoon and Laura.

"She was hardly welcome now, was she, after we ran her off yesterday."

Alice fell into step beside Calhoon's aunt, almost a head taller than she, but Alice was more interested in checking the whereabouts of her husband and his old lover than she was in keeping company with Naomi Polk.

"Laura is a part of Eli. She's in his blood and in his soul. He'll never get over her."

"Or he'll never get over her choosing his brother instead of him." She was trying her hardest to sound nonchalant, but she was hard put to keep the break out of her voice when Laura, being urged into her carriage by Calhoon, placed her gloved palms upon his chest and lifted her face to his. Calhoon took her hands in his.

"Andrew is dead. You're the only thing keeping them from marrying."

"Andrew was dead before he married me."

Naomi curled her lips into a smug smile. "He had his reasons for marrying you." Then she looked down at Alice. "Do not misunderstand me, dear. I don't believe Laura deserves him any more than you do. I am merely stating that he wants her." She shrugged. "Of course, being a Calhoon man, Eli probably intends to have his cake and eat it, too."

Meaning he intended to carry on with that Blackledge woman while married to Alice. The hateful old woman twisted her head. "I doubt Laura will agree to such an arrangement for long. She wants to be mistress of Camellia Creek, and she's certainly more deserving of it than a Northerner."

The wind rattled the dead leaves of the ancient sweet gum crowding the path, and with it, a chill froze Alice's blood. "I fail to see how my being a Northerner makes me undeserving, and if Calhoon had wanted to wed her, he would have done so."

There, Calhoon had Laura in her buggy. She turned from him and picked up the reins. Eyes straight ahead, Laura flicked the horse with Naomi and Alice's approach. She didn't look back. Naomi stopped next to Calhoon.

"She was late."

Calhoon started toward their wagon. Alice followed. "She didn't hear about it until early this afternoon," he said.

"Did you ask her to the house?"

"I told her to never step foot on Camellia Creek again."

"Is that so?"

Calhoon turned and almost bumped into Alice, who took a step back, but he locked his hand around her upper arm and drew her to the wagon, then helped her climb in.

"I don't want her at Camellia Creek, Aunt Naomi. If she comes, send her away."

That would certainly be no problem for Alice.

He turned and looked back to where Miss Elvie and a handful of Negroes lagged near the gravesite. "I'm gonna collect the others. Y'all go on home."

"You'll need the wagon," Alice said to him.

"We'll use Buck's."

Alice scooted over when he helped Naomi climb up beside her. The woman hollered for Miss Elvie. "She needs to help get things ready," she said to Calhoon when he frowned at her.

"She needs to stay with Brim for a little while longer," he said, "and so do I."

"We can do it," Alice said, looking around the statuesque Naomi Polk, who now glared at her.

Calhoon didn't say anything, but he did meet her eyes. Then he turned back to the small group of milling darkies.

"Mr. Cummings?"

The newspaperman took one look at Eli and closed his eyes. "Oh, hell, now it all makes sense."

Eli's gut tensed. "What makes sense?"

"Laura Blackledge."

So, it had been her. "Could you tell me what she told you?"

Poynter Cummings stepped back and motioned Eli through the door of his office. The rest of the building appeared deserted.

"She didn't actually tell me anything," Cummings said. "She came in late yesterday morning and asked me where she might find this Major Parker whom I'd cited in my most recent article on Alan Guthrie's murder."

"The one suggesting his death might be linked to cotton thefts?"

"That's the one."

"Did she tell you why she wanted to talk to Parker?"

"Oh, I asked." Cummings sat down at his desk. He raised a hand and offered a facing chair to Eli. "I am, after all, a newsman trying to get the scoop on the Alan Guthrie murder."

"Do you know who did it?"

Cummings studied him a moment, then said, "It wasn't you, was it, Calhoon?"

Eli grunted. "You're working too close with the Federals for me to tell you anything."

"But you were the man who hid the cotton Mrs. Blackledge disclosed to authorities, weren't you?"

"How do you know that's what she talked to Parker about?"

Cummings scratched thoughtfully at a nostril, then sniffed. "Yesterday evening—only hours after Laura Blackledge had requested his whereabouts—Parker told me about the find out at the Ferris place. Being the smart fella that I am, I put two and two together."

Eli said nothing.

"Look, Calhoon, I'm not working with the Federals because I'm for the Federals. I'm working with them to catch the bastards stealing from us. Helping them catch their own weasels is one thing—"

"Catching Southern weasels is different."

"Most assuredly. But I had nothing to do with their finding your cotton. All I did was tell Laura Blackledge that Parker's office is next to mine, and she was welcome to wait here for the major and his troops. She didn't want to wait, so I told her Parker had a room at the Port Gibson Hotel."

"Did Parker confirm she was the one who told him about the cotton?"

"Not to me. Like I said, I put two and two together. You did just marry, right?"

"I did."

"Laura Blackledge had her sights set on you?"

"So she said, but she's told me that before. This time I was no longer interested."

The newspaper editor leaned back. "Hell hath no fury...."

Well, Eli guessed he already knew that. He started to rise.

"You might be interested to know," Poynter Cummings said, "that Jon Franklin showed up this morning asking about that same link I'd made between Guthrie's death and the cotton thefts." Cummings shrugged. "It's nice to know folks are reading the paper."

"Did he want to talk to Parker, too?"

"I do believe that's who Franklin really wanted to talk to, but the major was out." Cummings shifted in his chair. "This isn't the first time Jon Franklin's shown interest in my reports on cotton thefts. Since there wasn't much new I could tell him in the way of Guthrie's death, I informed him of the find out at the Ferris place."

Eli narrowed his eyes on Cummings. "Why would you —"

"Look, Calhoon, Jon Franklin is a minor source of information. I thought he might toss me a bone in return."

"Did he?"

"No, but just to spice up the pot a bit, I told him about Laura Blackledge's wanting to speak to Parker."

Eli would have liked to smack the man, but instead said, "And we can assume Jon Franklin is smart enough to make the connection."

"I couldn't be sure, so I drew it out for him."

Eli blew out a breath. "Did you tell him I was suspect in the theft?"

"Like I said, I didn't make the connection between you and the theft until you walked through the door just now."

Well, Franklin would be aware soon enough. And since the authorities already knew about his role, what difference did it make? More significant to Eli was Jon Franklin's interest in Guthrie's murder.

"I admit I'm tastin' from a number of spoons." Cummings smiled when Eli said nothing. "Your showing up here this afternoon adds a whole new flavor to my simmering pot."

Alice didn't eat at the wake, and there'd been nothing prepared earlier at dinnertime. In fact, she couldn't even recall exactly what she'd been doing at midday. The new man, Buck, and his neighbor had pulled Sarah and little Sam from the house shortly after Calhoon rode off, and she and Miss Elvie had been preparing the bodies for burial when Naomi Polk arrived at noon. Though not the most grievous event Alice had to deal with in her life, it was certainly the most gruesome. Early in the afternoon, one of the men from the Freedman's Bureau sent to investigate the incident had gotten sick to his stomach. Subsequently, Alice had, too. Buck and two local Negroes, men Alice did not know, had built rough coffins from whatever wood they'd been able to scrounge up. After his impromptu talk with her mid afternoon, Seth Parker had forgone seeing the bodies. He trusted Alice's confirmation of Calhoon's story, and there'd been no need.

Lord, this was a forlorn place, and this had been an awful day.

Calhoon hadn't returned with the others from the grave site. Only a small gaggle of folks had attended the Solomons' funeral. Elvie told her that was because so many of the black folk had dispersed and hadn't gotten word. Mr. Bowen and Mr. Cleaver had been there along with one of their sons as had a few of Calhoon's white neighbors, who lived on the "back way," poorer whites who'd known Brim and had come in deference to Eli Calhoon. Few of the mourners, given the lateness of the service, had come back to Camellia Creek, and those who did had all been Negro. All had been quiet, reserved, and sad, and very respectful to her and Aunt Naomi, who was equally kind to everyone but Alice. A few brought food, which said something about these people, because all were limited in what they had to share. Miss Elvie knew where to return each modest plate.

"Where did Calhoon go?" Alice asked Elvie when the last old darkie started across Camellia Creek's bridge in fading daylight.

The old woman had pursed her lips and told Alice she didn't know, but believed the only thing that would have kept him away would have been something to do with Brim's death.

Alice bit her bottom lip. Still hunting his killer perhaps? She was tired and hurt. Hurt for the loss of the small family, and doubly pained by her husband's rejection of her offer of comfort, which he appeared to accept willingly from his old slave—and perhaps his lover.

Naomi walked to where they stood next to the dry sink and scraped dinner scraps into a slop jar. "He went to Port Gibson." She nodded to the bucket of rancid food leavings. "I'll take that to Emit Wilson's hogs on the way home."

"You leave it," Miss Elvie said clearly. "Eli's got hogs comin', prob'ly be tomorrow now."

Alice blinked at the old black woman. Naomi Polk, however, gave Alice a quick glance. "Things are looking up out here at Camellia Creek?"

"Yes'm," Miss Elvie said, taking the slop jar and placing it on the floor beside the stove. "Brim was s'posed to herd 'em ova today from Mr. Taylor Mills."

"Fine," Naomi said. "Leaves me one less thing to do."

"Main thing you needs to do is git. Clouds movin' in." Miss Elvie eyed Naomi. "And you don't want to be gittin' wet."

Naomi appeared to ignore her, but moved toward the cookhouse's rear door.

"Or lightnin' struck," the Negress added, her eyes on Naomi's retreating back.

Alice stuck her hand into a bucket of warm, sudsy water searching for the platter on the bottom.

"I made you a plate."

Alice turned to Naomi, who had one hand on the knob. The woman was looking at her.

"It's in the oven—still warm. In case you get hungry later. I saw you didn't eat."

The woman did seem sincere about making sure the people inhabiting Camellia Creek were cared for. Alice wasn't sure if she resented that fact or not. At the moment, she decided to simply be appreciative. "Thank you."

"You best eat it all. You're looking a bit peaked." She shifted her gaze to Miss Elvie. "Don't get too comfortable in this kitchen, Auntie."

"*I* think he might," Laura Blackledge said to Seth Parker, "but from what he told me, he's the only one that does. He said Wayne's murdering Brim had nothing to do with the cotton."

Seth Parker sat forward in the upholstered chair Laura Blackledge had offered him when he arrived. He came here, to her large, frame house on a secluded lot at the outskirts of Port Gibson because he thought that would be more discreet and keep her safe from the scrutiny of those who would not appreciate her collusion with the enemy. Seems that was a moot point.

"Do you know what it does have to do with?"

She appeared to give the question thought as she took a seat on the settee opposite him. "I only know that Wayne Hale and Brim had a falling out about work Brim was supposed to do, and Brim apparently stole Wayne's mule. But Brim returned the mule after Eli got back."

"Did you have the opportunity to broach the subject of Alan Guthrie's murder with Calhoon?"

The lovely Widow Blackledge shook her head, then looked to her lap where she twisted a handkerchief in her hands. "I forgot to ask. I was too upset over Brim."

Seth reached over and covered her writhing fingers. "He assured you that you had nothing to do with the Solomon murders, right?"

"But that doesn't change the fact Brim's dead." She looked

up, blue eyes welling tears. "Eli, Brim, and I played together when we were little. I've known Brim all my life."

The wrong person got hurt, directly or indirectly, as a result of her treachery, and now she was wracked with guilt…and grief, both real, he knew. Seth looked around the large room, pleasant enough despite the fading wallpaper and chipped chair rail. The carpet was worn, but serviceable, and even the plush chair he sat in was growing thin on the arms. Only shades covered the windows. There were no curtains or rods, only torn plaster where they should have been. The outside of the house could stand a good coat of paint, too.

He looked at her, watching him. "The furniture's second-hand," she said. "Your soldiers"—she glanced at his Negro troopers—"ransacked the place in '63 and '64."

There wasn't much he could say to that. Undoubtedly, she would not be able to make the taxes coming due, not even with a year's deferment. Albert Blackledge, her elderly spouse, had been a wealthy real estate investor and owner of a primary rail running from Meridian to Natchez and south to Baton Rouge. That rail line had been a victim of war, along with most of its cars and both its engines. An inadvertent asset of the Confederacy, according to the widow, The Meridian Southern and all future interests therein were now forfeit to the Union.

If he'd been the destitute widow, he'd have opted for a cut of that stolen cotton. Seth knew enough about the two older men involved, and her relationship with Eli Calhoon, to know they'd have likely brought her in. Instead, she'd turned the contraband over to their enemy, along with its prospective profit. Laura Blackledge had a grudge to settle, and from what little he'd learned from the locals, not to mention the inflection of the blonde beauty's voice when she said his name, that grudge was against Alice Shelton's groom, Eli Calhoon.

"Do you fear you're in danger from any of them?"

"Don't you?" she snapped.

"From what you tell me, only Calhoon suspects you're the one who talked. Do you think he'll tell Cleaver or Bowen?"

"Wayne would be the most dangerous," she told Seth, then followed him with her eyes when he rose.

"I think we can safely assume that the only talking Calhoon will be doing with Hale, if the man is still alive, will be with a gun." He started to the door. "I'd like to know if Calhoon had anything to do with Alan Guthrie's death, should"—he pivoted on his heel and met her gaze—"the opportunity arise."

She surged to her feet. "Eli Calhoon is a dangerous man."

He believed he probably could be. "How so?"

"He married that girl for her money."

Seth's heart skipped a beat.

"But I'm the one he loves and wants. He frightens me."

Seth frowned. "Has he ever given you reason to think he would hurt you…or Alice?"

Her eyes widened slightly, and inwardly he cursed himself. "You know her?"

"We've met."

"My first husband was Eli's brother. He died in battle," she said in a low tone, then pursed her lips, "under questionable circumstances. Eli was there."

"You think he had something to do with his brother's—"

"There is no doubt in my mind he killed his brother, so he could have me." She took an awkward step toward him and held her hands out in front of her. "He won't hesitate to rid himself of anyone else who stands in his way."

*E*li stopped at the entry leading from Laura's dining room to her parlor. There, pensively facing the cold hearth, sat beautiful, selfish Laura, the once-upon-a-time light of his life. This awful day had grown warm, and despite the onset of evening, there was as yet no need for a fire.

He'd followed Parker here. He had, in fact, been following Parker pretty much since he left Cummings' office, but when the major left here five minutes ago, Eli had given up the chase.

He leaned against the door frame. "A new lover?" he asked.

She grasped the settee and twisted her head with a shock akin to a cat terrified by a loud noise. He snickered, imagining a bushy tail.

"How long have you been in this house?"

"I was discreet enough to wait until they left. Given the look of shame on your pretty face, you must have filled Parker's head with all kinds of lies, and I bet they were all about me."

She rose, shrugging her shoulders as she did, the appearance of her old, confident self once more. Eli straightened with her approach. Lithe and tall, she stopped in front of him, then smiled with a coquettish cock of her head. "Only the truth, darling," she said, laying her palm on the front of his frock coat before walking her fingers up to its collar. "That you are obsessed with me, and you will go to any lengths to have me." She curled her fingers into the jacket and started to pull him to her.

Chapter Thirty-five

Wind shook the remaining leaves clinging to the deciduous trees surrounding the cookhouse. Alice had heard distant thunder minutes ago, but there'd been no flashes of light against the darkness, and the wind remained fitful. Tornado weather. Late by Ohio standards, but she was in Mississippi and the chill of morning had grown into a humid, overcast afternoon.

Her stomach growled, and she looked at the stove. Everyone was gone now, even Miss Elvie. The kitchen was relatively clean and neat. It smelled of food and wood smoke, which conjured memories of Brim Solomon's cabin and left a hint of nausea in its wake.

Another gust belted the rough walls of the building, then swept around the back corner with a subtle wail. A bad storm was moving in, and she wondered where her husband was, where he'd been all evening. He'd wanted Brim's wake at Camellia Creek, then he'd failed to even put in an appearance.

The wind grew and with it the short-lived wail. Thunder again, this time close enough to send a shudder through the heart-pine floor. If she were going to eat the meal Naomi had left her, she needed to grab it now and get to the dining room before the rain started.

She pulled off her apron and tossed it on the kitchen table, grabbed a towel, and opened the oven door. Still warm inside. A quick touch told her the plate was too hot to handle comfortably, so she folded her towel and seized the dish.

The dumplings looked dry, but they smelled good. The butter beans had dried out, too. Naomi should have left both in the cook pot, but they had wanted to get the kitchen cleaned up.

Everyone had been physically exhausted and emotionally drained. Alice turned and opened a drawer in the primitive breakfront behind her. She pulled out a fork, stirred the food into some semblance of an appetizing meal, then licked the fork clean and lifted the plate.

Outside the now familiar wail rose, then faded in the night, and Alice stilled. From the corner of her eye, movement tore across the swept floor. She squealed and stepped back, then juggling the plate she kneeled to see beneath the stove. A nasty, crapping little mouse was in her kitchen!

Overhead, wind filled the trees. No longer distracted by the mouse, but filled with prescient foreboding, she rose on her knees in front of the stove. From far away, coming closer, all the while swelling with woe, the screech of the gale advanced on her.

She'd just returned to her feet when the breezeway door exploded against the cookhouse wall and a whirlwind of frigid air swept the room, tearing at her hair and billowing her skirt. Sorrow, real enough to taste, bounced from wall to wall and back again, seeping into Alice's senses, freezing her blood and leaving her tongue thick with the taste of anguish.

The kitchen's rear door reverberated with a blow, and Alice whirled. A second blow followed the first, then another, and another and those bangs and their echoes swelled and throbbed inside her head, and Alice screamed, then raised her hands to her ears...

The china plate clattered to the floor.

Dead quiet. Alice sucked in a breath. She looked first at the back door, then dared to look behind her. The door to the breezeway remained open, but even the wind had stilled. Heart in her throat, muscles tense, she started toward the door, meaning to shut and bolt it, but as quickly as she'd started forward, she stopped. There was no need. She hugged herself, but despite her lingering chill, the room was warm. Whatever had happened was over. She looked at the plate, face down on the floor. Nausea assailed her anew. Given the day, she probably wouldn't have been able to keep supper down anyway.

Alice twisted around from where she squatted by the hearth. She couldn't build a good fire, not like her father and brothers. Sometimes she believed it really was man's work, but the chill lingered on her skin, in her blood. She'd been alone and frightened. But now Calhoon was here.

"Where have you been?" she called to where he stood hanging his coat on the peg next to the dining-room door. He looked across the expanse of the two rooms, then started her way.

"What's wrong? You look as if you've seen another ghost." He spoke casually, as if he didn't really believe his words, but paid her still closer attention when she scrambled to her feet and said indeed she had.

Sweeping his cavalry hat from his head, he stepped into the parlor and tossed the thing on the ragged settee, leaving a trail of water drops across the floor. "You did?"

He sounded skeptical. Well, of course, you fool, he would. "I didn't *see* anything actually, but I felt it."

At least he had the good grace not to laugh at her. "What happened?"

She told him without taking a breath, and he studied her before saying, "Probably a funnel cloud. I've heard the wind wail around the corners of this house all my life."

"And what was outside that back door?"

"The fright got the better of you."

She wrapped her arms around her torso. When he reached for her, she stepped back, but he caught her to him anyway.

"You're like ice," he said. "Do you feel all right?"

She pushed him away. "No, I'm not all right. I'm sick to my stomach with fear. I've been visited by a spook, and I was alone. Speaking of which, I asked you a question?"

Calhoon started around her. "We need to get your fire going."

She stepped in front of him. "Where have you been?"

He tried, gently, to set her aside.

"And with whom?" she said, holding her ground.

Not as gently, he moved her aside and knelt in front of the

hearth. "It's of no concern to you, Alice." He picked up the tin of matches she'd left there and lit one.

Her stomach quaked, which didn't help the prevailing nausea one bit. "If I bother to ask, it's of interest to me."

His gaze snapped to hers. "I will discuss my comings and going with you when it suits me. Tonight it doesn't."

"You are a horse's behind, sir."

The fire blazed. He rose and sat in his chair without glancing her way. "Any woman who can tell Dilbert to go screw his mules should be able to come up with something better than that."

"I intend to come up with much better than that, Calhoon. With every liberty you take, I intend to take one, too."

Whether he bothered to look at her then, she didn't know. She'd moved behind him on her way to the bedroom.

"I haven't taken any liberties, but even if I had, whatever you think those might be, you won't." After a moment, she heard his boots scrape the floor. "Come back in here."

"Go to the devil."

She heard a soft curse, then movement. When she heard him at the bedroom door, she looked up from where she was turning back the bed.

"Down here, husbands are not in the habit of accounting for every moment of their time to their wives."

"And how many wives have you had before me?"

His lips tightened. "Doubt men up north do either. Of course, a case could be made for the present state of the Union being the direct result of the Northern male being unable or unwilling to find their wives something useful to take up their time. Poor bastards probably hate to go home."

"That's right. The whole horrid war was to drive our men out of the house."

"They were nagged out of the house. I'm sure they've found robbing and raping the South much more amiable then being henpecked to death by puritanical, self-righteous shrews. Now those witches will have to find something else to complain about."

"For your information, the majority of Northern women are

not radical abolitionists, and they stay as busy with the home as Southern ones."

"Those that still have homes."

Her breath caught, and she almost choked. "That's right," she hollered, "but losses of family and menfolk worked both ways."

She saw the contrition in his eyes, but she screwed up her mouth and pointed a finger at him before he could snap back or apologize or say whatever it was he meant to say. "But I've got a replacement for the men I drove off to war. I've got myself a Southern male, who is apparently under some misconception he's going to run around doing whatever he pleases with whomever he pleases."

He cocked his head to one side.

She swallowed, small relief for a stomach burning with bile. "You insisted on marrying me, Calhoon. You should have con-sidered, given your in-depth knowledge of Northern women, that you were acquiring yourself a 'nagging' wife. And if you feel you have no obligation to tell me how you spend your day, then rest assured whenever you ask how I spent mine I will retain the right to respond accordingly."

"I think sitting through the litany of a woman's day would be extremely tedious," he said quietly.

"Today I prepared three young bodies for the grave. I went to their funeral and I buried your friend and his family. I hosted his wake—you weren't here. I cleaned up after the meal and put up with your hateful relation who pointed out to me"—she bit her bottom lip to keep her voice steady—"the comfort you and Laura Blackledge were providing each other over this grievous loss."

She saw his eyes flash, and she whipped around, making her way to the other side of the bed. She yanked down the quilt.

He came on in the room. "Believe me when I say I find no comfort in Laura as regards Brim's death."

"Another half-truth, Calhoon," she said, coming around the foot of the bed. She pushed him out of the way. "You sought no comfort from me, rejected it when offered"—he squinted at her and started to speak—"but offered her, at least, a little."

"She blames herself for Brim's death."

"Is she to blame?"

"No."

"Why would she think she is, and how does it involve you?"

He sighed, resolved it seemed, and her heart sank. "I'm not going to go into details with you, Alice. Suffice it to say I didn't have sex with her."

She turned back to the bed. "It doesn't matter. Today, tomorrow. The point is you found comfort with her you refused from me. It's only a matter of time, assuming your relationship ever ended to begin with. What would your now having a wife have to do with anything? Everyone knows what philanderers Southern men are."

"Those *everyones* are doubtless the same ones who so justly depicted the atrocities of Southern slavery."

She wiped her sweating palms on her skirt. "Philandering husbands, like slavery, is another male privilege down here. I cannot understand why Southern women put up with this."

"Because they're smart."

"Because they are meek and obedient and stupid."

"And what do Northern wives do with philandering husbands, Alice? Or do you expect me to believe such creatures do not exist up there. So who up north are meek, obedient, and stupid?"

"We shoot them." She said that because when she was ten, Henrietta Olson shot Abner Olson for sneaking about with some woman in Duncan Falls, several miles from her father's farm.

"I doubt that, else there wouldn't have been enough Yankees in the field to face us, much less defeat us, and you had us outnumbered ten to one."

"A bit overstated, don't you think? And we're talking about stupid women tolerating the faithlessness of their cheating husbands. Leave the war out of it."

"Let me tell you about stupid. Stupid is one small female provoking a fight with a man who is in no mood tonight to tolerate her yammering, much less her unjustified insults."

Alice studied him. He was angry, she could see it in his eyes, in the set of his jaw. But he wasn't threatening. More like he was trying to warn her off. Perhaps she was pushing him too hard, but she had a right, she was sure she had a right. He'd been gone all afternoon and into the evening, and he'd all but admitted seeing and talking to Laura…and he'd rejected her offer of comfort." She jutted her chin. "I think if a husband can be unfaithful, so can a wife."

"Well, I think a man wants to raise his own offspring."

Alice could hear her heart beating in her head. "He's sleeping around with every woman he can get his hands on. Obviously he doesn't care who is raising his."

"He's not sleeping around with every woman he can get his hands on, and depending on his feelings toward the mother, he does care who is raising his children."

"You're talking about legitimate offspring."

"Not necessarily, but in most cases, yes. But rest assured, he is most particular about whose children bear his name—and he wants them to be his own."

"He hasn't," she hissed, "the right."

"Oh, yes, he does, and any woman attempting to go tit for tat with a cheating husband in the bedroom is an extremely reckless one."

Alice clenched her fists. "How so?"

"Because he will probably kill her."

A warning. A veiled warning. "And he'll—"

"Be applauded by the legal system for doing so."

She stepped away from him. "By your prejudiced, morally degenerate, disgusting, *defeated* system."

He followed her only with his eyes. "Do you really think," he said softly, "the law here or anywhere regards female adultery differently than I do?"

She flexed her stiff fingers and allowed the thought of Calhoon and Laura Blackledge comforting each other in the wake of Brim Solomon's death to fill her senses, and her own hand freely offered, but rejected. "Seth Parker would."

Alice stumbled back with Calhoon's surge forward. Grabbing hold of her arm, he tossed her onto the bed, then stretched his body over hers, crushing her into the feather mattress. "Do you think it would be as good with him, Alice?" His warm breath caressed her ear, then his tongue invaded the orifice. She whimpered and pushed hard against his chest, straining with all her might to force him to let her go. He took her by the shoulders and pulled her up, shaking her as he did so. "Do you?" He thrust her back onto the mattress and brought his face close to her, a bitter smile on his lips. "But would there be anger, sweetheart? That perverse anger that sets your soul on fire?"

"It's not there!"

He stilled, as shocked it seemed as she at the vehemence in her voice.

"And it's not here either, Calhoon. There's only hurt. Mine and yours, and if you make me want you now, I will never, ever forgive you. Now let me up."

Abruptly he rolled away, and she scrambled off the bed. Straightening her clothing, she turned and looked at him, stretched across the bed watching her.

"And I'll let you know," she said, her voice finally breaking, "when I'm angry again."

Chapter Thirty-six

"You're sure you didn't eat anything?" Eli handed her a cool, wet cloth.

Alice shook her head. "Not all day." She covered her face with a hand. "I can't get the scent of…."

Burned human flesh out of her head, she'd been going to say.

"I dropped the plate on the floor when the ghost came."

The damn ghost again. She'd thrown up two minutes after she'd left their bedroom, leaving him there to ponder her cryptic words. One thing for sure, 'never ever' being forgiven was something he didn't want to rush into lightly.

He thought at first the vomiting was the result of her earlier fear and their subsequent confrontation, but minutes after her initial regurgitation, the diarrhea had started. Now, two hours later, he had her sitting on the chamber pot and holding a bucket, but she was getting too weak to sit there much longer. Vomiting had ceased to produce solid matter some time ago, but the dry heaves and stomach spasms were unrelenting. Eli, though he suspected only a stomach ailment, was worried. He'd seen people die of such. Cholera was another possibility, but there was no fever.

"Give her some broth." Aunt Naomi thrust a tin cup under his nose. Hot chicken soup. To him it smelled good, but looking at the greasy film floating on its surface, he knew Alice couldn't keep it down. "She needs something on her stomach," the woman said, "if for no other reason than to give her something more to throw up."

He wasn't sure if he agreed with the reasoning, but he took the cup and leaned toward Alice. Pale, her eyes sinking in her head, she stared at him, then the brew. "I can't."

286

With his free hand, he took the bucket from her and set it nearby. "Try."

She did, but the liquid had no sooner passed her lips when she pushed him away and reached for the bucket, heaving what little broth she'd taken along with green bile.

To his back, Aunt Naomi fussed about the waste of good food, then reached down for the cup. "Give it to me."

He did. "Would you get Auntie Elvie?"

Naomi snorted. "It's pouring outside. You go for her."

From where he kneeled on the floor, he twisted to look at the woman. Aunt Naomi was normally quick to do his bidding. "I can't leave her like this."

"I'll stay with her."

Again he wiped Alice's mouth. "If you go," she said, laying her head on his shoulder, "take her with you. She left hours ago. Why is she back here?"

Because she'd live here if he let her. "She said she planted flowers on the graves, then stopped up the road to see Celia Jenkins. She got caught in the storm and turned back."

"And where is the Jenkins' place?"

"Closer to here than Port Gibson going the back way."

"Take her to Miss Elvie's."

He rubbed Alice's back. She was so needy now…and sick as the proverbial dog. "Elvie and Aunt Nimi don't like each other."

"But you're bringing Miss Elvie here." She pulled back and gave him a drunk look. "So that will work well."

He opened his mouth to speak, but at that moment, Aunt Naomi stomped back in, pulling the hood of her cape over her head. "I'll go. I'm taking the wagon, then I'm going on home."

"The weather's too bad for you to go home."

"But not too bad for you to send me to Elvira's house. No, don't mind me, Eli. I'll send the witch to you, since you trust her with your little bride. But I have no intention of staying here and risking my own good health where I'm not appreciated."

And he'd been so bold as to ridicule Alice about nagging Northern women. He gazed at his wife's bowed head. Hopefully she hadn't noted the parallel. And at least he wasn't married to a Naomi Polk.

"Thank you," he said.

The woman snorted. Seconds later he heard the sound of pattering rain heighten, then fall as the back door opened, then slammed shut.

Chapter Thirty-seven

Aunt Betty stroked her cheek. "Are you certain you're all right? You look like death."

Alice smiled and blew out a breath. "Thank you." She wondered if her husband thought so, too. "I'm sure I'm on the mend. Calhoon thinks it was only a stomach sickness, but this kitchen has a mouse. I found droppings on the counter this morning."

Her aunt's head was shaking before she finished. "Was there a fever?"

"No."

"Then what you had was not a mouse-borne ailment."

"My point is, the kitchen may not be healthy."

"I understand your point. Now understand mine regarding a *rat*-borne ailment."

"I beg your pardon?"

Aunt Betty dropped her hand into her lap. "Alice, darling, are you sure they're not trying to poison you?"

For the first time today, Alice's stomach quivered.

"Seth Parker came to us," her aunt continued quickly. "He was my initial reason for visiting this morning."

Alice raised a hand to indicate silence, then stood. She and Aunt Betty were at the kitchen table, and for once Alice was glad the kitchen was separate from the main house; that made it harder for Calhoon to lurk unseen and listen in on their conversation.

She stepped to a window and peeked between the boards covering the shattered glass. He was still there, well away from the house, near where the barn had stood, talking to a man who had come to see him right after breakfast.

Alice relaxed and retook her seat. "What did he say?"

"He wanted to know how your marriage came about. He seemed to think you had wed, well..."

"Under duress. Calhoon told him that."

Her aunt knitted her brow. "Needless to say, I did not tell him the true circumstances—your Uncle Peter was sitting right there, so I let him answer."

Alice raised the cup of blackberry tea Miss Elvie had made for her.

"Peter said he could not begin to understand what had driven you to do such a thing, but attributed your action to that of a foolish young woman infatuated by a handsome and persuasive man."

He was persuasive, all right. "And what was Major Parker's response to that?"

"I could tell by the look on his face, he didn't believe that to be the case. He then pointed out that it was his understanding that you were worth a significant amount of money"—her aunt gave her an apologetic look—"and that Mr. Calhoon is reputed to be a ruthless man who, it was told to him, murdered his own brother so he could have his brother's wife."

The quiver swelled into nausea. The last time she'd vomited was yesterday morning.

"Are you aware of this other woman?"

"Laura Blackledge."

"Is he seeing her, do you know?"

"I don't know, Aunt Betty."

"I'm sorry, darling, but there's so much money involved and he's obviously desperate, and now this woman."

"How did Seth find out about my inheritance?"

"Jonathan, I think," Aunt Betty answered, "and I say that only because the next question out of Major Parker's mouth was in regards to your betrothal to Jonathan."

"My what? He'd only discussed such a thing with me the night before I—"

"I know," her aunt said, "but apparently Jonathan told someone that you and he were to be wed by the end of that week. Parker wouldn't divulge who."

"That was Jon's plan. What did Uncle Pete say?"

"He told Parker that Jonathan had been led to believe you had feelings for him."

Alice opened her mouth to protest, but Betty held up a hand. "Don't worry, I jumped in at that point and told Peter that if Jon had any such thoughts it was because Peter placed them in his head, because you certainly had never encouraged Jonathan. Peter didn't say anything more and the notion that Eli Calhoon had compromised you was never broached, though Seth Parker appears to be an astute man."

Alice closed her eyes.

"Three days you've been ill. A mere ailment of the stomach shouldn't last that long. For certain, you were given tainted—"

The back door to the cookhouse closed, and Alice followed the quick turn of her aunt's head. Together they watched Elvira Hinny start their way, and Alice, her stomach queasy again, wondered how long the woman had been listening. Aunt Betty raised her chin and turned to Alice. "I think you should consider a cat for this kitchen."

A discreet change of subject, but from the set of Miss Elvie's mouth she'd been standing in that doorway long enough to hear Aunt Betty's implication loud and clear.

You know I don't want to get another—"

"If I poisoned 'er," Miss Elvie said, "she'd be buried now. She ain't had a sick stomach since yeste'day mawnin' an' ate a good brekfes' right past sunup today." The black woman drew up abruptly beside Alice and nodded at her, all the while keeping her glare fixed on Aunt Betty. "Still in 'er belly best I know."

The initial shock on Aunt Betty's face twisted into anger.

"Yes it is," Alice said quickly, patting her aunt's hand. "I'm sure it was only an ailment."

Betty Franklin rose, but kept her eyes fixed on Miss Elvie's defiant face. "Or some disease from this filthy kitchen."

Though Alice herself had pointed her aunt that direction, she felt the sting of those words. She'd been working hard on this kitchen up until she got sick.

Miss Elvie cackled. "Ain't wo'ked in dis kitchen as a rule fo' years. Any sickness 'ere now yo' Yankee soldiers lef when dey to'e it up." She turned and pointed. "One moved his bowels right ova in dat co'ner der."

Good heavens, Alice hoped that wasn't true, and given the twinkle in Miss Elvie's eye, she suspected it wasn't. She stood and strategically placed herself between the two older women. "I'm getting better, Aunt Betty, thanks to Miss Hinny."

"Miss Hinny," her aunt said tightly, looking from Alice to the black woman, "works for Mr. Calhoon. I can only assume you are as safe from her as he wants you to be."

"An' him wants 'er well," Elvira said. "An' she be well."

"Ask and you shall be given," Aunt Betty said, hiking her skirts and stepping around the both of them. "I know where your loyalty lies, old woman."

Her aunt stopped at the back door and turned to find Alice, then nodded at Elvie. "That one is a witch who does what he commands." She narrowed her eyes on Elvie. "Now I'm going to go find the devil incarnate and let him know that under no circumstances is my niece to become ill and me not be informed immediately. I don't know what you people are up to out here, but Alice will not fall victim to it."

With that, she yanked the door open and disappeared, leaving it standing wide. After a moment, Miss Elvie ambled over and pushed it shut, and Alice again peeked out the boarded window and watched her aunt make her way to Calhoon. Lord, she hoped the woman was at least discreet in making her demands.

"You thinkin'"—Alice jumped. Aunt Elvie had moved up behind her without a sound—"dat Eli be tryin' to kill you?"

With a steadying breath, Alice turned around, found a chair and sat down hard. The night she'd gotten sick, Calhoon hadn't fed her anything to eat, and all his subsequent actions indicated he wanted her to get better. But now she'd heard this story of the death of Andrew Calhoon for the second time.

"Miss Elvie?"

The Negress didn't respond, and Alice looked up to find the old woman studying her.

"Who were some of the men the Calhoons served with in the Army? Someone who was with them at Shiloh?"

Chapter Thirty-eight

"He tell ya how long before they could start?" Dilbert asked.

"Soon as he can find some lumber," Eli answered. "It's in great demand."

"Yeah, reckon so. Probably being shipped from up north at record high prices."

Eli stopped at the edge of a now docile Camellia Creek, but for such a little thing, it could, and often did, become a raging torrent. Reminded him of Alice.

Her Aunt Betty had a thorn up her tail, too. She'd been put out at not having been told Alice was sick, and with her admonition, she'd subtly implied such was not to happen again. She considered him a threat to her niece, but he really didn't give a damn. She'd sold Alice—and he smiled to himself—downriver, in a manner of speaking, to protect her own daughter. Now she was trying to make up for it. It was too late. Alice was his, her fate in his hands, and Betty Franklin and her daughter had made it all too easy for him.

"Between the river's eating away at its channel and Camellia Creek's flooding moving farther and farther north, I'm afraid the Mississippi is going to find its way back into Lake Elizabeth."

Dilbert stopped beside him and looked. "Worried Holland, too. But Eli, that could be fifty years from now, or a hundred."

"Or this spring…or even the next good rain if things keep up like they have been lately. I'm afraid it could take the house with it."

"You need to talk to a geologist."

"Granddaddy did years back."

"I know, but things might have changed."

Eli shook his head. They'd changed all right, for the worse. The geologist had been the one to come up with the scenario he'd just described.

"What I need to do is steer Camellia's flood water more southerly. See this hollow?" He pointed northwest, then turned and faced southeast. "It merges right into the northern end of Lake Elizabeth."

"I know. It's the old river bed."

"A thousand years ago, maybe." Or two, or ten. "But Camellia Creek has found it, and with each heavy rain it's flooding up it more and more. I'm afraid the Mississippi is gonna take notice."

Dilbert frowned. "Surely that won't happen until the flood waters actually meet the river."

"Came within a mile of that happenin' with that big rain last month."

"Mile still seems a long ways to me. Whatcha thinkin'?"

"A deeper channel to keep all the water goin' into Bayou Pierre."

"That's a half mile of dredging…through woods."

"Can't be helped."

"Can't be done."

Hell, yeah, it could.

"And there ain't nothin' to say the ole Mississippi won't ignore the old channel, take the creek bed instead, and cut southwest to form up with itself by way of the bayou."

That would be the ideal. His front porch would then be sitting on a low bluff looking down on the river less than an eighth of a mile away. An already lovely sight made more so. Still, he feared, that same front porch might as easily be swept away if he didn't do something about that feisty little creek.

Which again dredged up thoughts of his wife. She was up with him at dawn this morning, first time in three days. That sweet body might be leaner, but he could still hope he might come up with something to "anger" her. He hoped she missed him, too.

Dilbert, who'd jumped the creek, nodded to the north. "I saw Franklin earlier over thataways."

Getting ready to clean up the fields for his spring crop, Eli reckoned. "Was his nephew with him?"

"He was. Thought I might mosey on over and find 'em." Dilbert grinned at him. "See if they're havin' any luck findin' field hands."

Eli figured not and started home.

Almost an hour later, he stepped out on the back porch and called Alice's name a second time. No answer. She'd gone somewhere. Her things were still here, though, first thing he'd checked. Aunt Elvie had left, too. Black-eyed peas and a few slices of last night's ham were on the kitchen table, covered with a cloth. They'd been eating good lately.

Eli folded up a piece of meat and stuck it in his mouth. He'd have to talk to his bride about her disappearing and not letting him know where to. Given their recent discussions on his accounting to her, *that* would raise her ire.

Chapter Thirty-nine

"You don't want her out there," Laura said.

Naomi Polk set the piece of pound cake in front of her. "I don't want you out there either."

Laura picked up her fork. "I know that, but I really don't care. You know I have more right out there than she does."

Laura didn't like the look Naomi gave her—it hinted at irritation, or plain disbelief. "Well, I do."

"No, you don't. You forfeited any right you had when you wed after Andy's death."

Naomi Polk pulled out her mismatched side chair and sat, much too close. Laura sipped her coffee. The dining room of Aunt Naomi's little house had always been dark. Like the rest of Port Gibson, it had been ransacked by Union troops on more than one occasion. Personal treasures were gone, mirrors and windows broken, chairs smashed. The place was not only dark, now it was desolate. Naomi was a stern, morose…generally unhappy person, but she'd been faithful to the Calhoons even after it became evident Holland Calhoon would never marry her. She'd contented herself with dominating the household, until at last Holland deferred to Hannah, by then a young lady, and moved his interfering sister-in-law from the premises of Camellia Creek into a house he paid for on the north end of Farmers Street in Port Gibson.

Laura tilted her head and studied the woman. Naomi noticed and stared back. Laura grinned and wondered, not for the first time, if Daddy Holland had ever slept with his sister-in-law.

She doubted it. Holland Calhoon's taste had run to the beautiful and decidedly feminine. He'd always been fond of Laura, he and her daddy being old, old friends. Long a playmate and adolescent sweetheart of Eli, the young woman she became caught the roving eye of Andrew, and she'd reciprocated by giving the older Calhoon boy a second look. When she'd wed Andrew Calhoon and moved to Camellia Creek as Holland's daughter by marriage, family life had not altered one bit; Hannah had remained Camellia Creek's mistress. But when Hannah married and left, Naomi again increased her presence on the farm, and Laura hadn't liked it.

"And with me gone and Holland gone and Eli home, all alone, you were set to take over as official mistress of Camellia Creek once more, weren't you, Aunt Naomi? Then Albert died and freed me to marry Eli."

"But Eli didn't want you," the old heifer said.

"He married that woman for the money."

Naomi laughed…a hateful snort, actually. "And you think he'd want you now that you've betrayed him to the authorities?"

Laura speared the cake—it was really quite good—and tore off another bite. "He doesn't need that cotton money now—"

"That's not the point." Naomi cut a bite off her own piece and put it in her mouth.

"And the point is?"

"You betrayed him. You betrayed his friends, and worst of all, you betrayed them to the Federals."

"Nothing will come of—"

"You didn't know that when you told," the woman said, her voice suddenly loud. "You didn't care. Even if Eli didn't want that Northerner, he doesn't want you." Naomi smiled, and Laura's stomach tensed. "But you fear he does want her, don't you? And that's killing you."

Laura slammed the fork down on the table. "I'll never forgive him for humiliating me."

"Like you humiliated him."

"I never did."

Naomi reached for her plate with a jerky movement. "Yes, you did. You betrayed him with Andrew, you betrayed him with

Blackledge, then you turned him into the authorities." Naomi rose, thrusting the chair away, and Laura looked up to meet the woman's glare.

"The Federals are looking for whoever killed that Treasury agent." Laura forced herself calm. "They haven't decided for sure whether Eli is involved."

Ah, what satisfaction she found with the tightening of Naomi Polk's lips.

"Is that what your new friend Franklin came over and talked to you about?"

Laura clenched her hand into a ball. She could hit this woman right now, just swing out and slap her stupid. "You're always skulking about, aren't you? Sticking your nose in matters that are none of your business.

Naomi lifted an eyebrow. "None of my business?"

"That's what I said."

Naomi laughed, a rare occurrence. "I only waste my time with the likes of you because you threaten 'my business' making time for the likes of that Franklin fella. What did he want?"

Now Laura sensed Naomi as an ally—what Laura had wanted when she'd come to Naomi's dreary house a half hour ago. "He wants that Yankee trollop Eli married, and I'm going to help him get her."

"He wants the money, and he can't get that now unless Eli's dead. Is that what you want?"

"Only certain times of the day, but that doesn't mean I can't pretend to work with Jon Franklin. He could prove useful." She simpered. "He likes to talk, and he brags about what he knows. I learned through him the Federals suspect Eli killed Wayne Hale. What do you suppose will happen when his body's found?"

"Maybe his body won't be found."

Laura smiled. "I did talk to May this morning."

"And?"

"Do you think Eli killed him, Aunt Naomi?"

The woman watched as Laura rose and faced her.

"Doesn't take much to set these Federals off," Laura said.

"'Specially when it comes to a Southerner who refuses to take the oath and one of their own being murdered."

"You'd really want to see Eli hanged?"

"Than be happy with that Northern bitch in his father's house, yes."

Naomi faltered. Oh, thank the Lord, she was having second thoughts now. Laura stepped forward, grabbed the woman by the shoulders, and shook her. "You don't want her there either. In *your* house. Help me get rid of her," Laura pleaded when Naomi looked her in the eye. "We can drive her off."

"Eli still wouldn't have you."

The hell he wouldn't. And they'd live rich as Midas, too. "The important thing is a Yankee won't be living at Camellia Creek."

"You must think me a fool, Laura, wooing me with something I know you want."

"I want Eli. If I can't have him, no one else will have him. But if you're so sure Eli won't have me, I see no problem with you helping me."

Naomi made a sibilant sound. "Mightn't hurt to join forces. I've already placed doubt in his young wife's head, by routinely invoking, of all things"—Naomi twisted out of Laura's grip—"Eli's relationship with you."

Laura stepped back. An alliance with Naomi Polk would be a mixed blessing, but it would strengthen the likelihood of an outcome Laura feared was still too tentative. There'd be another time to deal with Naomi. "Good," she told the older woman and turned away. "You take care of the Yankee miss, and I'll take care of Eli."

"How?"

"I think between me and the Federal threat, I can persuade him where his best interests lie." She lifted her coat from where she'd draped it over a parlor chair and looked back at the harridan. "In fact," she said, starting toward the front door, "I think I'll ride out to Camellia Creek right now."

Naomi moved, as if to follow. "You'll not force him into anything. Give us time to work on things together."

But Eli had hurt Laura's pride, not to mention she was running out of time. She needed help; she needed money; and she needed to know he was still obsessed with her. Her naked skin against Eli's hard body would do that. All their lives, she'd been the only one he'd ever wanted. He was hers, not some Northern woman's who didn't belong here.

She, Laura Calhoon Blackledge, was in control, and no matter how much Eli Calhoon denied it, she always would be. This was not the time for games and petty vengeance. He would accept her demands, or she would destroy him.

"We thought heaven an' earf of Andrew Calhoon. Sorrowful day he died." Caw Pruitt nodded to the Negro boy of probably fifteen or sixteen rounding the corner of the substantial cabin. "Jeb, he wandered off when he were three. We looked and called fo' dat boy fo' hours, didn't we, Willie?"

A frail Negress, not a day past forty if Alice were to guess, nodded with a small smile and kept rocking in her rocker.

"Fine'ly, I sent word to Holland Calhoon. We thought da boy was in da woods twixt his place an' ours. Low and swampy in places. Thick, too, and it be late Octoba. Was gonna get cold dat night."

"We be so 'fraid our baby dun drown," Willie Pruitt said, and the boy sat down on the porch step and listened. His daddy glanced his way.

"Fool chil'. Don't see to dis day how he lived to be as ole as he is."

The boy grinned at Alice, and she smiled back.

"Anyways, all three of da' menfolk come wif some of dem's darkies. Eli musta been thirteen or fawteen, Andy a little older dan Jebediah be now. We all fanned out searchin' dem woods, an' hollerin'. Mama"—he looked at Willie Pruitt again—"she were home cryin' and nursin' our new baby—"

"Fo' sho' I thought dey'd neva find 'im," Mrs. Pruitt said.

"Dark come upon us. When I got back heah, most of da rest had come out da woods, too, but Andy weren't wif da ones back.

We hollered fo' 'im, but he didn't answer. Mr. Holland, he be worried 'bout his own boy den. Went out paired up till moon set, den Holland Calhoon sent most of him's darkies home to wait daybreak. Eli went back out wif 'is daddy lookin' fo' 'is brudder."

Caw Pruitt looked Alice in the eye. "Gets dark in dat swamp, Miss Alice. Mighty dark. We know'd somethin' bad coulda happen to eitha of 'em. I went back in da woods to da no'th and looked. Didn't find nothin' but coons. 'Bout two in da mawnin', I come on home, heartsick. Mr. Holland come back down da road. He'd searched too, den he'd took Eli home.

"We hollered some 'mo, den gib up an' waited till fust light. Den full of coffee and whiskey Mr. Holland brought back wif 'im, we was ready to head out ag'in. Dats when Andy come walkin' outa da woods." Caw pointed across the narrow dirt road. "Right der'. He was holdin' Jebediah, sleepin'—"

"Lawd, I thought 'im dead." The woman laughed and wiped an eye.

Caw was shaking his head, a smile forming on his lips. "Naw, he were sleepin'. Andy say he be just nigh of the Mississippi itself when he heard Jeb cryin', an' when he hurried to git to 'im, he slipped in da swamp an' doused him's lantern. Couldn't see nuthin'. He followed Jeb's whimperin' an' got to him. Sayd he hollered, but none of us must've heard 'cause nobody hollered back. He tol' him's daddy he didn't want to attract anythin' to him he couldn't see—like I tol' ya, Miss, gits real dark and scary in dem swamp woods at night. Ain't no doubt Andy was a bit scared 'imsef. Climbed a tree he sayd, wrapped da baby in 'im's jacket and dey fell asleep. Woke as da world lighted, an dey come on home.

"No, Miss Alice, I cared deeply fo' Andrew Calhoon 'cause 'a what he done fo' me an mine. Cared fo' all da Calhoons, but I'da shot Eli mysef had he done anythin' to him's brudder."

The man's gaze met hers. "Eli loved Andy," he said softly. "He was behind 'im, him's arms wrapped unda'neath Andy's, doin' eva'thin' he could to pull 'im from beneath 'is hawse in da middle of a fiel'. Yankees was hid in da trees. I was beside da Calhoon boys, givin' 'em cover fire. Unit was leavin' da fiel'. Yankee bullet hit Andrew in da chest as he struggled up. Died in Eli's arms. Tom Nash had to come back and he'p me an' Eli drag Andy out, 'cause me an' Eli weren't gonna leave 'im. Colonel Butterfield wanted us to bury him up in Corinth wif otha' of our dead, but Eli wouldn't have it. He brung 'im on home to Camellia Creek."

He turned away, at the same time pushing on his rocker with one leg. Caw Pruitt looked tired, old and gray beyond his years. He was tall and thin, but Alice wasn't sure he'd always been that way. He'd lost an arm later in the war. Alice knew that because Miss Elvie had told her. The one thing she hadn't told her, perhaps because Miss Elvie had thought nothing of it, but it had shocked Alice silly when she'd met him, Caw Pruitt was a Negro. Born free into a freeman's household, he'd told her when her confusion gave her away. He must have realized then she wasn't from anywhere around here.

He'd lived side by side with the Calhoons all his life, he said, and he'd taken up arms against an invading enemy to protect his family and his property. He'd joined the same unit as the Calhoon boys to serve with Andrew. He had a rifle. He was an excellent tracker and a good shot. The Calhoons provided his horse—all he ever needed before then were mules.

"Was it Miss Laura or Ole Miss put da idee in yo' head Eli kilt 'is brudder?"

"Miss Laura," Willie Pruitt said before Alice could answer.

Caw turned to look at his wife, and she nodded. "Miss Naomi wouldn't accuse Eli of killin' Andrew, you know dat, Caw."

"I reckon not," he said slowly. He turned back to Alice, but he didn't appear to expect confirmation. "Miss Laura, she had her hooks in dem boys good. Figured Eli would marry 'er now dat 'er secon' husban' done passed on."

Now he did look as if he expected confirmation. Alice sucked in a deep breath, then blew it out. "Well, he married me."

"I wonder if she…?" He stopped cold.

If she refused him? Is that what the man had been about to ask, if Laura had refused Calhoon?

Caw furrowed his brow. "Reckon not," he said softly to himself. "Else she wouldn't'av lied to you."

"Lawd, man," Willie Pruitt said. "What you thinkin'? Look at dis girl heah. Easy to see why he wed 'er and not dat false woman done went off and married dat ugly ole man after she promised 'ersef to Eli when Andrew died. An' him at war. Shameful thing she done. For sho' dat boy washed his hands of Miss Laura long time ago. You thought so yo'sef."

Willie Pruitt leaned well forward so she could see Alice on the other side of her husband. "Dis girl be fresh and purty."

Alice felt her cheeks warm and gave thanks that Mrs. Pruitt didn't know the real reason Eli had married her.

The man's face lit with a gentle smile. "No, don't you worry none, Miz Calhoon. Ohio bullet fell Andrew..."

Alice felt the heightened color drain from her cheeks.

"...not 'is brudder's."

She bit her bottom lip and swallowed, trying to wet her dry mouth. "You were facing an Ohio unit?"

He nodded. "Accordin' to da pape'man."

"Do you know which unit?" Her fingers hurt, she held so hard to the chair arm.

Caw Pruitt was watching her, a question in his eyes.

"Nope, but I 'magine dat Mr. Cummin's at da paper do. He's talkin' to folks, tryin' to gather up stories on all da Claiborne County boys we lost. He come to me jus' a few weeks ago. Eli wouldn't talk to 'im 'bout Andy."

Did Calhoon know? She turned to the dirt yard and the road that disappeared beneath the pine, back down from where she'd come. She wanted to disappear now.

"Where you from, Miss?"

Alice rose, not looking at him. "I came here with my aunt and uncle from Chicago."

"Da Franklins?"

He knew them, or of them. It would be Uncle Pete he'd heard about. One of the damn Yankees that had moved into their midst.

"Yes," she said, clasping her gloved hands together and turning to face him. She could see Willie well from where she stood. The woman watched her.

"Eli married hissef a Yankee." It was a statement, softly spoken as if the man couldn't quite believe it.

She laughed shortly, then covered her mouth. She needed to leave this place. "I'm afraid so. Are you doing all right here, Mr. Pruitt?" Her gaze darted to the woman. "Has Eli been out to check on you?"

The man nodded calmly. He didn't seem put out. "'Bout two weeks ago be last I seen 'im. It's near dinna'time, Miss Alice. Won't you eat wif us?"

Her eyes filled with tears. "I-I can't, Mr. Pruitt, but I thank you kindly."

The three of them were watching her now, and she was certain she noted some confusion in, at least, the eyes of the man. "I tell you true," he said, "you be welcome at our table."

She blinked back the tears. "I haven't been totally truthful with you." She could not break bread at this man's table knowing how he'd felt about Andrew Calhoon. Not now. Caw Pruitt frowned at her.

"You ain't wed to Eli?"

"Oh, I'm married to Eli Calhoon, all right. And my aunt and uncle did bring me here from Chicago, but I'm not from Illinois, Mr. Pruitt. I'm from Ohio. My father and brothers were at Shiloh."

The images of the three watching her blurred before her eyes. Shaking her head she whirled and started down the stairs. "I have to find Mr. Cummings. I'm so sorry to have intruded on you like this."

Chapter Forty

"She wouldn't come here. Papa has made it clear she's not welcome," Cassie Franklin said and looked back up the road from where Eli had come. "He wouldn't like finding you here either."

She stood in the threshold of the front door, pulled near shut behind her. Eli watched her pull her shawl around her, fidgeting, then she widened her eyes.

"I know what you must think of me. It's my fault all this happened," she snapped. "And it is. I admit that."

"Miss Franklin, your indiscretion brought me Alice—"

"Alice's money you mean."

Eli flexed his jaw. He was about fed up with females at the moment. First he couldn't find Alice, and he'd be the first to admit—to someone he liked—that he was beginning to worry. Then he'd run into Laura on his way here. She'd been on her way to Camellia Creek armed with veiled threats, none of which concerned him much until she told him she'd had a long talk with May Hale this morning. That angered him, but he hadn't let on. He'd reiterated to Laura to keep off Camellia Creek. Then he'd continued east, leaving her sitting in her carriage in the middle of the Port Gibson-Rodney Road.

Now he had Cassie Franklin, the silly, vivacious twit with licentious hungers, as well as questionable judgment, telling him the reason he'd married Alice. Well, he knew the reason he'd wed Alice and didn't need the one person who could have stopped the nuptials, but for her own selfish reasons, casting stones at him.

"And again, I thank you for the sacrifice that made all that possible, Miss Franklin."

She bristled, then asked, "How did you know?"

"How did I know what?"

"The baby was Negro."

"Because the soldier who had carnal knowledge of you bragged."

"He was going on—"

"He talked immediately. To his fellow colored soldiers, to the hands on the boat, to everyone of his class who'd listen. Word was out about you before you ever stepped ashore in Vicksburg." He nodded at her. "Something you should keep in mind. Men boast when they enjoy sex with a woman they care little or nothing about—especially if she gives it away."

"You think he bragged because I was white, and he was Negro."

"I think he'd have bragged anyway, but given the bigoted world he lives in, sleeping with you may have been particularly sweet. Further more, he wasn't too smart. His big mouth could have gotten him castrated or killed."

Her chin puckered. "White men can sleep with a Negress."

"Miss Franklin," he said softly. "White men don't give birth to black babies. That's the key thing."

"And they don't claim them when they make them," she said sharply.

"Like your Negro wouldn't have claimed his." He made a sibilant sound. "It's not easy being a woman, I guess. Best to take care who you let between your legs."

She gave him a wide-eyed stare, then surprised him—though given what he knew of her, he didn't know why it should—with a laugh.

He wrinkled his brow. "Where's your Yankee captain?"

"He's transferred to the Arizona Territory. He's going to send for me."

Maybe, if the man hadn't learned of his fiancée's indiscretions. Eli glanced up the road. He didn't want a confrontation with Peter Franklin either. Best he hurry up. Resolved, he looked Cassie in the eye and asked, "Do you know where Alice is?"

Cassie frowned. "You've no idea where she's gone, do you?"

He swallowed. No, he didn't, and that made him mad as hell. Cassie's realizing it, made him madder. "I was out checking the creek. She left me a note"—that was a lie—"and said she was going into town. It's getting late. Lots of marauders about. I couldn't find her in Port Gibson and thought she might have stopped by here."

She didn't believe him; he could see that in her eyes.

"Your mother was at the house this morning. Could Alice be next door with her now?"

"She wasn't with Mama when she got home, so I think not."

"Copperhead?"

"No," Eli said, "she's Peter Franklin's niece."

"I know she's Franklin's niece, Calhoon," Cole Yeager said, "but that don't mean nothin'. Sure wouldn't be the only family torn apart by this mess." The older man looked over his shoulder as his young clerk descended the stairs to Eli's left.

"He ain't back yet, Mr. Calhoon."

"Knew he wouldn't be," Cole said with a shake of his head. "Too early yet. Him and his captain and sergeant didn't leave till near ten this mornin'."

With any luck, they wouldn't be back ever. "Rest of the troop here?" Eli asked Cole, then shifted his glance to young Deke Hampton, who now joined Cole behind the service desk.

"Yep," the boy said.

"He was going to Rodney," Cole said. "Overheard him talking to Cummings here at breakfast." Cole Yeager looked at Eli, who arched an eyebrow and waited. "Gonna talk to Isabel Hays from what I overheard."

Inwardly Eli cursed. He'd like to have killed Cummings at the moment. His one consolation was that he was now relatively sure Alice hadn't left him for Seth Parker. From what Eli gathered, Parker was still investigating Alan Guthrie's murder and the information that damnable newspaperman Cummings had given him had led the major to Rodney and Isabel Leigh Hays.

That complication, however, held less import for Eli at the moment than the whereabouts of his bride. He looked at Cole. "He'll have a hell of a time getting anything out of Isabel unless he gives her some good reason to want to give it."

"How about hanging for murder?"

Eli smiled. "That might get some cooperation out of her, but I don't believe she's involved in murder."

"Hard times, Calhoon. Hard times."

Eli swallowed. For sure, lotsa folks were stooping pretty low these days. "You'll know my wife if you see her?"

"I sure do," Deke said with a bright grin. "The real pretty one. I noticed her right off when they first come…"

The boy stopped talking, his gaze darting from Eli to Cole, who'd turned to watch the boy bury himself, then back to Eli.

"I didn't mean no offense, Mr. Calhoon."

"She is the pretty one, Deke. Thank you." Eli looked at Cole.

"I know her," Cole said, "and she wasn't here for lunch. If I see her…?"

Eli sighed, then putting up his best front—he didn't want these men to know he didn't know what had happened to her—he said, "It's getting too late for dinner. I imagine she's headed home. Looks like I missed her."

Cole nodded. "We'll send her on home then."

Of course you would, if she's of a mind to come. Eli stepped onto the hotel porch and looked down the street and up. First he'd let Laura know how things were going to be betwixt her and him from here on out, and May Hale would not become an issue come hell or high water. Then he'd find Cummings and try and find out what was going on with Isabel.

This time Laura was certain she heard the soft pat of a footfall. Perhaps he'd come back for more of her. She hauled herself from beneath the mussed sheets, and reached for the light cotton wrapper at the foot of the bed. Covering her naked body, still tingling with the satisfaction that came with conquest, she eased toward the bedroom door.

Her skin flushed with the memory of Eli's words when she'd met him on the road earlier. Poor lad. He'd actually driven her to use her wiles against him. Gone so far as to tell her she was making a fool out of herself. Well, she'd just made him the fool once again. Did he really think he was in control?

She stepped into the hall, then tiptoed to the dining room. Empty.

And if he was planning to keep that Yankee...and her on the side...he needed to think again. She was taking steps to get rid of his bride, and she wasn't waiting for his blessing.

Laura studied the spartan parlor, its moldings crushed, its wallpaper scarred. Situated on the east side of the house, the room was now dark and still. Laura's stomach growled, and she clutched it. She had food; she wasn't starving—yet. Preparing a meal was a different matter. She could cook, but she didn't like to.

"A game, dearest? I know you're here. Did you decide to stay the night after all?" She'd come to that place in her house where the hall led back to the master bedroom. Placing one foot in front of the other, quiet so as not to be detected, she walked to the threshold and gazed upon the tousled but empty bed. "Where are you, darling?" she sang out, then gurgled a pleased laugh.

"Behind you, *darling*."

"She knows something," Seth said.

"You can't get it out of her?" Jubal Summers asked.

Seth picked up his glass of water and took a sip. Long rays of sunlight, burnished gold, stretched across the stained carpet gracing the dining-room floor, then broke and climbed the table leg before jutting across the white linen tablecloth. The afternoon was waning. He was eating early, but he'd missed lunch, then declined Frank Zachary's offer of jerky on the road back from Rodney.

The hotel clerk, doing double duty now in the dining room, stepped over and lit the candle in the center of their table. The young man asked Seth if he needed anything, then shot a glance at Captain Summers, who shook his head. Seth waited till the teenager was out of earshot.

"I don't know if she's afraid of us or of someone else." He met Jubal's eyes. "I'm not really sure she's afraid of anything."

Jubal grunted. "From what you've told me, she ain't nothin' but a whore—"

"That's not the impression I meant to give, Jubal. Once she was the prized and pampered mistress of a very wealthy local planter. When he died, she struck out in business on her own. She's a high-class madam. She knows some powerful people, and I'd reckon, if I pushed too hard, she could call in some markers that would warn me off."

"She weren't born high-class or else she wouldn't be doin' what she's doin'."

Not what he meant by high-class, but... Seth cut a piece of chicken, then grinned at Jubal. "Whoring and moving cotton?"

"Whorin'. Don't figure a high-class white woman would find any great sin in movin' stolen cotton."

"Particularly Southern cotton." Seth frowned. "But I don't think she's doing much whoring these days either. I figure she belongs to one man and he's taking good care of her."

"Calhoon?"

Seth doubted it—at least from a "pleasure" standpoint. "That would have been the old man, Holland Calhoon, Eli Calhoon's daddy. I know about that connection, but he's been dead for over two years. Either someone else is keeping her or she's making her money elsewhere."

"Stealin' cotton," Jubal stated matter-of-factly.

"Stealin' something would be my guess."

Jubal picked up his coffee mug. He wasn't eating. "And you think she's in it with Calhoon?"

Oh, how he wished. And he wished he could catch them at it even more.

A hasty feminine voice, a male response. Seth looked over Jubal's shoulder to the front desk beyond the dining room. Moments later, Betty Franklin stepped through the portal, looked around, and spied him. Both he and Jubal Summers rose when she approached their table.

"Mrs. Franklin," Seth said, pulling his napkin from the collar of his blouse, "how pleasant to see you."

"Thank you," she said, out of breath. She nodded curtly to Jubal. "I'm sorry to interrupt your supper, but could I speak with you?" She again looked at Jubal. "Alone, I do apologize."

Interrupting his meal wasn't what bothered him. Interrupting his meeting with his subordinate was a bigger problem, not to mention the veiled slight. Jubal looked at him.

"It's all right, Captain."

Jubal saluted smartly—something he, as a rule, dispensed with—then nodded at Betty Franklin, who thanked him as he pulled out a chair for her. She sat, then turned and watched his captain walk away. Seth pursed his lips and reseated himself.

"Can I get you anything?"

"No, thank you," she said, that breathlessness still in her voice, and curiosity overrode his irritation.

"What can I do for you, Mrs. Franklin?"

"I'm sorry for being so…so pushy," she said, wringing her hands in front of her, "but I'm worried about Alice and I absolutely cannot go to Peter. He is terribly angry with her for marrying against his wishes."

Seth frowned. "Since your husband isn't here, and since you are so concerned for Alice, could you tell me the real reason she married Calhoon?"

The woman closed her eyes and drew in a breath, then leaned into him. "He compromised her, then forced her to marry him."

"I beg your pardon?" He didn't believe for a moment that impassioned defender of her father and brothers' struggle for the Union could be forced into marriage by a Southerner.

"It's true."

"He seduced her?" He didn't believe that either.

The woman blinked, then looked around the almost empty dining room. "I don't think so."

"He raped her?"

"I do not know," the woman said sharply. "For the love of God, Major, I don't know what transpired between those two."

He'd kill the bastard if he learned he'd raped Alice, but that was more impossible for him to believe than anything. The Alice he'd briefly gotten to know, or thought he had, would never enter a lifetime of marriage with a man who'd forced sexual relations on her.

"But suffice it to say, something compelled her to marry him against her will."

The woman was staring at him as she spoke, and he studied her right back. She knew what that "something" was; he knew it as well as he knew he was sitting in the shattered remains of a hotel dining room in Port Gibson, Mississippi. He was just as certain Mrs. Franklin wasn't going to tell him the dirty little secret (and he readily assumed a family secret) that landed Alice in the bed of a dishonorable man. At least Calhoon had married her.

"He was after her grandfather's fortune."

Well, hell, yes, no wonder he'd had the *decency* to marry her.

Betty Franklin grabbed the hand he'd laid on the table. "I fear her life is in danger."

Calhoon had the money…and a very beautiful young woman. "Why do you think he wants to kill her?"

She threw her arms wide in exasperation. "Did you not hear what I said?"

"Is there some stipulation that prevents him from controlling the money?"

"No, of course not." She was no longer trying to keep her frustration in check. Obviously, she considered him dense.

Gently he retook her balled fist. "He has the money, Mrs. Franklin. Why would he want to kill Alice? I know I wouldn't."

"You're not in love with somebody else," she ground out.

Laura Blackledge, the woman who claimed Eli Calhoon was obsessed with her. Obsessed to the point he'd murdered his own brother to have her. Perhaps he needed to check out how the lovely Laura's second husband had really died.

"She's not home. Calhoon indicated to my daughter earlier this afternoon that he didn't know where Alice was."

"And you believe he's trying to dupe people into thinking she's run off?"

"That, or she has fled for fear of her life, and he might find her."

He nodded, glanced at the remains of his cold dinner, then looked at the anxious Betty Franklin. "We'll find her. I need to talk to Calhoon anyway."

First though, he'd talk to Laura Blackledge.

Chapter Forty-one

"What's your best guess, Doctor?" Seth asked.

The diminutive man eyed him across the mostly nude body of Laura Blackledge. "Three hours at most."

Seth looked out the bedroom window at the waning evening light. That would've made it around two this afternoon at the earliest.

"Strangled," the elderly man said. He hadn't needed to point that out. The cause of death was obvious.

From where he squatted beside the corpse, Seth pointed to the burns around her neck. "Hemp?"

Doctor Ephraim Lester pulled his wire-rim spectacles off his ears. He too was squatting by the body. "A sound guess."

"Not too much of a guess, Doc." Seth lifted one of Laura's hands, which lay awkwardly at her shoulder.

The old doctor rubbed his eyes with the back of his thumbs and stood up. He'd been a doctor in Claiborne County for almost forty years, he'd told Seth minutes ago, and coroner for the past twenty-five. Too old for conscription in 1863, the man had not served in the Confederate military, but he had sworn allegiance to the Cause and helped many a wounded soldier when medical attention was required. Right now, he continued to serve as coroner. "I attended her birth," the doc said. "She grew into a beautiful woman."

Moved by the doc's words, Seth forced himself to study the bluish tint of Laura's once lovely face. His gaze passed over her swollen tongue visible at the corner of her mouth—as if she were drooling—then moved to her bulging, vacant eyes.

"Could we cover her up again now?" the doc asked.

Seth stood and took the quilt Frank Zachary had pulled from the bed when they'd first found Laura's body. Carefully, he replaced the cover over the corpse.

"Well"—and the old man sighed—"there's no guess either as to cause of death. Her windpipe is crushed. Asphyxiation due to strangulation."

All Seth really cared about was documenting that she'd been murdered—and the other critical item he was not capable of ascertaining for himself—the time of death.

"Any idea who did it?" the doc asked.

"Nope. How 'bout you?"

"I do not." He situated his spectacles back on the bridge of his nose and stepped to a small Queen Anne table next to the bedroom door, from which he picked up his hat and placed it on his head. "Do you want an autopsy?"

"I want her body checked. Give me your opinion on rape. Confirm for me she'd been with a man."

The doc nodded. "I'll go set up." His gaze darted to Jubal Summers, standing quietly at the threshold separating the bedroom from the dining room. "You get your boys here to bring her on over when you're done. I'll be waiting."

Jubal Summers moved up behind Seth when the doctor departed. "You think this ties to the cotton theft?"

Seth had no idea, but feared it might.

"Maybe somebody thought she sent you to that Hays woman in Rodney."

Seth scratched the stubble along his jaw and recalled the wide eyes of Betty Franklin, so worried for her niece. He glanced at the quilt-covered corpse on the floor, then, stomach a wee bit weak, he turned on his heel to face Jubal. "That said, Captain, I reckon I best mosey on downtown and try to find out how much Laura Blackledge knew of Isabel Leigh Hays' involvement with cotton dealing."

"You gonna talk to Cummings?"

"I am," he said and stopped at the door. "I hope I find him

alive. You get the men in here and get this body to Doctor Lester's. Then check the house and yard one more time before it gets too dark."

"*Mista* Eli been home 'bout two hours. First thing he ask 'bout when he gots heah was you."

Alice's worst fear since she'd stepped, heavyhearted, out of Mr. Cummings' newspaper office in Port Gibson and found the sun hovering just above the treetops to the west. All the way back, in increasing darkness, dragged along by the lumbering mule, she'd prayed Calhoon wasn't home. But then, when she got here, she would have had to wonder where he was, and there would have been no escaping the probability he was out looking for her. His homecoming would have been worse then. Alice massaged an aching temple. At the same time, the darkie Buck held out his hand to help her down. She reached for her cape on the seat beside her, then took his hand.

"You done got back jus' in time."

Her heart skipped the proverbial beat, but he nodded to the northwest. "Sto'm comin' in. Been downright hot today." He reached for the harness on the mule and unhitched it.

It had been spring-like. Alice's shoes sank in the soft dirt beneath the lean-to where they sheltered their meager stock, and Buck led the mule to the hay.

With some disgust, she pulled out her foot, then looked for Buck and found him busy with the mule, man and beast bathed in the glowing yellow light from a lantern hung on the rough support post holding up the lean-to. Storm or not, it was near dark, and she'd planned to be home long before now.

"Do you know where he went earlier?"

Buck looked over his shoulder, then pushed back on the mule that tried to nudge him out of the way. "Town, lookin' fo' you, I thought." The man looked away, shaking his head in what Alice took to mean reproof.

She closed her eyes. Her head pounded, had for most of the afternoon. She didn't want to deal with Calhoon now. The brief reprieve she'd enjoyed when she confirmed her husband had not murdered his brother for the sultry Laura Blackledge had been eclipsed by the additional information Mr. Cummings had provided concerning that fateful day in Tennessee and the implication that information held for her.

Anticipating Calhoon might be inside the kitchen, she bypassed it and walked around to the mud porch at the back of the house. There she shifted the cape to her left arm, then struggled, standing, to remove her muddy shoes. Giving up, she went on inside the dining room, tossed the cape on the table, and sat. Head bowed low, she concentrated on the laces of her footwear.

A floorboard creaked, and her stomach tensed. Steeling herself, she twisted in the chair to see the hall door and locked her gaze with Calhoon's, marked, she noted, with relief.

"Where have you been?" he asked.

She turned back to her shoe. "Helping Buck unhitch the wagon and put the mule away."

"That's not what I meant, Alice."

His voice had hardened, and she looked up into a face now tense with anger. She was alive and safely home, and she was going to feel the wrath wrought by an afternoon filled by worry. That was an agony she knew well.

But she'd loved the men she'd anguished over.

"Answer me."

She straightened in her chair as he approached her around the end of the table. What compelled Eli Calhoon? Property? Did he fear she'd come to some harm, or did he think she might have dared to leave him?

She looked at her remaining shoe and reached for it. "I'm sorry you were worried," she said with a calm she didn't feel, and slipped the footwear off.

"I don't care how sorry you are. What I want to know is where the devil you've been?"

"Oh," she said, rising so quickly she nipped his chin with her head, "I thought you might have been concerned something happened to me."

"I was concerned something happened to you," he bellowed as he stepped back. "But you're here now, and I know nothing happened to you. Now I want to know what you've been up to all—"

Pounding on the front door gave him pause, and as one, they looked in the direction of the racket.

"Open up inside," a man's voice demanded.

Calhoon narrowed his eyes on her.

"What?" she asked. Her heart was thumping, partly from Calhoon's anger, partly from the intrusion outside, and partly from the simple fact he thought she might be the cause of the intrusion.

"Open up," the voice cried again.

Calhoon started toward the hallway. "There's only one group of bastards in this day and time who'd pound on my door like that, Alice."

Union soldiers. She followed him across the dining room and into the foyer.

Calhoon yanked the door open. Seth Parker, flanked by his Negro captain and sergeant, stared at him. Seth acknowledged Alice with a blink, and his aggressive stance softened. He stepped inside, not waiting for an invitation. The two Negroes followed. Alice noticed Calhoon's hand tighten over the knob, but he said nothing. Even she found some offense at their bursting in without an invite, which her husband might well have made, given the chance.

"Alice," Seth said, removing the cap from his head. "It's a pleasure to find you well."

"It's good to see you, too." At least she hoped it was.

"Could I help you, Major?"

Seth turned slightly and looked at Calhoon, still holding the door.

"I have some matters I wish to talk to you about, Calhoon."

Calhoon shoved the door shut, but not too loudly. "Guthrie, cotton"—Calhoon stepped around the cluster of men gathered at the entrance—"Isabel Hays?"

Seth narrowed his eyes on her husband. "Initially, Miss Hays was the reason for my visit, but your relationship with her—"

"My father's relationship," Calhoon said and met Alice's gaze.

"Your family's relationship, if you prefer," Seth said, sounding annoyed, "has been superseded by more immediate events."

"Such as?"

"Laura Blackledge."

Alice saw Calhoon stiffen, and she tensed in response.

"And what has she told you about me now, Major?"

Seth was studying Calhoon with marked intensity. Chin high, Alice stepped closer to her husband. Both men appeared to notice, and it occurred to her that her subtle act of defense must have appeared silly. Seth refocused on Calhoon.

"She hasn't told me anything lately, nor will she ever."

Alice observed that for a moment Calhoon ceased to breathe, then he asked, "What do you mean by that?"

"She's dead."

Alice remained focused on her husband, who was staring at Seth. "What happened?"

"I found her in her home this afternoon," Seth said, and when Calhoon said nothing, Seth added, "strangled."

"She was murdered?"

"Indeed she was."

Calhoon turned and started for the parlor. Seth followed. Alice, her body trembling, trailed after them. Behind her, she heard one of the Negroes stir, then the captain passed her. Alice glanced back at the sergeant in place by the door. He stayed put. There were probably more men out back. Alice fell in step behind the captain and moved into the parlor, where Calhoon now squatted in front of the commode. He pulled out the earthen jug.

"Where were you this afternoon between two and three?"

Calhoon rose and placed the brew on top of the cabinet. "You think I killed her, Parker?"

"Did you?"

"I did not, and why would I?"

Seth twisted his head and glanced at Alice. He seemed reluctant to say what he needed, but she wasn't about to voluntarily leave this room.

"Because she refused your attention," Seth answered.

Now Calhoon looked at her, then back to Seth. "Despite Laura's delusions, I was not obsessed with her."

"According to what she told me"—Alice's heart was racing so fast, it pummeled her temples—"you murdered your—"

An unbidden groan escaped Alice's throat as she rushed in front of Seth Parker. "She was lying. He didn't kill his brother. You can talk to a man named Caw Pruitt." She stopped to catch her breath. Seth didn't say anything.

"Mr. Pruitt was with their unit," she continued, "and he was right beside them, providing cover fire for Calhoon, who was trying to pull Andrew from under a dead horse. That's when Andrew was fatally shot."

The silence was ominous. She looked over her shoulder at her husband. He returned her gaze with no expression. Drawing a breath, she turned to Seth. "He had no reason to kill that woman."

"That doesn't mean he wasn't obsessed with her," Seth said. "Nor does it mean he didn't have another reason for killing her."

From the corner of her eye, she caught a glimpse of the Negro captain near the parlor door. "What other reason?" she asked.

"It was Mrs. Blackledge who implicated your husband in the theft of that Union cotton."

"She couldn't implicate him any more than I could, and you know it. That cotton was stolen from the real thieves."

Seth tilted his head. "Someone killed a Treasury agent—"

"Guthrie. I know, you told me about him. Do you have reason to think my husband was involved in that?"

Seth flexed his jaw. "Alice, you sound like a legal defender, I'm the one asking the questions here."

"Your manner is a bit heavy-handed, sweetheart." Hands squeezed her shoulders, and she twisted her head around to see Calhoon's face. "It's all right. The major's trying to find out what happened to Laura."

She blinked. They were trying to take him off to jail. She had no idea what venomous lies Laura had told Seth Parker. He might believe anything. She didn't want her stubborn, Rebel husband at the mercy of a hostile occupying force that had already made up its mind as to his guilt or innocence based on the damning words of a dead woman hell-bent on getting even with him.

Seth looked from Alice to Calhoon. "Where were you at two this afternoon?"

"He was here with me," she said.

Seth frowned at her. "You were here all day, Alice?"

"Alice...."

She heard the warning implicit in Calhoon's tone. Yes, she was lying for him, but she didn't care. She would find out about Laura once she'd managed to get Seth and his overbearing troops out of here.

"I was," she said.

Seth's gaze passed to Calhoon, then returned to her with a pitying look. "Your aunt approached me this afternoon, Alice. Seems your husband was in town looking for you."

Alice felt her cheeks pale.

"She feared you'd run away from him because he'd threatened you, and she further feared your life might be in danger if he found you."

She closed her eyes, then breathed out before forcing herself to meet Seth's gaze again. What a damn fool she was.

"Did he find you and force you back here?" Seth persisted, but by the tone of his voice, she knew he didn't believe that to be the case.

She shook her head and looked straight ahead at the buttons on the man's blouse.

"I know for a fact both you and your husband visited Poynter Cummings this afternoon, roughly two hours apart."

Seth looked over her head to Calhoon. "You *were* in Port Gibson this afternoon?"

Calhoon lifted his hands from Alice's shoulders. "I was."

Alice trembled.

"Did you see Laura Blackledge?"

"I saw her on my way to town. She was headed out here to find me."

"Did she tell you why?"

"She wanted to talk about me and her."

"You and her?"

"That's right."

"As in a relationship, not in business."

Calhoon made a sound, then Alice felt him move. She turned and watched him walk away. "Laura was never part of my cotton business, Major. She overheard where we were stashing the stuff and took that information to you after I wed. She wanted to get back at me."

"Which was the reason for her version of your brother's death?"

Calhoon stopped near the commode, but he didn't reach for the jug. He turned and looked at Seth. "Actually, I think she was convinced I might have done such a thing. Laura set a high value on herself." Calhoon glanced briefly at Alice, as if pondering what to say next, then folded his arms across his chest and leaned his hip against the commode.

"What did she want out of you?" Seth asked.

"To marry me and become mistress of Camellia Creek."

Seth stepped around her, so that she no longer stood between him and Calhoon. "And that's not what you wanted?"

Calhoon smiled. "Not for a long, long time now, Major." He nodded at Alice. "And I already have a wife."

"Her solution?"

"We never got to that stage of discussion."

"Right. Someone killed her." Seth stepped closer to Calhoon. He was taller, more intimidating. Alice watched her husband.

"So you tell me," Calhoon said.

Alice breathed in, then out. He neither sounded nor looked intimidated.

"Did she ever threaten Alice?"

"No, but she liked to think herself a threat to my marriage."

"And you didn't like that?"

"Her threats were pathetic."

"Do you believe she posed a threat to Alice?"

"Not without me."

Alice studied her husband, then looked at Seth who shrugged. "So she intended to coerce you into killing your wife and marrying her?"

"She wasn't that foolish. She could never have coerced me into doing such a thing"—Calhoon glanced Alice's way—"if I weren't willing. Her confidence lay in that she thought I would be willing. Failing that, and she would have failed, she would have resorted to vengeance and come up with some ploy by which she hoped to destroy me."

"Such as?"

"Implicating me in murder."

"Guthrie's?"

"Maybe."

"Wayne Hale?"

Calhoon's smile didn't reach his eyes. "You found him yet?"

Seth's reciprocating smile didn't either. "Did you accompany her back to her house after meeting her on the road?"

"I told her, not for the first time, to stay away from Camellia Creek, then I left her on the road where I'd come across her, very much alive. I did go to her house later, though."

Seth cocked a brow. "Did you? Around what time?"

"A little after two, I'd guess. Well past dinnertime. I'd been at the Port Gibson Hotel talking with the proprietor."

"Ah," Seth said, then nodded. "That's how you knew I'd gone to Rodney to see Isabel Hays. I'll have to be more discreet."

"Did it need to be kept secret?"

"If Laura Blackledge died because of it."

Calhoon rubbed his chin with the back of his hand, pondering, it appeared, Seth's words. "Nobody answered her door," he said finally.

Seth's eyes narrowed. "I'd think you'd have felt at liberty to just walk in."

"I tried the doors, front and back. They were locked. A bit unusual, but these are troubled times. I figured she'd stepped out and locked up, though she didn't have anything left to steal, you boys-in-blue having already taken it all."

Seth seemed to ignore that. "Back door wasn't locked when I got there."

Calhoon watched the man a moment, then said, "Then somebody already inside came out between the time I left and you got there."

Seth flexed his jaw. "Then you went to see Cummings?"

"You noticed I didn't kill him."

Alice stepped closer, and Calhoon glanced at her.

"Yeah," Seth said, "he was pretty sore at me. Figured I was to blame for you showing up at his doorstep. If you didn't kill Mrs. Blackledge, do you have any idea who did?"

"I do not. As far as I know, she was a threat to no one but me."

They stared at each other a moment, then Seth turned to Alice.

"No," Calhoon said, then Alice heard her husband curse under his breath. "Her little hands couldn't—"

"The killer used a rope."

Seth hesitated a moment, then nodded to his captain, and with mounting dismay, Alice watched the latter head out of the parlor.

"What are you going to do?" she asked.

"Nothing now," Seth said a couple of steps behind his subordinate.

"You're not taking Calhoon?"

The handsome major stopped and turned back to face her. "You did your best to give him an alibi. Do you want me to?" His gaze passed to Calhoon behind her. "If you have some evidence that would lead me to believe he killed Laura Blackledge, you'd best give it to me now."

She looked at Calhoon, watching her. "I don't think he killed her."

Seth wavered, then said to Calhoon. "It's my understanding you didn't get home till late September, is that right?"

"It is."

"What took you so long getting back?"

Calhoon drew in a breath, subtle, but telling. "I went to Texas."

"You planned to—"

"After Taylor surrendered, I decided to carry on the fight, but surrender followed me there, too. For a brief, insane moment, I planned to follow Joe Shelby into Mexico, but as I sat on the north bank of the Rio Grande contemplating that Coahuila shrubland, I realized that wasn't the war I wanted to fight, and I came home."

"And are you continuing the fight you did want, Colonel?"

"In a manner of speaking."

"How's it goin'?"

"I've met the enemy, but I'm still advancing."

Seth flexed his jaw, then looked at Alice. "Your aunt is worried about you." He placed that odd cover back on his head, glanced at Calhoon, then focused his full attention on her. "Just so you know, Laura Blackledge was found in only her wrapper, in her bedroom. It appears she'd been with a man shortly before she died. I'll stop by the Franklins' on my way back to town and tell your aunt you're home, but you'd best be the one to tell her you're safe, because I'm not so sure you are."

<h1 align="center">Chapter Forty-two</h1>

"**I** wasn't with her, and I didn't kill her," Calhoon said.

Alice stood with her back to him, staring at the door Seth Parker had pulled shut behind him moments before.

When she didn't respond, Calhoon made a sibilant sound. "I don't think you believe I'm guilty."

She turned and looked at him. He shrugged. "'I was here with you all day' sorta gave it away."

"I didn't want them taking you to jail." She moved toward the settee. Her entire body ached.

"Now, given the implications of Laura's death scene, you're having second thoughts?"

"Which other man could she have possibly been with, Calhoon?"

"Whoever she was trying to manipulate at the time."

"She was in love with you. She wouldn't have been—"

"Alice, dammit, she was in love with herself. Laura used sex as a tool, a weapon even, and it no longer worked on me. I was not the man with her this afternoon."

"Do you know who was?"

"If I did, I'd have told your major."

"Not if you plan to mete out another dose of Southern justice on your own."

He let out a breath, then reached for the earthen jug on the commode. "I have no idea who killed Laura and no sense of personal justice to mete out."

"Please don't drink."

He uncorked the container and drank anyway, then hissed, she assumed because of the liquor—if that's what one could call the homemade brew. She wondered where his bourbon from Natchez was.

He set the jug down and pushed the cork back in its mouth. "Have you ever seen me drunk?" He started toward his chair.

"No," she said, and looked at the cold hearth. His one swig was a compromise of sorts. "But I haven't spent that much time with you, really, and tonight you could be more distraught than usual."

He sat in his wingback chair, away from her, but not too far. Still, she felt detached from him.

"Because of Laura, you mean?"

"Yes."

"Laura had become more like a sister with whom I had had an incestuous affair."

That sounded horribly perverse. The look on her face amused him obviously, because he laughed. Not loudly, but sadly.

"I have never been unfaithful to you with her, Alice."

She licked her dry lips. "And you didn't kill her?"

"A strange question to ask now that you've sent your knight in shining armor away. What if I said yes?"

"He's not my knight in shining armor."

He studied her a long moment. "I didn't kill her. Now tell me why you didn't want them taking me away."

Outside the boarded windows, branches scratched against the porch eaves.

"Can we fix the windows now?" she asked.

"I intend to. Tell me why."

"I don't think you—"

"Didn't."

She drew in a breath and stiffened her spine. "*Don't* think you're guilty, and I don't want you at their mercy. I think they would be too quick to believe you did it, and you're so stubborn and arrogant, they'd sooner hang you than try to find out the truth."

A smile curved his lips. This one reached to his eyes. "I'm not suicidal, Alice."

"That's why you told him you were continuing to fight."

"That was about you."

"About…?" She blinked at him. "Seth doesn't realize that."

"I think he does, which is why he decided to elaborate on Laura's death scene."

A wail rose with the wind, and she looked past him into the dark hall and the bedroom beyond.

"It's the wind," he said.

Her gaze found his. "If they'd arrested you, I'd be alone here."

"It is only the wind, that's all."

She briefly closed her eyes and massaged an aching shoulder.

"You're tired." Distant thunder echoed his words.

"Can't we afford a carriage now, too? I've fought with that buckboard all day."

"Doc Lester has mine. I'll get it back, but you might try staying home or taking Buck with you."

"Buck keeps busy with his own work."

"You are part of Buck's work. I'd prefer someone with you."

She bit her bottom lip as the wind again howled around the house. Calhoon shifted in his chair. "How is Caw?" he asked.

His expression was such that she couldn't determine if he were angry with her or not. "He seems to be fine. He said you'd been out to see him."

Calhoon nodded. "So, you found out what you wanted to know?"

That and so much more, but "yes" was all she said.

"Didn't want to take my word for it?"

"No," she snapped, "and you didn't tell me anything except that Laura was lying."

"I don't like to talk about the day Andrew died."

"And you didn't have to, so why do we need to talk about it now?"

They didn't, and that was fine with him. She reached up and pulled a pin from her hair. A silky auburn lock fell against skin he knew, even in the lantern light, was overly pale.

"Do you feel well, Alice?"

"I'm tired, as you said."

"Did you eat?"

"I have no appetite."

He frowned. "You've had nothing all day?"

Some distance beyond the house, the wail rose again, more ominous now. She didn't look at him, but listened.

"It is the *wind*," he said.

"It's different." Now she turned to him, and he shifted in his chair.

"No, it's not. I've heard that wail all my life. It's the wind. Answer me, have you eaten anything at all today?"

Again the cry rose. "We ate a good breakfast this morning, don't you remember?"

They had, at daybreak. That was a long time ago. "You've had nothing since?"

"No." Suddenly Alice grasped one arm of the settee and pulled herself forward. "Why did you marry me?"

"I thought we'd determined it was for the money."

"And vengeance?" she asked.

"Well, yes"—he squinted at her—"but you deprived me of that when you said you wanted me."

A new wail rose and whirled around the house, disconcerting to him only because it seemed to affect Alice so. She was squeezing the arm of the settee so tight her knuckles turned white.

"Unless the vengeance you wish to exact is of a different sort."

"Such as?" he asked. What was she was thinking, murder? He'd been unable to make her feel ravished—if he'd ever wanted to, and he had her money. What was left?

She stared at him for a moment, then rose, looking around the room as the wail faded.

"Alice?" he said when she didn't answer him. "Alice!"

Her head twisted to face him.

"What did you talk to Cummings about?"

She opened her mouth, but didn't speak; and anything she might have said would have drowned in the howling wind.

"It's her, Calhoon," she cried out above the turmoil. "Don't you realize it's her?" She jerked her head around and locked her eyes on him. "Why is she here now?"

Antsy with her unease, he rose, and she took a step back, away from him. "Alice," he said, his heart beating faster, "that sound is made every time the wind picks up."

She took another step back. "The wind didn't sound like that earlier."

"That wail only comes when the wind is from the northwest. Daddy always said it came around the northwest corner and passed through the…"

Quiet. The wind had stilled.

"Through the what?"

He swallowed. "The loft of the barn."

She bolted before he could think. Daddy'd been wrong, that's all. Whatever made that ominous sound was, simply, something else.

"Alice," he called as she disappeared into the dark hall. He started after her, then picked up his pace when he heard the back door open. "Where are you going?"

He caught her at the bottom of the porch steps. "It's her," she screamed above the renewed wind. The disconcerting wail rose again, drowning the roar in the churning crowns of the trees surrounding the house. "Let me go."

She yanked on her arm, and he released it from fear of hurting her. Lightning lit the sky, the house, and the entire yard where they stood. She hesitated a moment, giving him a long look as she did. The light flickered with the fading wind. "She's calling to me, Calhoon."

"You think it's because of me?"

He saw her shake her head in a brilliant flash of light, but she said nothing, and with the next flash she was running away. She didn't even have shoes on.

He ran to keep up, but he knew where she headed, and he wished like hell he had the good sense to go back and get a lantern. Not that one was necessary, given the on-and-off flickers of lightning, complemented with thunder, both highlighted by violent gusts of wind and its wails.

Lightning flickered, silhouetting the ancient oak. She stopped. He stopped, too, a few feet behind her. He saw nothing hanging from the lowest limb.

Alice turned and cried out to him above the tempest. "She's here. I can feel her. Can you?"

He could not. Light brightened the clearing, exposing his beautiful Alice, her hair wild and mostly down now, blowing in the wind. He approached closer. She didn't back away. A raindrop hit his cheek, and the light flickered out.

"You know whom you and Andrew and Caw and the others from the Butterfield Grays faced at Shiloh, don't you?"

"Yankees," he hollered.

Lightning struck close, illuminating her face. Her eyes were watching him.

Huge drops of rain pelted him for a moment, then lightning lit the sky at the same moment the wail rose around them. This time the hair on the back of his neck pricked. In the flickering light, Alice reached out to him.

"Make love to me."

He took her hand, more than ready to get them back to the house. The lightning was straight up and down now, and the earthshaking thunder, in tandem with the wails of the wind, were beginning to leave him doubtful as to what lurked in this clearing.

She pulled on him, trying to draw him closer to the tree. He resisted.

"Please, *Eli!*" she cried. In the darkness, he could feel her tearing at the buttons of her dress, then she kneeled on the ground and tugged him down. Deadly lightning exposed her breasts, and against his better judgment, he reached for her skirt the moment she reached for the buttons of his britches. Desire swelled, but what moved him, compelled him to risk both their lives in this chilling, violent place, and forced his surrender to her will, was his given name from her lips.

She ripped his shirt open and licked his breast. Heat surged through his veins, and he tore the clothing from her and laid his body over her naked thighs. He knew from her touch, her scent, her primordial moans when his tongue found a nipple… the way she arched her back when he thrust into her…that what drove her was not fear of him that only moments ago he'd been so certain she harbored. Nor was it hatred or anger or even the passion she claimed they begat. What she needed from him wasn't sex, but forgiveness. Forgiveness she'd already earned three times over.

Her nails pressed into his buttocks, and she pulled him hard against her, then cried out as lightning and thunder shredded the night in tandem. Heat and sensation obliterated the noise and numbed the frigid wet that pummeled them from the heavens. In the ensuing darkness, he rocked against her as his orgasm faded. A subsequent flash of white-hot light revealed her beneath him, her pale flesh wet and shimmering. She blinked rain out of her eyes and smiled at him before the light flickered out. He licked the water from her breast, and she forced herself up, circling her arms around his neck. The top of her rain-drenched head caressed his cheek. Lightning flashed. Out of the corner of his eye, he thought he saw—he brought his head up—something. But the light was out before he could confirm anything.

"Did you see her?" Alice said against his ear.

Again light flickered. Nothing was there. "No."

"She's here," Alice said, tightening her arms around his neck. He felt her forehead press against his breast, then felt her shiver. The temperature had dropped as the front passed through.

He grasped her face between his hands, tilted her head up and kissed her, her mouth sweet and fresh with the taste of raindrops. Then he forced himself from her.

Eli all but dragged her up the back porch stairs, cursing all the while that he didn't even have a fire lit in the house. He'd not once, however, admonished her for their lovemaking on the wet ground underneath the oak.

He stopped at the mud porch and grasped the door frame before searching for, she assumed, the bootjack. "Get on in, and get what little you've got on back off."

That would be her pantaloons. They'd found the dress, chemise, and corset, but those she held wadded against her naked breasts. She sat down hard on a bench beside the door and with one arm held the wet bundle of clothes in front of her.

"What are you doing?"

Alice reached for a foot. She'd made the trek to the tree in her stocking feet. Her toes were like ice, her stockings ruined. "Getting my stockings off before tracking up the house."

"We'll worry about the floor later," he said and took her arm. "Get inside."

Careful to keep the bundle over her breasts, she let him draw her to her feet, then looked at him when he chuckled.

"What?"

He nodded to the wet clothes. "Afraid I'll see something I haven't already?"

She felt her cheeks heat.

He dropped a boot onto the slick porch. "I'm fixin' to give you a bath, honey."

She raised her chin. "Maybe I'll give you one, too."

He grinned and, without another word, turned his attention to his remaining boot.

She reached for the door and stepped inside the dimly lit dining room. The house was scarcely warmer inside, but it was dry and there was no wind. Head bowed to see where she stepped, she turned and started closing the door.

Alice yelped as the tall hulk looming behind the portal emerged, and she jumped back into the dining-room chair she'd sat in to remove her boots when she'd first arrived home roughly an hour earlier. Naomi Polk's eyes raked Alice's body.

Eli grabbed Alice's arm and steadied her and the chair. "What are you doing here?" he asked Naomi.

Alice sucked in a breath. "Gracious, you scared me half to death."

The woman stepped forward. She'd not averted her attention from Alice. Behind her, Alice heard Eli close the door.

"Aunt Naomi, it's pouring out there."

"It wasn't when I left Port Gibson."

She was talking to Eli, but the woman still watched Alice. Lord, what a sight she must make, and what Alice had taken to be pure hatred in the woman's face was probably no more than moral censure.

"Why are you outside like that?" the woman asked.

When Alice didn't answer, Naomi's gaze shifted to Alice's right…to Eli. "Did she fall into the creek or into hay?"

"Why are you out on a night like this?" Eli persisted.

Disapproving eyes again moved over Alice.

"I came to tell you Laura is dead."

Alice felt Eli's cold hands on her shoulders. "Go on to the bedroom and start the stove. I'll get a fire started out here." He gave her a little push, distancing her from Naomi Polk. "We know about Laura," he told his aunt.

Alice slowed. The woman was watching Eli now. "You know?"

"Federal troops informed me a little while ago. They wanted to know if I knew who did it."

"They think you did it, don't they?"

"They haven't ruled me out."

The woman looked at Alice. "They'd never have considered you if you hadn't let *her* come between you."

Eli splayed his palm over Alice's bare back and propelled her more forcefully toward the door. "But she did."

The hateful woman bristled. "Do they know that if you were going to kill one of the two"—she nodded at Alice—"you'd have picked that one?"

Dread washed over her, and Eli stepped between her and his aunt. "That would be a lie."

Naomi Polk smiled, then let her gaze pass from Eli to Alice and back again. "Would it? You fornicated with her to force her into marriage. For the money, nephew."

The pounding in Alice's head heightened with the increased pulse of her heart.

"You have no idea why I married her."

Naomi sneered and stepped forward. "Laura's newly dead, and you're out in the storm partaking in some savage pleasure. Your wife's deviant enticements will grow old in time. Pity you can't talk to your father about her. He could tell you plenty about perverse women."

"Like he told you?" Eli shot back.

Naomi's hateful smile disappeared.

Alice was trembling—from the cold, from anger, from sheer defeat? She didn't know which. She had been wrong to seduce Eli tonight. He had lost, if nothing else, an old friend, and no matter how he and Laura might have fallen out over the last few days, their recent grievances could not wipe out a lifetime of friendship…and love.

He stepped in the direction of his aunt. Alice grabbed for his arm. "Eli—"

"Hush," he said. Then he looked at her. "You'll catch your death—"

The woman snorted. "You could wish, nephew."

Perhaps he did, but if tonight killed her, his good luck would be blind, because she'd definitely been the one to initiate the—she closed her eyes in self-disgust—sex.

"Go get warm," he said at her side. "I'll be in."

$\mathcal{F}$or the first time, Eli fully appreciated what his father, as master of Camellia Creek, had put up with from his sister-in-law, and he wondered, amazed, at his father's patience over the years.

Alice disappeared, and Naomi stepped toward him. He did likewise and met the woman eye to eye.

"She's nothing but a whore. I can't believe the things you're doing in your mother's house."

"My father's house, and Alice and I are married." He stepped around her. "How did you get here?"

"I came in Doctor Lester's carriage—"

"My carriage?"

She shrugged. "He let me borrow it when he came to tell me about Laura, so I could come tell you." She sniffed. "Obviously, you didn't care."

Whether she thought he cared or not didn't concern him in the least. He opened the back door and listened. Still raining pretty hard. He considered driving the woman back to town, then returning with his carriage, but Alice was warm to the touch, and he wasn't sure she was quite right in the head either. For certain he couldn't leave before he got her clean and settled down.

He shut the door. "If it slacks up, I want you to go home."

"Buck unhitched the horse, and he's gone on home now."

Bullshit, Buck had gone home before he and Alice ever left the house. Aunt Naomi was more than capable of hitching a horse to a carriage just as she was capable of unhitching it. He'd seen her do it a hundred times. "I'll hitch up the carriage if necessary. Otherwise, I want you to go on upstairs and go to bed right now. I don't want you around Alice any more tonight."

She fidgeted at that. Oh, she wanted to say something; he could see it in the glare of her eyes and the set of her thin-lipped mouth. But he was no longer the baby nephew. He was the master, home from four years of struggling for a lost cause, and he wasn't about to tolerate her heavy-handed antics, and he sensed she knew it.

"Have you eaten?" she said after a moment.

"I have not—"

"She doesn't even—"

"Nor do I wish to." He would like to get something warm in Alice, but he'd take care of that himself. He stepped around her.

"You'll catch your own death."

He stopped and looked down at his wet, muddy clothes. His shirt was open—there weren't many buttons left on it. He looked at Naomi Polk. "Go to bed or go home."

Chapter Forty-three

Seth set the kepi back on his head, pulled his frock coat closed at the neck, and peered beneath Doc Lester's porch at the rain sparkling in meager lantern light.

"Nasty night," Sergeant Zachary said, moving out of the porch shadows to stand beside him. Behind them, Jubal pulled the doc's door shut with a soft rattle.

Jubal moved forward, buttoning his coat. "Done turned cold again."

Seth blew out a breath and watched it mist. "Cold and miserable." He paused at the top of the steps and glanced at the men flanking him. "Y'all ready?"

"As we'll ever be, I reckon."

With Jubal's words they stepped one at a time from the protection of the porch and onto the doc's sidewalk.

"Doc doesn't believe she'd been raped," Seth said, head bowed and shoulders hunched against the frigid wet. "Except for the rope burns on her neck there's not a mark on her. He did, however, confirm she'd been with a man."

Jubal had fallen into step at his side. "Calhoon?"

"Given their history, he's the most likely suspect."

"You thinkin' the Calhoon woman killed Laura Blackledge after she screwed her husband?"

"Do you remember on the victim's neck, how the burns rose up behind her ears?"

"Yes."

"Whoever killed her was probably taller than she was and stronger. Alice Calhoon would have had to climb upon a chair to do that, and though she might have come up with some ploy to

lure Laura Blackledge into such a position, it's extremely doubtful. I was toying with Calhoon."

"You think he done it over the cotton?"

"I can't think of why he'd have killed her over the cotton since
it was already back in Federal hands."

"He was angry 'cause she caused 'em to lose the cotton."

"My gut tells me that if he's the killer, the reason is something
else."

"Like her threatenin' to tell about Guthrie if he didn't do what
she wanted?"

Cold water trickled beneath Seth's coat collar, and he shuddered. "That'd be more the kind of something I'm thinking of."

Behind them, Sergeant Zachary called out, "You think she
even know'd 'bout dat Guthrie fella?"

They'd come almost to the entrance of the hotel. Beneath its
overhang, Seth stopped, braced himself against the wind and
looked at the sergeant, who brought up the rear. At Seth's side,
Jubal also turned. Frank Zachary wiped rain from his eyes.

"Is there some reason you don't want to believe Calhoon did
it?" Jubal said to Zachary above the roar of the rain

"His woman don't think he done it."

That brought a guffaw from Jubal.

"If he got dere when he say, da Blackledge woman already be
dead," Zachary said.

"*If* he got there when he said."

Seth's shoulder ached, a frailty that went in tandem with his
shortness of breath and the bittersweet memory of lilac. His focus
passed from his sergeant to his captain. "You were watching him
when I told him Laura Blackledge was dead. What did you make
of his reaction?"

"He was blank."

The sergeant, his dark skin glistening from the rain, huddled
closer to the other two. "When you fust say to 'im da Blackledge
woman would neva tell you nothin' ag'in—dat got 'is attention."

Jubal Summers studied the sergeant. After a moment, Seth
said, "You don't think he knew?"

"All I can say, suh, is dat to me, he seemed su'prised."

Jubal snorted. "Surprised we were on him so fast would be my take."

The sergeant shrugged and stepped back. That seemed to mollify Jubal, who focused on Seth. "Major, should we even be workin' this particular murder?"

Seth sighed. "Laura Blackledge was one of my sources. Until I know for sure her murder doesn't tie in to Guthrie's, I've got to keep working it."

Eli pulled Alice closer in the dark. She smelled of soap and the lavender she'd placed in the ash-laden rainwater she'd used to rinse her hair after washing it with goat-milk soap. The rinse, she told him, made her hair soft.

He rubbed his cheek against the top of her head. God, he loved her hair. Still, he hadn't wanted her to wash it. But what the hell? She'd been soaked to the scalp already and being clean seemed important to her. If cleanliness helped her rest, the risk justified itself. So he'd warmed the cookhouse, heated buckets of water and helped her wash and rinse not only those luxurious auburn curls, but her body, too. Then he'd shaved and bathed and washed his own head, all on the back porch. He hadn't used that lavender rinse, but he liked her goat-milk soap.

"I'm not crazy," she said.

"Yes, you are."

She pushed herself up. "I did see her, you know I did."

"Honey," he said and pulled her supporting arm from beneath her, forcing her to the mattress, "for me to agree with that would make me as crazy as we don't want others to know you are. I will agree that you think you saw something."

He rolled her over and pulled her spine against his chest. "Now stay still. What I referred to when I said you were crazy was your passionate embrace during that lightning storm."

She stiffened subtly. "I am so sorry."

"I beg your pardon?"

"About Laura. I shouldn't have forced myself on you tonight."

"A short while ago, you considered I might have killed her."

"A short while ago I considered you might have *been* with her, not killed her."

"You don't think that now?"

"I think I proved that out by that oak tree."

He squeezed her arm. "I needed you tonight, too."

He felt her head move on the pillow, and he sensed she was trying to find him in the dark. "I wonder what really happened to Jocelyn all those years ago."

"She killed herself over a broken heart."

"I don't think that's what happened."

"If Jocelyn LeBlanc told you she was murdered, why won't she tell you who did it?"

"For Saint Peter's sake, she doesn't carry on conversations with me."

"Then how—"

"Because I do. There's more to the story. That's why she can't rest."

"Well, if it's some sort of violence or misery keeping her from rest, I would argue that the spirit of a woman, unhappy enough to take her own life, wouldn't be able to rest either."

Alice lay perfectly still a moment, then stirred. "But was she unhappy?"

"I don't know."

"Miss Elvie told me she was deliriously in love with your father."

"Aunt Elvie used the word 'deliriously'?"

"That's my word, Eli, but that is how she described her."

"However, daddy was displeased about the baby and told Jocelyn it was over between them. That's when she took her life."

"That's your Aunt Naomi's story."

"Aunt Elvie knew Daddy better than anyone, Alice. What did she tell you about how Daddy felt?"

Eli couldn't see her, but he could feel her body alongside his. She was feverishly warm. "The same thing you told me he said. That—"

"It wasn't true." He kissed her quick. "There's your answer."

"What answer? Something's true, and that's what Jocelyn wants me to find out."

Eli felt a chill rack her body. "Go to sleep, Alice."

"She's alone."

Dear God, what did she mean by that? Eli turned, forcing her to turn back also, then he cuddled her spoon fashion. "Is that why you ran out there tonight, to keep her company?"

"She was calling me. You heard her."

Calling her to the grave, he thought she meant. "If that was her, she's called me for years."

"And tonight you went to her."

He snorted softly. "And she rewarded me."

He splayed his palm across her breast and felt the steady beating of her heart. She coughed, not for the first time tonight. "I wanted you to want me."

He didn't respond, and she said, "Hasn't this been a horrid day, Eli?"

Not all of it. "What did you talk to Cummings about?" he asked.

She coughed again. "Shiloh."

"What did you want to—"

Without warning, she flipped over and buried her face in his chest. The hair on her crown tickled his chin. "I have a terrible headache," she said. "Let's not talk about death any more tonight."

That was fine with him, though he wouldn't have minded her bringing what bothered her out in the open and his dispensing of it once and for all.

Chapter Forty-four

"You know who you faced?"

Eli motioned her forward and fluffed the pillows behind Alice's head. "Lay back," he said. When she did, he placed his palm against her forehead. Hot, and he drew a deep breath before pulling a lock of hair over her shoulder.

She rolled her head in the direction of his hand. "I need to plait it. It's gonna tangle."

"Aunt Naomi should have already made it to your uncle's house by now. Your Aunt Betty should be here soon. She'll help you."

Alice coughed—hard and dry—then found his eyes. "How long have you known?"

"Quit worrying about this, Alice."

"Please tell me."

The fever was taking its toll, so was her anxiety. "Since the sixth of April 1862."

"That was the day before Andrew was killed."

"Yes."

"You knew all the time."

He swallowed. "I knew we were fighting the Army of the Ohio. I didn't know until the day after Andrew was killed that the unit we faced across that field was a unit from Ohio. I didn't know the regiment number and I sure didn't know your father and brothers were with them. Never even thought about it. I started to suspect last night when you brought up Shiloh. That's when I realized what was bothering you. It had nothing to do with my wanting to marry you." A quick knock sounded on the door. "If it'd been vengeance alone I wanted," he said, watching

Miss Elvie, cup in hand, step into the room, "I would not have married you."

"You'd have been happy simply to disgrace me?"

"Degraded and humiliated you." He turned to Miss Elvie. "What's in it?

"Quinine and onion water," the old woman said, handing him the cup. "Don't let 'er burn 'ersef, but make 'er drink it all."

He took the cup in both hands, then found the handle. Damn, the stuff was hot. He scooted closer to Alice. "Here."

She looked at the cup, then to his face. "Why would you have done such a thing?"

"I didn't."

"Would you, had you not wanted the money?"

His hand tightened on the cup, and he stifled a curse. Miss Elvie stepped back, out of prudence he suspected, and from the corner of his eye, he watched the old woman move to the stove.

"Would you have allowed me to?" he asked.

Behind him, he heard the Negress feeding the fire. The day had dawned clear and cold. *That's the real question, isn't it sweetheart? Why did you allow me to force you into marriage?* He relaxed a bit when Alice didn't answer.

"Be careful of your answer, my beauty."

"Maybe," she whispered, "I'm the one seeking vengeance."

Doing penance more likely. "If so, you're doing a poor job of exacting it." Eli extended her the cup, and she took it. "Do you blame me for the loss of your father and brothers?"

"You weren't at the battles where my father and brothers were killed." She breathed in the brew, but showed no reaction to its smell.

"Did Caw tell you that?"

"Mr. Cummings. I couldn't bear to stay in Mr. Pruitt's presence after I found out. He loved Andrew so."

"Drink it," he said softly, nodding to the cup she was holding. "Is what worries you the chance I think your father or one of your brothers shot Andrew?"

"One of them could have."

"By day two, the Army of the Ohio had over 40,000 men in it, so the odds are against that having happened. And even if it did, we're never gonna know. More importantly, it doesn't matter. Neither your father nor your brothers had anything personal against Andrew. We were at war with one another."

"I've not thought of the senselessness of it for days," she said, then winced when she sipped the brew.

"Senseless, sweetheart? You pure Americans had to destroy the evil South, which apparently was composed of something less."

She closed her eyes. Her body ached, her head pounded, and she'd burned her tongue on what was supposed to serve as healing brew. But there was no magic cure for what ailed her—only her own strength could do that, and that had weakened over the past week—else she'd not be sick at all.

But neither physical suffering nor scalding liquid had caused her downtrodden spirit.

Alice blinked when Eli shifted his weight, and she watched as he pulled the quilts up over her chest. His hands seemed strong and steady, but she thought there might be worry in his eyes, in the set of his mouth. "Who will you marry with Laura gone?"

He stilled. "I'm married to you."

"If I die, I mean?"

"Whoever I would have married if you'd never come down here, and she wouldn't have been Laura."

"Will you grieve long, do you—"

"Shut up, Alice."

His visage blurred. She thought if he were to die, she'd miss him. She wanted him to miss her, if only for a little while.

She bowed her head when she felt him move. Then he was very close, his palms cupping her jaws and pushing her face up. "Hush," he said, wiping the tears off her cheeks with his thumbs, "you're not going to die."

"I've never felt this awful in my life, not even when I was throwing up four days ago."

At Alice's side, Miss Elvie said, "Drink dat med'cine I made fo' you."

Alice brought the cup to her lips, and Eli sat back. Though still hot, the concoction was cooler now, and she managed it. Eli took the cup and handed it to Miss Elvie. Alice lay back.

"Auntie Elvie has pulled a number of people through pneumonia."

Alice closed her eyes and listened as the door closed. "But how many has she lost?"

He squeezed her fisted hands lying in her lap. "Can I get you anything else?"

"No answer?"

"I don't know the answer. She knows folk remedies, but she's not a miracle worker."

Her chest swelled with grief and remorse and perhaps a touch of anger, she wasn't sure. "Do you want me to die, Eli?"

"No."

"You'd have everything then."

"I have everything now."

"You're saddled with me." She sucked in a painful breath. She wanted him to tell her he liked her.

He leaned forward and kissed her forehead. "And you're a damn good ride."

She tilted her face to his and frowned, not sure what he meant, and he brushed her lips with his. Sex. He'd been speaking of sex. She opened her mouth to retort, but a brisk knock at the door drew his attention from her. She followed his gaze as Cassie, followed by Aunt Betty, stepped into the room. Miss Elvie, standing in the hall, nodded to Eli and closed the door.

Eli rose off the bed, and her cousin, pretty with cold-flushed cheeks and a bright smile, took his place beside her. "What is wrong with you, darling?" she said, taking Alice's hands in hers.

The chill on Cassie's glove-covered fingers felt good. "I fear I've taken ill."

Alice cast her aunt a furtive glance, but Eli was already approaching the woman, and her aunt, her eyes full of questions, did little more than acknowledge her presence before focusing on him.

"Let's talk out here," he said and opened the door.

Alice's heart sank. She wanted to know what he told her, but Cassie was already jabbering away and stopped only long enough to press Alice's fingers. Alice turned to her.

"My heavens, Alice, he is, I swear, the most handsome man I have ever laid eyes on. Is his lovemaking as good as his looks?"

"She threw up—"

"More Camellia Creek food?" Betty Franklin snapped.

Eli stared at her, stiff and indignant, her back to the closed bedroom door. "Blood," he said.

The woman narrowed her eyes on him. "Since she's come to live with you she stays ill."

Eli's gut tensed, not so much the result of Betty Franklin's finding fault with his care of Alice, but because the seriousness of his wife's ailment was sinking in. She was a little thing, but she'd seemed healthy enough when they wed. But the truth was he knew nothing of her general health growing up. He did know about stomach ailments—they weren't uncommon—and he knew about pneumonia—all too often fatal when afflicting a frail body.

"Is she prone to sickness?"

The woman's mouth tightened, souring her pretty face. "She has the constitution of an ox..."

That particular analogy didn't suit his petite Alice.

"...when it's not being tampered with."

Eli frowned. "Tampered with?"

Hands on hips, she leaned toward him so that the feathers on her hat almost touched his chin. "Come now, Calhoon. We both know that all you lose if Alice dies is an unwanted wife. You've gotten all out of her you can. Who has given her what to eat or drink?"

"She's had quinine and onion water." He nodded at Aunt Elvie standing several feet away, listening. "That's to fight her fever and the ailment. Last night, I got some chicken soup in her, which," he said between clenched teeth, "she told me you brought her yesterday morning.

"Let's review who has what to gain from her death, Mrs. Franklin. First, I haven't begun to get all out of Alice that I desire. Second, your land-lusting husband has his eye on Camellia Creek. If Alice dies and you manage to fix the blame on me, my family farm will be clean and clear for you to move in."

The slap would have stung more had she removed her gloves when she came in the door. "How dare you say such a thing to me!"

How dare he indeed? He brought his hand to his burning cheek. "I'll give you that one, *Aunt Betty*. I deserved it. Alice is hot to the touch, her skin is dry, as is her cough, and her spittle is tinged with blood. She hasn't been poisoned, and I don't need a physician to tell me she has pneumonia. I asked Aunt Naomi to stop by Doc Lester's after she saw you. In the meantime, we here at Camellia Creek are dealing with the disease the same way we always have. If you Yankees with your superior intelligence know another remedy you're welcome to try it. I'll not question you."

He turned on his heel and walked out the front door. Betty closed her eyes and folded her arms over her breasts. Her body shook. She couldn't believe she'd actually struck the man, but his allegation had been intolerable. She started to turn, but stopped when she noticed the old darkie Elvira Hinny watching her.

"He had no right to accuse me of wanting my niece's death."

Miss Hinny took a step toward her. "You shouldn'ta been accusin' 'im or me neither."

Betty dropped her arms. "You know he only married her for her fortune."

The old eyes narrowed. "Don't know dat a'tall. Have no idea why he wed into the likes of you mean, know-it-all people."

"You are an ignorant, ungrateful—"

The withered old black-skinned heathen cackled at her. "And what's I s'posed to be grateful to you fo'?"

"Your freedom."

"And what's an old woman to do wif dat?"

Betty bit her tongue; she was starting to sound like Eustacia. What was a poor old female darkie to do with freedom at her age? This woman simply needed to be cared for. Eli Calhoon's acknowledgment of her unwanted freedom would amount to abandonment. Dry-mouthed, Betty spun to the door. "Be happy, I guess. Enough men died to make you so."

Miss Hinny snorted. "Don't you try an' lay what happened at da feet of us niggers down here, tryin to find right in da murder and rapin' and destruction you all done an' all da time mosta you up der lookin' down on us lots mor'n our own white folk do."

Betty's heart was pounding in her chest. She could not believe she was hearing such opinions from the mouth of this woman.

Slowly shaking her cloth-covered head, the old Negress stepped around her, keeping her distance from Betty as if she believed her contaminated. "And I'll tell you somethin' mo'."

Good Lord, she didn't want to hear another thing from this old witch. Until the lunatics in the South seceded, threatening to permanently divide the Union, she never would have believed the last four years could happen. But they did. She glared at Elvira Hinny. Now all *these* people were free to run loose, unsupervised, and here she was, stuck, somewhat against her will, in a state full of them. "Say it," she hissed, "and be done with it."

"If you No'thern womens weren't so stupid and quick to judge dem you know nothin' 'bout, you'd know you ain't da only one scared for missy in dat room right now."

Chapter Forty-five

"Dem Yankees thinkin' you kilt Miss Laura, ain't dey?" Aunt Elvie asked Eli.

"I'm afraid so."

Laura's murder wasn't Eli's main concern this morning, but except for Alice's illness, it might have been. He sat on the bottom step leading to the back door of the cookhouse, arms on spread thighs, and stared down at the dirt.

"Would you have done that, Elvie?"

"Kilt Miss Laura?"

He looked up quickly. "No. Married a man you hated to protect someone you cared about?"

She turned back to the wash pot and stirred the sheets soiled with Alice's bloody vomit. Around sunup he'd failed to get the wash bowl to her in time. "'Pends on how much I cared 'bout da one and hated da other. 'Sides, Eli, don't you be askin' me. I rather be dead mysef dan tied to some fool man."

He chuckled at that. First time all morning he'd felt even remotely like laughing. "I remember Aunt Naomi trying to persuade Daddy to sell you to Harrison Lee over in Raymond, so you could marry his driver. You remember that?"

"Dat be Romeo Tatum." She shook her head. "Nimi wanted me gone from Camellia Creek."

"Romeo wanted you, too, I recall that real clear."

"No you don't. When yo' little white sef eva talk to 'im? You was scared to def I was gonna leave you wif yo' aunt."

"I wasn't afraid of Aunt Naomi, Elvie, but I did love you and didn't want you to go away. You didn't want to go either, did you?"

"Romeo be fine, but not to be stuck wif fo' a lifetime." She pulled up a steaming sheet with the stick, looked at it, then poked it back down into the water. This end of the building where they sat—and worked—was in shade, and the morning remained cold.

"Don't know what all's 'tween you two, but I can tell you dis. Next time you 'cide to stick in da knife an' twist—just to soothe yo' pride, best consider a woman who made a choice like dat might'n got much reason to carry on."

Eli averted his gaze from her scrutiny.

"Her heart like to give up as not. 'Dat ain't what she's needin', so make sure 'dat's what you want."

"You think I do that?"

"Sho' you do. Throw da war and da differences 'tween you two up like a stone wall eva chance you git."

Perhaps he did. Despite the sinking feeling that accompanied the admonition, Eli grinned at the old woman—she didn't see because she was bent over the pot. "Well, there is the war between us." He shrugged. "And her money uniting us."

"So's you don't need 'er no mo'," Miss Elvie said and poked out her bottom lip. "Her money, I reckon, hurtin' yo' pride mosta all."

Eli cursed softly, and Miss Elvie set the stick aside.

"You come he'p me now so's we can git dese dry fo' da sun go down."

He stepped off the porch as she stepped back away from the pot, wiping her hands on her skirt. "Ain't a soul lef alive knows you better'n me, Eli Calhoon."

Alive or probably even dead.

Eli pulled the gauntlets from his sweating hands and stuck them in the waistband of his britches. Despite the chilly afternoon, he'd managed to heat himself up traipsing through the woods between Camellia Creek and Bayou Pierre. He'd come to the southern end of that ridge and hollow, which paralleled a bend in the Mississippi for most of the distance between the two lesser waters. Here, he was a good fifty yards from Bayou Pierre, and now he debated the possibility of clearing up the hollow on both ends—subtly suggesting an alternate new bed for the Father of Waters, when and if the mighty stream decided to change course.

Fifteen minutes ago, he'd spied what he thought was a stranger on his land—about twenty yards inside dense underbrush that had grown up along the creek bank during the war years. Closer inspection had revealed it was Peter Franklin's nephew, Jon.

Eli hadn't hailed him—he was in no mood to deal with the man. The last time Eli saw him, Jonathan Franklin had been unconscious. But now Eli did consider seeking him out. He was curious as to what he was doing on Camellia Creek in view of the fact that Major Parker's Sergeant Zachary had shown up at the house earlier, seeking Betty Franklin, who he hoped could tell him where her nephew was. Maybe good ole Major Parker had started sniffing in the right direction.

Decision made, Eli stood and took a good look around. Jon Franklin had disappeared, and Eli concluded that was fine with him, after all. Franklin had probably seen him and meandered back to his side of the creek. Eli stole another look at the tree-filled hollow. These weren't saplings. Some of the oak and gum and pine had been growing, untouched, he wagered, well over fifty years. He might have to cut some timber to do what he was thinking, and for the moment figured he'd best stick with trying to control Camellia Creek.

He pulled off his cavalry hat, and wiped his forehead with the back sleeve of his coat. For a fleeting moment he considered he needed to make arrangements for burying Laura. As an ex-brother-in-law he was as close as could be found for next of kin.

The sun was west of him now, though he couldn't see it from the woods where he stood. He'd head on over the hill, hit Bayou Pierre, then continue east and home.

He'd been gone a good two hours, but it had gotten crowded at his house. In addition to Betty and Cassie Franklin's fussing over Alice, Aunt Naomi had shown up with a noon meal of fried squirrel and butter beans. That had caused some bristling in the kitchen, since Aunt Betty (left alone, on purpose Eli suspected, by Aunt Elvie) had been floundering in there looking for pots and pans to prepare soup for Alice.

That left Betty and Naomi sparring in the kitchen. Eli shook his head. Naomi Polk had never given quarter when it came to Camellia Creek's kitchen, and Betty Franklin was in no mood to kowtow to anybody. So when Sergeant Zachary showed up, he hadn't caught Aunt Betty at a good time. She didn't know where Jon was, and she told him to go ask her husband. Zachary responded he couldn't find Peter Franklin. The Franklin's cook told him he'd find the family here.

Well, he found only part of the family at Camellia Creek, and not the part he wanted. Eli figured Zachary's lack of wanting any part of Betty Franklin had grown with each tick of the clock as the man stood on his porch, forage hat in hand, doing his best to be polite. In fact, Eli figured the only thing the sergeant had wanted soon after he found "Miss" Betty was to get away from her. Go to the Freedman's Bureau in Port Gibson, she told him. Peter had made friends there.

The sweet-faced Zachary had nodded with a quick, "Thankee, ma'am," and was turning to leave when he spied Elvira Hinny at the corner of the porch. A friendly face, the poor soul must have thought. He started to speak to her, but another soldier Eli had heard addressed as Private Ball charged up the porch steps with Auntie's appearance, moved in front of his sergeant, and with a big smile on his face, raised two dead chickens, head, feathers, and all for her to see. "We'll share wif you, Miss Hinny," he said, "if you'll fry 'em."

Elvie asked where he'd stolen 'em, and he lowered the chickens, his smile gone, his face crestfallen, but Aunt Naomi reached out and took the birds. "I'll do it. One for us and one for you."

Aunt Naomi was disappearing around the corner of the porch headed for the kitchen, when Elvie motioned for the young men to follow her. Even the two listening in the yard grabbed the bridles of their four horses and started after her around that end of the house. The last words Eli heard as he pulled the front door shut and started down the porch in the opposite direction were Elvie's, admonishing the fellas for their role in inflicting misery on the poor folk they dared claim to be helping.

With the sweet sound of her words, misdirected though they might have been, echoing in his ears, he'd headed for the woods.

"Massa Eli!"

Buck, and he was calling from some distance away. Eli, heartbeat quickening, called "Yo" to orient the man to his location. Weaving back through the trees, Eli headed in the direction of the hail. He saw Buck about the same time Buck saw him.

"Dat aunt of yo' wife's done sent me to fin' you," he called.

"What's wrong?" But foreboding had already settled on his chest, and he quickened his pace.

"Yo' wife's done took a turn for the worse," Buck said, stopping when Eli reached him.

$\mathcal{D}$octor Lester stepped from the bedroom into the hall. He'd been about to pull the door shut, but Eli inserted himself at the threshold and looked at Alice, small and frail beneath the covers on the bed. He started in…

"She's sleeping," the doc said. "Let me talk to you before you go to her." With that, the doc pulled the door shut and pushed Eli back into the hall.

"It's not good, I'll tell you that. I don't know if she's going to make it through the night."

Eli's gut clenched. As many times as he'd been exposed to it, pneumonia's lethality never ceased to amaze him. He blinked at the older man, who watched him with sympathetic eyes.

"What do I need to do?"

"Keep her warm and as much water in her as you can. Her aunt and Elvie know. Other than that and whatever the hell Elvie has already given her, there's nothing you can do but pray. She'll make it or she won't."

Eli started for the bedroom, then stopped abruptly. "Laura's remains…?"

"Naomi's taking care of it," the doctor said. "You get in there with your wife now."

The bedroom door opened, and Betty Franklin stepped into the hall. "I'm going for Peter," she said to him. "He'll never forgive himself if she leaves us tonight"—her face contorted slightly, and she sobbed—"and him still angry with her."

Eli nodded—he really didn't give a damn if Franklin ever forgave himself or not—and started around her.

"I'll go, Mama," Cassie said, rushing to catch up with her mother. "You stay with Alice."

Eli maneuvered through the door and closed it. Quiet, except, he noted stepping toward the bed, for Alice's labored breathing.

Insides taut, chest heavy, Eli sat beside her and took her hand. For a moment he studied it, clammy as the mud along Camellia Creek's bank. He hadn't even given her a ring. Gently squeezing her fingers, he looked to her face, her skin so pale he could have traced the blue veins beneath its surface. Her hair was neatly plaited, though wisps had escaped their confines and curled softly around her face. She was so beautiful. Young and beautiful.

Leaning forward so that his lips almost touched her ear, he said softly, "Your enemy is here, sweetheart, waiting for you. Let's see some spunk or you're going to leave me a widower, and I'll spend your ill-gotten Yankee money on the South and easy women."

Chapter Forty-six

After midnight. Eli prayed Alice would just wake up and end this interminable nightmare. Twice he'd shaken her to make sure she was still alive. Betty Franklin had run him out of the sickroom minutes ago. He needed a break, she said, and he did. He relieved himself in the yard, then climbed the back steps to the cookhouse.

"Did you get more soup in her?" Aunt Naomi asked.

Eli shook his head and lifted the coffee pot off the stove. The woman had tiptoed around him all day. He hadn't forgotten the things she'd said the night before, and he was sure she hadn't either, but she hadn't broached the incident either. She handed him a speckle-ware cup before he had a chance to start looking for the mug he'd set aside hours ago.

"She'll not get better without sustenance."

"She's about out of her head with fever. She's not conscious."

Naomi grunted and moved from his side. "Elvie made corn-bread."

He could smell it, it and the chicory in the freshly-brewed coffee. If only he had an appetite. "It's in the oven?"

"Yes. Brought some buttermilk back with me, too. It's on the porch."

In a pitcher covered with a cloth. Kept good that way in the wintertime—well, part of the time it did—and he wondered where Aunt Naomi had gotten it, then decided he didn't care. "Maybe later. I don't feel like eating."

"You didn't have dinner or supper. You're going to need your own strength, if you plan to take care of her."

Eli stared at her, and she turned away. After a moment, he

opened the oven door. The chamber was still hot from making the coffee. The firebox needed to be emptied, he knew, because he'd heard Aunt Naomi tell Elvie to do it before breakfast. If his aunt had kept her mouth shut, Elvie would have done it on her own, but Eli figured the chances were slim Auntie had done it after Naomi Polk directed her to.

"Let me get it," Aunt Naomi said and pushed him gently out of the way. A minute later she'd cut him a long, crusty edge, and the piece looked and smelled so darn good he considered retrieving the buttermilk outside and breaking the bread up in it.

The breezeway door pushed open, and Peter Franklin stepped inside the kitchen. His gaze met Eli's, and he hesitated. Then he looked at Aunt Naomi, who turned her back on him.

"I was told there's fresh coffee out here," he said to Eli.

"There is." Eli took a bite of the bread at the same time he turned to the rough-hewn breakfront, now clean and neatly filled with a mismatched set of chipped mugs, cups, and speckle-ware. He pulled a mug out for Franklin and washed his food down with a swig of his own brew. "I saw your nephew earlier today."

Franklin poured coffee in the mug and, with a question in his eye, looked at Eli, who pulled out a chair and sat. He motioned for Franklin to do likewise. "He was on my land."

"Probably an accident," Franklin said. "Since you don't want your neighbors inadvertently wandering onto your property, I'll tell him to be more careful."

"I don't mind my neighbors on my land"—Eli was torn between calling him the less formal "Franklin" or being flippant and addressing him as Uncle Peter—"Mr. Franklin. I just wondered if there was anything in particular he was searching for."

"Wayne Hale's grave," Aunt Naomi said, setting a lidless sugar bowl down hard on the table.

Eli jerked his face up and looked at her. She was glaring at Franklin, who in turn watched her with his mouth wide open.

"I'm sorry?" Eli said to her.

She looked at him. "He's looking for Wayne Hale's grave, if you want my opinion."

Well, he hadn't even considered her opinion, but now, he had to admit, he was glad to have it.

"Everyone against you, Eli, is out to put Wayne's death off on you."

He wondered how many people were against him. He turned to Franklin, who'd managed to overcome his surprise and close his mouth. Such a ploy would benefit the man—with Eli out of the way, he could marry Alice off to that arrogant, two-faced, snake-in-the-grass nephew of his, and they'd have Camellia Creek. And maybe ole Seth Parker wasn't wising up after all. Maybe he'd decided to take advantage of the Franklins' easy access to Camellia Creek and had recruited Jonathan to gather information for him. Eli squinted at Peter Franklin. Maybe *Uncle* Peter, too.

Eli immediately dismissed the thought. Why would Parker resort to such? The United States government hadn't respected the Fourth Amendment in years. "I'm not sure the authorities are convinced Wayne is dead," he said instead. "Some members of Major Parker's troop were here earlier looking for Jon. Do you and your nephew know something I don't?"

Peter Franklin blinked at him. "I beg your pardon?"

Eli opened his mouth to speak, but a gust of wind rattled the back door. A wail echoed the wind, and Eli rose. Peter Franklin, watching him, asked, "What's the matter?"

Eli looked at him, but said nothing. The wail rose again, and Eli pushed his chair from the table, then stepped around it. Franklin's eyes darted to Aunt Naomi.

"It's only the wind," she said.

"No," Eli said, heading for the breezeway door, "it's a banshee."

And he'd be damned if he'd let her take Alice.

Chapter Forty-seven

Suffocating from excitement, Alice yanked open the door and blinked back tears at the sight of him. Giving up, she let the tears of joy come and threw herself into Michael's arms.

"How can this be?" she asked, her cheek on his shoulder. She could touch him, smell him, feel the coarse wool of his blue uniform against her skin, the strength in his arm around her waist. He was here.

"I can't stay long."

"You've seen Papa and Jason?"

He nodded. "Everything is all right, Alice."

With a heavy heart, she pushed away. "You've come for me?"

"No."

She sucked in a ragged breath. "You don't want me, because I betrayed you?"

"No, you haven't."

"You don't know what I've done."

"Yes, Alice Suzanne, we do."

"I have nothing to live for."

He pulled her close and kissed the top of her head, the way he had when he left at the end of his last furlough, Christmas, 1863. "He wants you. You must go back, and quickly."

She searched his face, but when she opened her mouth to speak, he caught her face in his hands. "There's nothing to forgive. We love you, now let us go."

A quick, rough kiss to her cheek, and he stepped from the threshold of their Ohio home. "Hurry," he said. "You'll have to fight to get back now, but he'll help you."

No, no, no... she reached for him, and he disappeared from the porch into a fog. Crying his name, she surged forward only to find herself alone *in the gloomy twilight of Camellia Creek's front porch. From the woods out back, a wail rose and a frigid wind chilled her bones. Dusk darkened to night. Holding her breath, she looked through the window pane to the lighted room inside. The wail expanded to a howl and the wind tore at her hair and whipped her skirt. She was fighting the storm to reach the door. She grasped for the doorknob, but when her trembling hand finally managed to seize it, it wouldn't turn.*

Eli.

At her back, the howl expanded, and the thing that made it moved closer. Inside, he cried her name. Cloistered by darkness, she growled and rattled the door, then caught her breath and cried his name in refrain.

Sweat burst from her fevered flesh. The door flew open. He grasped her to him, his arms strong and warm and inviting.

"Shhh. Hush, Alice." Eli rubbed her back as she burrowed her head into his chest and twisted her fingers into his shirt, pulling him closer yet. "Hush," he whispered again, then kissed the top of her head when she whimpered. "I'm here. It's okay."

Off kilter himself, Eli jumped when the bedroom door flew open. An ashen Peter Franklin looked first at him, then at his wife, standing beside Eli and Alice with her hand covering her mouth. From his stricken visage, Eli knew the man thought Alice had passed from them, and indeed, for the span of a heartbeat, Eli had been certain he'd held a lifeless body in his arms.

"She was dreaming, Papa," Cassie said, her voice breathless. The girl sat, wide-eyed, on Alice's other side. She'd been about to place yet another cold compress on her cousin's forehead when Eli rushed in. "She was dreaming about Michael."

Franklin stepped into the room. "Is she all right?" he asked.

Methodically shaking her head, Betty Franklin blinked back tears and dropped the hand from her lips. "Something happened." Betty looked toward the covered windows, then her gaze sought Eli's. "Out there. You knew, that's what brought you back here so suddenly."

Betty sucked in a breath, then looked at her husband. "She had a nightmare. That god-awful wind outside frightened her.

She was the one who screamed." Betty stepped to where Eli sat with Alice still in his arms and placed her hand on Alice's forehead. Closing her eyes, she pushed her fingers back into Alice's hairline, then slumped in obvious relief. "She's sweating," she choked out and, with a smile, looked over her shoulder at her husband. "The fever's broke."

Eli tried to lay Alice back onto the pillows, but she clung to him until she opened her eyes and surveyed the room with little glances. Making sure, he reckoned, of where she was and who she was with.

"Lie back," he whispered. "You're among the living."

She blinked at him, as if his words held some meaning for her and allowed him to lay her back on the pillows before her eyes sought her aunt Betty.

"Michael told me to come back."

Betty Franklin had taken the cool compress from Cassie and now washed Alice's face. "It was only a dream, darling."

"No, he was real." Alice rolled her head on the pillow and looked at her uncle, now near the foot of her bed. "The very fact that Uncle Peter has come to see me tells me how close I came. I was there. I was on the other side." She gave her uncle a weak smile and held out her hand. Sour-faced, Peter Franklin stepped forward and took it.

"Rather an extreme measure to go to, gal, to make your peace with me."

"I love you, too, Uncle Pete."

He smiled at her then and coughed—getting rid of the tears at the back of his own throat, Eli reckoned.

An hour or so before dawn, Eli got an exhausted Betty and Cassie situated comfortably upstairs. Betty was hesitant to leave Alice and told Eli point blank she didn't want Naomi Polk attending her niece. Hiding his irritation at the woman's barely veiled presumption to control the comings and goings of folk within his house, Eli told Betty he would be with Alice. Aunt

Betty's concern ultimately proved for naught, because Peter Franklin escorted Aunt Naomi back to town, from where he intended to return to his own house. Elvie took responsibility for the kitchen.

"I've slept for hours, but I'm so tired."

"The sickness has sapped your strength," Eli said, climbing into bed beside her. "You'll sleep a lot over the next few days. I do believe I've gained myself a sickly female."

"A rarity among you hardy Southern stock, I'm certain. You people prefer a sudden death for your women?"

"I will say this for them, when they get ready to go they git. They don't linger through one illness after another." Which, of course, was hokum.

She became very still. Sensing her anxiety, he wrapped his arm over her waist and snuggled closer.

"He told me you wanted me," she said.

Eli frowned in the darkness. "Michael?"

"Yes."

And how would he know? "It was only a bad dream."

"I touched him, smelled him. It wasn't bad. Not until he left and Jocelyn cried to me."

Or cried *for* her. Certainly that had been his fear when he heard the woe on the wind.

"I only came back because of what he said."

More ghosts, more doubts. He rolled onto his back so she wouldn't feel his erection. "Do you think I wanted you to die?"

He felt her turn so that she faced him. "If you did, then Michael lied to me."

"Maybe you wanted to come back to me, and you conjured up Michael to tell you to do what you couldn't convince yourself to do."

"He was real—"

A sob swallowed her words, and he crushed her to him. "I do want you." He felt her head upon his chest, her hand pressed against his nipple beneath his undershirt. She was warm and alive and vibrant despite the faint scent of sickness that permeated her skin. The smell of lavender-laced sweat filled his nostrils, the lingering essence from her hair, dull and limp in the aftermath of her illness. Gently, he rubbed her back.

"The day you saw Jocelyn at the creek, was she on your side or mine?"

"I saw her reflected in the water."

Eli felt her raise her head.

"The stream had become more a pool than a moving body of water. A mirror. She was reaching for me."

The hair along the back of his neck rose on end.

"She was on your side. She wasn't there when I looked up, but I saw you, too far away to be what I'd seen."

"That makes sense."

"What makes sense?"

He turned his body slightly toward her. "That she was on my side. Haints can't cross water."

"You believe me?"

He didn't know what to believe, but he'd just endured a horrific twenty-four hours and it was the specter, real or imagined, of Jocelyn LeBlanc that had drawn Alice, already feeling poorly, into the stormy night the evening before.

"Was she beckoning you into the creek?"

Alice was very still. "You think…? No," she said and lay her head back down, then pressed herself close. "She didn't beckon me."

"You said she was reaching for you."

"To help me cross, I think. I was looking for a way."

And how could an ephemeral spirit manage that?

"She warns me, Eli. She wants me to help her find her killer."

"She warned you about me?"

"Should she have?"

He chuckled, only moderately relieved by Alice's assurance that Jocelyn meant her no harm. "Well, you looked up and saw me."

"Maybe she wanted me to see you. Wanted us to be together. I can't help her if I'm not here at Camellia Creek, can I?"

"Mercenary, don't you think?"

He felt her shrug. "Maybe instead of believing I wanted to die, she wanted me to have something to live for."

"Her or me?"

"I only know that Michael sent me home to you. He didn't mention Jocelyn." Against his chest, her head moved, with some degree of conviction, he noted. "But she was there, Eli, calling to me, not to come to her, but driving me home to you. I've absolutely no doubt of it."

He wished he were that sure.

Chapter Forty-eight

"I don't need a search warrant."

The pork-faced lawyer propped one hand on the arm of his chair and situated his stout body to face Seth directly.

"You intend to invoke martial law to ransack my office, Major?"

Seth hadn't suspected Tobias Holbein would be so hostile, but then the man was a lawyer.

"Let me advise you that I am seventy-three years old. I'm a Whig. I opposed secession, and I was too damn old for the draft. You'll find no record of my supporting the Confederacy and I've spent my time since 1863 hobnobbing with occupying Federal officers. I have friends in high places, so I would advise you to tread lightly in attempting to intimidate me."

There might be no record of him supporting the Confederacy, but Seth had no doubt, when rhetoric turned to bullets, where Tobias Holbein's sympathies had aligned. Still, he probably did have friends in blue uniforms—just as Isabel Leigh Hays did. Seth narrowed his eyes on the defensive little man. Maybe this lawyer and Isabel had mutual friends.

Seth braced his arms on the surface of Holbein's desk and leaned forward. "I've got two men outside your front door, right now. They would love to tear your office apart and could before you covered a city block."

"And you could go home in disgrace."

"Not likely, unless General Wood himself is part of your plot."

Holbein's eyes widened in what Seth knew to be feigned surprise. "What plot?"

"The theft and resell of confiscated Confederate cotton."

The man relaxed in his chair. "And privately owned cotton and already consigned cotton and any other damn cotton Federal thieves can doctor the paperwork on, transfer, and accept illegal payment on." Holbein smiled. "I've heard of such goings-on."

"You've heard of Alan Guthrie."

"I knew Alan Guthrie."

"You were working with him?"

"Are you implying he was in need of a lawyer or that he was involved in the illegal sale of cotton and by association, so was I?"

Seth straightened. "Either. Both."

"Guthrie and I had mutual acquaintances. We knew each other socially, that's all."

"Appears he needed new acquaintances."

"Obviously."

"Are you acquainted with Isabel Leigh Hays?"

A crooked smile moved over the man's thick lips. "Only for about the last thirty years. She's a client and an old friend."

"And are you a client of hers?"

"Is that relevant?"

"Just curious."

"And as far as I'm concerned, you will remain so."

Seth smirked. "Is Elijah Calhoon also a client?"

The man's eyes narrowed. "Yes, and his father before him."

"Was he an acquaintance of Alan Guthrie?"

Tobias Holbein poked out his bottom lip in what appeared to be thoughtful consideration. "I don't know that they knew each other."

Seth could almost imagine the lawyer's mind working inside his shiny pate. "Are you thinking Eli Calhoon is involved in the cotton thefts?" the man asked.

"There is no doubt in my mind that Calhoon was involved in at least one such theft, Mr. Holbein. What I don't know is how far back, or how deeply, his involvement goes. Do you?"

"I'm sorry, Major, but I have no personal knowledge of the cotton thefts, but if you're trying to convince me that Eli Calhoon is working with Federals in any capacity, up to and including moving stolen cotton, then you must think me a fool."

"I agree with you, Holbein. That leaves him to work against us, which is my point regarding Guthrie's death."

"Do you have evidence implicating him, sir, or do you have orders to find a Southerner to blame?"

Seth blinked at the man, then flexed his jaw. "Did you know Laura Blackledge?"

The squat lawyer drew in a long breath. "Andrew Calhoon's widow. I did."

"You know she's dead?"

"I heard she was murdered four days ago. Do you think she was involved in the cotton thefts?"

"She's the one who told me of Calhoon's involvement."

"And you think Eli also killed her?"

"Can't rule him out."

"If Eli killed her, I don't think it would've been over cotton."

"I was thinking betrayal."

Holbein snorted. "Betrayal in love maybe, but I think if he were going to do that, he'd have done it years ago." He shook his head. "But not over cotton."

Seth studied the expectant gaze of the man a moment. Baited. The fat lawyer wanted more. Inwardly, Seth smiled. Well, as far as he was concerned, Holbein would remain "curious" in turn. Obviously, he knew more about the cotton-theft ring than he was letting on. That unexpected twist was something. Not exactly what Seth had been looking for when he approached the man, but it was something. The other something was that Holbein remained in Rodney. There was little left here. Sure, what was left of his clients knew where to find him, but Seth couldn't help feeling he had another reason for remaining in the vicinity.

And that particular something might prove much better.

Jubal Summers waited for him on the covered porch of Holbein's office. Sergeant Zachary was in the street holding their horses. He looked at his sergeant, then stepped off the porch and took Boone's reins.

"Well, men, I'm gonna mosey on up to see if my new lady friend has any bones to toss at me."

"You countin' too much on that Hays woman," Jubal said, putting his foot in the stirrup.

"I only count on her not to lie to me. She's too smart for that." He settled into the saddle. He was a good horseman despite his dislike at playing army. He was the son of a Kentucky plantation owner, after all. "The problem is her feigned ignorance."

"But if you ask the right questions, she —"

"I mean what comes out of her mouth is what she wants me to know or doesn't object to me knowing. It's something."

Seth turned his horse and started up the street. Jubal fell in beside him and Sergeant Zachary brought up the rear, listening, Seth knew, to every word they spoke. That was fine. The "sarge" actually offered good input from time to time.

They were about to enter the street leading to Isabel Hays' establishment when Private Ball found them. Sloppy in uniform, happy-go-lucky in demeanor, he sat a damn horse like a popped up jack-in-the-box. Jubal Summers had told Seth he didn't believe the man acknowledged a long, bloody war had just been fought, even though he'd partaken in some of it. He was dependable and eager to please, so Seth was glad to have him.

And he habitually rendered a smart salute. He rendered one now.

"Beggin' yo' pardon, suh."

Seth returned the salute. He'd left Corporal Peters and the remainder of his ten-man troop to loiter smartly in Port Gibson and watch the comings and goings at Poynter Cummings' newspaper office. It was something for them to do. He hadn't needed them with him today.

"Report, Private."

"'Bout an hour after y'all left, runner from headquawta's in Vicksbu'g come lookin' fo' ya. Dey got a telegram early dis mawnin' from da shurif in East Baton Rouge Parish, down in Lou'siana. Say a body done washed up from da Miz'sippi. Headquawta's say it might be dat fella Hale you been lookin' fo'."

Chapter Forty-nine

"You knew her," Alice said to him. "You were three, nearly four when she died."

Eli nodded.

Alice patted the settee beside her. "Come tell me about her, about her life."

She was up today. Good up. First time she'd actually dressed in six days. She had her hair pulled back tight and bound with a crocheted snood. She looked nice and kempt, but she wanted to wash her hair. He'd said no and had given Elvie strict orders not to help her and to tell him if she tried. Auntie had told Alice they'd wait till a warm day—early, so it'd be dry by bedtime. Alice had accepted that. "Please sit a minute."

"It's almost supper time. I need to wash up."

"From what? You haven't done anything all day."

He opened his mouth to protest.

"I mean to require washing up. I know you're working on your barn."

The design of it, that is. Actually he'd stayed close these past days because he wanted to keep Aunt Naomi and her aggravating presence away from his wife. He wandered off for short periods to study the creek bed and Lake Elizabeth or to supervise Buck, who required little supervision, but only when Aunt Betty was here fussing over the recuperating Alice. The Franklin woman's presence tended to aggravate *him*. Still he was grateful for it, in limited doses.

He sat by Alice. "What I remember of her deals more with scary ghost stories after her death than with her life."

"When was her ghost first seen?"

He looked at the ceiling, then at her. "First I recall, I was around ten. One of Daddy's old slaves was squirrel hunting in the early fall. Dark caught him out in a thunderstorm that blew up sudden. Uncle Jacob was his name, and I'll never forget him. Told the best stories to us kids, and Daddy, I think, figured his sighting was just another of his tales. But I do know Jacob never went near that clearing again.

"Over the years, there were sightings on Halloween, but those were more or less discounted. Kids from Port Gibson and neighboring farms actually camped out there one year on All Hallows Eve, me and Andrew included. Guy Thurston"—God, he'd been killed at Corinth—"actually claimed to have seen something, but me and Andrew didn't believe him. We didn't see anything, nor did anybody else. Besides, it wasn't even storming that night.

"Auntie Elvie, and you can talk to her about this if you like, says Bill Cherry, out there coon huntin' one fall night in the fifties saw something that scared the pooh-diddlin' out of 'im. He came yelpin' through the slave quarters 'bout three in the mornin' and set Daddy's huntin' dogs to howlin'. She didn't know who it was or what had happened for three days. Then Mr. Cherry's cook, Mamie, told her that the master had burst into the cookhouse around biscuit-makin' time before the sun came up on that particular mornin', white as the proverbial sheet and lookin' like a ghoul himself. His white hair was wet and"—Eli raised his arms to the top of his head and mimicked mussing his hair—"stickin' out every which-a-ways 'cause a storm had blown up on him. She said he grabbed his home brew he kept hid from Mrs. Cherry behind the cook stove and told her he'd seen Jocelyn's ghost hanging from that cursed tree over on Calhoon land. Forever after he denied telling her that, but she always swore he really said it and his denial was because he didn't want folks to think he was crazy."

He stopped then and grinned at her. "Now there's you."

"I've seen her and heard her and felt her."

"And you don't care if folks think you're crazy."

"But you do?"

"Care if you're crazy?"

"You know I'm not crazy, no matter what you imply. Do you care if folks around here think I'm crazy?"

"That could work to your disadvantage, darlin'."

"So you'd like folks to think I'm crazy in case you need to hang me from a tree."

"You said that, not me."

She studied him. "Who would have killed her, Eli?"

"I think she committed suicide."

"Then why can't she rest?"

"To answer that I would have to admit I believe there's a ghost."

"But you do believe. You asked me about her at the creek the night I was so sick."

"I was speculating."

Alice leaned toward him. "On her *actions*—all of which seem rational in your mind, if you believe her real."

He frowned at her. "Do you find comfort in my speculating that she might be beckoning you to an early grave?"

"I know she's not. I find comfort in your believing she's real."

"Or supporting my committing you."

She sat back. "I don't believe that."

He smiled.

"Let's think about why she would have killed herself." When he said nothing, she asked, "Another woman? You think she took her own life. She loved your father. Tell me what would have driven her to do it, if not something of that sort?"

His father's relationship with Isabel predated Jocelyn and continued after the young woman's death. How big a threat Jocelyn considered Isabel, or vice versa, he had no idea. He would have understood little of such things if he'd even been aware of them, which he wasn't. To him and Andrew, Jocelyn had been a playmate. Elvie told him years later that Aunt Naomi added fuel to that fire, doing her best to feed Jocelyn's doubts, but Elvie also said the girl ignored the woman.

"My father wasn't a saint when it came to women. There were others he knew after my mother died. I doubt many were the type of women that men of my father's class married, if you understand my meaning."

"That would have included Jocelyn?"

He shook his head and rose. He didn't know the answer to that question, not for sure, so instead he said, "Well, there's her father."

"Her father?"

"There was some speculation her father could have been responsible for her death."

"I didn't realize there was a father."

"Alice, of course there was a father. Everyone has a father. Jocelyn had a very wealthy father, Macon Treadwell. Jocelyn's grandmother was the most beautiful of octoroons. Treadwell, Jocelyn's father, lived south of Natchez, and Jocelyn's mother welcomed him whenever he could get away from the plantation, where his wife was busy birthing kids, raising kids, running a house, a farm, and—"

"Too tired to provide him sex when the sun went down."

"Passionate, perverse, prolonged sex, for certain." He shrugged. "Jocelyn had one full-blooded brother, born to her mother. Both those kids took their mother's name. She also had two half brothers born to Treadwell's legal wife. Jocelyn was the only girl and the youngest of all the children. All her brothers adored her."

"Did the three boys get along?"

Eli pursed his lips. "Like brothers, probably."

"Why would the father kill her, then?"

He shrugged. "Don't rule out the brothers, and the reason is they had higher hopes for her than being the mistress of a planter over twice her age. Her father had arranged a good marriage for her."

"And her prospective groom?"

"Indian trader."

Alice wrinkled her nose.

"The man was mixed-blood Choctaw, and wealthy. I'm sure Treadwell was considering alliances when looking at her future husband, but how important that was for him, I don't know. Supposedly, she rejected the fella."

"How did her father and brothers feel about your father?"

"I know how I'd have felt, but there were no threats or duels. I think she loved my father before Treadwell proposed the union with the Indian trader. Treadwell probably disowned her."

"So rejected by your father, abandoned by her family, she killed herself?"

"Does this mean you're agreeing with me that her death was a suicide?"

Alice blinked. "Of course not. I'm merely trying to rationalize the story as passed down."

His grin expanded, and he leaned down, planning to give her a kiss, but a loud knock sounded on the front door, followed by a hail.

Eli grimaced and stepped back. "Your boys-in-blue," he said.

Eli scrounged a side chair from the dining room and set it between his battered wingback and Alice on the settee. He looked back over his shoulder. "Your captain gonna join us?"

"This isn't a social call, Calhoon," Seth said and ignored the unspoken invite to sit.

"I didn't imagine it was."

Seth removed his cover and nodded at Alice, whose heart was pounding. She glanced at Captain Summers, watching from the parlor entrance. Sergeant Zachary stood at the front entry. They always did that. Made them feel trapped.

"Why then?" she asked, her voice soft, and turned back to Seth Parker.

"Official business, Alice," he said.

Eli bent and pulled his bottle of bourbon from behind the woodpile. A shot glass covered the top. "Cold night," he said first to Seth, then looked at the other officer, still hovering at the room's threshold. "Need something to warm you?"

"Captain Summers, you may," Seth said over his shoulder.

"I don't drink."

"Major?"

Seth looked at the bottle Eli held.

"Kentucky's finest."

"I'll not drink with you, Calhoon."

Alice felt her tension increase with Eli's shrug. He then removed the shot glass from the top of the bottle, uncorked it, then turned the bottle upside down and took a swig. He wiped his mouth on his shirt sleeve.

"It's been days since I last saw you, Parker. I was startin' to hope you'd gone back to wherever it is you came from. What brought you out here this evening?"

Alice's taxed heart quickened. Seth was going to arrest Eli, she just knew it.

"I've been out of town. Downriver, as a matter of fact, in the vicinity of Port Hudson."

Alice glanced at Summers.

"And does the matter relate to me?" Eli asked.

Immediately she focused on her husband. Seth was focused on him, too.

"Body turned up on the riverbank. Had to get it identified."

"No reason to hunker away from the campfire, Parker. Was it Wayne Hale?"

"Happens it was."

"Who identified the body?"

"Cummings."

"You've talked to Mrs. Hale?"

"We've told her."

Eli hesitated a moment. "How did she respond?"

"Mutely."

Alice watched Eli study Seth as if trying to ascertain the truth of his words.

"Coroner found six bullet holes in his back. Five exited out his front. Found one still in him. That sawbones downriver said there wasn't much left of his chest but a gaping hole, plus the body was in pretty bad shape from its trek downstream. Someone was pretty angry at him, I'd say."

"I'd say so," Eli said.

Alice's head was starting to pound.

"That one bullet indicates a standard-issue Colt."

"And I'd be willing to bet every other man in the area has one."

"Including, I'm told, Wayne Hale." Seth placed his cap back on his head and nodded. "Thought you might want to know." He started to pivot, then stopped. "By the way, May Hale wasn't totally mute when I went up to give her the news."

Eli continued to watch him, and Alice rose from her seat.

"She asked if I was investigating Laura Blackledge's death. I told her yes. She asked me if I had any idea who killed her." Seth narrowed his eyes on Eli. "She told me Laura had been up to see her the morning of the day she was killed."

Seth, the last man out of the house, closed the front door behind him. For a moment, Alice steadied herself against the side of the settee and stared at the portal fourteen feet beyond the parlor threshold. Then with an inward sigh, she turned to Eli in front of the fireplace. He had his back to her. "Intimidating son of a bitch," she heard him say. She came up behind him and touched his arm. He responded with a small twist of his head, and Alice's stomach squeezed. It had been a nice afternoon. They'd talked about Jocelyn LeBlanc and had been about to sit down to supper. Now the atmosphere in the room had chilled. Not with the physical cold that accompanied Jocelyn LeBlanc's hauntings or winter's dusk, but with a more sinister chill that lengthened the distance between her and Eli. It was as if the presence of the blue uniforms in his house reminded her husband of who she was and why he'd married her. She moved closer to him and hugged him. He wrapped his arms around her, and she laid her head on his chest.

"Go get our supper," she heard him say, his voice gentle.

She pushed back and looked at him. "You'll eat?"

"Despite my loss of appetite, yes."

She left him by the fireplace and prayed he wouldn't sneak out the front door while she was in the kitchen. Whatever shut him off from her now had to do with Wayne Hale's death, Brim Solomon, Wayne Hale's widow…and Laura Blackledge, and she knew her husband well enough to know he wasn't going to confide in her.

Chapter Fifty

"'Cause he didn't do it," Frank Zachary said.

"How come you say that?"

Sergeant Zachary closed his mouth and studied Jubal Summers. "Ain't no way dat man back yonder kilt another man like dat."

"Shootin' him in the back?"

"Shootin' 'im in da back six times."

Seth pulled his arm from the sleeve of his frock coat. "He loved Solomon like a brother, Sergeant," Seth said. It was a point. Seth didn't really need his sergeant's take on that point, but he would like to have it.

"Ain't a man in dis room knows dat better'n me, suh." Zachary watched Seth hang his coat on a rack near the door to the office Seth had commandeered from Poynter Cummings. The newsman, not too grudgingly, had moved into a smaller room adjacent to this one. He was gone for the night.

"But don't make no diff'rence. Killin' dat Hale fella like dat be a coward's way. Calhoon didn't do it."

"Why are you defendin' the man?" Jubal Summers asked Zachary, then glanced quickly at Seth. "And I don't believe any man could love another like a brother and keep him in bondage. More like a pet dog."

"Listen Jubal, I'm not trying to condone slavery to you, but trust me when I say these people care about one another. We're talking about boys that grew up together, played together, ate and slept together. Even got their scrawny little asses whupped together for doing something foolish, destructive, or just plain mean. Calhoon could have killed Wayne Hale over Solomon's murder, but I've got to agree with the sergeant that the way it was done makes me skeptical."

"I still think we should arrest him."

Seth pulled out the swivel chair to his desk and sat. Of the junior officers Seth had found hog-tied that night in Port Gibson last month, General Wood had sent three of them home—out of Mississippi. All had been, after all, innocent victims of armed men who'd beaten, stripped, and hogtied 'em for the fun of it. There was no proof they ever had any cotton, stolen or otherwise.

The newly arrived general had based that decision on the recommendation of someone in his chain of command. Seth had been unable, so far, to find out whom, and his protest had fallen on deaf ears. His continued protest was now beginning to elicit subtle warnings to ease off. He had to admit, after cursory questioning of the three, that they were underlings and probably had no knowledge of who killed Alan Guthrie, if indeed his death was even tied to cotton thieving.

More frustrating, the two mid-grades were to face a court of inquiry, but their misconduct had been deemed irrelevant to Guthrie's demise. They were under house arrest in Vicksburg and off limits to Seth, pending an investigation for conduct unbecoming an officer, which he sarcastically decided must have been their allowing themselves to be hogtied by disgruntled ex-Confederates, a conclusion based on the word of a dead woman.

Scapegoats, he figured, and he doubted, in the end, that anything would be done to them. If Guthrie hadn't been killed, and if his well-connected family were not making an issue of it, nobody would give a damn about Federal officers stealing Federal contraband—their gain ignored as a perquisite of war, but perhaps that wasn't the issue at all. Fueled by headquarters' interference in his investigation, Seth was becoming suspicious that the killer or killers served under the command at Vicksburg, or even more sinister, that headquarters had predetermined who it wanted the killer to be. That, or Guthrie had been the inadvertent victim of a bandit, and headquarters still knew who it wanted the killer to be.

Captain Jubal Summers stepped forward, forage cap in hand. Off the record, Seth had been advised he'd be losing his Negroes, too, after the first of the year. That bothered him, because he trusted this group of men implicitly, and they were loyal to a fault. Despite his personal misgivings, he did agree that getting the colored troops, as a whole, out of the South, or at least out of uniform, was imperative to the region's recovery. They were undermining the labor force, and people had to get back to work.

Jubal cleared his throat.

"Sit down, Captain." Seth leaned back. "Even if Calhoon's guilty, I think we'll learn more about what's going on if he's free to move about."

"He might run."

"I don't think so. Look, we don't know what, if anything, Wayne Hale knew regarding Guthrie's death. We don't know what he might have passed to his wife or what she in turn told Laura Blackledge." Seth shrugged. "Or maybe it was the other way around. All we have is a suspicion that Laura Blackledge's death stemmed from whatever she and May Hale talked about days ago, which, in turn, compelled Calhoon or someone else to shut her up."

Sergeant Zachary snorted. "If dat be da case, a smart man would kill dat Miz Hale. She be da one talkin' too much."

Jubal shifted in his chair. "But she's not the one threatening to tell."

Frank Zachary's mouth twisted contemptuously. "Not threatenin', bull. Dat woman ain't right, an' you know it. You two say she blurts out whatever she knows without thinkin'." The sergeant shook his head. "If'n she knows anythin', da woman's dangerous, and if I was da killer, I'da killed both 'em, not just da one."

Ruthless, but Seth agreed. If Wayne Hale's pitiful widow knew anything that could implicate a murderer, keeping her around would prove a liability. Briefly he considered putting May Hale in protective custody, then realized how absurd that would be. If the woman were a threat to the killer, she'd already be dead, and that was the sergeant's point. What Seth really thought—and Cummings agreed with him for the most part—was that Guthrie, as crooked as the mighty Mississippi itself, had a falling out with his cohort, or cohorts as the case may be. He was a threat to somebody, and his partners in crime killed him, and in so doing inadvertently disrupted the line of communications critical to their operation. At this juncture, the Union officials tapped their local contact, who Seth strongly believed was the beautiful madam, Isabel Leigh Hays of Rodney. This may have been the point where Calhoon was brought into the operation, but the Confederate cavalry officer could have been part of the conspiracy from the start. He could have killed Guthrie, then betrayed all of the thieves by forming a new group of his own. But that scenario brought Seth back around to the odds of Colonel Calhoon working with Federals in *any* capacity…and the disconcerting thought that headquarters, or was it Washington, really was looking for a Southerner to blame.

Chapter Fifty-one

ay Hale placed her hand on Alice's jaw — the woman had a gentle touch, despite the calluses on her finger tips. "You are so pretty and small, so much more to my liking for Eli than Laura." May's blue eyes twinkled, and she smiled a crooked smile, her mouth discolored with fading yellow bruises. She still had all her teeth, though, and once made a pretty woman herself, no doubt. From what little Alice knew of May Hale, she should be in her late thirties. Her dull, mousy hair already streaked with gray, she looked to be pushing fifty.

May dropped her hand. "You're near about the opposite of Laura, but I'm not surprised. I'm glad he outgrew his infatuation with her." She took Alice's arm and turned her toward the porch steps.

Alice looked back to Buck, still sitting in the rickety, miserable, hard-seated wagon she detested so. "I'll be a few minutes. Why don't you —"

"Turnips in the cookhouse, Buck. Cooked 'em yesterday for dinnertime. They're real good now. You go help yourself."

Buck tipped his slouch hat and climbed from the wagon as Alice, propelled by her hostess, climbed the three steps to the Hales' front porch.

"Come on in. I made myself some coffee and was mending some of Wayne's old clothes...." She met Alice's gaze. "There's plenty could use 'em."

The door closed behind them with a soft thud. The house was dark inside, despite open curtains. Like Camellia Creek, this neat, well-kept little four-room house, badly in need of whitewash, was surrounded by trees. Here and there, sunlight stretched across the bare floor in long, narrow streaks, and despite its dimness, the room was warm and neat.

May guided her to a rocker near the fireplace. "Union raiders never visited me up here. I was fortunate, but I still had to sell some of my furniture before the war ended. Used to have a lovely upholstered settee over by the wall." Taking her own seat, she affectionately fingered a crocheted doily on the small table next to her chair. "It was red." She sighed. "Sold it to the wife of one of the officers in Vicksburg."

"I'm sorry."

May looked at her. "Made her husband mad, I think. He thought everything we have should be theirs for the taking, but she was a good Christian woman and gave me more than it was worth. Some of you people are very kind, like us." The woman grimaced and looked away. "Kinder even than others of us."

"Mrs. Hale?"

"May, please."

Alice drew in a breath. "May, I'm sorry about your husband."

The woman studied her a long moment, and Alice held her breath. Finally May said, "Thank you."

Alice breathed only because she had to, then steeled herself. "Did Eli kill him?"

The woman reached for the service beside her. "Would you like some coffee?"

"No, thank you."

May picked up the pot. "It's chilly this morning," she said, pouring steaming brew into a porcelain cup. "You surely need something to warm you. Here, take this." She handed the cup and saucer to Alice. "You drink that now, and we'll have a nice chat about where you come from and your—"

"Please, Mrs....May, I have to know what happened here."

She was refreshing her own cup, no longer looking at Alice. "Nothing happened here."

Alice stared at the cup she held.

May looked up and smiled brightly. "I have honey. There is no sugar."

Alice nodded. May took back the cup and saucer.

"There's no milk either. I do apologize."

Alice was surprised there was even coffee. "I like honey."

With a pleased nod, May Hale spooned some into the cup, stirred, then returned the cup to Alice.

"Do you mean you know nothing of how your husband died?"

She didn't respond, and Alice swallowed.

"Do you know if your husband killed Brim Solomon?"

May frowned, then took a sip of coffee. "He said he did."

"Do you know why?"

The woman stared at her.

"May, the authorities believe Eli killed your husband."

Her eyes widened. "They've arrested him?"

"No, but…."

Alice watched the woman visibly relax and lean back in her rocker. "Eli told me not to speak of Wayne. Only to say that he was gone, and that's the truth."

"They've found his body."

"I know, but he's still gone."

Alice bit her bottom lip. "And you're glad?"

The woman's eyes glistened. "He was a strong, handsome man."

"I'm sorry I said that. I—"

"I am glad he's dead. There should be more to a man than strength and good looks." She pursed her lips. "Trust, respect." She cocked her head. "Does Eli trust you?"

Lord God, she didn't know, but she didn't think so or he'd tell her what was happening. Besides, that wasn't important now. She—

"Do you trust him?"

This time it was Alice's eyes that filled with tears.

"I trust Eli," May said, "and he told me not to talk about this."

Alice closed her eyes and pressed her fingers to her aching temples. "I want to know he didn't do any of this."

"Any of what?"

Alice ran her tongue over her parched lips, still chafed from her fever days ago. "What did you tell Laura?" she asked softly.

"That was a woman Eli could not trust."

Alice's heart skipped a beat. May Hale's demeanor ranged from mental frailty to stubborn determination. She could slip, and may have done so with Laura.

"Did you tell her what happened?"

"I—"

The clomp of boots resonated on the steps, then crossed the narrow porch. The front door opened with a loud groan, and Alice stiffened, her coffee cup suspended in mid air. Eli's glare locked on her face.

"I gave you Buck and the wagon to run errands."

Alice turned away and took a sip of coffee. Her hands were shaking so, she almost spilled it. "This was one of my errands."

"Bullshit! You were going to pick up grocery supplies in Port Gibson."

"Best to go to Vicksburg or Natchez," May said, looking at Eli. "There's nothing in Grand Gulf either, or Rodney. Miss Naomi told me so."

Alice swore Eli's face paled. "When did she come see you?" he asked.

"Yesterday. She came before the Federals."

Eli closed the front door and walked over to May, who sat staring at him. She appeared strained and so distracted by Eli's presence that Alice felt sorry for her.

"I-I—"

He held his hand palm up and mutely silenced her. "Shh, it's all right."

She smiled brilliantly then and nodded toward Alice. "Eli, she's so beautiful."

Alice dropped her jaw and turned to Eli.

"A beautiful, devious little Yankee witch."

He spoke the words with little emotion, but Alice knew he was angry. She opened her mouth to speak, but May laughed.

"No, she's not. She's concerned for you."

Eli reached for Alice's arm.

"I'm not done with my coffee."

"Or our chat," May whined, putting her own cup down.

"Yes, you are," he said to Alice, then glanced at May. "She is not here as a friend, May."

"She's here because of you," May said pleasantly. "Like Laura, but she doesn't want to—"

"May!"

The woman clamped her lips together, and Eli pulled Alice from the rocker, then started her toward the door. "Go home, and don't come back here."

With a quick breath, Alice jerked her arm from his grasp, then rubbed where he'd held her. "You can't keep me from coming back here. Do you intend to stand guard over me?" She looked around him and nodded curtly at May sitting in her rocker, watching them. "Or her?"

"I intend on talking to her."

"You should consider talking to me."

He leaned down so that his face was close to hers. "I don't want to talk to you."

She stretched her height. "You don't trust me."

"Not when it comes to this."

"Not when it comes to anything." She felt her chin pucker, and he must have noted it because he backed off just a bit.

"Go home," he repeated.

Alice drew in a breath, blinked, then turned to May Hale. "I thank you for the refreshment, May, and I'm sorry to rush off." She raised her chin and stared at Eli. "But I have some errands to run."

"You better go home."

She turned toward the door. "I'll be there when I get there."

Behind her, she heard him move. "Where's Buck?" he asked May.

"In the cookhouse."

Eli started toward the back of the house. Now Alice's head started to throb, and she whirled after him. "Don't you dare!"

"I will dare."

She caught him at the back door and pulled on his arm hard enough that he stumbled.

"Alice, I'm warning—"

"I will not be treated like a child. You can't keep me prisoner at Camellia Creek. Don't you dare tell Buck to take me home. I have things to do."

"I can't have you running around nosing into things that are not your concern."

"*You* are my concern."

"You have to trust me, Alice."

She shoved on him, then dropped her hand. "You're the one who doesn't trust me, Eli Calhoon, or I wouldn't have to resort to going behind your back."

$\mathcal{B}$uck set the brake and laid the reins on the seat. "Well, Miss Alice, don't look like he's back yet."

Alice rose from her hard perch on the wagon. Her rump was sore, and her shoulders ached. Johnny indeed was missing from the lean-to. She wasn't sure if she were dismayed or relieved over that. Eli had probably gone to Rodney to get drunk and find that whorehouse Cassie said Jonathan patronized.

"I'll get dese things in da cookhouse."

"I'll help, and thank you for talking to Mr. Pruitt for me."

"You welcome." He giggled, as if he'd heard a joke. "Sho' will be a su'prise for Mr. Eli come Christmas."

Which was coming up fast. She hoped he didn't stay angry with her till then, and having no idea what she would make for supper tonight didn't help matters. For certain, she needed to come up with something to appease the man and hoped Miss Elvira was in the cookhouse scrounging something up. She pulled a butter churn from the wagon bed.

She'd left Eli hours ago after he'd found Buck in May Hale's cookhouse. Her husband had studied the surprised colored man a moment before looking over his shoulder at Alice, admittedly livid, then told Buck to take her wherever she needed to go, but to have her home before dark or before she could get wet should the weather, as was expected, turn. "I don't want her sick again."

At the time, she'd been so relieved at Eli's relenting she'd almost wept. He hadn't spoken another word to her, but turned on his heel and gone back into the house to May. He'd probably stay sulled-up for a week.

Chapter Fifty-two

"**D**id you fry that chicken?"

From where she sat in front of the fire, Alice looked at Eli. Small talk. He'd scarcely spoken during dinner. Sulking, like she expected he would. Uncle Peter did Aunt Betty the same way. No doubt her father had acted the same toward her mother; she didn't recall, but it was doubtful she'd have been aware of the behavior, if he had.

If Eli was talking to her now, he was leading up to May Hale; she knew it.

"Miss Elvie showed me how she does it."

"And the cornbread?"

She shook her head. "I was too concerned with the chicken. Do you like collards?"

"And mustard and turnips." He glanced to the book in her lap, her spot marked with a finger. "Are you enjoying the book, Alice?"

She considered dog-earing her spot, but not a page of this volume of Machiavelli's works was blemished. She opened the book, made a mental note of her place, then held it out to him. "Here."

He shook his head. "I don't want it. I simply wondered if you were devising some strategy based on it."

"Machiavelli's reputation preceded my picking up this book, which you read like some people read the Bible. Based on what little I knew of the man, I was hoping for some insight on whatever ruthless strategy might be driving you, but after a brief perusal, I think you must be planning on founding a new system of government." She smiled. "More Southern sedition?"

He laughed. "Machiavelli's ruthless reputation does come

across as somewhat unjustified once you start reading his work. I guess I adhere more to the mythical philosophy of the man."

The end justifying the means, he meant. "So were you implying I wish to become as ruthless as you, Eli?"

"There are some things better left unknown."

"You don't want to know the answer to my question?"

He laughed again, not unpleasantly. Sweet, considering that moments before she felt he was going to light into her for her visit to May Hale.

"I know the answer to your question, sweetheart. What I was trying to get across was that you don't want to know the answer to your other question."

She swallowed hard. "What other question?"

"The one you asked May this morning."

"She told you?"

"I knew why you were there the moment I saw my wagon outside. What I couldn't believe was that you had the gall to go up there to begin with."

She tightened her hold on the book and leaned forward, but he raised a hand. "I made it clear, Alice. I don't want you nosing around in this."

"Nothing is clear, darn you. Did you kill Wayne Hale?"

He studied her with an unrelenting gaze, then said, "If I told you the truth, what would you do with it?"

"N-nothing."

"Nothing?"

Slowly she shook her head. "No."

A slow grin moved over his lips. "Now you're scared I will tell you."

Alice blinked at him. "No, I'm not."

"Yes, you are."

"I want to know."

"No, you don't, and that tells me so much about you, Alice."

She closed her eyes. "I *need* to know."

"Needing and wanting are two different things. Look at me."

She opened her eyes and found his.

"I will never tell you what happened that morning at Wayne Hale's."

"You think I would betray you."

He sat back. "Not necessarily."

She slapped the book down on the Queen Ann table beside her chair. He followed the movement with his eyes. "You must."

Slowly his gaze returned to her. "Leave it be, Alice."

"When Seth Parker lets it be, I will, too."

"Learning too much is dangerous."

She snatched up the book and held it in front of him. "Knowledge is power."

He frowned. "I believe that was Newton, not Machiavelli."

"I'm sure he says it somewhere in his own way. Did Laura know the truth?"

"She did, and now she's dead."

"And you think that's the reason?"

"What if she found out something I didn't want her to know? Something I didn't want anyone to know, and I had to kill her?"

Alice's stomach dropped.

"What if you found out?"

"I don't believe you would kill me, and I don't believe you killed her."

"Are you sure? Not even to save my own skin?" He stood then, the gleam dancing in his eye, the smirk back on his handsome mouth.

"I'm no threat to you."

He glanced at the book lying on the table. "She says, after reading my inspirational guide."

"You're trying to frighten me so I'll stop searching for answers."

He stepped toward her and held out his hand. "Maybe I don't want to have to hurt you."

"You won't." She placed her hand in his, and he pulled her to her feet. Her legs shook. He drew her close, and the scent of his clean white shirt filled her senses. Her world tilted. He held her, and his strength became her strength.

"What makes you so sure?" he whispered into her hair.

"Michael told me you wanted me."

"Ah, yes, you converse with the dead." He raised her chin and maneuvered his mouth to within a fraction of hers. His breath was warm, sweet. "But did Michael tell you why I wanted you?"

His lips covered hers before she could answer, and she closed her eyes, sinking into his embrace. He hadn't made love to her since her illness, and his kiss felt good. He abruptly pulled away, and she opened her eyes as she fell forward, him with a smug smile, steadying her. Damn him.

Liquid heat had dampened her pantaloons. They were both damned. She dropped her hand between his thighs and stroked upward. His eyes widened. "For the same reason I want you." She cupped him gently, and with a low growl, he yanked her hard to him, crushing her lips beneath his before lifting her in his arms and turning to the bedroom.

*L*ord, that was good. Eli rubbed his pelvis against her bottom, then suckled the curve of her shoulder. Alice rolled onto her back and arched when he found a breast. He kissed her eyes and lips before laying back and pulling her to him.

"I'm going to Vicksburg in the morning," he said, "then taking a packet down to Rodney. I'll take Buck with me."

"Rodney by way of Vicksburg?"

"I want to buy some laying hens. If I find any, they'll be in Vicksburg, and if you give me that bill of lading, we'll pick up your crates. I'll send Buck home after. We need to get to the Freedman's Bureau, too, and get a contract approved for him. He wants to stay with me."

"You can't do that here?"

"The agent in Port Gibson is being difficult. I own land in Warren County and that's where Buck is from."

"What about Elvie?"

"She's gonna stay, but she said the Federals could go to hell and take their Freedman's Bureau with 'em."

"She didn't say that."

"Not in those exact words, but that's what she meant."

Alice's soft sigh feathered his nipple. "They're only trying to protect the Negro."

"Perhaps they should consider protecting the Negro from themselves."

"It's different now, you know that. They need a place to live and work."

"They had a place to live and work. They need land."

Her hair brushed his chest when she raised her head. "You agree with redistributing the land?"

He heard the incredulity in her voice, but theoretically, as a student of Machiavelli, he could see the argument for providing them land—by the self-righteous hypocrites who for decades had mucked in something they didn't understand, nor, he knew, cared to understand. They echoed the pious beliefs of the abolitionists; it was their way or no way. And they'd won. But this had less to do with pious beliefs than rivalry over the wealth and power the slave system had brought the South. Power that since the beginning of the Republic had checked Northern greed. Old hatred, not something that came with the war. Deep-seated feelings that had driven the South to secede and caused the war. Radicals in the north would now do their best to destroy the South in total, including Southern beliefs and values, through destruction of the Southern economy. He'd go to his grave fighting them.

"If the bulk of the developed land is given to the freed slave to work on his own, Alice, the South will never recover."

"Do you really believe that?"

"I do."

"But the South has never made efficient use of its assets—"

"Your uncle's words, Alice, or your father's? Your Uncle Peter has been to me twice trying to figure out how to get Negroes to work for him. I've told him they don't want to work for him. They don't want to work period, first off. They don't feel free if they're working, and they sure as hell aren't going to work from sunup till sundown with no time for themselves, no patch of their own, six days a week, for a paltry wage all in the name of

Yankee efficiency. Despite your lying propaganda, they were never forced to work that way. 'Made efficient use of our assets,' you say? The difference between your people and mine, sweetheart, is that we know our *assets* intimately—what we expect of them and what they expect of us. Four years ago we had one of the strongest economies in the world—that's a good indicator we knew quite well what we were doing, and that's what the North couldn't stand. So they destroyed it rather than allow it to go off on its own. You can bet they'll do their best to keep it that way. Personally, I hope your uncle's endeavors bankrupt him and every other all-knowing Yankee peon who comes down here with the delusion he's going to 'improve' things. The true powers up North don't want things improved. They want it gone."

She was very still, and he curled her way so he could snuggle her closer. She didn't resist, as he expected she might.

"Have you taken the loyalty oath?" she asked.

"No."

"Which is why you're having trouble with the Freedman's Bureau in Port Gibson, no doubt."

He snorted.

"When will you?"

Dammit. He rolled away, onto his back. She responded by replacing her head on his chest and draping her arm across his waist, as if she meant to hold him there. "I won't," he said.

"Eli, you must. The war—"

"Two things, Alice. First, I'm a thirteenther, which means I require a Presidential pardon. I'd have to go to Washington and do penance in front of President Johnson."

"He's from Tennessee. The Radicals hate him."

Eli snorted. "I have my land, I don't require a pardon to get it back. But more importantly, the United States I believed in, was loyal to, is as dead to me as the Confederacy."

"The nation will go on. You need to be part of it."

He threw a shaking forearm over his eyes to shut out the haunting darkness. "Good Lord, woman, I can't even vote."

"But once you've re-sworn loyalty..."

"No," he said, rising on an elbow and forcing her up with him. "I'm not going to get my vote back. I'm not going to say I'm sorry I raised arms against the Union." He flopped onto the pillow. "*Against* the Union? To protect ourselves from the Union is what we were doing."

She wriggled a bit, snuggling closer. "I can't vote either."

Great, she'd put him on the same level as a woman. "The radicals desire civil rights for the Negro, including suffrage. They might as well let women vote."

"There might be peace on earth if women voted."

"Only if they each get their own way." He swallowed hard. "I was tired when the war ended. Tired and bitter. I knew things would be different, but I knew I could go on. I'm one of the lucky ones. One third of the male population of this state is dead or maimed. Except for near starvation and exposure, all I suffered was one clean shot through the side, which healed up fine. When I looked out over the Rio Grande and my prospects in Mexico, thoughts of home slapped me upside the head. I wanted peace, to begin again with whatever was left."

"Mississippi has its own civil government back, which is why you request your—"

"It's not over, Alice. I read it in the Northern papers. For three quarters of a century we caught the stench of Yankee malice wafting over the Ohio and down the Mississippi. It's closer now, rising among us, occupying us. Soon it will suffocate us. We're at the mercy of jealous, greedy people who hate us."

"People in the North are good people, Eli."

She spoke with conviction. She was, of course, speaking of herself and her aunt; her old neighbors, grieving now, who would never come south to see where their menfolk died. He should take her to Meridian so she could see how good her father and brothers could be when their restraints were removed.

"The people in your government aren't good people. By losing this war, the South has handed the Republic over to tyrants, and your good people aren't gonna do a damn thing to stop them, else they'd have never come South to begin with. Just sit back and watch what happens over the next year. You're fixing to see how bad good people can be."

"I want you to swear loyalty to the Union." A tear, unseen, resonated with her words. He wondered why she cared, but then she would. But he was every bit as stubborn.

"It will protect you, Eli."

"From what? A murder charge? Don't fool yourself."

"Your children will be American."

"*I* am an American, Alice, and I won't swear fealty to the flaming assholes who are responsible for the destruction of the nation our forefathers founded. To swear loyalty to a government that violated the Constitution in the manner they did is tantamount to high treason as far as I'm concerned. My sons will vote, but I swear they'll always be proud of their sire and what he stood for."

"And that is?"

At least she hadn't invoked that great moral vindicator, slavery. "State rights, the Constitution, and the balance of power."

"I want—"

A tiny puff of air escaped her lips when he squeezed her. "Shut up, Alice. When it comes to me and the loyalty oath, I don't care what you want." She tried to push away, but he held her to him. "Tell me something else you'd like to have and don't ask me about Wayne Hale."

Silence.

He nuzzled her ear. "I don't want to fight."

"Yes, you people down here kept saying that, but look what happened, and it was all because you were so hotheaded."

"We fought because you invaded us." Her stiff body was becoming more pliable with his every heartbeat. "You know, Mississippi is crawling with Yankees—"

"Mississippi has been *crawling* with Yankees for years."

"And I've captured me one and neutralized her." He tickled her ear with the tip of his tongue. "This one won't do any more damage."

Her arms moved over his shoulders, then tangled at the back

of his neck. "I believe if you were being fair, you'd say she's playing an important role in helping the local economy."

That she was, with her grandparents' fortune now in his hands. He kissed her lips. She kissed him back.

"Why are you going to Rodney?"

"It's come to my attention Parker has taken his investigation that direction."

"On Laura's death, you mean?"

"Or Guthrie's or Wayne Hale's or cotton stealing in general."

"Does any of it concern you?"

"I do believe I'm suspect in all three. I think Guthrie's murder brought him here, and he's trying to tie Guthrie's murder to cotton thieving. What I don't understand is his setting his sights on me."

"You stole cotton."

"I'm an exception. The cotton thieves are, as a rule, Federals." He rose over her. "Tell me this. The officers who visited your uncle while you lived with him and your aunt in Port Gibson…"

She remained unmoving beneath him, and when he didn't pursue his question, she said, "What of them?"

"Do you recall your uncle meeting with any of them in private?"

"They usually came at an invitation to dinner. The men retired to Uncle Pete's office after, but I never had the feeling they were secluded. Aunt Betty routinely interrupted them."

"Jonathan?"

"He was with them. You don't think Uncle Peter is involved with the cotton stealing, do you?"

Well, Peter Franklin was sure spending his days doing something, and it wasn't planting cotton, with his own hands, in December. Eli lay back. "I was hoping you would shed some light on that."

"He earned a living speculating, but I can't say he's involved in cotton speculation."

Was she protecting the man or did she really not know? For a long time Alice was quiet, thinking, he'd wager, on which of their discussions she wished to pursue. Goodness knows he'd offered her little satisfaction but, at least, some things to ponder.

"Givin' up the fight for tonight, darlin'?"

She squirmed beside him, then laid her head on his shoulder. "I want a milk cow."

Chapter Fifty-three

"If the conditions and the people in authority were not so dangerous," Isabel Hays said to Eli, "these tangents you and Major Parker are off on would be amusing. But the conditions, though ripe for easy profit, are dangerous for those suspect in the eyes of those wielding power. I will tell you, just like I told the major—"

"He asked?"

"Yes, he asked. I have never met Peter Franklin, though, thanks to his nephew, I am very much aware of the man's existence."

"Is Peter Franklin working with you and using his nephew as the nominal head man?"

Isabel smiled. "Again the major anticipated you, and I'll give you the same answer I gave him and that is I don't know, but I don't think so. If so, they're both buffoons, because Jonathan Franklin is an arrogant, conceited parasite, more brass than brains, and I honestly believe he's working only for himself."

"You told Parker that?"

"With him, I stopped at 'I don't think so.' To have told Parker the rest, I would have admitted an affiliation with Jon Franklin beyond the fulfillment of comfort in my humble establishment."

"What are you doing with him?"

Isabel furrowed her brow. "Why, providing him comfort in my humble establishment."

"Dammit, what business did he hope to conduct with you before I ran off with his bankroll?"

"Eli," she said, stepping behind her desk and taking a seat, "suffice it to say that Jonathan Franklin received information, from an undisclosed source, that I could put him in touch with individuals who might be willing to invest whatever capital he is willing to risk and that they could potentially increase it tenfold."

"Tenfold, Isabel?"

"His words. I was not there when he received this 'tip.'"

"Knowing what he would have had available to 'invest' from Alice Shelton's fortune, that comes out to a helluva lot of cotton."

"Cotton is your word, not mine."

Eli narrowed his eyes on the woman. "Something other than cotton?"

"You're not involved, Eli. Do you want to be?"

"Will it destroy the Republican Party and take the Federal government with it?"

She laughed. "It is a child of a like mind that created the Republican Party."

"Can I help thwart it?"

"Not through me, you can't."

Meaning she wouldn't allow it, which meant whatever she was involved with provided a profit for her; that or her life. Maybe both.

"Given your recent nuptials and access to your young wife's estate, are you in danger of insolvency?"

"No."

"Then let it be. Try to survive this nightmare with some degree of dignity and grace."

"I forced a woman into marriage and took her fortune, Isabel. I feel not one ounce of remorse. I don't know that I have any grace left in me."

She pursed her lips. "It doesn't matter. I desire neither your money nor your attention regarding this matter. And as regards other things with which I am able and willing to supply you, you've shown no interest, meaning you are proving of little value to me in every regard. Perhaps there's a little grace left in you, after all. Go home to your bride, darlin'."

He rose. "I'm not out of this mess, you know. Parker insists on keeping me in."

"He asks about you every time he visits."
"What does he ask?"
"The nature of our relationship."
"And what do you tell him?"
"That we don't have one."
"But we do have one."
"Yes, but he's neither privy to nor interested in that particular tie."

He turned his back on her and reached for the doorknob.
"Eli?"
He turned.
"Do you trust your wife?"
A pang twisted his gut. "Why do you ask?"
"Jon Franklin has made his way back here. He implies he's still in the game." She shrugged. "It's in his best interest to indicate such. The poor dear knows too much to rest easy, so I don't know how much is true and how much is bluster, but be careful."

Chapter Fifty-four

Alice thrust the broom beneath the stove, then bent at the waist, couldn't see, squatted, and thrust again. Darn the filthy, little beast. With a soft growl, she rose and rounded the side of the stove. Leaning her shoulder against the rough wall of the cookhouse, she strained to see behind the cast-iron monstrosity. Hopeless. Throwing down the broom with a clatter, she fell to her knees, flattened her palms on the floor and looked underneath it.

The mouse was gone.

She released a put-upon sigh and pushed herself to all fours. The back door opened, announced more by the thud of a booted footfall than the squeak of a rusty hinge. "I saw the thing again," she said, and she rose, dusting off her hands. She didn't look at Eli. She'd mopped the floor yesterday and already swept it this frigid morning, but far back, beneath the stove, soot and dust had collected for years. She wished she'd never looked, because she couldn't live with that filth another day, knowing it was there.

"What would you do if you caught it, Alice?"

"Kill it."

"With your bare hands?"

She turned to him. "Yes."

He studied her a moment. "If you could bear to touch it, you'd take it outside and let it go."

"And it would come right back in." She made her way to the wash pan. "I can do what I have to do, Eli, whether I like it or not." She looked over her shoulder and gave him a smile. "But maybe not with my bare hands."

He pulled off his hat and hung it by the door. He didn't wear his frock coat this morning, but a ragged wool jacket. Brown, not gray. Worn, but functional. He smelled of the cold outside, and guilt caused her cheeks to heat. She had checked his discarded drawers this morning. The musky scent of sex had been absent.

He didn't know she'd done that, and she was ashamed of herself, but he'd returned late last night, hours after Buck had gotten back from Vicksburg with four chickens, her requested milk cow, and ten pounds of sugar—not to mention three large crates of items that had been part of her Ohio home. Eli had gone on to Rodney as he'd said he was going to do. As she was very much aware, there was nothing much to visit in Rodney but that whorehouse Cassie alleged Jonathan patronized and Eli's 'old family friend,' who might well reside in the place.

"Our new cow isn't giving milk," he said.

"I know. That's why my coffee will be black again this morning."

He pulled out a chair and sat at the kitchen table. "Buck's hoping it's because she's upset with the move." He looked at her and smiled. "At least, your coffee will be sweet."

Alice stepped around him to get to the stove. *He* was being very pleasant this morning, which made her feel even guiltier. He'd told her before he left yesterday it was Seth Parker's investigation that took him to Rodney; perhaps she should take him at his word. Still, that was cause for worry in its own right.

She filled his cup with the chicory coffee she thought so little of and placed the china cup in front of him, then turned back to the stove. From the corner of her eye, she saw him move. He was watching her, she knew, but she didn't look at him.

"The fella I bought 'er from assured me she was giving milk. I don't believe anything anyone tells me these days, but there wasn't much to choose from."

"Once we've gotten some food in her, she should be all right."

"We'll hope. Come sit with me," he said.

Her heart skipped with the soft promise in his voice. She turned and found his eyes, then poured herself a cup of the bitter brew and sat. "I thank you for the cow. We can eat her if she doesn't start producing."

"She's not young. Wouldn't be anything but gristle."

"I imagine you're used to worse."

"That I am." He sat forward. "Have you checked the crates?"

"Not yet."

"I'll get Buck, and we'll get them in the kitchen. From what he tells me it's a good thing your uncle's name was on that bill of lading."

"Someone stopped him?"

"Negro troops outside Vicksburg. He was afraid they were going to take everything, wagon and mules included. Two of 'em actually climbed in the wagon and opened one of your crates. Started pulling things out before the one in nominal charge, who apparently could read, recognized Peter Franklin's name on that bill and made 'em put it back."

"Surely they weren't acting in an official capacity," Alice said.

"Their official 'capacity' is to mock and degrade us. I don't know what would have happened if I'd been in that wagon."

"You'd let them have the stuff, then take proper recourse."

"And you'd have never seen your things again."

Her stomach tensed. Her family treasures, most of which had value only for her, were all she….

Alice looked at one of the few cups remaining of Rosalind Calhoon's fine dinnerware. This morning it held her steaming coffee. Thoughtfully, she rubbed her finger over a chip in its rim. Items filled with memories, some passed down for generations. Grief washed over her, not for her father and brothers this time, but for an entire people. She looked up to find Eli watching her. "I'd have been heartsick," she said, drawing in a deep breath. "I asked Buck yesterday when he got back. He said a man at the Freedman's Bureau asked you about the oath."

"Then you know I told him I hadn't taken it."

"At least they didn't make an issue of it."

"Because a senior Yankee officer intervened and told his lieutenant it didn't matter." Eli appeared to hesitate a moment, then asked, "Had you given any consideration at all to Jon Franklin's proposal before I disrupted things?"

She frowned at him. "There was no proposal before you. You told me Uncle Pete wanted me to marry him, remember, there on the porch?"

"There'd never been any talk about it before that night?"

"Not with me, but Aunt Betty had indicated it was a secret hope of Uncle Pete's."

"So Jonathan had never spoken to you of marriage?"

"Not till the night you brought me home. He indicated he was willing to make the sacrifice—marrying damaged goods, I surmised—and that I should accommodate his mother. The fool actually believed I thought he was doing me a favor. If I hadn't already decided to marry you, Jonathan's obnoxious proposal would have been the convincing factor."

"Did you lead him to believe you'd marry him?"

"I didn't say yes, but I didn't do anything to make him suspect I was leaving, either. I told him he'd have my answer the following morning. He responded by telling me we'd be wed by the end of the week. I married you the next day. Why are you interested in Jonathan's proposal to me?"

He shrugged.

He shrugged. *Shrugged!* Alice gripped her cup, then hit it against the tabletop. Coffee splashed. "So we're back to that, are we? Don't tell Alice anything, and she won't do any harm."

Eli coolly studied the mess she'd made. Well, he could look down his nose at her mess all he wanted. She'd clean it up. She'd be the one stuck cleaning it up even if it were his darn mess.

He looked up. "I'd heard rumors, before I ever laid eyes on you, that he considered himself your intended."

"Well, he wasn't. Who told you he said that?"

He yawned, and she stood, scraping her chair across the floor.

He laughed and reached for her hand. "I'm not trying to provoke you. I really am tired."

Straightening, she yanked her hand from his, and he leaned back in his chair.

"I heard him say it myself, sweetheart."

"And where were you, to have overheard such a thing?"

He shook his head. He wouldn't tell her, but she could guess. "Was Uncle Peter with him? And does this have anything to do with your questions night before last regarding Uncle Pete and the cotton thefts?"

Eli rose. "No and yes. I don't trust Jon Franklin. I want to make sure he has no delusions regarding your feelings for him."

Her heart plummeted with the realization Eli might be considering she was working with Jonathan or her uncle against him. "All I can tell you, for certain, is that I regard him with contempt, stronger than ever now."

Eli nodded, then turned to the back door.

"And *he* knows I'll not have him."

Eli stopped in the open door, but he didn't turn around.

"Tell me I'm wrong to fear the doubt is yours, Eli?"

He closed the back door behind him.

Chapter Fifty-five

"Where is she?" Betty Franklin asked.

Eli watched the still graceful curve of the older woman's body as she placed a bundle of brown paper packages and a napkin-covered basket on the dining-room table. He reached for her coat, which she draped over a chair. Making herself at home, was she? For sure she didn't plan on leaving until she'd laid eyes on Alice.

"Still thinking I plan to dispose of her, Mrs. Franklin?"

"I can't rule that out."

Eli hung the coat on a peg. "Why would I?"

She studied him for a moment. "I hear things."

"And those things imply I'm a killer?"

"I'm told there's a good chance."

"Your source, no doubt, is your husband's nephew." His natural response, but Eli's gut twisted with his words. One reason for Betty Franklin to think he'd want his wife dead would be if she thought, or knew, Alice was working against him.

"To name one," she said.

"And is Alice another?"

"Mother...?"

Betty looked across the dining room and into the foyer, then started that way. Eli cursed under his breath and followed.

Cassie met them in the foyer. Hooking her arm through her mother's, she tugged the older woman into the front room. "Look what Alice has done to this parlor." Bright-eyed and smiling, Cassie looked over her shoulder to him. "It was Alice, wasn't it, Eli?" She turned away. "I know her touch. Oh...," she said and rushed to the front of the settee where Alice had moved his mother's ornate center table, its marble top cracked clean down the middle by a well-placed wallop with the fireplace poker in the hands of a Federal soldier. The top sat steady on its broad base, and Eli planned on having it professionally repaired one day.

Cassie opened the front cover of the large Bible, which Alice had placed there and subsequently surrounded with red candles and magnolia boughs. "It's Aunt Jenny's. I thought I recognized it." Cassie closed the book, then looked at the mantle, similarly decorated. "She's made this room look nice and festive."

Betty Franklin turned on her heel and almost bumped him. "I want her to go to church Christmas Day."

"I've already asked her about that."

"And?"

"She refuses."

The woman looked away. "If she were with us, I could convince her to go. The fact that she's gotten her mother's Bible out proves her faith is returning."

Eli stepped around the end of the settee. "She never stopped believing in God. She's mad at Him."

"Well, she must get over that."

And she would, in time.

"I want you and her to join us for dinner Christmas Day, too. Jenny always made a fuss over the holiday. Even as a little girl, Alice tried to replicate her mother's efforts for the sake of her father and brothers."

"Do come, Eli."

He glanced at Cassie. He wasn't sure what to think of her eager familiarity, but he was almost certain the girl was immune to insult after what he'd said to her about her Negro soldier. He looked back at the girl's mother.

"I'm not trying to ruin the day for her, Mrs. Franklin. I told her she could go alone. You and I both know I don't belong at your home—"

"Peter has agreed—"

"If he has, it's because you browbeat him into it."

She opened her mouth, but he raised a hand.

"I could deal with your husband. I know he wouldn't want me there any more than I'd want to be there. That would put us on equal footing. But my contempt for the asinine plot your nephew is concocting would tax my social niceties beyond my capabilities."

"Plot?"

"To implicate me in murder."

"Oh, that's not a plot, Eli," Cassie said lightly. "He's trying to determine your guilt or innocence for Alice's sake."

Eli turned to the younger woman. "And which murder does he believe I committed?"

"Cassie, hush!"

Cassie looked at her mother.

"He's probably looking at all of them," Eli said dryly, "and I have no doubt, *Aunt* Betty, you hope I committed them all."

"I consider the possibility that you committed murder, *Mister* Calhoon, but it's your protest that fuels my doubts. It occurs to me that if you were innocent, you wouldn't blink at Jonathan's efforts."

"To frame me?" Eli barked out a laugh. "Justice is falling a little short around here these days and it's meted out far too quickly. My concern is valid."

The woman sighed. "Where is she?"

"Delivering venison from a buck I killed yesterday. She and Miss Elvie left about an hour ago. They were only going to the old slave quarters. They'll be back soon."

The woman didn't say anything, and he nodded. "She's got a roast set aside for you, too. Have a seat and wait for her."

He fed the fire and left the room. He really wanted to get into those brown bundles on the dining-room table. For sure, Betty Franklin had food in that basket, something sweet, he bet. For all her Yankee faults, the woman was a fine cook.

He withstood temptation, though, walking past the parcels and going on to the cookhouse to prepare coffee for his "guests." Alice, cheeks glowing and out of breath, scurried in ten minutes later. She'd seen Aunt Betty's carriage out front. Yes, she'd delivered the meat. Yes, Buck would take a roast up to Caw in the morning, and yes, she had a package of goodies for her aunt and Cassie to take back home. She grabbed the pot of coffee he'd made and headed out the kitchen door. In the dining room, she collected her tea service, ignored his suggestion to look in the packages on the table, and had scurried off to the parlor. This time, he peeked inside the basket. Shortbreads with jelly centers. He took a cookie, hollered that Alice should come back and get them, then went out front to fish from Lake Elizabeth.

"*He*'s left the porch and gone down to the lake," Cassie said from the entry. She looked back over her shoulder toward the front door. "I'll keep my eye on him, Mama. You go ahead and talk to Alice."

Alice blinked at her aunt, next to her on the settee in front of the fire. For ten minutes they'd exchanged pleasant small talk waiting for Eli to leave the front porch where he could, possibly, overhear their conversation. Alice, at first, wouldn't have cared if he'd joined them, but Cassie's calculated movements in and out of the foyer coupled with Aunt Betty's furtive glances to her daughter were clear indications Aunt Betty had something to say and she didn't want Eli Calhoon overhearing it.

Aunt Betty reached for her hand. "Your husband was seen in a whorehouse in Rodney three nights ago."

Alice's chest tightened. It wasn't as if she hadn't known he'd done something. Actually, she preferred the thought of a whorehouse to an "old family friend." Prostitutes and their clients had a business relationship, she assumed, not one of mutual affection. Her aunt's knowing he'd visited a house of prostitution was what bothered her. The common knowledge of such behavior was an insult to her womanhood…and why had he needed feminine…?

But she knew he hadn't. She'd sniffed his drawers after all.

"How do you know?"

Aunt Betty leaned forward—as if she still feared someone might overhear them. Perhaps Cassie didn't know, but Alice doubted that.

"Peter told me."

Alice's mouth dropped open. "Uncle Peter saw him in a whorehouse?"

Her aunt reddened slightly. "Jonathan told him."

That made sense, didn't it? It could also help explain Eli's questions to her at the kitchen table two mornings ago.

"Did Jonathan talk to him?"

"To your uncle?"

"Of course not, to Eli."

Her beloved aunt sat back. "I said Jonathan saw him, not that Jonathan was there."

"Aunt Betty, do you expect me to believe you didn't ask Uncle Pete that very question?"

"Oh, all right, Jonathan was there."

"And did he talk to Eli?"

"I don't know, but I wouldn't think so."

Alice didn't know either, but she couldn't fathom Jonathan confronting Eli on a subject as sensitive as Eli's wife. "Do you know the name of the establishment?"

Her aunt screwed up her mouth. "No, and that's not the point. Who cares which house it is? What matters is it's a house where men go for perverse sexual pleasure."

"Perverse?"

Aunt Betty squeezed Alice's fingers. "Or men who are not happy with their wives."

Alice felt her skin blanch. She wanted to protest the slight, to tell her aunt that from best she could tell, Eli was, at least, sexually satisfied with her. But that was no one's business—including either the visitors to or the denizens of a house full of whores.

"How does he act with you?"

"Like a man." She pulled her hand from her aunt's and reached for the beautiful porcelain teapot that made up part of Jenny Shelton's service. She'd been so proud to bring it to the parlor and show it off to her female relations. She poured Aunt Betty another cup, then held her chin high. "Like a very healthy, happy man."

Her aunt grimaced. "I'm sorry, darling. I didn't mean to offend, but men can enjoy the sexual favors of a woman without caring anything for the woman herself."

"Are you referring to me or the whore in the whorehouse?"

Again, Aunt Betty covered Alice's hand with hers. "I'm worried about you. I haven't been too concerned since the night you were sick, and he sat so diligently by your side, but there's still the murder of that Blackledge woman with whom we know he'd been intimate, and now his visiting—"

"Perhaps it's the perversion you mentioned that he seeks."

Her aunt gave her a tearful smile. "Perhaps."

Alice didn't believe he'd had sex in that whorehouse, whichever whorehouse it was, but he had been there, and her aunt and Cassie and, no doubt, her uncle thought...

"Aunt Betty, do you know if Uncle Peter is working with the Federal authorities in any capacity?"

She frowned. "He visits the Freedman's Bureau daily, sometimes the provost marshal. He's trying to create a labor force for his spring planting. He does so want to become a farmer."

Alice hesitated, not sure how to go about her next question. Finally, she took a deep breath. "Could he be involved in anything...dangerous?"

"Dangerous?"

Alice swallowed. "Illegal?"

Her aunt's lips parted, then closed. "Whatever are you getting at, Alice?"

"Is there any chance either he or Jonathan or both are involved with this theft of Confederate property?"

Aunt Betty stared at her. She'd offended the woman, and Alice wouldn't have done that for the world.

"You mean like the cotton thefts, which authorities suspect may have cost that Treasury agent his life?"

"Or anything. It doesn't have to be cotton or involve murder. I'm sorry, Aunt Betty. I'm not accusing Uncle Peter of anything, but Jonathan's apparent knowledge of the comings and goings of Eli makes me suspicious."

"Suspicious of whom? Alice, we know *your* husband was involved in stealing cotton, even if it can't be proved."

"Who told you that?"

"Jon." Aunt Betty pursed her lips and looked away. "Maybe Jonathan is working with Major Parker."

For certain he was working with someone. Though he knew the truth, Seth Parker had never officially linked Eli to the cotton found at the old Ferris place, and the suspects' names had not appeared in the paper.

"Trying to trap Eli?" Alice said.

"Oh, honey, don't you see? We know Calhoon has been involved in illegal dealings. We know that without a doubt. Are you sure he trusts you?"

"I'm sure he doesn't."

Her aunt sighed. "What if he killed that Blackledge woman because she knew too much? What if he considers you a threat for the same reason? We're all so worried about you, Jonathan included. I truly have no idea of Calhoon's affection for you. Now this"—she threw out her hands—"whorehouse thing. I want you to come home."

Jonathan included, indeed. Alice had no doubt he had his own selfish reasons for attempting to undermine Eli. How dare he tell her family of having seen Eli in such a place? What if Eli ran and told Jonathan's hideous old goat of a mother her son had paid money for a prostitute? Whatever Eli had been doing in that place, he hadn't been there for....

Her heart skipped a beat. Eli had referred to a woman the night Seth came to Camellia Creek following Laura Blackledge's murder. A woman who had been friends with Holland Calhoon. A woman in Rodney. Alice met her aunt's eye.

"I am home, Aunt Betty, and I'll be home until Eli Calhoon himself tells me he doesn't want me here."

"Did you ask her about Christmas Day?" Eli asked Betty Franklin.

He was sitting on the low bridge that straddled the narrow

north end of Lake Elizabeth. The house was in sight, less than a hundred yards away. Betty and Cassie Franklin had to leave this way, and for that reason he'd chosen this spot after preparing his fishing tackle on the front porch. He'd hoped to catch snippets of feminine conversation, but he knew Alice had become wary of his eavesdropping, and he'd seen Cassie watching him from the foyer. Finally forsaking the chance of overhearing anything of value, he'd meandered down to the lake. Hell, he'd even caught two fish, a surprise given the time of day and the chilled wind.

"She won't leave you by yourself," Aunt Betty said. "For better or worse, you're her man now, and she wants to be with you."

There was a bitter edge to her voice, but he steeled himself to it. She could blame him for Alice's not being with them Christmas Day if she wanted, he didn't care. In the Franklin house he was behind enemy lines, for some reasons he knew, for other, more sinister ones, he could only speculate.

Camellia Creek was friendly territory. Oh, yes, he knew it had possibly been infiltrated, but if there was an enemy within, he could deal with her one on one. He waved as the women drove on, then picked up his two fish. Bass, and nice ones, too. A good mess for dinner. He started whistling *Dixie*. Alice could wring a chicken neck, skin a squirrel, and dress a deer. She could clean fish, too, and she'd even got Auntie Elvie to teach her how to deep fry, Southern style.

Time to put that little gal to work. He'd help. Might wangle a little information out of her while he was at it.

Chapter Fifty-six

"Miss Alice gonna be disappointed you found 'er. Wanted to show 'er to you 'ersef, I 'magine."

Eli patted the rump of the filly, then lifted a front hoof. "Never shod."

"Wouldn't think," Buck said with a grin. "She only be two. Caw got 'er from Mr. Bartlett Payne over in Madison County."

Eli raised his head and met Buck's eye.

"Yes, suh," Buck said. "You know she's outa Calhoon stock. Dat's what yo' woman wanted. Paid top dolla."

Eli clenched his jaw at that. The only way she could have done that was if she'd gotten access to money. He'd been, he thought, generous enough. She had a modest house fund to get Camellia Creek comfortable again. Maybe that's why the anticipated discussion of ordering new furniture had not been forthcoming. She'd spent the money on his Christmas present.

Buck took his tattered slouch hat from his head and wiped his brow. "She say you wanna raise hawses, so she gots dis thought in 'er head she'd start you off wif Calhoon stock. She thinkin' you gonna breed dis little filly wif Johnny."

Eli shot Buck a smile. "Did you tell—"

The old black man was already shaking his head. "Couldn't do it. I thought she were lookin' fo' a hawse fo' 'ersef. Caw'd already done da dickerin' when she told me why. Didn't have da heart to tell 'er den. You gonna have to. Her daddy had mules as I unde'stan' it, an' she don't know no diff'rence. Didn't think it be my place to educate her on such things."

"What things?"

Eli pivoted. She was there, bright-eyed and cheeks aglow.

Her hair was still down, and he knew she'd rushed to catch him once she realized he was headed out to the lean-to. Buck had sneaked the horse in a few minutes ago.

"I'd hoped to keep you away from here this morning." Her smile so anticipated his approval he couldn't help but smile in return. "I wanted to surprise you."

"I'm surprised." He really wanted to confirm which money she used. He was pacing himself pending procedural paperwork on her fortune.

"Do you like her?" she said and stepped nearer the horse's rump. Eli pulled her to the side.

"She's beautiful, but don't walk up behind a strange horse."

"She comes from Calhoon stock, I'm told." She glanced at Buck, apparently for his confirmation, and he nodded. "Caw Pruitt knew of a man near Jackson who'd purchased horses from your father before the war and raised them. He'd moved them around a bit, keeping out of Sherman's way—"

"And ole Johnston's, I 'magine," Buck said. Eli smirked and patted the horse's neck.

"Whoever," she said, "but he still has some of them. I thought you could breed her with John…."

She blinked at him, then turned to Buck. Must have been the looks on their faces.

"What's wrong?" she asked.

"Johnny's a gelding."

"You castrated your horse?"

"Years ago. Haven't you ever taken a good look at him?"

Apparently not, but she did then, stepping to her right and bending low to look at Johnny's accoutrements, or lack of them. She pivoted on him. "I'd have never thought…. I assumed, when you said you wanted to raise horses, you dealt only with stallions." She stamped her foot. "Why did you do that to him?"

"Because he was meaner than a damn cottonmouth, and I had enough to do fighting Yankees, often under extremely taxing conditions, without having to fight my horse, too."

"So I've accomplished nothing by buying the filly?"

"You've made the first purchase of my brood stock," he said. He drew her close and kissed her forehead. He'd have kissed her lips had Buck not been standing there. "She's a beautiful little filly, and I'll find her a good stud."

Alice pulled back and gave him a silly little smirk. "And won't Johnny be pleased with you then."

Buck laughed, and Eli smiled. His genteel Alice could be quite earthy, sometimes. That would have come from living in a house full of males, he reckoned. Despite her attempt to hide her disappointment over what she must now be thinking an inappropriate present, her eyes glistened. He felt bad, bad enough, in fact, not to try and track how she got her fingers on money. Tomorrow would be soon enough. No, tomorrow was Christmas. Maybe the day after…and hell…he'd paid no mind to Christmas. He hadn't bought her anything.

"Well," she said, and made a sibilant sound, "I'm going to bake some pound cakes. Buck, you make sure you get one before you leave this afternoon."

"Yes'm, I will."

"Hey," Eli said to Buck. Alice stopped and looked at him and would have continued on her way, but he told her to wait. "What did you do with that thing?"

Buck held up a finger, then reached over in the hay-filled trough and pulled out the kitten he'd shown up with this morning. He'd told Eli Mrs. Baker on the back road was trying to get rid of it, last of the litter. She couldn't feed another cat, she said, and she was going to drown it if no one took it. Eli asked him why he didn't let her drown it, but Buck had just smiled and shook his head. Gentlest soul on earth, ole Buck, and he knew there was a mouse in the cookhouse giving Alice fits.

Eli took the cat with one hand. Thing couldn't be more than four weeks old. The mouse would eat it. Calico. Female. Just dandy…. She'd have litter after litter of her own. Scrawny little thing could have at least been a male. A tom would leave after a while. "Can you…?"

But Alice's glistening eyes had already swelled with tears, and she made a garbled sound when she took it from his hand and hugged it to her. For a long moment she didn't say a word, her head bent over the animal. He watched her. Buck, standing stock still behind him, didn't say a word either. Then she sniffed and looked up, tears on her cheeks. "Aunt Betty told you."

Lost, Eli nodded, then lied, "Yes."

"I'm going to name her Mercy. Thank you." She choked on the words, then grasped his upper arm and tugged him at the shoulder. She kissed his cheek and hurried off, the poor little kitten bundled to her bosom.

"I do think she liked my cat," Buck said.

Eli turned and stared at the man, teeth shining against his dark skin.

"Let me see," he continued, rubbing his chin as if in thought. "What will I take fo' dat rare and precious kitty?"

"Oh, no, you don't." Eli wasn't sure he had enough money to ever pay for that damn cat. "You'd already given me that thing for the kitchen, but I'll come up with something fitting for you anyway to buy your silence. I think you might have just saved my ass."

Chapter Fifty-seven

"He isn't going to like you runnin' off like this," Naomi Polk said to Alice.

"That's why I'm going while he's gone."

More's the pity, for that. Christmas had been nice yesterday; they'd spent it together, mostly alone. Aunt Naomi had shown up at dinnertime with custard pie. Eli had invited her. Alice hadn't protested. It was Christmas after all, and the woman was family, and she was alone; and despite hovering over Alice in the kitchen while she prepared a venison roast, Naomi had been reasonably pleasant. She'd left in time to make it home before dark, driving Eli's carriage, the one on loan to Doctor Lester, over the "back way," an expanded footpath that entered Port Gibson on the north. Still, Alice would have preferred Elvie come, but Eli said traditionally the slaves had Christmas Day off to do as they pleased. The black church Elvie attended had potluck, and that's where she went. She always had.

Alice watched out the cookhouse door. "Here comes Buck."

Now she was going to anger Eli, but she couldn't think of an easier way around what she needed to do, short of his unlikely cooperation. She spun on the two women near the kitchen table. Darn she wished Naomi wasn't here. She showed up at the most inopportune times. "Please don't say anything to Buck. If he thinks Eli is against this, he won't take me."

"Your displeasing your husband doesn't bother me one bit," Naomi said.

"Why don't you get Eli to go wif you, girl?" Elvie said. "He can take you right to dat woman's house."

"I asked him to Christmas Eve, after you told me about her."

Alice walked back to the table and started pulling on her gloves. "You know what he said, Miss Elvie?"

"I reckon he said no, if you is runnin' off behin' him's back."

"He told me there was no way he would take me into Rodney to bother that poor old woman. Said she hasn't got enough sense left to tell me what street she lives on, much less recall Jocelyn LeBlanc."

Elvie chuckled. "Hmmpf. Dat's not as bad as what he tells folks wanna talk to Nimi."

Naomi walked to the stove, placed a cast-iron pot filled with a mess of collards and salt pork on a burner, then turned on Elvie. "Why did you tell her about Marguerite? He must be livid."

Alice silently cursed Naomi Polk. "He must visit her, don't you believe, Elvie, or he wouldn't know such?"

"He don't know such. He just tellin' you dat."

"I suspect so, too. He doesn't want me to talk to her."

Naomi settled the lid on the pot with a clank. "You think he wants people to know his wife converses with the dead? Doesn't want you making a fool of yourself."

Alice listened to the wagon lumber around the corner of the cookhouse. Naomi's arrival had put a damper on her talk with Miss Elvie and had increased her anxiety regarding the mission on which she was about to embark. She didn't need to have this conversation in front of Naomi Polk anyway. "I need to go."

"Well, if dat ole woman ain't got anymo' sense dan he say she gots, you won't do too much hurt to how people think 'a you."

Alice picked up her bonnet and smiled at the Negress. "Thank you." She had no idea how long Eli would be gone. Half the time he didn't tell her where he was going either, but on those occasions, he normally wasn't gone more than a few hours. Once she was on the road, she hoped he wouldn't force her back home.

Miss Elvie shook her head. "Used to be, she live on Cypress Street. She probably still do. I know she still be over dat way 'cause Eli took 'er squirrel when he first come back. Say she loves fried squirrel. But you should be able to find 'er, no matter what, 'cause ain't much left in Rodney to sift through now as I un'erstan' it. You be careful." Elvie rose when Alice opened the door to the breezeway, and Naomi stepped away from the stove to better see her.

"You need to take care getting home, young woman," Naomi said. "He's gonna be mad when you get back. Just remember I told you."

Alice knew he'd be angry, but she couldn't let that stop her. To hear him tell it, Jocelyn LeBlanc's story had ended twenty-five years ago. Yes, she'd had a family. Eli had even told her about some of those people, but that had been in the long forgotten past, and those folks all seemed to have conveniently faded away over the years. However, when Alice talked to Miss Elvie about Jocelyn two days ago, a different story emerged.

According to Elvie, Jocelyn's grandaunt, Marguerite Fortier, now in her eighties, still lived in Rodney, and she'd been known to the Calhoons for as long as Miss Elvie could remember. Jocelyn hadn't been, as Alice assumed, an acquaintance Holland Calhoon had hired as a nursemaid for his children. There had been a long connection between Holland Calhoon and Jocelyn's people. When Alice asked, Eli had acknowledged the existence of Mrs. Fortier, but he'd steadfastly refused to take her to "bother" the poor woman with an event that family had long since put to rest.

But Alice had to know more about Jocelyn and about the events leading up to her death. And then there was that niggling "old family friend." How much easier her mind would rest if that individual turned out to be a sweet, old woman.

At least, Alice assumed the poor soul was sweet.

"Bless it, Aunt Naomi!" Eli slapped his gloves on the kitchen table, but didn't let go of them. He turned back to the cookhouse door.

"Don't blame me. I told her not to go." Naomi looked up from where she sat at the table battering chicken in a big wooden bowl. "I knew you wouldn't like it." The woman snorted. "You and I know there's only one thing that would be of interest to her there, and that's Isabel's place. She's nosing around in your business." The woman returned to her chicken. "I hear the man she jilted for you spends a lot of time there."

Eli frowned, then said, "I guess he's lonely without Alice."

"Maybe he's not without Alice."

"Who told you Jonathan Franklin was making visits to Isabel's, Aunt Nimi?"

"I hear things."

"Who you hear things from is what I want to know."

She smiled. "I'll fry this chicken. I doubt your bride will be back to make you supper."

"Where's Elvie?"

Naomi rose and stepped toward the cast-iron skillet heating lard on the stove. "You know she won't stay long after I get here."

"Cover the chicken and leave it on the dining-room table when you're done."

She gave him a walleyed glance, and he considered that if it were him, he'd tell her to fry her own damn chicken. She didn't. He'd come as close as he could to asking her to leave short of tossing her off the place. He was mad as hell at Alice, but Naomi was intentionally trying to make matters worse for her in his eyes, and he didn't like that either.

"You going to Rodney?"

"How long ago did they leave?"

She shrugged. "Hour and a half. Maybe two."

Them in the wagon, him on the horse, he'd near about catch 'em. "Then I'm going, and I want the privacy of my home when I get back."

Eli slammed the cookhouse door behind him, bounded down the three steps, and headed to the pathetic lean-to where the impotent Johnny waited alongside the pretty little filly. The roads were dangerous, too, the western part of Claiborne County a relative wasteland since halfway through the war. Alice had her father's contract of service—he'd told her to carry it with her at all times—which would protect her from Federal harassment. But there was Rebel rabble about looking for trouble, too. He kept a shotgun under the wagon seat, and he'd once told Buck if any such approached him, particularly if Alice were in the wagon, to shoot 'em. He wasn't sure Buck could shoot another human being to protect himself, but Eli hoped he could to protect someone in his charge. Still, the man had to drag the gun out before getting shot himself.

Chapter Fifty-eight

"Come here in 1790 with my sister, Sarah Marie, and her man Raphael LeBlanc. I was eight. Sarah and me was orphans. She was twelve years older than me and already had a son by Raphael when we got here. The baby's name was Richard. She had a second son shortly after. They called him Hernan. Then come two daughters. Sarah was first. We called her Silky so we wouldn't confuse her with her mama. Silky was Jocelyn's mama. Angel was next, then come stillborn twins. Boy and a girl." The dusky-skinned Maggie Fortier tsk'ed and finally let go of Alice's hand to pour her a cup of tea, real *tea*. "Sarah grieved terrible, but Raphael gave her another daughter. We called her Izzie, after the name her mama give her. Such a beautiful little thing. I was wed myself by then. Lived next to them over on Church Street. Sweet little Izzie still takes care of her old auntie."

"She lives here in Rodney?"

"Oh, she always has. Never gave any thought to leavin' far as I know." The woman's green eyes smiled along with her lips, and she held up the delicate porcelain cup in mock salute. "This was a big town once, long before the war. A person would as soon live here as Natchez. Izzie's the one who brings me my tea."

Alice sipped the brew. The day was cold, and it tasted quite good. "Mrs. Fortier—"

"Aunt Maggie, please, child. You being Eli's wife, you and me are like family."

"Really?"

"Oh, my, yes."

"What is the relationship between—"

The woman held one palm up and set her cup and saucer

down with the other. "I'm not the person you should be talkin' to. If you're interested in Jocelyn, you need Silky's journal."

"Silky's journal?"

"Yes, the last one. She loved to write in her journals. She filled dozens of 'em over the years, but the death of Jocelyn is written in her last one. She only lived eighteen months after her daughter killed herself."

"Do you remember anyone at the time believing Jocelyn might have been murdered?"

"Yes, yes," the woman said and patted Alice's hand.

"Who—"

"That's why I'm sending you to Izzie, child. She knows so much more about what happened. Rather"—and the elderly woman shrugged—"remembers more. I fear my mind is growing feeble. Now listen, I'm gonna tell you where to find the plot." She met Alice's eyes, and Alice thought the woman anything but of feeble mind. "You saw the cemetery?"

"Yes, on the high hill above the river."

The woman smiled. "For sure, it would be hard to miss. My people are over the hill and to the south a little bit. It's a nice plot, enclosed by wrought iron. After you visit there, circle back down the north side of the hill and go right on Commerce. When the road forks, keep left, then left again on Spring Street. Izzie's house is a large structure, pink, overlooking the river. You'll see it. And Rebecca's here for a visit. You'll get to meet her."

"Rebecca?"

"Izzie's daughter. She's a war widow. Lives on her husband's plantation, or what's left of it, over in Madison County." Her eyes twinkled. "They'll both be so pleased to meet you."

Eli stepped around the side of Rodney's old Masonic Lodge. Sergeant Zachary stood at the opposite corner looking back down Church Street. For certain the sergeant was watching for him. Eli had doubled back on the man and now started his way.

"Is it me you're shadowin'," he said when he got within hearing distance, "or my wife?"

He saw the man stiffen, then his shoulders slumped slightly. Finally, when Eli drew up alongside him, the sergeant looked at him. "You," he said.

Eli looked up the hill to Rodney's impressive cemetery. "The captain's tailing my wife?"

The sergeant didn't say anything, but it was obvious. Eli himself had watched Alice climb the hill, then saw the blue uniform following discreetly from a distance. At the time he hadn't known he was being followed. He'd been trying to find where the devil Buck had gotten off to, because the wagon wasn't at Isabel's, and Eli figured Alice was still trying to find her way there.

Eli waited for Captain Summers to continue on over the hill behind Alice, and, he figured, down the other side. When the man disappeared, Eli looked over his shoulder at the sergeant. "Well, if you're to keep watch on me, come along. Maybe we'll both learn something."

The sergeant seemed to ponder that, then said, "Meanin' you think you'll learn somethin' from me?"

"I could hope."

Eli stopped on the other side of the hill, a bit removed from the cemetery proper. He'd been here many times as a boy, mostly in company with his father and Andrew. The plot was marked by a wrought-iron fence and contained a number of graves. He figured Captain Summers had taken at least a moment to look at these stones after watching Alice study them. Sarah Marie Dubois, 1770-1837; Sarah Marie LeBlanc, 1795-1842; Angel Elizabeth Peters, 1806-1828. He himself had told Alice that Jocelyn was from here, but he couldn't recall mentioning her being buried here. He figured Elvie was to blame for that.

Sergeant Zachary moved up beside him and read, "Jocelyn Marie LeBlanc, 1822-1840." He sighed. "You shouldn't be doin' dat, you know?"

Eli's heartbeat quickened, and he turned from the marker and stared at the man. "Doin' what?" he asked, his mouth suddenly dry.

Zachary grinned. "Hell, Colonel, you lookin' at me like you

done seen a ghos'. Followin' 'em, is all I meant. Rather, I ought not to be lettin' you."

It had been Zachary's words, them and the familiar levity, and for an instant, Eli had indeed stood in the presence of another ghost. "You and me," he said slowly, all the while watching Zachary, "we're workin' this together." Why he drew the scenario out, Eli couldn't guess, but he had. Just to see how it played out, he reckoned.

The grin remained on the sergeant's face, but he shook his head. "Oh, I don't know 'bout dat now."

"Unless he asks her, which he can't without giving himself away, your captain won't know why my wife stopped here."

"You think dey looked at dese graves?" the sergeant asked.

"My wife"—he tore his eyes from the sergeant and nodded at Jocelyn's headstone,—"looked at this one in particular, I imagine. You're from around here, aren't you?"

"Warren County."

"You didn't work in the fields."

He laughed. "My readin' gave dat away, I reckon. No, neva did pick cotton. Started my life on a suga' plantation down in Lou'siana, though. Was orphaned at six. When I be 'bout twelve, ole massa an' his two oldes' boys come down wif a feva. Don't think dey eva know'd what it was, but liked to kilt 'em.

"Doc Yancy, he floated up and down da bayous he'pin' folks, and he come to he'p da missus. All three of 'er men lived, but doc tol' me later he didn't save 'em 'cause he neva seen da like of what dey had. Say dey toughed it out on dey own.

"Anyways, da farm be down on its luck and Ole Miss didn't have no ready cash. Doc sayd dat be all right, but Ole Miss, she made 'im take me. Tol' 'im I be a good tracker an' know'd da swamps an' bayous close abouts an' I'd be a big he'p to 'im.

"Now, da doc, he were a young man, an' I know'd by da way he was actin' dat he didn't want no boy taggin' along, an' I sho' didn't want to leave da only place I eva know'd, but he took me. I guess I growed on 'im. He sho'nuff growed on me. Went with 'im up an' down da rivers an' bayous of Lou'siana an' Miss'ippi.

Had a place on da Big Black where we'd hole up in da winter an' early spring. Was with 'im fou'teen years. Den in da spring of '63 he went up da riva' a piece to he'p deliver a babe. Was by hisself. It rained heavy a few days befo'. Dat Big Black was still up some, but der was a ferry. Just had to go aways upstream to git it, but der was a place, too, we forded reg'lar.

"His hoss come to da neighbor's place midday. We found da doc a little downstream from our place, not a mark on 'im. Think he tried to cross at our ford, but dat riva' be stronger dan he thought." Zachary blinked and turned away. "He neva did learn to swim good."

"I'm sorry."

Zachary nodded.

"He taught you to read and write?"

"And some doctorin'. Me an' ole missus Hughes, she were da neighbor, an' all da ole folks left 'round buried 'im proper. Eva'body thought lots of 'im. Den I ask da missus what was I to do. She sayd to go home an' da shurif would come fo' me." He looked Eli in the eye.

"And you just kept walkin' till you came to the Yankee line."

"Dey was already in Grand Gulf." He shifted on his feet and looked away. "Doc Yancy had sayd not too long befo' dat he'd been thinkin' to join da Army. Too many of our young neighbors bein' kilt. He meant Confed'rate, and I thought 'bout dat befo' I went an' found dem Yanks." He bowed his head. "Felt bad 'bout dat, but I just couldn't see me belongin' to nobody else but da doc. Figured my chances of such a thing happenin' was better with da Confed'rates dan da Federals."

Eli figured those Rebs would have found a darkie who knew "doctorin'" right handy, but he reckoned Zachary had done the prudent thing.

"And they made a soldier out of you."

Zachary blew out a breath. "Dey wanted me to dig trenches." He grinned. "Dat's when I tol' 'em I know'd some doctorin'. Put me with da rest of da 'contraband' den, to he'p wif da sick."

"You served as a doctor in the Army?"

"Naw, I don't think dey eva would've let me be a real doctor. Dey put me to doin' da nasty stuff dey didn't wanna do. When things settled down a bit, and dey started formin' up da Native Guard, I talked my way into da 2nd Infantry, Warren County."

"And now this detail with Major Parker."

"Handpicked, I was." Zachary grinned again. "Just to follow you 'roun' dis ghost town."

Eli looked back at Jocelyn's grave, and after a moment, the sergeant cleared his throat. "Beggin' yo' pardon, Colonel, but I don't know what we lookin' at either, or why we lookin' at it."

Eli knelt down and pulled a blackberry sprig from near the foot of Jocelyn's grave. "This is Jocelyn LeBlanc, my father's alleged lover, who hanged herself from an oak tree at Camellia Creek."

The sergeant again looked at the headstone. "In 1840?"

"Yep."

"And yo' wife…?"

"Moved into my home a little over a month ago and has determined the suicide was murder."

Zachary looked at Eli, then back to the grave. "Oh," he said, then after a moment asked, "An' dat's all der is to it?"

"I'm afraid so."

"Do you think dis woman was murdered?"

Eli started off in the direction he'd watched Captain Summers trek. "Never gave it much thought."

"But now you do?" Zachary said, catching up and falling into step beside him.

"Got other things on my mind."

"Ah."

Eli looked at him. Like why his wife was here today.

"Miz Hale involved in da death of dat Jocelyn woman all dem years ago?"

Eli sure didn't think so. "No," he said, but then he *heard* the sergeant's question, and he repeated it in his mind. On his last visit a week ago, Parker had mentioned Laura's going to see May. No doubt Parker divulged that information to Eli to send him off to May's, but Alice had beat him there. And these Yanks had, no doubt, been watching. That could explain Parker on Alice's scent.

"Where's your major?"

Now Zachary turned straight ahead and kept plodding down the dirt road leading away from the cemetery.

At the base of the hill and back on Commerce Street, Eli looked up the road to his right. Up aways, Captain Summers was making the left turn onto Spring street, and Eli's gut quaked. That meant Alice had found her way to Isabel's. For a brief moment up on that hill, he'd hoped his wife's only reason for coming to Rodney was to pay her respects to Jocelyn. That no longer appeared to be the case, and assuming Parker wasn't already at Isabel's waiting for her, Captain Summers would soon let the major know Alice had arrived there. He looked at Zachary, who also watched his captain disappear.

"Sergeant, I think we can both assume my wife is on her way to the establishment of the lovely Isabel Hays."

The sergeant stood stoic.

"And I can assume you'll let Parker know I know it."

Zachary almost said something, but caught himself.

"Well," Eli said, "I have no desire to cross paths with more of you today, so unless you'd care to accompany me back to Camellia Creek, I'll say good-bye."

The sergeant nodded, then looked up the now deserted north block of Commerce Street. A good fifty paces later, Eli looked back at the sergeant, still standing in the same spot. He figured the man would wait until he lost sight of Eli, then he'd again take up the trail. He was the sergeant's charge. Alice was the captain's, and he didn't know who the devil Parker was hound-dogging.

Knowing he was being followed made it easier to lose the sergeant, and knowing the town and the now overgrown lots surrounding Isabel's house made it easier for him to stay lost to the man. He climbed the live oak he and Andrew used to climb as kids. Once this yard had been manicured all the way to the graceful monster's trunk. Today it was shrouded in high grass and shrubs, its low limbs resplendent with green foliage, which effectively hid him, and left him with a perfect view of Isabel's front door.

<h1 style="text-align:center">Chapter Fifty-nine</h1>

Alice raised a gloved hand to the door of the large and pristine town home, pink, indeed, just as "Aunt Maggie" had told her. It was a little past noon and the house appeared empty. That or its inhabitants slept.

Through the pines at the far end of the porch, she could see the Mississippi shimmering in the sunlight. She studied the door and couldn't help but feel she'd misconstrued something about this place. Then she drew in a breath, seized the brass knocker, and walloped it. A young woman of mixed blood and primly dressed in dark calico, opened the door. She peered curiously at Alice, then said, "Yes?"

"I would like to see Miss Izzie LeBlanc."

"Who?"

Oh, dear. Alice's heart sped up. She looked up, then down the length of the porch. Misconstrued something, yes, but she could not have mistaken the house. There'd been a daughter, Maggie told her, but Alice never thought to ask Izzie's married name. "Is there an Izzie here? The woman of the house?"

"Let me check with my mistress," the young woman said and allowed Alice inside. "Wait here."

Alice watched the woman travel down a hall lit by gas wall sconces, their flames reflected in the gold pattern woven into the red wallpaper. To her right, a stairwell of wide, oak footers and white-painted risers curved its way from the generous foyer to the next floor. Soft murmurs, then a giggle emerged from a room on her immediate right, and Alice started to peek in....

"You're looking for Izzie LeBlanc?"

Alice turned back toward the hallway where now stood a

431

beautiful golden-haired woman, amusement vying with curiosity in her eyes. She seemed so polite, refined. Alice licked her bottom lip and stepped forward. "Yes. Are you she?"

"Probably, but my dear Miss…"

"Mrs.," Alice said, "Mrs. Eli Calhoon."

The woman's eyes widened, and she extended a hand. "You are Alice Calhoon?"

"You know of me?"

The woman bubbled. "I know Eli, and I know he acquired a wife. I did not, however, expect her at my door." She laughed pleasantly and still holding Alice's hand, looked her over head to foot. "I thought you were looking for work, and I was going to hire you, too."

Alice glanced over her shoulder to the sunlit parlor, luxuriously outfitted in red velvet furniture. She saw no one, but heard soft murmurs interspersed with low male laughter. The rhythmic rapping of her heart increased. She was in a house of prostitution. Alice, of course, had never been in one, but she knew of them. She was in that very house, no doubt, which Jonathan and her own husband visited. Good Lord, what would Eli do if—Alice turned back to the woman—*when* he found out?

Trying to hide her dismay, she said, "I must be disturbing you."

"Not at all, and I am delighted to make your acquaintance. And so you know who you are talking to, there is no longer an Izzie LeBlanc. There never really was. There is an Izzie Hays, and there is only one person left alive who still refers to me as Izzie."

Alice blew out a breath. "You are Isabel Hays." Things were falling into place. They weren't making sense yet, but they were falling into place.

"I am indeed, Isabel Leigh Hays." The woman turned slightly and extended her arm in invitation. "Please."

And Alice led the way down the garish hall.

The woman was not the loud, coarse, painted creature of her imagination. This madam wore a gold taffeta dress with a white lace bodice, closed at the neck by a lace collar replete with pearl buttons. Her hair was coiffed to feminine perfection atop her head, and her skin, when Alice passed her, exuded the delicate scent of lilac—not gardenia.

"Could you bring us some tea, Dinah?" Isabel said to the girl who'd let Alice in the house, then ushered Alice into a spacious office, warmed by afternoon sunshine and a potbellied stove in a distant corner. A gaslight hung from a chain above a large desk.

"Let's sit on the sofa."

The sofa, long, leather, and very comfortable, sat against a wall near the stove.

Isabel sat beside her. "I am perplexed," the woman said. "I would have expected you to come about Eli, if you ever made an appearance here at all, but it appears Aunt Maggie sent you?"

"Yes, but she sent me to see Izzie."

Isabel frowned, and Alice continued. "I wasn't expecting Isabel Hays. I heard your name mentioned the night Laura Blackledge was murdered. You're involved in something and there are those who believe Eli is involved in it, too."

"I am involved in many things, Mrs. Calhoon."

"I fear Eli is going to be caught up in some investigation —"

Isabel held up her hand. "If I needed any information out of you, Mrs. Calhoon," she said with a touch of frost, "believe me, I'd let you continue. However, I do not. Be advised when talking to strangers, you do not know if they are friend or foe."

"But you are Eli's friend."

"You couldn't possibly be sure of that."

"He's working with you."

"You couldn't possibly be sure of that either, and as for that, you are mistaken."

Alice felt the blood drain from her cheeks. Isabel Hays must have seen it, too, because she reached out and patted the gloved hand in Alice's lap.

"But as regards the former, I am his friend. And because I care for him as the son of someone I loved dearly, I'm going to warn you to stay out of this."

"I hadn't expected this tie…"

"I've known Eli since he was born. His father and I were friends before Holland wed Rosalind."

"Friends?"

She smiled. "Yes, Mrs. Calhoon, friends. I was the mistress of a man named Isaac Baker. He had a plantation in Westside and a family. I met Holland through him when I was still a young girl. This house was Isaac's town home away from his family. Many of Isaac's associates joined him here for cards and business, but the only man I was required to serve was Isaac. He was a gentleman, and I loved him. He died in 1838. That was a very long time ago. He left me this house and little else. After, Holland was a client, shall we say, from time to time. But he was a good friend always."

Isabel Hays cocked an eyebrow. "Something else is confusing you?"

"I am sorry, but you're so…?"

"Yes?"

"Golden."

Isabel wrinkled her brow, and Alice, sorry she'd led the conversation this way, said, "You're very different from your aunt, I mean. In her I can see—"

A knock sounded on the door and the prim Dinah, tea service in hand, entered. She sat the tray on a black lacquer pedestal table at Isabel's end of the sofa.

"Thank you," Isabel said and took a cup from the servant, who was about to pour. "I'll do it. Would you ask Becky to come in here? She was in the library earlier."

While she poured the tea, Isabel didn't look at Alice. "Sugar?"

"And you have cream. Oh, please, yes."

"So much we'd taken for granted is missing from our lives, isn't it?" She handed Alice the cup and a shallow bowl filled with odd-sized clumps of brown sugar. "You were, of course, referring to the Negro blood before Dinah entered?"

"Yes. Your Aunt Maggie is beautiful," Alice said quickly. "I mean I'm sure she was when she was young."

"Don't feel awkward, Alice—may I call you that?"

"Of course."

Isabel smiled. "She was very beautiful. Both sisters were, as were the daughters. Silky's skin was light, but fell short of fair. My other sister, Angel, had green eyes and dark hair, wavy more than curly. Her skin was fair. She could have easily passed as white."

"Well, she had more white blood than Negro, didn't she?"

Isabel took a sip of tea. "It doesn't work that way."

Alice knew it didn't. Nowhere does it work that way.

"Angel wed a local merchant, the son of a wealthy fur trader, actually. He was a mix of Choctaw and Scot. She died in child-birth two years after they wed." Isabel set her cup and saucer on the table. "As for me, I have no Negro blood."

"I thought Sarah LeBlanc—"

"Dubois. Sarah Dubois was our mother. She was a freeborn octoroon, a prostitute from New Orleans, who at an early age became Raphael LeBlanc's woman. Raphael was a trapper, French by descent. He brought his small family here in 1790. For a brief period, many years later, he kept a second woman in Grand Gulf, where he conducted some of his business. That woman was my mother, a sixteen-year-old orphan whom he res-cued, shall we say, from a life of pure shame. She was white. Their relationship was short-lived. She died giving birth to me. The timing, if nothing else, proved fortuitous, because Sarah Dubois had just given birth to stillborn twins. Raphael brought me to her, and to her credit, she raised me as her own. Sarah Marie Dubois was as much my mother as she was Silky and Angel's. And despite what you must be thinking about my father, he was a kind, loving man, at least with his family, who provided well for us all until his untimely death in a knife fight in Choctaw territory. I was three.

"Aunt Maggie's husband had died of malaria shortly before that, and she and Mama returned to a trade to which they were very well suited. Silky and I eventually became mistresses to wealthy planters. Angel married, and of course you know her fate.

"Now, since you didn't know you were coming to Isabel Hays, is there some reason other than Eli that you're here?"

Alice poised the cup halfway to her lips. "I'm here because of Jocelyn."

"Jocelyn?"

"Yes," Alice said, nodding her head. "Your Aunt Maggie said you'd remember more of those days and that you have Silky's journals and perhaps you would let me review the one she wrote around the period of Jocelyn's death."

The woman studied her a long moment, then said, "May I ask your interest?"

"I believe she was murdered."

"Oh." Isabel tightened her lips. "And why do you think that?"

Alice wasn't sure how to answer that without indicating to Isabel Hays that she might be out of her mind. This was not the loopy aunt. She swallowed. "The ghost."

"The ghost?"

"You are aware some people have claimed, over the years, to have seen an apparition?"

"I am, and for the sake of discretion, I will not ask if you are one of those."

"I do thank you, as does my husband."

Isabel laughed softly. "You are not the first to have questioned how my niece died, Alice. However, you are the first lately." The woman rose gracefully from her place on the sofa and walked to a set of shelves behind her desk. She pulled a small volume from a set of books lining the middle shelf, opened the book at a point near its end, perused it, then turned to Alice, still on the sofa. "Her mother questioned it, for one."

"And you?"

She handed Alice the small book, then retook her seat. "Unfortunate as it is for my own peace of mind, I think she took her own life."

"But why?"

"My dear, naive niece miscalculated with Holland. She expected him to wed her."

"But…" Alice looked around the room. "Forgive me, Miss Hayes—"

"Isabel, please."

"Isabel. I'd been led to understand Jocelyn was his mistress, not unlike your relationship with—"

"Isaac, but no, they had no such relationship. Jocelyn was a deluded child. Her father and brothers had spoiled her terribly. Macon Treadwell could have made her a daughter in his world. He had made her a good match, but in her naiveté she forsook it all. She believed herself in love with Holland Calhoon and him with her, but you must understand Holland had known Jocelyn since she was a little girl. She visited me here often. After his wife died, and I lost Isaac, Holland took to bringing his boys here with him when he visited." Isabel smiled when Alice started to speak. "It wasn't a whorehouse then, Alice.

"Jocelyn took up a great deal of time with Andrew and later Eli. She played with them and read to them, much like a nurse-maid. Apparently Rosalind had doted on her boys, and that's how Jocelyn responded to them. Naomi Polk was not as giving.

"Suffice it to say, the boys loved Jocelyn. Eventually, she began visiting Camellia Creek for overnight stays. This familiarity continued past Jocelyn's eighteenth birthday and after Hawk Duvall, the match her father made, began courting her.

"Then one day in November 1840, Holland brought Jocelyn home to Silky and told her he felt Jocelyn was of an age that staying at his house, given his being single, was inappropriate.

"He didn't tell Silky why, but I know now he was sparing Jocelyn embarrassment. Not long after, Jocelyn turned up pregnant. She claimed Holland was the father. Holland denied it."

Alice glanced at the journal in her lap. "Her father and brothers, do you know where they are?"

"Her father died unexpectedly in 1847. His wife remarried. Her sons by Macon Treadwell, Jocelyn's half brothers, fought in the Mexican War. One was killed, the other never came home, choosing to make his home in California. I assume he's still there."

"That would have been after Jocelyn died."

"A number of years after. Silky's son Stephen was drafted into the Confederate Army at the age of forty-five. He was killed last year at Franklin." She looked away for a moment. "Sadly, there's little left of Raphael LeBlanc."

"I am sorry."

Isabel squeezed Alice's hand.

"If Holland wasn't the—"

A quick knock sounded on the office door, then it opened, and Alice cut off her query. Isabel rose with a flourish. "Becky, darling"—Isabel looked at Alice—"Alice Calhoon, Eli's wife."

A funny little squeak escaped yet another beautiful woman acquainted with her husband. This one was young, maybe a bit older than Alice, with honey blonde hair and green eyes. She was properly dressed in black, and Alice now recalled Aunt Maggie saying she was a war widow. A smile as pretty as the young woman herself spread across Becky's face, and she pushed the door wide, then crossed the room, her hands extended in welcome. Baffled, Alice rose to her feet. She still held her cup and could grasp only one of Becky's hands.

"Mother...?" the girl asked, stepping back after giving Alice a kiss on the cheek.

"I don't believe so," Isabel said in response to the cryptic question and took Alice's cup and saucer. Becky squeezed herself and a profusion of black crepe between Alice and the table and sat, pulling Alice down with her.

"Well, I'll have to talk to him, won't I? Shame on him for not telling you about Mama and me."

Alice assumed "he" to be Eli, and obviously he didn't want her to know about Isabel and Becky. That probably meant he was not going to be pleased that she'd found out... whatever it was she'd found out. Feeling a bit at a disadvantage, Alice said, "I did know about your mother."

"And what did you know?" Becky asked.

Alice swallowed, then nodded. "That she's an old family friend." Who wears lilac instead of gardenia.

Becky, who also wore lilac, laughed and took Alice's hands in hers before turning back to her mother. "Whatever are we going to do with our…?" She stopped, her eyes fixed on the door leading into the hallway, the one she'd just entered and left wide. Immediately her pleasantness slipped away. Alice's gut clenched. Beside her, Becky rose. Seth Parker, immaculate in his woolen blouse, stood in the entry, then came in, his presence dominating the room. He stared at Becky, who, face pale, stared right back, then he nodded to the women. Becky raised her chin as Alice bent her head in greeting. Finally, he leveled his gaze on Isabel, who smiled beautifully.

"I do apologize, Major Parker. I didn't hear you knock."

He removed the odd-looking forage cap from his head and tucked it beneath his arm. "That's because I didn't."

"To what do we owe this honor?"

"I came in pursuit of *other* business, and it was brought to my attention that Mrs. Calhoon was visiting you. I wish a word with her." He turned to Becky. "I wasn't aware that you had another guest."

"Well stated, Major," Isabel said. "This is my daughter, Rebecca Mackey, from Madison County."

He raised his chin. "*Madison* County, Mrs. Mackey?"

"Yes, Major Parker," she responded and turned to Alice. "It seems our visit has been interrupted. We'll chat later."

"I'd like to chat with you, also, Mrs. Mackey," Seth said, then stepped in front of her when she didn't stop. She stopped then and glared at him.

"You have no idea, Major, how little I care." She again started around him, and he looked over his shoulder at Captain Summers, waiting in the hall outside the door.

"Stop it," Isabel snapped. "Let her go. She arrived here last night, and she's not involved in any of my business. She never has been."

Becky had stopped at her mother's command. The younger woman locked eyes with Seth, who, after a moment, without taking his eyes off her, said, "Step aside, Captain."

Alice watched Becky disappear into the hall.

"I fear she doesn't think much of you Federals, Major," Isabel said and moved around him. The woman smiled. "Unlike me, she hasn't experienced the pleasure of your 'softer' side."

He snorted.

Alice looked down on the sofa, found Silky LeBlanc's journal, and slipped it into the pocket of her dress. She looked up in time to watch Isabel shut her office door in Captain Summers' face. Seth was watching Isabel, who stopped abruptly. "Unless you wish to speak to Alice alone?"

Chapter Sixty

"What are you doing here, Alice?"

"We were having tea, Major. Would you care to join us?"

Seth shot Isabel an irritated glance, then turned back to Alice. "Does your husband know where you are?"

His mind was working. Alice could tell that by the glint in his eye and the steel in his voice.

"He does not."

"You're sure?"

"Well, I didn't tell him I was coming here."

"That's interesting. Why didn't you?"

Isabel chuckled. "God only knows what he'll do when he finds out."

Alice looked at the shimmering madam. The woman winked at her. "And he will find out, my dear."

"Miss Hays, do you mind?" Seth said.

Alice's gaze slid from Seth to Isabel, then back to Seth. Isabel was finding the confrontation amusing, while Seth Parker's tone conveyed a patronizing superiority indicative of a man speaking to a woman he considered stupid. Alice was confused, not stupid.

"We were discussing murder, if you must know."

"Whose?"

"It doesn't concern you."

"I'll be the judge of that."

Alice glanced at Isabel, watching the two of them.

"Which one, Alice?" Seth said. "Wayne Hale's, Laura's, or Guthrie's?"

"You left out Brim Solomon's."

"We're pretty sure what happened to Solomon."

"So, one of the others you're determined to attribute to my husband." She waved her hand. "Take your pick."

"I'm not determined to 'attribute' anything to your husband unless he's guilty of something."

"Well, I wouldn't mind determining that myself."

"And if you do determine he's guilty of something?"

"If I were going to determine anything it would be that he's not."

"But if you discover he is?"

She clamped her mouth shut. She absolutely despised being bullied. Seth bent close, bringing his face to hers. "And here you are, talking to a woman up to her neck in this sordid mess."

Alice looked around him to Isabel, who gave her an innocent look. Of course, Isabel knew the real reason she was here, but either she was waiting to let Alice tell the handsome major the truth or she was content to leave him chasing his tail.

Alice frowned at him. She wasn't sure he'd believe the truth if she told him. In the meantime, he was doing a lot of talking on his own.

"If she and Calhoon are working together, Alice, where do you think that leaves you?"

Again, Alice looked at Isabel, who gave her head a subtle shake. Alice took that to mean say nothing.

"It could very well leave you dead."

What in the world was this "sordid mess" Seth referred to? "I'm not afraid," she said.

"And if I'm not working with your husband," Isabel said, "reckless interference on your part could cause him harm."

"I will try to remember that should I ever opt for reckless interference."

Seth stepped back, blinked at Alice, then pivoted to Isabel. "I'm aware that Franklin's here."

Alice's breath caught in her throat. "Uncle Peter?"

"Jonathan," Isabel said and smiled at Seth. "Though I've yet to meet the elder Franklin, I have heard much about him."

Whatever the woman implied, she meant it for Seth. Alice

waited a moment, hoping he'd say something from which she might deduce what these people were talking about, but he turned instead to Alice. "What's your relationship with Jonathan, Alice?"

Oh good Lord, not this again. "I haven't one."

"That's not the tale he tells."

"Oh?"

"He claims the two of you were to wed, before Calhoon stole you away."

"I've heard. It's not true."

"He seems to believe you may still have a future together."

Alice felt her cheeks warm. She would have responded, vehemently, but Isabel caught her eye. Again a subtle head shake. This time, Seth was quicker and noticed the woman's caution. He refocused on Alice.

"Did you come here today to meet him?"

She saw Isabel brace in an *oh my God* sort of way, but despite her heart belting her chest and pounding her ears, Alice managed calm. "Why," she said sweetly, "I thought he was working with you."

Seth bridled, then glanced at Isabel, who now sat forward in her chair, a look of marked interest on her face. He looked back at Alice. "I beg your pardon?" he ground out.

"Oops," Alice said with a smile, first for Isabel, then for Seth. "Perhaps I've inadvertently opted for reckless interference after all. I do apologize."

Seth's fingers dug into her bicep in a manner reminiscent of Eli's angry hold. He pushed her out the door, nearly into Captain Summers, then all but dragged her down the hall. In the foyer, she found herself face to face with Jonathan Franklin.

From inside the red-velvet-decorated parlor, someone hollered, "Did you rent her a room for the night, Franklin?"

His face reddened. She yanked her arm free of Seth's hold and charged toward the parlor to confront the filthy-mouthed buffoon who'd dare say such a thing. Seth caught her around the waist before she cleared the door.

"Alice," he said softly, "spare yourself the abuse. It's time you went home."

"Let go of me," she said to Seth. He let her go, and she looked around quickly for Jonathan. "Where did that snake go?" she asked Isabel, who stood in the foyer, with a smirk on her mouth. Captain Summers loomed behind Isabel. "Snuck out the front door," he said.

"You ran off my best customer," a pretty dark-haired girl at the foot of the stairs said to her.

"I apologize for your loss of income," Alice said, then pivoted and faced Seth Parker. She almost told the young woman that perhaps she could have this one, but she bit her tongue. He really did appear put out. She looked past him to Isabel. "I do thank you for the tea and the lovely conversation." She raised her chin to Seth, who was still watching her, and looked again at Isabel. "I will ponder the information you provided me, then I would like to talk to you again, if I may?"

"My pleasure."

"And do tell Rebecca it was nice to meet her and I hope we meet again."

"I'm certain you will, Alice, dear. Take care on the road home. You're not alone?"

"Eli's hand Buck is waiting for me at your aunt's."

Chapter Sixty-one

Sulfur stung her nostrils, and Alice held up the flaming match, a weary beacon in the cold darkness of her home. She lit the coal-oil-saturated wick and turned it up. A pregnant quiet met her ears. Eerie. The house breathed, and her heart jumped. She spun to see behind her, then gazed around the room, her eyes searching one dark corner of the parlor after another.

Nothing. Nevertheless, after she got the fire going, she'd check the entire house. She flexed her fingers, removed her gloves, and set the glass chimney in place. The lamp highlighted Silky LeBlanc's journal she had placed on the table, and she wondered where her husband was. A floorboard whispered to her, and again her heartbeat quickened. She called Eli's name.

Tugging at the ribbon securing her bonnet, she stepped around the settee. There was enough wood to get a fire started, but….

She tensed when the back door opened, then relaxed with the familiar sound of Eli's boots crossing the floor. He emerged from the dark recesses of the dining room and foyer, stared at her a moment, then tossed his hat into his chair. "Nice day?" he asked. "You haven't got a fire started."

She turned with him when he passed her. "I've only now gotten home."

"That would be obvious, even if I hadn't dogged your heels all day."

"You followed me?"

He tossed one log amidst the ashes and turned on her. "Yes, I followed you."

"Why?"

He looked up. "I can't be sure in this light, sweetheart, but I swear your pink cheeks have lost all their color."

"Why did you sneak around behind me?"

"Why did you wait until I was gone to leave? To Rodney, no less. I've told you the road through Westside is dangerous." He turned, bent, and picked up another log.

"It needs to be shoveled out, Eli."

He slammed the second log against the first sending ash over the hearth and onto the floor. "You do it then."

She dropped her gaze from his menacing stare. "I will."

Alice reached for the shovel hanging on the wall, and he grabbed her arm, forcing her to face him. "What are you up to?"

She whimpered at his hold, but he didn't relent.

"What? Tell me."

"Let me go."

He responded by grabbing her other shoulder, and her head reeled with the force of his shake. "Tell me."

"Let me go!" she screamed at him.

Cruel fingers bit her arms, and he pulled her face close to his, tight-jawed and hard-eyed in the dim light. "You are going to tell me what you're up to."

What *she* was up to? "I'm not saying a word till you let me go."

"You are talking just fine." He enunciated carefully, giving her a hard jolt with each word.

He stopped shaking her, leaving her head spinning. Nausea swelled her stomach. "Do you intend to beat it out of me?"

"If I have to."

"Well, if you don't let go of me right now, Eli Calhoon, you will have to, and I swear to God you'll not learn a thing."

He stared at her, his hands still bruising her biceps, his harsh breath fanning her face.

"Oh, yes, I will, darling, and what I want to know is why you went to the house of Isabel Hays?"

"You're bullying me." She blinked back tears. "And you're hurting me."

His brutal hold tightened. She didn't think that it could, but it did. She clenched her teeth and tried to twist away from him, but couldn't.

"I'm not compromising with you on this, Alice. Tell me why you went there."

She pried at his fingers, but when he shook her again and told her to stop she spat, "I went to see what you find so special about the place."

It was a lie, of course, but she didn't care. She'd done nothing to incur his wrath, not wrath like this.

"Is that why Parker showed up, tit for tat? Or was it Franklin you met? He scurried out pretty damn fast."

She'd assumed she'd run Jon off. Maybe—

"I told you I hadn't been unfaithful."

She widened her eyes and glared at him. "I would never whore myself to exact revenge from you."

"You said you would." His thumbs dug deeper in her biceps, and it was all she could do not to burrow her face in his chest to endure the pain.

"I said no such thing. I'd have to be in love with him."

"Are you?"

She folded at the knees, but he held her up. "Go to hell, you bastard! I've not been unfaithful either."

His hold lessened, but only a little, and she stood on her own.

"So is the vengeance you wish to extract of a different kind?"

"I beg your pardon?"

"Are you working with them?"

"Working with them?" she asked.

"Yes," he hissed, "working with them against me?"

"Is Isabel against you, too?"

He gave her a gentle shove, releasing her. She rubbed her bruised arms. He turned away and raked his hands through his hair, then whirled on her again. "What do you mean, 'too?'" He charged her. She wrapped her arms around her body and shrank into herself. "What did Parker say to you?"

He didn't touch her, and she looked up. "He was surprised to see me. He said I shouldn't be there."

"He wasn't surprised. Captain Summers followed you there."

She narrowed her eyes. "Why would he be following me?"

His gaze was accusatory, then he said, "Well, darling, perhaps he thinks you're involved in whatever it is I'm involved in?"

"What are you involved in?"

"Nothing. Why did you tell him you were there?"

"I didn't tell him anything."

He touched her again, and she hollered at him, "I told you, I didn't tell him anything. You think I want him to know you go to that place?"

"He already knows, and you are delusional, Alice, if you think I believe you didn't already realize that. Who told you about that place?

"You did."

"No, I didn't."

"Yes, you mentioned—"

"I might have spoken Isabel Hays' name in your presence, but I never mentioned her establishment." He shook her again. "Tell me."

She twisted away. "Aunt Betty."

He stared at her, then said, "Jon Franklin."

"Yes, he's seen you there. He told Uncle Peter, who told Aunt Betty."

"And she runs and tells you?"

"She's worried about my happiness."

"Does that make you happy, Alice, being told your husband fornicates in whorehouses?"

Alice glared at him. He was suspicious, suspicious of the Franklins. Well, that was reasonable; she herself had asked her aunt if Uncle Peter were involved with anything illegal. Alice raised her chin. "She thinks you are either unhappy with your wife or you like to engage in perverted sexual acts."

"Did you find the one that smelled of gardenia?"

Actually, she'd given that woman only cursory thought. She'd been focused on an "old family friend" she no longer considered a threat. Now he taunted her. She shifted to face him head-on, her arms so tense her forearms ached. Perhaps she should have looked for a woman wearing gardenia.

He chuckled. "Now what are you thinking, sweetheart? That my reason for going to Isabel Hays' whorehouse was nothing more sinister than perverse sex?"

She clenched and unclenched her fists. He glanced at her hands, then back to her face. "Would my desire for a bought woman be worse in your mind than plotting murder and mayhem against the United States?"

"You are despicable."

He narrowed his eyes. "As insane as that would make you, sweetheart, I would really like to believe that was your reason for going there."

"Meaning that would be better than my plotting to betray you?"

"Betray me, cheat on me, conspire against me with my enemies, your choice. Answer me."

"I think I should be the one to keep you satisfied."

He studied her face. "Are you sure?"

His voice was heavy with challenge, and her taxed heart, quickened anew. "Yes," she said, not at all certain that was the right thing to say.

With one quick step he brought his chest to hers. In the next instant his hands reached for her throat. She caught her breath when he grasped the collar of her dress and ripped the bodice open. The click of a button on the floor echoed Alice's gasp. One of his hands pushed the torn fabric over one shoulder, while the other reached for the ribbon securing her corset. He pulled her close, working the other arm of her dress over her shoulder and unlacing the corset. "Just so you know," he whispered in her ear, "I don't believe that's why you went there. Now get out of the dress."

He stepped back, and with shaking hands, she pushed the torn bodice over her hips. The dress, one of her nicer ones, pooled on the floor. The corset slipped, and she pressed it to her as she stepped out of her skirts. Still holding the corset in place, her body trembling, less from cold than anxiety, she looked up to find Eli a step away, watching her. He reached out and pulled the stiff leather corset from her breasts. She started to cover herself, but he commanded her not to. Obedience seemed prudent, she had accepted his challenge, so she did, and he stared at her breasts, then found her eyes. "You've got a body made to love, Alice."

She trembled violently in the dim lamplight.

"You should have left me be and let me make that fire when I wanted." He cocked his head and perused her body again. "Now I'm too busy."

"I don't think a fire would stop my shaking."

"What will?" he asked.

"Hold me." She needed to be held, to feel safe, as deluded as that thought might be, in his arms.

"Not yet."

She stepped toward him anyway.

"Stop it," he demanded.

Her eyes welled tears, and averting her gaze, she drew in a stuttered breath.

"Finish undressing." He pulled the shovel from the wall.

Gut taut with hurt, she kicked off one shoe, then the other. Damn him, damn him, damn him.

"Your petticoat and pantaloons."

Her nostrils flared, but she still didn't look at him. "I can use my hands?" Her voice sounded unsure to her ears, and she despised his knowing he'd managed to frighten her.

"You can."

His voice had softened, and she looked his way before grasping the ribbon holding her petticoat. He watched the undergarment fall to the floor.

"Are you getting undressed, too?"

"Hell, no," he said, "it's cold in here."

That was all she could take for the moment. Clamping her jaws tight, she reached for the petticoat on the floor and tossed it aside, then stepped to the wood pile and handed him a log. He frowned at her, glanced at her pantaloons, still on, and took the log. She handed him another.

"Is your plan to hit me in the head with one of those, Alice?"

She touched her dry upper lip with the tip of her tongue. "I hadn't thought of that." She squatted beside him. Keeping her breasts covered as best she could with one hand and arm, she used her other hand to place kindling among the stacked logs.

"Bring me the matches," he said.

She rose and did. Moments later he was glowing in golden light. The fire's warmth kissed her bare skin, and she prayed the flames would melt his cold resolve.

His eyes, black in the firelight, found hers. After a moment, his gaze dropped to the arms she held crisscrossed over her breasts. "You're starting to shiver again, sweetheart."

"I never stopped." She fought not to close her eyes, to shut out the cruel challenge in his and the doubts its hatefulness fueled.

"Stand up," he said. When she did, he pushed himself up on his knees in front of her. He pulled on her garters. "You should already have these off."

When she didn't speak, he looked up at her. She had twisted her hands together over her breasts, prayer-fashion. "Are you afraid of me, Alice?" he asked.

She shook her head. "Not of you." She lifted her foot, and he pulled her second stocking off. The touch of his hands on her waist surprised her, and she sucked in a breath.

"What then?" he asked, but before she could answer, he said, "Your skin is so soft," and he licked her navel.

Wet and cool and utterly delicious. A shudder raked her body, and he squeezed her hips at the same moment he sank his face into her stomach and kissed her belly. She arched slightly. "Nothing's wrong now, is there, darlin'."

Only the contempt she feared he held for her.

Alice felt his thumbs inside the waist of her pantaloons. With his quick tug on the ribbon holding up her drawers, she looked down and watched with mounting hunger the movement of his dark head so close to the apex of her legs. He dipped his head further and she tensed, relishing the velvet wetness of his tongue on the inside of her thigh.

Inner fire warmed her gut, then licked her womanhood. She reached out to steady herself on his shoulders, but he rose abruptly and, without warning, yanked her to him, pressing her nakedness against the rough wool of his frock coat. A gold button bit her nipple. He thrust his hand into her hair, and her carefully pinned coiffure loosened and fell around her shoulders. His fingers twisted into her locks. Pain scorched her scalp. She bit back a cry.

"Open up for me," he growled, and she did—the result of the stinging pain, not his command. Had she thought about it, she'd have forced him to tear her hair out rather than succumb to his sadistic force.

His lips covered hers, and his tongue plundered her mouth. Her heart was clamoring, her lips tingling, and her scalp burned where he held her still. He tore away and sank his face into her neck. "Goddamn you, Alice"—he nipped at her earlobe, then shook her when she whimpered and tried to push away—"nothing has ever tried my patience like you."

With his free arm, he circled her shoulders and rubbed his coat against her breasts. Heat pooled between her legs, and she moaned. His cruel fist unfolded against the back of her head, and his fingers gently caressed the hurt he'd inflicted.

He pulled back, but only far enough to see her face. She was still locked in his embrace. *In his embrace.* He was holding her and nothing else mattered. What kind of woman did that make her?

"Are you sure you still want to be the only one to please me?"

By allowing him to degrade and humiliate her? She shuddered and told herself he never would. "Can I please you, Eli?"

"I guess we'll see, won't we?"

She'd hoped for a more gracious response. "Will it hurt?"

"Do you want it to hurt?"

She shook her head.

He kissed her gently. "Then I won't let it hurt."

⋅⊱⋅

*H*e pushed his spent member inside his fly and buttoned his britches, then picked up the fireplace poker. "Are you ready to tell me why you went?"

"Not yet," she said from where she sat on the floor, naked, beneath a quilt. He prodded the fire, then threw on another log.

"I should take that shovel back off the wall and paddle your beautiful derrière until you howl for what you did today."

"That would hurt," she said softly.

"There're all kinds of pleasure, and all degrees of perversion."

"Spanking?"

"Very popular. More sadistic are cat-o'-nine-tails or a whip…and bondage."

"Did you use whips and cat-o'-nine-tails on the slaves?"

"Nary a one around. I don't recall there being any such on Camellia Creek in my lifetime. Daddy had a belt, though. Never recall him using it on a darkie. Used it on me and Andrew from time to time though."

She clamped her pretty lips together, red and bruised from the kisses he'd forced on her, given her, and finally, shared with her.

"Well, given your affinity for it, I'll spank you if you wish."

"Funny, sweetness, but I'm no masochist." He sat on the floor beside her. "And I'm happy to say I don't think you are either."

"That makes you happy?"

"I'm not a sadist."

"You don't like to inflict—"

"That was anger you felt, not sadism."

"Oh," she said.

"I made it up to you."

She bit her bottom lip, then turned and stared at the fire. She'd known pleasure, intense pleasure…and, he reckoned, what she might perceive to be degradation. That, he suspected, is what bothered her now. He'd tasted every inch of her naked flesh and suckled her breasts till she cried for him to stop. Then he'd kneeled, fully dressed, in front of her nude body, spread her legs, and performed oral sex on her until her petite body writhed in the golden glow of the fire. He'd made her happy, and he knew it.

Her returning the favor proved less palatable, but despite her barely veiled misgivings, she'd performed exceptionally, and he had spared her what he knew would have been the ultimate humiliation, ending that act early, tossing her belly-up on the cold floor, and possessing her in the traditional manner.

He'd been a supreme bastard tonight, but not as bad, given his anger, as he could have been. Her climactic cry of pleasure was his saving grace.

"I made Seth Parker almost as angry today as I made you."

Jealous heat swelled his cock. He wondered if the bastard had considered raping her as he had. "I still am. If you're not going to tell me what the two of you talked about, you'd be better off not mentioning him."

She pulled the quilt tighter around her shoulders and looked at him. "Isabel was with us. I don't think he knows what she's up to, and he doesn't know what you're up to either, but he said that if you are involved with anything illegal and I find out about it, you might kill me to protect yourself."

"And I've proven how ruthless I am."

"I've always known you were ruthless. I still don't know how much is ruthlessness and how much is an act."

And she didn't need to know.

"Isabel countered by implying that if you're not involved with her, my interference could get you killed." She scooted closer to him, then wrapped her quilt around him. "Why would that be?"

"Because Parker wants to believe I'm involved. He operates with impunity, Alice. Tyranny reigns, and I'm in a precarious position, though I'm not sure why. Did you tell him anything?"

"I don't *know* anything." She closed her eyes tight, and with one hand on the floor and the other holding the quilt in place, she struggled up. "And I wouldn't if I did."

"Wait," he said, and rose, then held his hand out to her. "Not knowingly, but Parker is smart. If you say anything at all, you give up information without realizing it."

"Which is why I mostly listened to him. Do you think I'm working against you?"

He started blowing out lamps, leaving one to guide their way. "It's a consideration I've had to accept since I brought you here."

She bowed her head. Her toes peeked from beneath the quilt. Cold, he bet. He needed to put her to bed and make tender love to her. Both of them naked. He touched her arm, and she looked up.

"Seth asked me a curious question," she said.

He cocked his head.

"He wanted to know if the reason I'd gone to Isabel's house was to meet Jonathan."

"Did you talk to him?"

"He left as soon as he saw me. One of the men there, I didn't see who, said something rude about me and him and a room." She blinked at Eli. "Along the same lines you and Seth are thinking, I gather. Seth told me Jonathan was telling people he and I still had a future together."

Eli swallowed. He needed to kill Jon Franklin.

"Is that why you asked me about Jonathan the other morning?"

"Yes."

"And what does all this mean to you?"

His heart beat a little harder in his chest. "It means good ole Jon expects me to be removed from the scene in the near future."

"That's what I think, too. Does he know anything about you that could make that happen?"

"There are three murders he'd like Parker to arrest me for."

"And Isabel Hays, would she help him?"

"No."

"You're sure?"

He grasped the poker and shoved it into a burning log. Sparks flew. "I'm sure."

"Does Seth think Jonathan is working with Isabel?"

"For all I know your entire Yankee get-rich-quick family is working with Isabel."

Her mouth opened, but Eli held up a hand.

"Or he might have been trying to find out if you were meeting Franklin for personal reasons."

"I thought that, too, but it seems rather indiscreet for me to meet my lover in a whorehouse."

"Jonathan Franklin is a client. Discretion can be bought in a place like Isabel's."

"My husband is a client. How discreet can that possibly be?"

"Your husband is not a client, and I'm trying to answer your question, that's all."

Her head was shaking stubbornly as she turned away from him, the quilt dragging behind her like a train. "That can't be the answer. Seth knows you have ties to Isabel, as does Jonathan, so he wasn't implying an affair. I believe he thinks you might be working with Jonathan."

"And you're thinking Parker might believe you're working with him, too?"

"Maybe—"

"Then why is Parker concerned for your safety at my hands?"

"Because he's not *sure* of anything. He's fishing."

"He's fishing, all right, with a net. Alice, Jon Franklin has a big mouth. Remember, before I came on the scene, he was telling people he intended to marry you. I know that's because he wanted to look like a serious investor for whatever dealings, legal or illegal, these people, whoever they may be, have going on."

"But you got the capital instead."

"That's right."

"So now you're the one who made the investment?"

"You fishing, too?" He turned away and banked the fire and set the screen in place.

"Have you considered you can trust me?"

"I have my own investments to make, Alice, and sound reasons for not trusting you."

Her eyes glistened in the firelight. He touched her lips. "Shhh," he said. "Self-created. I forced you to marry me. I don't dare forget that, because I doubt you have."

"I wish our trust was as strong as our passion."

A new erection rubbed against his britches. He picked the poker up from the hearth and stood it against the fireplace, then turned, scooping her, quilt and all, into his arms. "And I'm still angry enough to mete out another dose of passion, sweetheart."

Chapter Sixty-two

Eli stuck his head back inside the dimly lit bedroom. Alice was putting on her wrapper, her movements shaky. She looked at him. "Did you bring something with you from Isabel's?" he asked.

She stopped, frowned at him, then pulled her hair, its silken strands gleaming in the lantern light, from the neck of the outer garment. "Yes," she answered, her voice hushed. "One of Silky LeBlanc's journals."

"You need to come on out. Put on your heavy robe. I do believe every member of his troop is out here."

Eli returned to the parlor. He lit yet another lamp. Parker and five Negro troops had roused them from bed. It was after one in the morning. "She's coming. She says she did bring something with her." Eli took his seat in front of the fireplace, still smoldering, no flames, just embers. "Take a seat, Major."

"That won't be necessary."

Just like invading his home in the middle of the night wasn't necessary. Parker made half a pivot in the direction of the hall when Alice walked in. "What can I help you with, Major?"

Parker nodded politely. "I'm sorry to wake you so late, *Mrs.* Calhoon, but it was brought to my attention that you left Miss Hays' home this afternoon with a book of some sort. Miss Hays said it was a journal belonging to an older sister."

"An older sister who has been dead since 1842. What possible interest could you have in that journal?"

"Possibly the same as yours?"

"I seriously doubt that."

Eli spied the thing on the table that Alice had placed at one end of their worn settee. He reached for it, but she beat him to it. Parker extended his hand.

"Do you have a warrant?"

The major dropped his hand. "I don't need a warrant."

"Who says you don't? Mississippi has a civil government, approved by the president himself."

"My investigation includes the murder of a freedman and his family."

Eli watched her stiffen. "That gives you the right to act with impunity?"

He noted her use of his word, and he rose. "Tyranny" would be next. "Alice, let him have the journal."

She jerked her head around and looked at him. "No. It's Isabel's. She trusts me to take care of it and return it to her." She nodded at Parker. "This journal is of no value to him unless he's trying to solve Jocelyn's murder."

"Whose murder?" Parker asked.

Near the parlor entry, Sergeant Zachary shifted his weight. Eli met the man's eyes.

"Jocelyn LeBlanc, Isabel's niece. She was murdered twenty-five years ago," Alice answered.

Parker stole a glance at his sergeant, then cocked his head at Eli. "You know, Sergeant Zachary told me a little of your conversation in Rodney. I admit I'm not sure what to make of it."

Eli blew out a breath. "Jocelyn LeBlanc was found hanging from a tree near this house. Her death was ruled a suicide."

"It was murder," Alice said.

Eli stepped toward Alice. She should just let the bastard have the thing. Isabel would get it back. "There is no—"

"How do you know that?" Parker asked her.

"Because the gh…" She clamped her mouth shut and turned to Eli. He shook his head in defeat.

"I'm sorry, Alice," Parker said. "I didn't understand that."

Her eyes didn't leave Eli's, and he came to her side. Beyond his desire to protect her, guilt pricked his gut with the realization she hadn't gone to Rodney to spy on him. Guilt followed by relief.

"There's a legend about Jocelyn LeBlanc's ghost haunting Camellia Creek, Major. My wife has become enamored with the tale."

Parker frowned at him. "Somebody hanged her?"

"She hanged herself."

"You knew her?"

"He was a baby at the time she was murdered," Alice said, stepping between him and Parker. "He didn't kill her."

"I wasn't going to accuse him of the woman's murder, Alice, but you must trust me when I tell you I do not take Miss Hays, or you for that matter, at your word. I want the book."

Alice's lips tightened. "I told you when you interrupted Isabel and me today that we were discussing murder, that being Jocelyn's murder. You didn't listen."

"You were being disingenuous."

"I was visiting a family friend." She looked at Eli, then back to Parker. "An old family friend, and I owed you no explanation." Holding the book at her side, she moved to the overstuffed chair that had come in one of her mother's crates. "Sit down and I'll give it to you. You can look at it here."

Parker started to say something, but Eli put his arm around Alice's shoulder. "It's late, honey. Let him take the journal. He'll see that it's of no interest to him. I'll get it back tomorrow, and you can read it." Eli looked at Parker. "Right now, I want them out of here."

$\mathcal{A}$lice, rigid with what Eli dubbed righteous anger, watched the door close behind Parker. He rubbed her back, then walked over and locked the door. Five years ago he wouldn't have.

"I suffered a great deal for that book," she said.

He grimaced, then started back her way. "You went to Isabel about Jocelyn, not about me?"

"I went to Marguerite Dubois Fortier about Jocelyn. You wouldn't take me, so I went by myself."

He stopped in front of her. "Aunt Elvie told you where her house was?"

"Yes. It was Marguerite who sent me to 'Izzie,' who I assumed was Izzie LeBlanc. Isabel knew who I was before I realized who she was."

"Why didn't you just tell me?"

Her chin puckered. "You were being mean, cruel even, trying to force me when a simple request would have worked." Then her eyes glistened. "I told you I wouldn't tell you anything unless..."

He covered her lips with his when her voice broke. Dammit, he had to learn to deal differently with this woman. "I had a right to be mad. I told you I didn't want you to—"

"Just say you're sorry, Eli."

He crushed her to him. "I was wrong, and I'm sorry."

Chapter Sixty-three

Eli pulled the gauntlet from his right hand before reaching for the knob and pushing the rough-hewn cookhouse door open. Warmth from within washed over him, and he took the last step up off the rickety footer and entered the room.

Aunt Naomi, pulling a pan of biscuits from the oven, looked at him, then placed the biscuits on an unused burner.

"When did you get here?" he asked.

"I was here before you left. Thought you'd come to the cookhouse for coffee, but I saw you go on and saddle Johnny."

He pulled the remaining glove from his hand and the hat off his head. "If I'd known you were out here, I would have stopped in. I could have used a cup of coffee."

"Where's your wife?"

Eli didn't miss the contempt in the woman's voice. He didn't care. He was quite happy with his wife, and most mornings she did rise early to fix him coffee and breakfast.

"She had a rough night."

Naomi glared at him and set his cup down a little too hard. "You're acting like an animal, Eli."

He narrowed his eyes on her. "Not your concern," he said, and he pulled out a chair.

She snorted, then stirred whatever she had cooking in a cast-iron skillet. "I made biscuits and ham sop. You didn't eat the chicken I left for you yesterday."

Damn, he'd forgotten that chicken in the heat of last evening. "What time did you get here, did you say? 'Cause I left before six."

"Five." She set a plate of biscuits and gravy in front of him.

"Thanks."

Alice was sick to her stomach again, but not like the last time. She's the one, actually, who'd wakened him. He'd considered heading toward town and rousing sweet ole Aunt Betty, per her directive—it would have been rewarding to get her up and out in the cold before the sun came up, but Alice didn't want him to. Still, he was awake, and Alice's feeling poorly left him little incentive to loll around in bed, so he got up and got going.

Alice did want him to get in to Port Gibson and retrieve that journal, but he had his own agenda, and didn't even know if he'd find Parker in town, much less ready to relinquish the darn book. He told her they should give the man a little time. Still, he didn't want her going to town to retrieve the thing, and she just might. He hadn't noticed lights in here when he walked to the lean-to, but with the windows boarded on the kitchen's west side that wasn't surprising. Nor had he noticed an extra wagon or borrowed carriage out back.

"Mighty early for a walk," he said to Naomi. "Still not sleeping well?"

"Old age. Just don't need to sleep much anymore."

He speared a gravy-laden piece of biscuit and stuffed it in his mouth. He was hungry, and it tasted good. "Did you try to get in the house?"

"No. The place was dark. I figured y'all were still sleepin'."

They had been then. He chewed another forkful of biscuit and glanced to his right where morning sun streamed through the now pristine panes of the windows flanking the breezeway door and painted rectangles of light on the wooden floorboards of the cookhouse. Those two were the only kitchen windows untouched by the marauding Yankees.

He'd found the back door to the house unlocked this morning. He swore he locked it last night when he came in, mad as hell at Alice and ready to wring her neck. Maybe he hadn't, but he was more inclined to think Aunt Nimi had come in very early and, finding them asleep, had sneaked back out. She could say so, he wouldn't be bothered by it.

"You don't need to be out alone in the dark, that includes comin' the back way," he said.

Behind him, he heard the oven door close. "There's nothing on that back road but old neighbors, Eli. What's left of them."

"There's plenty these days for you to be wary of," he said, turning in his chair. "You don't have sense to know it."

She gave him a rare smile. "I've been making that trip way too long to stop now."

"Just do it in the daylight." He washed down the last of his biscuit with coffee. Aunt Naomi, cup in hand, sat beside him.

"What you lookin' for in the woods?"

"Checkin' along the creek. I'm thinking of clearing that back twenty acres. Been fallow too long. Might be ready for some corn."

"Buck gonna help you?"

"He's all I've got so far."

He looked around the kitchen. Despite Alice's complaints of the telltale mouse droppings each morning, the kitchen was as clean, if not even close to as well stocked, as it had been before the war. His bride wasn't going to like Naomi Polk's being in here again this morning.

"Have you seen Alice at all?"

"No, and I don't want to. How long before you tire of her, Eli?"

He stared at the woman and wondered at her effrontery.

"Well?" she demanded.

"She's my business, Aunt Naomi, and none of yours."

"You can't trust her. She'll betray you to your enemies, you think so yourself."

"Don't presume to know what I think." He rose. "And with that thought, I believe I'll go see how she's doing."

"You're a fool," she said with a hateful sneer. "You sniff after her like a dog does a bitch in heat."

His chest tightened. "I don't appreciate that likening."

She rose and met him eye to eye. "She didn't hear it."

"I did."

"I meant for you to."

"I don't want to hear it again or anything else like it."

After a moment, she blinked, then looked down at the table before stacking his plate on top of hers. "As you wish, 'Massa Eli.'"

"You brought me something?"

Alice was still in bed. She managed a smile despite her pallor, and he handed her the napkin-covered biscuit he'd pilfered from the kitchen.

"Elvie made you breakfast?"

He wished. "Aunt Naomi."

Alice's jaw tightened. "She's in my kitchen?"

"She is. Made biscuits and gravy and coffee and—"

"Oh, Eli, she makes such a mess, and she doesn't clean up after herself."

"She's a good cook, though."

"And I'm sure she made some point about me lying in bed while you get up in the predawn winter and go off to work with no food in your stomach."

"Well?"

"I think it might be your fault I'm sick, and I bet Naomi Polk didn't even wipe the mouse droppings off the counter before she started preparing the meal."

"I can honestly say I saw no droppings."

"They're probably in the biscuit dough."

"She might be used to having servants clean up after her, Alice, but she's sanitary around food." Eli watched Alice study the biscuit. "That one she intended for me. She didn't poison you. Eat the thing, you'll feel better."

"I already feel better." She took a bite.

"I'm going into Port Gibson later"—he raised a hand when she started to speak—"I'll try to find Parker, but I'm making no promises."

"It's absurd he took the thing from me."

"It is." But Eli was kinda glad the man had. If he worked its retrieval right, he'd have a chance to review Silky LeBlanc's thoughts on her daughter's death before Alice did. He might, in fact, have to return the journal to Isabel without letting Alice see it.

"The real reason I'm going to town is to check on lumber. I imagine I'll have to order most of the wood. I might end up having to go to Vicksburg, but Thornton's been expecting an order of glass. Maybe I can get enough to fix the windows."

"You'll cut it yourself?"

"Buck will."

She looked up at him. "He will?"

"He's a real handy fella to have around, fine carpenter. He learned from his owner, Nate Pike, who lived just north of the Big Black. He was a carpenter himself. Came here from Carolina in the twenties to raise cotton. Buck was with him from the time he was still a young man. Nate hired him out, usually during the winter when there were no crops to work. Worked for everybody around here goin' back as far as I can remember. Nate took half Buck's pay, but he was well paid when he was doing carpentry work."

"So you hired him to do carpentry?"

"Nah, he wants to stay here on Camellia Creek. He's getting old, and he's pretty much alone now. He's a good field hand, and he's got a way with animals, you've seen that."

"Where's Mr. Pike?"

"Died of a heart attack not long after the war started. His wife and two daughters died of cholera in '64. Got a son, but he's emigrating. Sold his land in Warren County to one of your uncle's cronies."

"Can you and Buck put the barn up together?"

"Years ago, we probably could have. Buck practically built Wayne and May Hale's house by himself, but Buck's almost sixty and my barn will be much bigger than the Hale cabin."

How did she get up there to jump off?

Or had there been some sort of stool or chair beneath her?

Alice closed her eyes and tried to recall the night she'd seen the body hanging from this tree. Nothing. She couldn't have recalled a stool or a chair if there'd been one.

Opening her eyes, she drew in a frigid breath. The clear winter morning was so cold she hurt. A few days ago the temperature had climbed over seventy. In a few more it would probably do so again.

Eli had left for town almost an hour ago. Alice had hoped he'd taken Naomi back with him, but when she entered the cookhouse, ready to clean it up, she'd found her still there. Despite her disappointment, Alice had greeted the woman cheerfully, but declined a sourly offered cup of coffee. She'd walked clean through the kitchen and out the back door and had come straight to this spot, hopeful the hateful being would leave before she got back.

Carefully raising her woolen skirts, Alice walked to the tree trunk and touched it with a gloved hand. There was no reason for touching it, no expectations it would talk to her—or that it would shrink or she grow. She simply touched it and rested her hand there, level with her head, and looked up at the broad limb a good four feet higher than her head. Jocelyn LeBlanc couldn't have reached the thing to tie a rope even if she'd had a chair. Alice stepped back and again studied the massive trunk. The woman would have had to climb up there somehow.

"*D*er was wood planks nailed in da trunk back den, a ladder. Massa Holland built Andrew what he called a fawt in dat tree."

Alice stirred the cast-iron pot on the stove. She'd returned from the woods to find Elvie busy in the kitchen making soap—a big job, and not one Alice had planned for today. This was an outside job, but the morning was so cold, and the wash tub out back was full of bed linens—the master's bed linens. Making the soap aggravated Alice, but those bed linens left her livid. As soon as Alice departed the house, apparently, Naomi Polk had gone into her and Eli's bedroom and stripped the sheets off their bed. The woman had left in a huff shortly thereafter, when she discovered there was not enough soap in the house to wash them.

Elvie had arrived as Naomi was stomping out the door. Alice was nowhere to be found, and the much put-upon Saint Naomi was being forced to go all the way to her house in Port Gibson and back, with soap, so she could get Eli's bed clothes done.

Elvie hadn't waited. She told Alice she'd stored hog fat back in October when Eli killed a wild pig. Given they were indeed about out of soap, Elvie started the process. Alice had wanted to scream, but she absolutely refused to take her ire out on Elvira Hinny.

The farm did need a large supply of lye, but unless Naomi came back, and Elvie told Alice she thought that was the woman's intent, there'd be no soap for linens today, not made at Camellia Creek anyway. Soap-making took more than a day.

"So they think she climbed up there, tied the rope—"

"Used da rope Andy had hangin' from dat limb. Da chil'en used it to climb down."

"Did it go all the way to the ground?"

Elvie stopped scrapping fat from the bucket and frowned. "Bes' I recall it be 'bout dis far off da ground."

Around two feet, the Negress indicated. "So," Alice said, "they think she climbed up on the limb using the ladder to Andrew's tree house, pulled up the rope, tied it around her neck, and jumped?"

"I reckon."

"Well, she would have had to cut the rope shorter, else she'd have jumped to the ground."

Elvie walked over and raised the bucket of fat over Alice's pot. Alice pulled out her stick.

"All I can tell you fo' sho' is she drawed up shawt." The old woman wiped out the bucket with her hands and flicked the greasy residue into the pot.

Alice put her stick back in and continued stirring, and Elvie crossed the room and pumped water in the bucket. "Sho be glad he got dis pump fixed," she said, then glanced over her shoulder to Alice. "Need to talk to one 'a da menfolk—shurif, docta. All I know'd was she be dead, and dey say she done it 'ersef. Now der was dem who sayd she didn't. Dem dat look at such things say she did, and dat's how it stayed all dis time." Elvie reached for a rag and turned to face Alice. "But I ain't doubtin' da things you say. Neva felt easy mysef near dat ole tree, not since it happened, like Miss Jocelyn still der, watchin' and waitin' to scare some po' soul."

"She doesn't mean to frighten people. She wants justice, and she needs someone to help her."

The old darkie stooped and turned the catch on the cabinet door. When the door fell open, she placed the bucket inside. "Maybe," she said, straightening, then reaching for Alice's stick, "she ain't lookin' fo' yo' he'p a'tall."

Alice stepped away, relinquishing her position as stirrer of the pot.

"Maybe she be wantin' you, missy."

"Eli asked if maybe she were beckoning to me. I've never felt she meant me harm."

"Might be in her mind it *ain't* harm she's intendin', but to the livin' it sho'nuff is."

"She lived once. She should know."

"Haints be selfish things."

A disconcerting thought at best. "Miss Elvie, I met a woman named Isabel Hays yesterday."

Ah yes, Elvira Hinny knew that name; Alice could see it in her eyes.

"Miss Maggie send you to 'er?"

"She did. I met her daughter, Rebecca. Do you know her?"

"What she say to you?"

Why were questions always answered with questions? "I got the impression they were close to the Calhoons."

"Yes'm. Dat girl, Becky, she be here offen. Her an' Hannah played togetha."

"She spoke that way about Eli, too, familiar, like she knew him very well."

"An' Andrew."

"We didn't speak of Andrew or Hannah. Just Eli."

"Dat's 'cause him's da one you wed."

"And our visit was cut short. Were they sweethearts, once, Becky and Eli?"

"No."

Alice waited for more, but Elvira didn't elaborate. Finally, Alice shrugged. "I was curious is all. I knew the name Isabel Hays. I didn't know Jocelyn was her niece."

"Dat were a mess for da massa back den. Now, if you he'p me, we'll get dis in da trays, den I needs to go and git me some colla'ds on fo' dinna."

Chapter Sixty-four

Isabel Hays and Eli Calhoon.
Isabel Hays, Eli Calhoon, and Alice Calhoon.
Isabel Hays, Tobias Holbein, and Eli Calhoon.
Isabel Hays, Jonathan Franklin, Alice Calhoon, and Eli Calhoon.
Wayne Hale and Eli Calhoon.
Laura Blackledge and Eli Calhoon.

Seth Parker tossed the pencil atop his desk, and it bounced off Silky LeBlanc's closed journal. He handed Jubal Summers the paper on which he'd scribbled his notes. "Our one common denominator is Eli Calhoon."

"That woman Rebecca?"

Seth thought a minute. Pretty, defiant Rebecca Mackey. What a surprise that had been. "She's a war widow from over in Madison. Her mother said she wasn't..." Seth caught Jubal Summer's jaundiced eye, and Seth said, "Just note her name."

"And you left off Brim Solomon."

"Brim Solomon, Eli Calhoon, and Wayne Hale." There, with the common denominator.

Sergeant Zachary stood over Jubal's shoulder and watched him add that grouping to the list. "You ain't got dat dead LeBlanc woman on der neitha."

"Well, she ain't got a recent tie to our common denominator, does she?" the captain said.

"We don't know that Guthrie does either, do we?" Frank Zachary looked at Seth. "Ain't that the killin' we s'posed to be investigatin'? In fact, you ain't got one tie on dat list to him."

Seth rubbed his aching forehead. "Thank you for your input, Sergeant."

The well-meaning sergeant looked at him, shamefaced, and stepped back.

"You're right. I don't know if we're looking at one conspiracy or five, and I'm not sure that I'm not working everything but what I'm supposed to be working."

Jubal straightened. "I think we ought to stop thinkin' about that LeBlanc case. First off, it was ruled a suicide, and even if she was murdered all them years ago, ain't no way it ties into the Guthrie murder now, and it appears to me, Seth, the Solomon and Hale deaths link together."

"I would readily agree, but Hale was linked to the cotton."

"But dat's not what got him kilt," Zachary interjected. "Da Solomon murders got Hale kilt."

Maybe, but what of Laura Blackledge's murder? Try as he might, Seth couldn't shake the feeling her coming to him is what got her killed. Did any of the murders—including Guthrie's—have anything at all to do with cotton thieving?

And other than the Solomons and Hale, did any of the murders fit together? And what was the relationship between his "common denominator" and the other people involved? Were Isabel Hays and Jonathan Franklin friends or foes? Hell, Alice Calhoon had intimated, in front of Isabel Hays no less, she believed Jonathan to be working with Federal authorities, specifically him. Of course he couldn't dismiss the possibility that innocent little, ghost-hunting Alice was actually devious enough to plant that seed in Isabel's mind.

Yesterday, when Summers informed him that Alice went into Isabel's place of business, Seth was certain she was trying to find out what her husband was up to. Now, given what Isabel had told him and what he'd learned last night at Camellia Creek and from Silky LeBlanc's journal this morning, Alice's purpose for journeying to Rodney appeared unrelated to whatever Calhoon did there.

The one saving grace was that Calhoon must have been thinking along the same lines as Seth in regards to Alice. From what he'd gleaned from Sergeant Zachary's conversation with the man, Calhoon had been following his wife. Obviously, he didn't trust her.

Seth suspected that if push came to shove, Alice would protect Calhoon, but her apparent loyalty to the man could prove a bad gamble on her part. Where would she stand if she uncovered a terrible truth? And finally, if Eli Calhoon considered his wife a foe, would her life prove forfeit in his hands?

A knock sounded at the door to his rented room. Summers turned, and Sergeant Zachary opened the portal to their common denominator.

Chapter Sixty-five

Eli tossed his cavalry hat on Aunt Elvie's rough table, then plopped into the cowhide seat of a homemade chair. He slapped Silky LeBlanc's journal on the table beside his cover. Aunt Elvie was heaping collards onto a chipped china plate. A lifetime ago that plate had been part of his mother's dinner set.

He'd left Camellia Creek around nine, Aunt Naomi still in the kitchen. He'd offered to drive her home, hadn't wanted to leave her there with Alice, but his bride was up and even feeling chipper, so he figured she could keep herself out of the woman's way.

As planned, he'd checked on lumber for his barn. Thornton told him he'd order it, but couldn't give him an arrival date. We need to rebuild the mill, the man told him, and Eli concluded he was right. It turned out he would have to order the glass for his windows, which he did. Then he made his way up Cotton Street to the Port Gibson Hotel. Eli figured he'd have trouble retrieving the journal from Parker, but the man had offered him no excuses to postpone turning it over, nor had he offered Eli any sympathy after asking if Alice actually believed in a ghost. Eli confirmed that yes, she did. He didn't tell Parker she actually claimed to have seen the thing and sure the devil didn't tell the man Alice believed the spirit was communicating with her.

Aunt Elvie removed his hat from the table and placed it on a peg beside the door, next to his father's hand-me-down. Briefly she touched the brim edge. "Won't be able to replace dis one when you done wo' it out."

"Don't reckon I'll ever need to, Auntie."

"You'll always want to keep it," she said softly.

"Maybe."

She turned and sidled back across the room, picked up the plate of collards and cornbread she'd made, and set it in front of him.

"I could throttle you for bringin' up Miss Maggie to her."

She moved back to the stove for her own plate. "She ask me 'bout Jocelyn. You ain't once tol' me not to talk to 'er 'bout dat girl. Needs to be you takin' da blame fo' dis, not me."

"How do you figure?"

"She tol' me she ask you to take 'er to see dat ole woman, an' you tol' 'er you wouldn't." Elvie sat down on the other side of the tiny table from him. "Whatcha think she gonna do, Eli?"

"She'd have never asked me if you hadn't told her about Miss Maggie in the first place, and I sure didn't expect her to take off to Rodney."

Elvie shook her head and picked up a two-pronged pewter fork with her right hand, then leaned toward him, her left forearm on the table. "I swear, I be da only person 'round here unde'-standin' da fu'st bless-it thing 'bout dat girl."

"And what the devil was Buck thinkin'?"

"You done sayd somethin' to 'im?

"Haven't seen him." Eli dipped his cornbread in collard juice.

"Have you eva' once tol' 'im to ask you befo' he takes dat gal somewheres she asks 'im to?"

Eli's eyes moved from his dinner plate to Elvie. No, he had not, though he had considered it. Just didn't seem practical for Buck to come get his permission every time Alice wanted to go somewhere, and she wouldn't have stood it for long.

"No, you ain't," she answered when he didn't. "So don't you be lightin' into po' Buck. He didn't know, an' she ask me not to say nothin' to 'im 'cause she know'd he wouldn't take 'er if you didn't want 'er goin'."

"Yeah, it's you I need to be lighting into."

She snorted. "Dat be da problem when dose you needs to be lightin' into be da ones raised you. Whupped yo' little tail too many times."

"You did. Maybe it's time I started whippin' yours."

"I'm shiverin' right down to my old toes now."

"Tell me this, Elvie, did Aunt Naomi know Alice was going to Rodney in search of Miss Maggie?"

"Sho' she did. She tol' her not to go, jes' like I tol' 'er. Nimi listened while I give Miss Alice d'rections."

Eli stuffed another forkful of collards, hot and spiked with pepper sauce, in his mouth. Well, he'd been pretty damn sure his aunt was up to no good yesterday, and he wished now he'd insisted on her leaving with him this morning.

"An' what's it gonna hurt, dat gal talkin' to Miz Maggie? Girl needs to put dat ghost in 'er head to res'."

"Aunt Maggie sent her to Isabel."

"She tol' me. She met Miss Becky, too, but I didn't plan dat."

"You had to suspect it could happen."

"She don't know nothin'." Elvie blew out a tired breath. "Eli, you married to da girl. How long is you plannin' on keepin' dat secret from her an' why?"

"As long as I can and the reason is I don't want her talking to Isabel, not about anything, including Jocelyn LeBlanc's death."

"Wouldn't think Miss Isabel be wantin' dat neitha."

"You're right, she's probably not happy about it being dredged up." He pushed his plate back and held up the journal. "This belonged to Silky LeBlanc. Isabel gave it to Alice to read. I want to look at it before I turn it over to Alice."

"You gonna read it here at yo' ole auntie's?"

He grinned. "Can I, ole Auntie, find refuge here for a couple of hours?"

"You know you can." She curled her hand into a relaxed fist. Her eyes softened as did her voice. "It's nice you comin' 'ere today. Reminds me of yo' daddy hidin' away from him's women-folk at da big house."

She tightened her lips. Watching her, Eli's heart weighed heavier in his chest. "I reckon I'm like him, huh, Ink?"

Tears filled her eyes with the endearment. Only one person had ever called her that.

"I sho' miss yo' daddy. You a lot like 'im, mo' so dan yo'

mama. Andrew, he were like Rosalind, him an' Hannah. But you, Eli, be yo' daddy's boy." She blinked back the tears and looked away. "Lawd, I miss 'em all."

He reached over and covered her frail hand.

She sobbed, a rare display of emotion, but not unfamiliar to him. "Ain't neva gonna be da same, is it, boy?"

Pressure filled the space behind his eyes. "No, ma'am, they've got what they wanted. They've destroyed the South. It's gone forever, it and the people who made it, and the bastards aren't done yet. God, Elvie, the Southern states should have never been part of the United States. We should have gone our own way from the start."

Chapter Sixty-six

"You changed them two days ago. Did you throw up that biscuit after I left?" Eli asked.

Alice looked up from where she tucked a sheet underneath the feather mattress on their bed. "I changed them three days ago, and no, I didn't get sick."

"Why—"

"Your Aunt Naomi saw fit as soon as I left the house this morning to strip the bed."

Eli frowned, and Alice straightened. "I can only guess that she thinks whatever we do in here is filthy. That or this is her way of protecting you from my contamination."

"Her behavior's always been bizarre. Don't worry about it."

"Don't worry about it!" Alice shook her head and started to the other side of the bed. "Bizarre doesn't account for that woman, Eli. She does things like this to offend me, and she's caused me unnecessary work."

"Where is she?"

"I've been expecting her since noon with soap to wash our sheets. Another of my failings. I didn't have soap in the house."

"So did you put the dirty ones back on?"

Alice fussed with the pillows. "These were my mother's. Ours will still be frozen stiff on the line by the time the sun goes down if they're even out of the wash pot. I know she's your aunt, Eli, but this is my...."

He arched a brow, and her stomach clenched, but he prudently fell back when she lunged toward him.

"...my house, too, and I'm quite capable of keeping it, darn you."

He couldn't quite hide the smirk, though she was sure he tried. "Well, the bed for sure is yours, sweetheart, and I don't want anyone messing with what you've created here."

She spun away and reached for the first quilt in the pile at the foot of the bed. Flippant horse's behind. "Tell her to keep away from our bed. You're the master." She drew out the last word. "If you don't, she'll not stop until she's crawled up in it herself and wallowed around."

"A horrifying thought," Eli said, turning away and going back into the parlor. "My guess is she won't be back today."

"You think she purposefully inconvenienced us?"

"Sabotage you is what she's trying to do," he hollered back.

She cast the bed, now neatly remade, one last appreciative glance. "Well," she said, following him, "she failed at sabotage, as you put it, but not at inconveniencing me. The wash is yet to be done."

"Leave it for her. She'll be back eventually."

"Hoping I'll throw one of your people's hissy fits." Alice entered the room and found him tending the fire. "And she's sure you'll take her side."

"How's the stove in the bedroom?"

"I fed it right before I started on the bed."

He rose agilely from in front of the hearth. "Gonna be real cold tonight. Did Aunt Naomi leave anything for supper?"

"I made black-eyed peas and cornbread."

"Aunt Elvie sent collards, already cooked. We'll need to warm 'em."

Alice stopped at the parlor entry. "I went for a walk this morning after you left the second time."

"Is that when Naomi invaded our—"

"Yes. I visited the tree. Do you know if there was a stool or anything nearby, which Jocelyn could have climbed up on to hang herself?"

"You know the rope—"

"Was already there, yes. It was Andrew's, and I know there was a ladder nailed into the tree. But, Eli, according to Miss

Elvie, the rope went almost to the ground. Can you imagine a distraught woman climbing up that tree…well, she'd have had to cut off the rope to shorten it…then making a noose and finally jumping off that limb?"

"I really can't say that I think she didn't do all those things, Alice."

She wrung her hands together. "I wish I could find out—"

"There was no chair or anything else at the scene for her to have climbed on."

Her eyes widened. "Are you sure?"

"Yes."

"How do you know, because Miss Elvie didn't remember and—"

"First, you've got to understand that Jocelyn was a playmate to us kids. She climbed that tree ladder with Andrew. And as far as the stool, I talked to Doctor Lester, but my thought was it would have been used by a killer if there was one—someone not used to climbing that ladder."

Her eyes widened. "You believe me, don't you? You know—"

"I don't know anything. I was curious, is all."

"You won't admit it, but you believe I'm right."

He shook his head. "Right about her being murdered? No, honey, what I don't want to admit is that I'm married to a lunatic. Doctor Lester was the brand new coroner at the time. According to him, the rope had been shortened, then simply knotted around her neck. Not a neat job and very much what a woman would have created—not a noose as you implied, which a man would more likely have made. That's one of the reasons they ruled out murder. All these questions you're bringing up he says were resolved twenty-five years ago. He seems pretty certain Jocelyn LeBlanc herself tied the knot around her neck."

"When did you talk to him?"

"This morning before I went to"—he sat on the settee and held up Silky LeBlanc's journal—"get this from Parker."

She smiled happily and rushed for it. "Oh, thank you. Have you looked at it?"

"Yep."

"Was there anything of value?" She sat on the settee beside him.

"I think you might have some questions when you go through it. Don't know if I can answer them all, but maybe Aunt Naomi or Elvie can."

"Elvie. I don't know that I'd trust what your Aunt Naomi tells me."

"Well, don't rule her out. She does have some strong opinions about those events, and I imagine her memory is pretty good."

Chapter Sixty-seven

"**H**er mother certainly didn't believe she took her own life," Alice said. "Reading this, I'm not even convinced they were lovers."

Eli looked up from the ten-day-old *Chicago Tribune* he'd been perusing. Alice held the journal in her lap. She wasn't looking at him, but he was pretty certain she wasn't talking to herself. "That was kinda my impression, too, when I read the thing."

If her daughter had been carrying on a passionate affair with Holland Calhoon, Silky LeBlanc hadn't known it, though the woman was clearly aware of the young woman's affection for the man. Eli had asked Elvie about that a few hours ago, and she reminded him that by the time Jocelyn LeBlanc was spending too much time at Camellia Creek for her own good, Elvie had returned to the fields. To this day, Elvie believed that Jocelyn was indulging in a school-girl crush on a handsome older man, but according to Naomi, the grieving Holland had succumbed to the virginal wiles of Jocelyn LeBlanc. He'd opted for a brief affair he soon regretted and, in the interim, got the girl with child. But, Elvie also reminded Eli that Nimi was inclined to spout the worst when it came to Holland and women.

"When are you going to warm up the collards?" he asked.

She looked from the journal to Eli, sitting across the room, comfy by the fire in his brutalized upholstered chair. There were things he could tell her about those events and, under different circumstances, probably would. The sticking point wasn't her interest in Jocelyn's death—that didn't concern him. It was that her prying would force her return to Isabel, and he didn't want her associating with Isabel. Hell, he didn't even like Rebecca in that house these days. His gut told him Isabel was playing a dangerous game with ruthless people.

Alice sat back. "Stove's hot. They've been warming for the last half hour. Everything's ready. It's still early, are you hungry?"

There was a good hour before sunset. His purpose had been to deflect her from this conversation. For how long he didn't know, but he knew she sensed his intent. "We can wait."

"Eli, listen to what she writes."

He didn't want to listen; he'd read the entire journal not two hours ago. He wanted to read his outdated newspaper.

"My darling daughter told me today… Alice stopped reading and flipped back a page. "It's the fifth of October 1840, two months before she died." She returned to her place.

"My darling daughter told me today that she believes Naomi Polk expects Holland to take her for his wife when a discreet period of grieving is done. I told Jocelyn that a discreet period of grieving is already passed and asked her if Miss Polk had confided that belief to her in an effort to discourage her visits to the Calhoon home. Jocelyn told me Miss Naomi rarely spoke to her at all and it was Elvira Hinny who told her Miss Naomi's expectations. Jocelyn says she asked Auntie Elvie, as Holland calls her, why Naomi believed that way, and the woman told her it was because things often worked that way among the big planters. Though Jocelyn does not appreciate the truth of such things, I know that they are so, and that is one reason Naomi Polk remains in Holland Calhoon's household. I told Jocelyn I wanted her to stop visiting there, she is of an age that such visits are considered improper, but she will have none of it, but will remain as a nurse for the Calhoon children as long as it pleases Holland. I fear she fancies herself in love with Holland at a time she should be giving Hawk Duval an answer to his proposal. The man is showing signs of discouragement, which will displease Macon. I will ask Macon to speak with Holland upon his return."

Alice frowned at Eli.

"Elvie thinks Treadwell was out of the country at the time, but doesn't know for sure," he said.

"I would imagine if her father had been here, he would have had words with yours."

"Alice, I'm not even sure my father was aware of the lack of discretion, and yes, I do believe if Macon Treadwell had spoken with him, Daddy would have made things right with Jocelyn and subsequent events would have never happened."

"Then do you think nothing hap—"

"I told you what Daddy told me, and I've always suspected that to mean he hadn't had relations with her."

Alice nodded, then read—inwardly, Eli groaned—aloud:

"The very fact she concerns herself with the possibility Holland Calhoon will marry his sister-in-law implies unwarranted interest in the man. Both Meg and Isabel share my concern. Meg believes Jocelyn hopes to marry Calhoon herself. Isabel dismisses the idea, but I do believe, with all my heart, the poor child believes he loves her."

"And I guess rejection for an eighteen-year-old who imagines herself desperately in love would be cause for suicide?"

Eli shrugged. "Seems foolish to me, and she did not spring from a foolish bunch of women, but I've never been an eighteen-year-old female."

"And what about this Hawk Duval her parents planned for her to marry? You told me yourself he was an Indian trader. No doubt he was coarse, violent. It's no wonder she wouldn't have wanted to marry him."

"You're assuming a great deal, darlin'. He was the son of a mixed-blood trader and a white woman in Simpson County. His paternal grandmother was a landed Choctaw of significant influence among her people. He was a prince among chiefs." Eli waved his arm for effect. "His people were wealthy, powerful, and quite civilized. He owned land, cattle, and slaves in addition to a two-storied, six-room house. He was much younger than my father. It was a good match."

"Who told you that?"

"Isabel, a number of years ago."

"Oh."

"Alice?"

She cocked her head.

"Can we eat now?"

Eyes on the writing in the journal, she stuck up an index finger. "One more thing. On the next page, Silky makes reference to Isabel expecting a baby, due in June of 1841? Do you recall that?"

"Yes."

She looked at him. "Was that Rebecca?"

"Her only child. I'm gonna go check on things in the kitchen."

"Wait," she called after him. "She told me Isaac Baker, her...her..." Alice waved a hand in the air.

"Benefactor?"

"Died in 1838." Alice thumbed through the remaining pages of the journal. "Does Silky say later who the father is?"

"She does not."

"Do you know who Rebecca's father is?"

"Alice, I can honestly say I never once asked that question of Isabel." He walked out of the parlor and crossed the entry into the dining room. "Come on, let's eat."

Chapter Sixty-eight

The kitten cried when Alice stepped into the cookhouse. Eli glanced at her, then it. He'd already removed the collards from the stove top and now sat on the table eating them right out of the pot.

"Stop that," she said and reached for the bowl she'd taken out earlier.

"Do you think Isabel would tell me who the father is?"

"I think she'd consider it none of your business, and it would be inappropriate to ask. But more importantly, I don't want you going back to Isabel's place, do you understand? Not without me."

"I won't," she said, "but do you think Isabel's baby could be related—"

"To Jocelyn's death? Why would it?"

Alice shrugged, then put her fists on her hips and looked down at her kitten, waddling around her skirts. "Did you feed her again?"

"I did not. She's your cat, not mine, and her stomach's so fat she looks like a swollen deer tick."

"I fed her earlier, but she acts like she didn't get enough."

"Probably has worms."

"No, she doesn't. I've checked."

"Then she wants attention."

Alice scooped her up in the palm of her hand. That little belly was, indeed, round and firm. She patted the furry head, took two steps, then squatted by the stove and put the kitten beneath it. "Go get it," she urged.

"What are you doing?"

She looked up at Eli, still sitting at the table. "Teaching her to hunt mice."

"Bullshit. First off, you can't teach a cat to hunt mice, they do it instinctively. Second, the mouse is bigger—"

The back door crashed against the back wall, startling Alice, who popped to her knees. Eli jumped, too, and spun in the direction of the door, its crash still reverberating through the kitchen. Naomi Polk, jaw set and eyes hard, thrust through the wide-open entry. Her gaze locked on Eli. Shock eclipsed the anger on her face. Hah, the woman hadn't expected to find the "ole massa" in here, and Alice knew from the look of contrition on Naomi's face, she regretted her grand entry. Without a doubt, the shrew had found the washtub in the back, water cold and full of this morning's linens, left for her, and she hadn't liked it.

Alice's gaze darted to Eli, who sat staring at his aunt. Defense in good hands, Alice looked for the kitten and found it huddled, tiny tail frizzed, against the wall at the back of the stove. The feline mewed softly when she reached for it. She coaxed it from its hiding place and rose, the cat in her hands. Naomi gave her a quick glance, acknowledged the cat with a look of contempt, then moved to shut the door...gently. It was nearly four in the afternoon and days were still short. Why had she come back here?

"There's never been a cat in this kitchen," Naomi said. "They jump up and walk around on the counters, get hair in the food. And you can't leave anything out on the table, covered or not, 'cause they'll get in it."

"She'll be a good mouser."

"Set traps."

Unasked-for advice. Naomi Polk was always quick to give it, and Alice resented it. Petting her kitten, she went outside and set it on the ground beside the stoop. "Go on and pooh, now," she said softly and left it. In the kitchen, she crossed her arms over her breasts and looked at Naomi. "I don't want to set traps. I want the cat my husband gave me to learn to be a mouser."

The hateful old witch snorted and glanced at Eli. "He doesn't like cats either."

"That only makes her more precious to me."

"That he'd go against his own likes to give you a filthy cat?"

Alice's heart skipped a beat. "Yes."

"You don't ask for much in the way of respect, do you, girl? What 'filth' do you give in return?"

Alice swallowed. On the other side of Naomi, Eli rose from the table. The woman may have gotten control of herself, but she'd hardly become a docile representative of Southern gentility.

"Did you have a reason for coming back here so late?" Eli said to the woman and stepped around his chair.

Naomi looked from him to Alice. "You need to make soap so you can finish those sheets."

"What sheets?" Alice asked.

"The ones out back in the wash pot." The woman straightened formidably, and Alice braced. From where Alice stood, Naomi Polk looked broader than Eli. "Didn't you notice they weren't on your bed?"

"We noticed." Eli stepped between her and his aunt. "We were told you'd be back to wash them, but we'd given up on you today."

Naomi stood eye to eye with him. "Isn't my place to make soap for this farm. She"—Naomi nodded at Alice—"should have had some."

"I would have, had I planned on doing wash today," Alice told her and bit her lip when Eli shot her a warning look.

"There's proper times for washing linens, and given you and him"—she nodded at Eli—"you should have soap ready all the time."

Alice stiffened, but before she could force words past her clenched lips, Eli said, "It's not your place to do our laundry, Aunt Naomi, and it's less your place to tell us when we need to do it."

"It's not a man's place to concern himself with laundry at all." Nostrils flared, mouth grim, she set her attention on Alice. "It's hers, and she ought to know."

"It's a man's right to have peace in his home, and he concerns himself with all threats to that. Alice is my wife. She keeps this house, and she knows when she wants to do the laundry."

The woman tried to stare him down, but Eli didn't blink or budge. Naomi Polk finally averted her eyes, then gave Alice one last hateful look. "Fine," she spat and stomped back out the door.

Eli stared after her. "Good Lord," he said and stepped away from the table.

"Our supper?"

"We'll try again in a little bit. Let's get her settled first." He reached for his hat hanging next to the door, then stopped short, studied the hat a moment, and turned. "Alice?"

"Yes."

"If anything happens to me, I want Aunt Elvie to have this hat."

Alice felt the color drain from her face. "Why do you think something is go—"

"I don't. But just in case, I want you to know to give her this hat." He yanked the door open and stepped outside.

Good, she was doing the sheets.

Eli heard the door open, then close behind him. The sun was still above the tree line, but it would fall fast, and it was darn cold.

"Here, kitty, kitty, kitty."

He glanced behind him where Alice had followed him off the stoop looking for that kitten. He turned back to his aunt, pushing sheets into the washtub with her… hands. She hadn't lit the fire.

"Where are you?"

Alice was on the ground, looking beneath the cookhouse. Eli took another look at Aunt Naomi. She didn't look at either of them, though she must have heard them come outside. His stomach tensed. She was concentrating on that…. *Damn.*

He shoved her roughly from where she worked. She snorted, but didn't try to stop him; didn't acknowledge his attack. Because the woman knew what she was doing, knew….

He shoved his hands into the frigid water and started dragging out sheets. "Where is it?" he yelled at her. He pulled the sheets and kept pulling, letting the things drag in the dirt. He yelled at her again, but she glared defiantly at him. Hate, hate, hate. It screamed back at him as surely as if she'd said the word out loud.

The kitten fell out on one of his pulls. Beside him now, Alice let out a little gasp and reached for it, unmoving on the cold wet linens at their feet. She started to kneel beside it, but he pushed her back. "I'll take care of it, Alice," he said roughly.

"No." She covered her mouth with one hand, then tried again to reach the kitten, but this time he grabbed her by the shoulders and gently pushed her back.

"I'll take care of it," he ground out. God knew he didn't want her dealing with this dead kitten, and he didn't want to deal with her sorrow.

Eyes wide, Alice stepped back, staring at him, her hand still covering her mouth.

"Go inside," he said more gently.

"How did it…?" Her gaze darted to his aunt, and he followed it. Naomi Polk stood where he'd shoved her, a look, without a doubt, of smug satisfaction on her face.

"You?" Alice said.

Naomi's look of satisfaction twisted into contempt. "Madge Baker planned to drown the thing herself had Buck not taken it."

"It was *mine*!"

"It was good for nothing." Naomi spoke each word precisely. "And it had no place in my sister's kitchen.

Her sister's kitchen, his ass. As he understood it, Rosalind Calhoon had never shown any interest in that kitchen and had, as Miss Elvie always said in the years following her death, happily left meal preparation to the cook with scarcely any interference at all. Naomi had been the one later, after her sister's death, who'd bulled her way into the domestic affairs of the farm.

"I want you off Camellia Creek," Eli said.

Naomi turned to him.

"I want you to get away from here now, and I don't want you to ever step foot on my land again."

The woman's eyes widened. He jerked forward and grabbed her arm, spinning her toward the carriage…*his* carriage.

"Buck!" He pushed her toward the lean-to in back of the house. She stumbled, then tried to free her arm.

"I can take myself," she said and tore her arm free.

"Buck will take you in the wagon. I'm keeping my carriage."

"To drive your tramp around in," she bellowed. She whipped around and took a step toward Alice, now kneeling on the ground beside her dead kitten. Eli took two more steps toward the lean-to in search of Buck.

Dry-eyed, Alice looked up.

"You are nothing but a slut," Naomi hissed at Alice.

"Shut your mouth, damn you," Eli said. Again he hollered for Buck.

A hateful grin contorted his aunt's lips, and she took another step toward Alice. He could see only part of his wife, the wash tub was in the way, but she'd returned her attention to the cat.

"Eli knows it, too. He hates you. Vengeance is what he wants out of you."

Sweet Jesus. He reversed direction, toward his aunt. Alice stood, limp kitten clutched to her bosom.

"You amuse him," she said. "A deviant whore who allows herself to be used like an animal to fulfill his lust. No Southern man who loved a woman would ask that of her." Then she giggled. "But he'd ask it of someone he despised. Her doing it would make him despise her more."

Alice, pale-faced, looked at him. He couldn't speak. Anger in the form of bile burned his chest and throat. He shook his head at Alice, then focused on his aunt, whose attention loitered victoriously on a clearly devastated Alice.

"Buck!" His strained effort this time made his head hurt.

Damn him for an idiot. If Buck were still at work this late, he was in the fields, clearing away the summer of '63's cotton crop for this spring's planting. Eli let loose a guttural growl and lunged for his aunt. He grabbed her arm and squeezed, but her heavy coat protected her. The grunt his yank forced from the woman brought only meager satisfaction. Behind him, he heard the cook-house door shut. He clamped his jaw together and silently cursed Naomi Polk with every overexerted fiber of his being. She was as tall as him, but dragging her toward the lean-to and the wagon wasn't hard. She didn't resist, and after a stumble or two, she told him to let her go, and she'd happily come on her own. He didn't let her go, though, until he'd reached the wagon. He shoved her and told her to climb up. She obeyed and that was good. He wanted to beat the hell out of her. He'd never wanted to knock the teeth out of another human being more in his life. "You stay put."

He stomped back to his carriage, unhitched doc's horse, and tied it to the back of his wagon.

"You'll be sorry, Eli," she said as he started hitching up the mule.

"What I'm sorry for, Aunt Naomi, is that Daddy didn't drive you off this place twenty years ago."

"I belonged here at Camellia Creek."

Eli reached for a tug and glanced at her. She was looking beyond him, to the woods and fields beyond the house. "I belong here still." She sneered at him. "I was here before you."

"Thanks to my father's generosity."

"Yes, but Holland didn't fulfill the promise."

Promise bullshit. The one where he was expected to marry her...where *she* expected him to marry her. Eli came around and climbed in the wagon. "I think you expected too much."

"He came to Tennessee to woo me. I was the oldest, but Rosalind stole him away."

Eli narrowed his eyes on her. Holland Calhoon had gone to Tennessee, at his father's request, to buy a quality stallion. Meeting and falling in love with Rosalind Polk had been inadvertent.

"So did you expect me to marry you, too?"

She turned to him and glared. "You are disgusting."

"Given your views on sex, I figured you might have been contemplating a celibate union."

Chapter Sixty-nine

Eli pushed the cookhouse door open and found the space empty. A brief respite. He hoped so, anyway, and went inside. He could use a drink before facing her, but his liquor was in the parlor, and he was sure he'd run into her before he got that far—his gut twisted as he reached the breezeway door—if he didn't, that could mean she was gone for good.

He'd been gone under half an hour. That's how long it'd taken him to hail Buck in the field and turn over his female relation. Take her home, he'd said. Return the doc's horse, and come on home yourself. He thought about asking the man to find him another calico kitten, but it was too soon, and he was pretty certain Alice would have nothing to do with it.

At the dining-room door, he stopped and listened, but heard only his anxious heartbeat—and that was in his head. When he maneuvered around the table, though, he could see through the foyer into the parlor. She was on the settee, facing the fire. Her back was to him, but he was certain she must have heard him.

She didn't look around when he came up behind her. Of course, she knew it was him. Over her shoulder, he could see she held the damn kitten, wrapped in a towel. He reached over her for it, and she moved suddenly, hugging it to her. Its eyes opened and its little ears lay back in confusion at her sudden move.

Eli closed his eyes and gave thanks for small favors. "It's alive?"

"She was unconscious," Alice said without emotion. "I think she's going to be all right."

When he didn't say anything, she looked up at him. "You told her what I let you do, didn't you?"

She couldn't read his face, as if he knew she would accuse him and had prepared himself to give nothing away.

"No, Alice, I did not."

"She knows. How else? I certainly didn't tell her." She put the kitten aside, and leaned on one arm over the back of the settee. "That's what she was talking about, you know th—"

"I know," he said roughly. "I know what she said. She was playing on your worst fears, and she was doing it on purpose."

He started around the settee. She grasped the central carving at its back and leaned forward, following him with her eyes. "It had to be you."

"No," he barked at her, "it does not have to be me. Dammit, Alice, a Southern man does not discuss his sex acts with his elderly female relations. For Christ's sake, she'd beat him with a club if she didn't die of apoplexy first."

Alice watched him pick up the kitten, still in the towel, and set it on the floor. He sat beside her, then leaned forward, elbows on his knees and met her eyes. Heartsick, she turned away.

"Look at me."

She didn't, and he sighed.

"I never have and never will discuss the intimate details that pass between you and me with anyone."

She did look at him then. "But isn't what she said true?"

"What?"

"That you despise me."

He straightened. "I do not—"

"That my allowing you to perform perverse acts on my body gave you some victory—"

"The satisfaction was sexual. The conquest was making you enjoy it as much as I did."

"Like a whore. A paid whore."

"My whore." He raked his hands through his hair, then tilted his face toward the ceiling. "Theoretically, you paid me."

"Then y-y"—her voice caught in her throat, and he blurred before her eyes.

He grabbed her hand. "Alice, don't do this."

He was the whore then, that's what she'd wanted to say, but couldn't get it out. With her free hand, she covered her mouth to stifle a sob. She found no amusement in any of this, and no matter how much she tried to twist things around and wrest victory from defeat, she couldn't. That was not what she wanted from him.

She pulled her hand free and rose, turning away so that she couldn't see him watching her with that unfathomable expression, and her wondering all the while how much gratification he found in her shame. She was outside his world, trying to break in. When had that happened? When had she started wanting in? She couldn't remember. And now she was thinking that not only did she not belong in, he didn't want her here, that he hated her for where she'd come from and for the color of the uniform her men had worn, and that he was using her to win some sort of tiny, hurtful, inconsequential victory that, in his mind, would make up for his loss. She swiped at a tear.

"Is it true?"

"Nothing is true."

"Of course there's truth, damn you." She jerked her body around so she could see him. "Is it true that I allowed you to do what no decent woman would have?"

He laid his hand on his thigh. "If you did, Alice, then for the sake of men everywhere, I hope there are no decent women."

Another answer that wasn't an answer.

He reached for the kitten climbing up his pants leg. "Git," he said and set it aside with a gentle pat on its tiny bottom.

She clenched her fists tight by her side and stepped stiffly toward him. "Give me an answer. Do you have any respect left for me at all?"

His face darkened, and he rose in front of her so she had to look up into his eyes. "What passed between us did not alter my feelings toward you one bit. If it's respect you want, as my wife, you have it. As for me, I want trust, and I want to be able to trust you in turn." He caught her chin when she started to lower her eyes. "And maybe when we've both realized what we *say* we want from each other, we'll have what we really *need*." He kissed her then, gently, his lips barely brushing hers, and he let her go. "I told her I never want to see her on Camellia Creek again." He started out of the room. "So if she shows up in that kitchen, run her off or find me."

"Eli?"

He stopped and looked at her.

"Do people down here change their bed sheets every time they have sex?"

"Or make love, either?" He shook his head and again started out of the room. "Only if they're as twisted as an unearthed worm."

Chapter Seventy

He touched the key hanging on a nail next to the back door. He'd locked it last night, he had no doubt now. Naomi Polk had been inside. She'd hid in his house and watched their perverse pleasure, as Alice called it.

"She'll be back," Miss Elvie said, stepping from the dining room onto the porch. He pulled the door shut behind them and followed her down the breezeway to the kitchen.

"I don't want her here." He stood aside and let Elvie, arms laden with table linens from Alice's mother's crates, enter the kitchen. "There'll be no forgiveness this time."

Elvie blew out an incredulous breath. "'Cause 'a dem dirty sheets, and you ain't—"

"I caught her trying to drown Alice's kitten in the washtub, Auntie."

The old woman turned and looked at him. After a moment, she pursed her lips and turned back to the linens. "Know'd she weren't gonna be happy 'bout a cat in da kitchen."

"It was more than that, and you know it. You know her better than anyone."

From where he stood near the stove, he saw the old woman grimace.

"You right. It be more'n dat."

"Have you ever known her to be so vengeful?"

Miss Elvie fingered the embroidery decorating a corner of a linen tablecloth. "Girl's got some purty things to show off heah at Camellia Creek."

"Have you?"

The old woman sighed. "'Pends on how bad she feel da slight.

Now dis, you runnin' 'er off Camellia Creek fo' good, she gonna take dat slight to heart."

Yes, he reckoned she would, but he couldn't very well leave her to wreak havoc in his household and kill the family pets because he feared she might do something *bad*.

"She's mean, Eli. Always been mean. Mean and jealous. Had to 'av 'er way, an' afta yo' mama passed, you know, she considered 'ersef mistress of Camellia Creek by right." She looked up at him and shook a finger before turning for the sink. "She'd been one 'a dem bad slave owners dem ab'litionists was always fussin' 'bout. Lawdy mercy"—she reached for the pump.

"Let me do that," he said and took the handle from her.

She started back to the table. "You recall how she hit Dolly dat day when she made dat lemon cake?"

Yes, he remembered.

"Hit 'er twice wif dat wood spoon…an' in da face. Had 'er lip bleedin' and all da while Missy Hannah had tol' Dolly to make dat cake. Oh, my Lawd, I can see it now, Hannah cryin' and yellin' and tellin' yo' daddy dis place done got too small for 'er and 'er Aunt Naomi and he better decide which one he wanted to keep."

Aunt Elvie turned to him, laughing so hard tears streamed down her face. "Po', po' massa, he weren't never able to deal wif woman's stuff…"

Gnawing pain, not unlike hunger, clawed his gut. Despite it, he smiled, too. Burgeoning grief he'd refused to face of late.

"But 'im gots Nimi outa heah dat time. He weren't standin' fo' no senseless hittin' 'im's people, not a'tall."

Elvie turned to him then, still laughing, still crying. She swiped at her cheeks. "Only time I eva recall 'im raisin' a hand to a darkie was when he whupped Brim Solomon's butt with da back of his hand, but dat was okay, 'cause he whupped yo's twice as hard."

"And twice as long." 'Cause he was the master's son, and he was the one responsible.

"Wonder you two didn't burn da house down wif dat lamp."

"It was an accident."

"Runnin' roun' da house like Injuns, da both ya, and he'd already tol' you once to stop."

"You got a bucket?"

She bent beneath the sink and pulled out a pail, which she placed beneath the water he had running. Elvie blinked, then nodded solemnly. "I b'lieve she might be real vengeful, Eli. Didn't know she tried to drown dat kitten. Does missy know dat?"

Eli stopped pumping, and Elvie took the pail and headed for the pot on the stove. Yeah, she knew all right. She knew that and feared so much more.

"She always like dat." Miss Elvie picked up the stir stick and pushed the boiling bed linens around in the wash pot. "Always findin' out what bothered folk, den pickin' at it till it bleed."

"Why did people tolerate her so long?" Alice asked.

"'Cause she family. My missy didn't want Nimi to come heah. She know'd how she be. But her uncle's wife weren't gonna have her in her house neitha." Miss Elvie nodded. "She know'd 'bout Nimi, too, and weren't gonna live wif 'er. My missy died less dan three years afta Nimi come. Nimi took ova runnin' da house."

"But you could have done that."

"Sho', lots I coulda done and did fo' a while, but sometime a white man need a white woman on 'is arm. Dinner parties and such. A mistress fo' da house."

"Why did she never marry? Her features aren't—"

"No, she ain't ugly. Pretty even when she be young, tall wif wide hips, good fo' breedin'. But she be real pa'tic'la' 'bout who she let court her. Reckon she neva found who she wanted an' him want her, too."

"But she hoped Holland Calhoon would marry her."

"She be jealous of Rosalind marryin' Holland Calhoon, then her daddy dyin' an' leavin' her with nothin' to be mistress of. When my missy died, Nimi wanted to be mistress of Camellia Creek. She sho' didn't want Holland wedded to nobody else and takin' her place heah."

"Then that's what she holds against me."

"She didn't want Eli to wed, fo' sho'. Doubt she even wanted 'im to come home, but she'da neva held onto dis place wifout 'im." Elvie looked at her across the pot. "Fo' dat, she needed 'im."

"She must not have been happy about Andrew's marrying Laura. Had things not turned out the way they did, Laura would have become mistress of Camellia Creek."

"But Miss Hannah had come between. Her was da mistress when Miss Laura and Andy wed. Think by den Nimi were content makin' as much trouble as she could, nothin' mo'."

"Then the war changed everything," Alice said. "Put her back into a position where she could be mistress."

"Oh, Lawd, and she were! From da time da massa kilt and young missy died till Eli come home in da fall, she acted da role. Weren't much to be mistress of. Slaves be free and most done run off anyways, and she neva would be mistress of me." The old darkie shrugged. "Prob'ly bes' she were heah, though. Empty homes and land was bein' squat on. Don't know what Eli woulda done if he come back and found strangers in dis house."

He'd be out buried by his father and sister and…and all the Calhoons going back three generations, probably. Queasiness unsettled her stomach, and she rubbed her belly. Eli was all that was left to carry on his family's name, but that was more than her father had. Jacob Shelton's blood would go on, but not his name. But she could have never given her papa that honor anyway. That had been her brothers' role, and they were gone.

With her stick, Elvie pulled up one of the sheets Naomi Polk had conveyed such umbrage over, and Alice blinked at it, bright white in the sunlight and smelling of lye. *Only if they're as twisted as an unearthed worm,* Eli had said in reference to the woman, but where, here, in this deepest of the Deep South, did the twisted people stop and the normal ones begin?

Chapter Seventy-one

"How high does it get during the heaviest rains?" the colonel asked.

"Water from the creek covered this entire bottom last month."

Lieutenant Colonel Alexander Wilson, U.S. Army Corps of Engineers studied the swath of land Eli indicated, then started walking north. Eli followed. From here, well west of the house, it wouldn't take them long to reach the creek. Wilson's lieutenant, who'd introduced himself as Thomas McKee, fell in behind, the three of them kicking up damp leaves as they rustled across the rough, if now somewhat barren, forest between Bayou Pierre and Camellia Creek. The colonel stopped on a low ridge overlooking the latter. He looked east, then back west, then south to the bayou from where they'd come. The day was sullen-looking, relatively warm, and dampness in the air hinted at rain.

"You say there's an oxbow in front of your home?"

"Just east. Small now. Formed a long time ago."

"How close is the creek to it?"

"Separated on the lake's northeast end by a land bridge less than ten feet wide."

"Creek flood into it?"

"Regularly."

"Lake oriented northeast to southwest?"

"Curves generally that direction for about a mile."

"Now looking at the flow of this creek here, I'm thinking it empties into the bayou somewhere downstream?"

"Little less than three miles up the bayou from the river, but it's here I'm worried about. Camellia Creek is starting to flood this old hollow, north and west toward the river."

"This old hollow could well be an ancient river bed," the lieutenant said.

"That's what a geologist told my grandfather years ago."

"Well," the colonel said, removing his hat and rubbing his forehead with the sleeve of his frock coat, "from what I'm hearing, I do believe you have more to fear immediately from the creek than you do from the Mississippi." He shrugged. "Maybe in a hundred years, or a thousand, a branch of the creek will find its way back to the Mississippi this way, and"—he nodded up the hollow—"*maybe* the Mississippi will decide to retake this route for its own, but I do believe it's as likely the creek would cut a new route to the bayou across the lake."

Colonel Wilson wasn't doing his reconnoitering as a favor to Eli—actually Eli had happened upon him and McKee this morning, the two of them stumbling around on the rougher patches of his land studying, they told him, the Bayou Pierre watershed on this side of the county. The Federals wanted to get boats, unhindered, inland from the Mississippi. There was rebuilding to be done, rebuilding in the best interest of the United States, if not necessarily that of the seditious inhabitants of the state. Still, the colonel had introduced himself with a handshake, and Eli had offered his to McKee in turn. Both were polite, helpful, and, given what little Eli knew of the subject, knowledgeable.

"The head of the creek anywhere near Port Gibson?" the colonel asked.

"No, turns due north just east of the lake."

"I'd like a look at it eventually, but for now the Corps of Engineers doesn't have much interest in this feisty little creek as you refer to it." The man turned and started retracing his steps. "This whole geological design with the river, the creek and the bayou is interesting, though, but there are higher priorities than Port Gibson and Bayou Pierre."

Eli fell in step beside him. "If you give the river a hundred years or a millennium"—from the very way it had been stated, that had to be a pretty rough guess in Eli's estimation—"perhaps the solution would be to dredge a new channel from the southern end of Lake Elizabeth to the Bayou, then knock a hole in that land bridge."

The colonel pursed his lips and nodded. "You say the creek is already flooding the land bridge between it and the lake?"

"Has periodically for years now."

The man stopped and faced east. From where they stood, they could see Bayou Pierre clearly to their right, Camellia Creek to their left. "Can we see the lake from here?"

"It's a good mile from where we're standin'."

"How far is your house from the lake?" Wilson asked.

"About a hundred yards. House is higher, up on an old bank of the Mississippi."

"That same geologist told you that?"

"Told Granddaddy, and yes sir, that would be the same fella."

"What do you think, Thomas?"

Thomas stepped around his senior. "If the creek ends up in the lake then this here"— he waved his hand toward the hollow that concerned Eli—"is no issue. What's it gonna do to your water source on this part of your land?"

Eli shrugged. "Creek's spring fed. I reckoned it'd go on, only calmer."

The colonel nodded, and Thomas McKee said, "I'd like to see the lake. The site sounds interesting and might help with that study we're doing on oxbows on the lower river." The younger man couldn't be past his mid-twenties. A little younger, Eli reckoned, than himself. Thomas grinned. "If there's a house there, sure makes the research easier than stomping around in a snake-infested swamp."

Wilson shot Eli a questioning look.

"Hell, I'm not lookin' a gift horse in the mouth. He's welcome."

Chapter Seventy-two

Seth Parker rose when Naomi Polk appeared in Private Ball's wake.

"She say it be 'bout Calhoon and da Hale killin', suh."

Seth motioned Miss Polk in, then said to the private, "Find the captain for me. Send him in when he gets here."

Ball nodded and closed the door behind him.

"Miss Polk…"

Tears filled her eyes, and she bowed her head. "I'm sorry, Major Parker, but it's so very difficult for me to come to you with this."

He did believe she'd just spoken more words to him with that sentence than she had in the brief interviews he'd had with her following the Solomon murders and that of Laura Blackledge. He moved to the front of his desk and patted the back of an upholstered chair, battered but serviceable. "Please, sit down."

She sniffed, delicately wiped her nose with the lace hankie wadded in her gloved hand, then gave him a grateful smile. With a heavy sigh, she maneuvered herself around the chair and sat.

"How can I help you?" he said, moving around his desk and retaking his seat.

She started that damn tearing and blinking again and averted her gaze. "It is I, unfortunately, who am here to help you."

"And I am most grateful for any help I might receive, no matter how unfortunate."

She closed her eyes as if his words pained her, then, chin high, mouth resolute, she blinked and looked at him. "I will be unable to live with myself if anything should happen to that girl."

"That girl?"

She swallowed and waved her hankie-clutching hand. "That poor, foolish thing my nephew seduced and forced to marry him."

He narrowed his eyes. "You believe she's in danger?"

The woman all but gasped. "Of course, she's in danger. Surely you've thought so from the start?"

That was one thing he hadn't completely ruled out, Alice's being in danger from Calhoon, though he had no doubt in his mind, Alice herself did not feel threatened by him.

"From whom?"

"Her husband, you f…" She snapped her mouth shut. "My nephew, Eli Calhoon. Who else?"

"Why do you believe your nephew means to harm her?"

"He wants to *kill* her." The woman snorted, looked away, then just as quickly looked back at him. "He found out about her relationship with that Franklin boy."

"She has a relationship with Jonathan Franklin?"

"Really, Major, you suspected that yourself."

How the hell would she know that?

She must have noted the intensity with which he was studying her, because she began fanning herself as if distressed. "Well," she said, "I don't know since she and Eli wed, but before, she and Franklin were promised to each other."

Only to hear Franklin tell it.

"Eli is insanely jealous, he —"

"Does he love his wife?"

Naomi Polk's eyes went hard. Much more like the woman he was heretofore familiar with. "I doubt it. He wanted her for the money. Nevertheless, Major, as I'm sure you are aware, she is his wife, his property. To cuckold him would be a dishonor."

To be righted on the field of honor, not by murdering one's spouse. Well, he conceded, maybe both. "Given that, Miss Polk, I would think your sympathies would lie with your nephew."

"Oh," she said quickly, "I don't know she's been unfaithful. However, Eli has convinced himself that she is conspiring with this young man, Franklin, to gather evidence against him for the murder of Wayne Hale."

"And once her husband has been convicted and perhaps hanged"—unlikely, Seth believed, at least in the case of Wayne Hale—"Alice and Jonathan Franklin can live happily ever after on Alice's fortune." Of course, Alice and Franklin could have accomplished that without Alice ever marrying Calhoon. And as if Naomi Polk sensed his doubt, she leaned forward.

"At Camellia Creek," she said.

A soft knock sounded on the door, then it swung open. Jubal Summers stood there. Naomi Polk glanced at him, and he came in when Seth motioned him forward.

"Pull up a chair, Captain Summers. Miss Polk has brought to my attention a threat she believes exists to Mrs. Alice Calhoon."

"From her husband?" Jubal asked.

When Seth nodded in the affirmative, Jubal reached for a chair and pulled it up beside Naomi Polk, who watched him, though she tried to disguise it, with silent contempt. "I, for one," Jubal said, "am pleased to learn anything that might take the likes of one Master Eli Calhoon out of circulation."

Good God, he hoped Jubal hadn't sabotaged Naomi Polk's resolve. She glared at the man, and Seth cleared his throat.

"I believe we were talking about gathering evidence against your nephew in the death of Wayne Hale."

She nodded.

"Does such evidence exist?"

"It must. That's why Eli was forced to kill Laura."

Seth's heart beat a little faster. Laura's brutal murder upped the ante. "He thought Laura Blackledge intended to use said evidence against him?"

"She wanted him to divorce his wife and marry her. She told him she would tell the authorities what happened the morning Wayne Hale was murdered."

Seth grimaced. "Miss Polk, I must be honest with you. I doubt your nephew's killing the murderer of a freedman and his family would even result in a trial, much less a conviction."

Naomi Polk's eyes widened. "But Eli doesn't realize that."

Seth gave her what he hoped was a skeptical look, and she

swallowed, blinked rapidly, then squirmed in her seat. "Very well, there is more."

Jubal sat forward in his seat. Seth did nothing.

"Wayne's death was about more than Brim Solomon," the woman said.

"Oh?"

"It had something to do with what Wayne knew about that Treasury agent's murder."

Seth glanced at Jubal, still as a statue, then back to Naomi Polk.

"You think Laura Blackledge knew Calhoon was involved in Alan Guthrie's death?"

"Yes, and that's what she was blackmailing him with."

"And did your nephew tell you that?"

She hesitated, then said, "Laura did."

"And did she tell you how she knew?"

The woman set her mouth firmly and raised her chin. "May Hale told her what was said the morning Eli killed Wayne."

Well, that was enlightening. Not much that May Hale had ever said to Seth made sense at all. Personally, he had doubted the woman's being of sound mind, much less a reliable source. And why, of all the people to talk to, would May Hale talk to Laura?

"What you are telling me," Seth said, "is that Eli Calhoon killed both Wayne Hale and Laura Blackledge to shut them up in regards to Alan Guthrie's murder?"

"Yes."

But did nothing to silence Laura Blackledge's source, May Hale. "Given your nephew's ruthlessness, Mrs. Polk, I would think you would consider your own life in danger."

"He doesn't know what Laura told me." She turned her face to heaven and closed her eyes. After a moment her eyes fluttered open, and she started to cry again. "Oh, my poor dead sister, that I have had to take steps to stop the rampage of her sole surviving child. And after the family has experienced so much tragedy.

"But please, Major Parker, it's that poor, stupid girl, who

probably means my nephew no harm at all. He confided in me just this morning that he is stricken by her subterfuge and betrayal, and he's determined to be rid of her and her alleged lover."

Seth's gut tightened. "He's threatened the life of Jonathan Franklin, too?"

"I do believe in his mind he has little choice. Laura had become…friendly, shall we say…with that Franklin boy. I believe Eli is suspicious of what she might have divulged to him regarding the agent's death and what Jon Franklin, in turn, has told Alice. I fear Eli is seeing enemies everywhere he looks. I've debated with myself all night over what to do and decided the only right course is to come to you."

The smile she gave him was oh so very sad and woeful. "Well," she said, and she rose. "I've other stops to make, and I understand we're to get a great deal of rain."

Both men rose when she did. "That's what I'm told," Seth said. "Perhaps I should get up to see May Hale before it starts."

"I considered that you might. I do not know when Eli intends to commit the deed, but by some hoax he intends to get poor Alice and Franklin together so that, if nothing else, he appears justified in his commission of murder." Naomi Polk extended Seth her hand, and he took it.

A weak shake for a strong woman.

"Have you considered warning Alice?"

"Oh, good Lord, no, I can't. You see, and I'm ashamed to say I was privy to the deceit, but Eli has tricked her into believing I am no longer welcome at Camellia Creek. He does, sir, trust me implicitly. I am his sole surviving relative."

Chapter Seventy-three

"Naomi Polk came to me after lunch," Jon Franklin said to Alice. "She said she feared for your life…and mine, as a matter of fact, and suggested I come and take you from here."

From the threshold of Camellia Creek's front door, Alice studied Jon, confident in an immaculate frock suit, the starched collar of his shirt brilliant against his tanned skin. He'd asked for Eli when she opened the door, then asked to wait when she told him he wasn't home. She'd said no, that she'd send Eli to her uncle's home if he needed to talk to him. Now Jon had broached the subject of Naomi Polk and her vague warning. It occurred to Alice now that it had been Jon's hope all along to find Eli gone. Or worse, and Alice's heart thumped a little faster, he'd known before knocking on the door. Her husband's horse was missing from the lean-to, after all.

Eli had gone off with Thomas McKee earlier in the afternoon. They were walking the creek, the lake, and the bayou. He'd told her he probably wouldn't be back until dark. They'd left on foot, but had taken their horses. Thomas—he'd asked her to call him that—planned to head into Port Gibson after they'd completed their observations. Alice considered impending rain might bring Eli in earlier; its threat had driven Miss Elvie and Buck to their cabins a while ago.

"Did she tell you why she said such a thing?"

The wind, from the south, gusted and roared through the pines. Foreboding swept over Alice, and she listened for Jocelyn. Lightning struck close, and thunder followed. Jon's horse, hitched to his carriage, shied with the strike, and the empty carriage rolled a foot. Jonathan cursed.

"It's going to storm," she said. "You should start back."

He looked at the sky and the lake, its surface rippling in the wind. Alice was stepping back from the threshold when Jon turned. "I fear I'll be caught in it if I leave now, and we do need to talk."

"I have no desire to talk to you, Jon, and you'll be better off caught out there than trapped in here. Camellia Creek is prone to flood." She was being inhospitable, but she wasn't going to let him in, not after the rumors he'd spread.

"I know it's prone to flood, but I must talk to you regarding this threat."

"Naomi Polk, I assure you, has no one's interest at heart save her own." Alice started to shut the door in his face, but he thrust it open, pushing her back, and stepped inside her home. Before she could react with more than a stifled gasp, he yanked the door out of her hand and slammed it behind him.

"How dare you force your way in here!"

"Stop this ridiculous attitude of yours, right now. We must talk." He smiled. "And I didn't force my way in. You invited me."

"Get out."

"Listen to me. Your husband has this bizarre notion there's some sort of relationship between you and me."

"And where did he get that idea, Jonathan?"

His eyes widened. "Certainly not from me. I've scarcely ever talked to the man and never about you. Now, could we please sit and have a civil conversation?" He moved around her. "I've never been inside. Uncle Peter does love this place, you know? Feels there's so much he could do with it." He turned at the parlor entry and found her eyes. "I had given up ever receiving an invitation to visit."

"You don't have an invitation now," she said following a few steps. Her body was growing tenser by the moment. "I want you to leave."

He held his arms out in supplication. "Please, Alice, I really mean no harm."

But harm is what she feared if her husband should come

home and find him here. And no matter what, she'd still have to tell Eli of the visit. He wouldn't like it, and this intrusion would add to the strain on their relationship...and their trust.

"Say your piece and go."

"I told you. Calhoon has threatened both our lives."

"There, you've said it, now get."

He laughed that snotty "foolish girl" laugh of his. "I can't leave you like this, knowing he's a danger."

"You don't know that, Jon, because I don't believe you would have come to Camellia Creek believing Eli planned to kill you."

"I would for you," he said, his voice gentle, and he moved toward her.

She stepped back. "Have no fear, Eli doesn't consider you a threat."

He stilled. "An insult, Alice?"

"A fact."

"He believes you were in love with me before he compromised you and forced you into marriage."

"Lies you spread." She held up an index finger when he started to protest. "Eli believes no such thing."

"That is not what his aunt told me."

"His aunt is purposely misleading you."

"She says you are terribly unhappy, that your husband routinely intimidates and abuses you"—his face took on a sorrowful expression, false by Alice's estimation—"that he humiliates you in the marriage bed."

Alice felt her color ebb. How much had that woman said to him? What was she telling others? Good heavens, how much did she know, and how did she know it? "I want you to leave my house right now."

"I won't leave you here to face him alone."

"Oh, for Saint Peter's sake!" She whirled in the direction of the door, but he caught her around the waist and yanked her hard against his chest. Air escaped her lungs, and the force of his hold around her waist soured her stomach. She grasped his arm to pull it away, and he pressed her tighter to him.

"Listen to me. You don't have to worry. I have this planned out. You and I can be rid of him for good. Then we'll have this place Uncle Peter wants so badly, and we'll have your fortune. Whatever threat he holds over you will die with him. I don't care how you behaved with the man."

Alice strained against him. "You don't care about anything but my grandparents' money."

"And I do need that money, desperately."

She pried at his arm, clenching her teeth with the force of her effort. "Let me go, you dog!"

His hold tightened. "Your relationship with my mother was the one thing holding me back with you, Alice, but now you're going to have to come to terms with her, and she with you."

He turned her in his arms and held her by the shoulders. "But I would like to know why you married him in the first place. What hold did he have over you? Cassie wasn't it." He laughed when her eyes widened. "My army friends talk. Seems my cousin has quite the reputation. I feared Nathan would learn of it, and he will if you don't work with me."

"Go to hell."

"You always did come across as a little less than a lady. Must have been the lack of a mother's guidance."

She twisted and managed to force herself to arm's length, but couldn't get free. He shook her.

"Calhoon's aunt says he's a jealous man. That's why she's so concerned for your safety. She says he killed Laura."

Laura. Alice narrowed her eyes. "You knew her?"

"Yes, I knew the trollop." He twisted his face into what she took to be a triumphant smile. "Intimately. Naomi says Calhoon knew about me and her. Says he couldn't take any more of her cheating. He married you for money. To him you're chattel. They all think that way down here. Think what will happen when he comes home and finds you and me alone together in his house." He clamped his mouth over hers. Bile burned her stomach and her throat. She tried to push away, struggling desperately to twist her mouth from his and keep his—she grunted and pushed—

filthy tongue out of her mouth. With a quick tilt of her head, she found his bottom lip and bit down. He managed a garbled growl. She bit harder, and he struggled to push her away.

Full of fight and heady with victory, no matter how tenuous, she grabbed his hair and pulled; she tasted blood. He wrenched his body, and when he failed to free himself, he tangled his fingers into the hair on top of her head and crushed her scalp beneath his hands. Pain tore across the top and back of her head and neck, then across her shoulders when he shoved her away, freeing his bottom lip from between her teeth. He bent at the waist and raised his hand to his mouth. Her scalp stinging, she watched him, then reeled as blood dripped over his fingers onto the floor. She reached for the coal oil lamp on the table she'd placed beside the settee, picked it up, and slammed its heavy base against the back of his head. He fell forward. She dropped the lamp base, which landed with a thud. Its chimney shattered beside him.

With a whimper, she circled around the settee, grabbed the poker from the hearth, and whirled back toward him. He was on his feet, after her, but stopped short when he saw what she held. How quickly he'd recovered. She hesitated only a moment, then feigning a blow to his head, she wielded the poker, with as much force as she could muster, to his knee. Michael had told her once, years ago, to never aim any type of club at an opponent's head. "If you aim for the head, he'll take it away from you."

Jonathan buckled, and this time she hit his left shoulder with a force that rolled him to one side, then she hit him high across the back of his shoulders, sending him sprawling flat to the floor before walloping his elbow. He cried out with the blow, and she hit him again. Hard...she chopped...hard...again...harder. He'd stopped trying to grab for the poker now, choosing instead to protect himself with arms that appeared more and more useless. Don't stop. Don't stop. As long as he's moving, don't stop hitting him.

"You will not say anything about Cassie," she cried, her voice jerky, rat-a-tat in consonance with her chopping blows, hitting his torso and legs and arms, never his head. "Do you under-stand?" Again and again, as hard as she could, clenching her teeth and growling and spitting as tears rolled down her cheeks, until she heard him crying, begging for her to stop, that he was done for and would go. She stopped and looked at him, pathetic, rolled up in a fetal position, head curled to his body, arms cover-ing his chest. "I'll go. I'll go. Just stop!"

Straining for breath, she came to herself, then hit him again when he tried to rise. "Crawl out!" she screamed. "You slither out like the snake you are."

And he did. As best he could, he dragged himself out of the parlor and across the foyer. She made him reach up and open the door; she wasn't about to get within his grasp. He'd surely kill her now. She slammed the front door and locked it when he cleared the entry. Then leaning her back against it, she closed her eyes and sucked in a breath. Through a crack in the boards covering the front window, she watched him rise gingerly, then stumble and half-fall down the porch stairs before struggling into the car-riage. It had started to rain. Awkwardly he reached for the reins—he didn't appear to have good control of his left arm— and, hunkered low in the seat, he started off.

Clammy, her body shaking, she rushed to the dining room, locked that door, and no longer able to fight the sickness, she grabbed a large serving bowl off the buffet and retched.

Alice sank into a dining-room chair. The house was large, filled with indefensible windows and doors, mostly boarded. She thought of Holland Calhoon's Colt hidden in Eli's dresser. In the world they lived in of late, he kept it loaded, and if he hadn't taken it with him, his rifle would be above the door in the cook-house.

Her chin itched, and she licked her lips, caked, she realized, with Jon Franklin's blood, which she attempted to scrub off with the sleeve of her dress. What sort of creature must she look like? She buried her head in her hands, and whispered Eli's name.

Outside the wind rose.

And the wail of Jocelyn LeBlanc echoed in refrain.

"*D*amn!" Thomas McKee hollered at Eli above the fading thunder. On their left, the waters of Bayou Pierre rippled from bank to bank, and above them, the treetops roared in the gale. "I'm not believing this electrical storm this late in the year."

After introducing McKee to Alice, who fed them lunch, he and Thomas — per the lieutenant's request — had started with the land bridge separating Camellia Creek from Lake Elizabeth, then moved south along the lakefront. At the south end of the lake, they spent some time studying the best place to start a trench to the bayou, only a quarter mile away. After some rough speculating, they moved on to Bayou Pierre and followed it two and a half miles downstream to where Camellia Creek emptied into it. They turned back at that point, but in the interim, an expected front from the south had collided with one from the north, and the anticipated storm had formed, followed them east, and finally overtaken them.

Eli squinted, the gusting wind effectively countering the protection from the rain normally offered by the brim of his cavalry hat. "Believe it. Let's get on back to my place."

Thomas shook his head. "I'll stick to my plan. It's not that much farther to Port Gibson. Might be marooned at Camellia Creek by morning. Colonel wouldn't be happy." He grasped the saddle horn and mounted. "Maneuvering around the south end of the lake will be easier, too. You cuddle up with that pretty little wife of yours."

A pleasant thought, or should have been, were things different. Eli gave the man a two-fingered salute and, tugging Johnny behind him, turned for home. The frigid rain hit him full in the face, and he sucked in a breath between clenched teeth. The thought of Alice waiting in his warm home eclipsed his misgivings. It was past time to make things right between him and her.

*S*eth pulled the sleeve of his frock coat up his arm and started buttoning. He'd meant to get out of here right after Naomi Polk had left over two hours ago, but a visit from an acquaintance at the Freedman's Bureau, another officer, had sidetracked him. The man's visit, dealing with the case of a freedman accused by a local of cotton theft, was unrelated to what Seth was working on. Still, this previously established contact at the Bureau could one day prove valuable, so Seth didn't want to put the man off by appearing unappreciative, and they'd lunched together at the hotel. Now, the damn storm was on them.

Seth had been of a mind to wait until tomorrow to visit May Hale, but Sergeant Zachary had returned twenty minutes ago, unable to find Jonathan Franklin—or Peter Franklin. Earlier, at the Franklin house, he'd been told Jon Franklin's mother was napping, and she'd refused to rise and talk to him. The woman had sent word, via the servant Zachary sent to roust her, that her son had an unknown visitor after lunch and had left. The woman requested Zachary leave also and try back later. Franklin's mother did not appear amenable to wasting any more time with a Negro sergeant so he did leave. The Franklin household was a loyal Union one after all, not a Southern one to be bullied about.

Seth's not knowing the whereabouts of Jon Franklin at first aggravated him, but now the darkening sky conjured a sense of forboding, and his aggravation had blossomed into apprehension, which had spawned an inexplicable need for urgency.

"We'll be at the Hale residence, then we're heading out to Camellia Creek," he said to Private Ball, standing behind a make-shift desk consisting of two flour barrels and an old table top. He really should confiscate a desk for the entry.

"In this rain, Camellia Creek's gonna flood."

Seth looked across the front room of the newspaper office to where Poynter Cummings lounged in the door of the room Seth had allowed him to keep as his own. With all the commotion, the editor had sneaked out of his back hole.

Outside, lightning crackled and the building shuddered with the strike. Seth hunched his shoulders as did Private Ball. The rain outside was making almost as much noise on the porch roof, and Seth turned. They had the door open, water was blowing in, and in the street, the horses were whinnying in protest. What the hell was he thinking, going out in this mess.

"Daws, close the damn door!"

The corporal obliged—went outside instead of in, and Seth cursed. Maybe he liked being cold and wet. Seth pivoted around and looked at Cummings. "There's got to be a way on and off."

"Hasn't ever gotten so deep a horse can't make it over the bridge, but you've got to know where the bridge is."

Seth knew where the bridge was, at least he did when it wasn't covered with water. "Is it too rough to swim?"

Cummings frowned and shook his head. "Not if you cross the lake, and with cavalry horses you should be okay if you don't stir up any cottonmouth nests."

"Scare my man from New York, Mr. Cummings. I'm from Kentucky."

"And meaner than any old cottonmouth I'm sure."

Seth laughed, though he wasn't sure why. Odds were a lot better the lightning would get 'em than any snakes that might be living in Lake Elizabeth."

Cummings meandered into the front office. "You gotta do this now?"

Seth yanked the door open—the gusting wind helped—and rain pelted his face. "Corporal Daws, get your ass in here." He glanced back at Cummings. "I'm afraid I'm running out of time."

Seth turned to Daws, drenched and dripping water in the door of the office, then stepped around and closed the door behind him. "Soon as the lightning lets up a bit," Seth said to him, "you and Private Spain get out to the Franklin house. If Jonathan Franklin still isn't there, find out where he is and escort him home, and I don't care if you have to interrupt his mother's nap to do it. If anyone wants to know why, tell them it's because I have reason to believe someone is going to make an attempt on his life—that should wake his mama up."

"You think that someone is Eli Calhoon?" Cummings asked.

Seth turned and motioned to Jubal and Frank Zachary, already bundled up and getting warm by the stove, then glanced at Cummings. "How much of my conversation with Naomi Polk did you overhear earlier?"

"Everything." Cummings cocked his head. "These walls are thin."

All the more reason to lunch at the hotel. "What's your take?"

"Somebody's done gone an' made dat ole woman mad."

All eyes turned to Zachary. He shrugged, and looked at Jubal Summers. "Sorry, Cap'n, but you wrong on dis. You always been wrong 'bout dat Calhoon fella."

Seth set his havelock-covered kepi on his head and fastened the chin strap. He wasn't absolutely convinced about that "Calhoon fella," but he did agree with his senior noncom on one point. Somebody had gone and rubbed Naomi Polk's fur the wrong way.

Chapter Seventy-four

Alice rose and turned slowly toward the back door. The wail died. Outside the wind gusted, whipping the wood siding and rattling the sparse window panes. Lightning struck brilliantly, and she covered her ears, cringing at the exploding thunder that shook the foundation of the house. Eli had no business out in this, even if she didn't want him home so fervently.

Something slapped the wall of the mud porch. Alice jumped, but garnered the courage to peek out the window. Eli's razor strap slapped in the wind. Identifying the source of the racket would have been enough to resolve her anxiety, but for Jocelyn's haunting cry. Again, she checked the porch, bleak and gray and damp as water misted between the modest columns defining it. She saw nothing but muddy boots and shoes scattered on its floor and an old wool jacket hanging from a nail. She opened the back door and checked. The porch was deserted. Deserted, but cold and wet, the weathered wood floor slick with rain water. Drawing a breath, she stepped onto the porch, then covered the brief distance to the gyrating strap and took it down. To her right stood the covered breezeway, through which the raging storm passed unimpeded. At its other end stood the cookhouse, and inside the cookhouse a lamp burned.

She moved back into the dining room, shut the door, and locked it. That kitchen lamp could keep burning, too. She wasn't going out there until Eli got home.

The temperature was dropping. She needed to tend the fire, then check the stove in the bedroom. She blinked. Then the gutted library at the far end of the hall, and Hannah's old room next to hers and Eli's, and then the bedrooms upstairs. Her head was starting to hurt. She forced herself calm. In a minute. She'd do all that in a minute. First she'd tend the fire in the parlor.

She had just set the poker aside when Jocelyn's wail rose in tandem with the wind.

The spirit had come closer. Alice turned to the foyer and looked at the front door beyond. Heart in her throat, she crossed the entry and checked that door once more. Fool, she told herself, peeking between the boards covering the door's window, there were five busted doors on the first floor of this house, and not one was secure. If someone wanted in, there was little defense. Still, boarded as they were, entering in silence would be impossible.

She moved to an adjacent window, and her heart began to pound as a carriage emerged through the veil of rain. It crossed the bridge at the north end of Lake Elizabeth. Would Jonathan be so bold as to…?

Overhead, the unrelenting rain roared over Camellia Creek's cedar shingles, and Alice, hand at her throat, hurried into the dining room and watched the dark form of the carriage, like a hearse, make its way to the lean-to behind the house. She lost sight of it when it drove behind the kitchen.

In the bedroom, Alice opened Eli's top dresser drawer and reached inside. Her stomach tensed when repeated searches failed to uncover Holland Calhoon's Colt. She'd seen Eli put it here. He'd told her it was here, darn it. Told her after that mysterious visitor, who he claimed not to believe in, invaded their home the night he'd gone to Rodney.

A new sound, and her heartbeat quickened. She shoved the drawer half-closed. Someone was at the back door.

The storm had darkened the afternoon, and the house was dim but for the fire in the parlor and the gray gloom that fell languorously through those windows not boarded. She'd yet to light the first lamp.

Her hand on the door frame leading from the bedroom, Alice listened. She heard nothing now except the violent noise of the horrendous storm. Bad enough. Mother Nature was, conceivably, covering the sounds of an invader. Alice looked across to the parlor. The poker was lost in shadow, but she remembered where she'd placed it not ten minutes ago after stoking the fire.

She drew a steadying breath. The thing had served her well once today, and she was no longer sure Holland Calhoon's Colt was in the bedroom. She glanced around the corner into the quiet, and apparently empty, foyer, then up the dark stairwell.

Heart clamoring, she crept to the end of the hall, where it entered the foyer, and peeked to her left into the dining room…

"There you are."

Alice jumped and would have hid behind the wall, but the woman had seen her. Alice stepped into the foyer proper and watched a tall woman, shrouded in a dark cape, turn back and close the back door.

"I saw Jon Franklin," the woman said, turning now to face her. "He says you beat him with a poker. I didn't tell him so, but I'm sure he probably deserved it. He said he couldn't go home under the circumstances, so he was coming to see me."

The woman turned to one side in the dark dining room and pulled a slouch hat from her head. "I was on my way to Port Gibson, but I told him to go on. My girls will take good care of him." She hung the hat on the back of a dining-room chair, then removed her cloak and tossed it in the seat. "Given the way he looked, I decided I'd best check on you. I wanted to talk to you anyway. But you, my dear, appear to be fine. Shaken, but fine."

"I locked the door," Alice said with a small voice. "How did you get in?"

Isabel Hays in all her shimmering beauty stepped into the dubious light and frowned at her. "I did knock. No one answered. I feared you might not be able to get to the door, so I took the liberty of letting myself in." She held up her hand, displaying a brass skeleton key. Her smile and ensuing shrug implied an apology. "Holland gave it to me. I've had it for the past twenty-five years."

Chapter Seventy-five

"It's nice here with him gone." May Hale was looking out her window, beyond the gossamer sheers, at the pouring rain drenching the dark afternoon. Periodically lightning brightened the darkness, and the sky grumbled, but mostly it pounded out a steady, frigid rain. Seth and his small troop of Jubal Summers and Frank Zachary had ridden hard despite the elements, but they'd still spent a good forty-five minutes getting here.

"It was nice during the war, too," she said. "Sad to say, so many women prayed their men would come home safe to them, and they didn't. All the while I prayed mine wouldn't, and he did."

Seth sat back in the cushioned chair she'd offered him. May Hale didn't cry. She never had in front of him.

"Mrs. Hale, did you hear what I said?"

"I heard you." Her gaze passed over him to Sergeant Zachary, by the door. She straightened and called to him. Zachary looked at Seth, who nodded.

"Come down here," she said and sat forward. The sergeant knelt on one knee in front of her. She touched his face. Jubal Summers, who'd lingered quietly since they arrived, watched.

"How old are you?" she asked Zachary.

"'Bout twenty-nine, I think."

She dropped her hand. "I thought you were around that. Brim Solomon was twenty-nine. You remind me of him." She drew in a stuttered breath and looked at Jubal. "You came here asking about him a long time ago. Do you remember?"

"Yes, ma'am."

"He was such a sweet man. He had a woman and a little boy."

Again she turned to the window. "Sally and Sam. Sally was going to have another baby, Brim told me. She wanted to come home to Camellia Creek." May Hale closed her eyes. "She thought their life would be better."

Seth glanced at Frank Zachary. The sergeant shot him a frown. Seth leaned forward. "Mrs. Hale, did Eli Calhoon kill your husband?"

She opened her eyes with a start. "I told you I don't know what happened to him. He left. He never came back. You told me yourself they found him in the river way down in Louisiana."

"I told you earlier, Naomi Polk said you confided in Laura Blackledge that Eli Calhoon murdered your husband."

"I said no such thing to Laura, and that's the honest truth."

"We need to arrest him then, sir," Frank Zachary said.

Seth blinked at the man, and Jubal Summers stepped closer, his forehead furrowed.

"Arrest Eli?" May Hale whispered.

Seth glanced at his sergeant, pursed his lips, then stood. "I think so. Perhaps Miss Polk was mistaken as to where Mrs. Blackledge got the information, but for certain she's convinced Eli Calhoon murdered Laura Blackledge to keep her quiet."

May Hale grasped the arms of the rocker, her gaze roaming from Seth to Zachary and back to Seth. "You think Eli murdered Laura to keep her quiet about Wayne's death?"

Frank Zachary rose.

"He's always been our number one suspect, Mrs. Hale," Seth said. "Now his own aunt has come to us of her own free will and accused him."

"Naomi Polk is a liar."

"You couldn't possibly be sure of that."

"If he felt it necessary to kill Laura, he would have needed to kill me, too."

Seth's heart was beating a tad faster. "But you don't know who killed your husband."

She closed her eyes. "Yes, I do."

Seth sat back down. "Was it Calhoon?"

May Hale smiled at him, then twisted her head to one side. "Eli would have never killed Laura to protect himself."

"Laura thought he did it, didn't she?"

May's head shook slowly. "Laura knew who killed Wayne."

Seth reached out and took one of the woman's hands, fisted in her lap. She looked down at his hold. "Then he killed Laura to protect who, Mrs. Hale?"

She looked up with glistening eyes. "I'm not as big a fool as you might think, Major Parker. You need to ask that question a bit differently."

"Who killed your husband?"

She pulled her hand from his, then twisted hers together in her lap. After a moment she rocked back.

"Wayne came home at daybreak. He told me what he'd done. He beat me when I covered my mouth to keep from crying out. Beat me bad.

"Late last summer he hired Brim for field work. Brim was a good worker. Eli wasn't back. No one knew if he'd ever come back. Camellia Creek had no seed for planting, no tools for farming. Wayne, at least, could pay somethin'.

"Brim came up to the house one afternoon. He found Wayne hitting me. He'd found out I'd had an abortion, my third." She turned and met Seth's gaze. "Don't judge me too harshly. The baby was my husband's, as was the one before that and the one before that, but they were not my first pregnancies. There'd been babies before those." She closed her eyes. A tear slipped out and trickled down her pale cheek. She licked it with her tongue. "I told my family and neighbors I miscarried every one." Again she met his eyes. "But he beat them out of me, all but the ones I destroyed so he wouldn't."

A cannon ball sat in Seth's stomach. "I'm sorry."

She gave them an uncheerful laugh, then raised her face to the ceiling, blinking back tears she couldn't stop. Finally she wiped her cheeks with a fist. "He was determined they weren't his, and in truth the first one wasn't. I was pregnant when he wed me. Pregnant when my daddy, who was fairly well-to-do, paid

Wayne to marry me. He knew I was damaged goods, said that was all right. My daddy gave him these eighty acres and two hundred dollars. But Wayne never respected me and never believed I was true to him." She looked down at her hands, then back up. "But I was.

"That day last September, Brim made him stop. Hit him, knocked him out." May had stopped crying and now turned to look at Frank Zachary and Jubal. "We owned or borrowed a darkie from time to time, when the crops were doin' good and we could afford it. Wayne was never abusive to them. He worked side by side with 'em in the field, but to be hit by a Negro…" She closed her eyes and shook her head. "And to have that same man know he beat his pregnant wife. Wayne couldn't abide that. He went near crazy. Like when he was angry with me. He said he'd kill Brim. Accused him of being my lover. Good Lord, Brim Solomon and Eli used to bring me their fish from the time they were old enough to wear britches.

"Brim took Wayne's mule as payment for the work he'd done, and he ran. He come home to Eli last month. That's when Wayne killed him. Him and Sally and little Samuel."

She tightened her lips. "I let him beat me year after year. Destroy our babies when we could have been happy. I did make my mistake as a young girl. I paid for it ever since. I thought I deserved to be punished and should keep on deserving it." One by one, May Hale met their three faces. "But Brim Solomon and his little family didn't deserve nothin' like that, and I knew I'd waited too late to do what had to be done.

"Wayne pulled his revolver out of his waistband and laid it on the dry sink by the kitchen door like he always did. Kept his rifle with him. Went out back to chop wood. He leaned the rifle by the shed. His back was to me. I walked up close behind him. He heard me, because he asked me what I wanted. I must have shot him twice before he hit the ground. Then I walked up over him and fired till that revolver just clicked and clicked and clicked.

"I dropped the gun by him and went back into the cookhouse and sat on the floor. That's where Eli found me."

"He took the body?"

May nodded. "He didn't tell me where, but said he hoped it would never be found." She smiled sadly at Seth. "But that old river can do such funny things sometimes. Keeps them you want back, throws up those you don't. Guess the ole Mississippi didn't want Wayne any more than I did.

"Eli told me to tell anyone who come lookin' that Wayne had run 'cause of the killings. He said if anyone suspected Wayne was murdered, they'd think he did it. I didn't want that, but Eli said not to worry 'cause if I hadn't already killed Wayne, he'd have done it when he got here."

"Did you tell Laura that Calhoon killed Wayne?"

"Lettin' people think Eli killed Wayne as long as nothing could be proved is one thing, Major. Tellin' people he did it is another. I'd have never done that. Laura knew that I had to have known what happened that morning. She was so angry at Eli for marrying that pretty little Northerner. She wanted to hurt him however she could, but mostly she wanted him back. She told me she was going to tell you Eli killed Wayne. Said you already thought so anyway. So I told her the truth. Told her it would do no good because I wouldn't let Eli take the blame."

"Then he killed Mrs. Blackledge to protect her," Jubal said to Seth over his shoulder.

Out of the corner of his eye, Seth saw Frank Zachary shift his weight.

"Eli would not have killed Laura to protect me. He'd have confessed to killing Wayne first."

"But he knew you wouldn't let him take responsibility for your husband's death," Seth said. "That would have left you in jeopardy."

Jubal Summers snorted. May Hale looked up at him, then at Seth with a plea in her eyes. "Eli wouldn't kill one woman to protect another. He would have found another way. You must believe me."

"Mrs. Hale," Seth asked, "did you ever hear your husband or Eli Calhoon mention a man named Alan Guthrie?"

"No, but Laura asked me that same question."

Seth's gut squeezed, and he glanced at Jubal, who frowned at him. Hell, he himself had asked Laura to pursue a connection between Calhoon and Guthrie. "Did you tell Calhoon she asked that question?" Seth asked May.

May Hale blinked at him, then nodded. "But," she said, when Seth sucked in a resolute breath, "I didn't see him to tell him until after Laura was dead."

Murky, but one thing was clear, and it said a lot regarding Naomi Polk and her whole cock-and-bull story, she'd lied outright in her attempt to tie Wayne Hale—and Eli Calhoon—to Alan Guthrie's murder.

Jubal Summers raised a hand and slowed his mount. Beside him, Seth did the same and swiped at the water dripping from his havelock into his eyes. Damn, regulation or not, he was gonna get himself a felt hat.

"Private Spain, sir," Jubal yelled above the driving rain.

Lightning lit the darkening road, and water shimmered all around them. The road Spain navigated at a churning clip was little more than a shallow, muddy stream. Seth reined his mount in, as did his two subordinates.

"Cawp'ral Daws sent me to fin' you, suh," Spain hollered as he raised his hand in a salute.

Seth returned the greeting. "Report, private."

"We done found dat Franklin fella, suh, but we was too late."

Seth could have swallowed his tongue. "He's dead?"

"Yes, suh."

Sweet Jesus. He really hadn't expected this. Considered it a possibility, but not this quickly. "What happened?"

"Found him on da Pawt Gibson-Rodney Road. Was in a carriage. Cawp'ral said to tell you it be pourin' rain when we gots to 'im. Nothin' in da way 'a tracks."

Seth glanced at Sergeant Zachary who'd moved up beside him and Jubal. "How did he die?"

"Gunshot to da chest. Cawp'ral Daws found it, easy to see.

Da cawp'ral say to tell ya he been dead a little while, but not too long. Say looks like he been beat, too."

"Where's Daws?"

"Took da body to dat doc in Pawt Gibson. Said to ask if you want 'im to tell da Franklins."

"You'd been by there?"

"Stopped der fu'st like ya tol' Daws to. Franklin's mama say he'd gone to visit at Camellia Creek."

What had Naomi Polk said? *I considered that you might.* Sweet heaven! *I considered that you might.* That calculating old haint had factored in the time she'd have when he insisted on talking to May Hale. *I do not know when he intends to commit the deed, but by some hoax he intends to get poor Alice and this Franklin person together so that, if nothing else, he appears justified in his commission of murder.*

Seth cursed. The hell she hadn't known when. She'd been setting the stage right there in his office.

Seth squinted at Spain. "Well, doesn't look like he made it does it, Private? Good report. You tell Corporal—

Spain raised his hand. "Der be mo', suh."

More?

"Cawp'ral Peters come upon us 'bout time we come 'cross Franklin. Lawson an' Price was wif 'im."

"They were following the Hays woman?"

"Yes, suh. Say dey give her 'bout a fifteen minute start outa Rodney, but dey know'd where she was goin', 'cause she tol' 'em befo' she lef'."

Seth sighed. Sometimes he thought Isabel Leigh Hays considered his efforts a game.

"But Cawp'ral Daws done tol' 'em dey musta lost 'er, cause she hadn't passed us an' she woulda had to unless she passed by while we was talkin' to da Franklin woman. But we thinkin' dat was too long befo'."

Would have been if she were only fifteen minutes ahead of Corporal Peters' troop. She told them where she was going, then... "When you found Franklin's body, how close were you to the turnoff to Camellia Creek?"

"Suh, when we come up to da turnoff, we could see da carriage mired in da ditch up ahead on da Rodney Road 'bout fifty yards. Checked it fu'st."

"You didn't go to Camellia Creek?"

"No, suh, didn't see no need. We'd done found Jon Franklin."

A gnawing heat clawed Seth's gut, and his thoughts turned to Alice and her husband's role in this.

"Where's Peters?"

"Went on to Pawt Gibson lookin' fo' dat Hays woman."

Damn, Seth wished Corporal Peters and his men had gone to Camellia Creek. That's where he was betting Isabel Hays had gone.

"Tell Daws I'll inform the Franklin family," he called to Private Spain, then returned the man's salute. He turned to Jubal Summers and Frank Zachary. "Gentlemen," he got out before another lightning strike forced him to settle his skittish horse, "we need to find out what's going on at Camellia Creek."

Chapter Seventy-six

"I wouldn't accept it," Isabel Hays said to Alice. "Carnal knowledge of a young woman whom he'd once bounced on his knee was not the sort of thing I imagined Holland capable of."

Alice finished stirring Isabel's coffee—she was a bit embarrassed not to be able to offer tea, since Isabel's Rodney whorehouse seemed so well appointed, but she did have her mother's lovely tea set, and she had sugar, *and* the cow was producing milk now. "Thank you, darling," the woman said, took a sip, then set the cup on the broken marble-top table in front of the settee.

Alice sipped her own. All in all, she'd managed an acceptable cup of coffee, and a pleasant atmosphere. A blazing fire warmed the room—Isabel was responsible for that—and Alice's initial anxiety at Isabel's surprise entry had melted away with the burgeoning flames.

"Suspicious of my sometimes willful niece, I took it upon myself to seek out Hawk Duval, her father's choice for her husband, if you recall. He'd been in Rodney for weeks, patiently courting her. When I told Hawk she was pregnant, his response was they would wed immediately."

Alice narrowed her eyes. "He wasn't angry about—"

"He wasn't surprised, Alice. He'd slept with her. He never questioned the babe's being his, didn't know at the time she thought herself in love with another. He was thrilled they would finally wed. Failing to coax Holland to bed, Jocelyn had purposefully seduced Hawk, planning to trap Holland. She believed her father and brothers would force the union if Holland resisted."

"I never considered her being the kind of person who..."

Isabel touched her hand. "She wasn't as wicked as she seems, and in her defense, Holland failed to see the warning signs. She was young and spoiled. Perhaps he misled her, playing her game, but I've no doubt he did so without thinking, and he never violated her parents' trust. Jocelyn believed herself hopelessly in love and certain only she could fill the void Rosalind's death had left in his heart. Holland's rejection humiliated her." Isabel picked up her coffee and drank as if the stuff fortified her, and Alice considered offering her some of Eli's bourbon.

"Then she found out he intended to wed another. The night she died, she'd returned to Camellia Creek without Holland knowing. I followed her. He wasn't here. He'd gone to Jackson and planned to return the next day. I told Jocelyn she was making a fool of herself. We had a bit of a row. I feared our confrontation would upset the children. Hannah and Eli were too young to understand what was going on, but Andrew was almost seven. Naomi wasn't pleased with the invasion of two feuding women. She told us to go, then hurried the children out to the cookhouse for their supper.

"I took that opportunity to inform Jocelyn I knew the truth about her baby, and her ruse had failed. I asked her why she thought Holland would want a spoiled, selfish, girl such as she and how he could ever love her once he learned of her attempt to embarrass him by implying he'd bedded a mere child. I was cruel to her. Still, she refused to leave, so I decided I would go and hoped she would come to her senses. Holland was a grown man, after all, more than capable of dealing with an infatuated girl, and Naomi was there to chaperone.

"I left her on the floor of this room, distraught and crying. Devastated. She didn't want Hawk Duval, who loved her and would have made a fine husband. She wanted Holland Calhoon.

"Holland returned to Camellia Creek a day early—around nine that same night. According to him the children and Naomi were sleeping. Jocelyn, he claimed, was not here. He went to bed, not knowing she'd even been here. One of his darkies found her the next morning. The doctor and sheriff said she'd been hanging from that tree all night."

Alice tilted her head and studied Isabel. "And Holland didn't marry the other woman."

She shot Alice a sad smile. "That gleam in your eye tells me you realize the other woman was me, and no, we did not wed."

"Did Jocelyn know?"

"Oh, yes. I'd told her that before she returned to Camellia Creek. That was one of the things that compelled her to come. She was very angry with me."

"Why didn't you and Holland wed?"

Isabel paused, then took another sip of coffee. "The whole mess with Jocelyn proved quite the scandal, but worse, in the days immediately following Jocelyn's death, I harbored doubt as to whether or not Holland had indeed seen her that night. Holland sensed my wariness. Trust is important in a marriage."

Alice swallowed. "Yes, it is."

"Just as important, he blamed me, and I blamed myself. I was too hard on her, he told me so, and the truth, on top of my grief, hurt. He might have spared me that, but he was hurt, too. For a long while after, our relationship was strained. In time it improved, but it was never quite the same."

"It amazes me it survived at all."

The woman looked at her.

"Would you tell me the name of Rebecca's father?"

She smiled. "Holland McGillivray Calhoon. Eli didn't tell you?"

Alice blew out a breath. "I asked. He told me he'd never discussed the subject with you."

"That rotten imp. And indeed he hasn't. There was never any reason to. All the children knew. Hannah and Rebecca roomed together at school in Noxubee County. She spent most of her summers here at Camellia Creek. Holland gave her his name and orchestrated her marriage to James Mackey." Isabel chuckled. "Eli wouldn't have kept it secret long. Rebecca wouldn't have allowed it." The woman sobered some. "She wants to get to know you. She has so much less now, as do we all. All her husband's people are gone, but for a six-year-old niece."

"Will she not return to Rodney with you?"

Isabel laughed. "Oh, my dear girl, my house is not a place for her, much less appropriate for a six-year-old child."

"No, of course not, I wasn't thinking."

"And she still has the Mackey plantation. The house is gone, but the land is there and, many of her darkies have stayed with her. She doesn't want to abandon them. They were very loyal to old man Mackey."

With that, Isabel Hays smiled and stood. Alice stood, too. "I must rush," Isabel said, and strained to see the yard and the lake through a crack in a boarded foyer window. "I keep forgetting the damage," she said and turned back to Alice. "I wanted to confirm Jonathan hadn't harmed you and finish the conversation Seth Parker interrupted."

"After hearing the full tale from you, suicide does seem the most reasonable explanation. Now I don't know what to do to help her."

"Help her?"

"She's not at rest."

The woman looked at her a long moment, then nodded as if she understood. She turned on her heel and started for the dining room.

"Jocelyn's death," she said, pulling on her gloves without looking at Alice, "settled over me like a shroud. I'm sorry, actually, you've brought it up again."

Alice felt her stomach squeeze. "I apologize. I had no idea—"

The woman turned, and grasped Alice by the shoulders. Bending lower, she kissed her cheek. "Oh, my dear girl, I wish you could prove there was a killer." She pushed Alice back and looked at her. "That would lift the shroud. Now if I don't get out of here, I won't be able to." She picked up the slouch hat, damp, but no longer dripping, then held it up for Alice to see. "Not very fashionable, but indispensable against conditions such as these."

Alice smiled. "I've learned that myself." She followed Isabel onto the mud porch, wet and blustery, and together they looked through the open breezeway to the misty lake beyond.

"The bridge is flooded," Alice said.

"The land bridge isn't, but it won't be long before the creek overflows into the lake, then it will be impossible to get out with a carriage."

"And you're alone. Why don't you stay?"

"I've got business in Port Gibson, and I could hope I'm alone."

Alice frowned, and Isabel winked. "Parker's men have been following me for days. I'm never alone." She turned to the muddy yard. "I'll go the back way from here. I may have actually managed to lose them."

A gust of wind filled Alice's skirt and doused her with rain. Two minutes later, she moved back inside the house and watched Isabel's covered carriage maneuver over the narrow piece of land between Camellia Creek and Lake Elizabeth. The ridge was grass-covered, else Alice was sure the carriage would have bogged down. Isabel maneuvered beautifully, and Alice watched until her guest and carriage faded out of sight in the pouring rain.

Behind her, a floorboard creaked. Alone again, Alice turned from the dining room's east window and looked into the dim foyer. Outside, distant thunder echoed a flash of lightning. Another front moving in. The wind gusted, and Jocelyn LeBlanc whispered her name. Unease crept up Alice's spine, and for the first time, Alice considered that perhaps it was she, all along, whom Jocelyn wanted.

Chapter Seventy-seven

Alice eased into the parlor and into a wall of frigid air that prickled her skin, and she saw her breath. Foreboding warped her senses and weighted her body. Her fingers chilled, and now Jocelyn's agitated presence billowed her skirt and tore at her hair, causing Alice to wrap her arms around herself as she fought the urge to cry in tandem with the spirit. And Alice knew that here, in this room, on this very spot, Jocelyn LeBlanc had died.

Grief lulled into a woeful moan, long and low, then surged into a wail before shattering into a mind-numbing screech that bounced from wall to wall and sliced Alice's soul, but at the same time set her free from the debilitating trance.

Quiet.

Alice pivoted in the cold dimness of the parlor. Something evil watched and waited.

She heaved in a breath and crossed to the hearth. The fire, though subdued, still burned. What had she done with the poker?

Isabel had been the last to use it. It wouldn't be where Alice left it. But it wasn't on the hearth, either, where Isabel should have put it. She spun and searched the floor, behind the settee, and every dark corner of the room. The poker was gone. Alice looked across the room into the foyer. Now the gun, allegedly squirreled away in the bedroom, appeared her only defense.

Making a conscious decision not to burden herself with the lamp, she started back to the dark cavern of the bedroom. In the hallway, a soft pop in the dining room brought her to a halt, then as quickly as it had stopped, Jocelyn's wail filled the room, expanding the air and swelling her eardrums.

The front door rattled in its frame—writhed by the wind—

and Alice whirled to face the portal. In the hall behind her, she heard movement and turned in time to raise her hand, only partly warding off a vicious blow from her lost poker. Hand stinging, shoulder aching, Alice stumbled back into the parlor.

The twisted face and glaring eyes of Naomi Polk, glowing a hellish amber in the firelight, emerged from the hall and filled her vision. The woman's arm pulled back to deliver another blow. Alice, reeling from the first attack, fell to one side, and Naomi's second strike only grazed her temple, but smashed into her left shoulder. Pain circled her neck and radiated down her arm, numbing the fingers of her left hand. Alice braced her fall with both hands, but her left arm gave way, and she would have crashed onto her face but for the strength in her right arm. Naomi screamed in triumph, and Alice looked up. The hideous old woman held the poker frozen above her head and listened to Jocelyn's malevolent cry reverberate through the room.

"You can't harm me," the woman cried, pivoting as she searched the dark, unseen void of Camellia Creek's high ceiling. "You'll never drive me from this place. I know you haven't the power."

With Naomi Polk's distraction, Alice moved. Pain scorched her injured shoulder, and she floundered.

"Where do you think you're going, missy?" Naomi said and eased closer, poker raised.

"You killed her, didn't you?"

"Who?" she asked with faux innocence.

"Jocelyn."

"Yes," she hissed. "I killed her and hung her body from the tree. Holland intended to marry again, a matter of duty, he said. He never discussed such matters with me, but he told his friends, who told their wives, who told me. Then that stupid little whore told Elvie she was pregnant. I figured she was his 'matter of duty,' and I knew Holland didn't want to marry that stupid child. He didn't want to marry anyone. He still grieved for Rosalind. So I fixed things for him."

Naomi stepped toward Alice, who scooted back.

"But as you now know, I was wrong as to who he planned to marry. It was Isabel." Naomi spat the name. "But my mistake served me well. Each blamed the other for Jocelyn's death, and they never wed."

Alice continued to push with the heel of her shoe until she came up against the back of the settee. Naomi closed on her.

"And Laura?"

"She was determined to have Eli arrested for killing Wayne Hale. Conniving against him, sleeping with that dandy Franklin, trying to force her way back here. I didn't want her here and neither did Eli. She'd become dangerous. We don't want you here either."

Naomi Polk took a step forward, the poker on her shoulder. "I watched you beat up your boyfriend. I'd have been pleased, but you messed up my plans. For the past two hours, I've been wondering about what I should do now."

Alice tried to turn her head. Fire gripped her shoulder, and when Naomi moved closer, Alice scrunched tighter against the settee. "Your plans?"

"The plan was for Eli to kill you both when he found you together. That sissified Yankee couldn't even —"

"Whose plan was that?"

The woman loomed over her, studying Alice's face through half-closed eyelids. Then, suddenly, she raised her chin and smiled. "*Our* plan, you little fool. Eli's and mine. He plotted it all from the start." The woman leaned closer and sneered. "Even to making you think he'd run me off for good. It was his idea to drown the cat."

Alice's heart, already strained, pounded harder. The woman was lying, she had to be. "What would be the point of killing me?"

"Why, to be rid of you, of course, but still have your fortune."

"He'd be hanged."

"For killing a cheating wife and her lover? Even the Federals wouldn't fault him."

"But you don't have Jon Franklin. I drove him off, still alive.

The hateful creature poised for a chopping blow.

"What lie will you and Eli conjure now? Certainly no one will believe I beat myself to death with a poker."

Alice braced, ready to twist if Naomi brought the poker down. The woman hesitated. Then her expression changed, and she looked over her shoulder to the dining room.

Alice rolled to her stomach. Pain ripped through her shoulder, and she grunted. Her chin hit the floor and jarred her neck, starting it stinging. Behind her, Naomi growled. A floorboard creaked.

Pain exploded with light.

Chapter Seventy-eight

"Left him on Bayou Pierre, well off the road, about a mile west of the lake's south end. You know it?"

Seth shook his head, then hollered out "No" since he doubted the lieutenant, who'd identified himself as Thomas McKee, could see him well in the last of the storm-shrouded daylight. "How long ago?"

"Little over an hour, I'd guess."

"We're not that far from Camellia Creek," Seth yelled above the driving rain.

"We are if you end up swamped and have to fight your way back to the road," McKee countered. "He's probably home by now, and I wish I'd accepted his invitation to join him."

"And he's been with you all day?"

"Since late morning. Took the noon meal with him and his wife."

"Thank you."

"You need me to go with you?"

"Why don't you tag along?" Seth turned in the saddle. Even in the near darkness and rain he could see Frank Zachary's I-told-you-so grin stretching from ear to ear.

"He didn't do it," Zachary called out.

For sure Eli Calhoon hadn't killed Jon Franklin. Still, where was Isabel Hays? "But that doesn't mean he wasn't party to it," Seth hollered back.

Alice sensed being moved, then being half-laid, half-dropped onto a hard surface and finally shoved and kicked. Jammed into something. Her compelling need to vomit brought her to, and she jerked up and hit her head. Wherever she was, it was dark as a crypt.

She heard movement. Eli's footfalls. Her heartbeat quickened, and she almost called for him, but then she remembered she might shouldn't.

Nausea threatened again, and she lay back down. Good Lord, he'd hear her retching and know where she was.

But he should already know where she was, shouldn't he? Otherwise there'd be no need to hide from him.

She closed her eyes and fought back the sickness. A soft thump sounded above her, and this time, when she opened her eyes, dim light greeted her at her eye level. She'd been stuffed beneath her bed.

The room brightened more. She heard Eli curse. He was moving about. Had he put her here or Naomi? If he had, staying here served no purpose, and careful not to make a sound over the driving rain, she eased herself, using her good right arm, from under the bed, opposite where he was slamming drawers.

"Dammit," he said softly. She heard him pull out another drawer.

Biting back a groan, she raised her head. He was at his chest of drawers, his back to her, pulling out clothing, searching. In the center of the lovely quilt that had been her mother's lay his revolver. That's what she'd heard plop there. He slammed the second drawer shut and pulled out the one below it. She rose on her knees, fought back a bout of dizziness, and reached for the gun. She closed her hand around the butt at the moment he turned.

His eyes widened at the sight of her. "Where have you been?" He looked from her face to her hand and watched her draw the pistol across the bed. He didn't try and stop her. "I've been calling for you for the last fifteen minutes." His eyes narrowed. "What happened to…?"

She scrambled to her feet, clumsy, and he started around the bed. With two awkward steps back, she fell against a nightstand, then caught her breath when she almost dropped the pistol. "No," she barked and regained control of the weapon, pressing the butt against her palm and leveling the pistol on him. He stopped and looked at the gun.

"Wash you looshing for?" she said. She didn't know why she asked, and in her mind, she giggled. To relax?

He narrowed his eyes. "I noticed the drawer was open and someone plundered my things. My father's gun is gone."

"Zhat wush me." Goodness, did she sound as funny to him as she did to herself?

His gaze moved from her face, to the pistol she held, and back again. "You took my father's gun? Something frightened you?"

"Zhis is your gun. I plungered your shings." She closed her eyes and fought for control.

"Honey, let me—"

Her eyes flew open, and she cocked the hammer.

He held his hands palm up. "I haven't made a move, sweetheart, not one. I'm not going to try and overpower you, but you need to sit down before you fall."

Her eyes welled tears, and his face blurred before her. "Are you parsh of zhis?"

She blinked, but despite the trouble she had focusing on him, she thought he might have paled. Thunder rumbled in the distance, and outside, the rain still poured. She looked him down, then up. His pants were soaked from mid-thigh to hem. His face looked as sick as she felt.

"You think I did this to you?"

"I know who did zhis to me"—she snarled—"zhis." She shook her head. Sweet Jesus, that had been a mistake, but she sucked in a breath, placed her tongue against her front teeth and forced out, "This. *This* to me." Now she spoke slowly, carefully. "I want to know what you had to do with it."

"Nothing, and I'll kill the son of a bitch who did."

"Who did you plan for it to be, Eli?" she said, trying her hardest to keep her voice cool and confident. Telling him she knew the answer in case he did, too.

"Who did I plan for it to be?"

"Quit repeating what I say and tell me the truth, damn you."

With her outburst, her heart started pounding in her head, and her head couldn't take much more pounding.

"Admit to a lie?" he cried out. "Dammit, Alice, I don't even know what you're talking about, much less what's going on inside your head. You've got blood running down the side of your face. Will you please put that gun down and let me help you?"

"Then make something up." Good God, she needed to hold her head, but one hand held the pistol, the other lay at the end of a useless arm. "I need to know that you care for me, at least enough that you're not conspiring to kill me, too."

*H*is heart raced beneath his breast. "Conspiring to kill you?"

"You're repeating me again."

He winced at the pain that washed over her features—physical pain as well as emotional, and he held his hands out in offering…and submission. "I'm sorry, baby, I didn't mean to, but how could you ever believe that I'd want to hurt you? Me, Alice? *Me?*"

The nightstand was supporting her now; she tipped slightly, then flinched when she tried to support herself with her left arm. She managed to straighten.

"Why wouldn't I believe it?" she said. "You say you married me for my money, you hold me and mine in contempt for what we fought for, and you despise me for succumbing to your will."

He looked at the gun.

She followed his gaze. "Such a monstrous thing I'm holding between us, Eli." She looked up. "But not as monstrous as our doubts."

"Your doubts, Alice, and yours only."

She shook her head. "You don't trust me."

"The hell I don't. Looking at you now, hurt as you are, I'm scared to death. You have no idea how hard it is for me to stand here and not take that gun away from you, because I know you'd never use it on me. But I don't want to make you any more frightened of me than you already are."

"I'm not—"

"Yes, you are."

"Bullshit! I *love* you. How can a body love someone she's afraid of?" She eased back on the hammer, then stumbled when she tossed the gun onto the bed. She grabbed the corner of the bedside table with her right hand and looked him in the eye. "And if I made that big a mistake in giving away my heart when I had nothing left to live for, then I might as well be dead. Now you either tell me what I need to know or you beat me to death, or strangle me, or"—she nodded, painfully if the look on her face meant anything, to the revolver lying on the bed—"shoot me."

His eyes stung, and he said softly. "I'd rather kill myself. Sweetheart, the reason I refused to tell you who killed Wayne Hale is because I knew if you had to make the choice, you'd repeat the truth." He leaned forward at the waist so he could see her glassy eyes. He had to get her off her feet. "Repeat the truth to save me. I couldn't let that happen."

She closed her eyes in obvious relief and mouthed May Hale's name. Whether or not she suspected that all along, he didn't know, nor did he care.

"As for your fortune, that was my excuse for forcing you into marriage. I wanted you since that morning I saw you wandering along Camellia Creek, so full of grief and unhappiness. You looked like I felt. You were sweet and beautiful and so sad. I knew you'd never have me, not with me in gray and you dressed in mourning. Mourning for some man, who I figured you'd blame me for taking from you. You have no idea how often I've prayed you'd forgive me the losses of your menfolk."

She pressed her good right hand against the base of her throat and blinked back tears.

"But no matter what," he continued, "I couldn't help wanting you. You sealed your fate that night on your uncle's porch when you asked me where my horse was. Maybe I fell in love with you at that moment. Maybe I already loved you back on Camellia Creek, but I knew for sure I was hopelessly lost on our wedding night when you seduced me with your innocent bravado, so afraid I considered the surrender of your virginity my victory, and all the time I knew you were giving me a treasure. Every intimate moment, *every* one that has passed between us since that night is a moment I cherish."

Her breaths had deepened as he spoke, perhaps an effort to control her emotions, but he feared she was near to passing out. He started toward her. She brightened and fought to straighten in anticipation—ah, yes, his sweet Alice did like to be held—held by him.

He caught her in his arms, and she fell against him. The blood on her face drained from a wound on her scalp, above the temple. "I love you, Alice. I want us to grow old together and have lots of kids and grandbabies I can tell war stories to." He wrapped her tight in his arms. Her beautiful, battered body, so warm and soft. He kissed the top of her head. "Embellished war stories."

"About how Yankees crapped their pants when they heard a Rebel yell."

He laughed gently. "I'll make those boys-in-blue appear brave as best I can. That will make us look even better. And I'll try my hardest to downplay their numerical superiority."

She tilted her face to his. "Their mom, and someday grandmother, will help daddy and gramps keep things in proper perspective."

He kissed her lips, lifting her as he did. He needed to get help, but he didn't dare leave her. He laid her on the bed. "Who did this?"

Her eyes widened. "Naomi," she said and grabbed the hand he used to push her into the pillows. "Eli, she killed Jocelyn, and she killed Laura."

Immune to shock, given Alice's condition, he didn't even flinch. "She told you that?"

"Yes."

He tried to roll her so he could check her, but a painful grimace twisted her pretty face, and he stopped. Blood stained her mother's pretty pillowcase and Eli tensed. The initial shock was passing and the truth of Alice's words was setting in.

"She hit me with the poker and meant to kill me. You were to take the blame for my alleged affair with Jonathan Franklin."

Alice closed her eyes, and he shook her. "Don't go to sleep," he said when she looked at him.

"I think it must have been you who stopped her. She heard you out back."

He rose from the bed. "Let me get something to clean your head with."

"No," she cried.

From the back of the house, the wind rose, and with it, an eerie howl. Alice seized his bicep and pulled herself into sitting position. "She's here."

"The ghost?"

"No…yes. The ghost is here because Naomi's here."

Seth spun his gelding in the pouring rain and looked behind him at the other three men, their glistening ponchos and havelocks shimmering in the deadly lightning. In front of them lay a wider and no doubt deeper Lake Elizabeth than they'd before encountered, and the water on this end of Lake Elizabeth was churning.

"The land bridge is flooded," Thomas McKee hollered over the storm. "Camellia Creek's flooding into the lake. It's a torrent here." McKee moved around Seth. "Let's try to cross a little farther south. The lake will make for a longer swim, but the going will be easier. Horses shouldn't have a problem."

Two minutes below where they'd first encountered it, the lake appeared more placid, at least the part of it they could see when lightning flashed. In the dark Seth didn't recognize one familiar thing, but he wasn't sure he'd recognize anything in daylight either, so significant were the changes wrought by the water.

"Here looks good, Major," McKee said to him, then called over his shoulder to include Jubal and Zachary. "Need to be careful when we get near the center. Watch the current from the creek, it could be strong." McKee urged his horse into the water. Zachary followed.

"Since you're taking the lead on this, lieutenant," Seth hollered after him, "give us a shout when you come upon a cypress stump."

"Or a cottonmouth," Zachary rejoined.

"'Specially a cottonmouth," Jubal Summers called.

"They're sleepin'," McKee called back from somewhere up front. "They don't like being out in this kind of weather."

Sleeping, hell. Cottonmouths sure might not like being out in this weather, but Seth would bet his next paycheck Second Lieutenant Thomas McKee was lovin' it. He gave Boone a gentle tap with his heels, and the horse lumbered forward, shied, balked, then charged in. Within ten yards of the bank, the horse was swimming.

Forging a body of water wasn't new to Seth, but he hated crossing a strange one in the dark and in a storm. On the other side of Lake Elizabeth, the dim lights of Camellia Creek blinked at him in the pouring rain. Within its walls, he suspected a killer lurked, and he feared a lovely young woman, one he admittedly cared for, was in danger.

Seth looked behind him and watched Jubal Summers follow. In front of him, his commandeered lieutenant and Frank Zachary led the way. Above the hollow plopping of the rain on the lake's surface, a terrifying wail rose around them. A shudder raced through Boone, and Seth tensed. Just in front of Seth, Zachary's mount screamed, then careened sideways almost tumbling the sergeant from the saddle. After an anxious moment, Seth heard him comforting his frightened animal, while in front and behind him, McKee and Summers let loose a series of curses. Seth figured their animals had reacted in kind.

"Sweet Jesus," Jubal hollered after a moment. "What was that?"

"Dat be da ghos' you don't b'lieve in."

The sergeant laughed as if he didn't really believe his own words, but Seth, disturbed as much by the history of Camellia Creek that he could now piece together as by the otherworldly cry, thought the man might be right.

Chapter Seventy-nine

Minutes ticked away inside Eli's head. Alice was determined he would not leave her side, but he needed to check the house. If his aunt was here....

A cold chill crept over his skin, and he shuddered. Naomi Polk would have killed his beautiful bride. Laura must have confided her plans to Naomi. She would have wanted an ally in crime. Naomi, however, needed no ally. She wouldn't have wanted Laura here any more than she wanted Alice. Naomi needed Eli to validate her presence at Camellia Creek, and she certainly thought he killed Wayne. Eli's arrest for murder was a risk Naomi would not have taken, and she'd undoubtedly killed Laura to put an end to her ploy.

Not for the first time, Eli touched Alice's head. The outer swelling above her temple was extensive, indicating there was little or no swelling inside her skull. Still, she was fighting to stay awake, and God, he was scared for her to sleep. He needed to find Naomi, put a stop to her, and he needed to get to Buck or Miss Elvie and get one of them to town.

The rain. He hadn't looked lately, and wouldn't have been able to see if he had, but without a doubt, his home now sat on a large island.

He squeezed her fingers when he rose, determined to do what he had to do despite her.

"Let me go with you then."

"I'm going to find her, then I'll take her with me. I'll get Miss Elvie over here with you, and I'll get to town and find the doctor."

"You know I'm going to be all right. I came to the first time."

He didn't care if she had. He knew little about such things, but he was painfully aware that sometimes blows to the head resulted in people going to sleep and never waking up. He'd found the promise of his love and his life tonight. He wasn't going to lose this woman now.

"She's hiding somewhere in the house. I know now that's what she did the night we made love in the parlor. That's why she knew what we'd done, and what worried you. She played on your mind." He kissed her forehead and tried to coax her back down, but she wouldn't go.

Hell, he thought, moving around the foot of the bed, the horrid creature had probably lurked in the dark corners of this house off and on for years listening, watching, weaving plans.

At the doorway leading to the parlor, he heard the bed creak, and he glanced back at her. "Alice, do as I—"

He watched with mounting horror as her eyes widened. Jocelyn's sorrowful wail fell from the ceiling, then swirled around him as he spun in what seemed like slow motion to see his aunt explode before him from the dark recesses of the hall. Her eyes blazed with hate, and her mouth screamed in righteous anger in defense of her irrational needs. With his left arm, he thrust upward, deflecting the weapon she had aimed at Alice on the bed. The shot exploded, momentarily deafening him. The smell of saltpeter filled the room.

Aunt Naomi slammed her body into him, thrusting him into the door. Pain whipped across the back of his head. The woman straightened and started raising the gun. Alice screamed. The front door crashed amidst a hail of shouts and booted feet. Alice rose off the bed at the same time Eli moved. In the foyer, he could hear Seth Parker screaming for him to halt. Halt. Halt!

But he couldn't halt. Naomi had the gun pointed at Alice. He moved in front of his aunt at the same moment a blast exploded in the room. He flew back, insides blazing. He stopped with a force that popped his back, pain enough that for an instant it eclipsed the burning in his chest. He heard a second blast. His aunt flew past him, the gun in her hand pointed harmlessly to the floor. She crashed into the back wall of the room. He would have hit the floor full force, but Alice was already beside him, breaking his fall. His chest was on fire, but he could no longer feel the pain in his back.

Alice was touching him, crying, tugging at his shirt. The face of Seth Parker loomed over him. Beside him swam the image of that black sergeant—Zachary—who was always with him…the one who reminded him of….

Eli turned his head. He wanted to see Alice. Ah, there she was, tears streaming down her face. "Eli, don't you leave me," she cried, but her face was growing dim. She took his hand and brought it to her belly. He could feel her, but he had no control to help her. "I'm going to have a baby, Eli. Our baby." In the fading light, he saw her bow her head closer to him. "Don't you dare die on me," she ordered. He couldn't keep his eyes open, but he tried to talk, to tell her he wouldn't if he could help it.

That sergeant was yelling at all of them, telling them to get back. He thought the man might be tearing at his shirt, he wasn't sure. He no longer cared. He wanted Alice. He wanted to hear about their baby.

"Our baby, Eli, I need you to help me raise him. O God, don't take him from me, too!"

He felt her lips against his ear. "Eli, listen to me, I promise he'll always be proud of you and what you fought for, state rights, the Constitution, and the…" her words…his words…garbled into sobs. She was kissing his closed eyes, his lips. He felt her tears on his cheeks. "I remembered. I'll always remember. He'll always remember. He'll know every battle you fought in…. Noooo." Her voice was growing faint. He wanted to help her, but no longer could.

"Eli…?" He felt her hands shake his shoulders. *"Eli…!"*

His name from her lips. He would hear it, he thought, always and forever.

Epilogue

Camellia Creek Plantation, South of the Chittaloosa, Claiborne County, Mississippi. March 1866

Alice glanced once more at the postmark on the letter, then laid it on the tray next to the porcelain teapot.

"Major Parker goin' back to Rodney?" Miss Elvie asked. She pulled a pan of biscuits from the oven.

From where Alice stood in the cookhouse, she could hear the workers hammering away on the barn. "He leaves for Jackson sometime this morning. I'm a bit worried for him. This case he's working seems to become more complex with each passing day. He's not sure who to trust. He trusted his Negroes, but doesn't feel the same way about the white officers. I'm glad he still has Jubal, at least for a little while."

Miss Elvie set the biscuits on the cooling rack above the stove, then shuffled back to the sink. "Barn done gone up fas'."

Alice joined her at the window, a bright, clean, glass window. Indeed, the barn was almost finished. She turned and looked at the tray on that rough old table, sleek with two new coats of paint the color of the Bonnie Blue Flag. The kitchen, itself freshly whitewashed, looked clean and smelled clean. She hadn't seen a sign of a mouse in weeks. Mercy, drenched in late winter sunshine, slept curled on a chair.

Late winter. It had been warm the past three days, and Elvie told her yesterday winter was about done. There might be a few surprises left, but Mississippi herself wasn't expecting any, because spring was budding out all over.

Budding and blooming. But then cruel surprises from the north weren't unheard of here. Alice rubbed her belly where Eli's baby grew. She turned suddenly and caught Miss Elvie watching her with knowing eyes.

"Ain't been sick for how many days now?"

"Five. Maybe I'll start getting fat."

"You be fat soon 'nuff, then you gonna wonder why you wanted it so."

Alice picked the sugar bowl up from the counter and carried it to the tray. Buck pushed the back door open, found her and smiled. "Found a right pretty azalea," he said and held it up. "Dey be in full bloom in a couple mo' days."

"Thank you," she said and walked over and took it from his hand. "It is lovely." She sniffed it, and he laughed. "Ain't known fo' its smell now. If that's what you be wantin', need to wait on the gardenia and magnolia."

She smiled. "I want something pretty to adorn the tray this morning. Thank you for getting it for me."

He saluted her with two fingers.

On the stove, coffee steamed, and she retrieved the brew and poured it into her porcelain pot.

"Tell 'im I gots ham sop if'n he wants brekfes' befo' he gets out."

Alice nodded and headed to the dining room. The morning air was cool and fresh along the breezeway, the day green and filled with life. Back in the house, she set the tray on the dining-room table and retrieved two porcelain cups belonging to her mother's tea service. Eli's cavalry hat hung beside the door. How many times had she passed it since that terrible night and recalled his request that she give it to Miss Elvie should anything befall him. She touched it, smelled it, then swallowed the tears that collected in the back of her throat. It was as if he'd known something terrible was about to happen.

She said a silent prayer to her God, and with a calming breath, checked her reflection in the glass doors of the china cabinet. Perhaps a bit more provocation was in order, and she untied the belt to her robe and adjusted the décolletage of the gown beneath. Blue. She primped a moment more, then smiled, picked up the tray, and headed for the bedroom. He'd made love to her last night, the first time…

"You're dressed," she said. She came on in the room and tapped the door shut with her foot.

"You were gone," he answered, pushing on the heel of his boot. He grunted. "I didn't know you were coming back."

"Well, I was, and I've brought us coffee—to drink in bed on this lovely spring morning."

"It's not spring, and there'll be cold days yet."

"Yes, come November." She set the tray on her dresser. He picked up his other boot, but she snatched it from him and tossed it in the corner opposite the door. "Stop that."

"As late as April and 'stop what?'"

"Quit dressing."

He grinned. "Looking for a repeat performance?"

She smiled and shook her curls.

God, he loved her hair.

"Do you think you're up to it?" she asked.

He'd always loved her hair, and he always would. "I am at the moment, Mrs. Calhoon, but I'm likely to have a relapse if you insist on my loving on you morning and night."

"Well, Mr. Calhoon, I have no intention of going through another two months like the ones I just endured."

She took a letter from the tray, then pushed him into the mattress. He was tired of this bed, even after being able to get out of it regularly for the past fortnight. Last night was the first time since Aunt Naomi shot him he'd enjoyed being in it.

"We don't have to make love," she said climbing in beside him. "You've another letter."

"From Warrenton? He could just come visit. I think he's practicing his handwriting, holding out for a commission."

"This one's postmarked Memphis."

She cuddled close to him, and he glanced down at the top of

her head. "My getting comfortable in this bed, sweetheart, is contingent upon our making love."

"That is fine with me," she said, and she sat up and kissed him.

He ripped the envelope open. This was his second letter from Frank Zachary, ex-sergeant, United States Army, who ten weeks ago had stuck his hand in Eli's chest and checked the bleeding, then supervised treatment for three hours until Thomas McKee braved the flood and retrieved Doc Lester from Port Gibson. For three days after, his life had hung in the balance and for three days Alice, his little pregnant, battered wife had stayed awake, talking and reading and bathing him constantly, afraid to even doze, fearing, she said, quiet in the house would give Eli pause to embrace eternal rest. When he'd opened his eyes early on that third day, she, exhausted, had started to cry. He told her he'd been to some strange place where some fella called Michael had kicked him in the butt and told him to get on back where he belonged and take care of his baby sister. Of course that wasn't true, but he figured Alice would sleep easier after that, thinking Michael wasn't going to allow him to "embrace eternal rest" while he was riding picket. He'd finally told her the truth, and that was he couldn't remember dreaming at all. But he did recall fighting hard to get back to the beautiful woman, who squeezed his hand constantly and was forever whispering her love in his ear.

"What does he say?" she asked.

"He got your letter. Glad to hear I'm up and about. Says he'll let us know later where to send the next letter 'cause he's not sure where he'll be." Eli squinted at the writing. "Rumor has it, he says, that Congress is supporting the recruitment of the freedmen into the regular Army. Needs men out west to fight the Indians, and he wants to be part of it."

"Do you think he really wants to fight Indians, Eli?"

Eli looked up from the letter and shrugged. "Out there, Alice, doing his soldiering, he's a man like any other."

"I think he should pursue medicine. Doctor Lester asked him to stay with him."

"I don't know that he'd have the same opportunity for respect amongst his peers if he pursued medicine. It would be tough. But the good part is, he doesn't want to be a doctor, he wants to fight Indians."

"And now he can."

Eli smirked at her when she looked at him. "What's funny?" she asked.

"You. Our black folks have been fighting with and against Indians for as long as we have. Did up north, too."

"Now he can fight Indians on his own instead of being told to."

"Alice, listen to yourself. He'll be in the *Army*."

"But it's his choice to join the Army."

Actually the United States Army would have a big say in that, his joining as well as his being allowed to fight. "His choices are pretty limited, but I guess if there's anything gained from it all, that would have to be it."

She pulled back and studied him.

"Don't get maudlin on me, honey. The consolation prize isn't worth the price paid, and when it comes to the winner, the North isn't even done reaping its spoils, but it will justify its wrongs behind the end of slavery."

"Hush," she said and laid her head on his chest. "He liked you, you know?"

Eli rubbed her arm with the palm of his hand, then relaxed against the pillow.

"And I think he sensed you liked him, too, despite 'the color of his goddamn uniform.'"

Eli had given no thought to how he responded to Frank Zachary. He just had. The man's size, his appearance—the easy manner with which he fell in beside Eli and talked with him that day in Rodney.

"I wish he'd come back here and work for me. I could use him. Hell, I'd give him forty acres and Brim's mule."

"He reminded you of Brim, didn't he?"

"Yeah. Brim's attitude toward this whole mess would be on

the order of 'get to work, Eli, the sun's still gonna come up tomorrow.'"

"I think so, too."

He looked at the top of her head, lying on his chest. "You think what?"

"I think the sun will come up tomorrow."

"Do you now?"

"I do, and it will brighten all our tomorrows."

Eli suspected they had a lot of dark tomorrows ahead of them.

"*You* are the bright spot in my tomorrows," he said, "You and that little creature growing in your belly."

She raised her head, looked at him, and smiled. "We're your sunshine then." She lay back down. "I listened for Jocelyn during the storm last night, did you?"

He had and probably would from now on. "She's crossed over. I figure she found Michael on the other side and they'll exist happily ever after."

"You are impossible."

"You're right." He rubbed her back. "And since it doesn't look like I'll be 'embracing eternal rest' anytime soon, I'd best prepare to get up with my sunshine from now on."

She sat up and reached for the top button on his shirt. "Your sunshine may not always be in a hurry to rise. We may as well make our hell here on earth worth it."

He tugged on the belt to her robe, and it opened. "I love you, Alice."

"I love you, too, Eli."

Historical Note

My story opens with the not-so-sovereign state of Mississippi hovering in an uncertain status between civil and martial law, seven months into Presidential Reconstruction. During this brief period (in Mississippi, May 1865-December 1865) President Andrew Johnson, Abraham Lincoln's vice president and successor, tried, in vain, to hold the excesses of the Radical Republicans in check. That is not to say the policies of Lincoln or Johnson were constitutional in their dealings with the South, just more moderate than what ultimately occurred.

Claiborne County on the Mississippi River was formed from the northern half of Jefferson County in 1801, but British settlers had begun settling the east bank of the Mississippi and lower reaches of the region's waterways in the 1770s following Britain's victory over France in the French and Indian War (1754-1763). The territory, which today comprises Claiborne, was part of British West Florida's Natchez District.

In 1772, twenty-four-year-old Samuel Gibson arrived in the almost untrodden wilds of Bayou Pierre, eight miles upstream from where it empties into the "Great River." There he joined (Jacob) Cobun, a fellow South Carolinian. At the time, panthers, bears, wolves, and Indians inhabited the forests and cane brakes along Bayou Pierre. In December of that year Samuel Gibson wed Cobun's daughter Rebecca. It would be fair to assume the immigrants had known one another in South Carolina, since extended families and neighbors often emigrated together.

British West Florida fell to Spain, ally of Britain's rebellious colonies, near the end of the Revolutionary War. Documents record Samuel Gibson receiving a Spanish land grant of 850 acres for a tract of land on Bayou Pierre in 1788. Cobun had received a similar grant for 800 acres, adjacent to Gibson's, the year before. It is possible these Spanish grants validated ownership of lands that had belonged to these men since British times.

The Gibsons and Cobuns (there was at least one son in addition to the daughter, Rebecca) lived in a state of what has been described as "rustic wealth," subsistence farmers possessing cattle for meat, milk, and butter; hogs for cured ham, bacon, lard, and soap; wild game aplenty; bee hives for honey and pollinating; and fresh fruit for eating and drying. Both cotton (I am discussing the historical period before the cotton gin) and wood were grown on the farm—though I doubt the need for "growing" wood at that time; it would have been plentiful.

Sam Gibson boasted a library of 150 books, but his wife was uneducated. The reader can speculate as well as I as to whether Sam kept her that way by design, but it's as likely she was content. Goodness knows she had enough to do managing the home of a subsistence farmer and little time for "book learning."

As of 1802 "Gibson's Landing" on Bayou Pierre was home to a private ferry where Robert and George Cochran's trading post may have already been built. Samuel and his family lived in a log home roughly three-quarters of a mile from the bayou in the northern section of what the territorial legislature in 1803 dubbed Port Gibson. Incorporated in 1811, by the 1830s Port Gibson was a backwoods cultural center boasting banks, hotels, a fire station, churches, doctors, lawyers, a printing office, a post office, as well as a stage line. The stage line eventually gave way to the train (Grand Gulf-Port Gibson Railroad) linking it to the thriving Mississippi River cotton port at Grand Gulf, which was built at the confluence of the Big Black (Chittaloosa) and Mississippi Rivers eight miles to the west. Port Gibson's import/export businesses linked the town not only with the north and east coast of the United States, but also with Britain and Germany.

Westside, an area in southwest Claiborne County, became the site of numerous plantations, with land grants going back to the late 18th century. The Rodney-Port Gibson Road passed through it, and in the 1830s wealthy plantation owners built opulent homes along this road. By the time Alice travels the route in the winter of 1865, the beautiful homes have been burned or abandoned, casualties of war. Westside was also the site of Oakland Presbyterian College, prestigious before the war. It closed its doors in 1871 and sold its property to the state. That same year, the buildings and grounds became the site of Mississippi's first Negro school of higher education, Alcorn University, today Alcorn State University.

On 30 April 1863, General Ulysses S. Grant, with a force of 40,000 men, landed southwest of Port Gibson in the vicinity of Bruinsburg, another thriving Mississippi River cotton port. Grant defeated the Confederate force at Port Gibson the following day and spared the town, inhabited by women, children, and old or sick men, the able-bodied being at war—and in retreat—calling the town "too beautiful to burn."

Though Port Gibson was not burned, it did endure raids from Federal forces stationed in the area. From the summer of 1863 until the end of the conflict, Federal soldiers came into town on more than one occasion and plundered it. Not merely thievery of every item of food, clothing, and bed linens, but wanton, purposeful destruction of furniture, mirrors, family heirlooms, windows and doors, the gardens, wells, sheds, etc. On at least one occasion, the white troops came in one day, leaving the colored troops (probably Native Guards) outside town, and after plundering what they wanted, let the Negro troops take or destroy what was left the next day.

At the time my story opens, Mississippi is occupied primarily by Negro troops—Mississippi "loyal" Native Guards formed up by county from ex-slaves either captured or emancipated by Federal forces, or who defected behind Union lines. Native Guards made up the bulk of Negro soldiers in service to the United States and are not to be confused with United States Colored Troops (USCT), who were members of the regular Army, if one does not take their segregation from white forces into account. The Native Guards were part of the volunteer service. It was from this group of men that Seth Parker's troop investigating the cotton thefts and the murder of Alan Guthrie was drawn. I wanted Jubal Summers to be an educated black man from the North, who was originally a member of a USCT regiment. Putting him in Mississippi at that time, with those criteria, required a little imagination. I hope I've suspended disbelief.

The other members of the troop were drawn from Native Guards in Claiborne and Warren Counties. The story that Sergeant Frank Zachary related to Eli Calhoon about his last master is based loosely on the story of Henry Clay Lewis, who practiced medicine in the swamplands and bayous of Louisiana and Mississippi. Lewis wrote a humorous semiautobiographical work, *Odd Leaves From the Life of a Louisiana Swamp Doctor*. The book was published shortly before his premature death in 1850.

James Garner states in *Reconstruction in Mississippi* (1901) that President Johnson reported to the House of Representatives that as of 5 January 1866 there were 39 white commissioned officers in the volunteer service in Mississippi and 338 Negro officers. The number of enlisted men was 1,071 whites and 8,784 Negroes. There were no regular troops in the state. Garner's narrative records that with the mustering out of the last Negro regiment on 20 May 1866 there was one battalion of regular infantry in the state. By August, General Wood, Commander of the Department of Mississippi, had abolished the district organization of the state and reformed the state into the Mississippi district with five companies of regular white troops in Vicksburg, one company in Natchez, one in Jackson, and one in Grenada.

My fictional Caw Pruitt would have been one of an estimated 90,000 black Confederates who fought, fully integrated, with Southern units across the South. Today, history relegates the black Confederate to the status of a body servant and laborer, the concept of his having fought under that Battle Flag politically incorrect. However, Holt Collier of Teddy Roosevelt/Teddy Bear fame was a Confederate sharpshooter and tracker. Further testimony to the existence of black fighting Confederates is well substantiated. From the time the Negro first came to the South, he fought side by side with his white masters and neighbors against foreign armies, French, Spanish, and even British, who held designs on North America, and he fought for and against the native peoples—some of whom owned him. And there were free blacks such as Caw, with farms and families of their own to protect against invading Yankee soldiers—and there was no shortage of bigoted Northerners among them who didn't hesitate to kill, maim, and ravish black Southerners, whom they despised.

My point is that for almost two and a half centuries before the Union onslaught, black and white Southerners had faced common threats, and they had fought them together.

As regards Alice's menfolk, the 78th Ohio is real, Company J is fictional (at least I didn't find one in the order of battle). The 78th was with William Tecumseh Sherman (and/or Grant) from Fort Donelson (February 1862) through Sherman's "march to the sea." Ohio units are well documented on Union websites and catalogued by county, which made it easy for me to pick a place of origin for the Shelton family in south-central Ohio. Sherman's abuses are anathema in Mississippi to this day. They would have been more so in 1865, leaving Alice Shelton particularly sensitive to perceived hostility, and heightening her doubts as to Eli's motives regarding her.

I had a little more trouble with Eli Calhoon's mounted infantry unit. The Third Mississippi Infantry distinguished itself at Shiloh, and Claiborne County formed up several cavalry units. However, no cavalry units from Claiborne County were present at Shiloh. I made up the 20th Mississippi Regiment, then placed Andrew and Eli Calhoon and their neighbor Caw Pruitt along with the rest of Captain Uriah Butterfield's company (the Butterfield Grays) in an unremembered farmer's field facing the 78th Ohio on day two of the battle.

As the war progressed, combat experience and attrition earned Eli the rank of lieutenant colonel and the assistant commander's billet of the 20th Mississippi Regiment.

—❦—

Built on the natural gulf formed where the Big Black enters the Mississippi, Grand Gulf in the 1830s was one of the richest cotton ports on the Mississippi. In 1843 it exported more cotton to foreign ports than Vicksburg and had a thriving population in excess of 3,000 people. The town had been built along a ledge of iron sandstone, the only cliff rock in the area. July 1858 began with a series of landslides lasting for weeks with major parts of the city and areas north and south of Grand Gulf melting "away like snow" into the muddy waters of the Mississippi.

But stability did return, with a lesser Grand Gulf determined to carry on. Then in May 1863 Captain James A Hoskins' Confederate battery, situated to the rear of the city, inflicted heavy damage on Admiral David Farragut's U.S. Navy fleet. Damage done, the battery prudently retreated. The Federals retaliated by shelling the town, giving the population no advance warning. Grant subsequently burned what was left standing of the town. At the time of my story, the valiant citizens of Grand Gulf are in the process of rebuilding, or trying to, with much bluster. But despite its bravado that Port Gibson must give way to Grand Gulf's determined industry, the city's comeback was not sustained. The destruction of war had been but one factor contributing to the town's demise. Steamboat travel was falling away naturally, giving way to rail. Life on the Mississippi River was changing.

In the fall and early winter of 1865-1866, efforts were under-way to reestablish reliable stage service between Port Gibson and Grand Gulf, as the railroad was insolvent and not operating. Telegraph service had been reestablished between the two towns.

I highlighted the fate of Rodney, in Jefferson County, south of Claiborne, in the historical note to my earlier book *River's Bend*. Though Rodney's days were not done at war's end, it was, at the time of *Camellia Creek*, little more than a ghost town—a direct result of the conflict. No businesses (Isabel Hays' house of ill repute is, of course, fictional) reopened in Rodney until 1868 and regular steamboat service didn't resume there until the 1870s.

From my research, it does appear steamboats still stopped there, but the service was unreliable, so Eli and Alice would have either gotten lucky on their wedding day, or more likely, Eli hailed a passing steamboat from the shore. Of course, the trip back from Natchez would have been easier, Eli merely requesting the boat captain to stop at the Rodney landing.

Camellia Creek was a typical Louisiana plantation home. The two-storied house was built eight feet off the ground on the remnants of what was once the west bank of a more ancient Mississippi River. The house, boasting a series of casement doors and floor-to-ceiling windows on the first floor, had a deep, wraparound porch with square pillars, broken in the back by a mud porch with access to a breezeway leading to the kitchen. The home sat at the end of a secluded dirt drive off the Rodney-Port Gibson Road. Residents would have crossed Bayou Pierre to reach it and, for the sake of convenience, a narrow wooden bridge spanning the north end of the fictional oxbow, Lake Elizabeth. North of the house and separated from the lake by a narrow land bridge, feisty little Camellia Creek meandered southwest to empty into Bayou Pierre, roughly three miles upstream from where Bayou Pierre enters the Mississippi. For the purposes of my story, there was also a secluded foot trail leading from Camellia Creek to the north end of Port Gibson, five miles east as the crow flies, and traveled primarily by locals familiar with its existence.

The theft of Southern cotton confiscated by Federal authorities ran rampant among Union officers stationed in Mississippi, and the rest of the South, and was a problem in the occupied territories throughout the war. In order to give the reader some idea of the motivation driving my not-quite-ready-to-give-up-the-fight Rebels, I opted to figure out the value of the property they stole that rainy November night in 1865. Given the bed size of an army wagon and the size and weight of a bale of cotton, I calculated six bales of cotton to a wagon, each bale weighing 480-500 pounds at

$1.25 a pound (roughly $600.00 a bale) for 24 bales on each of two runs, or 48 bales total. That came out to $28,800.00 divided four ways for $7,200.00 each. That's on the order of $90,000.00 by today's standard. Not too shabby, and would have certainly paid for Eli's new barn and helped with the state's back taxes.

November 1865 finds Lincoln dead seven months, Mississippi's infrastructure devastated, her economy in shambles and her labor force dispersed, endangered, and undermined by the presence of undisciplined Negro troops, mostly ex-slaves, who discourage the freedmen from returning to their former plantations or even securing new work contracts with different employers. A spring, summer, and fall have passed with no significant effort to get the agrarian economy moving, and the entire South is headed toward its third hungry year. The strain on caring for what has become an indigent, lawless class of vagrant freedmen is now beginning to tell on the Federal government, and President Johnson struggles against the excesses of the Radical Republicans, whose skewed views of republicanism and the Constitution did much more to destroy the federal republic founded by our forefathers than the South's independence would have. In fact, I would argue that the South was the true successor of our founders' nation and that the North willfully destroyed it.

Under the leadership of Judge William L. Sharkey, a pre-war Whig against whom no blight of disloyalty to the United States could be spoken, a provisional civil government had been formed in June of 1865 with the blessings of President Johnson. From what I've deduced about him, Sharkey was a Union man. By that I mean he opposed secession, not necessarily the South. Neither did he appear to be in agreement with the beliefs of the Republican Party. He was, however, pragmatic, and no doubt angry and frustrated by the state of affairs resulting from the actions of the secessionists and the devastation those actions had visited upon the state. Sharkey's provisional government acceded to freedom for the Negro and nullified, rather than repealed, the Acts of Secession of 1861. In so doing, the provisional government acknowledged that the state had no legal right to secede. This provision remains in the state constitution (adopted in 1890) to this day. In my opinion, the existence of such a provision in a state constitution is unconscionable. The right of secession is inherent in the Tenth Amendment.

Elections were held for the governor and the legislature in October 1865. President Johnson was somewhat disappointed that the constituency of Mississippi chose General B. G. Humphreys, ex-Confederate States Army, over Judge E. S. Fisher, an old-line Whig, who had played no role in the secession or the war. Nevertheless, Johnson recognized the new governor and legislature in December of that year, hoping the new civil government would recognize an end to slavery (already adhered to by the provisional government under Sharkey) and ratify the Thirteenth Amendment. The Northern view was that the people of Mississippi preferred Confederates over Union men. I'm not sure why that should have been a surprise.

This legislature did not ratify the Thirteenth Amendment, but acknowledged the end of slavery (section one of the Thirteenth Amendment). The legislature's refusal to ratify the amendment was due to section 2, which the new civil government believed ceded too much power to Congress. The United States government under force of arms, therefore, would be credited with ending slavery in Mississippi, and not the state itself. Mississippi officially ratified the Thirteenth Amendment on 7 February 2013, the egregious second paragraph no longer acknowledged as a problem.

It was Governor Humphrey's legislature which met in October 1865, prior to the state's new constitution being blessed by President Johnson in December, that passed the notorious Black Code, the first of the Southern states to do so. Notorious? Yes, *notorious* is the word often attributed to the first civil effort to gain control of a vagrant population exceeding, probably, 100,000 people. The black population of Mississippi in 1866 was 381,258, but they would not have all been vagrants.

A better term to describe the Black Code was "imprudent." A

sovereign state exists at the consent of the governed (citizens), which means a state has the right to establish its own government, create its own constitution and laws as long as (according to the United States Constitution) it is a republican form of government. Now, this is where the imprudence kicks in. Why the duly-elected legislature of the state of Mississippi and her people would assume that persons who had just waged vicious, total war against them, and still had their heel on their necks, all in direct violation of said U.S. Constitution, would respect Mississippi's right to write its own laws eludes me. For some odd reason the Republicans and the North invoked the 1776 Declaration of Independence from Great Britain as the legal document that "holds" us together, which makes right, based on the "all men are created equal" clause, their aggression and their destruction of not only the Confederacy, but also the Federal Republic.

But, by the United States Constitution—the soul of the Republic and the law which in fact does hold us together, or once did—the 1865 Constitution of the state of Mississippi, Black Code included, was legal—imprudent, but legal.

One should remember that in the fall of 1865 the Negro was free, but he was no more a citizen in the South (and most other states and territories) than the Indian or the Chinese coolie making his way to the west coast.

If I might rehash the infamous code, not to be confused with the Jim Crow segregation laws, which came later, it regulated the relation of master and apprentice as related to freedmen, free negroes, and mulattoes, making it the duty of civil officers to report to their respective county probate court all Negroes under eighteen years of age who were orphans or were without means of support. Their former owners, if considered competent in the eyes of the court, were given preference for what was indenture, males up to twenty-one years of age and females to eighteen years. Masters were empowered to apply moderate chastisement for misbehavior and judicial remedy was available in the case of abuse and in cases of runaway apprentices and those judged to perpetrate such incidents. The masters provided food, clothing, medical care, and instruction in reading and writing. This act was in no way different from the then-current treatment of orphans in the North, nor, historically, in the North or South.

The laws against vagrancy, provided that Negroes, mulattoes, and whites over eighteen in the state as of the second Monday of 1866 without employment or business could be fined a maximum $50.00 and ten days in jail (whites were fined $200.00 and up to six months in jail). This vagrancy law was not inconsistent with vagrancy statutes existing in Wisconsin, New York, Maine, Massachusetts, Indiana, and Connecticut.

Though not full citizens, the Negro could now sue and be sued, own property and dispose of it like his white counterpart, but was expressly forbidden to rent or lease land except in incorporated towns or cities where authorities could control the privilege. He could now sit on a jury and bear witness in civil and criminal trials, but only those not involving a white man.

Contracts for labor of more than one month were to be in writing, and it was a criminal offense for the employee to abrogate the agreement without just cause, and if he did so, he could be captured and returned to the employer at the employer's expense. The employer could then add time to the contract to offset his cost. Both employee and employer had access to the court to address the cause for the employee's abandonment of employment and other grievances in regard to employment. Likewise, anyone attempting to entice an employee from fulfilling his or her contract was subject to a fine of $25-$200 and confinement of no more than two months.

Efforts to care for displaced slaves/freedmen that ultimately solidified into the Freedmen's Bureau had been ongoing in Mississippi since the summer of 1863. As of the fall of Vicksburg in July of that year, General Grant had 50,000 displaced slaves in the environs of his camp and was at a loss as to how to support them. He called upon the United States government and benevolent societies in the North for assistance. Subsequently, the Negro was utilized in the war effort against the South, ranging from growing and harvesting crops to military service.

Camps were established on abandoned and confiscated Southern property, and plantations were leased to "loyal" citizens (those would be white) and the Negro was contracted to work, all under the auspices of a provost marshal who monitored the well-being of the labor force. Those Negroes were not allowed to leave the plantation, and Negro soldiers—roughly 79,000 from Mississippi alone were in the U. S. Army—were not allowed near this labor force contracted to "loyal" citizens. Advising the freedmen not to work on the plantations, the soldiers continued to undermine the labor force in Mississippi until they were finally disbanded in 1866.

In 1864, under the Department of the Treasury, Home Farms (Negro colonies) were established on confiscated property for Negroes who wished to cultivate their own land. The site of Mississippi's Home Farm was Davis Bend near Natchez, the bulk of the Jefferson Davis family plantation. The home site had been plundered, then destroyed by U.S. Marines in 1863, but 10,000 acres of fertile soil was still there. On the first of January 1865, all whites not directly connected to the colony, those being the military, were expelled from the colony and were not allowed on the property without written permission. It was to be restored at the end of hostilities "if the owner could furnish satisfactory proof of undoubted loyalty throughout the war." (A bit of Yankee humor. The owner died a man without a country. President Jimmy Carter restored Jeff Davis' citizenship in 1978.)

For the purpose of my story, Eli Calhoon was a member of one of fourteen excepted classes, his class being that the value of his taxable property exceeded $20,000. Thus classified, the pardon required for his return to full citizenship and for the return of any confiscated property could only be granted by the president, who liberally granted such pardons. Abandoned property was particularly vulnerable to confiscation. Since Naomi Polk returned to Camellia Creek after the deaths of Holland Calhoon and Eli's sister Hannah,

Eli's property was not seized by the Federals. Eli had, however, lost his citizenship, thus his right to vote, and he had no desire to swear loyalty to the powers that be in order to regain it.

On 2 March 1865, Congress officially established the Bureau of Freedmen's Affairs, using revenues from abandoned lands and sale of confiscated property to partially fund it. General O. O. Howard, Sherman's right wing in the Army of the Tennessee, served as the Bureau's commissioner. An assistant commissioner headed each Southern state. Mississippi's first assistant commissioner, headquartered in Vicksburg, was Colonel Samuel Thomas, who headed three sub-districts: Northern, Southern, and Western. These sub-district commanders, all white, were commanders of Negro regiments and had a myriad of subordinates serving under them. As of December 1865, the time period of my story, the Bureau had 58 local agents in Mississippi, all military officers, and 67 teachers.

No small degree of conflict existed between the Freedmen's Bureau and the civil government in Mississippi. Basically, the Bureau replaced the plantation master regarding the welfare of the Negro. The Freedmen's Bureau issued marriage licenses until civil authorities took over this responsibility under the provisional governor, later codified by the Constitution of 1865. The Bureau was also responsible for establishing schools for the freedmen's children, the earliest teachers being chaplains from colored units. Shortly thereafter teachers were contracted, mostly from the north and paid by missionary societies. These schools were quickly augmented by planters' schools, established on the old, struggling plantations as an incentive to a somewhat tenuous labor force.

On October 12, 1865, days before Humphrey's government assumed responsibility for civil administration from Provisional Governor Sharkey, a "secessionist" judge in Vicksburg allowed Negro testimony in court. This act prompted Colonel Thomas to move that civil courts assume responsibility for all court actions involving the Negro. Unfortunately, the "Black Codes," passed by the legis-lature shortly thereafter, qualified the criteria by which Negro testimony was allowed in court—that being he could only testify in cases restricted to Negroes, freedmen, and mulattoes. Preventing the freedmen's testimony in court in cases involving whites gave General Howard, head of the Freedman's Bureau in Washington, pause before ceasing to monitor civil infractions levied against the freedmen, and the Bureau, under military tribunals, assumed responsibility for all civil and criminal cases involving the Negro. White Mississippians regarded the Freedman's Bureau as abusive, unjust, and guilty of allowing black criminals to walk free. Ironic, when one considers that for decades white murderers of other whites "walked free" when the only witness was a black man whose testimony was disallowed. Of course, in the Old South, family and friends of the murder victim could always resort to "Southern justice," and in some cases, I'm confident they did.

Another source of friction between the Freedmen's Bureau and the white Southerner was the Bureau's regulation of Negro labor. This was not the result of the Bureau's discouraging labor, which some low-ranking minions did and for which they were removed from their positions, but because of the rules involved. Under the bureaucracy, contracts had to be blessed by military authority, a requirement considered belittling, time-consuming, and generally inconvenient by the prospective employer, since in some cases, the nearest agent was up to 50 miles distant.

Negro labor was another problem with which the Federal government had been dealing since the days of Grant's camp followers back in 1863—hence the rules forbidding intermingling between the "leased-plantation" workers and the Negro soldiers before the war ended. Relying on their newly-granted freedom, many laborers believed they didn't have to work the plantations if they didn't want to, and this sentiment was encouraged by the Negro troops stationed in very large numbers throughout the South. Theoretically, that was true, but they still had to eat, and to eat they had to work, and their opportunities were pretty much limited to farming (or a short-lived army career).

Numerous threats by the military authority that subsistence would cease and the freedman must contract work fell on mostly deaf ears, though hearing was loud and clear when colored troops told the freedmen that all the abandoned and confiscated land would be divided among them at Christmas 1865. That did not happen; in July of 1865, President Johnson had overturned the Bureau's policy on abandoned and confiscated property, directing its return to its owner upon presidential pardon. Still, as late as August 1866, ten months after the state legislature had passed its black vagrancy code, General Wood was compelled to issue an order expelling all non-working Negroes from Vicksburg.

The Federal government provided subsistence to the freedmen through the summer and fall of 1865, but Assistant Commissioner Thomas reported in December of that year subsistence was not needed since there was plenty of work for all and for an additional 50,000 persons if they could be found.

The freedmen's interests were closely monitored by agents of the Freedmen's Bureau, thus the Bureau's insistence on a written contract for the laborer. The freedman, however, was reluctant to sign a written contract, believing it would return him to slave status (see my comments on the "loyal lease laborer" before the end of the war, i.e., he couldn't leave the plantation. Of course, at that time, the Negro was considered contraband).

What the written document did do was tie him to his contracted crop from planting to harvest. Throughout this period, many laborers failed to honor the contract, planting the crops, but moving on before harvest. Families were normally contracted for a year; however, the Freedmen's Bureau, in its zeal to accommodate the Negro, specified that single males might be contracted by the month, an agreement of little value to the Southern farmer, who knew that no help at harvest time rendered the crop of no value. This the Southerner attributed to the ignorance of the agent. The South's agrarian economy couldn't work that way.

As of December 1865, Colonel Thomas issued a circular to

freedmen advising them to enter contracts in time for the spring planting. Thomas stated agreement, in principle, with the vagrancy laws and advised the freedman to enter contracts or be arrested on vagrancy charges and forced to perform public works.

At the end of Colonel Thomas' tenure as assistant commissioner of the Bureau in early 1866, he stated that the Bureau was "working in perfect harmony with the state government and the department commander" (Governor Humphreys and General Wood). General Thomas J. Wood, who became the new Department of Mississippi commander in November 1865, echoed this sentiment in early 1866 when he stated whites were "acting nobler than could be expected."

In December of 1865, Governor-elect Humphreys, sent ex-Mississippi State Judges William Yerger and Joel Acker to Washington and asked President Johnson to identify which of the Mississippi legislature's measures he would direct the military to disregard. Johnson stated there would be no nullification of the code unless done by the courts. One can only surmise what Humphreys would have done had Johnson been more forthright, or in control. Humphreys might very well have called the legislature back in session to right the egregious passages—whatever they were. But to his credit, President Johnson had given guidance, via the provisional government and even after Humphreys and the legislature were elected. He requested the Thirteenth Amendment be passed by the legislature, he requested freedmen who owned property and paid taxes be admitted to the franchise, and he requested Negro testimony be allowed unconditionally in court.

Johnson was not a strong President, but despite his disappointment in Mississippi's legislature, he was a Southerner and can assume by his actions that he knew the Constitution and knew Mississippi was right under it. He also knew he was the President of the United States, tasked with bringing the late states of the rebellion back into the fold. In the next year he would endure an impeachment trial. Perhaps he was as "impru-dent" as the rest of the South. The actions of the legislature, though legal, had undermined the president vis-à-vis a Congress that had no regard for legality.

In January 1867, the office of assistant commissioner of the Freedmen's Bureau was consolidated with that of the district mili-tary commander. In that capacity, General Alvan C. Gillem assumed General T. J. Wood's responsibilities as both District Commander and assistant commissioner of the Freedman's Bureau. Gillem was the last assistant commissioner of the Freedman's Bureau in Mississippi.

Note that while all these readjustments were occurring, Mississippi and the entire South were crawling with northern newspaper correspondents who reported everything happening in the occupied South.

In July 1868, Congress directed the Bureau withdrawn from several states and its operations, except in the cases of education and bounty, discontinued after 1 January 1869. The freedman was advised to look to civil authorities for redress and assistance for food, clothing, medicine, transportation, and contract assis-tance. Of course, by that time the Radical Republicans had swept aside the post-war civil governments, which the taxpayer across the South had elected during Presidential Reconstruction. The civil authorities referred to were the republican puppet govern-ments, and there was no need for the protection of the Negro — the Radicals had taken over responsibility and given power to the Negro. I guess the assurance of Federal officers, northern lawyers, and powerful newspapers that all was proceeding well in the post-war South did not ring true to the radicals, who, with their prudent choice of the popular Ulysses S. Grant as their presidential hopeful, gained control of Congress.

For eighty years the South had served as a bulwark against the threat of an all-powerful federal government. Truth is, the reports from the South did ring true, and that was the problem. With duly-elected legislatures and Congressional representatives from the South, that bulwark against Federal tyranny remained in place. That had to end, else the war had been for naught. Now reduced to the status of banana republics, the Southern states and the illegally-elected representatives usurping their statehouses, as well as the puppets sent to Washington in their name, are on record for passing the most egregious desecrations to the Constitution of our forefathers.

And you really think the War for Southern Independence was about slavery? The economy derived from slavery, yes, but not the morality of it.

But that follows Presidential Reconstruction, dear reader, and belongs in another historical note, for it should be obvious that though the novel *Camellia Creek* ended, the story did not, literally as well as figuratively. The murder of Alan Guthrie, which brought Seth Parker to Mississippi, as well as the death of Jonathan Franklin near the end of the story, are yet to be resolved, as is the story of Southern Reconstruction. Ultimately, Reconstruction would strip all the states, not just the Southern ones, of their coequal rights vis-à-vis what became a stronger central government. The Northern states blindly sacrificed their rights in order to strip the South of hers, not incomprehensible considering the North and the evolving Republicans showed little respect for the Constitution from the beginning—hence their unjustified war against the South. As a result, *Camellia Creek* will be my first novel to have a sequel. I prefer to wrap up all my loose ends neatly at the close of each work, but the nature and structure of *Camellia Creek* are better suited to another novel than a saga. *Honor's Banner* will begin where *Camellia Creek* proper ends, with Eli Calhoon fighting for his life and Seth Parker in search of two killers.

And the sun setting on our Founders' Republic.

If you enjoyed *Camellia Creek* don't miss Charlsie Russell's award-winning first novel

The Devil's Bastard

Natchez on the river, 1793. The Spanish Fleet controls the Mississippi, and the Dons rule their rowdy British and American subjects with a patient hand. The location is strategic, the land fertile, and within two decades, cotton will be king. Into this web of international intrigue, the rich and powerful Elizabeth Boswell welcomes her orphaned grandniece Angelique Veilleux and introduces the impoverished beauty to a world of privilege. But power has enemies and wealth demands a price. Rumors state that Elizabeth's success stems from dalliance with a lustful demon that still prowls her family farm of De Leau outside Natchez.

At the center of this ominous legend is Elizabeth's grandson, the handsome and dangerous Mathias Douglas, who saves Angelique from degradation and death near the end of her journey to Natchez. Mathias is the son of the doomed Julianna,

Elizabeth's only daughter. Mathias's father, locals whisper, is Elizabeth's demon.

Despite the dark legend, Angelique cannot quell her feelings for Mathias, for whom she would make any sacrifice. An outcast, Mathias is cruelly tested by Angelique's affection. Determined not to dishonor her, he callously puts her aside. But Elizabeth has other plans and offers him the family farm at De Leau to marry the girl. Soon Angelique finds herself desperately in love with the man who has conquered her body and possessed her soul.

But something in the swamps surrounding De Leau stalks her, and nightmares invade her dreams. What she perceives as Mathias' indifference to the threat leaves Angelique isolated and afraid. She begins to doubt her grandaunt's motives for sending her to De Leau, as well as Mathias' role in Elizabeth's plan. Resolving her doubts means uncovering the secret of Mathias' sire.

From Mathias and Angelique's first meeting to Elizabeth Boswell's revelation at story's end, *The Devil's Bastard* is a splendid read. First and foremost a sensual romance, it is also a well-researched historical with a haunting mystery.

Don't miss Charlsie Russell's second award-winning novel

Wolf Dawson

Ten years after the Confederate Army reported him killed in action, dirt-poor Jeff Dawson returns to Natchez, Mississippi, a wealthy man and purchases White Oak Glen, the once opulent home of the now impoverished Seatons, the aristocratic family that years ago shattered his own.

Burdened with her drunken brother, Tucker, and besieged by greedy relatives, Juliet Seaton struggles to hold on to what remains of her farm. Now she finds her family faced with a new menace in the form of a marauding wolf that slaughters valuable stock and assails the mind of her alcoholic brother. Tucker Seaton warns his sister that the man occupying White Oak Glen is a ghost, who in the form of that vicious wolf seeks to destroy what is left of the Seatons.

An infant when events occurred setting her family against the Dawsons, Juliet appears pitted against a neighbor hell-bent on avenging his sister, who died in childbirth after being violated by a Seaton male. Jeff's grandfather was part Creek Indian.

Local legend states he terrorized unfriendly neighbors with tales of his ability to shape-shift into a deadly wolf. Unidentified persons lynched the colorful old man following the savage killing, apparently by a wolf, of the Seaton who raped Jeff Dawson's sister.

But Juliet finds the handsome Jeff a living, breathing man. Hot-blooded, to boot. His seductive touch weakens her resolve and blinds her to the danger he poses. Jeff, however, is no longer compelled to destroy the Seatons, if he ever was; they have destroyed themselves and left the vulnerable Juliet to his mercy — mercy he's quite willing to give, though he's not ready to let the feisty beauty know that.

Into this explosive mix of fear and distrust comes a sadistic killer, and what this fiend kills is not Seaton livestock.

With the countryside ablaze with suspicion directed toward Jeff, he and Juliet overcome mutual distrust and strip away a lost generation's hatred as quickly as the clothes covering their bodies. Old lies give way to new truths, lust to love, and together, the lovers set out to uncover not only a killer, but the identity of the spectral beast haunting the countryside.

Don't miss Charlsie Russell's third award-winning novel

$\mathcal{E}pico\ \mathcal{B}ayou$

In the fall of 1897, a grand old gentleman of Handsboro, Mississippi dies a very wealthy man, and much to the chagrin of Lionel Augustus's siblings, he leaves the bulk of his estate to his estranged bastard son, Clay Boudreaux, and his beloved step-daughter, Olivia Lee. There is but one stipulation to Lionel's will, the two must wed.

For reasons of their own, the two young people agree to marry, sight unseen, but only days after her marriage by proxy to Deputy Sheriff Clay Boudreaux of Galveston County, Texas, Olivia learns her husband has died in a house fire and her ex-tended family intends to contest the terms of the will. Exacerbating her situation, a mysterious stranger, claiming to be the dead Clay, but who her family warns is Clay's older brother Troy, invades Olivia's opulent home and accuses her of hiring Troy to kill Clay . . . and yet another henchman to eliminate Clay's killer.

Olivia and the handsome stranger, whoever he might be, both have sound reasons for confusing their roles in the plot to murder

Clay Boudreaux, reasons dealing with duty, justice, and survival. Neither is sure of the role the other plays in the Machiavellian plan of Lionel's siblings, nor is it clear if Lionel's brother and sister are the only subversives working to sabotage the terms of Lionel's will. So clear is the present danger, it overshadows the dark secret driving Lionel's bizarre stipulation that Clay and Olivia wed.

Set on the Mississippi Gulf Coast at the close of the nineteenth century, Charlsie Russell's third novel is both a romantic charade and a compelling mystery, pitting the wit and will of one wary lover against the honor and sheer determination of the other, even while the sinister machinations of dangerous foes force them into a grudging alliance.

Though the tangled mystery sets this novel apart from her edgy Gothics, *The Devil's Bastard* and *Wolf Dawson*, Ms. Russell's *Epico Bayou* still features those tried and true elements of suspense, sensual romance, and historical setting that characterize her work. Pure escape. Don't miss this journey!

And if you like what you've read so far, look for

River's Bend

Rafe Stone came back to Mississippi seeking justice and the house irrevocably linked to everything that makes him who he is. But the magnificent structure that began life as a one-room, French-Dominion log cabin and grew into an antebellum showcase south of Natchez has fallen into disrepair and into the hands of a savvy Mississippi City businessman by the name of Josephus Collander. The astute Collander has no use for the tax-draining piece of real estate; moreover, he needs to unburden himself of a recently acquired orphaned niece who, through no fault of her own, is wreaking havoc within his household. The house is not for sale, Collander tells the disappointed Rafe...but he can have it for nothing, if he'll accept it as Delilah Graff's dowry.

Rafe's desperation, coupled with Delilah's beauty, makes the decision, albeit a reckless one, easy. But what secret in the siren's past would cause a seemingly kind and responsible kinsman to barter her to a stranger?

Tragedy, followed by a difficult childhood, has left Delilah jaundiced toward life, bitter toward men, and eager for the independence she is sure is coming. Instead, the financial support her beneficent Uncle Joe promised is suddenly forfeit, and he has called in his markers, compelling her to wed a man she does not know. Worse yet, her uncle doesn't appear to know much about the handsome Rafe Stone either. Adding to her discomfort, this Mr. Stone takes her to Natchez, a city where her name is synonymous with disgrace. There he moves her into a house rumored, over the course of its nearly two hundred years, to have hosted treason, robbery, adultery, and murder. A house still reputed to harbor the specter of a vicious killer.

And who is Rafe Stone, the man to whom she has sworn her troth and under whose roof she sleeps at night? A man who claims to be a stranger to Mississippi, yet knows more about the ominously majestic River's Bend, and its past, than he should? What is his link to the dark legends haunting River's Bend and to the ghost walking its rambling halls? Is he the personification of her nightmare or an unbidden dream come true?

Mystery, suspense, romance, and history, dear reader. Enjoy this look back to the time when the memory of the Old South blossomed into legend.

About the Author

Charlsie Russell is a retired United States Navy commander turned author. She loves history, and she loves the South. She focuses her writing on historical suspense set in her home state of Mississippi.

After seven years of rejection, she woke up one morning and determined she did not have enough years left on this planet to sit back and hope a New York publisher would one day take a risk on her novels. Thus resolved, she expanded her horizons into the publishing realm with the creation of Loblolly Writer's House.

In addition to writing and publishing, Ms. Russell is a mother and homemaker.

To learn more about Charlsie Russell and Loblolly Writer's House, visit www.loblollywritershouse.com.

Loblolly Writer's House

<u>**Order Blank**</u>

Tear this sheet out and mail order to:

**Loblolly Writer's House
P.O. Box 7438
Gulfport, MS 39506-7438**

<u>Item</u>	<u>Price</u>*	<u>Qty</u>	<u>Total</u>
The Devil's Bastard	$16.00	______	______
Wolf Dawson	$16.00	______	______
Epico Bayou	$16.00	______	______
River's Bend	$16.00	______	______
Shipping free:	<u>0.00</u>		

Total payment: ______

Would you like a signed copy?
Tell me how:________________________________

____

<u>Send to:</u>

____

____

____

*Price includes 7% Mississippi sales tax

For Bookseller rates visit: www.loblollywritershouse.com